"Marge Piercy's new novel is one of the first to explore the variety of life-styles that women in our time are adopting in order to give meaning to their personal and political lives. The novel depicts a new reality . . . the chaos and confusion women have faced . . . the courage and strength many of them have found."

—THE NEW REPUBLIC

SMALL CHANGES

Marge Piercy

54971

FAWCETT CREST • NEW YORK

SMALL CHANGES

THIS BOOK CONTAINS THE COMPLETE TEXT OF
THE ORIGINAL HARDCOVER EDITION.

Published by Fawcett Crest Books, a unit of CBS Publications,
the Consumer Publishing Division of CBS Inc., by arrange-
ment with Doubleday and Company, Inc.

ISBN: 0-449-23671-4

"The Happiest Day of a Woman's Life" was first printed in
Works In Progress VII. "Marriage Is a Matter of Give and
Take" appeared in The Boston *Phoenix*. "Mothers and Daughters" and "The Rhythms of Two Households" were published
in *aphra,* Summer 1973, Vol. IV, No. 3.

Printed in the United States of America
First Fawcett printing: September 1974

17   16   15   14   13   12   11   10   9   8   7

For me.
For you.
For us.
Even for them.

CONTENTS

SMALL CHANGES

ONE

The Book of Beth

1

The Happiest Day of a Woman's Life

Beth was looking in the mirror of her mother's vanity. The mirror had wings that opened and shut. When she was little she used to like to pull them together around her into a cave of mirrors with only a slit of light. It isn't me, isn't me. Well, who else would it be, stupid? Isn't anyone except Bride: a dress wearing a girl.

Beth could not help seeing herself in the mirror: could never call up a glamorous image as her younger sister Nancy could. Nancy was sulking in the bathroom because her best friend Trudy had called her a dishwater blond. Like Beth, Nancy had naturally curly, almost kinky light brown hair. They were the little ones in the family. Just yesterday she had picked off the floor a piece of paper with gum stuck in it written in Nancy's fancy new backhand: *Nancy Phail is a petite vivacious blond with loads of personality*. Nancy could look in the same mirror and see faces from those teen-age magazines she brooded over. But Beth saw Beth lost in a vast dress. She felt like a wedding cake: they would come and slice her and take her home in white boxes to sleep on under their pillows.

With their married sister Marie's help, Nancy had written a description for the paper and mailed it in, though they never printed that except for people like, oh, executives' daughters from the G.E. plant where her father worked at the gate. "Schiffli embroidery and ribbons dip softly over an organza skirt and bodice, with sheer daintily puffed sleeves," Nancy had written. "The train comes away." That meant the thing that dragged could be taken off, with a little timely help.

"What are you frowning for? Mooning around, just as if it was any Saturday. Now let your sister Marie use the mirror, don't be standing there making faces." Her mother clucked

12

and nudged and peered at her with that familiar worried look. "Oh, if you aren't covered with freckles the size of pennies!"

Jim and she had gone to Verona Beach on Lake Oneida last Sunday and now she was freckled on her face and hands and arms and even her back, though nobody could see through the yards of white fencing. Only her thin arms and hair stuck out, her hair not anything like its fluffy silly self but turned into a stiff coiled mass that smelled chemical and had sitting on it pearls and lace and imitation flowers rising from what looked like the doilies her Grandma Phail used to keep pinned to the arms of her overstuffed mohair couch.

Everything was to be pink and white. Her mother, nudging her from the mirror, was wearing a rustly old rose dress that was too tight. It was left from Marie's wedding, but Mother said nobody would remember what she wore four years ago —though it was clear she had put on weight. Marie's dress was in a color called cerise and she was matron of honor. Marie was one of the big Phails, like Dad and their brother Dick, big-boned and now filled out wide in the hips to balance her shoulders. Nancy was bridesmaid in pale pink and so was Beth's girl friend Dolores in a dress the color of salmon from a can. There had been some fussing because Dolores was Catholic, but Beth insisted on her. It was the only thing she had insisted on. Dolores and Beth were not as close any more, both spending so much time with their boy friends and both having to work after school their senior year, but there had been many times—especially in junior high school—when Beth felt nobody in the whole world cared for her except Dolores.

Dolores had not liked the dresses that Marie and Nancy picked out, and they had fought for a whole week. Dolores had ended up taking hers home to let out the bodice, which meant she made it come out lower so her breasts showed some. She always said, if you had it you might as well flaunt it. Salmon was not Dolores' best color, but she looked more definite than anybody else. Dolores had taken over from Mother to work on Marie's hair, all the while flirting with herself in the mirror over Marie's broad shoulders. She made Beth smile for the first time since waking up.

Why did Marie look strange? Beth realized she had not seen her dressed up since—when? Her own wedding? Mrs. MacRae's funeral? Marie had lived upstairs since Mrs. Mac-

Rae died and poor Mr. MacRae moved to his sister's house.
Gene had been out of work, long, too long. They had lost
their house. Marie's baby Lucille had been put down on the
bed, where the everyday clothes people had worn over were
piled. Lucille was spitting up on the cotton dresses and pants.
Joey was out in the yard with Dick's kids dressed up in their
little suits and the last time she had seen them they were
rolling in the grass playing Indians.

Nancy flung out of the bathroom. "Look at me! I'm a
wreck! My hair didn't come out right. And how can I wear
such stupid clunky earrings?" Nancy and Dolores were
jockeying at the three-sided mirror. At the window she started
to look out but Marie yanked her back. "It's bad luck to be
seen on your wedding day."

"You could just wrap me like a package." To give her
away. It was funny how they celebrated her going off with
Jim, when for a long time Mother had not let her see him
and she had used to meet him secretly after work. His brother
raced stock cars and Jimbo liked to hang around the cars
and her mother thought he had a bad reputation. Last month
her mother had been worried and kept shaking her head and
saying, "If this is what you really want." Of course she
wanted to marry Jim. She could hardly believe that she was
really his girl. From one day to the next, she was always
scared of losing him.

Weddings and funerals. All through Beth's childhood Mrs.
MacRae had lived upstairs. She was plump, with flesh like
mashed potatoes, put on make-up at home in the evenings and
did not wear housedresses like Mother and now Marie did.
She had a pink naked-looking dog Honeybun. Her mother
had told Marie that Mrs. MacRae wasn't really a woman, for
she had had her organs removed. That was why she didn't
have children like everybody else. The MacRaes had a little
more money than their neighbors, and Mrs. MacRae was
always inviting the other women in for Pot and Pan Parties.
She would have games and demonstrate products and give
door prizes and they would buy pans. Mrs. MacRae also gave
parties for cosmetics and wigs and shoes. Those were the only
times women in the neighborhood got together. Beth had
loved to tag along. Her mother had bottles of apricot throat
cream in the hall closet she would never remember until

they dried up. But an imitation party was better than no party at all.

"This is the happiest day of your life!" Mother came and pinched her arm below the puffed sleeve. "The happiest day!"

The day was already hot with flies buzzing at the pane but she felt cold and strange. Finally she ran to the bathroom and waited till her Uncle Bob came out. It was impossible to sit on the toilet in the dress. It took ten minutes to get into position. When she came back to the bedroom, Marie started fussing that she was getting the dress wrinkled.

"No, you can't sit down!" her mother snapped. All the funny curls danced. Usually her mother had her thin gray-brown hair pulled back in a hairnet. She always wore a hairnet, Beth didn't know why. Now her hair was skinned into tight rings like something you might use to clean a pot. "Don't you want things nice, on your own day? That dress cost enough, so you might as well enjoy it while you can!" Mother gave her a poke. They never did embrace much. She had not thought about that before she hung around with Dolores, whose family was always kissing and yelling. People in Beth's family turned things in and carried them off to brood on. When her parents argued, usually over money because there was never enough, they argued in low voices that would begin hissing and rise with anger like a saw cutting into wood and then compress again so that the children would not hear, although of course the children always heard.

"You'll get plenty of time to rest later. In the car I mean!" Dolores giggled and hugged her around what were usually her ribs.

"Don't muss the dress!" Mother warned. She had been lost in a fret of anxiety for days, seeing disaster in each broken glass.

"Why, you'll get to lie down flat for days and days on your honeymoon—I mean in the sun!" Dolores said singsong.

She made herself push her lips into a pretend smile. Getting dressed up meant being uncomfortable. Putting on extra underwear that bound you and shoes that pinched or clopped and dresses in which you could not move. Putting stuff on your face and watching the wind did not get in your hair and make it look as usual. Trying to appear as little like Beth as could be arranged. She felt embarrassed, whether it was for a party or the senior prom with Jim, as if she were caught out in the open trying to be someone else. Getting dressed up meant everything about her was saying LOOK AT ME when she would just as soon nobody would bother.

Mostly people didn't. She was small, like Nancy and Mother, although Mother by this time was so wide she wasn't exactly invisible. Mother was round and had trouble with her legs, bursitis. But Beth was five feet one and weighed a hundred pounds exactly and Jim's sweet name for her was Little Girl. Of course she could look in the family album and see photographs of her mother looking just as slight. Her mother would refuse to eat potatoes at supper because she was watching her weight, and then in midmorning she would sit down to a snack of coffee with cream and sugar and a danish and at three o'clock have coffee with cream and sugar and Sara Lee cake. A sweet tooth never filled, a hunger for sugar greater than a hunger for food. In repose the expression on Mother's face was a worried sadness, a look of things missed and wasted, a look of bills coming home to roost and nothing gained.

Beth had always felt the wrong size. She was convinced she had been bred to be miniature, like a toy poodle or a dwarf peach tree, in the world where everybody else was twice her size and ready to push through her like a revolving door, ready to step on her and overlook her and keep her from seeing whatever the rest of the crowd was yelling about. In chairs her feet never quite touched the floor. If she sat forward, then her back was without support. Shelves were out of her reach and she was always groping impossibly for straps in buses and clawing at luggage racks and she never could shut windows. Now her littleness was swallowed by a dress standing as if on a padded hanger.

"You can still see her freckles, Mom." Nancy was squinting in Beth's face. So they got towels from the bathroom to protect The Dress and painted on more make-up slathered over the old make-up. They told her to close her eyes and open her eyes and make faces and be still. When they finished, her face looked like rough plaster but they all had to admit, you could still see her freckles.

"Well, it's because she has such a fair skin that she freckles," Dolores said protectively.

"Now, that's true." Mother rubbed idly at the rose taffeta where an old stain faintly showed. "She bruises easily too.

Why, you lay a finger on her and it shows. She's the sensitive one."

"And hickeys," Dolores whispered, giving her shoulders a squeeze, because when Beth had been seeing Jim on the sly she had used to worry that her father would see the marks on her neck. "The headpiece is coming untacked!" Dolores wailed. "Mrs. Phail, look, it's coming off of her!"

"It's almost one and I have so much to do, and you keep undoing what I've done already. That's a thirty-five-dollar headpiece, Bethie, so hold your head up proud and stop dancing around like a flea on a hot griddle."

"Mom, don't worry!" The sour waves of anxiety coming off her. "Mom, what does it matter? It will be all right." Beth tried to smile.

"Yeah, take it easy," Marie said with a sigh. She had been looking in the hand mirror with a puzzled smile at the way Dolores had done her hair. It did look nice. "It's too hot to get so excited. Beth'll do fine."

"Did you ever see a girl fidget so? Your family's giving you a real wedding, and don't you forget it," Mother said. "We haven't cut any corners. This is no hole in the wall at the courthouse or in the front room to save on the trimmings. You're getting married in church with flowers and bridesmaids and your father rented a hall for afterward with real caterers. And I want *you* to remember this, Nancy Rose Phail—that's how it's supposed to be. Just like we're doing for your sister Bethie, if you're a good girl and do right by your parents, your parents will do right by you."

Of course Dick's wife Elinor had come swishing in and Mother had been talking as much to dig at Elinor as to warn Nancy. "Where's the blooming bride?" Elinor cried out as if she hadn't heard. "Why, doesn't she look good enough to eat! Whats wrong with the veil? Is it supposed to stick straight out that way?"

"Oh, she's jiggling around so much she's twitched it loose again. How many pins can we put in her? It stays or it doesn't. I wash my hands of it." Mother made a hand-washing gesture.

"Poor lamb, she's all excited. Well, you got quite a day for it, happy's the bride the sun shines on, they say. What are you going to do with those three blenders? What a shame."

"She's going to take them back and get an electric knife and a bathroom scales!" Mother's warning voice rose to a whine. Elinor wanted to help herself, and Beth would just as soon she did. All that heap of stuff to write letters for, strange silver thingies and glasses that cost too much to use. It had been going on for weeks. "Your Aunt Emma could have done fairer than that! Why, I saw that vase on sale downtown for five ninety-five and I'm going to let her know she can't pull the wool over my eyes!"

"What's that big china contraption Jim's sister-in-law gave you? She told me it's an antique soup tureen, but I'll tell you, cross my heart and hope to die, I think it's a big old chamber pot!"

"Isn't it an eyesore?" Mother forgave Elinor for saying that because she already didn't like Jim's relatives. Dad made a practice of liking his in-laws, on principle, because they were family and you always put up with family. Mother made a practice of disliking in-laws on principle, because they were only pretending to be family and they were making comparisons and out to take advantage.

The day was sunny and hot. Beth was sweating in her gloves by the time they left for church. Mother had spread out a sheet in the back seat of the car and they sat on it very stiff, Dad driving with Nancy and Mother in front, and Marie and Dolores on either side of her in back. She had not seen Jim since yesterday. It was strange that she was not permitted to talk to him, to know how his morning had been. He was supposed to be the one to hold her when she felt frightened, she was supposed to be the one to understand and make him feel all right. "Why can't men and women see each other before a wedding?"

"Maybe so the groom won't take a last look at the bride and change his mind, ha-ha," her dad said. He was wearing a gray hat that smelled of dry cleaning and he could not see his face.

The scent of the mock oranges in the church was overpowering. Across the street kids were playing softball. It was crowded in the little room with everyone babbling and Aunt Susie bawling. Someone had been drinking. Gin crept under the mock orange and grass clippings from the church lawn and the smell of camphor heavy from a closet where vestments were stored. An invitation lay on the table and she picked it up. "Mr. and Mrs. Charles L. Phail are pleased . . . their daughter Elizabeth Ann to James Hayes Walker . . . June 22,

1968." She saw herself start down the aisle and trip on her train and go rolling headfirst over and over to end up sprawled on her back, dress piled over her head at the altar. She could not make the picture go away. Again and again she saw herself rolling like a snowball of stiff organza over and over down the aisle to end up sprawled knees apart, legs spread, and dress up over her head in rape position.

Nancy would love to slip into this gown. In Dad's and Uncle Bob's jokes at the family dinner, there had been such a sense of relief at only one more girl to marry off, and that the pretty one.

Nancy was the pretty one, everybody said, and Marie was the one who wanted to be a nurse and wiped their noses when they were little and helped in the kitchen. Everybody said Marie would be a good mother. Marie was twice a mother and Beth could hear her yelling all day long, "No! No! No! Now shut up your lousy mouth, Joey, or Mother will shut it for you! Will this stupid baby ever stop crying? Now shut your face and keep it shut, or I'm going to cream you, Joey, you hear me? I'm going to wring your neck!" Her voice sounded like a teacher's. Her mouth was getting pinched. The flat upstairs was too small but what could they find? Gene had been out of work for close to a year before he finally got hired at Carrier.

She remembered Marie saying to her when she had panicked, two weeks ago, "Now look, Jim's not perfect, no man is. But you'll get away from home. Right? Just don't start having babies before you have a little saved. Have some fun together first. At least you'll have a place of your own!"

Yes, Nancy was the pretty one and Dick was to be the success. He did okay as a salesman in an appliance store downtown on Salina, but he was always pushing Elinor around and they kept moving into houses a little farther out of Syracuse than they could afford. Marie had wanted to be a nurse but everyone said she was the Little Mother. Beth was the quiet one. Such a good girl. She was the one who liked school and did well but nobody said she was smart because she was too quiet. She had wanted to go to college. For all of her junior year she had brought home catalogs. Mother's *good* little girl. You don't have to bother to love the good ones.

But now she would be loved. Now it would be safe to love. Here was the real beginning. Now she would have her life. She would be loved for herself and would love Jim without being afraid things would turn ugly and jagged and painful. This day was the narrow gate through to Jimbo and she must go on to the thumping music. She must stand while they twitched at her veil and pinched her hair, while they pulled at the skirt, while they flapped the train. Inside the marshmallow she endured their tweaking and tugging. Now Marie was shaking the train like a scatter rug so it would float properly and the music was booming into the processional and Nancy was parading back and forth looking haughty with a sly smile.

> *Here comes the bride, big, fat and wide.*
> *Look how she wiggles, from side to side.*
>
> *Here comes the groom, lean as a broom.*
> *He would wiggle too, if he only had the room!*

That's what they used to sing when they were children, and sometimes they would stick pillows under their dresses to make themselves pregnant. Like Dick's wife Elinor. To have to get married. If there were other words to that music, she had never heard them. Going to be given away. Her father grinned bleakly, tugging at his bow tie. Take two, they're small: ad from an adoption agency in the bus she used to take to work after school. But love came after this. After.

She had been taught to count going down the aisle, trying hard not to feel how everyone was looking. The air was thick hot pudding. Her hands were damp. Her scalp felt sticky under the headpiece. She could make up a ceremony prettier than this in half an hour, but nobody had asked her and she understood prettiness had nothing to do with it. They were giving her away. When she wanted to go to college—she had wanted badly to be a lawyer, like Portia in the play, like Perry Mason, and everybody thought that was funny—they had told her there was no money. But they had spent enough money on this day for two years of studying. She must not think about that. She would be married to Jim, and that was the important thing.

Jim looked like somebody else. His face was red and his long hair was cut to just brushing his shoulders and he was dressed in a rented outfit of striped baggy trousers. Frankie, who worked with him at the garage, was got up the same way.

She looked for Jim's eyes. His eyes were gray with a green tint that made her think of stones and water and ferns that grew in the woods. Once they had driven all the way to Watkins Glen with his brother Dan and his wife. Jim had a beautiful smile like a huge daisy but now he was not smiling. She could not find her way into his eyes. After all, he could not open to her any more than she could to him: they would run out the door together from all this strange nonsense.

Dad was wearing his best suit—he had two, best and second best—tight as Mother's rose taffeta. They looked like salami and little sausage, sweating and breathing heavily in the heat. Now her father was giving her away when he'd never had that much to say to her. Dick was the apple of his eye, and, sometimes he said, his biggest disappointment. Nancy was his favorite among the girls. Mostly he just called them The Girls, including their mother. But Nancy was the one he let sit on his lap and teased till she giggled and sometimes till she cried, and the one he threatened the most. He was scared Nancy would go bad, he said often enough. The bouquet in her hands was wilting: her nervousness was shriveling it.

Cars outside were hurrying past from the city to the Finger Lakes or farther to the mountains. An ice cream truck, a Mr. Softie, rode by playing its jingle as the minister spoke to them. She tried to fix her mind on what she had to say. She could not hear the words over the roaring in her ears. Magic words that made things happen or go away, recipes like I Love You, and I'm Sorry, and I Pledge Allegiance, and God Bless Mommy and Daddy, and Will You Marry Me, and Fine, Thank You, and I Do. The way through to Jim. Jim spoke up clearly. He kissed her, but his lips felt hard and closed. Then they were going out. She tried to match his stride. They were supposed to go out slowly, but they weren't going as they were supposed to.

Rice tossed and ribbons and big signs on the car, shoes and cans dragging. Frankie blew the horn as they went, ta taaa ta ta. Jim was hugging her in the car but again for show. Still the radio had turned on with the ignition to a rock station, and the air felt more alive. They passed a lawn where in those silly two-piece bathing suits hung on little girls three children ran under the sprinkler with a brown woolly dog chasing with them woofing and leaping high and shaking himself. Suppose they could run now under the hose, wet her dress down to size, pry off the white shoes that gripped her feet and dance together. The worst was over. They were really married. They could not dance under the hose with Dick and Elinor and Marie and Dad, and not even with Nancy, who would say her hair was ruined. But in just a little while all the noise would fade and they would be together as they wanted to be, their own lives. Soon it would begin to be beautiful.

"I'll be glad to get this thing off," she said softly to Jim.

"Yes, baby." He squeezed her hand. Her face heated and she was afraid she blushed because he was grinning at her. You were supposed to hold out, you were supposed to or everyone suffered: then you got caught and you had to get married and Mother lay on her bed having headaches for weeks, like Mother and Elinor. She had to make up for that. This big church wedding was the certificate that the Phails were not ashamed this time, not in a pig's eye, as her father said, no baby in five months, they had invited the neighbors in to look this time.

The reception was at the V.F.W. Hall. The bar was set up along one wall and Frankie and Jim made a dash for it, Jim yelling, "Charge!" On the other far wall was a buffet arranged with the wedding cake in the middle. "Save the top layer—keep an eye out that nobody cuts into it," Marie whispered to her. The cake had three tiers. Now she and Jim cut it with a knife that was a wedding present from Jimbo's Uncle Victor which said A Slice of Life Knife on its pearl handle. "Now you can cut the mustard, ha-ha," Frankie said. All the wedding presents were piled up. Mother and Dad and Marie were to cart them afterward over to the apartment they had rented, so they'd be there when Beth and Jim got back from their honeymoon a week from Sunday.

The cake tasted just like store-bought sawdust white cake, but she had to eat it because the photographer her father had hired was taking pictures. Spots danced in her eyes. She and Jim had to feed each other pieces. He liked chocolate cake the best and so did she, but the baker said nobody ever had chocolate wedding cake and her mother acted as if there was something dirty-minded in wanting it. So they had what the baker called Lady's Cake. It had pink rosebuds and green leaves and a chubby bride and groom holding hands under an archway.

The four-piece rock group from her high school had

started to play and she and Jim had to dance together first in front of everybody. They had to waltz. They had never waltzed together. They didn't do it well because she only came up to the middle of his chest. She felt smothered, not able to see where she was backing to, with the stiff jacket pressing her nose. When they danced to rock music, their different sizes did not matter. They could look at each other and her feet did not always end up planted under his coming down. Finally the waltz ended and they could stop. The musicians too looked relieved.

Except that, when she went to sit down, people kept coming and she had to get up. The champagne was okay, it was like pop only not as sweet. It didn't bite like the bourbon Jim drank sometimes and it was not sour like beer. Jim and Frankie kept bringing her champagne. She never did get to eat but after a while she did not mind. It was so hot the fans could not seem to move the sluggish air and people kept going outside and standing on the sidewalk with their drinks. There was an enormous press around the bar. She heard Dad talking to Mother about the liquor bill. "We've got to get them out of here by five," her dad said. "How are we ever going to get them to leave? Look at them lap it up."

She could smell the sweetish odor of grass, but nobody offered her any. It was hard to really dance inside the marshmallow. Jimbo had said this group wasn't really good, but they were very loud and that helped.

Dick looked as if he might be drunk. He kept saying that his baby sister had got married, although of course Nancy was his baby sister. Nancy looked more grown up than Beth did, everyone said so, because she was good at putting on make-up. Nancy's cross in life was that Dad wouldn't let her bleach her hair. She was dancing with Frankie too close and Marie and her mother were arguing about whether to go say anything. Then Marie had to go off to the women's lounge to breast-feed the baby and Mother made Nancy come and say hello to some aged second cousin, which she did for thirty seconds. Chuckie, Dick's five-year-old, was throwing up by the band from too much ice cream and maybe a little champagne.

Then Elinor was clutching her by the arm saying, "You wait and see if you think it makes so damn much difference! You wait and see! I know how they've always thought of me.

Some families have a heart, they accept you and make you feel at home, but your mother has never let me forget a thing. But just you wait and see how much fucking difference it makes when you come down to it!"

Frankie asked her to dance and she kept dancing with him for a while, it was so good to get away from all the people she had to make a stiff smile for and say oh, thank you for whatever it was. Then Mother came and hissed in her ear that she shouldn't let Frankie pinch her that way. But she hadn't felt anything through the dress. She didn't much like him kissing her, he tasted like alcohol. Men kept kissing her all afternoon, especially uncles. When her new Uncle Victor was slobbering on her she thought, suppose she suddenly bit him, and then she began to laugh. The champagne went up as bubbles into her head and made her laugh a lot.

Dick was yelling at Elinor about Chuckie when a big fat old walrus of a man she had never seen before passed out and had to be carried away. Under the stairway, Nancy was kissing Tom. Tom used to go with her but now went steady with Trudy, and Trudy ran upstairs crying. Her mother came and told Beth it was time for her to go up and change. Jim was dancing with Dolores, who had succeeded in making another alteration in her bridesmaid's dress so that now most of her breasts showed. Marie was still feeding Lucille in the lounge, with Frankie's mother fallen asleep beside her with her mouth open, but Dolores and Jim were finally pried apart. Dolores came to help her out of the marshmallow. By this time Beth was damp with the heat and felt dizzy and clammy under the layers and layers.

At last she was unpeeled and Dolores and Nancy and Trudy, who had stopped crying, stood around making jokes about brides getting undressed all the time, as if she hadn't petted enough times with Jim, and Dolores anyhow knew that. Mother and Marie had tried to make her get a suit, but she had picked a little print dress without sleeves that felt soft and looked like flowers that had run a bit, flowers that were not color-fast in a light rain. Then they all kissed her good-by and Mother sniffed and pretended to cry and everybody came to kiss her for yet another beery, smelly, balony time, taste of foods she hadn't got to eat, chicken salad and ham and mayonnaise, and the guests went right on drinking and outside on the sidewalk Frankie and Tom were getting ready to fight each other and Uncle Vic was blowing and yelling. Then they got into Jim's car at last and drove away.

They drove toward New Hampshire, toward the White Mountains, which sounded cool but turned out to be too far. They were both tired by sunset so they stopped at a motel in Vermont. Because there were no doubles left they had to take a room with two double beds, which cost more than they had figured on. They ate supper at a restaurant up the highway where drinks were served. Jim had pork chops and a couple of shots of Jim Beam, and she had chicken and a whiskey sour. By the time they finished she was sleepy but Jim was waking up. She had two cups of coffee. When they drove back to the motel she was almost too tired to be nervous. After all, it would be just like always, only better.

"You know, Little Girl, I was stoned." Jim unbuttoned his shirt sitting on the bed. "Couldn't go through that otherwise without freaking out, no way. But Frankie and I had a joint right outside and I just floated through. I didn't get your old lady mad at me even once—a world's record."

In the room next door the people had the TV on loud and the laugh track kept clattering through the walls. She told herself the noise was protective. She liked the motel. Oh, it was ugly and plastic but it was a room that didn't belong to anybody. For one night it belonged to her and Jim together. At last they were out of sight of everybody. It was beautiful that there were rooms people could rent to be alone. Here they were in a town whose name she had not even noticed, in a room for the two of them.

He said they should go to bed. "I mean, who wants to watch TV, what's the point, right, Little Girl? You get ready."

She went off to the bathroom and did not know if she should put on the black nightgown Dolores had given her. Always they had been together in Jim's car, or on the couch at Dolores' when her parents were out, or at Marie's when she would baby-sit and Jim would sneak up. They had done what she thought of as everything except that ultimate dangerous, culminating act. But they had never been all the way undressed. Somebody might return home early or come along and shine a light on them. It wasn't as if her body were strange to him but it felt brazen to walk out there naked, as if she were expecting something. Finally she put on the nightgown and brushed her hair till it lost its strange frozen shape. Then she came out barefoot with her arms folded and paused beside the bed. "Jim, love, here I am."

It was over in fifteen minutes, the whole thing. Then he lay on his side breathing softly in sleep and she was lying there with a new hole torn in her, oozing softly into the mattress. She was stretched there still wound up as if whatever she was waiting for had not yet happened. She felt much less satisfied than she had after one of those fumbling long-drawn-out sessions on the couch or the back seat of his Chevy. It was accomplished. That was it, the whole thing. They had made love finally, but where was the love they had made?

2

Marriage Is a Matter of Give and Take

The days were long but blurred except for weekends when she and Jim could be together. Often they went shopping or to the stock-car races, especially if Dan was driving. Usually they went out with Frankie and the girl he was seeing that month. She was thrown together with Frankie's girl friends. Some she liked and some she didn't, but she had to get along with all of them while becoming attached to none: because in three weeks he would be through with that one. Then the suddenly dropped girl would be calling her to cry and wonder what she had done.

She looked at Jim at the table, in the shower, lying beside him in bed, studying him and her feelings, trying to understand what this was, this marriage, this loving. A pain bloomed in her flesh sometimes when she looked at him, a beautiful frightening jagged pain of loving. Why? Because of his straight nose and his gray eyes and the way one brow slanted higher than the other and the turn at the corner of his mouth?

What did such a sweet pain mean? For a year she had schemed, lied to her mother and father, used an elaborate code on the phone like a heroine in a spy movie, all to be with him. Now here they were married, month after month. She had loved him and been sure she knew him; every day it hit her how little they knew each other. Yet they seemed to go on exactly the same.

Every day she had to go to work too early. She wished she could arrive at nine-thirty when she had to punch in, but Jim had to be at work by nine and he wanted the car with him. Where they were living in East Syracuse, there really was no other way to get downtown to Edwards, where she worked. So every day she had half an hour, forty-five minutes to kill before work. The downtown had been urban-renewed and there were benches, especially in the square in front of St. Mary's and the County Courthouse, where sometimes she could read for a while without being pestered. Or she wandered past the parking lots paved over rubble and looked at the fancy new yellow stucco townhouses, the high-rise apartments, and wondered what it would be like if they lived near things she might want to do, instead of so far out. By the museum a playground had an elephant slide, and even at that hour children were crawling through the elephant's belly and sliding down his trunk. Watching, she felt a peculiar nostalgia; not for her own childhood certainly. For children she would have?

She did not like selling in Daytime Dresses where a nervous manager was always breathing down her neck, telling her to fold boxes or work on stock if she lacked a customer. She hated being checker at the fitting rooms, pulling clothes out of women's hands and counting to make sure nothing was stolen.

In March, after she had been married and working full time for nine months, she was transferred to Notions, on the ground floor. Notions tended to be quiet and mostly she just had to show customers where hangers or sewing supplies were located. All day long music engulfed her. Records were in the middle of Men's Wear, just through the archway. In June she began to notice the music more. The person who put on the records now was a college boy pretending to be his brother just graduated from high school. If the store had known he was twenty and in college, they would not have

hired him. He called her Mrs. Walker and seemed to think
that was funny. She called him Larry. He told her she was a
child bride, that she had been married at age thirteen and
would have ten children by the time she was thirty.

She liked the music Larry played. Sometimes it was soul,
sometimes it was people saying things sharper and cleaner
than people ever talked to each other in her life. She had
always liked music but mainly as part of the ambience of
dating. She had had an AM radio to share with Nancy but
never before a record player. Her mother could not see buying
records when she could turn on the radio free. Jim had a
phonograph and with her discount she began to buy some of
the records Larry played. It was like bringing home a mood,
a thick potent mood. She was beginning to listen carefully
to the music and to the words too, hearing the records over
and over all day while she stood by her cash register. Music
stopped being background for dancing or driving in the car
or eating pizza and began to be great charges of feeling,
someone and then someone else talking to her with power.

It seemed to her that the music was a messenger from
another place, some level where people lived more fully, felt
more strongly, reached out and experienced in a way that no
one about her ever did. Sort of how she had imagined being
with Jim would be, beforehand. She tried to explain that to
Jim, but he thought she meant the life that rock musicians
led. Sure, he said, they had a lot of money and different girls
every night and all the drugs they wanted and cars and great
clothes. That was the life.

It wasn't just rock music. Sometimes Larry played piano
music or violins with orchestras that spoke of completely other
inner and outer landscapes. When a customer suddenly asked
for a folding umbrella, she found it hard to disconnect. But
of course she did. All her life she had been polite and service-
able. After a customer had taken out bad temper on her and
called her stupid and blamed her for things that did not work
or were out of stock, she scarcely knew she was angry until
she found herself shaking.

Jim was not interested when she tried to talk about the store,
and she had to agree, her days were empty. She liked Larry.
She liked to look at him. He had even longer hair than Jim
and gentler features. He talked differently, though he preferred to talk to several of the other girls. She was fifth or

sixth choice. She should not mind that. She was married. She was not supposed to mind if men ignored her, and besides, they mostly always had. But she did mind that he didn't like to talk to her as much as she liked to listen to him. She wished she knew all the names that danced through his talk. If she had been able to go to college, of course she would. Often Larry carried books with him and sometimes he would loan her a paperback.

As a child she had loved to read. She had especially liked novels about history or faraway countries or animals. The other girls used to tease her. Historical books were for girls, *The Little Maid of Bunker Hill*. But books about dogs and the sea—*Spike: Dog of the North* and *Treasure Island*— were supposed to be for boys. For a long time she had even gone on reading in high school, randomly in the school library and at the branch. If she liked a book by an author, she would read everything else by that name. Nobody paid attention to what she read, unless they were paperbacks. Then her father sometimes would pick up one with a sexy cover and throw it in the garbage pail. She read a lot of Frank Yerby and Galsworthy, but she also read all of Aldous Huxley and Iris Murdoch. On such books she formed her notions of what was out there, past Syracuse.

Gradually she had stopped reading. Partly it was knowing that they weren't going to let her go to college. The books had betrayed her, leading her to want what she could not approach. She had to work downtown selling after school her senior year, and it was hard enough to get homework done. Her grades should have suffered, but she was known to be a good if unexciting student, and no one seemed to notice that the work she did had fallen off. She spent any free time trying desperately to see Jim or managing to see him, or discussing him with Dolores, or covering up for having seen him. Withdrawing her energies from school and the world glimpsed in books, she had put everything into her romance. Then getting married had been a full-time occupation for weeks.

In the evenings now Jim watched sports on TV, baseball and basketball and football and racing when there was any. He also liked the comedies where the set kept laughing, so she would sit in a chair across from him and read while he watched, taking care to keep an eye on the set as she turned a page so she would know what to say when he spoke to her. She had begun bringing books home from the downtown library. She had originally gone in to kill time during bad weather, and besides she had walked over the whole downtown so many times she was tired of it. She spent her lunch hours picking out books to bring home.

Nancy clipped magazine articles for her about fixing up the apartment with what they called unusual accessories to give it a bold, dramatic look, but the few times she tried, all she created was a mess that made Jim ask, "Now what the hell is that?" She decided decorating would have to wait for that magical time when she could stop working. For now it was hard enough to keep the rooms straightened and moderately clean. She wished Jim would not drop his socks beside the bed when he took them off at night or scatter the paper on the floor or leave beer cans under his chair. But when she spoke to him, he got touchy and said she was nagging just like his mother, and she'd better quit it.

She was studying him, learning him, trying to please him. She picked out clothes mainly in blue now because it was his favorite color. She learned to sleep with the window shut and to iron shirts. She was friendly but not too friendly to Frankie's girls. She suffered his brother Dan to maul her. Yet Jim seemed to please her the same ways as before, or less: he aimed to please her with ritual gestures addressed to Any Girl. In bed he took her pleasure for granted. Before, when they had petted, he had made her come, but now he just pushed in and pumped away for a while until he had his orgasm. He always mumbled, "Um, was that good for you too, baby?" She was embarrassed to say anything, but she started wondering if that wasn't a form of lying to him. Finally she told him one night that it wasn't good for her. He called her frigid. "You better start shaping up as a woman!" He said he had been with plenty of girls, plenty, and they had all told him how good he was. In fact, they had scratched his back and moaned.

Finally she asked Marie. Marie told her that men expected you to act a certain way. She told Beth to notice how women acted in movies. That was how you were supposed to be, and Beth had better start doing it right, or she'd find herself out in the cold.

"But don't you ever feel pleasure? I mean, can't we?"

"That's a bunch of nonsense," Marie said with a grimace. "Just get it over with. Do you want him looking for it someplace else?"

Jim stayed mad at her until she began making noises like the movie actresses did. Then he loved her again.

She had never masturbated. She would have been afraid to touch herself there before, for fear she would rupture her virginity or get a disease. Now she began to make herself come with her finger as he used to before they were married. She would do it in bed after he fell asleep, so that she could slip free of the excitement trapped in her limbs and tissues. Then she too could sleep.

Since she was married, her mother and Marie talked to her differently. They complained about their husbands. They assumed a common level of grievance. That was being married. They saw a certain level of war as normal: women had to get things indirectly, wives had to plot and manage and evade. "You have to make him think he's getting his way," Marie warned. "Don't cross him directly. You have to coax him along." If she thought Jim was a slob, she ought to see Gene. Then Marie would begin tales of women whose husbands had left them suddenly after a month, a year, twenty years, forty years. Formerly Marie had been her ally against her mother, to escape to Jim; now Jim was suddenly the one to get around.

Their second summer together came to its height and died away brown. Larry returned to school, where he told her he lived in a commune with three other men and two women. She would have liked to ask him questions, but they all seemed too personal. Another young man was hired in records who played only the Top Forty. Though she was sorry when Larry said good-by, she guessed he would not remember her in a month. Never had fall seemed sadder, more full of things dying and flying away and fading. She took walks sometimes near their apartment and watched the blackbirds gathering above the weedy suburban fields that stretched between their bulldozed development and the next. Really there was no place to walk. One house was like another, and out on the highway people tooted and roared past in a smell of exhaust.

Something, something hung out there in music and birds wheeling against the dusk and crickets chirping in the weeds. Standing at the sink doing supper dishes on feet swollen from selling all day in Notions, she watched the moon rise orange and tarnished between two identical brick two-story apartments across the cul-de-sac. She was lonely. She felt she was perishing of loneliness. But how could she be lonely when she was married to Jim? Was everybody really lonely? Was Larry lonely in his commune? She asked Marie about loneliness and Marie snorted. "Lonely? Wait till you have children! Oh, I'd give my right arm to be alone for a day, just once!" But she was lonely with Frankie and Jim and Dan at the speedway in Cicero, and she was lonely with Jim sitting in the living room.

"Hamburger, spaghetti, macaroni, meat loaf—don't you know how to cook anything else? I might as well eat in a diner. Didn't your mother teach you one damn thing that's useful?"

"I'm tired when I get home—the same as you are."

"You think standing around in an air-conditioned store all day is work? Jesus, you ought to be out there doing some real work for a change. Now I don't want to come home to any more of these short-order meals. I didn't get married to eat shit!"

She could not understand the fuss he made about supper. For her it was something to be got out of the way so that they could have the evening to enjoy. She would just as soon eat some tuna fish, a peach, and a bit of cheese. He wanted meat, but then he lost his temper at the amount they had to pay at the supermarket and said she didn't know how to shop. She found it hard to believe how much he cared. After all, even if she fussed for an hour, supper was all eaten up in ten minutes and they were full and the difference between making something difficult and something easy was only in how tired she was afterward. His ideas of big meals seemed designed to rob her of the precious bit of energy left after eight hours standing behind the counter, the energy to suppress her aching feet and aching back, to steal a little of something sweet from the fading day.

When he looked at her that way, his gray eyes narrowed to slits of contempt, when his voice took on that edge of a saw, each tooth catching one by one in her throat, she had to hold tight to herself. A shrill of pain sang in her. She wanted to promise anything to make him look gently at her again, to make the lover reappear. The terror at the absence of love: coldness, coldness. If she got angry too, it did not work the same way. Experimentally she tried yelling back at him when he yelled.

"Why should I have to fix a six-course meal? Your mother, your mother, I'm tired of hearing about how great a cook she is! She doesn't have to work all day. You want me to quit? Fine! Let's live on your pay check."

"You throwing that in my face?" His hand gripped her shoulder, burned into it. "You talk like that and you won't see a pay check of mine till next Christmas!"

He did not grow fearful before her temper as she before his. Her attempts to express anger, to defend herself, ended in tears, in begging forgiveness, in taking back her words abjectly, in a sense of humiliation and insulted flesh and bruises. The upper hand, he called it. Keeping the upper hand. A man wore the pants, he said, or he was henpecked. After they fought she despised herself. Her mother and Marie were right. If she could never win, if fighting had such a price attached to it, then it was better to avoid the open fight, to turn aside, to make the soft answer and pretend not to hear and not to see and not to understand.

She felt as if he had developed jagged spikes that stuck out into her, so that she must retract not to encounter them. It seemed to her he became spinier and more angular and she became smaller and denser and compressed into a shape that would not touch off his alarm system. He was expanding and she was contracting. She began to suspect he enjoyed his temper, the temper he could not use at work where he was bottom dog. He was working at a garage owned by the man with the Ford dealership who was backing Dan—enough to get him hired but not enough to keep him from being subject to the other men's jokes and expendable. At home he got noisier and she got quieter. He seemed to shine when he was angry. After a fight he ate with a good appetite. He slammed out of the house to see the boys and had a few beers and came home to sleep soundly. She cried and clutched the pillow and rehearsed everything said and unsaid, what she would have said if she dared. Then one evening when he had slammed out, she picked up a novel about a married woman in France, by a Frenchwoman who had only a first name, Colette. The night before she had started it, and now she forgot everything in it—until she heard his car and leapt up, suddenly guilty.

That was the small miracle of that night, to discover that pain could be obliterated. Some of the records were as good if she concentrated on them. That gave her a measure of detachment when they had bad scenes, to think that she could sponge them at least briefly from her mind with something more real. How could a book be more real than a marriage?

Often now she found herself daydreaming while she was sweeping or waiting in the laundry room of the building across the street, or ironing or chopping vegetables. She had used to daydream, yes, in early and middle adolescence. But for three years she had lived in direct emotional weather, thinking about boys she went out with, thinking about boys she wanted to go out with, fingering her last encounters with Jim and imagining the next.

Now, as Jim's old lady, sometimes she was taken along and sometimes she was left home. Football games he tended to go to alone with Frankie or Dan because of the cost of the tickets and because they liked to drink. That Saturday she was home alone and started to sort a box of stuff her mother had dropped by, odds and ends from cleaning out her old room. Lots of photos of Dolores and herself in their bathing suits trying to look worldly wise, in back yards with their arms around each other, squinting against the glare of the Finger Lakes.

She got no further than the diary she had kept during her junior year. Somehow there had been no time for it her senior year, she was too tired at bedtime to write for half an hour to herself. By then she was oriented toward Jim. But all through the year she had turned from sixteen to seventeen, she had kept a diary. Reading it through, what struck her so sharply that she kept pausing and walking around the room holding it out from herself was how different, how exactly different her memories were from what she had written in the diary.

She had lied to herself. She had lied by omission and by alteration of the truth, constantly, daily, fervently, with many exclamation points. First of all she had lied always about how and when she met boys. All occasions were described in her diary as formal dates, when she could remember perfectly well that what she was writing about was her and Dolores hanging out someplace until some guys picked them up and they went with them, casually, dragging along. She had lied to the diary just as she lied to her mother. Because mothers had fixed ideas about the world that had nothing to do with the way things really were. No, it was not quite like lying to her mother, because all the boys got mentioned and there were details of kissing So-and-So and details of drag races where she was not supposed to be. She had not truly worried that her mother would read her diary. She might not always feel her mother loved her enough or was sympathetic with her, but she never thought her mother would pry in her dresser.

No, it was not her mother she was lying for. She remembered months when Dolores and she were twelve, thirteen, too young to go out with boys in any usual dating scene but obsessed with them. They had always been planning parties they were going to give, they had drawn up lists of boys and girls to invite and exclude. But of course it was all pretend, though they never admitted that. The parties came from movies, TV, Archie comics about teen-agers. None of them had family rooms. Where would they have had parties? Where would they have found the money to spend on refreshments? Things were supposed to be a certain way, and in her diary always she tried to pretend that they were. Never did she admit on paper more than kissing. Everything coarse and painful was censored from her life. Her diary was the record of how it was all supposed to be.

It seemed to her that always from the age when the great pressure began—eleven, twelve, thirteen?—until her wedding day she had been teetering on that verge between how everyone said things were and what really happened that you did not talk about, except a little with Dolores. The magazines said boys liked you, boys fell in love with you, and they wanted to but you waited and then it was beautiful. But it always seemed that a girl needed a boy a lot more than he needed you: your rating depended on him. He might be good at any one of a number of things and that would win him points. But no matter what else a girl did well, no matter what they said once a year on Honors Day, what counted was pleasing boys.

If your hair didn't please, you cut it or you curled it or you straightened it, and if your parents let you, you streaked it or dyed it. If your voice didn't please, you went around trying to talk in your throat. You did exercises supposed to make your breasts grow and your waist shrink, and always you dieted. You shaved your legs and under your arms and bought creams and lotions and medicines to fight pimples. The constant message in the air was that, if you didn't attract boys, you must change your body, rearrange your head, your personality, your ideas to fit in with what was currently wanted. Or else you were a failure. You were a dog.

So she had had little to bargain with. If you didn't satisfy a boy, he would drop you. If you had sex with him, he might drop you anyhow, and then if he talked, you'd have to go on doing it. So you had to work something out, as she had. It was a dangerous game with the prize marriage. And then what?

So she had won her love-and-marriage, but somehow that too was not the way it was supposed to be. Saturday night she put her old diary away, but she remained at odds with herself. She did not lie to herself in a diary now, no, she carried around daydreams like knitting, like the scarves and sweaters some girls used to carry around in high school and sit in class working on when they were supposed to be listening to the teacher. She carried her daydreaming with her in the car, to work, to bed.

Sunday morning she was straightening the house while Jim sat in his favorite recliner reading the funnies. She was also on a hill in Spain and the Fascists were closing in and planes had just flown over strafing them. Every one of their guerrilla band was dead except for her beloved and herself. He was dying of a wound in the chest and she too was badly wounded though not in any particular place. As she held his noble head in her lap looking like the photo of Hemingway on the back of the book she was reading, she made a speech about how good and beautiful it was to die under those particular circumstances. "And I regret I have but one life to give for my country and my beloved," she was saying when Jim's voice cut through. "What the hell do you think you're doing? Have you flipped out?"

She looked. It took her a moment to understand. Then she saw that, with the fine gesture of relinquishment with which she had waved away surrender and welcomed death with her beloved, she had emptied the ashtray filled to overflowing with butts and roaches and pistachio shells neatly into the open drawer of the end table, and the playing cards which she had gathered from the table she had tossed into the waste-basket.

She knew there was something shameful about living so much in a daydream, not only because she was returning to a period she thought she had outgrown in meeting Jim, but because there was something second rate about an imaginary life. Her best thinking was going not into living but into making up lives. All the rest of that Sunday she forced herself to fight daydreaming. Yes, daydreaming was a drug. It kept her quiet, it made the time pass better than being stoned.

By refusing to let herself dream away that Sunday she remained conscious of it. Conscious of the housework and how weary she was of doing it while he sat and watched her, littering the floor she had just cleaned and then complaining if the litter remained. Tired of spending Sundays at the races with his buddies and their girls. Tired of watching Jim drink himself bloated and silly or bad-tempered. Tired of him climbing on top of her. Tired of the whole mythology of love and marriage, which seemed much of a piece with the rest of her daydreaming. She had never known Jim and he didn't know her. Perhaps they did not even like each other. "Jim" was a character made up as she used to make over her daily life for her diary.

There had to be more than this! They were not really together. This could not be what they had wanted. She must get through to him. She could not let his annoyance smash her to silence but for once she had to touch him, to make him hear her out.

He wrinkled his forehead at her over the kitchen table. "What is it now? You don't like living here? This apartment?"

"I don't care where we live, honest. This is okay."

"What do you want then? Do you know what you're talking about?"

"Us. How we are to each other. What we want in our lives."

"You want to have a kid? Is that what it is?"

From the terror that touched her she knew that, whatever she wanted, that wasn't it. Why so afraid? Just a couple of months before she had imagined that very soon they would have a baby. She had brooded over names. Because then she would be trapped. Because then she could not leave.

Till that moment at the table she did not even know she had imagined leaving. Getting away. Escaping. From what? Him? Her family? The box. It was all the box. There had to be something more to living, there had to be, or there was no point.

She felt the undertow. What he was saying to her, her own trained obedient self said too: that she could not specify what she wanted. How could she want something if she couldn't even give it a name? All right, but if she had been so confined she had never seen the sun, the sky, she would still know there must be something beyond four walls.

"I want us to talk to each other! I want us to know each other! I want us to be . . . more people. To grow!"

The upshot of talking to Jim was that he had sex with her insistently and often and much of the time now his eyes watched her as she moved about the kitchen and the bedroom.

Staying together as they were meant that they would have children and buy a house and buy things to put in it. It meant never growing up. It meant never finding out what she wanted. It meant never entering into the heart of feeling except secretly through music, through the drug of daydream, for Jim through booze and drugs. She had never been on her own. She had learned none of the small skills by which people got around in the world. But everybody started ignorant. She was making excuses from the timidity she had been studying all her life, believing that she could not do anything, that she was not worth anything. Mittens pinned to her coat in grade school, Jim not liking her to drive their car, Mrs. James H. Walker, that strange opaque name she was supposed to sign, the softness of her hands and the weakness of her wrists, that had never learned to do anything useful.

Jim watched her. His gray eyes were wary and full of suspicion. He asked questions about phone calls and where she went and why and for how long. In bed he tried being violent, kissing her till her teeth ached and clutching her breasts so hard that in the morning there were bruises. Then he tried being gentle. He caressed her with his fingertips. He tried kissing her vagina. Through all the experiments he watched. Because he watched she tightened. She was aware of him waiting and she could not respond. Her body felt like a watch ticking. She wished that he had tried some of his experiments earlier, but now with those suspicious eyes and his anger banked and gathering interest, she could not breathe in bed with him. Her body mistrusted. She had to resume making the passionate moans she had learned.

She felt caught in the gray web of his gaze. His anger was muted but growing. She was something that was not working as it was supposed to. He was still trying to fix it. Soon he would lose his patience. Then would he return it or break it? One night as she was trying to fall asleep beside him she remembered something from the summer when she was ten. One Saturday at a company picnic that G.E. had every year with sack races and three-legged races and egg tosses and horseshoes and softball, there in the path Nancy and she had found a box turtle. He had a beautiful shell, divided into sort of shingles above and polished wood on the bottom. They brought him back and made a home for him in the yard. They put up a chicken-wire fence and built a house of broken bricks. All day the turtle went round and round the chicken wire, butting his head against the fence and standing up awkwardly on edge and flopping over backward trying to escape. In a book on reptiles she had taken from the branch library, it showed a picture of a turtle just like Roxy and said box turtles were easily tamed and made good pets. Round and round the fence Roxy went making a trail in the dust and rolling like a sad tank through the water dish and over the lettuce and grapes they had put down, and around again. Finally she felt so sorry she could not stand it. She bargained with Dick to drive her out to the country to let the turtle go where she had found it in return for the contents of her white piggy bank.

During the next week she kept thinking of the turtle. She was the turtle going round and round the chicken wire searching for a way out. But she did not want Jim to take her back where he had found her because that was a prison too. She studied herself as turtle. Turtles were not glamorous creatures. They were slow but dogged. Maybe it took them a long while to get someplace, even to figure out where they wanted to go, but then they kept stubbornly at it. They were not beautiful but they carried what they needed. They were not particularly brave and the idea of running from a wild

turtle would make a child laugh. Threatened, they had a
shell they could draw into and tuck up inside. They were
cautious and long-lived. No one could teach a turtle to do
tricks. They were quiet and could be mistaken for something
not really alive, a rock or a piece of wood. Sometimes they
aroused sadism in people. No great power had ever marched
out to conquest under the emblem of a turtle.

Real turtles had an advantage over self-proclaimed ones:
a real shell. They could shut out questions. Jim told Marie's
husband that Beth was not acting right. Now she was getting
a lot of flak from Marie and her mother. Every day one or
the other or both called her and gave her a dressing down.
Her mother turned up at work to mutter at her over the
scissors and pins. Thursday evening Marie and Gene came
over with the kids and told her she ought to have a baby,
what was wrong with her now? Somehow everything had got
simplified into Jim wanting her to get pregnant. Everyone
agreed that was both problem and solution. Her mother told
her that every woman was afraid at first, but every woman
went through it, that was what God had made them for.

Both Marie and her mother closed themselves off to her.
She would think they were responding, she would try to talk
to them. Once she started to cry and her mother touched
her on the shoulder and said, "There, there." But they were
the arm of authority. The next moment her mother was
calling her a crybaby. They had to press her back in line.
She was not behaving as a wife was supposed to. She sensed
that she scared them. She touched something in Marie, a sore
spot that made Marie nervous, until Marie responded by
yelling at her in the same voice she used to scream at her
kids. "Now you shape up, Bethie! We're ashamed of you!
Everybody has babies and nobody else makes a fuss!"

Her mother and her mother-in-law came over together.
Her mother spread herself smack in the middle of a blue
sofa. Her mother-in-law sat in Jim's favorite chair, the recliner. It had three positions. Mrs. Walker sat up straight
in it. Beth did not want to sit next to her mother so she sat
on the hassock that matched the recliner, which put her
down near the floor. They both told her loudly that it was
her duty as a wife to have a baby.

"He doesn't want a baby, either. He's just insisting on it
now because he's mad at me and he doesn't want to listen!"

"Don't spout nonsense," her mother said. "What should he listen to you about? What do you know? He wants what's good for the marriage."

"Jim does too want children. He always has," Mrs. Walker said. "And you let on that you wanted children too before you got married, so I don't know where you're getting all this now."

They glared at her and each other. Mrs. Walker said her mother had spoiled her. Her mother said she never had. Up until Bethie left home she had been a good girl and minded her mother and kept her room clean and never ran around the way some people's children did.

Friday she came home from work and made meat loaf. When they sat down at the table, she couldn't find her pills. She looked all over the table and then under it and then all around the kitchen counter. Finally, afraid already, she asked Jim.

"I poured them down the toilet." He made a gesture of flushing. "All down."

She ran into the bedroom to look in her dresser. He followed. "I flushed down next month too. No more pills. Now you'll have to shape up and do things the right way."

"Why are you doing this to me? I don't want a baby! I don't want one right now!"

"Well, you're going to. Because you're my wife and I love you, and you're supposed to love me. So you're going to have my baby, and from now on we're going to have a real marriage."

Her hands shook as she tried to eat. She could not swallow. She put down her fork and began to cry. He was willing to comfort her. He came and put his arms around her but she pulled away. "Don't pretend to be sympathetic! Don't pretend I'm just crying! I'm crying for what you did!"

"Okay, if you want to cry, cry. Look ugly if you want to. I don't have to sit and look at you." He went into the living room and turned on the set.

Sitting at the table, after a while she began to eat, chewing the meat loaf a bite at a time. A trapped animal eating a dead animal. She chewed and swallowed. He was willing to trap her. That made him the enemy. Who then was the ally? Only herself. Only the records and books that gave her energy. Only the Turtle Flag she was flying secretly.

That private morale-building was all very well. Turtles laid eggs in the mud and walked away, but she was going to be stuck. Always she liked to think in images, as if that were thinking! She chewed on the meat loaf, cold chunk by chunk. She was a lousy cook, he was right. The cafeteria where she sometimes ate lunch made better meat loaf. She would rather be cooked for than cook, which made her an unsatisfactory wife right there. She must not forget that again, if she was lucky enough to get out of here. Remember the cold meat loaf. From the refrigerator she got the ketchup and doused it liberally. Then it was less obnoxious. Meat, a dead animal that had been alive. She felt as if her life were something slippery she was trying to grab in running water. She could not stop thinking in pictures. She ground her teeth, tasting ketchup and gristle. She must think clearly about a course of action.

Come on, come on, she had been clever enough intriguing to see Jim. But although the weight of her family had pressed her one way, the weight of needing to have Jim, someone she belonged to, love and marriage, had pressed her even harder the other. Then she had been marvelously inventive in ways to get out of the house, in ways to explain where she'd been after work, after school. She had been stubborn enough when she refused to keep it hidden longer, insisting she had the right to see him and marry him. Come on, come on!

Okay, this was the second week of her cycle. If she did not take the pills she might ovulate. So she must not let him take her. She must get through the weekend. Monday she would escape. She could run away.

He did not like to have sex when she was menstruating. The month before last when she had forgotten to take the pill one evening, her period had started early. Could she persuade him that her period was starting tonight? Dipping a finger in the ketchup, she carefully worked her finger into herself, smearing ketchup on her genitals, on her panties. He would not disbelieve unless he could smell the ketchup. But he smoked and his nose was not half as keen as hers. She must take that chance.

After she washed her face and changed to the blue pants he liked the best, she came in the living room. "Would you like to do something tonight? How about a movie? Or we could drop in to Marie's or over to your mother's?"

They went to see Frankie and Jo. Jo had been Frankie's girl for three weeks. They talked about going to a movie or maybe going out to The Haven on the highway for dancing. They drank beer and played cards with the television on. Jim told Frankie the story of what he'd done to Beth. Everybody laughed and agreed he'd turned the tables on her. She just needed a little sense knocked into her, Frankie said, and Jo said that she could tell Jimbo was a real man. Frankie said that she was acting like the old Bethie now. She'd been getting too big for her britches but Jimbo had cut her down to size, and he put his arms around her and lifted her way up. Jim said he should watch whose wife he was putting his hands on, but they were all laughing and nobody minded but her. She was worried that Jim was drinking too much so he wouldn't care about her saying it was her period. But when they got home he was in a good mood and pinched her backside, saying she was his Little Girl again. She kept laughing nervously and trying to remember how she used to respond.

When it came time to undress, she went through the whole thing about "Oh dear, my period's starting! Now what should I do? I just had a period!"

"So what's the big deal? Once we're under way you won't have one for nine months, right?"

"I don't know, it seems kind of heavy. I hope nothing's wrong."

"You didn't take the pill, so it starts. That's happened before. If you're worried, call up the doctor Monday, ask him."

The weekend crept. Saturday he stuck to her all day, but she was acting submissive and she made a fancy meal in the evening. Even though the chicken came out leathery he seemed satisfied with the effort and relaxed his vigilance a little. By Sunday a light bleeding did begin and she could ease up on the ketchup. Sunday afternoon he had tickets to a football game with Frankie at Syracuse, and he did not even suggest that he wasn't going. The minute he left she began to plot her course.

She had forty-two dollars housekeeping money. She must risk going to the bank on Monday right after he dropped her off downtown—she would not go to work. She would head straight for the bank, sign his name as she often did— they knew her by now, she would choose a teller who cashed his pay check for her—and draw out half their money. She would take two hundred dollars. The important thing, she suspected from crime stories, was to get across a state border. She could not go to New York City. If only she could run away to college. . . . Of the girls in her high school who had gone to college, most had gone nearby to nursing schools or teacher's colleges. But when all the Spanish students in Syracuse had a fiesta, she had met a girl named Naomi Burns she had liked a whole lot. Naomi had said she was going away to Wellesley to school, outside Boston. . . . She would go to Boston. She had never been there, but she associated it with schools and music and symphony orchestras and historic sites and books and learning. Maybe there she would meet people like those in books, who lived as if they meant to do something.

How to get there? Jim kept the car with him. She must take a bus or a plane. She found Greyhound and Trailways in the yellow pages and called them up. She expected them to ask questions, but they just told her the schedule and how much tickets cost.

With airlines it was more complicated. The first one she called did not go to Boston, nor did the second. But the woman at the second told her to call Allegheny. It cost a great deal to fly, but there was a plane at eleven. She thought she would be less frightened to get on a plane and be in Boston in an hour and a half and disappear into the crowd. If she went by bus he might catch up with her, it took so long. A plane seemed more decisive. She would fly to Boston.

Packing: she could not carry a suitcase to work. For a moment she was dismayed by how little she could take. Then she mocked herself: she was lucky to get out with her skin. She would wear her raincoat Monday with the lining in. Carefully she sewed her best underwear and panty hose and a blouse and her bathing suit into the lining. She hesitated over the bathing suit, but it was a dark cobalt blue and one of the few things she had really loved, and swimming was the one sport she was good at. In the water, everyone was the same size.

Into the pockets she packed gloves and scarves and photos of her family and her own baby picture and herself at age ten on the swings in the park and herself with Jim last spring. Into the bottom of her purse she crammed her favorite summer dress—the one she had worn when they left the reception—rolled up in rubber bands with her favorite sweater.

Then she took a box that came from the department store where she worked and, folding carefully, managed to get into it two winter dresses, a pair of boots, a pair of shoes, and two pairs of pants. She put rubber bands or string around each item so nothing would bulge. Then she tied up the box and hid it under the bed. That plus whatever she could wear in various layers on Monday would have to do. She felt bad about leaving the records. But she would not have a phonograph. If she could ever afford to buy a record player, then she could buy the records again too. They were too bulky.

Mainly she worried about not taking her winter coat. It was a strange blue and green check her mother had got on sale, but it was a lot warmer than no winter coat. She paced and worried but could come up with no scheme by which she could smuggle a winter coat past Jim in the morning.

Again she did her best to make him the supper he seemed to want and again he accepted her efforts as gestures at making up. She was too excited, too apprehensive to eat. She kept up a stream of questions about the game and Frankie. It occurred to her that she was supposed to write a note about why she was leaving. She could not think of anything that she had not already tried to say, and she could not figure out where she could hide it that he might not see it before she was gone. Write a letter? No, it would have a postmark.

Sitting across from him, she did not hate him but she was gravely aware that he could still keep her, that he could still make her pregnant, that he could call her parents and they would not let her run away. She would forgive him once she was safely gone: she did not think he would forgive her. She was the sinner, the criminal. He had meant well, he said he loved her, though she had grown so mistrustful of that word she did not think she would ever again be able to use it except as she might say, I love to swim, or I love strawberries. I love to eat up Bethie. Bethie is mine. No, she would steal his property from him and belong to no one but herself.

In the morning he asked what the box was.

"Oh, a coat Marie bought. It's too big on her and I'm taking it back for a refund."

"I didn't think they made coats too big for that cow."

She coughed the fearful giggle that answered his jokes about her family. He thought he was obligated to make jokes. That was how a husband was supposed to talk about his in-laws.

When he dropped her off she got out of the car and waved as he drove away. Then she walked rapidly in the direction of the bank, three blocks down. Going past the closed doors of the department stores, she felt that scary excited feeling of cutting class.

At fifteen after eleven she was sitting in a window seat on a small jet. She had watched the businessmen ahead of her. Unless they were charging tickets, no one asked for identification. She said her name was Naomi Burns. The woman stamped her ticket and wished her a pleasant trip and told her to go to Gate 7. She asked Beth if she had any luggage, and Beth-Naomi gave her the tied-up box. The woman gave her a red stub and said she could reclaim her luggage at Logan Airport.

At eleven-fifteen the jet made noise and shook itself up as if it were about to explode and then it began running forward and went up into the air, tilting steeply. It was her first time, but she was not frightened. She said to herself that if she died on the airplane it would be better than not being there at all. She stared at the ground. The airport, the university, the highway that led to the thruway. The day was cloudy and soon she could see nothing but white and could not tell if they were upside down or right side up. She kept swallowing. Then they came above the clouds. Up here the sun shone and the sky was a dark hard clear blue like the bathing suit sewn into the lining of her raincoat, stowed above her in the rack. She clasped her hands and joy pierced her. She was wiry with joy and tingling. How beautiful to be up here! How beautiful was flight and how free (even though it cost money). She was the only flying turtle under the sun.

3

Welcome to the Sexual Revolution

In Boston she was lonely, but her loneliness for the first four or five months was a positive thing, a free space she thrived in. With everything she tasted and tried, she studied herself suspiciously: do you really like this? She must never again choose by what tasted good to somebody else, even what tasted fine to everybody else. "You can't taste with anybody else's tongue," she wrote on the wall.

The first time it had occurred to her to write on the wall beside her bed, she had stood with a marking pen in her hand for twenty minutes, unable to deface the surface. Not that it wasn't ugly, cracked and crisscrossed with scars and scabbed with plaster and caked with layers of paint. The top layer was scum green, with pink showing through. Her room was in a warren of a building in Back Bay near the subway —not the Back Bay of neat brick row houses but the blocks of large decaying tenements. The subway was a funny one where trolley cars ran in the ground pretending to be a subway train. She took it five mornings a week to connect with a real subway, which in turn took her to M.I.T. where she worked.

She had a bed and a dresser and a small desk and a wobbly metal table and a hot plate and a small refrigerator and a lavatory for washing dishes and herself. The wee bathroom was equipped with a shower stall and toilet. The only window faced a building six feet away. Mice ran in the walls and nibbled her cereal and crackers. Traffic from the street echoed in the alley.

Nevertheless she loved her room. She loved the mattress with bloodstains and a circular hole and a ravine in the middle. She loved the dripping shower and the hot plate that took fifteen minutes to get warm and never did get too hot to sit on. She loved the closet with the door that would not shut. She loved the man's plaid bathrobe that had been hanging there when she moved in and that she wore even though it was too big. At least the robe was woolly and warm, while the room was frigid. She made love to her room by writing mottoes on the wall and by making patchwork curtains out of remnants from the sale tables downtown at Jordan Marsh. Those curtains glowed and kept out the winter wind. Slowly she was filling the room with books. She had discovered secondhand stores where used paperbacks were cheap. On Saturday she liked to go to the bookstores and search the tables for her next week's reading.

At first she ate from cans, but gradually, wandering on Newbury and Boylston, she discovered health food and natural food stores. The revulsion toward eating flesh from the night of the meat loaf remained. It was part superstition and part morality: she had escaped to her freedom and did not want to steal the life of other warm-blooded creatures. She ate brown rice and whole-grain breads and granola and muesli and cracked wheat and lentils and navy, lima, mung, marrow, kidney, and turtle beans. She learned from a clerk at Erewhon how to sprout beans on a dish. Always she had liked breakfast, cereals and breads and eggs, so now she would eat breakfasts all day long, instead of the fuss her dad had called dinner and Jim supper. Whatever they called it, she had always hated it. Her dad ate rapidly, bent over his plate, but he kept an eye on the kids and told them to mind their manners. It was the time of day he came home and became boss. It was growl time for him, complaint time for Mother, whine and poke and nudge time for the kids. No, every person should eat quietly, without fuss.

She found cheeses she savored: port salut and camembert and boursin. For many years her mother had used frozen vegetables, and she was surprised how good raw vegetables tasted. She discovered yogurt and sour cream and ricotta.

She carried a lunch to work that she could eat gradually, nibbling through the day, and on her lunch hour she audited classes. Much of what went on at M.I.T. was incomprehensible but she had found subjects that interested her. Mondays, Wednesdays, and Fridays she sat in on Shakespeare, and Tuesdays and Thursdays she listened to European History from 1640 to 1900. Three mornings a week she came to campus an hour early for a small class on Cervantes, conducted in Spanish. At first she had trouble following the lectures. The registrar's office had told her she could not be a student, but she had only to be unobtrusive or, as with Professor Hernandez, to beg permission.

When she returned to the computer center, she passed over an invisible boundary. Students had a way of acting toward each other that she experienced as she walked around campus carrying her books, chatting before class—the way that the few students who recognized her from class spoke to her when she ran into them. But she became an invisible robot when she entered the center. All the troubles with the computer were visitable on her head; the nuisance of misplaced runoff or lost data, suddenly active bugs in the programs and being bumped from the computer, could all be blamed on her because she was no longer a person but a function.

In January she got a less harassed job over in Tech Square, as secretary to a project involving biochemists and a graduate student in computer sciences. Instead of dealing anonymously with hundreds of students who treated her as automatically stupid, she had only to take orders from eight people. Professor Owasa had hired her. She had lied to him about her age and education, taking the chance that he would not bother to check her references. He hadn't. Yes, the job was less harried and less unpleasant, but gradually she began to feel her isolation.

She sat at the little desk out front of Professor Owasa's office, off a corridor up in the tall office building. When she walked along the corridors with the brightly colored doors that reminded her of kindergarten blocks, she saw many other rooms in which one or two secretaries sat at desks like hers, secretaries to professors or to projects. In other rooms students sat typing at electric typewriters connected over phone lines to one of the big computers upstairs. Here and there were small lounges. The building was in use twenty-four hours a day, and in some of the offices she saw cots and couches. The atmosphere among the almost entirely male students and faculty tended to be loose and joking, but it was not easy to get to know other secretaries isolated in their offices.

The younger secretaries told her about their sex lives, for

she had become an automatic older woman as a divorcee.
Saying she was divorced saved explaining. She imagined Jim
would divorce her for desertion eventually. She did not feel
secure enough to let him know where she was. The older
secretaries worked much harder at their jobs and were nice
to her though they thought her peculiar. It was funny to be
an older woman. Most of the girls had had more experience
with men than she had. But she liked to listen.

At least two of the people who worked on the project were
friendly to her and did not treat her as a robot. Tom Ryan,
a fourth-year graduate student, had lived in her building
briefly in between separating from his wife and moving into
an apartment in Cambridge. He was unusually small for a
man, barely taller than Beth and slight: but he was twenty-
five and close to his doctorate. The other person who spoke
to her in a personal way was a big flamboyant woman who
was a graduate student in computer sciences.

She could not remember exactly when Miriam Berg had
first singled her out to notice. But one day while Beth was
eating a fig surreptitiously, Miriam tapped her shoulder. "If
you give me one, I won't report you to the campus cops. Why,
you can't do anything as human as eat on this project."

So Beth gave Miriam a Calmyrna fig and Miriam ate it.
She said figs looked funny when you really took a look at
them, they looked like candied balls, didn't they?

Beth looked at the white fig she had bitten and smiled.
"I never looked at balls that carefully. If I ever get a chance,
I'll try to notice."

Miriam, who had perhaps been seeing if she could be
shocked, because that would be like her, smiled more broadly
and after that always stopped to chat with her. Sometimes
Miriam brought her little gifts of a pear or an apple. Miriam
was the only person in the world who knew she was a vegetarian, because no one but Miriam had enough curiosity
about her to find out. Miriam reminded her of Dolores—and
perhaps that was why she had not been shy with her—with
her long black hair and her extravagant full body and Dolores'
way that if you had it you might as well flaunt it. Miriam
dressed vividly and moved like a dancer. She was taller than
Dolores and her clothes were more exotic. She was halfway to
a doctorate and always referred to as brilliant, although
with that word often went something disapproving like "bitch"

even from some of the men on their project. She exuded a
sexual aura she seemed well aware of, and one she enjoyed
as much as any passer-by. She annoyed people. Sometimes
the other secretaries on the corridor gossiped about her, but
although Beth listened with interest, she learned little except
that Miriam was supposed to have too many boy friends at
the same time.

In Beth's classes, when students found out she was not
really a student, they seemed to lose interest. From jokes she
overheard she knew that the men who worked on the projects
in her building thought the women worked there looking for
husbands. They looked her over without interest in the corridors, at the coffee machines, but never started a conversation. She began to feel she was going to spend her life
traveling the subway between M.I.T. and her room without
ever making a friend, that if she disappeared or were run over,
no one would even know. Her head bubbled with ideas and
the solitary pleasures of her new fresh life, but she had no
one to talk them over with. She felt as if her voice were
rusting.

Then the first Tuesday in April Tom Ryan asked her out.
He had sent her upstairs to pick up his print-out. He was
pleased with the results and held out the sheets to her, an
accordion-folded pile of perforated paper with writing on it
all in numbers and capital letters. "By God, it's true you can
make anything look good with numbers if you keep at it long
enough, Beth my girl. If you're just a bit clever . . . Aw, the
wonders of science. . . . How would you like to take in a
flick tonight?"

She felt scared for a minute. Dating. Back to the fence-
walking of high school. She did not find Tom Ryan particularly attractive, a thin small man with reddish hair and a
pointed face like a fox. But she was curious what a man who
was twenty-five and so educated would be like, and she was
grateful too because he often spoke to her. She hesitated, not
saying yes or no.

"Now, I'm not into that dating crap. There's a good Czech
film at the Orson Welles. Wait a minute, I'll check the
schedule. You can meet me there."

"Yes," she said quickly then, in case he might change his
mind. Maybe it would not be the same as high school. Maybe
men and women could be friends here and do things together

and have long good conversations. When it became clear she had never been to the Orson Welles and had in fact been nowhere in Cambridge except M.I.T., he said he would take her this time, because obviously she must not have her passport in order. He explained at length that he usually had a car but tonight it was in the garage being tuned.

After the movie he said, "Come on, we'll do the guided-tour bit, the Square, Harvard and environs, walk along the Charles by moonlight, phantom sculling, Georgian brick, etc. You aren't one of those overdelicate females who can't walk on their feet, are you? One of those held together with little gold wires and hair lacquer? Good, good, I thought you were put together a little solider. Walking's good for you—healthy, cheap, what have you." He gripped her by the elbow, his fingers like clothespins. Propelled her along. She hardly understood half of what he was saying but he would not let her interrupt for questions. The only pause in the swirl of words was when he chuckled at one of his remarks.

She had never walked much except in the development where she had lived with Jim, and there she had felt thwarted. Then she had walked for escape, in search of another world on the next street where there stretched only identical two-story buildings or a ragweed-grown field. Walking was something she could manage even with her short legs. Along the Cambridge bank of the Charles they marched along, on the grass just getting green between the slow-moving smelly river and the cars whizzing past on Memorial Drive. The night was mild and soft, one of the first sweet nights of the spring.

"Boston has a low silhouette—like a European city, like Paris or Florence—except for the ugly towers they're putting up every chance they get. That Prudential monstrosity was the first."

"Have you been to Paris?"

"Of course. Though only as a tourist. I'd like to spend a year working there. I meant to do that before now, only I got married too young and that was stupid. Don't you think you were stupid to get married so young?" This time he did pause for a reply.

"Not stupid. I think I was well trained."

"But you think it was a mistake, or do you? Or do you think that was just Mr. Wrongo and now you're looking for Mr. Right to slip it on again?"

"I don't want to marry again, if that's what you mean. I didn't care for marriage."

"It's two people trying to wear one shoe at the same time."

"Or a three-legged race." The company picnics of her childhood. She had to explain that. He attached a sexual meaning to three-legged.

He took her to the subway station in Central Square, where he went back toward Harvard Square and she went into Boston. He had not touched her except for that bony grip on her elbow. She had enjoyed the evening and in the next week she thought of him as she did her work.

When she did see Tom again it was on a day when he was running more data through the computer. Just before five, he came to her. "If you aren't doing anything exciting for supper, you ought to come home with me. Yes, come on up and see my etchings. I'll introduce you to my fifty roommates. Even if there aren't any etchings, I can show you the worst, the totally worst and biggest nudes in all of Greater Boston, green as grass and ugly as a horse's back end."

"Green nudes? Do you mean paintings?"

"I mean throwings. Why, a chimpanzee with a paintbrush would do better. You coming?" When she nodded he guided her out with his fingers gripping her elbow again. "Him and his girl friend Chlorine. He paints her nude. Though she doesn't look any worse that way than with her clothes on."

"Is her name really Chlorine?"

"Would I lie to you, Beth my girl?"

He lived on Pearl Street in a three-story shabby tan house that appeared not quite straight in the lines of the floors, the walls, even the windows, as if the whole building had slipped somehow to the south. In this neighborhood there were mostly two- and three-story wooden houses set right up against the brick sidewalks and close to each other. She climbed the stairs behind him as he chattered on, all the way to the top floor. The door was unlocked. A man sat with his back to them. In khaki pants and a shirt hanging open on his tall wiry body, he bent over a desk made from a door on iron legs. "Hi, Tom."

"Well, are we inviting all the neighborhood junkies in? Iron bars do not a prison make, nor locks a cage. Would it be hopelessly bourgeois to go down to the locksmith and get a new lock put on the door?"

"Haven't you introduced her because you're afraid to? Or does she maybe not have a name?" He had a slow and patient way of speaking, as if translating from another, internal language. Slowly and gently the words came out and stood awhile, waiting.

"Jackson, Beth, etc. Be careful not to shake hands with him, Beth, or you'll get a social disease. How come you're home tonight?"

"Because I was fired last week, as I told you, if you ever listened. I'm working on a paper for one of my many incompletes."

"Are we disturbing you then?" Tom took two quick steps in the direction of the room beyond.

"Disturbance is something I always like, along with interruptions and diversions and anything except work. Besides, I'm just typing the paper—if you can call it typing. Lennie hawked all his papers early and got back, so I sent him to the store."

"Jackson, you order Lennie around too much. Just because he's younger." Soft voice from the doorway. She was only a few inches taller than Beth but fuller-bodied, with bittersweet chocolate hair frizzed around her ears and a heart-shaped plaintive face.

"Come on, Dorine." Jackson screwed up his forehead. "But he can't cook, you know. I cook, Tom here fixes things."

"I've noticed that," she said sharply, then looked embarrassed, seeing Beth? "Hello?"

Jackson introduced them, tilting back in his chair. His age was hard to guess, except that he was older. His eyebrows were raised a little habitually, cutting a sharp line across his forehead. His dark brown hair was long and straight, caught back in a rubber band, and under the overhead bulb a few silver hairs shone. A shadow of dark stubble emphasized the lines at the corners of his mouth and eyes. The lines belonged. Gazing at him in a series of quick, cautious glances, Beth could not help but guess patience, suffering, an honest intelligence. His eyes were a light sandy brown, with the kind of gaze she kept finding herself tangling with involuntarily until she would again drop her own. He was so homely she found him attractive, and instantly suspected that such must be the case with many other women: dangerously homely. She found herself inclined to trust an attractive homely man over an attractive handsome man, especially since she knew she had loved Jim with her eyes.

"Where's kitty? Oh, here you are." Dorine scooped up a dusty gray kitten from the desk. With piercing mews it skittered up her arm, clinging with tiny sharp claws. Kneeling on a daybed covered with a yellow and black Mexican blanket, Dorine caressed the kitten and watched Jackson peck at the keys. "You really don't know how to type."

"Inadequate again. Been at this since noon."

"If you want me to, I'll do a few pages while we're waiting for Lennie to get back."

With no pretense of reluctance, Jackson sprang up. "You're saving my life. Meantime, I'll get started on supper."

Tom followed Jackson back through the rooms and Beth trailed after, looking right and left and up and down. The second room was larger but of a staggering disorder. From the central light socket a web of heavy extension cords wound among and under the furniture. Bright green jagged nudes on canvases were stacked against one wall and more leaned against the wall of the corridor beyond. Bookcases up to the ceiling. Records without jackets, cups with dregs of coffee, plates serving as ashtrays. Off a narrow corridor, one bedroom was relatively neat. "That's my room," Tom said over his shoulder. "The one that doesn't stink." Then a second room with a mattress on the floor and all other space taken up with canvases. Then three steps led down to the kitchen. The kitten chased after them, attacking her feet.

"You will notice that Dorine washed the dishes this afternoon," Jackson said, running water into a pot.

"Is that good for them?" Tom walked past the sink, shaking his head. "Won't they wear out?"

"By the by, Laverne called."

Tom stopped abruptly. "When?"

"About five-fifteen."

"Why didn't you tell me?"

"I just did."

"Sit you down, Beth my girl. Watch the master chef perform. I have to make a business call, just a quickie."

As Beth sat at the round oak kitchen table, the kitten climbed her leg and rolled over in her lap. Jackson was cooking and paying her no attention. She felt awkward, parked there in a strange kitchen. Only the kitten perceived her, seizing her hand in four dusty gray paws and beginning to gnaw. She finally thought of something she could say. "What do you call this kitten?"

He did answer her, although he did not turn around. "That depends, that depends. Named Orpheus because we fished him from a sewer."

"What was he doing in a sewer?"

"Drowning." Jackson paused with spoon lifted high, scratching himself slowly over his bare chest. "How he stank. Incredible for something so small."

Still he faced the stove and said nothing more. Minutes crept over her. Something to say, something! "You're a graduate student?"

"At B.U. I was out of school for years. I wouldn't like you to think my hair was turning white in the struggle."

"Why did you go back?"

"A friend talked me into it." He stirred the pot round and round and said nothing else for five minutes. Then he mumbled, "I was out of my mind. So was she. So was she."

At least if she kept asking questions he answered something. "What are you studying?"

He did turn then and suddenly tousled her hair with his hand. "You're out of *Alice in Wonderland*, all those questions. Political science—which is not science and neither holy, Roman, nor an empire."

With his gesture and his way of talking mainly for himself he made her feel ridiculously young—as if she had looked out through his sandy eyes and saw herself on a par with the kitten. She held the kitten on her lap and gave up trying to talk to him. Finally Tom Ryan came back muttering to himself, and the third roommate, who was called Lennie, arrived behind a bag of groceries. Lennie was thin and bony, with a dark kinky beard, heavy glasses, and large sad nose, though his hands were well formed. Dorine stuck close to him. Jackson took out shrimp and carried them to the stove. By luck she would be able to eat everything. That was like a blessing on her excursion. It was a new and curious world. The men talked to each other as a kind of playing. Instead of slapping each other and poking and punching the way Jim and Frankie and Dan did, these men poked and tickled and slapped each other with words. Mainly she and Dorine sat on the sidelines and watched the words go by.

At supper everyone ate buffet style in the middle room. Apparently the first room at the entrance was Jackson's, and the cot with the Mexican blanket was his bed. "But how can he have any privacy?" she asked Tom quietly.

"Aw, but now Jackson sleeps alone." Tom smiled at something.

But that wasn't what she meant. Privacy was precious to her. Never until Marie married had she had a room to herself, and even then nobody bothered knocking. The walls had been paper thin and she could always hear every cough and shoe dropped and flush of the toilet.

Lennie had put a blues record on the turntable. They did not have a phonograph but what they called a system, which had parts: turntable, speakers, amps. The music that emerged was rich. To listen to music that full was sensuous and electrifying: it was swimming music, it could almost be drowning. As they ate, from the open windows mild spring air sifted through the rooms rustling papers and swaying the matchstick bamboo blinds.

Lennie dug into the pockets of the army surplus jacket he had not removed. "Anyone for anchovies? Or fancy mixed nuts?"

"Hey, Raskolnikov, we're going have to bail you out," Tom warned but reached for the nuts. "Why boost anchovies? They taste like the canned food we give that miserable cat."

"Because I love them." Dorine took the can. "Thank you, sweetie. Why do you call him Raskolnikov?"

"Because he looks like a wild man hatchet murderer. Ask our dear neighbor downstairs. She faints at the sight of him."

"Okay, Napoleon," Lennie said. "Little and mean and crafty, a general nuisance and generally devious."

"Now I may be little, I may be mean, but I'm an Irishman. And no Irishman was ever caught dead at a place named Waterloo. Unless he thought it was a urinal."

Jackson looked at Tom sadly. "That, I think, is a joke you shoplifted from Phil."

"One Irishman is like another. Just like people say about Chinese, they all look alike," Lennie said.

"I'll give you an easy way to tell us apart." Tom started to grin. "I still have my head. Philip Francis Boyle's is nailed to the wall of a certain lady collector—"

"Who am I?" Dorine chirped nervously. Something lurked

under the talk. Dorine was trying to get them away safely. "Sonia? Am I Sonia, if he's Raskolnikov?"

Jackson came around with a bottle, refilling glasses. "You're Lady Godiva. For your kind heart, of course."

The jagged green nudes. They had bodies you could cut yourself on. Women of broken glass and metal: nothing like Dorine. She was soft and squishy and nervous to be liked, sitting there apologetic for taking up space.

"Who's Jackson?" Lennie asked. "Socrates?"

"I fancy myself a Christ figure." Jackson posed against the wall with arms outstretched. "For my saintly humility, my absolute Christian poverty, and my patience with all of you sinners."

"No, man." Ryan smiled. He had the look of a fox sometimes, a tame slightly seedy fox, perhaps one born in a zoo. His eyes saw a great deal out of the corners. She was not used to a man who observed people carefully. "I know the parallel. Tannhäuser."

"Who?" Jackson looked blank.

"Jackson lacks culture, don't you think?" Tom clucked to Lennie, who nodded sadly. "Tannhäuser was a knight who escaped after being held prisoner a long time in the Venusberg."

Jackson looked at Tom steadily and his skull seemed to harden and come forward in his face. "Not very original, man. That too is Phil's baggage. Don't you get weary of dressing up in other men's ideas and other men's wit?"

Tom looked young and sullen. "You take yourself too seriously. Phil only thought up calling her Venus. The Venusberg is a higher-level joke."

"Who am I?" Beth asked. But Jackson was giving Tom that unwavering stare and Tom was acting out being unmoved and Lennie was looking worried. No one heard except Dorine, who smiled at her with a shrug. Almost immediately they broke up into the two couples, leaving Jackson. Fingers on her elbow, Tom led her to his room. "What was that all about?" she asked him.

"Oh, just a ball breaker Jackson was mixed up with. She left this guy Phil—a drunken would-be poet—for Jackson and then vice versa. You know her—that big loud-mouthed Miriam Berg. See, that was the pun that got to Jackson. To me it's just a joke. You know how a woman like that makes it. She gets her grants flat on her back. . . . Jackson too, he comes on like Abraham Lincoln. But he's just a fringe academic character. The coffee shops are full of failures like him, all words and no publications. Pretensions and empty pockets and a résumé full of jobs like janitor and ditchdigger. Don't let him fool you with the somber gaze and the big words."

She understood she was to ask no more questions about Jackson or he would allow his jealousy—of what? Jackson's presence? style? what Tom would call moral pretensions?—to annoy him into being unpleasant to her.

He had seized the wine bottle and taken it along, and now he poured more for each of them. He pressed the harsh red wine on her insistently. She had sat down in the only chair, a comfortable leather swivel armchair that seemed a different order of furniture from everything else in the apartment. Well, he had been married. "Did you bring this from your house when you moved?"

He nodded. "Pretty good chair, isn't it? But why don't you come over here with me?"

She hesitated. He was sitting back on the bed. So far except for gripping her elbow he had not touched her, and she had not sensed desire from him.

"Come on, you aren't going to act coy now, are you? I mean, we're both consenting adults and you don't expect to be courted, I hope? You know why you're here. Let's go to bed."

"I don't know if that's why I'm here. Maybe that's why you asked me. But I came along because I'm curious about you and your friends."

"Well, how do you expect to get to know me, sitting over there? Come on, don't play games with me. I can't take that. You're interested or you're not—no music is going to start to play or roses pop out of my ears. I'm not going to force you into anything. You want to or you don't, and I'll take you home. It's your choice."

People here went to bed with each other much more quickly than she would have permitted anything beyond kissing back home. In a way she was glad to be relieved of the responsibility of metering herself into doses, deciding if she could permit the hand on the breast through the sweater, the hand under the sweater, the hand on the thigh. Fear had always been mixed with excitement, the fear of making the mistake. But to decide before she even knew someone that she was going to pop in bed with him—men had surely invented that rule. She felt no desire toward Tom. She could not imagine wanting to be touched on her body by someone she did not know well. However, there did not seem to be a great deal of choice for women here any more than there had been at home. Either she refused, and then she would never come here again and explore the new world that had opened—for she could just imagine appearing on the doorstep, hi, I've come visiting, can I stay to supper—or she accepted as an instant lover this strange foxy man sitting on the bed fixing her with his bright narrow blue eyes and waiting for her to deliver herself to him. She still knew no one in Boston. It might be months before anyone else noticed she was alive. Sighing, she got up and went over to sit beside him on the bed.

He kissed her a few times pleasantly and she was just beginning to think perhaps she could enjoy being with him when he left off and began to remove his clothes. So she got undressed too and they climbed into bed. She noticed that he did not have an erection. Once they were in bed he put his arms around her and began to caress her, but he began talking again, compulsively, bitterly talking.

"That was Laverne who called, my ex-wife. She says I can't see my children this Sunday. Bonnie's invited to a birthday party. Laverne makes out it would be this terrible deprivation, this social disaster, for Bonnie not to go. As if a four-year-old kid knows what a birthday party is. It's the mothers who dig that sort of thing. Kids couldn't care less, they end up throwing the cake at each other and fighting over the toys they're supposed to give to the birthday boy. And she says my baby, Tommy, Jr., she says I gave him a cold last time. Which is a lousy lie."

His fingers cruised on her body, hard and grasping and nervous. His bony shoulder pressed on hers, his mouth was against her ear. It was almost as if he caressed her to compel her to stay and listen. As if she might run away if he did take off her clothes and nail her down to the bed. People were stranger than she had ever realized. She wished there were some way she could communicate to him that she would willingly listen to his troubles sitting across the room in the comfortable chair. Perhaps he could not talk that way. Perhaps he needed the touch of vulnerable naked flesh.

"She's making Bonnie into her. And she'll do the same to Tommy if I don't stop her. See, Laverne is beautiful, nobody could deny that. When I met her she used to do occasional modeling for the department stores. You know, she's a bit taller than me, but that never bothered either of us. A man is as big as he feels. When she walks into a room, even today, after she's had two kids, every man turns around to look. I like a woman who can wear clothes, a woman with style. Not one of your fleshy cows like Miriam Berg. But Laverne's trying to make Bonnie a little fashion plate too. She wants to keep both kids near Mama and make them just like Mama and deny me my rightful share in my own flesh and blood."

He did not actually enter her that night but made her come with his hand and had her do the same. When she got up to dress, he urged her to come back to bed.

"I'd just as soon go home. Besides, I have an eight o'clock class."

"Didn't know you were in school. Okay, okay, I'll drive you to M.I.T. in the morning. Please. Come on, stay with me. I don't like to spend the night alone."

Sleeping with him was difficult on account of restlessness. Mumbling, grinding his teeth, he rolled and bucked and occasionally his outflung arm would strike her. Still he seemed vulnerable in sleep. She thought to herself, as long as she was clear about him and did not confuse convenience and curiosity and fringe benefits and ordinary human concern with real affection, no damage would be done. Curled in a tight ball way on her side of the bed, she fell asleep playing a Bach concerto for two violins that Larry had used to put on sometimes early, just after the store opened.

When they got up everyone else was still asleep. He seemed to expect her to make breakfast so she did in a perfunctory manner. He shaved while she got things on the table and then he turned on the news. They ate across the table like a couple married ten years or two strangers sitting beside each other in the subway. The kitten mewed and begged till she put down some cat food.

As they left, the front end of the apartment was still heavy with the smell of grass. She would have preferred to share some rather than drink the cheap harsh wine all evening. Sometimes she had smoked grass with Jim. As she followed Tom out to the door with the broken lock, she glanced at Jackson asleep on his cot with only a sheet pulled over his long body and the yellow and black Mexican blanket folded at the foot. He was breathing in deep sleep. The kitten climbed the cot, galloped across his chest, and curled into his armpit without waking him. One long arm was clasped over his chest holding the sheet to him, and the other was hanging off the cot's edge. His left shoulder was seamed with a strange purplish scar. His hand dangled open, not quite limp, as if it were grasping at something in the air. Tom going ahead of her into the hall was already into a monologue about his thesis adviser and his peculiarities and the handles by which he could best be manipulated, and she was glad he never looked over his shoulder to catch the fascination with which she stopped to examine Jackson sleeping.

4

Come Live with Me and Be My Love

Two or three afternoons a week Tom would arrive at the office at a good time for bringing her back to his place for supper and the night. He said her room was a rathole. She was glad he did not want to sleep there, leaving her privacy intact. Much of her interest in seeing him was wanting to spend time in his apartment with the relaxed meals, the strange banter, the music she could immerse herself in. They had more than a hundred records. The third evening she got Jackson to show her how to work the system. Saturday mornings she no longer went religiously to browse the second-hand books. On the shelves of the Pearl Street apartment she could find books as rapidly as she read them. Usually there was grass. She drank the wine with supper but not afterward. Now that Tom understood she would go to bed with him on demand, he did not press the wine on her.

They teased her about not eating meat. Jackson called her Peter Rabbit: they had chosen an identity for her. Still they let her eat what she chose and did not hassle. Except for Dorine, who tried to pressure her into sharing the housework.

"If you get married, you'll get cleaning out of your system," she said to Dorine firmly.

"Do you think Lennie will? Marry me?"

Dorine told her Lennie had been in love with a girl who had died, either committing suicide or O.D.ing, Dorine was not sure because Lennie refused to talk about it. The girl had been blond and beautiful and Lennie had painted her—perhaps he still was. Dorine would always be second best, but she accepted that. Perhaps Dorine thought that was all she was worth. Desperately she wanted Lennie to want to marry her, so desperately she could hardly bring up the subject with him. Two months earlier she had moved in. She knew that Tom Ryan did not like her, and she was glad he was thinking of getting an apartment alone. This was news to Beth.

"I'll tell you something else you don't know," Dorine whispered in the kitchen, motioning her closer. "Tom isn't divorced the way he tells you. He's just separated from Laverne. I think he'd go back in a flash—Lennie thinks so too. We don't want you to get hurt."

She thanked Dorine. However, if Dorine could have heard Tom muttering on and on about Laverne and Tom, Jr., and Bonnie, Dorine would not have bothered warning her. Beth was Tom's hot-water bottle. She believed Tom had sex with her mainly to assert his possession, his right to her ear and comfort. Sometimes he would put her hand on his cock, sometimes he would push into her. Either way he was not with her but off in his head, sweating and trembling and going rigid as a board and clenching his teeth. Whether he was coming into her hand or inside her, they were equally unconnected.

Often they saw movies. He chose them, in part because she knew nothing of Czech films or old thirties comedies; but she did not think he would have consulted her if she had. Anyhow, she enjoyed going. She was uneasy about him paying their way. Certainly he had little more money than she did. However, she settled it as fair since he chose the movies and since that was the only expense he did come by in seeing her—she kicked into the supper fund and gave a few dollars whenever Jackson went to make a deal for dope.

Once in a great while they did something else. They heard an all-Mozart concert that Professor Owasa had given him tickets to. One Thursday night in mid-May they went to a coffeehouse to see someone perform they all seemed to know, since Lennie and Dorine, though not Jackson, went with them. When they arrived the singer had not yet begun. The room was only twice the size of the apartment and people were buzzing to each other. Dorine hurried to a table up front where Miriam sat, who jumped up and hugged her. The man who had been sitting with Miriam, head on hands, paid no attention. All Beth could see was a shaggy blond head and a dark blue turtleneck and the hands dug into his hair. Those fingers would have looked gaunt and spidery if they had not already been tanned. Tom was gossiping about his department with another man and Lennie had gone behind the small stage, so after a while she got up and drifted over to the other table.

"Well, of course it would be better if there were just the two of you. Maybe I can get you that job, so you'll be able to afford it. But if Ryan does move out, it won't be nearly so tense, right? I mean, you get on with Jackson," Miriam was saying.

"Oh, Jackson's easy to get along with. . . . I mean . . ."

"As long as you don't try to come close," Miriam said dryly, shifting the rough multicolored shawl more closely about her. She was wearing a long red gypsy dress with her glossy black hair curling over the shoulders and tangling over the shawl. Her large dark eyes were fixed intently on Dorine, her hand resting on Dorine's shoulder. Her coloring seemed ruddier than ever, perhaps from a day's exposure to the sun: she glowed like a light bulb.

At Miriam's remark the man looked up. His eyes stared at her back, flicked briefly over Dorine and Beth, returned to Miriam: blue-green eyes in the new tan of the face, shocking as a splash of sea water. She could not help gaping. He was probably the best-looking man she had ever seen close up. He was about Tom's age, in his twenties. Pulling a bag from under the table, he took a swig and put it back, still watching Miriam. He seemed to be pretending not to be in the room, not to be visible, not to be knowing that others were there. He was making a pane of glass around him, except for Miriam.

"Bethie! How are you?" Miriam, turning from Dorine, saw her. A warm bath of attention spilled on her, the sudden satisfying of an unknown hunger. Beth moved forward involuntarily, into that warmth. "You're going out with Tom Ryan now, umm?"

Beth nodded. Large eyes seeing her over the high Tartar cheekbones, enormous eyes dark brown with flecks of light.

"Beth, don't let him set you against me. We don't get on, as you may have noticed. That's a dull story. But, like all stories, there are two sides. Don't let him persuade you I'm all claws and fangs."

She was surprised that Miriam should care what Ryan said to Beth: after all, they were not yet friends. That was how she put it to herself: not yet. "I don't expect people I like to like the same things I do or the same people."

"Don't you really?"

"It would be like expecting you to be vegetarians too."

"I always want to make everybody tangled up with each other. I want to be sharing good things. It's an awful compulsion."

"It's the Mama Mountain in you," the man said. "A dogmatism of the blood. Drown you in warm milk."

Miriam introduced him as Phil and he mumbled acknowledgment. Once more he looked around the room warily from table to table, counting or searching. Then he seemed to relax very slightly and, unfocusing his eyes into the distance, lit a cigarette. Miriam watched with obvious anxiety. "Phil, are you all right? Are you sure you want to stay?"

His face became a mask of cold irony. "Indeed. Why not? One good trip is like another, but each bad trip is unique and irreplaceable."

"Especially if you decide beforehand it will be bad."

"Aw, but how I avoid disappointment. Besides, it takes a certain amount of gall for a man to sit down to listen to the spewings of his dead self."

"Indeed!" She mocked his tone. "You seemed alive today. We were out on Hal's sailboat, all day. But since you're dead now, Philip, I guess there's nothing to be done but bury you under the table."

"Bury me no place but in your body, Miriam. Take me all in and let me be born again."

Beth realized he was drunk. He sat so neatly and spoke so clearly in a voice that climbed and dipped and sang a bit veined with coldness or suddenly furred with sex, that it had not occurred to her till now that he was very drunk.

"Look, Hal's getting ready. You want to come up and sit with us? This is a good spot. I'll put up with Tom Ryan for an evening for your sake, if he'll put up with me."

Tom seemed eager to join the other table. "Well, well, what made the great bitch extend herself? This ought to be interesting. Phil is, I presume, drunk? I mean, it's evening and I've seen him sodden at ten in the morning. Not that he's anything so archaic as an alcoholic. He puts it all in, anything to fog the mechanism. Grass, hash, acid, coke, even heroin. Nothing so selective as being an alcoholic. One time last year he got really sick from taking too much aspirin—can you believe it, aspirin?" Tom muttered all the way to the other table.

Phil came into focus as Tom pulled up a chair. "Well, well, if it isn't Mr. Ryan himself, the lace-curtain third-generation boyo. God Save the Dean, Mr. Ryan, tell me, are ya a doctor yet?"

"If it isn't the Stage Irishman, drinking his whiskey in his brown bag under the table and blathering to the ladies about what he would do—if he only could."

"For that matter, we could ask the lady present which of us truly can. I mean, if you want an objective opinion." Phil was grinning. He had a long straight nose, thin well-formed lips, a fine jaw. When he grinned she could see a tooth missing just to the right of his canines. His teeth were poor, apart in front and that one missing, which made him more human to her.

"So Hal's agreed to perform a few of your songs tonight—your few, few songs. We could do a sing-along, those of us who have heard those old familiar ditties so many times. Unless you've written something new?"

The singer had started:

"I am your bride of Ivory Soap.

Select my model by horoscope.
Breasts of chromium, platinum womb.
My brain is a dentist's waiting room.
I do not age, I do not tire.
I am the product you desire."

"And ruin my image? Who would you academic creeps scorn, if I wasn't around displaying my gutted body and burnt-out brain? I'm a local monument, the hunchback of Harvard Square. I should be given a retainer. Every time you see me you make a resolve to kiss ass a bit harder."

"I am white as lavatory tile.
I wear a no-iron dacron smile.
Buying is my favorite sport.
Consumer research men report . . ."

"Shh, Phil. Would you both shut up? I want to hear Hal, even if you don't." Miriam sat listening to the singer, a pudgy, cherubic-faced man with an enormous mane of streaked blond-on-brown hair and a big barrel voice. He played acoustic guitar and was backed up by a drummer and a bass player.

"I am stumbling here
with gulls' cries in my ears,
hunting a lost key,
lost coin, lost year. . . ."

Although Hal announced his songs he did so with a drawled mumble unlike his singing voice. Thus all the songs sounded as if they were Gumpty Grubble written by Muddle and Mutter. Still she knew the moment Hal started one of Phil's songs, because a shudder of pain would go through Phil, while everyone else at this table seemed to draw tighter.

"Here is the golden place
where I lay down to sleep.
Here I dreamt until I felt
the sharp salt wavelets creep
about my feet
and woke in the day's debris,

papers, driftwood, seaweed
and rotting spawn.
That other body gone,
my golden love is gone,
only the setting sun here with me,
only the sunset
floating like an oil slick
on the sea."

That had a flowing melodic line. It was pretty. But so
self-pitying. Though Beth listened to Hal, she watched
Miriam, sitting with her arms crossed as if she were chilly,
pushing her heavy breasts higher against her. Why should
Miriam prefer this man to Jackson? Perhaps she did not know
as much about men as she seemed to. This one, Phil, was
handsome, but what could you do with him? Jackson was
solider: she longed to give Miriam advice. Miriam's big
florid body seemed to make her more vulnerable as well as
more visible. Now Hal was playing a bluesy song. Tom was
drumming his fingers, looking around. He winked at her,
mouthed something to a friend two tables away.

"The stinking Hudson
runs deep and wide.
That's Jersey smoking
on the other side.
I smell like a loser
but I'm mean with pride."

Besides, Beth thought, maybe being married had given her
some insight. Miriam was loving with her eyes, as Beth had
loved Jim. Perhaps Miriam had had a quarrel with Jackson
that Phil with his ready tongue had taken advantage of.
Tom was always ready to needle and gossip and spar, but
with Phil he became embattled in an ugly way. Perhaps Phil
had made Tom dislike Miriam. Though the talk implied
something had happened between them.

"I like that one," Dorine said when the blues had ended.

"It's a song, you can say that," Phil said. "Not a poem set
to music. Maybe that's all you can say."

Hal began a minor flamenco-like introduction. Immediately
Miriam sat up straight and pulled the shawl close, glaring at

Phil. "Here comes my unfavorite. Goddamn you, you are a complete brass piggy!"

Tom was grinning. Everybody else at the table seemed to have sunk into a hot miasma of discomfort for the duration of the song, which Hal sang with great relish and many guitar decorations:

> *"Let the night come down upon my back.*
> *Let the clocks close their staring eyes.*
> *I will have her in my bed again."*

Phil winced. "Think of it this way: I suffer too. When I am bad, I am very, very bad."

> *"Close the doors of your arms on me,*
> *lock your arms around my neck.*
> *I name you hope, I name you despair.*
> *Wind me in your hair, your hair,*
> *wind me tight in your black, black hair."*

Could Miriam and Tom have been involved before he got married? But that was five years or more. Further, Miriam had told her she had grown up in Brooklyn and gone to school in the Midwest.

> *"The squalid lusts of little men*
> *hammer at you, Venus of distress.*
> *Night mare, night witch, dark madonna,*
> *coffin angel, whore of loneliness."*

Tom nudged her. "Venus Berg—get it now?"

Anyhow, Beth was sure Phil had made it worse. He sat there vain and self-centered and made glass walls grow up around him and sucked his own invented pain like a pickle inside. Perhaps Miriam thought his writing songs was romantic. Would Miriam put up with him if he made change in a supermarket instead of songs for a coffeehouse?

> *"Close the doors of your arms on me,*
> *dig your nails in my back.*
> *Do not promise, do not swear,*
> *Just wind me in your hair, your hair."*

Miriam was sitting with a mask of non-expression, turned outward to the room and apparently fascinated by Hal's performance. Phil was faintly smiling, his mouth drawn out thin and his brows lifted. Beth found herself sweating. It was ghastly.

> *"Let the night come down and bury us.*
> *Go on loving me and go on lying.*
> *Venus, you pulse with life and I am dying. . . ."*

As Hal finished, Miriam turned back to the table with an audible sigh. "Wow! Does that really get longer every time?"

"Do you get tired of tribute?" Phil asked gently and she glared.

"It's not about me! It's about your mythical nonsense."

"Didn't I invent you?"

"You won't believe how angry you make me when you say that."

> *"Oh, I went down to the river last night*
> *just to throw my body in.*
> *I left my soul to the F.B.I.*
> *and I left my love my skin . . .*
>
> *"I held my nose and said, Here goes,*
> *and jumped right off the bank.*
> *I choked and coughed as I rolled down,*
> *the smell was pretty rank.*
> *I hit the waves with a thud and thump,*
> *but you know, I never sank."*

Miriam's face opened in a big grin. "Phil, Phil, that's new! Why didn't you tell me?"

"I thought for your patience you could use a small surprise."

> *"For the water it was solid*
> *with garbage, oil, and shit.*
> *No matter how I banged and kicked, I*
> *couldn't penetrate it.*
> *I did not sink, I did not drown.*
> *I walked on the water to Boston town."*

"But I like it, Phil. It's funny."

At the end of the set Hal announced that he was off to New York next week to sign a contract, no shit, folks, for his first record.

"That song is something new for you," Lennie said. "First time I ever heard you putting your politics into your songs."

"That ecology crap, it's not political. It's every place, like garbage."

"A muse of ecology, that's a new turn for Venus," Tom said. "A broadside, by God."

"I never call Miriam that old rot any more." Phil seemed less drunk. It was as if his energy level had trebled and burned out the alcohol in sudden efflorescence. "It's spring— you'd only know that by the university calendar—but everything's going to turn out all right, all right. . . ."

Miriam came over behind Phil and tickled him under the arms, saying something in his ear.

"Is that for real about the record contract?" Lennie asked. "What about the rest of Going-to-the-Sun?"

Phil shrugged uneasily. "He's trying to make it as a single. Terry and Rick are getting a new group together. . . . Hal says he's going to do some of my songs."

"Phil, think you've absorbed enough glory and we could depart?" Miriam lingered over him. "Let's go home before you start coming down."

"Just like a woman, to drag you off," Phil grumbled but he got up. Slowly from clot to clot of people she got him out the door.

So much of the new lives Beth touched through Ryan puzzled her. At least her room was cheap, but she was shocked to learn that Jackson paid two hundred and fifty dollars for the apartment rented in his name. Tom paid shares on the first of the month and Lennie whenever he could scrape his together. During his stint as a C.O. Lennie had served in hospitals as an orderly. Afterward he went on working until he had got involved in an attempt to organize a union of hospital workers in Boston. He had been badly beaten and then fired. Now he was making a living hawking underground papers around Harvard Square.

Their apartment was considered a bargain, although whenever anyone slammed the bathroom door too hard another portion of the ceiling fell into the tub. The wiring consisted of extensions plugged into hanging light sockets in gross webs or run against the baseboards from one plug to the next. If Dorine forgot to unplug the refrigerator before plugging in the iron, the fuses blew. Often they blew randomly, and sometimes the whole house went dark and the ice would melt in the refrigerator. Then the milk would spoil and the meat would begin to smell and everyone would have to study by candlelight or hang out in the all-night diner where the police were always drinking coffee and telling stories, watching the neighborhood longhairs come and go with a hostility that coagulated the air. Regularly the plumbing quit, and Tom would have to get out his tools and make it work again. Tom's father was a plumber and the tools were an old set from him. She learned that fact from Jackson, not from Tom.

Saturday night she invariably spent with Tom in the apartment, and then he would get her up early Sunday and drop her off on the way to pick up Bonnie and Tom, Jr. The third Sunday in May Beth did not leave with him, since she had promised Dorine to hang around and help her mat some of Lennie's drawings and frame some canvases. Memorial Day weekend there was a Cambridge street fair, and Lennie was hoping to sell something. They always got up late and so she sat on at the breakfast table drinking smoky Lapsang Souchong tea and reading *Swann's Way*, until Jackson emerged from the bathroom scratching himself drowsily over his chest.

Strong homely face. Lines etched the mouth and eyes, making a texture that drew her fingers to want to touch lightly, like carved wood. Jackson discomforted her, a reaction she hid away. She felt he looked upon her as if she were a child or a pet cat, while she was all too aware of him as a man. All too aware. Often she did not speak to him when she wanted to, because the remote kindly quality of his answers made her feel invisible.

He asked her, "Do you think Tom's going to move out?"

"He's found a place in Brookline that sounds good, but he hasn't actually seen it yet. Do you mind if he moves?"

Jackson shrugged. "This is a kind of halfway house. People come in here and stay for a while till they can get it together.

From busted marriages and bad trips and exploded communes. They can take it easy here and keep to themselves if they need to, or have company if they need that. Once their heads are together, they move on. At least that's what I like to think on good mornings."

"On bad mornings what do you say?"

He laughed silently, almost a grimace. "Then I think we all live in narrowing circles, round and round saying our pieces. Like a cartoon I saw during the last Harvard strike. One of the deans had his head up his own asshole saying, 'Now we're beginning to see the light.' "

"If Tom moves back to Brookline, he'll be closer to his kids."

"Close to Laverne too." He puzzled on her, his forehead wrinkling. "You don't care?"

"He belongs to that marriage. That's where he's . . . glued together, somehow."

"Suppose he goes back to her. You wouldn't miss him?"

"We miss each other every day, by about a mile."

"What a cool child you pretend to be." His eyes searched her, sandy and narrowed. "You ought to at least *think* you're in love at your age."

"I did that once. And got married."

"You're awfully young to be so cynical. To go drifting along with such a measured thing."

"Maybe I'm not so young that I don't prefer to know what I'm doing!"

His bread popped out of the toaster and he spread grape jelly on it. "The young learn the words early. But wait. You'll turn on again." He was smiling at his toast.

His easy patronizing assurance, you'll fall back into love, wheel turning, natural as the seasons. How dare he assume that she would do what she did not want, did not accept? Looking up from his plate, Jackson winced as if he had bitten on a stone. For a moment he met her stare with his sandy gaze questioning. Then he pulled an old wallet from his pocket and unzipped the picture compartment, shaking out loose pipe tobacco before handing the photograph across. A small boy stood wobbly-legged, his sunflower face open in a blaze of grin.

"Who is that? You? No. Your baby brother?"

"Jerry Magnusson, born Jerry Jackson."

"He's your son?"

Dryly, "He was."

Dorine said from the doorway, "What's that? I didn't know you had a kid. I didn't even know you'd been married. Nobody knows, do they?"

"Sure. Phil and Miriam do. Phil's met him many times. The courts are something wonderful, when you get caught in their net."

Dorine handed the photo back and went to take a shower. Beth came around the table to look again at the picture.

Jackson said, "It's easier for him, having the same name as his brothers. And his new father, oh, he can do a lot for him." He slammed the wallet and shoved it in his pocket. "You kind of look like him, freckles and coloring. Who the hell knows what he looks like now?" He sprawled back, glaring at nothing.

Slowly Beth returned to her side of the table. The splatter of Dorine's shower came through the closed door. She felt a sore sympathy with him that she was too timid to offer, but also a sense of wrong . . . as if the picture were a license, a degree in suffering. "You used that on me to say you know more about pain than I do. . . . Okay! . . . But you don't know me. . . . I mean . . ." Words so flat. Tempest of emotion and thought churned through her and issued in words like a handful of gravel.

"Whereas you know yourself through and through." He grinned bleakly.

"But I can try to live the way . . . according to rules I believe in. To live . . . right."

"Child, life isn't played that way. Matter of fact it isn't played at all. It's endured. Your cool is all on the surface. Scratch you and you get mad as a tiger kitten."

She dropped her gaze, convinced he could see in her what she most wanted to hide, her attraction. Her eyes stung. She feared for a moment that she would cry. She took a deep breath, placed her palms together under the table, pushed tight and relaxed, then slowly forced herself to meet his gaze again. He had been looking at her with an open brooding sadness that he instantly ironed from his face. It was just her luck that she probably did remind him of his son Jerry: turning what had perhaps become a convenient role—that pose of absolute detachment, the man with the ancient wound, the total bachelor—into something more real again. Well, let him rest with his honorable wounds. She could not grapple with him.

When she was working with Dorine and Lennie in their room, choosing drawings to mat, Dorine told Lennie what she'd heard in the kitchen. "Did you know he'd been married and divorced?"

"Christ, no." Lennie rubbed his kinky beard. "If he isn't close-mouthed. Now how come he told you?"

Friday night Tom went to a party which he told her would be a great bore: which she had come to learn meant that his wife would be there. It was also true that she would find the party not so much dull as an attack on her nervous system. She had not figured out how to cope with the smoking that made her sinuses swell, the drinking, the talking that had no purpose, the looking each other over in that blatant sexual window-shopping that made her want to hide in a closet. No, he was better off going alone.

Saturday morning when he picked her up he took her to Brookline first, to three empty sunny rooms he had rented in a yellow brick apartment house on School Street. "Now isn't this an improvement? The toilet actually flushes, the windows open and shut in a normal manner, and there is even a lock on the door. Pretty nice kitchen, good stove, what do you think of it?"

"It looks fine."

He seemed disappointed at her lack of enthusiasm. "Well, I hope you like it. After all, you'll be the one spending your time in it, ha-ha."

A chill settled on her. "I'm not much of a cook."

"Practice makes perfect. Besides, we won't spend all our time in the kitchen." Hand on her elbow he walked her to the bedroom door. "Cross ventilation. Could be attractive, once we get it fixed up. The landlord's going to paint it next week. Says I can move in by Friday. I told him paint all the walls white. But I can still change it. I'm meeting him at three. What do you think?"

"Paint them whatever you like best."

"Thought you might have a preference. Look, Bethie." He locked the door, pocketing the key with satisfaction, and they started down the carpeted stair. "No reason for you to live in that rathole. I mean, if you want to keep up a separate address for your family, cool, but it's a waste of rent. There's plenty of room for both of us here. All this coming and going and getting you and bringing you back is a drag. Like dating and other horrors. I couldn't ask you to move into that menagerie—like moving into the Park Street subway station— but this is more like it, isn't it?"

"Tom, I like to live alone. I was already married once."

"Well, who says we have to go through that nonsense? You know what I think about the ring game?"

"But I don't want to live with somebody either. It's easier to cut out then, but that's the only improvement I can see."

"It's a whole different scene, Beth. It's being together because we want to, not because some guy in a black dress says it's okay to do it in bed." They got into his VW. "Got to meet the landlord at three. You really want to go to that freak show in the streets?"

"I would . . . really. I've never seen a street fair. . . . Besides, Lennie would feel bad if we didn't come by." She felt itchy and uncomfortable. The situation was sticky. Yet the day was so beautiful, so summery, she could not stay worried. On the corner of his street a magnolia was in full bloom. The smelly rank puddle of the Charles, the river that hardly flowed, reflected the sky blue as a country lake from the B.U. bridge, busy with sculls and kayaks and sunfish and sailboats.

He grumbled about parking. "Freaks panhandling, lot of losers like Lennie selling nonsense to each other." But they did find a place, a car pulling out just as they drove up.

It looked like any other Saturday and she was disappointed till they came around the corner to Garden. At first it just looked like a street full of people milling. She had imagined lights and structures, perhaps rides and games and she did not know what else. Garden Street was closed to traffic and booths and tables had been set up, and ahead she could hear rock music. Men with carts were selling ice cream on a stick and hot dogs and soft drinks and balloons with peace symbols.

"Look, there's Phil the Failed." Tom waved. Phil was slouching with his hands in his pockets looking bored while Miriam was chatting with a woman selling loaves of whole-grain bread, spread out in ornamental step pyramids about her as she squatted on a red blanket, wearing what looked

like an old tablecloth. Miriam was in wide elephant pants in a
soft blue tie-dye print. The top was cut low in front and in
back consisted only of yarn ties. The line of her tanned back
was graceful and the soft fabric moved as she moved,
flowingly. He hair was plaited in a fat glossy braid.

"If that little string should break, two more loose balloons,"
Tom said. "Let's get a hot dog."

Beth had a lemon slush: syrup poured over crushed ice.
She began to enjoy the fair. Everything was dancing, the
flickering trees, the people walking with rangy grace to the
jingle of ice-cream bells and the sputter of a motorbike making a slow way through the crowd, the throb of rock music
ahead. Green and gold and blue: the sun was hot, a fore-
taste of summer. All along the sidewalk paintings leaned and
hung, rectangles of color claiming as they passed, Look!
Look! with the artists sitting on the ground or folding chairs.
On occasional tables or spread on the ground as in photographs of native markets, jewelry, pottery, leather belts and
sandals, macramé, hand-woven fabrics, elaborate candles of
dripped and molded wax were set out.

"Look here, Beth, this part-time thing is silly. We're both
adults, we've been through the marriage mill, we know what
we want. It's a great thing to sleep with a woman and wake
up with her."

"But I don't want to live with anyone. I've never before
had a door that really shuts and a place only for me. It
wasn't till both Dick and Marie got married that I finally got
a room of my own. Even then, I had to share it with Mother's
sewing machine and everybody's off-season clothes."

"Hey, please. I don't have any place to crash, I didn't eat
last night. Give me a quarter?" The girl looked fourteen. Tom
ignored her, but Beth fumbled for change in her pocket.

"There's one every ten feet," he snorted, and he was right.
Hare Krishna chanters passed them, orange and white with
their shaved heads glinting, moving like butterflies through
the crowd. Their music came back through the thickness of
people like a rhythmic echo. Phil was bargaining at the curb
with a burly guy in a yellow T-shirt that said HOT TUNA and a
grotesquely thin girl in a man's white undershirt and torn
bells. A folded bill and a matchbox changed hands. Phil
popped the pill and ground the matchbox under his heel.
Miriam was down the block where some street musicians

were playing while the next rock group set up their vast system of amps and cables. She was dancing with another woman, big and ruddy and somewhat pregnant, and a young willowy horse-faced boy, all laughing in a round before the musicians, who were playing country style with guitars and a fiddle.

"So we'd have three rooms. That's two more than you have." His fingers released her elbow and for once he put his arm around her. They bumped along through the crowd. "You can't tell how great that place is going to look once it's fixed up—decent furniture, a few groovy lamps and posters, the walls painted. I'm ready to put some effort in—tired of living like a bum."

"Have you let Jesus into your heart?" A pale grublike boy with a sweet set smile stretching his face and enormous brown eyes that seemed to see glory or nothing, seized her arm. "Tell me, sister, have you tried Jesus?" Hal passed them with his guitar on his back, carrying what looked like a cage full of pigeons. By the time Tom had disentangled them from the Jesus boy, her pockets were full of smartly printed exhortations about sin and salvation and how Africa and China were going to invade Israel and launch Armageddon as it said in Revelations, and they had come upon Lennie's green nudes. Sitting on the ground, Dorine saw them and jumped up to wave. Leaving Jackson with Lennie, she came to meet them.

"How's it going?" Beth asked her.

"Sort of awful. Jackson took over for a while and we had lunch and walked around. That was okay."

"Lennie hasn't sold anything?"

Dorine shook her head. "Don't ask him. He's kind of down."

Jackson had been standing beside Lennie staring into the crowd, and as they approached he started off slowly. She did not think he saw her, though she waved. He was watching something behind them, where the rock group was still setting up and the fiddler playing a hoedown.

"What happened to spring?" Lennie mopped his forehead. For once he had taken off his leather jacket. He looked gaunt and pale. Ever since his beating when he was working as an organizer for the hospital union, his back hurt him and he stooped. "It's summer already. I wish the wind would come up."

The sun laid a metal hand on her head. She could feel her bare arms beginning to freckle. They drifted on in the crowd till Tom stopped ostensibly to watch two exhibitors playing chess. He returned at once to Topic A. "I don't get it. What are you afraid of? That your parents will find out? You're a big girl now. What's the point of this two, three times a week bit, when we can live together?"

"I said I don't want to."

"You're being stubborn. I think we should look at those irrational fears and deal with them."

"Why do you want me to live there so bad?"

He glared. "What's the use getting an apartment if you don't?" As his irritation mounted he began to plow through the crowd again, more quickly. He had let go her waist and his fingers pinched her elbow.

"I have my place without living with anyone. I don't see the connection." But she did. Warm body, how do you like the kitchen?

"Jesus!" He snorted and stuffed his hands at the pockets of his pants. They would not fit in, the pants being tailored too tight, and he again gripped her elbow. For five minutes he steered her through the crowd in a bristly silence and she could look around. A woman was handing out leaflets about the air war in Laos, a man was stringing beads without looking at anyone, a big oaf with a movie camera stomped on her toe and did not even turn when she yelped. She tried to imagine herself sitting on a mat selling big coiled pots she had made, like that woman nursing her baby. She had never seen anyone breast-feed a baby outside. She felt excited and confused by the street, smells of grass and vegetables cooking, and the mutter of drug deals going on all around her. Just at the other curb Miriam's blue print flashed. She was walking alone now, slowly, looking around with a basket rocking on her hip. Behind her a balloon popped and she jumped, swung around, walked on more quickly. About ten feet back and a head taller than anyone in between Jackson strolled, his denim sleeves rolled up. Tracking her? A breeze stirred dust, but the sun beat down without relief. She could feel her arms beginning to burn. They had reached the end of the fair where a first-aid tent was set up. A woman shaking all over was being led in one step at a time, muttering and shivering.

They turned back. "Look, I'm a grown man. I don't want to live by myself. I want to live with a woman."

"Any woman." She pulled her arm free. "Ring room service for a woman."

"I didn't say any woman. I said you. You need speeches?"

"But, Tom, I might as well be any woman. I'm a warm body, I listen to you, I make breakfast. I'm a toaster with a cunt." It took effort to say that word. All the real sexual words were ugly.

"Oh, I see." He looked skyward. "I haven't demonstrated enough interest in your mind."

"I haven't asked you to. I like things the way they are. But I will not live with you."

"If you want me to know you better and treat you differently, isn't this a fair place to start?"

"I don't want to live with you! I don't want to! I don't want to be closer!"

"I guess you don't." His face seemed pinched toward his sharp chin and his eyes squinted. "I guess you're scared to be a real woman with me, and that's all there is to it. Well, take it or leave it, because that's the way it is."

"You don't care what I want. You just care what you want!" But she could not work much conviction into her anger. That was, after all, what the small thing between them had been based on. "Tom, try to understand. I just don't want to live with anyone."

"I'm tired of this part-time crap. I want a woman, not an adolescent I have to date. Either you live up to it or we call it quits. I mean it, Beth."

She did not know what to say, because she had said it all. She stood awkwardly on one foot and tried a smile. He got angrier. "You think I don't mean it. Think you can get around me. Think again! It's forward or backward or get out of the road." Turning, he pushed off into the crowd. He did not look back. His narrow back seemed to vibrate outrage.

She wandered back toward Dorine, stopping to watch a street theater group doing a play about landlords and high rent, but she felt too unhappy to get interested. Past a table where people were explaining how to set up food co-ops, past two men quarreling loudly about which had ripped off the other, she felt exhausted before she found Dorine and began telling her what had happened.

"You'll make it up." Dorine took her arm. "You know, I think you're getting a burn."

Beth nodded. "I can feel it. I guess I ought to go home."

"Lennie, want to go back? You look so done in." Dorine patted his cheek.

He shrugged her off but got up. "Yeah, what's the use. All those tourists making jokes. But how can we get the stuff back without Jackson?"

"Beth can help. It's not so heavy. Beth, you'll help?"

Tom was supposed to go to the landlord at three, so she did not think she would run into him. Or maybe she still hoped he would change his mind and come back and let them go on as they had. Besides, Dorine and Lennie really could not manage the paintings without her.

On the way back they did not talk much. It was a long walk. The paintings were heavy and awkward to carry. The twenty blocks felt like an all-day hike. Lennie was grumpy and Dorine was fussing over him. Beth was down too. The relationship with Tom was not much, but it was a lot more than nothing. She felt lonely already. She wondered if she would ever see any of the people she had met through him. Hauling Lennie's canvases blocks and blocks and blocks felt like a heavy penance for something she had done wrong. After she had done this, surely she would have a right to come by sometimes. But Dorine and Lennie were totally involved in Lennie's depression.

Lennie was trying to cheer himself up as they finally climbed the stairs. "What the hell, people would always rather buy jewelry or pots, they don't feel they're putting their taste on the line the same way. If they pick out a canvas, they're scared somebody else will look at it and say, '*Ark,* you're an idiot.' It's exposing yourself." He pushed the door ajar, thrusting his load in. As Dorine and Beth crowded after into the cool dim room, the two bodies stretched on the bed—Miriam lying on her stomach with her black hair half tangled over Jackson's chest, he with one arm around her buttocks, the other lying palm up at his own side—jerked convulsively and froze. Lennie made a surprised noise in his throat. As they halted halfway into the room, Jackson yanked his arm free and, arching himself with rough speed,

pulled the sheet from under him and over her, as she was
struggling to sit up and cover herself. As Beth backed out
the door, she could see vividly Jackson's lean body with its
hard, almost scarified muscles, dark wiry body and pubic
hair, the limp condom swinging pendulum-like in the haste
of his motion. Jostling, they plummeted downstairs, leaving
the rest of the paintings outside the door.

"Damn it!" Lennie struck his forehead. "He'll never forgive me. Why did it have to be him?"

"People . . . Hey, stop a minute!"

They looked up. Miriam stuck her head out under the
matchstick shade. "Leave your stuff where it is and wait ten
minutes. Okay?"

Lennie kept his head down. "We're sorry. Honest."

"Don't worry. Everything's cool. Come up in ten minutes."
She ducked in under the shade.

"Should we really go back?" Lennie bobbed nervously.
"Jackson doesn't lose his temper often, but when he
does . . ."

"Why not give them a chance to gloss it over?" Beth
wanted to see them together. "Besides, what will we do with
all your stuff? Take it back to the fair?"

As they sat on the porch steps she kept thinking of how
Jackson had immediately covered her, a chivalry of the re-
flexes more attractive than any amount of door opening or
ritual complimenting.

This time Lennie knocked. Miriam opened the door smiling gravely, in her Pakistani pants and top, barefoot still with
her hair once again braided. The little hairs on the nape
were wet: she smelled of soap. Carrying in a pitcher, Jackson
motioned for them to sit on the neatly made bed. "Vodka
and orange juice and lots of ice. Get them glasses, Miriam."

Back and forth on her bare feet she went, bringing glasses
and then a loaf of Italian bread, plates, bologna and cheese,
setting them on his cleared desk while he watched with a
sucked-in smile of which only a little escaped. As everyone
took a turn in the bathroom she moved gracefully around
him in a parody of feminine subservience, a playfully over-
acted domesticity. She sliced the bologna and bread and
cheese and arranged them, wheels within wheels, with mustard
and horseradish, before she sat down on the edge of the desk
beside Jackson on the desk chair. Dorine and Lennie and

Beth were lined up with their plates and glasses on the bed.

"Beth, Beth. Were you named that, or are you really Elizabeth in soft disguise?" Miriam's voice was low and rich and a little gritty, teasing.

"I'm named Elizabeth, but nobody's called me that except in grade school."

"God is your oath—that's what it means, you know."

"She could use an oath if her parents had decided to nickname her Lizzie instead." Jackson crunched an ice cube between his teeth. As Miriam offered the plate around, he followed her movements with that slight smile. "Miriam's a little insane over names. What did you tell me yours meant? Rebellion?"

"Or bitter. I've seen it explained that way too."

"Not bittersweet?"

"Not by the books."

"The books don't know everything. It's bitter and sweet."

"Like you." She gave him a slow smile that was mostly in her eyes set deep and wide. Bending then, she gathered the dishes. Something Beth was groping for. If Dorine had been serving them, nobody would have noticed, though the actual act would have been the same. By playing servant with that conscious touch, Miriam made it more flattering to Jackson, to them. She wasn't quite sure what in that disquieted her. Miriam asked, "Did many stop to look at your work, Lennie?"

"To make cracks, sure."

Jackson stretched his feet halfway across the room, tilting the desk chair back. "People are afraid of the pain in your pictures. They don't want anything that isn't easy."

"Jackson . . . " Dorine rested her head on Lennie's shoulder. Jackson and Miriam sat only a few inches apart but had not touched since the others came in. "You know, after all this time of being your roommate, I still don't know your first name?"

"That's my only name. Jackson Jackson Jackson."

"No, it isn't." Miriam held her glass to her cheek. "He has a secret first name, like Rumpelstiltskin."

"What is it?" Dorine sat up. "Ebenezer? Zacharias? Is it a girl's name that they give boys sometimes like Shirley or Evelyn?"

Miriam shook her head sternly. "It's a piece of Americana. He'd disappear if I told you—he does anyhow. You have to love this idiot for years on end to find out his secret name."

He tapped his finger on the desk beside her hand. "How do you know, woman, that's really my name?"

Under her low brows she looked at him, the light from the window shading her face under the cheekbones. "It would be like you to fool me. Do you know what I'd do if I found that out?"

His face was a wary mask. "Yes."

They go so well together, Beth thought, that to see them is to find them immediately a couple, the clear answer to a series of muddled questions. Yet tensions sprang out. Watching them she felt a pang of loneliness and then remembered. "I must go. Tom will be coming back, and I shouldn't be here."

"We have to go too. We'll walk with you." Miriam padded across the room to her shoes. "Jackson, this time we have to find Phil, immediately."

His face was wary, his eyes questioning, but he got slowly to his feet. Lennie and Dorine exchanged uneasy glances.

"We have to find Phil, we have to come back here, and we all have to talk." Miriam faced him, looking into his eyes insistently. "Don't shut me out and don't shut him out. You can't make me choose any more. I can't stand it. We can't stay apart, all right, we can't, but I can't punish Phil for that. I won't be the club you use on each other! Never again."

Slowly Jackson put his hand on her shoulder. He did not smile, no muscle in his face moved. "Phil was my friend long before I met you, long before he met you. Remember that."

"Stay open, Jackson. Stay open and talk. That's all I ask."

"Woman, that isn't enough?" But he nodded again, opening the door and following her down the stairs, one hand resting lightly on her shoulder. Going after, Beth wondered. What was happening? He was so thoroughly there with her, what could it be he denied that she needed Phil too, that drew hungry shadows down her cheeks from her watching eyes? She wondered if she would ever arrive at watching lovers without some pang of wanting to be loved too, for all of her analysis.

Well, one thing had been saved for her out of the day. If Miriam did become involved with Jackson once again, she could continue to come here and visit. Miriam would justify her presence as somehow Dorine could not. And then she would come to know Miriam at last too.

5

Women's Soft Voices on a Summer Day

SCENE: *The Cambridge apartment. The room that had been Tom Ryan's is now Miriam's. On the double bed is an old patchwork comforter made by Miriam's mother's mother, Rachel. Phil is at work tending bar: he has two part-time bartending jobs at the moment, Oggy's and Finnegan's Wake. Jackson is off with Terry and Rick from Going-to-the-Sun commune, and nobody knows where they are or when he will reappear. Lennie is out hawking papers. It is Saturday afternoon. Miriam has just trimmed Beth's hair, cut Dorine's, and had her own mane thinned and evened by Dorine. Now all three lie on the bed in a wilted row. The air over them is another feather bed.*

MIRIAM: Well, you guess wrong. I have a brother Mark, younger by a year, and a sister Allegra, younger by three. Not only wasn't I an only child, I got stuck being a mother a lot.

DORINE: Oh, I bet you dug playing mother.

MIRIAM: Sure, playing it. But not having to do it day in and day out. When I was little my mother always had to work. My father was blacklisted for a long time and he couldn't get a job. He was a folk singer and he'd signed his name to a lot of things.

BETH: But at least you must have admired him.

MIRIAM: When I was little, oh sure. He had us all conned. I mean, don't get the idea he was a Communist. He was an opportunist, he just wanted to be a big-name folk singer. I'll always wonder to what extent he was martyred to his associations, and to what extent he just thought it fine that my mother should teach and support him. But don't imagine that meant he hung around the house taking care of us and doing

85

the housework, oh no! I was raised to think he was a hero.
When he was home he was always composing awful songs
about civil rights that must have made the blacks embarrassed,
or he was practicing. The only real radical in the family is my
grandmother, who made this quilt, and she's crazy now.

DORINE: Being an only child isn't such a bed of roses. You
think, sure, an only child gets spoiled. But some people have
one kid because that one was an accident. Okay, they're going
to live with that accident. How would you like to feel like a
fucking accident? You're only there because she didn't put the
diaphragm in right one time, and they were too scared to get
an abortion or maybe they didn't know where to go.

MIRIAM: Bethie, are you an only child?

BETH: Two sisters, younger and older, and a brother. The
big event in our family was when my brother had to get
married, because Elinor was pregnant four months. My older
sister Marie was eased into that mother routine. We always got
on. I think mainly I resented my youngest sister, Nancy.

DORINE: You know, my parents used to call me The Kid.
'What are we going to do about The Kid?' they'd ask each
other. They'd be talking about going to a movie or out for
a bite to eat, as they always called it. Or going on a little
vacation. They called all their jaunts Little Vacations. Little
Vacations and Bites to Eat and Smart Little Dresses and
Another Wee Drinkie.

BETH: I think I always resented Nancy. She was pretty
from the time she was a baby. The youngest and the prettiest
and she always got everything, it seemed to me.

MIRIAM: Oh, you too. My sister Allegra. I mean, take the
name. You know how come I have such a lumpy old-
fashioned Jewish name as Miriam? Because my father named
me after his mother's mother, so Grandma Berg would give
them some money. In other words, friends, he sold me out.
Times weren't so tight when the other kids were born, so
they got groovy names, Mark and Allegra.

DORINE: I never thought Dorine was such a hot name
either. It sounds as if I should be working in a dime store.
You can't believe how angry I used to get with Tom calling
me Chlorine all the time, as if my own name wasn't bad
enough.

BETH: But you never acted as if you were mad. I didn't

know it bothered you—I mean, I never thought it was nice of him.

DORINE: Well, what was I supposed to do? Slug him? I mean, what can you do? When men start teasing you that way, if you let on it hurts, they only do it more.

BETH: I've never seen you get angry.

DORINE: Sure I get angry! . . . I guess I get depressed more.

MIRIAM: It's not just a matter of names. Allegra was pretty all ways. Maybe every family in this society that has more than one daughter, they pick one girl to love and make her a baby doll, and the others are just raised to be lowered, made to feel inferior all of the time.

BETH: But you're beautiful. How could they make you feel that way?

Miriam makes a sour face, pushing her heavy hair back.

DORINE: You are. Everybody says so.

MIRIAM: Ever stop to think that's what makes somebody beautiful—other people? I wasn't pretty when I was growing up. Let me see your teeth. Come on, both of you. No, you didn't go through that (*to Beth*) but you did, Dorine. Braces. Right? How long did you wear them?

DORINE: Centuries. Ugh, I hated them. Into high school. I never smiled except this little simper. I was so homely!

MIRIAM: Well, I was fat. Fat! I wore braces and I was fat and I had pimples and they put glasses on me when I was nine or ten. So don't talk to me about beautiful. Inside I am still fat and I wear braces and my nose always runs and I have pimples and the only boy I like in seventh grade calls me Four Eyes. And ugly orthopedic shoes my uncle fitted on me free, because it was all in the family. There wasn't anything wrong with my feet! But I had to wear those clod-busters because they were free, when all the other girls wore patent leather T-straps and darling red boots. It still makes me mad, I can remember that and still get furious.

BETH: Is Allegra really more beautiful than you are?

MIRIAM: Now who am I to ask? At home she was. She photographs better. I come across coarse in photographs. She hasn't got my coloring, but then nobody thought that was an advantage when I was growing up. Allegra looks— you should excuse me—more like a *shiksa*, more like you, Bethie. She hasn't got such a big bosom and she hasn't got such a big nose. She's more like the size a woman is supposed to be—she's five feet six and she has a good figure but it's within reason, and she can wear clothes off the rack, tailored clothes, anything.

BETH: I never thought it was possible to have breasts that were too big. The bigger, the better.

MIRIAM: Oh, Bethie, that's not true. Nothing fits you. You go around bowed over and embarrassed for years. I used to spend vast amounts of energy in search for a perfect bra until I stopped wearing them altogether, except under itchy things. What a relief! I always bounced anyway. How my mother used to glare at my boobs. I felt so ashamed. It was as if I'd done it on purpose, it was part of being too fat, too tall, too gross. The worst thing was some guy suddenly deciding to pinch them to see if they were real. In grade school already, by the eighth grade, I was getting that. I don't know how I ever went out of the house. It was like this terrible embarrassment suddenly hung on the front of me that was in the way and which everybody else looked at before they looked at me—maybe it was all they saw.

BETH: I've always gotten it the other way. I used to have this awful fantasy in high school, when it was clear I was just never going to have much. There I'd be and I would get married and then I'd take off my clothes. Then my husband would look at me and say, 'Well, is that all?' Then he'd throw me out.

MIRIAM: That's so ugly! Why do we hate ourselves so much? We all go around hating ourselves because we don't look like the women in the ads.

BETH: Nancy didn't look like that either. She's almost as thin as I am. It's as if the family game is set up so that, if she wins, I lose. I guess there's always a favorite. If there's two kids, each can be one parent's favorite, but if there's more, then somebody gets left out.

DORINE: But at least you feel there's somebody there. I mean, I get money from them sometimes but I feel as if I was born lonely. I feel sometimes as if I'll go through life and never belong to anyone.

BETH: But you aren't a dog, why do you want to be owned?

MIRIAM: Mark's in law school now, but Allegra's husband hunting. The minute she got to be a senior she started turning over eight cylinders and got engaged to a pre-med student. His family wasn't big on him marrying, and the prospects of putting him through four years of medical school were dreary. Now she's engaged to some guy who works in the personnel department of a company that makes peanut butter. I call him the Peanut Butter Crumb. Every time she sees me she asks me the first thing: Are you getting married yet? Do you have any prospects? You mean you're still *seeing Philip!* Oy, oy. . . . Forgive me, Allegra would never say oy. She has our father's gentility, excuse the pun. He always pressuring us how to talk.

DORINE: Does your family know about Phil and Jackson?

MIRIAM: Not Jackson. But Phil. He was the scandal of my college years. I used to come running into New York every vacation to see him and my family would start screaming and yelling and carrying on. Oh, how they hated him!

DORINE: My parents know I'm living with Lennie. They don't make a fuss, they like to be modern and up to date and that jazz. But every so often my mother will say something really nasty. How she can get under my skin.

BETH: You started going out with Phil in college? How old were you?

MIRIAM: Nineteen. We never really went out. It wasn't that way.

BETH: I don't understand about him. What way was it?

MIRIAM: Oh! (*She shrugs, running her hand through her heavy hair, tugging on it. Then she smiles widely and sweetly, shaking her head.*) It was all the doors in the world opening at once!

TWO

The Book of Miriam

6

You Ain't Pretty
So You Might as Well Be Smart

The first home Miriam remembered was her grandmother's apartment, long, wandering, and rent-controlled in a vast building on West End Avenue on the Upper West Side of Manhattan. Everything appeared at least as old as Grandma, and the furniture was large and Germanic and stiff. Grandma Berg and Grandfather Berg, who was in the shirt-making trade, and Aunt Yette, who was not exactly her aunt, all lived there.

Before, her parents had lived in Canarsie. Then her father had gone to the Army to fight the Nazis to protect the Jews. The Russians had pushed from one side and her father from the other, and then the Nazis had to let the Jews not yet burned up go free, as in the song her father sang about Moses. When her father came back after winning, she was born and Mark was born. But then the troubles came and her father got blacklisted and fired, and they had all moved in with the Bergs. Nobody thought her father was a hero any more except her mother, Sonia, and her. Grandma Berg said it was all Sonia's fault, but even when Miriam was little she knew her mother was not political. Rachel, her other grandma, yelled at Sonia that she had false consciousness and a petty bourgeois mentality. Her mother and father always said that you could not argue politics with Rachel, because she was a Trot.

So when Miriam first remembered, they lived with the Bergs and went out on Sunday to see Grandma Rachel. When Sonia complained how oppressive it was to live at Grandma Berg's, Rachel would always tell her she could move back home, even now that Allegra was born too. But Grandma Rachel had a boy friend even though she was an old woman,

and Sonia thought that was not right. They fought about
everything. Fighting with Grandma Rachel was different
from fighting with Grandma Berg. Grandma Rachel would
start yelling and wailing and sometimes she would throw a
cup on the floor or pound on the wall. She made a lot of
noise when she was mad and sometimes she cried.

When Grandma Berg was angry, it was something cold.
It was something in the food and in the walls and in the air.
It meant whispering and trying not to make noise and it
meant that little smile of hers and iron poking through her
voice. It meant discussions instead of fights, quiet shiftings
of forces, invisible maneuvers. Grandma Berg did not believe
in politics: she said in America you had to do like an American. She said, Look, did the Communists save the Jews in
Germany? No, your Stalin signed a pact to deliver them to
the butcher. Here you work hard and you can have what
you want.

Miriam had shared a room at times with Aunt Yette, and
at times with her parents. Her warmest memories were of
the piano which she was sometimes allowed to bang on, and
of a hall that led from the dining room back into the wing with
the bedrooms. Miriam had loved to shut all the doors that
led off, the door to Aunt Yette's room, the door to her
grandparents' room, the door to her parents' room where baby
Mark slept, the door to the bathroom (there was another off
Grandma's bedroom) and the doors to the linen closet and
dining room. Then she would dance, singing to herself and
whirling round and round in the wonderful dark till she
keeled over. The hall smelled of lavender. In an herb shop
that sold spices and ingredients used in European baking,
Grandma Berg bought camomile and *lindenbluten* for tea,
and lavender to strew among the sheets and pillowcases and
blankets. She said it made them smell clean and kept moths
away. Her mother would make faces when she had to shake
the dried flowers out of the linens.

Sonia hated living with Grandma and Grandfather and
Aunt Yette. Sonia was always saying, whispering as they did
in their room even though the walls were thick, that she
would rather live as a family in a flophouse than to stay
any longer with her in-laws. She kept talking about Grandma
taking a pound of flesh from her every day, though it seemed
clear to Miriam as she was plodding through her childhood

that what had been given up to Grandma Berg was her.
Miriam was always understood to be her favorite grandchild:
not in the sense that Mark was, of course, because he was
the son, the name-bearer, the carrier of light. In fact Miriam
had disliked the word "future" since she was little and had
always imagined it stamped with Mark's face. The only
time people ever talked about the future in her household or
later when they were visiting the West End apartment was
when they were arguing about Mark's schooling. Mark had a
future before him; Allegra and she had only prospects, which
meant husbands.

Even Sonia's mother, Grandma Rachel Abrams, twice a
widow, said that Grandma Berg was a *berrieh*. She managed
for everybody. That wasn't all Rachel said Grandma Berg
was, of course. They looked down their noses at each other.
"We'll never feel like *mishpockeh*," said Rachel. Grandma
Berg did not use Yiddish in her daily conversations, reserving
it for communication with Yette. Nobody knew what she
spoke with Grandfather Berg. Their relationship was formal.
He worked and worked and worked and worked. He had a
small business always on the verge of disaster, and he was
perhaps the most harried human being Miriam had ever
watched. What money could be leached out of that business
had gone into the education of the children and into insurance and burial plots. Lionel, Miriam's father, was always convinced there was more and always trying to get some of it.

Grandma Berg did not quite trust Allegra's prettiness. She
was always telling Sonia and Lionel that they had spoiled
her. She never recovered from her austere amusement at the
name. "You wanted a fast girl, Lionel? Let us give thanks
you didn't call her Largo or Fortissimo. Never did I think,
all those years paying for music lessons, you wouldn't make
a living and you'd visit such names on the children." But
Miriam was what she called a good girl: lumpy, overweight
(a good eater), pale, with a big nose and a perennial head
cold. It seemed to Miriam she had been born with her sinuses
swollen. All through grade school she had coughed and
wheezed and sniveled, with infected tonsils and raw throat
and the constant steady drip of snot. She often felt there
could be nothing else inside her. In how many processed
forests she had wiped her leaky nose: a mountain of paper-
mâché could have been built of her used tissues: a monument

the size of the Statue of Liberty to a deep and persistent discomfort. She was always sick, right up until she left home.

Grandma was blunter than Mother, but the message was the same. "You're not pretty, Miriam mine, so you better be smart. But not too smart. Don't get your head swelled." Little fuss was made over her grades, though they were always better than Mark's. Big, awkward, shy, she felt like something acquired at a rummage sale, one of those awful coats her mother got from resale shops.

"Aunt Yette *would* take her to Gimbel's and buy her a yellow dress. Lionel, what am I going to do? Yette didn't give me the sales slip, and they'll expect to see it on her. It looks like she's wearing a whole circus tent!" Her mother would look her up and down and sideways in the yellow dress, wringing her hands, and her father would laugh and say, patting Sonia's shoulder, that they should count themselves lucky it didn't have purple polka dots and green lace trim too. They should be thankful it didn't also have a neon sign that went on and off saying Buy Bonds for Israel.

By that time her father had a job. He was teaching music in a high school in Canarsie. He had given up trying to make a record, but he was still writing his songs and sending them to *Sing Out* and *Broadside*, hoping they would print one. For several months he took up electric guitar until the neighbors made the landlord threaten to evict them. He was a man with more charm than she had ever needed in her father: he could always charm her, but so often he was laughing at her. She could still remember one time when some younger faculty from his high school were over and they were commenting on how pretty Allegra was. Her father had replied with that smile that meant he was anticipating saying something witty, "Well, she's the youngest of three: practice makes perfect!"

At one time in her childhood she had determined to conquer her father with music and she had practiced and practiced, but the harder she tried and the more she sweated over her Chopin waltzes, the more irritable he became, the oftener he winced and stalked out. She was terrible. "That's a waltz, Miriam, a waltz. You know, a dance, a light beautiful dance. So why do you play it as a lament for the zombie's return? You must have a natural sense of lack of rhythm!"

But she did sense rhythms. She had always danced. First

she stood in her room and listened to the music, not with her ears but with her skin and muscle, feeling it swell through her until it moved her from within. Whenever she was left alone in the house or when she went to stay at her grandma's and had a room to herself, she would dance until the sweat ran down her body and her heart beat in her fingers like enormous wings. She learned to be light on her feet for a big woman, so that no one else in the house would know she was dancing. If someone did burst in, Mother coming to tell her to go to the bakery, Allegra dashing in to change, they would gape at her and say, "What on earth do you think you're doing?" She learned to answer that she was doing exercises. Thus she grew up fat but never weak.

Grew up: strange word. By the time she was twelve she was as tall as she would ever be. Her body was a pale heavy cocoon. Inside, though apparently passive she was actively changing, remaking herself.

She never imagined herself as having flaming red hair like the most popular girl in her eighth-grade class, Sheila Kellermann, or blonde like *shiksas* and Christmas angels: she never imagined herself petite or willowy: she imagined herself HERSELF but beautiful. It would be a magical transformation. Sometimes she made up other names, Anita, Shelley, Adrienne, convinced that would alter the way others perceived her. She would sign them in her diary. That was a notebook that had a few homework assignments in the front, just like all the others, so as not to attract the curiosity of her mother or Allegra. She was convinced that if one of them ever looked at what she wrote there she would die of shame instantly, turned to a pillar of salt like Lot's wife.

Often she fell painfully in love. For two agonizing years she loved the president of the Math Club (she was secretary, although she was better), who was also in the Chess Club with her. He was thinner and shorter with already a slight stoop, but he had beautiful luminous brown eyes and a smile that seemed to pass like slivers of fire through her bones. Beyond little jokes about extending the fief of their club and defeating other schools, their relationship was confined to setting each other problems or riddles (the cannibals and the missionary with the boat) to solve. Once for two weeks she deliberated and seethed, before she summoned up her courage to ask him if he had seen a certain exhibition yet. He said no. She asked him if he might like to go with her. He said he had promised his girl friend, regarding Miriam as if she had gone crazy. She went back to her diary.

Spending half of her waking hours in a state of deep fantasy, she was never as happy as when she saw a new movie or read a book or saw a story on television that she recognized as usable: a hero, a situation, a motif she could borrow. She was always exhausting old motifs. Though in most stories there were good roles for men, for her they were one-shot affairs. She could embroider the heroine's role but basically the hero overcame difficulties and then you were won or captured or whatever, and that was that. Basically, to get more mileage she had to make up a new role that was more active. Sometimes she could adopt a male role and then import favorite heroes from another fantasy to people the new landscape. For instance in westerns the only satisfactory role was to be a woman outlaw: everything else wore thin too quickly: the rancher's daughter, the sheriff's wife, or standing around a smelly saloon in feathers and beads looking like a dyed pigeon in a draft.

Most plots consisted of a hero going through adventures. Once in a while there was a heroine instead, but her adventures then were men she met and got involved with. Everybody said it was bad for a woman to have affairs with a series of men. Therefore women were supposed to be dull and good. Miriam decided that she would rather be bad and exciting, but she was not sure she would ever get the chance.

Her favorite self was Tamar De Luria, who was a real witch. Tamar was a student of anthropology who had acquired her powers by helping a tribe of beautiful primitive people on a south sea island fight off the attacks of white colonialists. In thanks they had adopted her into the tribe and taught her all their ancient tribal wisdom. She could pretend to be dead by reducing her breathing and heartbeat below the detectable level. She could hypnotize people, causing them to see things that were not there or to forget things they had seen. Miriam had studied hypnotism out of a book she got from the library. On her second attempt she actually hypnotized Allegra. Lionel cut off her permission to go to the library for a month.

Tamar could track people and walk so silently she never broke a twig and climb trees like a cat and scamper over buildings and fight as well as a man. Sometimes Tamar could read thoughts. She had that ability or not depending on the plot. When Tamar danced, men fell in love with her. Because of the need to conceal her occult powers, and because she never knew when a message would come from her island saying that her people were in danger again and she must return to save them, she could never marry.

Whatever Tamar was, she was never afraid. She confronted the men, with their files and their agents and their laws and their detention camps, who had blacklisted her father, and she made them take it all back. She burned their files so that nobody was afraid, the fear that sat in the house, that cold persistent gnawing fear that had yellowed the air of her childhood. It seemed to be equal parts fear of sinking into poverty and fear of the government, fear of the knock on the door, fear of the agent's report, fear of prison and fear of the neighbors, fear of disappearing, that cold whispery shadow of repression that lay over them for years and years.

Sometimes Miriam had Tamar die heroically. Sometimes she went back to her island and did a lot of native dancing and rescued her people and hunted wild animals. In the beginning, perhaps when Miriam was twelve or so, Tamar had a great many special powers that Miriam would think about in class: she could kill with a glance and make people think what she wanted them to. As Miriam endured through high school, Tamar shed her powers and acquired a social conscience and a tragic love life. Tamar had numerous affairs, satisfactorily passionate though vague in their physical details. Miriam had been given sex education books by her father. He thought it was important to give children Sex Education the Right Way, which meant dreary books written for teenagers with a whole chapter on Why It Is Right to Wait and a whole chapter on Why Women Are Naturally Monogamous, and no clear colored pictures of penises. She remembered what Mark had looked like as a baby when she used to give him his bath, but she doubted if that was what all the fuss was about.

When Miriam went to college, Tamar stayed home. During her freshman year at Michigan, Miriam's head cleared. Perhaps she had been allergic to her family. Anyhow she breathed deeply and her head and voice emerged through the fog. Always she would associate that slight harshness in her

voice, that huskiness, with seventeen years of coughing and
sniveling.

Eating dormitory veal birds and wan garbagey soups and
hamburgers extended with potato peelings, the dietitian's
salads of carrots and raisins and celery in raspberry jello, with
no one to fuss about how she ate or prey on her sense of
guilt, she promptly lost weight. She dropped twenty pounds
the first semester and her skin began to clear. All her clothes
were too big. She had always favored shapeless sweaters and
baggy slacks and extra cardigans over them, to disguise that
embarrassing body.

No longer overweight, her energy level rose. Suddenly she
could sit up till two in the morning and still make an eight
o'clock class. Because the agility of her new body turned her
on she even got involved in fencing and house volleyball for
a while. But she remained painfully modest. She never ran
around naked in the shower room with the other girls. She
had a long pink flowered flannel robe she wore at all times.
The girls on her floor pretended to think she had a hideous
birthmark. She was only ashamed.

Through her freshman and sophomore years she worked
hard and got straight As and was active in the left-liberal
campus groups. Occasionally a friend would fix her up with
a boy who was usually shorter and at least as shy. She would
try to make conversation and her hands would sweat and
turn cold.

Mark had his bar mitzvah and Allegra had her Sweet Sixteen party, but Miriam's puberty ritual was getting her braces
removed. But by the time Allegra had her party, Miriam in
New York for the summer did not care, did not care at all,
not even that Lionel had taken up the sitar, because something had finally happened. She resented being sent out to
look for work and did not look hard. By now the perennial
bad times had eased and she was tired from studying. Allegra
was going steady with the president of the high school Sportsmanship Council, and the family put no pressure on her to
waste her summer in an office. Miriam worked for a few
weeks at a temporary typing job and then spent most of what
she had made on contact lenses, without asking.

She did not care that the lenses made her eyes water and
sometimes when she took them out her lids were sore. She
didn't care that she seemed always to be getting dust and

cinders in her eyes and weeping. She did not care that once a week she dropped a lens and had to go crawling on her hands and knees about the floor, in the public street, looking for the little saucer of glass. She did not care that they made her sensitive to smoke and grime. She passionately cared that she no longer needed to wear glasses in public, that the last piece of ugly teen-age Miriam was exiled, and that she could see clearly. Being extremely myopic she had never seen well through her thick glasses. They distorted the size and shape of objects. Once she began to get accustomed to the lenses, she walked in a state of wonderment, staring. Since she had normal vision for the first time, she no longer tended to walk with her head bowed, afraid to look up for fear she would look straight at someone she knew without recognizing her. She developed a more stately walk. She stared at everyone. In the Museum of Modern Art on Saturday afternoon she stared at Philip, nonchalantly leaning on a piece of metal sculpture in the courtyard, striking a match off it to light his cigarette, and Philip stared back at her.

Then he came right to her. "I've been waiting for you all afternoon," he said. "Why are you so late?"

She began to laugh. "I didn't remember it was here I was supposed to meet you. I've been looking in the wrong place."

"This isn't the right place yet. Come on." Putting his arm around her, he led her out. It was exactly like a daydream. It was a fantasy, so she knew just how to behave. She did not hesitate, she did not worry that she would not know what to say. She went with him laughing and gazing at him, looking and looking at him while the world changed colors. He was beautiful and that made her want to laugh and touch him. She did not really believe he existed. Instead all that energy invested in daydreaming all those years had not merely dissipated. That would be bad physics. No, her spent energy had gathered itself and created this being who appeared to be flesh and blood but who was really her condensed wanting of years. She did not doubt she would go to bed with him. She was only afraid he would not ask her before she had to go home for supper, or before it was time for him to disappear and to turn back into an English 31 lyric or a movie poster.

PHIL (*He is talking to Jackson in Jackson's basement rooms, where he lives because he is janitor of three buildings*

*on East Tenth Street. Phil has just helped Jackson take out
the garbage cans and now they are smoking dope together.*)
So you know I picked her out right away, I mean you couldn't
miss her sailing in like the Russian Navy. That is a woman that
is built, I said to myself. She was wearing a shitty college
girl outfit consisting of dirty laundry bags, but you just
couldn't miss that body if she was wearing a barrel. Caught
her eye right away and it didn't take thirty seconds to execute
the mission. I decided she was ripe for it and I didn't need to
hang around with the tourists for an hour rapping about
"kulchur," though I was prepared as usual, man, to surround
us with a dancing cloud of words all the way. And she took
it like a winner, she came right along as easy as can be.
Along we sailed right out the door and down the sidewalk.
Man, I was so scared she'd think twice or be stolen away I
hailed a cab. I kept my hands off her in the cab and kept up
the steady patter till I got her upstairs. Then I opened a bottle
of rosy from the icebox—Donald the Duck, he's always got
some kind of wine on hand, little tins of S. S. Pierce goodies,
it's the place to live, my man. He's a high-living dude, is
Donald the Duck. By this time I'd had a hard on for forty-five
minutes or so. I figured, this is it, gold or a ringer, and I sat
down beside her on the daybed. So I reached for her and she
kind of hung her head, you know, all apologetic and big eyes.
She started off saying, "You know I've never done this
before."

I thought, hot damn, why every time you pick up a chick
does she have to pretend like it was written into the Constitution that nobody's ever picked her up before? Sweet Jesus,
why can't one of them say, "Gee, I pick up guys every day
and get laid, that's what it's all for"? But what she said was
that she didn't exactly know how to kiss and would I please
not mind, but I could show her and she would try.

I almost fell off the couch, it was so beautiful. Then I knew
I'd found it, the pot of gold, the end of the rainbow. The
poet's delight! I mean, she wasn't kidding, she didn't know
one end from the other, but with a body like that who requires expertise? Jackson baby, I'm telling you, this one is
out of a convent, a Jewish convent, she just has to be, they
don't send them out on the streets like that any more. She
was a stone virgin, but she was willing. I mean, lying there,
letting me take her clothes off. It became clear that I wasn't

going to have to seduce her a piece at a time, she wasn't
going to play it out with me by the inch. She had only one
question, did I have some means of contraception. . . .

No, those were her words. She has a formal way of talking,
as if she'd learned everything out of books. She's the only
live human I've ever heard refer to the sex organs since we
got out of the Army. God, her lying there watching me with
those huge brown eyes. I could have wept! You know, Jackson, she's bright too. She's a fucking mathematician! Man, she
gets straight As. She's a Jewish princess from Flatbush and
a goddamn meal ticket. She's going to support me in my approaching decline and keep me warm through the long dark
night of the soul. Jackson, think of it. There she was newly
hatched from her piggy bank. Think of the wrong dudes, the
make men, the nincompoops, the optometrists and errand
boys and stocking salesmen she could have met that day.

Now don't give me the eyebrow. You think it could have
been anyone, could have been you. Why not? I'll tell you
why. Sure, you'd have noticed her sailing in. But you would
have stood there in a deep study contemplating her, you
would have considered her carefully and classified her and
analyzed her from across the room. You would have considered the whys and why nots and the ins and the outs and
the pros and cons and the whys and wherefores, the economic
implications and the eugenic ramifications. You'd have
scratched your head and your chest and your left testicle
for half an hour. Then by the time you got it together
and came sauntering like a hobbled camel across the room,
she would have been long gone back to Flatbush on the subway shrugging and reading Henry Miller for kicks. But I
am always ready to embrace the possibility—put that in your
clay pipe and smoke on it. So if fifty-one in a row are dogs,
I have got at last into my long and interesting hands a
princess. . . . Sexually, Jackson, consider it coolly for one
moment, if you can leave off drooling. You're still getting it
from the bag in 4B, right? Sexually, a tabula rasa. No experience, no traumas, no shadows, no one has been there before,
but also no inhibitions. All that lovely equipment ready to
function when you plug in. And she's mine, Jackson, to mold
into a fit companion for one whom J. Singleton Proxmire
has called the most promising lyric poet of his age. . . . All
right, the most promising *young* lyric poet. Did you ever

hear of a promising middle-aged poet? Put that in your crapper: The finest slightly senile lyric poet of his generation will speak tonight at the local Y . . . No, you cannot, you shall not meet her. Not this trip. By and by, amigo, by and by. . . .

She could not fit together her memories of his apartment that afternoon with what it was like on later visits, when she actually looked around. Her images of that afternoon were too vivid to correct with observation. So forever the walls that afternoon were a pale gold, although on all other visits they were white. She did not look around or pick up the books lying on the coffee table or look at the records by the phonograph. She looked at him. His eyes were the sea. Ultramarine, aquamarine, cold and breaking light, startling against the tan of his face. No one in her family had blue eyes. They seemed to her unnatural set in the flesh, but beautiful. They were changeable too, now blue, now green, glinting like metal. There was texture in his face, gold wires of stubble, old shaving nicks, a scar at the hairline where his falling hair hid it. He said it was from a fight.

The worst moment was when he went to kiss her and she realized he would figure out she was not as experienced as she was pretending to be. She was also afraid he would think she was plain incompetent. So she decided to confess right away, before he decided she was an idiot. She was astonished then to realize he did not believe her.

"Why would I make that up? You confuse me."

"Oh, to make it special."

"But how could it not be special to me? I'm not proud of never having anything to do with men. I have to start somewhere."

"Pigeon, pigeon." He put his arms around her again. "You've picked the right place to start, believe me."

It was not as complicated as she would have thought, holding and touching, as it would have looked watching the coil of bodies from across the room. She was soon as excited as when she made up the vague but passionate stories, and soon more excited than she had ever been. The nuisance was the clothing, which made it hard to touch, and though it occurred to her quickly that it would be better to take off her clothes, she kept quiet and waited with what patience she could muster for him to undress her. He did that finally, stopping to kiss her as he uncovered her, and she felt that he seemed pleased. She asked him about contraception and he said he had a condom. Everything seemed to go smoothly until he was lying on her and pushing against her. He tried for a while and he stopped and explored more carefully with his finger.

"You really are a virgin."

She sat up, exasperated. "I warned you! You can't just give up now!"

"I've lost it," he said. It took her awhile to understand he meant that his penis was no longer erect. "Oh, my incredible great baby," he moaned, "You're so beautiful! I can't make it, I just can't stand it!" He laughed and wept at once. Tears rolled out of his eyes as she held him against her breasts. Understanding that he still was not displeased with her, she held him and rocked him and stroked his skin. It was wonderful that she was allowed to touch him, that she was given this male body to hold. He was nowhere as pasty white as her breasts and loins but had a coating of tan every place, though his arms and back and chest and face were bronzed. In height they were exactly matched, so that their bodies fit together face to face, or face to back. His buttocks were small and hard compared to hers, and hair grew abundantly on his chest and belly. He was muttering words she could not make out into her breasts. Cautiously her fingers trailed over the limp little organ drooping against him. "Touch me," he murmured. He took her hand and closed it over his and showed her how to caress him. Slowly the little worm began to fatten but still it curved and hung on itself until she learned how to take it in her mouth.

She had read a great many stories about women losing their virginities, and she had expected to be somewhat frightened. There seemed always an element of brutality, being torn, thrust open, rent apart. But it became clear to her that her defloration would not be even slightly scary. She was more in charge of it than was Philip. He taught her what to do with her hands and her mouth, but it cost considerable effort and patience to get him to the size and hardness required to enter her. Eventually, however, she heaved and he pushed and they battered their way into penetration. By that time

Phil no longer had a condom, so he withdrew to put it on and promptly lost his erection again.

"Look, you're bleeding like a stuck pig, darling. Let's call it off for the day. Tomorrow we'll continue your lessons, same time, same place. You're a darling, you're a real find, you're a rare and living beauty, Miriam. Will you come back to me tomorrow, from Flatbush and Dreary Farther Brooklyn?"

"I will, I will." She threw her arms around his neck and they embraced, kneeling on the bed smeared with her blood in a large comma. Phil seemed happy. He put on a record and without deciding to, she got up and began to dance. After watching a moment he came and danced with her. It was new, dancing with another person instead of alone. She enjoyed the dancing more than she had the sex. They danced roles and attitudes, they danced flirtation and fight, they made faces and picked up props to embroider their attitudes— a pillow, a feather, a vase.

"I can play with you!" She held his face between her hands. "We can play together. I've never played with anyone."

"We'll play a great many games, pigeon, wait and see. I'm as full of games as Santa's bag."

He walked her to the subway and, standing outside the turnstyle as she went through to the Seventh Avenue express, he said with sudden gravity, "You will come back? You won't turn chicken?"

"Oh! No! I tell you, if there were a subway strike tomorrow, I'd walk, I'd roller-skate. But I'll come back."

She was born to herself. She had become beautiful and a woman and the Queen of Sheba and Merciful Mary and Holy Aphrodite. The dancing remained good and the sex improved. The last of her pimples vanished. She felt herself walking differently, moving with the joy she had always felt in her secret dancing.

Phil worked evenings tending bar, but they had the days together. Every day during the week when she was supposed to be looking for work, she got up early and went into Manhattan with the paper. She went directly to his apartment and let herself in and climbed into bed with Phil, who would wake up gradually and hug her and cuddle and make up nonsense. Donald, whose apartment Phil was staying in, was at work by the time she came and did not know she had a key. By the time he came home from work she was gone. Phil's bed was a studio couch in the living room but sometimes they used Donald's big bed. He never seemed to notice. In the mornings they made love and talked and told stories.

In the afternoons they went out to play in the city. Never again would she love New York as she did that summer, never would it seem so like a stage setting painted in with bold luminous strokes, such a fair that burned all day and all night with booths of all conceivable games and pleasures. Never before had she lied to her family, though she had always been secretive out of a fear of being mocked, especially by Lionel. But she understood she must protect her relationship with Phil from their scrutiny. Some days she announced she was going to the library to study. In August a friend who made films came through and Phil went off to spend a week with him and someone named Jackson out on the Island. He wanted her to come but instead she got a temporary typing job, to prove to her parents she was looking.

Going to him on the subway, she felt lucid in her joy. He was the right man at the right time. In September she would return to school and probably when she came back to New York he would be gone or he would have another woman. She sensed a lightness in him: he might as easily drift off as stay. He had started school, then he had been drafted and sent to Vietnam. Now he was studying again at N.Y.U. She tried to be quite matter-of-fact about the likelihood of losing him when she left.

They touched on so many changes in each other. She grew with him. He must be shielded from her mother, who would ask immediately what were his prospects. She would wail he was not Jewish, she would point out how unfit he was to be her husband. They would not understand that she did not want a good gray husband with a pay check. She wanted Phil, who made her open wide to sights and sounds and tastes and the feel of things, who made her sensual and beautiful, who made her mind spin and made her laugh and made her adventurous and daring, as before only in fantasy. It was the right time and the right man. Summer was all too short, like fireworks.

"You have no idea how to dress, pigeon. You're a slob. You dress like a Brooklyn high school social studies teacher, just like your mother, right? Your idea of getting dressed up is to attach a few rhinestones and put on uncomfortable shoes. Princess, only a poet could have perceived the woman through your Flatbush army uniform. You look so much better when you take your clothes off, it's ridiculous. However, until the fuzz develop a more enlightened attitude toward beauty naked, we'll have to put clothes over you in public."

It was drizzling and drab, a head cold of the air, but they did not mind. Donald had started out for work before the sky clouded over and left his fancy English umbrella that opened by touching a button in the leather handle. "Instant erection," Phil said. "Machine over man." He had also left his English raincoat, which would not fit Phil but looked elegant draped over his shoulder or held over his arm carelessly, with the label showing. Phil took her to a boutique, instructing her en route on general strategy and communications.

He found the right dress at once and had her try it on for him. Attended by a saleswoman, he slumped in a chair. "Well, the style is pleasant but the color is dreadful on you."

The saleswoman tried to assure him that Miriam looked devastating in that dull dark yellow.

"If you care for red Indians," he said, fixing her with a stare.

Miriam tried on five more dresses. She liked all of them, but she could tell from his eyes that he did not. However, he selected one to try again and to pretend he was deeply considering. In the meantime that yellow dress had been returned to the rack and removed from the rack to his side, under the raincoat. He got up abruptly. "Get dressed, Cecily. That blue number is the only possibility. How late are you open? . . . We'll likely be back."

"Do you want me to put it aside for you?"

"Yes, why don't you do that?"

The yellow dress was almost backless and made her tan glow. She walked back and forth in the apartment in it. She could not wear a brassiere with it because it would have shown, but somehow it worked anyhow. "I can't take it home, you know."

" 'You know' is what I say. Do not pick up my mannerisms. It cloys."

"Phil, your mannerisms are sticky. Besides, I'm sure you picked up some of them yourself. Don't be such a thorny prick."

He laughed. "I can't push you around. Why not? Why don't you quail at my frown?"

"I'm too heavy to push around. You can't lift me either."

"You're so sure of me, sometimes I want to kick the shit out of you."

"Listen to me. I can't take this dress home."

"Indeed, I'm sure modeling it for your parents would be a waste of your time. So park it here. Other wonders of the Western world will join it."

He taught her to wear funky colors and bold colors and cloth with an interesting texture. He taught her to look first at how the cloth lay against her body: how it lay when she stood, when she sat, when she moved. Walking wrapped in his long arm she would catch a glimpse of herself in a store window and be startled. She could have been any age. She looked as she probably would for years, matured and wearing her full body like a flag.

Through Labor Day weekend and early September, a veining of sadness tinted the days. Sonia was putting pressure on her to spend more time at home. She could no longer pretend to be job hunting. Allegra was back in high school and Lionel was teaching full time, but Sonia was home and wanted her there. Sonia was not teaching this year. She was into her psychosomatic illnesses again. She *kretchzed* all day long of fatigue and stomach aches. Kept home by guilt, by pressure, Miriam quarreled with her. Why should Sonia want her around when all they did was fight?

"Let me cut your hair," Sonia would croon in that husky voice that wanted to wheedle her back to a pliable child again. "At least put it up! But you *should* want to go with us to Winkleman's, he's a nice boy. What's wrong, you're too stuck up to meet a nice boy? Running out of the house, running down the street like a wild wind, you're just trying to get away from me!"

Sonia was lonely and Miriam knew it. But it was tricky too. The husky croon urged her to remember how they had conspired in her early childhood, how Sonia had confided in her, how together they had managed and cared for their family. But Miriam felt that ever since Sonia had handed her her first sanitary napkin with a horrendous list of things she must not do (leave it in the bathroom, get blood on her clothes, flush it down the toilet lest she block the plumbing) they had been at war.

Sonia was overweight, always overweight and ashamed. Lionel was not fat. He told her she had no self-discipline. He was always pointing out women her age who were gorgeous: even while they watched television he would point out actresses and he would tell Sonia this one was forty-six and that one was fifty-two and that one was twice a grandmother.

Miriam felt as if Sonia were secretly angry at her for losing weight. She felt as if her mother were engaged in a campaign to overfeed her, leaving cakes and candy bars out and tempting her to nosh between meals on just a bite of this or that. "You eat all that *chozzerai* at school, and at home nothing's good enough. You'll get sick, mark my words, you'll come down with mononucleosis like your cousin Michael."

Miriam resented being kept home, she resented feeling guilty when she escaped. She did not want to give up a moment of the precious time running through her fingers, time to be spent with Phil in bed tangling their bodies, through the parks and museums and over the bridges, to be flaunted through all their games and codes and confidences. It was a sweet honeydew melon to be eaten down to the rind. The second week she had got herself a diaphragm she kept at his apartment when she was not carrying it in herself or hiding it in a rolled sock, and she felt safe and glad in her body.

In September Donald the Duck stopped going out to Fire Island every weekend, and they could no longer have the apartment to themselves all the time. She finally met him. He was stout and he waddled and he was meticulous in all of his habits, setting her teeth on edge. Yet a sequence of elegant bony model types came through the apartment to dine with him on gourmet meals he rustled up, as he put it, and to share his bed. On weekends Phil and Miriam had the studio couch and no privacy, but still they made long slow love and told stories and carried on, negating Donald and his elegant partners.

Yet the time ran out. Instead of returning to school early

as usual, she made her departure the last day before registration began. The afternoon before her plane she went into Manhattan, saying she absolutely had to do some last-minute shopping and would be back in a couple of hours, and no, Sonia could not come along because she complained too much about her feet and was slow in the stores.

The afternoon hurt. It seemed covered with fine sticky hairs that secreted a substance sweet and poisonous. Twice they almost quarreled. He had done up her clothing in a neat parcel and rather formally he presented her with four poems he said he had written about her. They did not leave the apartment. It was a Tuesday and Donald the Duck was at work at the credit card corporation where he was a minor executive. They lay naked on the open couch and held each other, but all her best and most intricate efforts could not produce an erection in Phil.

"You don't want me to go away?"

"No, I don't want you to go away. I want you to throw over everything for me. I want you to quit school and come live in my closet and we'll subsist on old rubber bands. I want you to want to, and if you wanted to, I'd be terrified, I'd run like hell."

"But I do want to. I love you, I love the person I am with you. But how can I explain to my parents about the winter? How will I support you in your old age if I don't get my degree?"

"Fly away, pigeon, fly away home. Your house is on fire, your books will all burn."

"What do you want, Philip?"

"I want to be miserable at the top of my lungs. I want to scream and yell and break things. I want to fuck you, and I can't even do that."

"But you have so many times and you will again. I'll come and find you next summer."

"Are you going to keep yourself pure for me?"

Sideways she looked at him. "Is that a trick question?"

"As many tricks as you can learn. I'm sending you out to try what you've studied with me, pigeon. Unless I'm mistaken—and as you know, I am never, never mistaken—back at the school you'll find it a different scene this year. You will try out what you've practiced and write me about your adventures. I want a letter every two weeks, each more outrageous than the last."

"Will you write me too? Please?"

"I'll send you poems, which is better, and I'll tell you lies, which is worse. I'll write, Miriam, hastily, badly, wildly, nastily, and unsteadily. Now get the hell out of here. And don't look back!"

7

Is Sex More Fun Than Pinochle?

Miriam wrote Phil every two weeks—the compromise between her craving to communicate with him, her massive class schedule, and her fear of seeming too dependent by flooding him with letters. She worked on the letters as carefully as on her problems for class, deleting the many paragraphs of longing and trying craftily to get reassurances from him that nobody else had quite replaced her, striving hard for a tone that would make her interesting. At the same time, she wanted to tell him everything about her life and extract his opinion on how she was conducting herself.

DEAREST PHILIP,

If you had not given me explicit orders, I would not bother with extracurricular activities here. I miss you. There is no one like you. It is all second rate and drab. But I am doing my best to carry out instructions. I'd still rather be with you in darkest Flatbush than with anybody else in Paris. It would be more interesting.

I am living in Martha Cooke, which is better than my old dorm. It's for women with high grade point averages and active on campus: elitism pure and simple. Still the accommodations are pleasant, the rules not so tight, and it's right on campus.

I have discovered something alarming. Being
attractive is a con game. Men are so brainwashed in
this society, they want to buy any product that comes
well recommended. If you convey by how you act
that you expect a man to find you irresistible and
devastating, nine times out of ten he acts that way too!
It's ridiculous. When I think of the men who looked
right through me last year—those same idiots are
falling over themselves. It makes me want to belt them
in the jaw, frankly. You could see me as I was,
and the only difference is that now I'm a good con artist.

Still I enjoy it sometimes. If I could get rid of
the sense of conjuring trick, I would enjoy it more.
All the time I was growing up I wished every day to be
suddenly pretty like my sister Allegra. I think you
were always handsome. You were born grinning. But I
was lumpy and dreadful, and I was made to feel
twice as lumpy. Now you're my good fairy godmother
—now don't get angry. Neither the adjective nor the
noun is appropriate! But the magic is.

It's other people make one beautiful or ugly. So
if you know how to manipulate their reactions, if
you do a good selling job, they decide you're
beautiful. Women are so dreadfully unhappy when they're
losing, which is 90% of women 90% of the time.
My mother always felt that she isn't attractive
enough for my father, I think. That's easier for me to
see now. He's good-looking in his way, I guess, though
he doesn't turn me on, I mean incest taboos aside.
He's too self-pitying and he takes advantage of her.
When I was younger I always took his side because
I wanted so badly for him to love me.

I think my mother believes the only reason he's
stayed is because she supported us all—I guess it was
only four or five years but it looms large. Because
she felt she had to be this terrific housekeeper besides
and glamorous too, and she hadn't the foggiest notion
how. He's had affairs, I guess everybody in the family
knows. When he was giving guitar lessons, he
got involved with a girl and another time my mother
was crying her eyes out because she found a letter

from a woman singer he met at the Philadelphia folk festival.

My mother has always felt inferior and while I was growing up she put that on me. I had to be twice as good at everything, nothing was ever good enough, but at the same time she assumed in her bones that I would be inadequate. They put that on me till you came and cut the webs away.

Well, this is tedious, isn't it? I just keep thinking now about things I never saw so clearly. To the attack again. I went out for a while with a guy I had a crush on all last year from a math class. He has beautiful long lashes and the look of a wasted Renaissance prince. Alas, he turns out to be a virgin and impotent, or a virgin because impotent. I think about once a month some woman gets him almost to it and fails. I tried, dear Philip, I tried. I have put him back where I found him. It occurred to me that perhaps in his ascetic condition he has a vitamin deficiency or is actually undernourished. He appears lacking in energy. A good Jewish mama would fix him in no time.

While playing my rotten game of tennis with a girl from my house, I picked up my second. He appeared a bit weak in gray matter but equipped with muscles and energy and willingness. Indeed the first time we were alone he jumped me. It was rather like being made love to by a cement mixer. I went through the proper demurrals he seemed to expect and allowed myself to be mauled and carried off—figuratively speaking, as the whole scene took place on a couch. Alas, again: he did not lack enthusiasm but staying power. A four-stroke man. For two weeks I tried to get him past that point. He doesn't seem to grasp the the idea that intercourse consists of more than putting it in and coming. By the end of my fourteen days of patience I was becoming an irritable bitch. Lack of orgasm makes one nasty, I think, and his conversation lacked content and variety. So I dumped him.

A great willingness and some idea of how to connect with men doesn't seem to give one a satisfactory sex life. Let alone establishing Relationships. The Renaissance

Prince was totally non-verbal except when discussing
Abelian groups and the Four-Stroke Man was great on
basketball and television and how he kept in shape with
Tiger's Milk.

I am trying to seduce my section man in political
science, which I am taking to fulfill my social science
requirement. He is about your age and, although
not as attractive, has some wit. I think he might actually
talk. He is wary and suspects a trap. (Bulbs flash,
the dean's man and the campus police jump out from
under the desk, catching him with his hand on my
breast). However, I think he is susceptible, and tracking
him is more fun than my last two non-events.

I actually like him. He has progressive ideas and
doesn't seem to think women are for putting down. I
think I will not try again unless I like somebody,
because otherwise there is not enough to pass the time. I
never had the feeling that the Renaissance Prince
or the Four-Stroke Man were capable of dealing with
me at one and the same time as sex object and as human
being. If I talked too much they got upset, because
that turned them off. It reminded them too heavily
there was a person there, me, and not just a body.
If you don't like somebody and he doesn't like you,
then if the sex doesn't work out, as it frequently seems
not to, the whole evening is blown. Then I get the
feeling I'd be better off back at the dorm working
on a problem.

One of my professors, the one in topology, is
brilliant if a little hard to follow. He puts stuff up on
the blackboard so fast I know that someday he will go
right off the end and fall on the floor and continue
scribbling without pause. I like him the best of
anybody but he's married and totally abstracted. I don't
think he needs me in his life when he has topology, a
more interesting mistress when you come down to
it, love, and I wish you were here to come down
to it. I am obeying you but would rather be with
you. Send me poems and a less facetious letter next
time. You write all metaphors and no facts. I cannot
tell what you are talking about half the time. I am
sure you were right to quit that new job if you didn't like

it, but what is an S-M bar? Please have mercy on my
mathematical mind and tell me things straight, with
a glossary maybe.

                                        LOVE!
          XXXXXXXXXXXXXXXXXXXXXXXXXXXXXX
                        YOUR MIRIAM

8

Mothers and Daughters

Sonia's letters tended to be dreary. Typically they began with
a complaint about the weather: it was always raining or
sleeting or sweltering. Miriam once wrote an imitation for
Phil of a Sonia letter:

                                        Monday, 11 A.M.

It is a cold rainy day and the streets are flooding
and the sewers backing up and your father has just
tracked mud all over the clean kitchen which I just spent
the morning cleaning down on my hands and knees. The
scrub brush broke and so I had to clean the floor
with my toothbrush. It took me four hours.

I will have to buy a new scrub brush and I just
don't know where the money will come from. In
addition we must re-cover the living-room couch and
your sister Allegra needs a new Dior original dress to
wear to her class picnic this Sunday, and your father
needs a new sitar, gold plated this time. He says
it is very important to have a gold-plated sitar to have
a good tone, and you know that your father is very
particular about his tone! Therefore I am having to cut
down your allowance this month, I know you will
understand our situation.

I can hardly write this letter, my hand is so sore and red and raw and bleeding from the knuckles because of having to get down on my hands and knees and spend four hours cleaning the kitchen floor with a toothbrush because your sister Allegra used the scrub brush to splatter-paint her wall. She says all of the other girls in her club at school splatter-paint their walls. It is a very exclusive club, all the other girls are the children of doctors. Haven't you met anybody at school yet? Don't you go out? Perhaps you should join a sorority. There are good Jewish sororities nowadays. If it is not too expensive. Perhaps that way you could meet a nice young man. Remember you are not getting any younger, daughter mine, and Opportunity is passing you by. Never again will you have such good opportunities to meet nice young men as right now, today, while you are attending a good college. Remember not to stay up too late at night studying, you don't want to get skinny and unhealthy and catch a cold. You are very susceptible to colds, remember your chest and do not stay out when it is wet and cold like today.

Your brother Mark got Bs and two Cs this semester, isn't that wonderful! We are lucky to have such a smart boy as our Mark. He doesn't write too often but he sends his laundry home every week and I can keep in touch with my loving boy by looking at the stains. Your brother makes such wonderful stains! Each one is special and I know he is thinking of his mother every day.

Remember your loving mother and be a good girl. Your father and your sister Allegra send their love and also Aunt Yette. She is very sick. I am not feeling too good myself. I have pains in my stomach all the time. Your father says it is my imagination and I eat too much. Well, I am getting older and I guess I should not be surprised to have pains in my stomach. Allegra will not eat at all. She is on a diet of grapefruit. She read about it in a magazine. Be sure and eat well and be careful about eating out. You can never tell in restaurants what they put in the food.

YOUR LOVING MAMA

In every letter Sonia complained of her stomach. She was always *krechtzing*. Miriam suspected that her mother would have thought it downright immoral to feel good. Nobody paid much attention, it wasn't like Mark having an infected wisdom tooth or Lionel getting laryngitis. Then the first week in May she got a phone call from her father, just as she got back to Martha Cooke at ten in the evening.

"Hello there. How's the girl?"

"Fine, Dad. How are you? How come you're calling?"

"I've been trying to reach you all evening, but they said you weren't in."

"Yes, I was studying at the library." She had been seeing her section man of last semester. He had held out till after finals: a man of principle. She liked the relationship. She went out with other men but saw him only at his apartment. She would go over, he would cook supper, they would sit and talk or listen to music and then they would go to bed. Of course she would have to get up again and go back to the dormitory to sleep. He was writing his doctoral thesis about an abolitionist paper and she learned a great deal about that period. He was mildly radical and reminded her a little of her father: his politics was a kind of intellectual decoration and admiration of others who were more committed, and it would never intentionally affect the course of his life or career. She thought he should perhaps be warned that, like her father, he might find at some point that a wave of repression would grind him too, but what was the point? Her father had retreated into safety and was a worse person for that withdrawal. He had lost the only counter to his self-indulgence.

"I was trying to reach you all evening," her father repeated and cleared his throat.

"Is something wrong?"

"Don't get upset. You know how your mother is."

"What's wrong now?"

"Well, they don't exactly know yet. It's nothing to worry about. But she has to go into the hospital for a visit."

"Into the *hospital?* What for?"

"Well, they have to take a look inside."

"Inside what?"

"It's just a diagnostic procedure. Her small intestine, I think it is."

"Mama has to have an operation?"

"Don't overdramatize! You sound like your grandmother. They're just going in for a look."

"What kind of a look?"

"To see what's wrong. Now let's not get ourselves all worked up. There's no reason to behave irrationally. She'll be in the hospital for a week or so while they carry out their diagnostic procedures. That's the way they do things. She has a good doctor."

"Should I come home?"

"I don't see any reason for you to leave school so late in the semester. What time do your classes end?" He mulled it over nervously. "You'll be coming in June anyhow, she'll be out of the hospital. But you should write your mother regularly and why don't you send her a card? Something to cheer her up. Let me give you the address."

After finals in June when she arrived in Brooklyn, her mother was still in the hospital and what was wrong had been diagnosed as cancer. A cold wave of panic passed over Miriam, leaving her disbelieving. Sonia was not old, she was not quite fifty. She was too young! Rachel didn't even have cancer, although her husband had died of it. How could Sonia have cancer?

When she came to sit in Sonia's room in the hospital, her mother was her mother—pale, yellowed, bloated and wasted, but the same *kvetch.* Sonia immediately launched an attack. "What kind of outfit is that? Miriam mine, are you wearing a brassiere or not? Do you want people to see you in the halls looking like a . . . a gypsy? *Es passt nit!*" Sonia clucked and wrung her hands.

"Mother, all you've got to worry about is what clothes I got on? I'm here, never mind the window dressing."

"It isn't like you're a little girl any more, nobody would mind. You're big as a horse and you want to go around hanging out like a bum!"

"Mama, I look good this way. I don't need a bra! It feels good not to wear one."

"What do you care how it feels? That's disgusting. How can you run around with people looking?"

Her mother with cancer was still her enemy. Her mother thought the best she could hope for was not to be looked at. Don't draw attention, double-lock the door, don't speak to strangers. "Mama, leave me alone! Don't tear me down!"

"If you're satisfied. None so blind as them that will not see. I wouldn't let somebody in my classroom looking like that! What should you care what people say behind your back?"

Her reflection hung enormous and bulging on the water pitcher. Listening to her mother, she began to feel fat, huge, oozing flesh. She found herself hunching forward to hide her breasts, fingering her nose for length. "Mama, I do fine! Get off my back!"

"You mean people stare because they can't understand how your family lets you run around like that. Is that what you learned going away to school? No wonder you don't have prospects. Even your brother agrees you look like a slob."

"The feeling is mutual! He doesn't even clean the tub after himself! He shaves and he leaves his hairs all over the sink!"

"Now look at your sister. She keeps herself neat. I'm not saying she isn't too thin, she eats like a mousie. But she's neat and she looks nice and the boys respect her and they ask her out. Did you see her new boy friend? That's Dr. Moshman's son Roger. They got tickets to a musical next week, in the balcony."

"Mama, I don't want to go to a musical and sit in the balcony with a dentist's son with all his teeth capped!"

"Who'd ask you, running around with your bosom flopping and your hair hanging like a hippie? Miriam mine, listen to your mother, you're not getting younger and opportunity is passing you by every day. Listen to me, make your mother happy before it's too late! I worry about you, I lie here and worry about you so I can't sleep. They give me pills but I can't sleep."

"Mama, don't worry about me, because I can take care of myself. I'll have a profession. I'm the only woman in my department who gets As. Worry about Allegra. If she doesn't get a husband, if she gets married and divorced—"

"Don't say such things! Don't wish such things on your own flesh and blood!"

"What will she do then? Look in the mirror for fifty years?"

"You think you're so smart because you get a few good grades. You always could get around your teachers."

Oh, section man who had committed the brave public act of borrowing a car to take her to the airport. He had helped her off on the cheapie midnight flight to LaGuardia with her suitcase, typewriter, and books.

"When you learn to cover up some of that smartness instead of being so pushy with people, you'll catch more flies with honey than vinegar. Nobody wants to marry a walking encyclopedia!"

"Mama, I don't want to get married!"

"You want to be like your Aunt Yette? What kind of life is that? Listen to your mother and don't be so proud. You want to end up living in other people's houses, on charity?"

She left the hospital feeling swollen and numbed and exhausted. She could not make contact. Sonia could not leave off playing policewoman, could not stop trying frantically to batter her back into line. She could not express her caring to Sonia. They clenched and grappled but nothing real was exchanged.

The next day she went to see Philip. He was living down on East Tenth Street in a basement apartment that belonged to a friend, off to Mexico for the summer. Phil was living in his tiny apartment and doing his job, being janitor to three buildings. He took out the garbage cans, swept the halls, accepted packages and made minor repairs, and once in a while laid the woman in 4B—which Phil insisted was part of the job.

The apartment was peculiar. It was mostly empty. There was a mattress on the floor, the usual kitchen and bathroom equipment, and a formica table and two kitchen chairs. That was all: no chairs or sofas or dressers or end tables or desks. With the white cement walls and the starkness, it made her think of a jail. Phil laughed at that: he said it was nothing like any jail he had ever seen. For one thing, the toilet worked.

Phil shook his head, sitting cross-legged on the mattress. "A hermit's cell, my child. Vows of poverty and chastity—except for 4B, which is part of the job—that's Jackson's style."

Kneeling before him she put her hands on his shoulders and slowly rubbed against him. "I hope you're not thinking of taking up his style with his house and his job?"

Yet when they began to make love, Phil was impotent and she could not rouse him. She lay beside him helplessly and all of a sudden she began to cry. "Phil, I know what it is. You sense something wrong in me."

"That's what I've been looking for." He spoke quite remotely. Turning on his side he lay with head propped up staring at her. His eyes were cold and watchful, ice blue.

"My mother has cancer . . ." She said that much and then her throat closed tight and she wept and wept. His eyelids sank and his face relaxed. Then he opened his eyes again and held her against him. He stroked her hair and her tears ran over his shoulder and into the pillow. She could not speak, she could hardly breathe. Her throat was closed and she gasped for breath and still the tears ran out of her like blood to soak the pillow.

She became aware his impotence had vanished when still lying beside her he guided his penis gently between her labia and slowly began to slide into her. She tried to say no, but she could not speak. She shook her head wildly and tried to push him back, but he held her with the full strength of his hands and arms until he was buried in her with his legs scissored about hers.

"Don't, Miriam, don't do a guilt trip. I have to unwind you. Let me bring you out. Don't push, don't fight me. Just lie still and let me draw you out." Slowly he moved in her and she would not move and did not want to feel. "Us being together doesn't make her pain worse. I'm real too, pigeon, and loving you is real. Don't deny me with your body. Don't ever close yourself against me." She realized she was breathing again, the knot was dissolving in her, the ragged pain in her chest was easing its constriction. "Don't you dare feel guilty, I won't let you put that on us. Feel guilty only if you deny me. Loosen, loosen. Give yourself back to me."

Why the resistance in her? Because she had not been able to love Sonia for years and Sonia had not been able to love her, she should not love him. Because inside her was a core memory of loving and being loved in the mama-center, the lap, the baby milk and warmth. It seemed a sin to loosen to a man, Philip, to let her love open to him, to have sex in the region of death and pain; to love now felt obscene and impious. To feel toward Philip was to deny her mother and her mother in her flesh: her mother, somehow in her Miriambody as well as her own sick Sonia-body. Her mother was in her flesh scolding and whispering she must reject him even as shamefully she loosened and warmed to him. "Come on, Miriam, come over to me, open to me, come back to me, come . . ."

Afterward she asked him if sensing in her the struggle over her mother's sickness was what had made him unable to take her at first.

"Maybe." He shrugged. "Maybe it was more smelling the other men."

"The other men? You mean at school? But you told me to!"

"Sure. You would have anyhow. There is more dignity in telling you to do that which you would do anyhow."

"But, Philip! You told me to! I wouldn't have. I think I had relationships as much to have something to write you about as for anything in them. I wanted to please you!"

"Nevertheless I have burned with the green fire of jealousy. Aw, don't stare at me with big bruised eyes. All that was interesting and productive of poems. And that's what lasts."

The bedroom was stark, nothing but the mattress and Phil's suitcase. But one morning Phil saw a perfectly good mattress thrown out on the street, and together they moved it into the bedroom beside the other so that the whole small room was carpeted with mattress and became a room-sized bed to roll on. It was dim, with the only light filtering from an airshaft in which rumbled toilets flushing and electric razors and songs and curses and radios and babies. The grimy light made the room feel under water. They painted the walls with sea creatures, with fish and squids and mermaids and strands of filmy seaweed. Phil said they could paint it over white before Jackson returned. Back in the utility part of the basement they found leftover paint in partly used cans. What they tired of they blanked out and replaced. Sea horses and whales and huge clams and a purple lobster walking on its tail. A woman fucking an octopus. Whales in the act. One day at the Aquarium in Coney Island they watched two white pilot whales engaged in hours of flirting foreplay and graceful afterplay and brief turning bouts of energetic fucking. "Their whole bodies are erogenous zones," Phil muttered. "I want reincarnation as a whale. To whom should I apply, do you think?"

"Moby Dick. Now I understand that name!"

But the days of wandering and games playing were few. She needed him, she needed him dreadfully. Afternoons they stayed home, smoking hash in his water pipe and lying naked on the bed and painting on the walls. Often he read to her his own and other poems and they lay forehead to forehead dreaming and touching and talking. She began to understand that he had feared losing her when she began to have sex with other men. For all his boasting, often he could not make it. He had feared she would discover that not all men required to be coaxed to erection and that she would not return to him; or worse, she would return with scorn, with pity, with secret contempt.

She feared she would never make him understand that she did not mind the extra effort. She came easily with him. She was relaxed and totally there with him, and she had the confidence that if one thing failed he would try something else, he would not withdraw from her. With other men sex was sometimes satisfactory and more vigorous, but only with him was it magical. Only his body held in her arms seemed beautiful and precious and intricate and wiry and frail. He was the Player King. He was a wan knight-errant come at once for succor and battle. He was wounded and subtle and he floated in her body as in a river and brought up treasure. Sex was a speaking, and no matter how much more endowed her section leader had been, sex with him had been dumb by comparison. Sex was only a part of the touching with Philip, an intensification of touching with the fingers and tongue and memory and intelligence.

"Sometimes I have a secret myth, Philip. I imagine that we're really brother and sister."

"I don't know how in that lovely family of yours you would have developed a taste for incest."

"Philip! Don't you know what I mean?"

His face was shadowed, half turned from her. "I understand better than you do. Now shut up."

Sores in him she stubbed on, hurting both of them. She felt as if she were growing out of him in a union more comradely than lovers and closer, if less violent. Only alone with him could the grief within her cut loose. She could not comprehend her pain. Guilt and pity and grief and loss. She felt lacerated, crying to exhaustion. She came and went from the hospital. Sonia had good days when she was lucid and demanding, bad days when the sedation blurred her mind and she cried and talked randomly. Days of greater pain and lesser pain. But from week to week she was visibly decaying. Sonia was dying. Her mother was slowly dying.

Nobody in the family would acknowledge what was happening. She hated her father and her brother and her sister and she felt impacted with them in mutual guilt. Not one of them had listened when Sonia talked of her pain. She had satirized her mother's complaints. Dr. Steinbaum said, "I don't understand how Mrs. Berg could have waited so long before she came in. The pain had to have been considerable for months. It's impossible to understand what makes these women wait so long when they know something serious is wrong."

But Miriam understood. None of them had listened. All of them told Sonia she was a drag, always complaining. They tuned out, till she could not believe in the legitimacy of her feelings. Who was she to have serious pain? Who was she to feel anything real? Only Sonia, who never did feel quite right. She must have been afraid. She must have thought of cancer and her father dying. She must have brooded, but she could not speak because no one wanted to listen.

Now Sonia was gradually and miserably dying from operation to operation in the hospital room she shared with two others. The women in those beds came and went, came in for an operation and walked out, came in for an operation and went behind the screens and were wheeled out, but Sonia remained. The room was hot in the long summer days. Sonia lay slightly yellow and with her flesh loosened from her bones against the mound of pillows, with the flowers changed once a week beside her and a red geranium plant and a couple of best sellers that never changed and her rented TV at the foot of the bed. She would leave the room only for another operation. Yet her father continued heartily saying, "When your mother comes home, we'll have to do something about that couch in the living room."

Nobody made Miriam work that summer, but she was getting on so badly with Lionel she would not ask for money and he did not offer her any. Phil got her a job posing for an informal class doing figure drawing. Posing paid better than typing and was not quite as boring. Phil was penny-pinching because he had been accepted into graduate school at Boston University in the fall. A former teacher of his had moved there with a full professorship and had got Phil in. Phil wavered about going. Sometimes he said, "Aw, I've got to be able to gouge a living from those academic factories. I figure I should knock down a degree in three years. I'll treat it like any other job. Anybody that can tend bar on Saturday night can handle a department of English. My only problem will be hiding my contempt for those soft damp bastards." Other times he said he was being co-opted. That spring he had got friendly with Joe Rosario, a bright economist just getting his Ph.D. at N.Y.U., who had grown up in East Harlem, and they argued about revolution and went to the anti-war demonstrations that Joe helped organize. Joe made a fuss about Phil being a Vietnam veteran who was against the war, but that embarrassed Phil. After all, he said, he'd gone. Phil's politics confused her: they seemed all emotion and reaction.

She wondered where her father thought she got the money to exist that summer: did he think she printed it on a press in her closet or begged it on the subway? She felt hostile to him. In childhood he had been her adored parent. She was always trying to please him and failing: her good was never good enough. He was obviously superior to the fathers of her friends: had suffered more, had more friends, was better-looking and had a wonderful voice and talent. Even as a high school teacher he seemed special, popular with students, always arranging something exciting for assemblies, with friends among the younger and less hidebound faculty.

She kept wanting him to ask her where she was getting the money to spend on subway fare and clothing and books. But he had the habit of not permitting practical matters to intrude. It was convenient for him to forget to give her money. It was a fierce struggle carried out entirely on one side. He was oblivious and she could not make him ask the questions to which she could deliver the crushing replies. She realized for the hundredth time, although with diminished pain, that she did not loom large in Lionel's view of the world.

He expected her to take over the housewife role Sonia had always played, even when she used to work. When Miriam was little she had naturally filled in with Mark and Allegra, keeping an eye on them, wiping their noses, changing their diapers, giving them milk and cookies after school till Sonia could get home. But the idea of taking over Sonia's place now made her sick. She mutely refused. She refused to see the lint on the rug and the laundry overflowing the hamper.

Mark had worked the summer before at a camp up in New Hampshire. He had liked being a camp counselor and obviously he did not like spending the summer in Brooklyn. His room always smelled of grass, but nobody else in the family seemed to notice. As far as she could figure out, he spent his time looking at nudie magazines and masturbating with the radio turned to the Top Forty. He got out the stamp collection he had used to cherish in the eighth through tenth grades and pored over it for a couple of weeks, tearing stamps off the occasional letters that arrived. Then one day he took the two books into Manhattan and did not bring them back.

"Did you get enough for a nickel bag?" she asked him politely when he came home.

He did a suspicious double-take. "Don't try to sound smart."

She shrugged and turned away.

"Hey, Fatty-Pan, when are you going to iron my shirts? Off your *tuchis* and get with it."

Fatty-Pan was an old affectionate family name for her, and it struck her that she had never found it particularly affectionate. "Mark, if you found it beneath your notice, I might point out I am no fatter than you are."

"So when are you going to iron my shirts?"

"When are you going to iron *my* shirts? I don't like to iron. Why don't you take your shirts to your friendly neighborhood laundry and get them done? Or why not learn to iron yourself?"

"You can kiss my ass, Fatty. You know you're supposed to be doing the ironing in this house. You think you can sit around taking it easy just because she's in the hospital."

"I haven't noticed you doing much. I haven't seen that you're too busy to trot down to Flatbush and Nostrand to the laundry. I don't see why I should make your bed and wash your clothes or iron your shirts. I am not your maid. What am I asking you to do for me?"

"Not to tell the old man how late you get in at night."

"Kiss off, Mark. You'll tell him the same day I tell him what makes your room smell so good. It's not incense, baby brother mine. And no use looking in my room, because it's clean." Must she quarrel with everyone in her family? She felt alienated from them, sick of the family roles, stuck together in mutual guilt. "Mark, I don't want to jump on you. Smoke what you please. It's a terrible summer and I know you're bored."

"I suppose you're having fun?"

"No. I hate it. I hate being in the house."

"Is that why you go running into town all the time?"

"What I do in town is my business, just like what you do in your room. Don't hock me, Mark. I don't want to play mother. I don't want to take care of you and Allegra and him." She put her hand tentatively on his arm.

He shook it off, glaring as if she had done something disgusting. "You're going to shape up. Don't try to blackmail me with Dad. Because you won't win. I will. Mother's mad at you too."

Lionel was a sociable man and he continued to be invited out to dinner and to attend concerts and sit in on folk sessions. He was out in the evenings more often than he was home. He would never have considered checking up on whether Miriam was in her room when he got home, since he generally had no idea she had gone out. The first time Miriam spent a night with Phil, when the alarm went off and she got up in the pale yellow dawn to take the subway home, she was sure she would have a scene with a shocked Allegra.

Indeed Allegra did wake up when she came in and watched her undress and climb into bed, but she said nothing. She did not speak about it until the next afternoon when they were making supper. Surprisingly Allegra with all her identification with the feminine hated to cook. "When I get married, I'll have a cook or we'll eat out. How can you knock yourself out cooking every night the way Mama did and not get fat? Oh, I suppose if I really have to, I'll learn. That's what cookbooks are for. But nobody is going to marry me because I'm a whiz with a mixing bowl, no matter what Mama thinks. That's not where it's at."

"Where is it at?" It seemed to Miriam that she had never before been able to look at her sister, because of jealousy.

She was beginning to like her. It was a strange and fragile pleasure. Allegra was shorter and built more delicately. Her eyes were almost the same but not set above the high and strong Tartar cheekbones. Allegra's face was oval and her hair was lighter and more toned with red, though that was partly the rinse she used.

"It's a matter of being desirable to a man—but never letting him feel too sure of you. That was Mama's problem—don't you see? She never felt sure of him but he always felt sure of her. So he didn't have to bother trying hard to please her, and she was always shaking for fear she wasn't doing right by him. Yet she was a very attractive woman."

"Mama?"

"Come in the living room a minute. I want to show you something." Allegra dried her hands on her shocking-pink apron and led Miriam to sit down on the couch (still threadbare with exposed foam leaking crumbs), where Allegra spread out over their laps the contents of a box of old family pictures. Rachel and husband and friends lined up in the Catskills when it was a roughing-it, *kibbutznik* circuit. Lionel in a private's uniform too big on him standing very straight on West End Avenue, looking determined and scared. Herself gasping like a fish in the Coney Island sun, holding one sister and one brother by brute force for the camera. What Allegra passed her was a brown-toned photo of Sonia in her college graduation robes—Brooklyn College, Class of 1940—so young and bright and happy that Miriam could not meet the paper gaze.

"You're right. I can't look at it."

"Why? Everybody gets old. I know someday I'll get old and lose my looks. Every woman has to face that."

"But not every man?"

"Our looks wear out sooner. Consider Dad. Besides, she didn't take care of herself. She hasn't been to have her hair done or a facial in all the time we were growing up."

"What *mishegoss*, Allegra. Do you really like those Bergs we never see out in New Rochelle, those ladies with the pink and blue hair and the corsets and the ironed faces?" She made herself look at the picture. The difference was in the hopefulness in that face. A curly eager girl with great earnestness and hope and energy looked back. The nose, the eyes, the chin were Sonia, but the message was different. She remem-

bered her mother answering a question once. "Social studies,
I thought, what could be more important? To teach kids the
truth about history and government. But you get in the classroom and with the Regents and the paperwork and the
principal and the hoodlums, you're lucky you don't get
trampled to death." A young idealistic woman who had
thought she found in marrying a young idealistic man who
was going to make people's music a mission higher than the
teaching which had begun to disappoint her. "She must have
believed in him with a passion. Then slowly and painfully
she must have let go of that. Maybe that's why she was so
frantic for us. We weren't allowed to let her down too. Something had to come out."

"Don't talk about her in the past tense."

"She's dying, Allegra. For once admit it."

Allegra put her hands over her ears. "Don't say that to
me! You can be so ugly when you want to!" She marched
back into the kitchen. Miriam put the box away on a shelf
in the Danish-type room divider that housed books and hi-fi
and television and miniature bar and knickknacks and plodded
back to Allegra, who was peeling carrots with the languid
fastidiousness she always affected with housework. Miriam
considered it affected because it meant she ended up doing
more than half of the work.

After a while Allegra said, "You got a boy friend, mm?"

"Is that an official family question?"

"I should care? I only think you weren't studying at the
library till four this morning. All that studying you're supposed to do, I'm beginning to wonder."

"If I tell you, who are you going to tell?"

"Why should I? Maybe I'll want to stay out sometime. But
you better make up some cover story, like a girl friend you
stay with, and you better let me know where you are in case
something happens at night."

"How is that different from what I said about Mother,
Allegra? Okay, say I'm staying with a girl friend. When you
call, let the phone ring once, hang up, and dial again. So
I'll answer instead of Phil."

"Who is he?"

"A friend. My best friend."

"Oh, sure, you're staying out till four in the morning with
a friend! You must think I'm super-backward."

"What I'm doing is obvious. But he's still my friend. I like best to do that with friends."

"Has he asked you to marry him?"

Miriam grinned. "If you knew him, you'd think that was funny. Marrying Phil—it would be like marrying the Fool in the Tarot pack. Have you seen that?"

"Those cards people tell fortunes with. Thelma in my sorority did a reading for me just before I met Roger. But I'm not going to marry him. He's only a summer romance. Is that what Phil is? Maybe he won't ask you because you gave in too quickly."

"I guess he'd marry me if I had a good reason. It would be pointless. He'd never be a husband. He'd still be my friend."

"You mean like he hasn't got a career?"

"Well . . . no."

"Oh. Well, I wouldn't marry Roger either. Mother thinks he's wonderful, but I don't want to be a dentist's wife in Brooklyn. He's going into practice with his father. If he'd consider moving out to California, for instance, I'd take him more seriously. But I don't want to live and die in Brooklyn!"

"Allegra, do you ever have sex with any of your boy friends?" Funny stiff question in a stiff household.

"What do you mean? Like going to bed? In-the-bed sex?"

"Fucking."

"You love ugly words don't you?" Allegra made a face. "Do you think I'd do it with Roger? What a waste! He hasn't even made me pet with him yet. Once I almost did it with Stan—it was very, very close. I almost got carried away."

"Stan? Which one was he?"

"You don't notice anybody, do you? Imagine not remembering a dynamite guy like Stan! I went out with him all last summer. He was president of the Sportsmanship Council and the veep of our senior class. I'm glad I didn't get carried away, because we broke up. What does Phil look like? Show me his picture."

"I don't have a picture of him."

"Why not? You can get one taken. Even in the subway, they have those booths."

"If you're curious, maybe you can meet him sometime. He's my height and fair and he has blue eyes—"

"Is he Jewish?"

Miriam shook her head. "Irish."

"Catholic!"

"Well, he was raised Catholic. He's violently anti."

"Oh, Miriam, you've done it! No wonder you can't marry him. I mean even if he asked you. Mother would have a heart attack! He isn't married already, is he? That would be the limit."

"No, not married or engaged. And he loves me. And he's beautiful."

"Men aren't beautiful. Unless they're queer."

"Oh yes they are. I often find men beautiful. And oftenest of all I find Phil beautiful."

"Do you love him?"

Miriam nodded.

"I don't know what's going to become of you." Allegra stared out of eyes so like her own. "I guess you got carried away because you never had a boy friend before. But it's really the limit! An Irish Catholic without a career. Does he work?"

"As a janitor. But he's going to graduate school in the fall." She hated herself for saying that. Why did she need to persuade Allegra she wasn't a complete jackass by Allegra's terms? In a moment she would tell her sister about the poetry prize he had won as an undergraduate, and about the poems he had printed in literary magazines.

"Well, a college professor wouldn't be too bad. You're into mathematics. Maybe you could both teach till you have a baby. Dad wouldn't care half so much as Mother about him not being Jewish. But I wouldn't tell him about the Catholic part. What's his last name?"

"Allegra, I'm not going to marry Phil! I don't want to marry anybody! I don't want any marriage I've ever seen!"

"What do you want? Just to be a teacher?"

"I want to be me!"

"Oh." Allegra made a face. "Groovy. You'll get tired enough of that. Nobody wants to be an old maid."

The Flatbush flat was the world of boxes. Little boxes of pain. In one was old term papers Sonia had saved from her favorite students. In another was clippings about HUAC and frantic letters from Lionel to people who had suddenly stopped being his friends. In another was Sonia's cut-off brown hair. In another the love letter from the woman her

father had laid at a folk festival. In another were Mark's baby
shoes and his merit badges from Boy Scouts. In another was
the white dress Allegra used to wear to parties when she was
thirteen and fourteen until once her period started and she
stained the dress. She came home weeping hysterically as if
she would die. Convinced she would never be able to leave
the house again, she took to her bed for three days. In
another was the goldfish—the only pet Miriam was allowed as
a child, as all other animals were classified as dirty—she had
overfed till it died and floated belly up and she had wept
with guilt. Nothing touched, nothing rubbed, nothing was
connected. She could not learn from anyone else or take comfort from them or give to them. Fear had killed the past and
the world was all boxes and cans.

With Phil was the world of changing shapes. Of dreams and
images and words flowing and flowing bodies. It was hot in
the basement though not as hot as outside. Summer festered
in the dirty streets of the Lower East Side. Firecrackers
went off all of the time like a barrage, like the real war in
the streets. Most of the time they did not wear clothes. The
only comfortable place was the bedroom. When they ate and
when they quarreled, they sat at the formica table in the
kitchen in two tubular chairs: chromium and formica and
hard edges and white enamel.

"Your friend Jackson has a talent for discomfort."

"You wouldn't understand. Women love lushness. He likes
things simple and straight. He's trained himself to feel as
little as possible."

"Why doesn't he shut off altogether? Turn on the gas and
turn off the world?"

"You can't stand the idea that there might be one man
who prefers being alone. Who prefers his own mind to a lot
of complicated relationships and women crawling over his
flesh. Men respect the differences of other men, but women
want to make every man over into their child. What you can't
devour, you want to destroy."

And other ravings when he was irritated or depressed,
when various of his overly intricate plans for money or dope
fell through. They would get dressed to quarrel and move instinctively to the uncomfortable chairs tipping too far forward or back on their chromium tubes. They would face each
other across the formica. When they had finished their spat

they would drift into the bedroom again, take off their clothes, and sit or lie or kneel or prop their backs against a wall on the two mattresses that covered the floor. Sometimes they smoked hash or grass and sometimes they drank wine or gin and tonic or beer. One Monday they dropped acid together. One evening they swallowed peyote buttons which carried Phil high into a talking jag and made Miriam painfully, violently sick for three hours of the wet and dry heaves. The hot city stewing in its garbage and sputtering with violence turned them off. They went out mainly to fetch supplies and see an air-conditioned movie.

Sometimes when they talked they lay forehead to forehead. Sometimes they lay side by side staring at the ceiling painted with ripple marks, only their fingers touching. Sometimes he talked with his chin dug into her shoulder and his hands playing with her breasts and as they talked her nipples would harden and he would knead her breasts while a slow timid desire spread in her. Often for hours she was partly turned on with him, as if a state of some excitement were the norm for her body, a background to everything else going on inside and around her. Her level of responsiveness and arousal had risen severalfold over the weeks. He lectured her on her capacity for multiple orgasm. There was a streak of pain in his will to find out how much pleasure she could experience, but she had to trust him in his exploration of her. Their loving would never be simple. She must trust him, for she needed him. Only with him could she loosen her emotions, separate the strands of her desperation. She carried herself like a knot to him, her hand clasped sweating on the book she was toting with her to his apartment, to the hospital, back and forth: what she was supposed to be studying that summer for her fall course, the Theory of Complex Variables.

He liked to be inside her often long before they would actually begin to move and as long afterward as he could keep from sliding out. Their best game was called Home Movies: it was the giving over of chunks of past life from one to the other. Nakedness and proximity made for vivid exchange. In a half-roused state her nervous system seemed more open to his, readier to receive, to form images. Often she imagined afterward that she had actually watched parts of his life and shown him on the screen in his head long sequences from hers.

Phil was seven. He was living with his mother in the chunky red brick barracks of public housing, a whole area that felt as if it stood behind barbed wire with guard towers at the corners. When his mother tried to get on welfare, they told her she could not get relief unless she gave them all the information they needed to trace her husband, because first it must be proved before the law that he could not support them. So the law caught his father, gone for years, and brought that loud-mouthed, hard-drinking loser home again to the wife he probably hardly remembered marrying. He could go to jail or live with his family. He said all day long that it was close to half a dozen of one and six of the other, but he couldn't get booze in jail so he chose living with his loving wife and loving son instead.

One afternoon Phil was sent with some change to the store across the street from Roosevelt Towers to get a loaf of Wonder Bread and some frozen fish sticks and tonic— that's what he had grown up calling soda. He was supposed to get orange but the store was out, so after great deliberation, not wanting to disappoint his mom or himself, he chose root beer. He went back across the street and around the long way so he wouldn't go past the benches where the kid who called himself Shitkicker had his gang. They would get him down and take the tonic and break open the bread and stomp on it. The project was called Roosevelt Towers but only the big building in back was a tower, the rest were long blocks three stories tall with benches and cement and a little grass in between.

When he came running up the dark stairs the door of their apartment was funny. It was hanging wide and awry. That scared him. When things got broken they stayed broken. They would get robbed of the money in his mom's purse and the little radio. He began to call, "Mom! Mom!" He heard her groaning and she half sat up and tried to tell him with her hand not to come in. She was lying on the floor with her dress ripped open and he was scared to see that her breasts were hanging out, and that her jaw was funny. She could not talk. Blood ran down her face onto the torn rag of her dress. Her cheeks were swollen and her jaw was stuck on at a queer angle and she was holding a piece of tooth in her hand, as if maybe it could be put back in. The room was knocked every which way too. His old man was gone, with all the money in the house.

The would not send an ambulance to the housing project for a woman with a broken jaw so they had to go on the bus. They were hours and hours in the fracture clinic before she could go home with him. All night long she had groaned with pain. He had felt frightened of this strange woman who no longer had his mother's face and who was wired together and could not talk clearly, and he had shrunk from her when she reached out to him.

The caseworker brought a policeman who was jolly about it and said, "Now come on, these people are always fighting, it's just a man taking a hard hand to his wife. Now do you really want to swear out a complaint, Mrs. Boyle?" She was scared to death of the police and she stammered and turned away. The next time the old man was hauled home, he disappeared more quietly. That was the good time. He just took off.

His mother decided that welfare was too expensive and she would just have to leave Phil alone days after school and get some work. She got a job cleaning for a woman in Brookline and another two days for a family on Clarendon, in Back Bay. She would leave him the money to go to the store and get Hostess Cupcakes for lunch. But they could not really make ends meet and by and by it turned out she was pregnant. The caseworker told his mother she could get a divorce from his father on the grounds of cruelty and desertion but his mother could not get a divorce because of the Church, just as she was afraid to do anything about the baby coming that nobody wanted. Nobody except God. He was ten by then and had a big lip and he called it God's baby that she was carrying. That made her wail and carry on.

So his old man, who didn't have the brains to leave Boston, was once again summoned to the bar of justice and united with his family. The old man seemed a bit scared this time. He was in other trouble too. He started working as a scab painter and brought home money for a while. In fact they were about to get kicked out of public housing because the old man was making too high a wage, when the old man beat up his mother again for whining too much about the pains in her back and giving too much lip. She began to bleed on the kitchen floor and the old man took off again. Phil was lying thrown against the bedroom wall through the whole scene with his shoulder dislocated, and this time they got to the hospital in time for her to lose the baby in the emergency ward while they were waiting for the nurse to dig out their records.

Finally his mother had sense enough to give false information after that, and apparently the old man did not immediately return to his favorite bars and old cronies. He might have thought he had killed Phil's mother that time and was lying low. Or he might have thought nothing at all.

The last time he saw his father was at the funeral. His old man was run over by a truck in the Haymarket area where he had got a temporary night watchman's job at some construction. Amazingly there was an insurance policy to pay for the funeral and a bit over, from some Irish Brotherhood he had belonged to back in the old neighborhood. His mother put on her black dress that she wore to mass on Sunday and went very straight and white. Phil, who was thirteen, strode up to the grave and very deliberately spat in as they were lowering away. His mother slapped him. Nobody else said anything. There was a good feeding at an aunt's afterward.

When he was fifteen his mother got married again. He should have been happy. She married a solid fat electrician, a steady worker named Jerry Flynn. He had two children to take care of from his wife dying of a mistake in the operating room during the third birth. The pains had come on her early and unexpectedly at a union picnic. Her stomach had not been empty. They had put her out with anesthesia and she had choked to death on her own vomit. The baby had died the first month.

Flynn's sons were younger than Philip and much healthier. Phil was then five feet eight but so thin his skin looked like Gorgonzola cheese and his bones squeaked and clattered when he ran. He should have been happy. His mother had a beaver coat. She did not sit on a kitchen chair with her bottle of beer staring into it with that look of iron despair. She seemed years younger. She cut her hair and wore bright aprons. She did not have to do other women's housework any more, and she bubbled around the house cleaning and recleaning and polishing and rubbing and shining. The house was a real house, like in the movies, it was called a colonial on a street in Medford lined with trees, and had two floors

and a stairway and a back yard. Phil had a bedroom to himself which had been the guest room. He felt like a guest.

Phil had a closet of his own full of clothes like the boys
in family shows on TV. Like the Others. His new supposed-to-
be old man took him along with his real kids to football and
baseball games. He was supposed to dig all that. They had
a yard where the previous wife, No. 1, had planted some
flowers on bushes and in beds, before she choked to death.
His mother could not relate to all that green stuff but the
electrician went out and stood around with the hose in his
hand. Phil was supposed to mow the lawn. It made him
sneeze. He turned out to be allergic to green stuff. So Tim,
the older of the new supposed-to-be brothers, had to go back
to mowing.

Phil felt like a ghost in the neat room with its blue walls
and filmy curtains hung there by No. 1. He was surly and
blank. He did okay in school but he was quick to anger and
quick to take to his fists. In spite of his shortness of breath
and his fragility, he could beat up most of the guys because
of training and practice. He knew how to fight: he had never
in his life been able to afford not to know how. They were
soft, the boys in his school, and he despised them.

The girls were something else. He discovered he was attractive from them. He liked middle-class girls with their
clear skins and their clear voices and their soft clothes. His
sex before that had usually been in groups: the gang would
get a girl and they would all lay her. Or a bunch would go
over to Peggy's in the afternoon when her mother was at
work, and Marilyn might be there too. They would bring
some tonic and some ups and downs, it didn't matter. They
took whatever they could buy. It was all something to numb
you. It took you up above the lousy stinking world of the
school prison and the barracks project and you floated there.
It took you back into the funhouse of your head. It took you
deep into the caverns of the body. It took you way up and
out to ride a sense of power: you were someone after all.
Coming into Marilyn was something quick like stepping into
the head to take a leak, somebody was always waiting.
Nothing ever worked in the world of the project, not the
toilets, not the lights, not the doors, not the screens, not the
stoves, not the phones, not the heat, nothing. It was all solid
crap.

"But I missed something in Medford, I missed something. I didn't know who I was. I had always had a tight connection to my mother. Maybe she was the only thing I had and I was all she had, but I had her. I didn't have her any more. God help me, I began to hate her. I began to despise her. I'd make her weep just like my old man. She would tell me again and again she had only got married for me, for my sake, so I'd grow up right and not go to the devil like my dad. I felt evil. I felt mean. I began to believe I was just like my old man and that I only felt alive when I was hurting people. God, how I hated myself then." His head rested on her breasts, his eyes open toward the ceiling. "It was the old sexual repulsion routine. Sure, my old man had had my mother, but it was obviously abuse. She was pure anyhow and suffering. But here she was sleeping every night with this fat satisfied electrician, that she had chosen of her own free will. She was doting on him.

"I was jealous. I was playing *Hamlet* and grinding my teeth. I was ready to deal out punishment and seek relief on the soft bodies of the girls of Medford. And I'll tell you, one of the most powerful aphrodisiacs known is a bad reputation in a man. It's damned lucky I didn't knock up any of them but, unlike my mother, I believed in contraception. The line ends here." He smote his chest. "If you ever get some sperm of mine growing in you, I'll uproot it myself. No babies. I hate them. You hear me?"

"Loud and clear. After all, you are yelling. I have no wish to bear babies into this fucked-up life, I assure you. Sometimes I feel as if my mother's too much in me already. I feel a dreadful useless connection. And I can't reach out. I can't comfort her."

There was a law in operation that mothers and daughters could not teach each other, could not inherit, could not relate. They must continually react against each other, generation against generation. Out in Far Rockaway Grandma Rachel was freaking out over what she could find out or could not find out about Sonia. She smuggled out a letter accusing Lionel of poisoning Sonia.

Miriam thought she might be able to relate to Rachel. As she had often heard as a little girl, her mother came from a real working-class family with a radical tradition. Lionel was fond of saying that on appropriate occasions. Rachel was a

Trotskyist who had been active in the needleworkers' union. She had emigrated from Lithuania just before World War I to the Lower East Side.

Sonia, the youngest daughter, had resented a working mother. Sonia had resented the politics and rallies and campaigns and strikes. She had hated the meetings in the living room and the organizers sleeping on the couch and the floor. It made her mad that when there was never enough to eat well, there was always enough to feed somebody else who said he was hungrier. Rachel gave away her own coat, she gave away the last dollar in the house, she gave away her bed to a sick comrade to sleep in. Grandfather had terrible arthritis and had to stop working years before Rachel, but still he was folding leaflets with his cramped claws. He had died of cancer too young for Miriam to remember, except for his hands. Rachel wept and mourned and carried on, and then suddenly there was an old man living with her! At her age! He was eight years younger than Rachel and he had his nose flattened and his face thickened by fights in the streets, on the picket lines. He did not talk as much as Rachel but he looked at her a lot and he teased her. That ended in a political schism in the McCarthy years: a division between those who were more angry at the Communists and more willing to fight them and put the finger on them, and those who were more angry at the capitalists and the government, and would not co-operate. For all Rachel's contempt for Stalinists, she said that Stalin would die and somebody else would come in and the line would change, but Rockefellers bred Rockefellers and went on forever getting richer. Then Rachel was alone.

Now Rachel was stuck away in a Jewish old folks' home out in Far Rockaway. Rachel had always despised Lionel for his unformed politics, and she used to call him every name the Committee had. Then she would taunt him for never joining the Party and say they wouldn't have him, he was a schlump. But when Miriam was growing up, Rachel was the grandma she preferred. Rachel had no money to give them and not much else. She had causes and bills and too many grandchildren and pains in the chest and the head. Miriam had her cheekbones and eyes and complexion. She suspected she also had her temper and her will and her sensuality. Now Rachel was about to outlive Sonia, who had reacted against her and told Miriam all through her childhood how lucky she was to have a real mother instead of a politician for a mother.

Always Sonia had taken them out to see Rachel in Far Rockaway, but in July Miriam and Allegra went by themselves. Rachel was under sedation in the room she shared with four other old and sick and defeated women. Her head seemed heavy on her thin shoulders and drooped first to one side and then to the other. She told them the Communists were in control of the nursing home and putting arsenic in her food. They were coming to murder her as they had Trotsky with his beautiful lion's head. Rachel had loved Leon Trotsky with an unstinting full-blooded devotion. She had loved her husband and clucked and fussed over him long after he was wizened. She adored her sons above her daughters, consciously a man's woman. Now she asked insistently after Mark, who did not bother to come. Her father had been an orthodox Jew who prayed every morning his thanks that God had seen fit to make him a man and not a woman. Rachel had been born a woman, but she made it clear she would not identify with others in that condition unless they shaped up. She could only admire heroes, and heroes were men.

Miriam doubted the arsenic, but the tranquilizers were bad enough, stupefying Rachel and surrounding her with a querulous cloud they could not pierce. They sat with her for two hours but only sometimes did she recognize them. She kept calling Miriam Masha and Allegra Sonia. "Masha, where's the baby?" Rachel kept demanding. "Is something wrong with the baby?" When she did recognize them, she scolded them for not bringing Sonia, she begged them to take her to Sonia immediately.

So Miriam was cast back on herself and her only connection—to Phil. She lay beside him and they tangled their bodies and histories and wove images on the dim low ceiling.

"Phil. Should I apply to graduate schools in Massachusetts?"

"Are you thinking of that?"

"Shouldn't I be?"

"Not if you have any brains. But why not? We'll live together. We can move back to East Cambridge and raise rats for the hospitals."

"I don't have to apply around Boston. We'd still have summers."

"Crap. New York is ceasing to be a summer festival. A pile of rotting meat and decaying circuits in the center of a dying empire. Summer of love, my sweet prick! I was solicited yesterday by a kid who must have been all of fifteen. She said she was hungry and I say she was on smack. If it wasn't for you, do you think I'd be sweltering like Job on his dung-heap here? If I can bring myself to play janitor in this hellhole for you, you can damned well move your ass to Boston for me. *Princess.*"

9

To Each According to Her Need

"Mama, we don't know how to talk to each other. You always did it for us. You were the soft stuff in between, so we wouldn't bump, so we wouldn't rattle or jab. You always said what each of us should buy for the other's birthday. You'd tell me that Allegra was mad because I made fun of her new haircut, or Mark didn't want me borrowing his drawing pen. Now we don't have a common language."

Her mother lay in the hospital bed against the left wall, yellower, limper after a third operation. There would be no fourth. In the middle bed was a fat woman with a daughter just a bit younger than Miriam, who sat beside the bed while they whispered and giggled like friends. Miriam saw their closeness as an emblem of what she could not guess how to reach for.

Against the right wall an elderly woman, Mrs. Katz, was under heavy sedation. She lay mumbling to herself. Often the

restraint bar was up on her bed, making it a crib. Miriam
never saw anyone talking with her except a nurse giving her
pills, taking her temperature, changing the bedpan. She lay
under the sheets like a bundle of straw, tiny and inert except
for periods of tossing and querulous whining. Perhaps she
was dying, perhaps she was not. Miriam heard a doctor
bleating jocularly at her, "Why, you have an iron constitution, Mrs. Katz, you'll live to be a hundred!" Perhaps she
was a widow. No one came.

Sonia talked sometimes with the woman in the middle bed,
but she was a divorcee and made sarcastic remarks about the
doctors that upset Sonia's sense of decorum. Sonia had seldom
been interested in people beyond the family—except for her
students. Just as she had loved Miriam best when she was
little, she fussed and worried over her favorite students. The
slow ones who tried were her special care. But she regarded
excessive interest in others as gossip: perhaps it reminded
her of Rachel. Sonia expressed contempt for women who
could not find enough to concern themselves with in their
proper work, their family, and had to worry about neighbors
or strangers. Certainly Sonia was shy with adults she did
not know, so tended never to get to know them. For years
they had feared their neighbors. They had been forced out
of one apartment because the neighbors were hostile and
called them Reds. Sonia would not go down to get the mail
because of threats in the box. Her "girl friends" were from
her earlier life, before marriage: the ones who had not
moved from Brooklyn, Judy and Gussie and Barbara came
in faithfully to see her and brought flowers and best sellers
and funny cards. They met together to try to play bridge, but
Sonia could not keep up her end of the game.

Miriam could remember feeling peeved when she would
hear her mother on the phone to Judy: her mother would be
laughing like herself chatting with a girl friend. That was
wrong: not how her mother was supposed to act. Lionel
would groan at the mention of their names. "All the interesting people you meet in the world and you still want to get
together with those *yentas*." Her father used few Yiddish
words, for he thought them parochial and clannish, but that
one he used. Sonia would wince.

"I got nothing in common with your friends. I know they
all think I'm a nobody."

"Ten years a teacher and you say, 'I got nothing.'"

"Am I in the classroom now?" She would arch her short plump neck in an attempt at dignity. "I know how to talk in front of a class, do I need you to tell me? Am I in front of a class in my own home?"

"You think it's more important to teach a stranger's children than your own. Perhaps you don't care if they grow up sounding as if they'd never left Flatbush, but I care. You had an education, but no one would know it to hear you. I don't want my son growing up with a voice like a comedian on the borscht circuit."

"So be ashamed of me. Teach my own children to scorn me. Someday they'll understand what I went through to keep a home together for them!"

As Miriam sat in the stuffy hospital room with its acrid smells, she thought that swimming in the humid air were all of the words that had ever been spoken in family. All those words like tiny sharks swam through the yellowed air snapping at her, food of anguish, food of bitterness, the seder bitter herbs and dry bread: all the pain she had grown up with and taken for granted as the normal daily bread of living together. Nothing was lost. Nothing could be assimilated. Their words would not dissolve and be forgotten but, like aluminum shreds, like the pop tops of soda containers, would lie where they had been tossed and never decay, but be ready in fifteen years to tear the foot of a passing child. Yet she had always considered that she lived in a happy family. Her parents had always assured her that she was lucky to have both parents living together. All the children had been wanted, had been intentional. Children of broken homes, unwanted children, were to be pitied.

"What are you talking about, you can't speak to each other!" Sonia rolled her head back and forth. "Your father tells me you're staying out late at night and you won't keep up the house. How can you treat your mother that way? Don't you think I'd keep the house clean if I could?" Sonia motioned her closer and took her arm caressingly. Sonia had always been the affectionate one, who held, caressed, comforted. Wait till Mama comes home from work and then you can cry. . . .

"Mama, I'm doing my share and so is Allegra. We keep our room clean, we make supper every night and do the dishes. But Mark won't do a thing! He doesn't even want to make his own bed."

"Mark's a good boy. You're the oldest daughter and it's your responsibility to keep up the house." Sonia let go her arm, arching her flaccid neck against the pillow. "What's wrong with you? It's too much to expect you to act like a *mensch* and do a little work around the house when your mother's too sick?"

Miriam sat up stiffly. Always drawing love away to punish me! "Why don't you ask Mark to be a *mensch?* Why don't you tell him to do his part?" The bitter tang of injustice. She felt twelve: So don't love me! I'm right anyhow!

"What's this staying out late at night? What's going on the minute my back is turned?"

"I have a friend, that's all. I like to be with him. I don't like hanging around the flat. I'm not getting along with Mark or Dad. I am getting along with Allegra, by the way, for maybe the first time in my life."

"You've always been jealous of your sister."

"I admit that. But not any more."

"Your sister loves you and your father loves you, and if you're not getting along, it's because of how you're acting. Where did you pick up this new way? Where did you get such a swelled head? You're such a smart aleck you can do anything and you know better."

Sonia attacked from the bed, and from the bedside table came the whine of the Theory of Complex Variables. She had had discipline, always. At school she was always up to date. All her adventures were fitted into the interstices of a careful schedule. Now this summer she had done nothing but lie in bed and fuck and weep! She could not read that stupid book: it was the single most boring object she had ever encountered. Ten minutes with it and she felt embalmed. Her discipline had eroded.

"I bet that's some friend! Why doesn't he come out to the flat and see you, if he's so friendly?"

"He's working as a janitor. Besides, I like going into town."

"I'm beginning to get the picture. Miriam, daughter mine" —Sonia motioned her near to whisper—"is he black?"

"No, but he isn't Jewish. And I don't want to marry him. And I don't want to bring him home to Flatbush. I just want to see him and talk to him and spend time with him this summer."

"Is the wool so easy to pull over my eyes? You aren't staying out late at night talking. One thing leads to another. Pretty soon, you'll be in trouble deep."

"Who told you? Was it smart Mark who told you?"

"What do you care who told me? It's a thorn in my side lying here that I can't trust my own daughter when I'm not keeping an eye on her."

"Mama, I spend nine months of the year at school. What do you want from me? Only that I not be me. I'm not ashamed of how I look any more. Or that I'm good in math instead of something supposed to be feminine. Or that I'm too tall—too tall for what? I'm not too tall for me!"

"Just so long as you're satisfied with *bubkes!* Why should you care how your mother feels?"

"Mama, I don't want them to bother you. It's a hard summer, we're worried about you, we don't get along."

"That's my fault, of course! Blame it on me! You were a good girl when you were growing up, now look at you!"

"I don't want you to worry! There's nothing to get excited about."

"Okay, so if it isn't important, do your sick mother a favor and don't see this man any more."

"I didn't say seeing him doesn't matter to me. I said it wasn't important from your point of view. I'm not going to marry him! He's my friend, Mama. I just like him enormously."

"You know how I feel lying here? Staying out late with some janitor. Who knows what you're doing? Refusing to clean up so when your father comes home from work he finds a nice house. Not a nest of vipers and daughters running back to the Lower East Side to hang around all hours of the night! I grew up there, I know! How glad we were when we could move to Brooklyn and get away! Thieves, rapists, women selling themselves! How can you go back there?"

"Mama, I do care that you're sick! I don't want you to be unhappy over me! I don't want you to feel pain! I know that you're suffering and I want you to feel that I care."

"Sha! Keep your voice down. You want them to hear in the next bed? So act like Mother's good loving daughter!"

"I want to show you I care but I don't want to pretend I'm somebody else! Don't make me lie. I'm not shoving my life in your face. I don't want to make a fuss. Just let me love you in my own way and be me."

"You won't do me a thing. You won't cross the street for your mother. Words are cheap. Actions are what count. Actions speak louder than fine words. I hear you saying to me that some janitor you're ashamed to bring home is more important to you than your mother lying on her bed of pain, suffering day and night and worrying!"

Allegra watched Miriam's troubles with an ironic eye. Lying on the rug between their beds doing exercises for her abdominal muscles designed to make her gentle tummy vanish, Allegra panted, "You needn't have got . . . into all that hot water . . . with Mama. She has no way of figuring out what goes on unless some little bird tells her."

"I was sure it wasn't you."

"Why should I? It only makes trouble for me. She gets on that questioning *shtik*. 'What are you doing with Roger? Are you letting him take advantage of you?' As if he'd know how! I can't wait till I start school in September. I expect to meet a new type of man. But it's really your fault. If you don't rub Mark the wrong way, he never pays attention to us. You think he wasn't hocking me to iron his shirts? I just took one and burned a hole in it. I was so apologetic! He won't ask me again! You don't know how to get out of things, big sister. It's easy if you do it right."

"I never thought of that." Miriam felt large and unwieldly beside Allegra.

"You feel superior because you don't think of things like that. As if it's moral to do things head on. It's just messy. Daddy would never make a fuss about dating some guy. I mean, he hardly pays that much attention unless you shove it in his face. He only wants to go on his way, and we shouldn't be a drag. We've always been her kids, and only his when he felt like it. You know what I mean?"

Miriam nodded. "Sure. Father's Day and Thanksgiving. When you were dressed up extra cute. When Mark won a prize or had his bar mitzvah. When he wants us to listen to some song and admire him."

"It hurts to admire? So of course he wasn't going to keep

anything from her about us. I mean, it's her *business*. So you had to stay out of his path. I don't want to get stuck with the housework either. I don't see why we can't have a woman come in once a week like everybody else. But the way to get that is to demonstrate how hard we're trying but it's too much."

Miriam began to laugh. "But, Allegra, I can't maneuver that way. It takes a kind of energy I lack. I blunder ahead."

"Big sister, you sure do!" Allegra smiled at her. "Don't fret. She's out of it, stuck in the hospital, and Dad lacks the taste for grand family confrontations. He'll make rules but he won't enforce. Now just take it easy for a while, would you?"

Labor Day came and Labor Day went, but Jackson did not return. Although Phil wanted to cut out for Boston to find a place to live, he was wedged into the basement until relieved. Jackson had promised to be back Labor Day at the latest, but no word had come after a postcard from Oaxaca dated August 1 which was a long joke about dope.

"He's probably rotting in a Mexican calaboose on a drug charge, and I'll spend my remaining years baby-sitting a rotting building. Just because for once in my life good old J. Singleton Proxmire is lined up to be my meal ticket. Just because I get a break finally, my old buddy has to sit on his ass too stoned to observe the date."

Sometimes Phil turned paranoid and suspected that Jackson was purposefully blocking him. "He's jealous because I got my shit together. I got my letters of recommendation marshaled, I got my transcripts patched, I got my benefactor lined up. He didn't think I could get up early enough in the morning to make the appointment, but I did it. While he's still fucking around playing old Jack Kerouac games. You know, he had Advantages, Jackson did. His father's a big-shot businessman in some small-change town out in the Great American Desert. Sofa, Nebraska, or Chaise Longue, Idaho. After a little time in the war, instead of advancing steadily up the escalator, he turned around and started backward. Now he's doing me in, his best friend. Doing me dirty. I should have known he wouldn't get back on time. Secretly, deep down inside, he doesn't believe time exists outside, that there's really an independent world with clocks that run while he isn't looking. He probably isn't convinced I exist

when he isn't with me, so why the hell should he sweat it
getting his ass back here and taking over his own stupid job
and his cellblock just because he solemnly promised me on
June 21 he'd be here?"

Phil got some tabs of acid called Electric Lady which were
supposed to be the best stuff since Sunshine. They were red
and long. He kept them in a little round carved wooden box
shaped like an egg that came apart at the waist. Whenever
Phil opened it, the spicy odor of sandalwood escaped. He had
saved one for each of them to drop that Monday, but she
felt too nervous, too tense in her body.

She was annoyed at him for wanting to trip: she had been
looking forward to being with him after a weekend when she
had not got away from her family. Acid was something else
than being together, really together. She had little time left.
Why was he bitterly impatient to be off to Boston? Her
family was screaming about him night and day. When she
managed to come to him, she could not stay long. Sonia was
drugged all of the time, incoherent and sometimes unconscious. The third operation had accomplished nothing. The
cancer had reached too many organs. Sonia was getting cobalt
treatments with side effects as bad as the disease. She was
losing her hair and control over her body.

Miriam wanted to be held and comforted and listened to.
She wanted a concentrated message of mutual strength and
reaffirmation that she was who she thought she was and
Phil was her friend and her love. But he wanted to run back
into his psyche and escape the anxiety of plans falling like
plaster from the damp ceiling.

She did not drop the acid with him but sat sullenly on the
mattress cross-legged drinking cream soda and eating macaroni salad from a deli and an orange section by section,
sorry for herself for all she wanted from him that she wasn't
getting.

"Jackson would describe your state as excessive attraction
to particular forms." Phil spoke coldly. He was disappointed
in her too and waiting for the first rush of the acid to take
him.

"That particular form is my mother. I seem to recall that
your own had considerable power to upset you."

"I would not deny that I am excessively attached to

particular forms. That extravagant attention, for example, I pay to your skin. Fetishism."

"Since I live in that skin, you don't expect me to agree? Excessive as measured against what? The lady in 4B?"

"That's no lady, that's my tenant. Even positing that the physiological pressure produces a natural urge to put a prick in something, why the frenzy about where? The saint would put it in anywheres, a tree, a chicken, an old woman—"

"Pardon my Jewish ignorance, but I'd expect a saint wouldn't put it in anywheres at all."

"I mean a saint with balls. He'd give his sperm to the universe."

"And expect it to thank him? Deposit twenty spermatozoa for the next three minutes, pul-lease."

"Tell you a story. It's beginning. Coming on. Story I read in Jackson's book. About this Buddhist monk. To wean himself from excessive attachment to the things of this world, he contemplated day by day the rotting, the putrefaction of a corpse of a beautiful woman he'd been attracted to. Saw her go from beauty into shit."

"All he found out was that she was a body too—just like him! Did he think he'd smell better? All things smell when they die, especially male philosophies about women! I won't represent the world. Or physical being. Or procreation. Or spring. I'm a person just as much as you are!"

"You don't see. I'll show you." He crawled over to root in a box of books. Slowly he turned pages, muttering and frowning. "Why do these books smell like basements? Books rotting too. It's not here. Never step in the same river twice, never pick up the same book. I know it was in this book, *Buddhist Texts*. But it's gone. . . . Been taken away. Impermanence is all, see?"

"You made it up, just to hit me over the head. Don't you see what you're doing with it? Saying you're a spirit living in your body, but I'm an animal because I am a body."

The book dropped. He was staring at the wall. "Dozens of them baking in the sun. Bellies split open. Guts cooking. Saw dogs eating a kid once. . . . And his arm came right off on my lap. . . . And the nurses, V.C. nurses the Marines had worked over. Just pieces of them left. . . . Just bloody pieces . . ." He crept toward her. Stopped, shook his head, looking from side to side. As if swimming through thick water, came on toward her to put his hand at last on her thigh. "Frozen. Cold. White. Take off your clothes. Why are you sitting with clothes on? I want to come in. Keep warm. Hurry! Why does it take so long? Why are you doing this to me? Don't you want me to be safe? Hurry!"

When she was undressed he sprawled against her, his cheek to her belly, his eye to her navel. "Trying to see in. I remember a story about a man who got shot in the belly and the doctors put in a glass window. . . . Wouldn't that be weird?"

"Better a door in your head so I could watch your brain change colors."

"What color is it now? Look and see."

"Silver. A kind of silver gray like a sea gull's wings."

"They're dirty. They're always over Boston. In the winter you look at the Charles, it's all frozen, and there they are sitting on the ice all facing in one direction as if they were listening to a speech. They face right into the wind, all of them sitting in rows on the ice. Hold me. Hold me!"

She held. For long periods it was as if she were alone. He withdrew into his head. He would begin staring at wrinkles in the sheet or fine hairs on her leg and get lost. He would mumble. She would lose contact. Was Allegra right in saying that she made quarrels happen? Early in the summer she had wanted confrontation with her father. But that wish to meet head on had guttered out. What was the use? She had no more stomach for bad words. She wished she had gone the quiet way of the summer before.

But lying was sour in the long run, even lying by omission. Yet telling the truth was a bucket of worms. Give in or lie: those seemed the only options. She could not decide which horn was less painful to hang on. Lying was immediately more comfortable but in the long run less tolerable: or was it? She tossed and turned in her life and seemed not to fit any longer.

Was it right to choose a graduate school by proximity to Phil? Wasn't that weakness? To attach too much importance to the relationship could crush it. Perhaps that was what Phil's ascetic ramblings meant. Was she really applying to M.I.T. because of Phil? Or was that the logical choice? Her hand came and went in his fine blond hair. His lips were parted. He stared at the wall, panting. She did not know where he was. Not with her.

Churnings in her, flotsam and jetsam, anguish and guilt. Maybe she really was hurting her mother. Maybe Sonia really did lie in pain over her. For the first two years at Michigan, she had put the strongest part of herself into her classes. This last year she had begun to direct some energy into relationships. But as she proceeded into polar realms of abstraction and cerebral landscapes of more awesome complication, the demands were greater. If she were really to go on in mathematics, she must commit the bulk of her energies to it. But she was no longer sure that was what she wanted. She had awakened in her senses. She was curious about the persons behind the faces she encountered.

But if she did not march on to graduate school, what would she do? A B.A. in math was worth nothing. She did not want to teach high school like her parents. She wanted something interesting to do with her head, but perhaps no longer to pledge her life to those grand Platonic forms. She felt stymied, a hand resting idly on Philip's thin, well-turned shoulder. He had a good chin, firm and slightly squared, precise and almost delicate. Probably his mother's had been like that: easy to break.

"S'a kind of contempt, think of it. Forgetting a promise. Shows he didn't take it seriously. I hate people who make promises and don't take it seriously. He didn't believe I'd get my shit together. Didn't believe 'cause he thinks I'm a loser."

He sat up, frowning. His hands pounded at each other, turning and knocking fist on palm. His hands fought. She felt in herself a muscled hostility to the invisible Jackson. Damned ascetic blowhard. Older than Phil. She imagined him sour and self-righteous. Sitting on a bed of nails scowling. If it were not for Phil's dilemma, she would wish Jackson in Mexico forever.

"He's jealous of me. I won't let him meet you. I do that to bug him, because he gets curious. Intellectual curiosity is his cutting edge. He's kind of possessive of me. . . . I want you to relate through me. Through my body. Through my mind. Through my eyes. But he's jealous too because I have a thing with a woman like he thinks he wants. He was married to the sort of girl he was supposed to marry. WASP from Homewood, Illinois. He met her at Northwestern, they got

married and had a kid. No kids! You hear me? No repro-
ducing. I don't want any more of me. That's all, you hear
me?" He tried to push his hand up into her.

"You're hurting me! Be careful."

"You be careful too. No babies."

"I want a baby inside me even less than you do. Can't you
get that straight?"

"You be straight with me. I put it in you. How can I be
sure you aren't keeping some there? Making babies with it.
The queen bee, you know about her? When the male bee
fights it out with the other males for the great privilege, they
go up and away. Then he puts it to her and, the poor bastard,
it breaks right off inside her. He dies. She rips it right off
him and flies away with it to make babies."

"You're hurting me, Phil. Now quit it! I'm not a queen
bee! I'm not a crocodile. I'm not a monk's corpse. I'm me!"
She twisted his wrist free of her and pulled away.

"Don't pull away from me, don't ever pull away from me!
Don't thrust me away. Don't close yourself to me."

"You were hurting me."

"I won't. Hold me." He dragged himself over. "Don't
pull away. Got to be inside."

"I don't like to be hurt, Phil. Understand that. It doesn't
turn me on. It makes me close up tight."

"Healthy Miriam. Whereas we both know who's the mas-
ochist in this room. You're my soft padded luxury torture
rack. My lioness with the velvet tongue who bites me to the
bone."

Sighing, wincing, she put her arms around him. "I'm a big
girl from Flatbush who loves you and likes to fuck. I'm not
Queen Bee, and I'm not the Great Devouring Mother. I'm
not something you read about in Jung's *Symbols of Transformation!*"

"Changed and unchanging. I wear myself out on your
marble belly. I turn into sperm. I cream away. You are unmoved."

She began to giggle. "Idiot, child, nincompoop! Dear
Philip, have I ever complained? You have standards of virility
in your head that have nothing to do with me."

"It all begins here. The whole thing." He had his cheek
on her belly again, his eye at her navel. "Here it begins."

Life? He was mumbling and staring, his fingers flexing. "All begins here." He was flushed and excited. "Round and round. In circles. Break the magic circle. Follow me in. Follow me out. But can't return. Where it begins and begins." He kept mumbling about beginning and circles and magic stones. Sweating heavily he complained now and then of cramps in his gut. "When he got his, I told him I'd get him out. But it came off in my hand. I couldn't get him back. It wouldn't fit together! It wasn't my fault!" Time leaked away. He was caught in a loop of his psyche and could not break out. He responded obliquely to whatever she said when he heard at all, so she could not comfort him. He seemed more frantically to beat to and fro in his loop, mumbling about beginnings and circles and somebody's arm, something that wouldn't fit back together.

Lying beside her purse was the blue textbook for her fall course on complex variables, which had sweated on it the print of her palm. She had wept into it and sweated upon it but learned nothing. Some of the hypercompetitive men in her math classes were always talking about cracking the books. She got a picture from that phrase of the books as nuts that they split open, gobbled the meats and tossed aside, ravaged and empty. That seemed a predatory way to feel about books.

Why did she call them hypercompetitive? They saw her the same way, from things they dropped from time to time in conversation, but she did not feel herself competing directly with them. She suddenly saw herself as if from a great distance, playing a game with grades. Women were not supposed to compete, she was not supposed to compete, she could never compete with Mark. So she saw herself rather as trying to do things as they should be done, learning ideally, proceeding upon a Platonic hierarchy of ideas and levels of abstraction. That is, trying to please Daddy again. She moaned aloud, disgusted.

"What, what?" He was sweating heavily, tossing to and fro.

She felt a rising panic coming off him. She began to be a little afraid. "Phil? What's wrong? What is it?" He did not seem to hear. He clung and stared at her with a remote paranoid glare, muttering nonsense.

"You want to push me out!" He sat up glaring. "While you stay inside waiting. Eating it all up. See how it looks like a hill but it's really a cave. What is it that's inside? What's really waiting?"

"There's no it! There's only me. Phil, don't look at me that way. It's Miriam, me, just me."

"*Me.*" He smiled in a crafty conspiratorial way and turned to the wall. "Me. Ha."

"Phil!" Now she was afraid. She took a deep breath. Then she knelt beside him and put her arms around his shoulders and began to stroke his back and chest. "Phil, Phil, it's me. Relax."

Slowly, slowly he relaxed and after what felt like an hour he leaned against her, very slowly. Leaned against her his full weight until they were lying with him sprawled partly over her. "She pushed me away. Don't do that. Let me stay."

"I'm holding you. It's all right. Philip, don't go so far off. I don't know how to help you then."

"Not far. Right here. Hold me and I won't disappear." His face was seraphic and mild, his eyelids half shut. His hands drifted over her flanks and thighs gently, curiously. Gently he tossed her breast so it bounced back. "Ridiculous. All round in handfuls that bounce. If you squeezed my balls like that, they'd fall off and roll under the bed. If there was an under." He began to laugh with his whole body loosely. "A bed with no under. Nothing but the cold bedrock. Full of cables and subways and sewers and F.B.I. men. Do you know that every telephone in Manhattan is bugged?"

He did not want her to caress him. He said that was too much. He came into her and very slowly, pausing and stopping altogether for side trips and more mumbling and resting, he went on and on. She felt nervous. She was afraid he would shoot into a paranoid tangent again if she relaxed her wariness. She did not come for a long time. Finally she got too excited to control her responses and got launched and came. Still he went on until she began to feel supersensitive and then sore. Eventually one of the times he paused, he seemed to forget what he was doing altogether, and still never having come, slipped out of her, could not get back in, and lay beside her instead.

About what must have been suppertime, although Phil would not eat and she felt too tense to do more than nibble, the phone rang. It rang once, then stopped. Next it begin to ring again. Miriam felt something cold slide in her, like a congealment of fear itself. She also thought as she ran flat-footed into the kitchen to the wall phone, how ridiculous for Allegra to use the code, now that everybody knew about Phil. Or perhaps Allegra was shy about speaking directly to him. "Hello?"

"Is that . . . Miriam?"

"Yes, Allegra, who did you expect? What's up?"

"We have to go to the hospital right away. She's gone into some kind of coma."

"No!" Strange how distant the formica table top looked. She was standing with her naked right shoulder to the wall, feeling the sexual damp drying on her thighs, one ankle crossed over the other. Gripping the receiver between hunched shoulder and twisted neck with a quick stiff finger she drew in the crumbs from his breakfast that lay on the formica. Her finger kept drawing a zero or a circle. Where he said it all began. In mother. "Is this it?"

"I guess so. How do I know! We have to go now. Can you get there right away, to the hospital?"

"I'll take a cab."

"If you can get one."

She felt cold. Something was coming to a sharp point, like a drill bit. "I'll try. I can get there on the subway in an hour and a half. Anyhow, I'll see you there."

"Hurry. I'll tell Dad you're on your way. We have to find Mark."

"I didn't know he was lost." The dry gasp of a mirthless laugh, like the beginning of someone vomiting.

"He's playing baseball in the park. I think I know where. Wouldn't it be like this? If my period hadn't started I wouldn't be home myself. I was supposed to go to Jones Beach with Roger, but I got cramps this morning."

When Miriam came to the bedroom door, she ran against a pane of electrified air. He was scowling that furious glare. His eyes were chips of broken glass. "Are *they* calling you here now?"

"That was my sister."

"That's what you say." He nodded, smiling ironically.

She knelt on the mattress, taking his chin in her palm. "Phil, that was my sister Allegra. My mother is in a coma."

He turned his face away. "You pulled away from me. Two can play. Two can be as cold as one."

She felt like screaming, Come off it, Phil, this is no time to play games! But she realized, staring into the chips of glass that were his eyes, that he was too far into his trip to understand. A queasy horror settled on her. She wanted to lie down. She wanted to turn to the wall and close her eyes. If only the phone had not worked. If only Allegra had lost the number.

"Phil, listen to me. Sweetheart, listen. I didn't go away because I wanted to. My sister called. My mother is very, very sick now. I have to go to the hospital where she is."

"Why?"

"She's dying."

"She's been dying all summer. Let them all die. Do you think they care about us?"

"Phil, she's my *mother*. I have to go. She's in a coma."

"Unconscious. But I'm conscious . . . That's the sharpest pain . . . Time is static and I'm stuck . . . like a fly in honey. . . . Petrified. Time . . . is glass. If you leave me stuck here, I'll be stuck forever, forever stuck, forever and ever and ever stuck." He was breathing heavily, kneading the folds of his belly.

"Are you in pain?"

"Yes. Pain. Terrible cramps. Inside the tunnel in waves."

She could not tell if he was in physical pain or frightened into pain: but that was a meaningless distinction.

"I think . . . I'm dying. I'm very sick, Miriam. Something terrible is happening to me. I'm being carried along. Something terrible like a storm is carrying me. I'm afraid, listen! Something's gone wrong! I can't get back."

"Sha, Phil, shhh." She cradled him against her, kneeling, facing him. He was hurling himself to and fro and she had to hold on with all her might. Fear came off him pungent as ammonia. She tried to control her own rising panic. What could be wrong? Sometimes the acid was cut with other drugs, bad drugs, sometimes with strychnine. Perhaps he was poisoned. Perhaps the pains in his belly were from poison and not from bad vibrations or bad visions or tensions. She did not know what to do. She wanted to run out of the room and get help, but she had no idea where to turn. She could not leave him like this: she could not stay. Should she take him to the hospital with her? "Phil, maybe we should get dressed."

"Clothes bind the body. No clothes. Close the body's eyes.

Keep-out signs. Can't get into you, can't touch you. No more clothes."

The hospital would not do. He might start to freak out there. She would not be able to protect him. She could not take him with her. She was briefly furious with herself for considering the possibility: false hope that she could meet all obligations, satisfy everyone, make it all come out well. Do every duty. It was now forty-five minutes since Allegra had called and she was not out the door. She remembered a piece of folklore to the effect that vitamin pills would bring somebody down from a bad trip. She disentangled herself long enough to search the medicine cabinet and the kitchen. She found only vitamin C against colds. She fed that to him and he took it placidly enough with a glass of water, but nothing happened.

Seven twenty-four. She was sitting cross-legged on the mattress and he was lying with his head on her thigh, weeping occasional fat tears and blowing his nose copiously. "I see it now. Yes. For both of us. How we have to open. Give birth to ourselves, to each other. Then we can love all the way open. Trusting, that's been hard. Because of my old man. Because of her going and turning into some damn bourgeois housewife after all we went through together. Jackson running off after he promised me. Now you want to leave me. Everybody wants to leave me."

If only she could know how far into self-pity he was, how objective the need, how violent the pains. To measure people against each other was distasteful. But there was only one of her, feeling guiltier every minute. Her body made goose pimples when he stroked it. Suppose Sonia was dying right now. Suppose Sonia was already dead. Suppose Sonia was calling for her. Suppose she got dressed and he ran after her naked into East Tenth Street and got hit by a truck. Suppose she never saw him again because he could not forgive her for deserting him on a bad trip.

He had dropped the acid about two-thirty, three. He could be up for hours. He could be up for the rest of the night. She could not wait. If only she could step outside the time stream and see what would happen and make the wise decision. Each would weigh her decision as weighing her love, but she was only trying to judge their needs. She did not think she actively loved Sonia any longer, but she could remember loving her. She could remember Sonia as the sun that warmed her world from the center, the milky heart, the lap of roundness and comfort. There was still in her the little girl who could not lie to her mommy.

"Phil, I'll be right back. Five minutes. I'm only going upstairs. Phil, I'll be right back." She got dressed and ran up the dim steps, past the charred railing from the fire the janitor before Jackson had started while drunk, up to 4B.

"Who is it?" Woman's voice close to the door, suspicious.

"I'm a friend of Phil's. You know, the janitor. He's sick downstairs. Please come."

With a clanking of bolts and turning over of locks the door at last opened on its chain wide enough for an eye at the crack. "Who is it? Who's there?"

"I'm a friend of Phil's. He's sick downstairs. I have to leave now. Please come down."

"What's wrong with him?"

"He took a pill that's made him sick. He's upset."

"Who are you?"

"Just a friend. I'm Miriam."

"Oh, the collegiate princess from Flatbush, how do you do?" The woman pulled out the steel rod of the police lock and swung the door open. Miriam had expected her to be middle-aged, the way they talked about her, but she was at the most in her late twenties, probably not even as old as Jackson and three or four years older than Phil. She had been sitting on the fire escape eating peanuts and she still carried the bag, wearing faded shorts on good tanned legs and a white T-shirt. Bleached hair and soft brown eyes and brows plucked thin, her face was anxious with suspicion. A slight limp showed as she followed Miriam down. Phil was lying awry against one wall, his eyes clenched shut and his hand scrabbling at the sheets.

"Naked as a jaybird." With that limp she minced across the mattress on high-heeled sandals to poke him with a foot. "What's wrong with you? Anything real? Come off it."

He sprawled on his back holding the side she had kicked. He stared at her blankly, then cowered. "Kill me. Eat my guts out. Suck my body dry."

"Whats' wrong with him? Some pill he took! Are you sure he isn't drunk? Sounds like the D.T.s."

"He took acid." When the woman went on looking at her, she continued. "L.S.D., you know."

"Oh well, no wonder. That stuff's illegal. They're always peddling that crap down on the street. Well, what are we supposed to do with him?"

"My mother's in the hospital. I got a phone call. I have to go there—"

"I'll bet." The plucked eyebrows raised. "How many times do you think you can get away with that one? Who gave him this L.S.D.?"

"Look, she's been in the hospital all summer. She's got cancer. My sister called me here an hour and a half ago. I promised I'd leave immediately, but he won't let me go. I'm scared to leave him alone. Please, just sit with him. Don't let him harm himself. I'll come back as soon as I can. I don't even know if she's still alive—but if I don't go now she'll never forgive me and I'll hate myself."

4B reluctantly agreed, though she kept her face screwed up to indicate she wasn't taken in by any such stories, and Miriam ran toward Second Avenue to get a cab. The first one that stopped pushed her out, telling her to fuck off when she asked him to go to Brooklyn. The second wouldn't let her in till he found out where she was going, and when he heard he gunned the motor and charged off, leaving her to catch her balance. The third she jumped in and started screaming hysterically that her mother was dying! The cabbie was furious but he was young and not as experienced at the game as the others, so he agreed to take her to the hospital for an extra two bucks over the meter.

Everybody was sitting in the hall waiting: her father, Allegra, Mark still in his ball-playing clothes, and even her mother's friend Judy, who had been there since late afternoon.

"So you finally got here," Lionel said. "Well, well. We couldn't expect you to hurry, of course."

"I couldn't get a cab to take me. I had to come on the subway. How is she?"

"Bad. Very bad. Who knows? They don't tell you a thing."

About three in the morning the night nurse came by to say that they might as well go home, because Sonia's condition was not likely to change. She promised they would be called. Early in the morning Sonia regained consciousness briefly. At least the woman in the next bed thought so, although the nurse doubted her. By the time they arrived again she was back under. Miriam went to a pay phone in the lobby to call Philip.

No answer. But there had to be an answer. Phil had to be there. It was early. She dialed again. Again. Still no answer. Probably the stupid phone wasn't working. He had to be there. But she believed he had run off. She believed he had disappeared. Something terrible had happened. He had run into the street and been hit by one of the cabs that would not stop for her. The woman from 4B had called the police. He was in jail. He had hitchhiked off to Mexico to join Jackson in myth.

She had not even the satisfaction of crisis. Sonia had not died, or, if she had, not technically. It was becoming evident that Sonia might never regain consciousness. She was being kept somewhat alive by machines that had taken over the duties of her failing organs. They digested for her and excreted for her and cleansed her body of its wastes. The nurses tended her vacant body. Sonia might wake up at any moment remembering nothing. Or she might come to and call for her family. Or nothing at all might happen but that the machines would go on changing her fluids and what had been her mother would lie there in the rented bed.

Lionel had a social engagement in the Bronx that night. He went home first to change. As soon as he was gone, she ran to the subway to go into town. She had to find out what was happening. Probably Phil was too angry at her to answer his phone. She would appear there. She would make him love her again. She would make it all right, somehow, somehow!

When she buzzed him there was no response. She let herself in with her key. Boxes tied up on the kitchen table. "Phil! Phil!"

A man came out of the john zipping up his pants. "Who the hell are you?"

"I could say the same, but I won't. You're Jackson."

He was taller than Phil and thin but more solidly built, darker and grizzled. He was homely and glaring at her, doing up his belt. A loose washed-out blue work shirt hung open. "I suppose you're his girl. That was a hell of a trick, running out on him in the middle of a bad trip."

"You make a lot of assumptions. Where is he?"

"What do you care?" He rubbed his head vacantly. He seemed idiotic, drawling his words and scratching himself all over his hairy chest while he gaped at her.

"What I care is nothing to you. Where is Phil?"

"Where did you expect him to go?"

"Do you always play stupid games?"

"He thought a lot of you. You let him down."

"Go fuck yourself, you stupid prig! What do you know what happened, you creep! Were you here? No, you were farting around Mexico, leaving me to take care of him alone on a bad trip—caused by his anxiety over going to Boston and his so-called friend who didn't get back when he promised to! My mother is in the hospital dying of cancer and I had to go there, you creepy, self-righteous, tight-assed schmuck!"

"Your mother?"

"Why do you suppose I had to leave? I left him with that woman in 4B you fuck. She was supposed to stay with him. Now I want to know where is he and what happened."

"He's in Bellevue."

"Oh, no. What's he doing there?"

"Under psychiatric observation. Your friend—"

"Yours, if you mean 4B, you—"

"I wouldn't leave a sick kitten with her. Anyhow, she freaked when he started running around. He tried to slash his wrists, though I don't think he tried hard."

Why didn't you get back on time?"

"Who said it was like catching a plane? School doesn't start for two weeks. Anyhow, I'm fired. I'm out of a job and Phil's in the hospital, and if it isn't your fault, who can I blame? In situations of this sort, someone is traditionally a scapegoat. We could use Wendy—that's 4B."

"I'm sure she did what she could—how was she supposed to know what to do? Did you ever give her lessons?"

"Why didn't you give him some B vitamins?"

"Why didn't you fly a kite? What are you being so smart-assed about, with him in the hospital now too?"

"It's not the first time nor, I expect, the last. I was growing tired of being a janitor anyhow. I'm too tall for basement work, and the damp was starting to mold my books. And maybe me. It's as well to clear out."

"How can you stand around here scratching yourself like a senile monkey? How do we get him out?"

He began to laugh. "Maybe you are something else. Maybe."

"Just shut your face about me. I have enough troubles. Now take me where he is."

"We can't get in to see him today. However, tomorrow. How would you like to take a senile monkey home with you?"

"Are you crazy?"

"Never saner. I'm kicked out. I'm fired as of two days ago. Looking for a place to sleep."

"Not with my family. You wouldn't appreciate, they wouldn't appreciate. Enough trouble. What happened to that guy Phil used to live with, Donald Duck?"

Jackson shrugged. "Possible. Let me call. If I end up there, we can go see Phil tomorrow."

"I don't want to hang around. I'm going back to the hospital. Here, this is my home number. I'll go in with you tomorrow."

He took the slip of paper and tried to hold her gaze, seeming about to speak, but she did not wait to hear. She left at once for the subway. It was a hot day, like summer again, in the nineties. The streets were crowded, people jammed on the sidewalks, men lounging at the corners and in the doorways and on the stoops. Every five steps some guy tried to pinch her, invited her to suck his prick, made loud wet noises with his lips, talked about her as pussy and tried to block her way. She had to walk faster and faster and by the time she dived hostile and jittery into the smarmy murk of the subway she had broken into a heavy sweat. She could not decide whether she should go back home or to the hospital, but having a reservoir of guilt that never seemed to run dry, she decided on the hospital.

They finally extracted Phil from Bellevue, looking starved and pallid. "That's a hellhole. But what a drug traffic. If all I wanted to do was get high, I'd never have to leave."

"Phil." She rested her hand on his shoulder. "Do you understand what happened? About my mother?"

"Still alive, isn't she?"

"Yes, and so are you, no?"

"Phil's card in the poets' union requires this sort of thing once a year," Jackson said on Phil's right side.

"What happened is that you betrayed me. Yes. You two met, without my permission. Over my drugged and tied-down body. In secret. In the farthest realms of my paranoid imaginings, you met and signed a devil's pact against me."

"Phil, I wouldn't even say we got on."

"She called me a senile monkey," Jackson drawled. "A tight-assed self-righteous creep. She insults with energy but lacks your style."

"Maybe she sees through you. You are both forgiven." He made a sign of the cross. "Forgiving is a pious hoax. Who ever forgives for something they haven't forgotten? Every time you remember a thing that hurt you, you charge that account a little more. Dig this: we'll go around with wee laser guns. When we mean to forgive somebody we'll put the laser gun to our skulls and blow out that memory: gone. Forgiveness will enter the world. Until then, I forget nothing."

She saw them off to Boston together, in a rented car loaded with their few boxes and suitcases. They both traveled light. Their massed possessions did not quite fill the trunk and back seat. On the sidewalk outside Donald's apartment on West Eighty-second, she stood and waved while they careened off through the maze of double-parked cars. Jackson was driving, Phil had his feet on the dashboard and his head hanging out waving back to her. Bye-bye, bye-bye, bye-bye. She found herself sniveling as she walked away.

In the next ten days she finally got into the Theory of Complex Variables. She carried it to the hospital where she sat beside her mother's body for several hours a day. A woman with a tumor in her throat lay in the middle bed now, though the old woman Mrs. Katz was still penned in her crib.

Miriam's eyes would glide off the dismal pages to her mother's slack yellowed face, to her hand lying limp with the wedding ring thin and gold and worn almost smooth from a filigree pattern, cutting into the finger. Sonia's face looked bitter in abandonment. She imagined entering her mother's head telepathically to communicate—what? Mother, I love you, let me live . . . differently? The better afternoons were those with Allegra sitting there too, both of them feeling strongly their mother's daughters and talking quietly. Remembering. Merging their childhoods.

When school reopened, Lionel decided they should go.

Allegra said to her, "Besides, he's tired of having us around. We're noisy. Suppose he got stuck with us living here with him forever—two unmarried daughters. He'd *plotz*."

Allegra and Miriam kissed good-by with affection for the first time. Allegra was going to a small liberal arts college in upstate New York near Cornell but rather less demanding. They agreed not to write unless they had something to tell.

Back to Ann Arbor Miriam went, to her comfortable room in the elite murmur of Martha Cooke with its blind statues and the nervous click of pills like worry beads, the hilly streets of tall oaks and maples just beginning to turn salmon and orange and gold and flame, the white wooden houses with big front porches and towers perched at the corners. She went back to her quiet affair with her ex-section man with its once- or twice-a-week meals and to bed with music and reasonable conversation and a certain amount of history of the Civil War era freely taught. She plunged into her classes and found the Theory of Complex Variables every bit as hideously stony and arid as it had seemed when she was sweating her palm print into the book all summer. For the first time she was not only doing less than well in a math class but loathing every minute. However, Theory of Discrete Systems was delighting her. She began to consider changing the direction of her studies to something involving computers.

Lionel kept saying how little money there was, and how he could not send her anything to live on above the dormitory. She cast around for a way to combine curiosity about computers with making some cash. She found a job building mathematical models of enzyme systems on a computer for a professor in bio-chemistry. It was all right. It was even interesting. She enjoyed that kind of playing. But working fifteen to twenty hours a week for him and taking a full load of classes left her little time for exploring her fellow humans. That would have to wait awhile. She was subdued and depressed still. She was surer than ever that she was going to move into computer science when, midway through November, Sonia officially died, and she flew back to Brooklyn for the funeral.

10

Just off the Freedom Trail (Phil)

Phil came back to Boston with anxiety and mixed urges. Something snotty in Boston stuck in his craw, cozy and stratified and damp at the core: he hated to come back, he hated to be away too long. Cambridge was even worse: the imperial domes of M.I.T. fading into its industrial fringe, separated by careful demolition from the nearby slums where he'd spent his lousy childhood. But this time he returned on his own terms, with a meal ticket, a synecure, a niche.

He even managed to visit his mother every two weeks with only minor friction. The older of his stepbrothers was married and living in Schenectady. The younger had dropped out of school and the old man had got him apprenticed in the union. He was still at home, but he'd grown his hair long and smoked dope and Phil liked him all right. The old man was having trouble with his heart and Phil tried to behave himself. His mother was looking older than she should and tired. Arthritis knotted her hands till she could hardly comb her hair. He thought of the years of her life spent cleaning other people's floors and chattered about how well he was doing for himself.

He and Jackson rented a floor-through on Pearl Street in Cambridgeport, a mixed-up area where nobody was in the majority. The old frame houses crowded the rambling brick sidewalks, but in spite of the tides of through traffic, the neighborhood felt green and pastoral, especially in the summer. Big maples and horse chestnuts. Kids sitting on steps playing guitars, children with their wagons and bikes, dogs in back yards. Fences every place. Every front yard the size of a tablecloth had a wire fence or a privet hedge around it. Jackson was driving a hack, Phil picked up a part-time bartending stint and they eased into life in Cambridge.

People drifted through their apartment, crashed there, came and went in that ebb and flow Phil liked. Jackson was loosening too, took readily to the traffic. He was dropping his monkish withdrawal. Getting more into his old army role of father confessor, listening and nodding and mumbling in his chest and scratching his balls and looking wise.

On and off girls lived with them. Of the women Phil brought home, a certain tithe would always fall for Jackson, hoping and hanging on and maybe sharing his mattress for a while. Jackson was bone and steel and brain: he couldn't be caught. Once in a while they would get into a little momentary tug-of-war over a piece, but it never lasted. It was a game. With a regular kitchen, Jackson took up cooking and they started eating well. Jackson got involved in the local food co-op and guys from that came through talking and arguing and eating and turning on together. Always they had food to eat and dope to smoke and wine to ease the body and friends to rap with and things happening and warm bodies to take off to bed. After the tensions of New York and the manic din and weird funky anomie, it was all easy. He was doing okay hustling J. Singleton Proxmire, professor of English, and making it in his department. Two of his poems got accepted by the *Hudson Review,* where J. Singleton Proxmire had an in, and three by a little poetry mag called *Barking Dog.* He felt good. Things were coming on for them.

They weren't that far from East Cambridge, where he'd grown up in Roosevelt Towers. But he put off going by. He had some funny notion he had heard coming out of his mouth one time he was stoned with Jackson. He would go over there and he would meet himself, fifteen, mean, sore, halfway to a junkie. And *zap,* he would be transferred back to his undernourished asthmatic adolescence, simmering with hatred and self-hatred, back on the corner hanging out, shooting up in the hallways, getting laid among the garbage in the vacant lot behind the high rise, marked KEEP OUT, though it held nothing even they could find to steal. . . . His buddy Joe Rosario was the only person he could ever talk about class and poverty to without fudging it in rhetoric, without exaggerating one way or the other. Joe was in Boston too, teaching at Northwestern, but he was knocking himself out in the anti-war movement and went to seven meetings a week. Phil only saw him when Joe had a drink at Finnegan's Wake.

Then in early June Miriam turned up. Since she was starting graduate school at M.I.T. in September, she had decided there was no point spending the summer in Brooklyn. She had a job lined up and she obviously expected him to live with her somewhere.

Nine months, long time. He remembered how she had left him when her family whistled. Remembered her crying and crying like a busted hose. As he met her at the airport and brought her back to Pearl Street, he realized he was no longer in love with her and experienced a wild sense of liberation, like a wrecking ball swinging free. She sensed that quickly—she was always quick—sensed him holding back. The next morning she started looking for a place. She lucked into a sublet from an Italian-American social worker who was going to Europe for the summer. But in a week of installing her at the acute angle of Hanover and Charter in the North End, he was hooked again. Back to wanting her. Caught in that sense of intimacy.

It didn't burn and pinch in the old way, but it was strong. He still wanted to be with her, he wanted her a lot, and the talking was better. She was getting tougher, chewier. He liked sleeping at the sublet. But when he thought of them living together in the fall, he felt it as a narrowing. Suppose he wanted to bring home a girl from the bar. Would he call up first? He wanted Miriam to move in to Pearl Street. She'd be on hand for him and so would the rest of that easygoing scene. And she'd be out-numbered.

She and Jackson didn't get on. They rubbed each other the wrong way. She brought out all of Jackson's latent Midwestern uptightness. After all, he remembered Jackson's ex-wife: Sissy and Miriam had nothing in common besides being female. Sissy had been slim and long-legged and narrow-hipped, blond and athletic and polished, cool and expensive. She moved artfully, climbing stairs, sitting down: he had never seen her awkward till the end, when she was scared and angry.

But Miriam with her flamboyance and her earthiness and her sensuality put Jackson right up against the wall. It tickled Phil to see him bridling and setting his jaw: her presence caused him to brood about sex more than he liked. Still, they spent far more time at her place. Days when she wasn't working they would sleep late, then run down five flights to shop for lunch. In the yard of the Eliot School across the street, kids would be playing baseball or basketball, and he would stop to kibitz. Old men sat out in chairs on the sidewalk, there were little old women in black gossiping in Italian.

Miriam would have her shopping bag on her arm and they would stop at the bakery for fresh hot bread. The markets spilled out onto the sidewalk with fruit and vegetables that never any place else looked so fetching, so vivid. He swore the fish was more beautiful, the squid, the crabs, the flounder, the eels, the blowfish, the steamers and quahogs, the cod and halibut, spread out in rainbow splendor on the ice. Always at noon the narrow streets were jammed, and there were even a few pushcarts. The butchers had luscious veal and furry rabbits hanging outside. They drank espresso at shops patronized by middle-aged men who eyed them curiously. But the neighborhood was still the old working-class Italian island; and not even enough freaks had moved in for people to have started being hostile. When he spoke to people in the street they answered him. Always a grand wash seemed to be in progress, sheets and shirts and tablecloths whipping in the wind off the nearby and mostly invisible bay, suspended over the narrow passageways. Miriam's progress through the streets did not go unappreciated. Phil was constantly amused, though Miriam was not.

They spent a lot of time out of doors. They strolled past the dusty monument maker, past the workshop where the man and his son made plaster figures of swordfish, angels, mermaids, and madonnas. Miriam greeted her neighbor underneath, who had lived there for forty-three years, as she often repeated. Phil liked to rap about Boston. He felt it was something he was turning her on to, though sometimes she complained he was cramming it down her throat.

"The first draft riot occurred in the North End, you know that? They try to tell us fighting the draft is new, but that's bullshit."

"Was that World War I?" Miriam was eating lemon slush out of a paper cone.

"You scientists know nothing, ha. Civil War. The federal marshals handing out draft notices were attacked by a woman who thought they were after her husband. A crowd beat them up and then started fighting the police. Aw, they attacked a police station and the Cooper Street Armory. The troops fired into the crowd and charged with bayonets. The protesters broke into a gun shop in Dock Square but the police busted obvious leaders. Twenty people were killed and five sent to prison for 'causing' the riot. Sound familiar?" He strolled along with his hand on the back of her neck, under the fall of her hair.

They scrambled through the hole in the fence up into Copps Hill Burying Ground and sauntered among the worn old gravestones, with the kids riding tricycles and their mothers talking and an old man reading a newspaper in Italian and a couple holding hands. It was a neighborhood park, essentially, useful and green, in spite of the tourists following the signs for the Freedom Trail from Christ Church past the bocce players. They crossed the street and stood in the shade of the old trees looking down on the play ground and across the inner harbor to the Charlestown Navy Yard, where his old man had briefly been employed, and the three masts of the *Constitution* sticking up behind the squat mass of the Port Authority building. Then they wandered back home full of goodies and laden with bags of more, well sunned and walked out, and fell into bed. They had a nice big double bed and there they would fuck under a big reproduction of Rouault's sad-eyed *David the King* until Phil revolted and threw it in the closet. "Jesus, it reminds me of a spaniel sitting there wanting some too, with those sad soulful entreaties. Enough to take the edge off."

"I hadn't noticed that," Miriam said, smiling. It was a good summer based around her sublet.

"Smoking dope and tobacco in the same pipe. Jackson, you have no style. Why don't you pour a little chocolate in too? Or mayonnaise. Everything in the Midwest comes covered with a thin pale greasy layer—salads, bacon, sandwiches, hamburgers. When a boy baby is born to a family like yours, he's slapped on the behind and coated with mayonnaise."

"Listen to the gourmet. Why, before I met you, you thought a meal was a hot dog, and a seven-course dinner was seven hot dogs."

"Remember who turned you on in the first place."

"My Uncle Sam. You were just a scrawny nineteen-year-old, too stupid to use his asthma to stay out of the stew."

"A lot of good your conniving did you. Three years in the reserves, and you ended up in Nam anyhow."

"And that," Jackson said soulfully, with his hand on his belly, "is where I went wrong. Led astray. Where the lures of the wicked lay in wait and tempted me. I always tell that to my father, on the rare occasions we hold converse these dark days. It's usually good for a twenty."

Phil had been drafted, but Jackson had been caught by surprise. Old Jackson had had things worked out in his life. Very fancily he had taken concurrent M.A.s in sociology and business administration, married his girl friend Sissy, and gone to work for a conglomerate. Their parents kicked in lest they live in squalor on his measly salary of sixteen thou, and helped them into a split level in the woods outside St. Paul. Soon enough Jackson wiggled upward, they moved to a suburb near Dayton, had a baby, while Jackson switched his reserve duty to his new location. He had joined the reserves after college, figuring his deferments might come home to roost. Then the President called up Jackson's unit and he found himself in it for real.

"Man, you know, in the reserves you can just ooze up from rank to rank," Jackson had told him long ago. "When they activated us I was a top sergeant. Hadn't done more than clean rifles in years. The next thing I knew I was jumping out of a helicopter leading an attack and landing in a rice paddy, sinking up to my hips in the muck. . . . I hated the Army. It was two weeks of hyped-up shit every summer. All the guys saying to each other as we crawled through the woods on our bellies slapping at mosquitoes, 'If my secretary could see me now,' while some nineteen-year-old with stripes on bellowed orders." Jackson's stripes did not last long, with a little help from his friends. The Army had been, as they say, a radicalizing experience for Jackson.

Phil hadn't needed any pointers on how shitty things were. But they had locked into each other strengths and weaknesses and somehow the pattern fit, meshed. Jackson had turned him on to books. Jackson was big then on Hermann Hesse and gave him *Steppenwolf* to read. That was Jackson identifying, the lean gray bookish wolf of the steppes who was going to bring them through somehow alive and fight the brass to save their skins. Bunch of kids, lot of them from college, painting peace symbols on their helmets but following orders just the same. They called the company hangout the wolf den. Less than half of them came back to the world.

Jackson had tried to return to his life and pick up the leads where they had been cut from his hands. He tried. Sort of. But he was full of anger and bitterness and depressions he could not handle and rages that spilled out and a boredom he could not hide. Phil went to a better school than he'd quit, got into N.Y.U. in English. He went into a brief incandescent dream in which books seemed more real than his life—hard now to remember his idealism about departments of English and the teaching of literature. Vacations he'd go to Medford a couple of days and then off to Jackson's. Each time the tensions were rawer. Sissy stopped being polite and then she stopped flirting and bared her teeth. She was scared. She was losing what she thought she needed. She was fighting for what she felt entitled to. He was a messager of chaos come to wake in Jackson all she could not understand or accept.

And they were bad together, baaad. Phil left at school his earnest new scholarly identity, his passion for Keats, and arrived in fatigues and street-corner leer, the lining of his jacket hiding the magic pills. They traded atrocity stories, their own, ones they had merely heard told as their own. They reminisced about whores for hours in the kitchen till Sissy barricaded herself in the bedroom. She refused to cook for them, and they brought back take-out and filled up the house with bags of french fries, the bones of barbecued spareribs and gnawed chicken, paper plates and cups of half-drunk Coke and 7-Up. They spread their untidy feast over the pale carpeting and the glass and chrome Design Research furniture and Phil pissed in the potted avocado tree. On weekends like those Sissy could be made to represent Mom and apple pie and the American Dream and the vast pile of crap waving at them from every plastic ad with a blond selling a refrigerator. The last time he went to visit, Jackson left with him, after breaking up the living room and trying unsuccessfully to flush Sissy's mink coat down the toilet.

Jackson went into a strange violent scene in New York, holed up in a commune supported by a couple of dealers and some girls who hustled, on Third between C and D. When Jackson climbed out of that, he withdrew into ascetic monkishness. Jackson had the basement cell on Tenth Street and the janitor's job and was into needing nothing, no one, self-sufficient and lean and bony and ogling the death's head in the mirror, all established as a way of life by the time Phil had picked up Miriam at the MOMA.

"I'd never have gone to school if you hadn't pushed me," Phil said. "But while you were nudging me into the system, you were climbing out."

"Does anybody really influence another? Maybe it's all genetically determined. If we could read the DNA, who knows? I was programmed to zig, then zag. I am all zagged out."

Unconfrontable Jackson. They had talked for years about sharing rooms. But always before something had precluded it. "Miriam's sublet will be up soon. She's starting to look. I think she kind of expects I-might move in with her."

Jackson tapped his pipe out. "I could get somebody else to split the rent. If you're into the domesticity routine? I guess you could get used to it. Might as well get it over."

"Yeah. I just don't know if I want to."

"What's the matter, you scared of some other guy cutting you out if you don't set up house?"

"Don't project that shit on me. She's free. So am I. I do what I want to whoever I want when I want to."

"Sure," Jackson drawled, grinning. "Have fun. They're all so easy to get on with in the beginning. Women are always agreeable. For a while, for a while, for a while."

"Not that she's pushing me. She knows better than to try that. But I told her, how come she doesn't move in here. Would that bug you a lot?"

"I don't have to deal with her. She's no worse than the other chicks you've let loose in here."

"Aw come on, Jackson, they're not in her class."

"She's smart, or so she tells us. But I'll bet you a nickel bag she'll never move in while I'm here."

"She says she couldn't work here, there's too much traffic."

"It's your worry. Just so she splits the expenses when she eats here, it's the same to me."

"You're so scared someone's going to cop one meal without putting into the kitty, I can't believe it."

"I didn't know you'd inherited a fortune. Or is your princess keeping you these days?"

"Aw come on, we get by. It gives me a large pain to hear

about voluntary poverty around here, when everybody has bread to buy dope and clothes and bikes and records. Poverty my sweet ass! Poverty is when you don't have it for food, man. We live pretty well, if you ask me."

"It is because I do not ask you that we live well. And small thanks I get for my clever managing."

"Sure, Jackson, you're the best housewife on all of Pearl Street!"

Jackson punched him in the chest not quite playfully, then shambled off to his room before Phil could get his breath back. He was always susceptible in the chest. Dirty pool. He'd get back at Jackson later. One way or the other. Noisy sex scene. Bring some of the political heavies home from the bar tonight. Maybe Joe Rosario, who always got Jackson uptight when they argued by making him feel like a liberal. Joe would get more and more vehement and more and more militant and finally he would stand there pounding and roaring and representing the whole Third World in their kitchen. Besides, Jackson liked politics in words and Joe liked to do it in the streets. Phil hated all those meetings where people jawed at each other in their stupid factions, but he was drawn to Joe's energy and anger. Phil got his breath back and smiled to himself. Jackson wasn't always right: though Phil could remember when, at nineteen, that thought would have seemed disloyal.

11

The Competition

Miriam tried hard to locate a permanent apartment in the North End but she could not find anyone who would rent to her. As August progressed, Phil suggested frequently that she move in. She did not take that idea seriously. She was no longer the Complete Scholar she had been, but M.I.T. was a place that habitually set students a rigorous schedule and

she liked computer science. Above all she had found a
project to work on, which was not only supporting her but
could probably be mined for a thesis subject eventually.

Before school started she found a one-room apartment in
Cambridge on Upland Road. It was twenty minutes by bus
from Phil's apartment but she bought a bicycle and sometimes she pedaled to M.I.T. or to Phil's. Her room on the
top floor faced small yards where housewives hung out their
laundry and put their children to play. Past the back fence
the Boston and Maine Railroad ran, shaking the house. The
room was light and clean and free from bugs and only typically exorbitant in rent. The street outside was lined with big
trees whose branches almost knit.

She was working for a project that was just getting started
with a number of biochemists plus her providing the computer
know-how. M.I.T. was not like Michigan. It lacked a campus
people gathered around, easy meeting places, comfortable
hangouts if you overlooked the F & T Diner. She was on
campus some, among the modernistic slabs of building, but
most of the time she was over at Project MAC, in Tech
Square. It was a total environment. Some computer freaks
almost lived in. The big computer and the artificial intelligence
labs were on the ninth floor but her project office was on eight.
Her part was to work on developing an artificial language
which biochemists could use to describe such entities as enzyme systems: a language which they would find easy to
use without having to know anything about computers and in
which they could directly express their problems. She was
also working on computer software which could operate with
that language, to turn it into machine language, and run
simulations of those enzyme systems that the scientists were
describing. The computer would simulate them and give
the results back to the biochemists. It was an interesting set
of problems, way more interesting than the mathematical
models she had been diddling with at Michigan.

For one thing, she thought that this work felt real. During
her senior year, purer mathematics had come to seem more
and more alienated and alienating. She did not want to spend
her life manipulating concepts almost nobody understood and
nobody could relate to. People might not understand exactly
what she did now if they weren't in her field, but at least
they could relate to the products of that work. She thought

that her mind was really more suited to this work than to pure mathematics, and the feedback with the machine at one end and the biochemists on the other end was interesting in itself. Even debugging the programs that she wrote was fun.

Because she liked her work, she had essentially different needs than Phil or Jackson. Too many people came percolating through Pearl Street. She wanted a place where she could shut Phil out when she had to, where she could spread out her books and her papers and her flow charts, and come back and find them undisturbed. When she came skipping in from class or from Phil her work waited, beautiful and inviting her to grapple with it.

Phil could be home engulfed in that steady gregarious hum he craved, friends, acquaintances, just faces to turn on with and drink with during all those hours when she worked on her compiler. The structures she generated gave her aesthetic pleasure: there was a neatness, an economy, an elegance to a good program just as there was to a good piece of music, although she could never convince Phil. That sense of economical and functionally elegant shape pleased her, satisfied something that had been hungry for use inside her. She felt surer than ever that she had made a good choice in changing fields.

Tech Square had been built for NASA under Kennedy and now housed corporations like Polaroid and cold-war entities like the Cambridge Project, as well as M.I.T. offshoots. It stood in a vast parking area that had been a working-class neighborhood when Phil was growing up, and towered over two mostly black housing projects from which trashing parties and entrepreneur thieves came raiding. 545, the building she spent so much time in, had a big fancy lobby with security and seemed to have been designed like a lot of M.I.T. to minimize the environmental shock students would experience in moving from school to industry. She shared an office with three other students, windowless and painted luridly, full of science fiction and mild anti-war slogans, with a cot and a hot plate and a calendar run off by computer with Snoopy saying FUCK YOU RED BARON. If she wanted to kill time, she could do it endlessly.

For all of her careful irony to Phil about the place and her sense sometimes of "What am I, daughter of a HUAC victim, doing in the brain of the military-industrial complex?"

she was having a good time. Just one floor up were the most exciting toys she could imagine. Besides the big old GE 645, there were elegant small computers, two DEC 10s and a 6 lashed together, and graphics terminals for dynamic modeling. Not to mention the computer-directed robots in the lab where there was so much wiring that the floor quaked when she walked on it, floating on a mass of circuits.

From Brooklyn she had brought whatever clothes she still wanted. Allegra told her she thought Lionel would move out of the flat, and Miriam rather hoped he would. It depressed them all. Even Mark sighed and drooped there. She hung her room with dripping subtle colors, for Phil had got into tie dying. The bare bulb of the ceiling fixture in his room now was muted by a canopy of sheets dyed with golds and browns and reds. He had made a canopy for her ceiling in red and blues he said had the tonality of stained-glass windows that neither of them had ever seen. They would go and see, someday. . . . They went to rummage sales and the Salvation Army and Good Will on Mount Auburn to get used sheets and plain white curtains and T-shirts. All of these they tie-dyed in big spaghetti pots on the stove.

"I don't give a shit what you brew up like witches on my stove, so long as you clean it up. I will not have cobalt blue stew poisoning me." Jackson inspected every pot.

At home her biggest meal was of hamburgers or hot dogs, but Jackson turned out to be an exacting and inventive cook. On their meager budget he produced good soups and stews and casseroles. In the stores he watched the prices with a sharp eye. He was deeply involved in the local food co-op and always knew when they had paid too much for produce. That was a strange side to this somber man: he always knew how much everything cost. Sonia would have adored him. It piqued her how little he seemed to think of her. Most of the time he ignored her, as if she were some pickup Phil had scraped off the barroom floor.

"You're a tight bastard, Jackson, when we come down to it. And we always do. You count pennies. You could dwindle into an old bachelor miser saving foil and old twine and with twenty thousand dollars under the mattress in crumpled singles while you tie your pants with an end of rope." Phil leaned on the refrigerator drinking a beer, whose quality he had just been complaining of.

"Whereas you have a hole in your pocket as big as your mouth. Until we pay the rent, there's no Tuborg or even Pabst."

"This Old Bohemian is just Charles River water. Nice and brown."

"Hmmm." Jackson regarded him gravely. "I could go down with a bucket and get it directly. Do you fancy the taste of the sewage on the Boston or the Cambridge shore?"

"Aw, the Cambridge sewage is the tastiest. It's all that academic shit going out to sea. Pound for pound, you can't beat it. . . . I know you don't mean to be tight, Jackson. It's just your Midwestern toilet training."

"Yes, we did have them. I expect you've found it hard to adjust."

Phil tensed, coming straight off the refrigerator. Miriam, washing up at the sink, turned quickly drying her hands on her dungarees. "Personally, I think we should eat it for supper. Recycling, Jesus saves. Ecologically sound. Eat shit and cram the empties up your ass."

"You have a vulgar woman, Philip old buddy," Jackson drawled, trying to make contact. He had seen Phil tighten also. In their constant sparring, one often pushed the other too far. "Where did you say you found her? Cruising the Square?"

"Wherever I found her, I know how to keep her. And you can jam that up your ass." Phil stomped into the john and slammed the door. Hunks of the ceiling were heard to fall into the tub. Miriam's and Jackson's gazes collided and rebounded. Industriously she scrubbed the mashed potato pot from supper.

When she let out the water, Phil was still sulking in the bathroom and Jackson had quietly laid out the chessboard on the kitchen table. When Phil sauntered out, they were already playing.

"As soon as I've finished off this slow-motion general, I'll come," she said. They were always playing nowadays.

She thought of it as a kind of heaviness, as if the room tipped or she swelled. It had to do with the way Jackson watched her sometimes. The game was half played. She had two pawns on Jackson, but she had allowed her mind to wander, that wooziness to creep in, and now her bishop had been exchanged for his knight and he was threatening her rook. The same gaps appeared in his game from time to time. Playing chess was something they had fallen into as a war they could legitimately wage on each other.

Phil she could beat easily because, although he played a cunning game at first, he would forget his own grand strategies in flashes of bravado and wild vendettas. He would launch an attack on her queen and in that pursuit sacrifice four other pieces if only he could effect her capture. Jackson was more nearly her match. If he would have accepted handicapping her a pawn or two, he would have beat her a good percentage of the time. But he did not believe in handicaps, he said, and would not enjoy the game if they did not start out apparently even.

She did not really like to play chess with Phil. But in her uneasy facing of Phil's roommate, chess was useful. It filled the space between them with mock battle. Phil wanted the pleasure of winning, but he wanted it quickly. If she looked away from the board, sometimes Phil would move the pieces, and then laugh like a kid when she caught him. If he lost his temper he would clean the board with a swipe of his forearm. A couple of times when she patiently got the pieces and set them up as they had been, he was amazed. He no longer remembered.

Playing with Phil was playing, not competing. They had so many games. Sometimes an object would start them off: a flowered, flounced dress she got at the Salvation Army while browsing for surfaces to dye, that they would try on each in turn mincing and posing. A torn and ragged suit of tails in which Phil was a magician failing to produce rabbits from a bottomless hat, in which she was a mad conductor leading the orchestra of Phil. Comb and tissue paper could prompt them to kazoo serenades and outlandish versions of Beethoven that sent Jackson howling to a bar. Even when they were in bed what began as love-making might turn over into teasing or acting out an elaborate seduction, one of the other.

But Jackson truly wanted to win. He deliberated maddeningly. He was a slow player and she was fast and sometimes she would fetch a clock and impose a time limit, or bring a book and ostentatiously read while he was brooding. If she let him wait her into fidgetiness, he sometimes won through lapses on her part. When she faced him across the board, it mattered each time who came out on top. It was ridiculous that they cared, but they did. She noticed one morning when she brought up the mail and knocked on his door to give him a letter from his parents in Davenport, Iowa, that on the wooden box beside his mattress now lay *My System* by Aron Nimzovich and Griffith and Sergeant's *Modern Chess Openings*.

It was a bare ascetic room, replica of the New York basement cell. His books were still in boxes, his socks and underwear in laundry bag or suitcase. Covered with an army blanket, the aged mattress lay on the floor with his boots beside it. A broken shade hung partway off the window that he seemed to leave open three or four inches now in November just as he had when she had first seen the room, in June. It was a room she entered seldom, and never without knocking and identifying herself and her purpose.

Her feelings remained sore that he was not friendlier. They always seemed rivals for Phil's attention and respect. Chess was the one thing he would admit wanting to do with her, the one opening he gave her, and that was a poor way to win him over. Obviously he found her presence in the flat an irritant. Phil and she had been used to wandering around naked and it was difficult to remember always to wrap herself in a sheet or put on Phil's shirt before she trotted to the bathroom or got a beer for Phil or ran into the living room to change a record. Phil did not bother. He marched out as he was regardless of who was sitting in the kitchen. Not defiantly or ostentatiously, just without thinking.

Now Jackson forced her back from that naturalness. He forced her into a false modesty. He dropped remarks and comments and made hard faces. He forced her to become conscious of her body in a bad way, as if it were something he must be protected from, a time bomb in his eye that might explode if left uncovered. He did not treat Phil's nakedness as aimed at him, a weapon, a taunt, but for her to walk about as she was he regarded as an act of aggression.

One afternoon in December Phil was putting Jackson on about being inhibited. "You can't touch anybody. Can't ever give me a pat or hug. It's like you have a barbed-wire fence around your skin, or one of those force fields from science fiction that nobody can cross. Look at old Miriam. She's a toucher. Watch her make out sometime with dogs and cats and kiddies. But you're scared. All the time she's around here, you've never put a finger on her."

Miriam laughed. "It's true, Jackson. Everybody else comes through, they kiss hello, they shake hands, they give a pat or a hug. I've never seen you touch another person. I'm not quite sure you touch yourself. Except for scratching!"

"Oh. You want me to touch her." Jackson looked very tight and mean. "Fine. How about this?" He walked up behind her where she sat at the table and ran his hand slowly and deliberately along her throat and into her shirt to close over her breast. She sat stark still. His hand felt hot and bony and more callused than Phil's. She did not think she remembered to breathe for several minutes. Jackson was glaring at Phil, who was glaring at Jackson.

She got up abruptly and pushed Jackson out of the way. "I am not a tool with which to beat each other. If you want to touch me, you may not do so in lieu of hitting him. Is that clear?"

"He was provoking me," Jackson said mildly and sat down at the table with his head in his hands.

"Only because you claim you cannot be provoked." Miriam went to stand by Phil. "Come, Philip, come. I have to go home soon and do my duty to God and Computer. Cuddle with me and leave Jackson in the solitude he so richly deserves."

"If you ever do that again, I'll kick the shit out of you," Phil said between gritted teeth.

"Are you sure you can?" Jackson still had his head in his hands. "Why should you care? She isn't faithful to you anyhow."

"What do you know about what or who I'm faithful to?" Miriam stepped forward, clenching and unclenching her fists. "What do you know about us as a couple? How I care for Phil or how he cares for me?"

"I see him chewed up by jealousy."

"But you don't see him suffocating with boredom. There's a choice. We made it consciously."

"She's on target." Phil stretched himself, suddenly less angry. "You want to fit us in your notions, put the strait jacket on whether it fits or not." He put an arm around Miriam. "I'm not going to fuck one woman for thirty years, or pretend that's what it's all about. Don't you understand

I found her and I taught her? I opened her into the woman she is, the woman that suits me."

When Phil spoke about her as if she were a clay doll he had found lumpish in Brooklyn and molded into a woman, she felt uncomfortable. But after all he had been her teacher. He could open her up to what was on her mind as nobody else ever could. Besides, he liked to sound off in an exaggerated way, and especially he liked to boast in front of Jackson.

"Maybe. And is that what she wants?"

"Jackson, you grew up among WASP ladies who are all raped virgins at heart, and you just can't believe in a woman with juice."

"A fool and his honey are soon parted." Jackson leaned back·in the kitchen chair, scratching his shoulder.

As they lay face to face in Phil's bed she asked, "What was that all about?"

"Oh, he gets the itch around here—the two of us going at it like jack rabbits day and night." Phil was grinning, golden and wicked and proud of himself. "He just needs some pussy. He always gets very moral when he's horny."

Her body still prickled, her pride was sore. So coldly deliberate. Or was he attracted to her? She felt he was always punishing her for being alive. "He doesn't like me. Thinks I'm no good for you."

"Aw, he's a bit jealous. We've been friends a long, long time, pigeon. I was a punk kid, and I wouldn't have come through Nam alive except for him. We been through a whole lot of different scenes. Lots of women have come and women have gone. Like Sissy, his wife. She never could stand me, though I'll say she was a good-looking piece, and one time he accused me of being after her, one time when he was drunk. It's the fact that I can talk to you, that's the rub. He thinks I take you too seriously, that's what he says."

"Too seriously! Am I some kind of joke?"

"He thinks you take yourself too seriously."

"That's just what men say about women who don't giggle and play dumb. He's always setting himself up as some kind of judge! How will I support you in your old age if I don't have a profession! . . . But I don't understand the two of you together. The way you poke at each other."

"That's just fooling around. What do you want us to do,

kiss each other? He's my old buddy, old Jackson. We both know where the other one's at."

"Do you?" She put her finger on his lean aquiline nose and pressed gently. "I'm not convinced."

"It's beyond you, girl." He brought his mouth down to her breast.

Saturday night between Christmas and New Year's she sat facing Jackson at the kitchen table over a chess game while Phil was tending bar. He would come home after work. In the meantime she had taken the first game with style: for once Jackson had conceded long before the end game. Sometimes he was stubborn, but as he read his chess books, less often he insisted on prolonging a game whose outcome was clearly charted.

"Come on, two out of three." Jackson began to set up the pieces again. "We'll have time for another game before he gets home. If he can find his way. Some nights he swallows as much as he sells."

"Okay, two out of two."

She hoped that Phil would not drink too much. She wanted badly to unwind with him. She had worked hard all week, debugging a program on the computer. The night before, something gratuitously nasty had happened. She had run into Barnett from her course in compiler generator systems and he had asked her how she had done. At her answer he had given her a mean squinty smirk and said, "Maybe if I had tits to shake in his face I'd ace it too." He had walked off leaving her feeling daubed with vomit. As if she hadn't been eating and sleeping and breathing that course.

Women did not get turned off by a man because he knew how to do things they knew how to do. At least it was a basis for communication. But men seemed to prefer that women sit in some nether land in suspended animation crocheting doilies while waiting to be fetched out. In going from undergraduate to graduate school she had crossed a boundary: before, no matter how good her grades, she had been minimally threatening. But to go to M.I.T. was to announce herself as meaning to get a good job in her field: not to be kept, not to go to school four years and then take a job typing, but to do real work she could live on.

Now men responded to her differently. Even if they were

attracted, and some men she worked with obviously were, they seemed to resent that. It baffled her. Other new students as good as she was were already treated with respect: she was not. When she met someone who seemed to have a good mind and ideas and a flavor to his talk, she wanted to be with him, but men did not react that way to women. She felt hemmed in. Just as this one, Jackson, kept himself closed to her. With everyone else he was so damned sympathetic, listening to their troubles, but some stupid prejudice kept him from perceiving her. He would not be her friend and she bristled back. Repaid insult with insult, coldness with coldness.

The phone rang halfway through the second game. Jackson answered. "Yeah, she's here. Playing chess. What? Sure, here." Jackson handed her the phone.

"Pigeon? Listen and forgive." Phil's voice came over slurred with excitement. He must be calling from the pay phone. Sounded like a roomful of people. "Got to make this fast. Chick in here tonight, strange, I'm telling you. A purseful of coke and dressed like a leather queen. First I wasn't sure she *was* a woman and not in drag, I mean, she's too elegant. Passed me an invitation. Pigeon, I want to follow this. Maybe it'll be a bad scene and I'll clear out. But I'm itching to follow my nose."

"Sure. But watch out. She could be a sadist, she could be a nark."

"They couldn't pay enough for her to dress like that. Three-hundred-dollar vests, Daddy knows. I can take care of myself. Listen, maybe I'll get back there, maybe I won't. Don't hang in if you don't feel like it. Sorry to pull this on you so late."

"It's okay, Phil. I'll go home. Be careful and tell me all about how leather tastes tomorrow. Take care." She hung up.

"Your move," Jackson said. "Come on, you get feisty if I take too long."

"I should leave. It's getting late."

"In the middle of the game? You can't do that to me."

Because she wasn't especially eager to go out and stand around the dark windy corner waiting for a bus and warding off approaches, she easily persuaded herself it would be mean not to finish the game. Besides, it shouldn't take long. She could map out a strategy of quick victory and be out of here in plenty of time to catch the last bus that started from the end of the line at midnight. She tried a daring attack involving a queen sacrifice that should have hooked him. Instead, Jackson took the game with a line of play she had overlooked, an immediate countersacrifice of his own queen. She had tried to entice him with a strategy that would have worked better on Phil.

As she stood, he reminded her, "Two out of three."

She pointed to the clock. "I'll have to hustle to catch the last bus. I don't like hitching this late."

"Stay. You do it often enough. Besides, Phil might still show."

"On cocaine? Don't bet on it." She picked up her purse from the chair.

"Come on, sit. I'm going to beat you tonight. Why leave me lonely on Saturday night? I think I've pulled my game up to where I can take you. I want to prove it." He spoke emphatically for him, leaning back in his chair as if relaxed but watching her closely, smiling for once at her. "Come on, we never get this long to play. When are we going to sit down and play three games again? I improve in long sessions, whereas you do better marshaling your energies for one game."

"What nonsense! I played tourneys in high school, all day. . . . It was a form of escape to a world with rules. Master the rules, remember history, and you win. Life was rather less satisfying."

"It still is, I find . . . Miriam."

How seldom he addressed her directly, by name. Still she looked at the clock. A problem sat on her desk that she could be working on, if only she were transported there instantly. His insistence puzzled her. Was he really convinced he could beat her? No, she didn't accept that. Something funny between, around, something buzzed. She looked at him levelly and waited. That remote monastic abstraction was missing tonight. He was actually there across the kitchen table seeking to confront her in some manner. He did not scratch himself or slump there but sat gathered in his muscles, watching her with his steady gaze. Not ignoring her, not fending her off, not insulting or looking askance at her. But there.

"Tell you what," he said. "Let's have stakes."

She shrugged. "Five bucks?" She sat down, tentatively.

"No. Covered stakes."

"What do you mean?" She felt irritated. Now he was slipping back into games playing, aloof gestures, hints.

"A chess game shouldn't be played for money—"

"*Mishegoss*. Romanticism." She snorted. "What do you think masters play for? Like athletes. You learn to do something specialized really well, how else would you make it?"

"We are not masters, Miriam. But we can play for something real."

She sat chin on knuckles, frowning. "What is this, Jackson? Don't dodge back and forth."

"It's you who keep getting up. . . . Covered stakes. You must have something you want me to do or not to do. Likewise." He leaned back, his sandy eyes crinkled up but measuring her.

"I'm awfully curious what you have in mind." A hook pulling.

"I can only think of one way to find out." He began setting out the pieces, white for him and black for her.

If she had any sense she would go home. But an opening finally. She had a now-or-never sense that she might force Jackson into dealing honestly with her. She did not want this hostile prickly skirmishing with him, this endless playing of formal bouts, this scarcely covert struggle for Phil's attention and friendship. This was a strange confrontation. The two of them were never alone except waiting for Phil. They had no basis of contact or communication except Phil and the endless games of chess. "What do you want, Jackson? Can't you just talk to me like a person? Do you want me out of here?"

"Wrong guess. No more free guesses. Your move." He opened with his knight to king's bishop 3: Nimzovich's attack. He had indeed been studying.

She smiled and he smiled back. As they played she was aware of the silence in the flat, the little noises that reinforced the silence. She began to wish very hard that Phil would come. But he was off on his adventure. She should have left. While she still could. Trying to make someone like her who was set against her from the beginning, who was so judgmental, always weighing her and putting her down, what odds on winning that? What could she do but bribe him with victory or her body? Oh, she was being superparanoid. He was even attractive in his grim way, but she blamed him for Phil's not living with her. Why should she be so nervous?

Just because they were here late at night where she must
sleep now, just because she was playing chess with Jackson,
who resisted her for the fortieth time, just because he was so
cocksure he would beat her for a change. Why should she
have such a strong sense of having gone far into something unknown?

"Your move." His voice cut into her. "You're playing
slowly."

"I must be tired."

"I doubt it. A woman of your energies?"

She tried to concentrate on the game but that heaviness
engulfed her. He was right: she did not feel tired. She felt
strange. His will to win was enormous. Normally he was
withdrawn, gently remote. Tonight he was stubborn and will-
ful. He played solidly, carefully, following the principles he
had learned from Nimzovich's book, gradually bringing all
his forces to bear on the center squares. She could feel his
intense will to beat her flowing over the table. She did not
have an enormous counterweight to that will. She was disappointed that Phil had gone off with a woman. She could
not let herself react to that disappointment. It was part of
their bargain, their rapport, not to drag one another from
side trips and curiosities. Having so little of Phil's attraction
to chemical changes rung on the body, she sometimes found
it hard to empathize with his adventuring. She felt, and
judged it ridiculous to so feel, that he had deserted her. By
now she could have been curled up in his bed telling him
that scene with Barnett at Tech Square, looking into his sea-
colored eyes, rubbing her cheek against his. But Phil was off
pursuing a handful of white powder.

Jackson was wanting and wanting to win. It was like a
pushing against her. She did not want to win nearly that much.
It was as if Phil were slipping farther and farther from her
into the side show of his head, into the strange labyrinths of
another woman, leaving her alone with Jackson's desire to
overcome her. She tasted again her curiosity. What would
she ask for if she won? She would ask him for less uptightness, more acceptance. But was acceptance something he
could provide on demand? Could he feel more tolerant of her
just because she asked him to? He would try hard for a day,
perhaps. Then he would resent her all the more for having
made the effort.

It was not that she ever decided to let him win. It was not that she made a decision. It was that his will to win pushed on her, and losing was simply not pushing back. Her mind kept wandering. She felt almost anxious to get it over. She played out short strategies without much interest. Still, the game was long-drawn. She played a defensive game, trying to reduce his pressure on the center, and most of the exchanges were even. He gained only a slow advantage which she would normally have experienced as a stimulus. It was like very slowly letting go of a grip, a finger at a time. Sliding in sand. She never said to herself that she was losing. She only did not feel that she was winning. She only thought defensively and almost automatically continued to hold him off, until he seized control of the seventh rank with both rooks. Then she realized she was at a point where she should concede, and yet she did not and ritualistically they continued until checkmate.

At that moment the heaviness slid from her and she felt herself alert again. She leaned forward, tapping on the table. "Well, now what? What *do* you want from me?"

His eyebrows raised. His sandy eyes seemed sad beyond any cause. "Now you defend yourself."

They were both quiet. Silence itched in her ears. The house was creaking to itself. It felt as if everybody else in the city had gone to bed to leave them facing each other across this table. "You don't seem particularly pleased," she said ingenuously. "I though you'd enjoy winning. I could have conceded the game, but you seemed to want to act it out. Were you gaining time?"

"I was. And I don't seem to have gained enough. I thought the words would come to me." He was rubbing his head, setting the hair on end.

They sat on in the 'abrasive silence until she began to laugh. "For heaven's sake, you can't really expect *me* to make a pass at *you*, no matter how long we sit here!" It came out. As if all along she had known what he wanted. She was horrified as soon as she said it, hot with alarm.

He began to laugh too and got to his feet. "It would simplify matters. But if you won't, I'll have to. Miriam, Miriam!" She had the impression he stepped over the table because he was suddenly upon her and gripping her almost in a wrestling hold, his lips against her, his tongue thrusting into her mouth. One arm was against the back of her waist like a bar of iron, the other closed on her buttock. She felt the start of a reaction of pain and anger, just the start of that reaction, and then she went under to him. His body felt hard against her, violent. The intensity of his desire to win turned into an intense desire to take her that she caught at once as if catching fire.

Kissing him back, she was suddenly, totally delighted. Ha, he did want her, he found her attractive. It was like an enormous vindication, a proving of her. It was like the first time with Phil in discovering she could be what she wanted to be with a man. All the soreness of the last six months, the insults and jostling, the bad vibrations coming out from him, abrading her, all fused seamlessly into her victory. She briefly remembered then that she had wanted him to like her, not to want her.

Did I want him? Did I want him all along? No, this wanting that boiled up against his hard body, thin and strong arched against her, feeling him erect against her belly, was something she caught from him. No one had ever wanted her so much. The violent wanting excited her, she felt caught in it as if she need not think any more about him, need not agree, need not work things out but simply let go and be carried on it.

She had time to think that much as he picked her up and carried her into his cell and dropped her on the mattress and fell on her. It was not that he was brutal or rushed or perfunctory. It was just that the wanting was strong and she caught it at once. It was an abdication. She need only go with him. She need only let go and let him. She did not let herself think but willfully went under to him, she wanted and thrust and wanted. After the rough act, she felt peculiar as she came to herself in the dark—he had not even paused to turn on the overhead light so they could see each other—with his weight on her and his hand seized on her nape. She felt dazed. She felt lost, battered. Yet something in her stretched and purred: see, he wanted me, he did. And called that reality.

12

Love Is a Woman's Whole Existence

She felt like a battlefield. She felt as if an enormous force had picked her up and turned her around, moving the masses of her along new fault lines, fracturing her being. "I forgot to do anything. I didn't put in my diaphragm."

He held her foot. "Why don't you take the pill?"

"It's not good for you. All that blood clot evidence. Anyhow, it's probably not serious. My period ended four days ago." But she was disturbed. She detested sloppiness, letting events carry her, determining action by consequence. She had always found sympathy hard when she heard women at Michigan worrying about being pregnant because they forgot to do anything, as if they had never heard of the mechanics of conception or thought natural laws would be suspended for them.

He rose on his elbow beside her and looked into her face, laying his warm callused hand along her cheek. "How long and how often I've wanted to do that."

"You have to believe me, that I didn't know how attracted I was to you. That is, I would never—"

He put his hand over her mouth. "Another story to tell Phil when he comes home?"

She freed her mouth. "Do you think I can reasonably not tell Phil?"

"If you're planning to get up and walk out that door as if nothing happened, tell him, don't tell him. Is gossip that important?"

"Jackson." She knelt, putting her hand on his shoulder, where a jagged scar ran. "You're picking a fight. Was fucking me a way of putting me down? And it didn't quite work out your aggression?"

He glared at her lockjawed. Then he put his arms on her

189

shoulders and pulled her down, rolling over on her. "Nothing can work out my aggression. Don't come at me so rational-like. I don't believe it." He put his hand on her belly, rubbing in low circles down into her hair. "Do you want me?"

Her body magnetized around his hand. "Yes."

"Good. Because I want you. I'll still want you in an hour. When I wake up with you in the morning I'll be wanting you."

A conversation that was another sort of struggle. She got up to get her diaphragm before anything more happened. She found it in Phil's top drawer and put it in. She had a moment of queasy guilt, looking at Phil's socks. What had she done? What had she got into? Yet she was pulled immediately back to Jackson, the sense of him waiting hard and heavy on her. She wanted him. She had never wanted in such an intense gathered way. Maybe it was only physical: the tension between them snapping finally. But already she did not believe that.

Feeling inert and passive, she flung herself down on the mattress. Waiting for him to take her. They did not speak. Falling into a river where the currents took her and spun her around and dashed her onward, a river where she rose and fell under an alien power, where she might drown. . . . Against his scarred shoulder she smiled at her nonsense. Alien power: it was only desire. She tried a little to get her mind around it. No one had ever wanted her as powerfully. She wanted to be wanted this strongly. It felt good, like a myth born full-fledged within her. She fell into it, she leaped into it. Something in her came to and snapped, saying, He is The Man. He is it. This is more real than anything gone before.

When he drew back and looked at her, she could not sustain his gaze. She reached forward to bury her face against him. His face bruised her in a new vulnerability. Such sharpness in him, angles and pikes and jagged escarpments. Stony places and thorns.

He had a sexual confidence and a simplicity that got to her. Perhaps it was like her own. Jackson was intellectual and withdrawn, but when he got into bed with her, he was there. Here I am, I want you, his body said against her and did not require support or encouragement or assistance: only that she respond. No, his body said more than Here I am. Phil was knowing her; Jackson was having her.

That scared her, but part of her rose up from under and flowed with it. Caught, hooked, tangled with him. Something in her said, This is how it is supposed to be. This is a man. This is loving. His possessing was a current that seemed to require from her only that she let go: then she would be held firmly in him without tension, without decision. Let go into him. She would be carried on that wanting that came out from him. It was the memory, the strong image of him carrying her off to bed in his arms. Like the letting go in orgasm, she thought: it felt powerful around her. It was a deep image present from earliest adolescence of the strong man who would want her, who would find her, who would carry her off, who would be a world in which she floated, whose being would contain hers.

In the morning they sat dressed and nervous at the table, expecting Phil. Sometime around noon he called, telling Jackson he'd see him Monday, remarking he hadn't been able to reach Miriam. Nothing more was exchanged. Yet she did not go home, she did not leave. She remained with Jackson feeling like an opened package, loose, half spent, vulnerable. Waiting. Why had Phil gone off? She wanted to blame him, she wanted to tell him he had thrown her at Jackson. With other men she had had an ease, based on desiring nothing more than respect and consideration. Some relationships were good and some were disappointing. But she had never been hurt beyond a quiet sadness when things did not work out, or the sadness of departure when they could not continue and yet the end was not ripe. Phil was always with her, her friend, her lover, her guru. He sent her out to learn of others and she returned with that knowledge to him. Now what? Now what? She felt raw in her nerve endings as if she had been torn loose. She could not endure thinking about Phil.

Jackson and she sat on the cot in the front room, his hand tangled in her hair. "So you think you're confused?" His hand dropped to her nape. "Don't lie to me. You aren't confused about us."

"I'm not confused about *feeling* for you—"

"It's a plain thing, a man and a woman. People invent fancy things when they're bored with each other. Do you think I'd have taken you from Phil—hell, do you think I could have if he'd wanted you the way I do? He wants you and a dozen other things. He wants you sometimes and sometimes he wants no connections at all. His relationship to you is no different in kind than his relationship to me. That's not what you need as a woman. That's not what I want from you."

Weeping. All day she kept weeping, dissolving into water and whimpers. She had not cried like this since the summer of her mother's dying. She felt like a child, seeking blind comfort in his flesh. There was a terrible simplicity indeed about him.

When she awoke Monday morning he was still asleep, and she lay in the crook of his arm unnaturally still and sick with anxiety. Phil would come home. Phil. She must think. Jackson's eyes opened, sandy, slightly bloodshot, vague at first then focusing on her. Their second night together. She felt that heaviness gathering.

"Still here." Voice with a morning harshness in his chest.

She put on her rumpled clothes. The wrinkled tie-dyed shirt she had been wearing: a slow bolt of sadness passed through her. A butterfly design Phil had made of soft opulent purples and bronzes.

"Go to school. I doubt if Phil will be back early but it's conceivable."

"Jackson, I have to talk to him."

"No." Slowly he shook his head. "I'll wait for him. Better that way."

"Jackson, I've been involved with Phil for years. He's been my closest friend. I can't let you do it for me."

"He's been my friend for more than twice that long. I don't want you to talk to him. I've been jealous enough, Miriam, jealous enough."

"But I have to talk to him. It isn't in me to go along home and twiddle my thumbs while you two have it out."

"You have to find it in you. Don't you see that, with you here, it will become a fight? I'll be asking you to hurt him, to reject him. I don't want to do that to you or to him. Don't do it to me."

"But I owe it to Phil. He has a right to be angry at me. I haven't got the right to run and hide and leave it all to you as if I hadn't the guts to admit what I've done."

"Doesn't have anything to do with guts. Can't you see that? Has to do with my telling Phil that you used to have a relationship with him and you don't have it any more. Decide.

You can't have both of us like puppets on a string."

"You're pulling me apart!"

"You can't have things both ways. Miriam, I've gone through the pit of jealousy watching you with him and every other idiot you feel like playing with. You're not going to play games with me. You're mine or you're not, but I'm not dancing through hoops." He took her face in his hands. "Trust me!"

"You ask a lot!"

"Just everything. Are you woman enough to give me that?" She leaned into his arms and began to weep.

Where so much had been, plans and projects and curiosities and relationships and speculations and histories, was now everything and nothing in one: this painful hollow wanting, this fierce turbulence, this centering about him white hot and icy, cold and dark and bright. Lying on her bed and waiting for him to call, waiting for him to summon her, she understood that she was in love and did not know whether to label it good fortune or catastrophe. She had never before fallen in love, obviously. She had loved. She knew that she still loved Phil, she worried over him, she wrote letters to him she dared not send for fear of Jackson's continuing jealousy, she sought the smallest scrap of news or gossip.

Jackson was alone on Pearl Street. Phil had moved out. Why hadn't she moved in? The answer was no longer all the reasons she used to have, good reasons having to do with her work and her interests. It was because he had not asked her. He took for granted that he would find some male roommate and she would continue living where she was. She felt ill at ease but uncertain. After all, those good reasons she no longer felt were still reasons. She needed her room. Yet she felt as if he demanded all of her and then took only a piece and went away, that he shut the door leaving her outside still vainly offering herself.

He scorned the diaphragm. "How can you decide beforehand? Making an appointment to fuck. All that machinery in there with me. The damned jelly tastes like soap."

She went to a gynecologist and was put on the pill. It swelled her up. She rose in the morning belching and farting and her ankles turned watery. The doctor told her those were temporary symptoms and would subside. She felt vaguely uneasy. Her contact lenses began to give her some trouble when she wore them her usual length of time. But to be able to have sex any time he wanted was an enormous convenience. She did not have to be stopping to think where she'd left it and did she need to put more jelly in for the second time. She did not need to tell him to wait while she ran off to the bathroom, returning to find him reading a book. He disliked being reminded of the mechanics of contraception. When she talked about the swelling and flatulence he showed his disgust.

"Why must women talk incessantly about what is, after all, a matter of plumbing? Little minds wondering where the turds go when you flush the toilet." He could be quite sarcastic.

The act itself was beautiful, was joining without the seam. She needed it as tangible proof of his love. Yet she had the feeling that her very responsiveness would sometimes turn him cold. As he sensed her need, he drew back. He went into ascetic phases, said he needed all his energy, and shut her out for three days. She waited, empty.

She lay on her bed in embryo position curled round her obsession. So much of what she had thought of as her self seemed to have vanished, to have dissolved. She was a loving. She was occupied entirely by him. Alone, she dreamed about seeing him, she re-enacted their last scenes, she made up things to say to him and things she wanted him to say to her, she made up things she was terrified he would say to her and she wept. She examined and re-examined, analyzed and memorized what he had in reality said to her to discern the inner hidden meaning and proper interpretation.

When she did her work at all, she did it perfunctorily. Only occasionally when they had been together and it had been wholly good, she returned feeling cheerful and cleansed. Then she sat down with her neglected compiler and suddenly once again had ideas. She felt revitalized. Once again she could think and act and turn outward. Those times were rare. More often it cost such a battle to stop brooding about him that she used up her energy in the struggle and had nothing left to spend on real work.

This was what she had always been told would be the true center of her being, the central act of her life. A woman loving a man. Now it had happened. The more she gave herself to her obsession, the more she loved him, the more she felt herself to be in love. The rougher things went, the more pain she felt in her loving, the more obsessive it grew. It was totally new, this sense of being out of control, occupied, taken over. Everything else in her life had been a doing, a deciding, a working, but this was something different. This became the content of living.

With others she was elsewhere and impatient. In the middle of a conversation with a colleague, she would suddenly think of Jackson and she would resent the trivial chatter about programming languages that made her for a moment unable to loose her whole energies on her obsession. When other people came to see him, she could hardly enter talk with them, for she only wanted them to go away. It was a cold fierce winter in Boston. Every day the cars were parked a little further out into the street, as the glaciers pushed out from either curb toward the narrowing center. The sidewalks were deeply rutted in ice. She had no desire to go anywhere, to do anything except to be with him. She felt as if the rest of the world were frozen solid. Except for the minimal reading she had to do for courses, she could concentrate on nothing. She would begin to see his face, to hallucinate his hands, to study a tone of voice or gesture for what it hid of his feelings.

Much of the time she felt lucky, chosen, exalted. Her life seemed infused with intensity, a plenum, shining and holy. She was never bored. Her previous life seemed vacuous by comparison. At other times she felt ashamed, that she had become a zombie. She seemed to have nothing left for anyone else, anything else. She was stupefied in general and in that one touch point intensely burning like a laser.

Did he love her? He did not say so. She told him she loved him. She told him incessantly. It seemed to her impossible not to say it to him again and again. He did not answer her. A knife went into the same wound all of the time.

She would cry out in bed, "I love you!" He would hold her to him. But something in him would clench against her. He would not speak. She could feel that locking in him, that stubbornness.

"It's because that woman hurt you, the woman you married. You're punishing me for her."

"A fool sticks his hand on the chopping block once to feel

if the knife will really lop off a finger. Only a complete idiot does it twice."

"I'm not a knife! I'm not a chopping block!"

"I'm not a complete idiot."

She sensed in him a huge will to failure having run its course. She could not trace the history of it, but the janitor's job and the cold sexual trade-off with the woman in 4B had been a bottom, and he was ready now to want to do something in the world. He would not admit to wanting much. It was she who had to send for his old transcripts and write letters to graduate schools and get his file of letters of recommendation together. Yet the activity was not her idea. She was responding to quiet pressure from him. He wanted to be made to do something. He felt it was appropriate for her to want him to return to school.

Maybe it was just as well she couldn't see Phil. She feared she would have nothing to give him. She seemed to have nothing left over. What did they do? They made love. They ate meals. They quarreled. They walked together. In pauses in the long icy winter, in the occasional thaws of February, on frigid clear nights in March, they walked. He liked especially to walk in the evenings past the lighted houses on the hilly tree-lined streets of Cambridge and Somerville. "So many little lives," he drawled. "Look in and try them on for size. Window-shopping. Would that life fit you, those apple-cheeked kids, that TV set, that lamp with its tutu in the window? That book-lined study and 1917 posters and the oak table? That black light and the strobe and the purple walls and mobile of the solar system going round under the huge speakers?"

"Who'd walk into anybody's life? Like sticking your feet in somebody's old boots. Too loose in the places you curve in and too tight in the places you stick out."

"You think people's lives fit them? Maybe they all feel that way. Silent screams going up like smoke, Get me out of here!"

They listened to music a lot, mildly stoned. Often he would cook them a good meal and then they would sit about replete, listening to records. See, she would tell herself, it is an equal relationship, for he does the cooking. But she knew she lied. He had too much heavy will for controlling her.

One Friday evening she was to spend with him, when she

arrived and let herself in, he was not there. She waited. She waited two hours, while anxiety and resentment wound her tighter and tighter. She tried to fight her tension. After all, how many times had she waited for Phil, casually relaxed, knowing he would come or he wouldn't and never attaching that much importance to one time in an open series? Why couldn't she achieve that grace with Jackson, that looseness? Why must she sit like—like a woman was supposed to, stewing? Her anxiety stripped away her sense of herself as a strong person moving through things in her own style. She became grasping woman. She became dependent woman. She became scared woman. This waiting had teeth.

When she heard him on the stairs, a great relief loosened her. Now to find the strength to suppress what she had felt. She came to meet him, reaching up to kiss. He tasted of whiskey.

"You've been drinking it up." Keep the voice light.

"Dropped by Finnegan's Wake, got to talking."

"Finnegan's Wake. Isn't that where Phil works?"

"Yeah, he was on duty. Being as it's early, he wasn't that busy yet."

She searched his face. "I'm glad you saw him. It's bad, never seeing each other, never talking, never knowing how he is."

"Old Phil? He's fine." Jackson set his jaw, put a record on loud on the phonograph, got out his hash pipe. Every line of his body told her what they had said was none of her business.

"Did you talk about me?"

"No." His gaze asked her scornfully why they would.

"Is he really all right?"

Jackson did not answer.

She began to shout. "You're just going to sit there, right? Closed off. No communication, no warmth, no contact. I can sit and twiddle my thumbs and freeze to death."

"You might try listening to the Mozart. It's a new recording of that horn concerto," he drawled.

"Go fuck yourself!" She bounced up. "If you're going to pretend I'm not here, I'll save you the trouble. Good night!" She felt like a fool. Going for her jacket, putting it on, making the motions of leaving, she kept waiting for him to stop her, to protest, to save their time together. But his stubborn silence held. He sat and sucked on the pipe, presumably engrossed in the music. She slammed out.

At home she could do nothing but brood and weep. Perhaps she had been unreasonable. Perhaps he had had little conversation with Phil beyond How are you doing, okay, keep on trucking. Perhaps he had really wanted to listen to the record. Perhaps he had been depressed and, instead of trying to reach him, she had attacked. Perhaps he did blame her for his estrangement from Phil. She had hurt only herself storming out. But she had to draw the line someplace in what she would endure. She felt wrong on the left and on the right, no matter what she did or didn't.

She kept getting glimpses of the man who had wanted her so much, of the man who could love her. Was it Jackson she saw then or only a trick of the light falling at the right angle on what her wishes projected? Sometimes he would open to her. He would push aside his fear that she would get too close to him, gobble him, possess him, to reach out and meet her suddenly.

One mild night in April she took him to a party someone in her department was giving in Watertown, a married student and his wife who worked as a nurse, on the ground floor of a late Victorian house. Uniquely among such parties it turned out to be the kind she enjoyed, with lots of dancing as well as the inevitable shop talk by the men and house talk by the women. Jackson never danced but he found some men to talk to. After she had danced for an hour she felt good through her body and was ready to leave with him, both of them pleased till they got outside and found it was pouring rain. The wind was blowing from the east, smelling of fish and bringing torrents. Her apartment was closer and they decided to spend the night for a change. He seemed to like the idea.

"You sure were busy with those vats of colored water," he remarked, but he still seemed relaxed. He sat on her bed, back to the wall and one leg flexed, rolling a joint. For once the memory of her intimacy with Phil did not jog him into withdrawal. He held her ankle with one hand and the joint with the other and sucked smoke and sighed and relaxed.

"My father grew up in a house like the one tonight. He thought it a horror. He couldn't wait to live in an up-to-date house. He's always building another one. The one they're in now, the guy who threw it up, he's into a Machine for Living rhetoric. It's big as a shopping plaza and just as garish. All angles and glass walls that birds kill themselves on. Nothing works. The doors don't shut, where there are any. The fireplace fills the living room with smoke. You can hear any noise. The plumbing kicks like a mule. I'd live in a trailer before that."

"Did you grow up in that kind of house?"

"Smaller scale. We lived out in a fancy suburb. The thing that used to impress the other kiddies was that we had our own tennis courts. I broke my wrist out there once. Fell on it. I don't fall well—I never have."

"Want me to attach metaphorical meaning to that?"

He grinned. "As you wish. I've seen Phil fall down a flight of stairs and get up and walk off. If I did that, I'd break my back." He heard himself speaking Phil's name and stiffened, his eyes going up to the softly patterned canopy over the light bulb. "Arabian nights fantasy, the two of you. He wouldn't chop off your head and throw you out with the other chicks because you kept bringing stories home."

"Do you really want to talk about Phil and me, or do you want to toss out one of those barbed remarks and go back inside?"

"Toss a remark and run. No." He let go of her ankle and pulled her down to him. "Do not pass go. Do not collect two hundred dollars or two hundred sorrows. Just go directly to bed."

"What were you like as a child?" His sad-eyed face was framed in her hands like a permanent question.

"A snot. I was one of those awful children who beat up others who don't admire their daddies enough."

"Don't you want me to know you? You hoard your past. You feed me one dry dog biscuit at a time."

"No. I want you to love me."

"Do you? But you don't want to love me."

"Miriam, Miriam, I do. But freely. Not under compulsion."

"Who's compulsing you?"

"You are. When you ask me to do what I do."

"I don't understand."

"What do you think I'm doing but loving you?" He

gathered her against him. "Come on, take off this frippery stuff."

She wished she could ask him what made this sex loving and other sex cold to him, but she did not want to destroy the closeness and therefore kept quiet.

Afterward she sat cross-legged, still naked, and took his wallet from the pants lying over the foot of the bed. Reading his driver's license: "Douglas M. Jackson. Why can't I call you Doug?"

"That stands for Douglas MacArthur Jackson. Can you imagine going through the reserves and into the Army with a name like that? Christ, how did I survive? I loathe and detest that name more than you can conceive. My old man's hero. Not that he served under him—you can bet your boots on that. Essential war industries, getting rich on the home front. He almost sent me to military school."

"If you had a child, what would you name him or her?"

"I have a child." His face stiffened.

"Jackson, Jackson, I forgot. I forgot for just a moment."

"I never forget."

"Why can't you ever see him? What is it?"

The words were chunks of iron dropping from his mouth. "Her name was Cecily but I used to call her Sissy. She wanted what I seemed to be. What I thought I was. What I was trained to be. She had her sights on me and I went along. She wanted a ring, I got her a ring. She wanted a wedding, I got her a wedding. She wanted a house, I got her a house. She was a good-looking woman, a thorough-bred from a family that regularly coughed up college presidents and bank managers and even a senator. They all live to be ninety and stand six feet tall and are always right because they laid down the rules. Then I stopped producing, so she got a divorce." He laughed dryly. "I knew she'd been with another man but I couldn't prove it. She took me to the cleaners. The judge practically wept for her, married to such a degenerate drug addict bum. He was probably her uncle. Then she pulled the real sly one. She agreed to a cash settlement, no alimony. That was supposed to be a great gesture, I wasn't going to be pinned to the wall for thirty years. Then she married the lawyer."

"The lawyer who got the divorce?"

"I had another lawyer on paper, but I wasn't contesting

it. It was supposed to be such a generous deal. He wasn't a
divorce lawyer, he was the family lawyer doing the divorce
as a special favor. Then she married him. Haha. Chuck
Magnusson. I try to get anywhere near Jerry and they can
put me in the can. We don't fight in the same class, Magnusson and I."

"Did she hate you? Is that why?"

"She pretended to be scared of me. We had some ugly
scenes. The only way I could shut her up was physical. And
I suppose she was really scared about how I'd changed. Any
change scares people like that. She kept saying she couldn't
talk to me any more. I didn't notice her trying to listen."

"Had they set you up from the beginning? Was she involved with him before?"

"I'll never really know, will I? I was pretty sure I knew
who she'd been seeing—a real estate developer. But Magnusson was a way superior catch. He'd been divorced himself three years before—very different scene. Visitation rights,
friendly going back and forth, no scandal, no menace,
everybody polite. I understand they all get together for bar-
becues and other social occasions, all the half brothers and
half sisters and half-wits and half-truths and bitter halves."
He sat tight, his arm wooden under her touch.

"Jackson, you know I am not Cecily. Do you really in any
part of your mind think we're the same?"

He looked at her. Then he said in a gentle voice, "You're
both cunts."

She tried to abate her anger. "You and I both have livers,
large and small intestines, kidneys, spines, blood vessels,
nerves, spleens, stomachs, hearts and, I had thought, brains
in common. What conclusions do you draw from anatomy?
That I am about to take you to the cleaners? Wow, Jackson,
I might as well develop the paranoid fantasy that you want
me to keep you." She brushed the hair from her eyes. "After
all, in a couple of years I'll be able to. What on earth do you
think I want from you, that you're so concerned to hang
onto?"

"Possession."

"What are you talking about? The first thing you wanted
after we went to bed was to separate me from Phil."

"Now you're jealous when you know I've seen him."

"You're damned straight I am. Why should you have the

privilege and I be denied it? I miss seeing him!"

"I'm sure you do," he said flatly.

"What a drag you are! You think you invented friendliness."

"You think you're not always pushing at me? Why do you think we struggle so much? You're always trying to shove me around."

"If you don't want to be open with me, what do you want with me? I'm in love with you and I'm starving to death."

"That's what it is: I don't want to be eaten."

She shook her head. "I fell into that. Right into your hands."

"What better place? All this talking, it creates flak. When you shut your mouth and open your legs, we do much better."

She ran into Phil in a bookstore off Harvard Square. A feeling of being watched made her raise her head from the table of remaindered books she was leafing through and turn slowly. Phil was standing by the poetry books still holding whatever he had been reading and looking at her, his intense stare crossing the store. She immediately dropped her gaze. Stifling hot in her red poncho. The first time in the museum courtyard, that gaze asking her questions. Now more pain, more anger, but still questions. She could not turn away. She met his gaze again and felt her lips part as if she could say something across the distance. She could not move. She stood transfixed, the glossy book of Indian sculpture growing heavy in her sweating hands.

Suddenly Phil grinned, while something tore in her. He looked beautiful and funny grinning at her rigidity, till he crooked his index finger and made a Svengali face. "Come," he mouthed at her. "Come!" Playing hypnotist. Obediently taking the part he offered, she played zombie. She came walking toward him with hands stuck out past students who turned to look at her and then away (drug episode).

"All right, buddy," she said, "I saw you put that book under your coat. Stealing pornography again."

"I'll go along quietly, sir or madam, but don't take my dirty book. . . . How about a wake at Finnegan's? A drink is surely in order."

"Phil, Phil, it's been so long—"

"Not by my choice."

"He didn't exactly give me a choice, Phil. I wanted him. Those were his terms."

He did not take her arm. It was strange to walk with him and not touch, through the streets where a south wind smelled warm and a little smoky, stirring papers in the gutters and promising more rain. The sun was in and out, drying the morning's puddles. Across Mass Avenue the Yard looked busy. It was a relief when they were sitting in the booth in the dimness of the bar. They ordered dark beer and faced each other. His legs grazed hers under the table. Her knees felt watery. She kept staring into his face looking for estrangement, hatred.

"Phil, I don't underestimate my guilt. I can't get my mind around it. It's such a relief to see you again!"

"Seeing is believing, as they say. Would you believe I knew it would happen?"

"Why, then? Why let it?"

"He's my friend. We're bound up together too. I thought I'd kept you apart long enough so the thing with me was very strong. I thought we'd got to the point where we could handle anything."

She put her face in her hands. Shame was the taste.

He tugged gently at her fingers until he had pried her hand loose. He held it lightly in his only half-closed hand. "Come on. No suds, baby. You love him, huh?"

"You know it."

"That figured. So, is it good?"

She shook her head. "It's awful."

"Shit! He's closed himself up, right? I thought he couldn't do it to you. Thought he'd be too scared of losing you."

"He's more scared of me than he is of losing me, Phil. It's rotten to complain to you about this. How are you?"

"Getting it on. I hung around with that leather chick for a while. Wasn't much of a trade, Miriam. I got the short end of the stick. She had money and drugs, but she was a bad fuck. Nothing in bed but whining and do me something. The energy level of a maggot. But she bought me things and turned me on to anything. She couldn't make coffee in a pot, but we could go down to the S. S. Pierce and buy pâté de foie gras and smoked trout in cans. You aren't such a great companion on a trip, but when I got up there, I'd just want to step on her. But she got me this vest—nice, uh?"

Miriam was astonished to find herself mildly jealous of the woman. She felt that was in the worst of all possible taste and unjust, but she had the uncanny sense that Phil knew and that was why he was grinning again.

"You can have it if you want to." He made to take it off.

"No! It would look ridiculous, all that fringe hanging off my boobs. It looks handsome on you, or you in it, whatever one's supposed to say."

"You're supposed to tell me I'm devastating and ask for the next dance."

"I would if I could." She smiled for the first time. "I can never remember your eyes—that color."

"I can never remember how hard it is to keep my self-righteous anger against you. You're always sacrificing me to someone you think is bigger."

"Phil, don't say that!"

"You lack respect for me. Maybe 'cause I'm no good." He took her hand again, just the fingers, his finger against the tips of hers. "But I'm learning to live with my mean self. You know McGeorge Bundy is lecturing at B.U. tomorrow?"

"What has that to do with the price of fish?"

"I want you to go and hear him."

"*Nu,* Phil, are you handing out penances?"

"Something will entertain you, and I don't mean his speech. They think they're off the hook now Nixon's in, all those bastards who used us and sent us over there to rot and die all those years, they're all fading back into the foundations and corporations and universities. Chalk that one up to experience, boys, and we'll write another book about it. Memoirs by and by. They're war criminals and we can't forget it. . . . Will you go?"

She nodded, taking down the time and place.

"I'm late now to meet Joe Rosario. Can you go my bail?"

"I'll be ready. See you there."

Miriam could not get in. They were checking tickets carefully, but obviously Phil and his friends had provided themselves with tickets. But she heard the uproar. In the middle of the speech they began to play tapes of bombing and Phil stood up holding aloft the papier-mâché figure of a burned child. A mob of campus and regular police stampeded them at once and they never got to finish their guerrilla theater.

Miriam collected Phil from the Charles Street jail the next day. He had been roughed up but he was in high spirits. As he had had nothing to eat for eighteen hours, she took him to Jackson's by cab. There Phil washed and got into Jackson's shirt and pants, complaining about their tackiness, while Jackson cooked up a garlicky spaghetti and sauce. The evening seemed to flow all right.

"It's time to make those power brokers feel they aren't safe either." Phil leaned on the refrigerator rubbing his sore head.

"And who gets their head bashed? Bundy? Or you?" Jackson sucked on his clay pipe, smoking his favorite gingery tobacco.

"Someone's got to be willing. You lost years to them too. Do you want to let them get away with it?"

Miriam kept quiet. She wanted the evening to glide gently by and establish precedents. She wanted them to be together and friendly. She would look and see Phil gesturing and grimacing, Jackson tilted back sucking on his pipe and slowly scratching his chest, and she could almost believe in the surface ease.

Two nights later the bill came due, when she mentioned something that had been troubling her. "I know I'm being irrational. The doctor told me I might skip a period or two before my body got over reacting to the pill. But honest, it makes me nervous."

He gave her a long measured stare. "If you've taken the pill every day, you can't be pregnant. If you haven't, why haven't you?"

"Jackson, you know damned well there was one night I missed, when we went to bed early and never got up again. I took it in the morning, that's supposed to work. But how can one ever be sure, playing around with hormones? I've been getting a bad reaction to the pill, and I suppose this is just part of it, but it's gruesome to have to worry."

"You're starting early to worry out loud. What kind of reaction are you expecting? What reassurance do you want from me?"

"I want you to tell me with great confidence it can't possibly be so. I guess just mainly it's better to share a worry. Don't you find that natural?"

"I find the whole thing a little too natural."

"What does that mean?"

"We'll discuss it when it's relevant. If you really are pregnant. If it's not just your body wanting to be. I'm assuming that, in telling me, you are assuming that it would be mine?"

The jagged ugly insinuation trailing worse arguments was lurking there just under the surface waiting for her. She could feel the suspicion, the fear, the hostility from him. It was too ugly. She had no stomach for it. She shut into herself and went home early to lie in her own bed, brooding and wondering.

Saturday afternoon, shortly after two, Phil appeared. He posed against the door, arms outstretched. "Pigeon, I been crucified!"

"Can they make that assault rap stick?"

"For that I have a lawyer. It's the university. I'm out."

She came and put her hand on his shoulder. "Can't you appeal. Won't your sponsor Proxmire help you? He has clout."

"J. Singleton Proxmire has decided I'm one of the unwashed hoodlums the gates must be barred against. Barbarian, he called me. Said I don't understand the fragility of academic freedom and the importance of the exchange of ideas. I said I'm more into real freedom for people, and as for expression of ideas, I'd been expressing mine. Aw shit." He flung himself on the bed and spoke muffled into her pillow. "Looks like Joe's in trouble too. A faculty type, even worse, and not at his own school. They may really go after him. They put four times the bail on him they had on me, and Wanda, his wife, had to go running around all night to raise it, so pregnant she looked like she might drop the kid in night court."

"The woman who was yelling at the police?"

Phil laughed. "That's Wanda! Pigeon, I was never cut out for the academic strait jacket and that's the truth. I've conned my way as far as I can. I'd never have been able to write that asinine thesis on George Herbert. My Catholic background was supposed to be a big help. My Catholic background consists of Irish wakes and St. Patrick's Day parades— a great day for the bar business—my mother's fear of abortion, maudlin tenors singing 'Mother Machree' and 'The Croppy Boy,' and a big to-do on election days." Phil started to laugh again, shaking the bed. "Old Singleton, he's a converted Catholic, fills his house with religious paraphernalia and always gassing about the beauties of this or that missal. He's a big one for looking into my baby-blue eyes and squeezing my knee, but I heard him call one of the other profs a disgusting faggot for actually getting laid."

She sat down on the bed's edge and tapped his shoulder. "Why did you do it, really?"

"Told you." He mumbled into her pillow. "Besides, been impotent for a month."

"You're turning my questions."

"No! S'true. Buried anger makes maggots, pigeon. I've been swallowing my rage too long and it's eating me. It's shit to grow up poor in the supermarket. I carry my childhood in my bad teeth there was never money to get fixed, in my poor bones, in the lines of calcium deposit you can see in X rays for the times when, by god, I got enough for a stretch."

"I carry my childhood too. I've learned with Jackson how hard I carry it. . . . Unloved, dreaming of the love that would prove me, vindicate me. . . . But you wanted to be in school!"

"I can push the words. I can pretend to be an intellectual. But inside I'm a street kid, and I don't believe what those smug pricks do is so fucking superior. I hate them because they're so comfortable. Sweet Jesus, are they comfortable with their tasteful lives and tasteful wives and bright kids and trips yonder and interesting food and interesting books and interesting friends, so comfortable, and they don't care for five minutes, Miriam, who's screaming outside. I'm sick to dying of all those cracks about the mindless boobs who watch television and put themselves in hock to buy a new car. What the hell do they think is the choice? They watch the news on TV and feel superior to the people who watch Lucy, and don't figure they're both watching situation comedy. They feel so damn nose-in-the-air about the folks in South Boston trying to keep blacks out of their schools, then they send their kids to private schools 'cause they're so sensitive. They feel contempt for hardhats who won't let blacks in their unions, and they squawk and scream about Black Studies actually run by blacks. I'm dying of hypocrisy, pigeon, dying of it. I had to throw up. Can't you understand?"

"I'm trying. I see your anger. But the gesture seems futile."

"Any gesture is futile that isn't victory. Assassination is futile. But acting my anger makes me less dead."

Affection welling up in her. An old strong loving that was a choice, not a destiny, that didn't engulf her. Feeling meek, she asked, "Do you think I'm the same kind of hypocrite?"

"No. You're a real intellectual. You like to push things around in your head. Besides, that's the point of a girl from even a wishy-washy pink family. You're trained right. Social conscience may be a weak guilt, but it's a hell of a lot easier to live with than the downright open contempt I put up with every time one of those johns opens his trap about those who haven't made it through to join the club."

"What are you going to do?"

"Go on tending bar. Write my poems. I've been into songs, lately. Hal was giving me lessons and Rick has been showing me some things. They think I'm onto something. One of them you won't like at all." He chuckled. " 'Litanies to the Deadly Venus.' "

"Oh? Is that supposed to be me?"

"If the shoe fits . . ." He turned onto his back. "Aw, I don't know nothing about nothing. Maybe I'm dead already. I walk in a fog of pain. I fog myself up inside to bear that. I swallow fog in pills. I shoot fog in my arm."

She pulled back the Indian cloth of his sleeve. "Damn you, Phil, what's the use of that?"

He began to laugh loosely. "Only you could ask a question like that! Why, I'm acting out my self-hatred, what do you think?"

"Idiot child. What will become of you?" Somehow she had put her arms around him and he was curled up, his body pulled into embryo position, his head coming to rest against her.

"You'll take care of me. Or won't? Will you, won't you, will you, won't you?"

"Ya-ta-ta-ta, ya-ta-ta-ta. Want to hear what's scaring me?"

"Not me, I hope."

"No, *nudnik*, not you. In me. I went on the pill—"

"Your belly's bigger." He patted her.

"Made me swell up. And belch and feel nauseous and bloat."

"Your breasts are bigger too. Bury me between them."

"As if they weren't ridiculous before."

"I like them. They're warm. There are too few warm big soft things in this mean world." She laughed and he put his arms around her. "I like to feel you laugh. You do it from the belly, not the throat or the head. For an intellectual woman, you're pretty physical. Ha. It must be kind of nice on the pill, no apparatus. Just pop right in."

"If you had to take pills that made you swell up like an elephant with elephantiasis, you wouldn't think it was cute. If your balls got sore and your legs swelled. Besides, I haven't had my period this time. Nothing happened. I'm scared."

"Think you're knocked up?"

"Not really. But I don't like my body playing tricks. I can't help worrying."

"Tell you what we're gonna do. I've got a book on hypnosis. After I leave here today, I'll brush up. I tried it a couple of times and I'm pretty good. It takes real charisma, real projection. But I can do it. I'll hypnotize you into your period."

"I hypnotized Allegra once, when I was a kid. . . . Why do you think it happened? Jackson is suspicious. Thinks I'm trying to pin a baby on him. It's so ugly. I start suspecting my own body of dark female plots. It makes me feel divided against myself. Is my own body really saying it wants to be pregnant?"

"Maybe it's saying it's scared to be pregnant. Or it doesn't like the taste of the pills. Or it misses me, coming in and out and saying hello." Under her sweater his hand reached up. "Haven't you missed me?"

"Now what are you trying to hypnotize me into, Philip?"

Gently he put her hand against his jeans. He held her hand there and she did not pull it away. It would have felt, oh, silly, melodramatic to pull loose. She could not remember exactly what was supposed to be wrong about being with Phil. In her was a deep exasperated fatigue with Jackson's rules and prohibitions and jealousy. How could she not be affectionate with Phil? Was she supposed to be suddenly installed with an On and Off button?

"Feel, Miriam, for you. I'm alive again. Aw, let me in, what the hell. Who's to know, besides us?"

She could sense her body preparing. She wanted to feel him again. She wanted to hold him: he was Phil, her friend and her love. She wanted to play with him again, she wanted to be with him. She could not want to refuse. "It doesn't matter, Philip sparrow. Jackson and I have been on a bad trip and it's better over and done with."

"That was why he sent you away that morning. Because you couldn't have said good-by to me face to face."

She was not sure of that, remembering the fearful joy, the total submission she had felt. But she was done sacrificing Philip to abstractions or to anyone. "I'm filled with mistrust for myself."

They were wriggling out of their clothes and into bed. The room was chilly and she pulled up the quilt over them.

"Because of not refusing me?"

"No. This part I trust. It's what's been struggling with him I mistrust."

"Home free. George Herbert up the flagpole, this is my mystical experience."

"I thought you'd been having problems. Tricky Dick doesn't know it."

"The only problem I have is just getting solved. I mean, aside from being kicked out of school and likely to end up in jail."

That evening she went to see Jackson, not less desperate but clearer in her mind. When she met his gaze, she waited to see if guilt would surface. No. She felt only calmer, as if being with Phil had drawn her at least part way off that iron hook she had been impaled on. "I brought you a small thingie." She gave him a pipe she had bought several weeks before. "I was waiting for an occasion, but why shouldn't this be it? I like the shape of it. It's comely in its heaviness and that made me think of you. Use it or throw it away, in good health."

"Beware the Greeks when they come carrying gifts?" He hefted the gnarled pipe.

"The Greek was your other girl friend. I'm the Jew. We're always bringing bribes. We want to be liked."

"Like breeds like. Do you still think you're carrying another little present in there?" He looked hard at her belly.

"Jackson, I'm also the girl friend who learns from experience. I got hurt the other day. I'm not going to repeat that mistake."

He sat down in the kitchen chair and stared impassively. "What does that mean, for instance?"

"What it says. I'm willing to agree it's none of your business."

"Oh." He put the new pipe down on the table and leaned back. "Let's parse that one. *None* of my business? None of *my* business? None of my *business?*"

A slimy despair filled her and she sat down in a chair, hard. She tried again to find the clarity she had brought. "Whatever in fact you meant when you responded that way."

"I meant I was not to be caught quite so easily."

"Jackson, we've got to stop! These are awful games we play! I don't like the person I'm becoming with you!"

Some of the guarded tension dissolved from his face and it seemed as if he really looked back at her. "I don't know what it is. I just don't know. Before you come, I want you to be here. I miss you when you're gone. I miss the vitality, the life in you. Then as soon as you walk in the door something snaps shut. Something closes down. I start defending myself."

"I'm becoming a shrew. It's like I was given something beautiful ever so briefly. I was promised something. I was promised you, the man I can love with all my heart and soul. I was promised and given it just long enough to make me want it, and then it was taken away. So I get into this *schlemiel's* game of trying to get it back. Oh, Jackson, it's an ugly game, and I quit it!" Her eyes were burning and she carefully did not blink them for fear tears would fall. Carefully she snuffed in her nose to keep control. If she cried, he might comfort her, and then they would start the cycle again.

"I don't know what it is, that I can't be with you. I want to be with you. You can't know how I want to be with you."

"No, I can't. I think you more want to be sure of not getting hurt. I think you want to punish your ex-wife for what you feel she did to you. Jackson, I know you could love me and you don't, and that's what hurts."

"If you'd be patient and not push me. Just sit back and let it happen."

"But my life enters too. I wasn't a loved child, and I have those mechanisms of the woman who gets hooked on trying to make someone love her. You become the father I was never pretty enough to please. You become the mother who never found my best good enough. You become the piggy bank that I put the dime in and I'm going to shake you and shake you till I get it back." She laughed wryly. Philip would never say that was a laugh that came from the belly. That was a laugh from the head.

"It makes me feel manipulated. After all, I came after you. If you didn't ride me so hard, don't you see that I'd come through?"

"Through what? Into what? We have to make it together or it doesn't count. All this performing in front of a statue of the other is beside the point." Here she was waving her hands around. He sat still, rocking back on the tilted chair. Occasionally his fingers drummed on the table. "Don't you think the way we started out has something to do with the bad smell?"

"Sure. I stole you from Phil. How can I not expect that Phil will steal you back? Or somebody else?"

"You didn't 'steal' me from Phil, because Phil didn't 'have' me in the sense you mean. I'm sick of this having. I can't hack it. It doesn't work. You insist on possessing me, and then you get scared I'll possess you back. I can't survive. But what you don't see is, neither really can you win."

"You want out." He looked at her levelly, rubbing his chin. He had not shaved. His cheek was stubbled.

"I am out, Jackson. I can't stay in here."

His eyes narrowed. "Seeing Phil?"

"Of course I am. He's in trouble. And how can I not *see* him? He isn't exactly invisible."

"What can I say?" He made a business of filling his pipe, his old clay pipe.

"A lot. I can say lots to you too. But we don't listen to each other, we don't get closer. Jackson, I'm not trying to break off with you tonight."

"No, you're just doing it." He tamped the tobacco down methodically, struck a kitchen match on the bottom of the table, sucked flame into the bowl.

"I'm just saying, here I am, myself again. I can't stand the way we've been. That woman is awful. I don't want to be her pushing on you. I love you, I want you to know that."

"Sure. In your own comfortable way."

"If you don't want it, sugar, you don't have to have it! I don't want to turn mean. I want you to love me. But you can't. I'm not going to stop caring for you, but I'm not going to hang around here trying to get a response out of you as if my worth as a human being depended on it."

"You're just going to go back to Phil and the old life."

"*My* life. Yes, I'm resuming my life. If you want me, you know where to find me. I hope you do, because I want you. I really want you."

His hands flexed with anger on the table. The knuckles made white peaks of contained anger. "Don't hold your breath. If you're leaving, you might as well leave."

She got slowly to her feet. She wanted to kiss him, she wanted to touch him. She wanted to pull them both back from this jagged edge. His eyes burned in his taut face. She did not dare. "So long."

He would not answer. She turned, fumbled into her red poncho, turned back. Still she watched him for a sign, any sign. Then she walked through the long hall past the bedrooms and out, shutting the door quietly.

13

Stills from a Year

Almost, she could hang out her front window on Raymond Street and call to Phil as her grandma used to call to her neighbor Mrs. Ganzman, out her kitchen window over the lines on the pulley where Rachel hung out her wash and the bedding to air. How Lionel had laughed at that: Grandma Rachel hooting out the window about her company, about her bowels, about her arthritis. "No, my daughter's boy is here! Sonia's boy!" *Tsatskeleh der mama.* Not for Miriam the child lump did anybody yell.

Phil was living across Raymond Street and down three houses, in a triple-decker wooden house that a commune was renting. He had a room on the third floor up under the eaves like her little studio apartment. Everyone called it Going-to-the-Sun House, although it didn't so much look as if it were going to the sun as slowly down in ruin. It had been a rooming house before, and the present occupants were not a together commune.

Going-to-the-Sun was a mountain peak in Glacier, where Hal had worked one summer, and Going-to-the-Sun was the name of a country music group he had formed with Terry and Rick. Now Hal had moved out and was trying to make it as a single, doing some of his own stuff and some of Phil's songs and songs his manager picked out. Terry and Rick were still in the house, trying to get up a new group that would hold together longer than a couple of performances. But everybody still called the house Going-to-the-Sun.

People in the house boasted about Hal and felt ripped off by him. Phil was caught between. Hal was doing his songs and seemed on the verge of getting a record contract. Phil dreamed of getting rich soon with Hal recording his songs, and then he could retire from the bar. But while he saw Hal sometimes he was always hanging around with Terry and Rick, and they resented Hal's leaving the group.

To have Phil nearby but in the commune worked fine. She need not worry about him the way she used to. It was not the solidest commune in Cambridge, but the people took care of each other minimally. They could handle a bad trip or a depression or a drunken messed-up Philip appearing in the middle of the night. If things were extra bad, Dorine or Rick would get her.

Three of four nights a week she ate there: it was a convenience. She had no time to cook. The food was minimal too, but better than the places she ate out. She was thinner than she ever had been, overcommitted, overextended, always on the run, never enough sleep or time to catch up on her laundry or to finish the novel she had borrowed from Phil in the summer. Time she lacked but not energy. She had come out of the sad passage with Jackson with a wound of being unloved when it really counted, but with a rebirth of strength and curiosity and the will to open herself to people, to ideas, to sensations, to relationships. Work was the center and the center held.

Phil had a beautiful bed in his room, with a head and foot of iron arabesques they had painted with blue enamel. A tie-dyed canopy hung over it and beside it sandalwood incense curled feathery smoke upward. Phil loved the scent of sandalwood, he said it smelled like Keats's poetry. Cuddled up with him, she was saying, "People are content to know so little of what they handle, it amazes me."

"What do you care how a radio works, so long as it plays music?" He was lying on his side with her pressed to his back.

"Nobody knows yet what a computer can really do, you know that? Nobody has any idea how much of the programming it could take over. That whole artificial intelligence thing really turns me on. But take even a person, for example."

"Which one should I take for starters?"

"I get the feeling so strong sometimes that I'll never get a chance to bump against my limits. How many people could I love at once, and really love each one? How many children would I have if I had all I wanted? How much could I learn if I put all my energy into some new field for six months, say? How fast could I learn Greek or Russian? Could I suddenly become a painter?"

"You're just saying, pigeon, that you get only one life to live, something I've been noticing for a long while. You shoot your wad and that's it. You're depressing me. I think you're growing and I'm shrinking, every day."

"Don't start that, Phil, I beg you. Things are going better for you now—aren't they?"

"Maybe. Seems like I just tread water."

She held him closer. "Philip darling, I wouldn't let you drown." He was at a disadvantage in survival techniques. Not in a knock-down, drag-out fight—he had a bruise still from a fight with a nasty drunk in Finnegan's: he was supposed to throw the bums out as well as mix drinks and play psychiatrist and regulate the sexual traffic—but ill equipped to take care of himself year in and year out. She wished there was a way she could politely say to him that she was perfectly willing to be his social security.

Vi started bellowing from halfway up the stairs. "Food's on!"

Phil seemed reluctant to get off the bed but she nudged him. It was important she get some food into him before he went off to Finnegan's. He never ate enough for the booze he swilled on the job. "Bartenders are all bottle freaks," he said, hand in the small of her back as they sauntered down. "If you don't guzzle, the smell turns you green. Your throat dries out, and who wants to stand there setting a bad example with water?"

Eliot had built the table that stood in the living room, massive and splintery like a picnic table with rough wooden benches. Lately the top had finally got sanded and painted, in the likeness of a large dollar bill with George Washington winking and giving the V sign. Supper was fatty hamburgers, potatoes mashed with the skins left on, and head lettuce cut up with an underripe tomato passing as salad. They ate fast, shouting over the wan little TV with the evening news on. Dessert was a tray of brownies. Desserts were the best part of the meal because everybody in this house had a terrible sweet tooth, and the only part of the meal anybody wanted to put effort into, the only part the girls got praised for, was sweets.

The pipe went around while they were still at the table and Phil got too involved in a shouting argument about some football player to go back upstairs with her in any hurry. Instead she trailed Dorine into the kitchen, helped to clear, and took up a towel. She wouldn't let herself be pressed into kitchen service often: it was important to her to refuse that role, and by and large she got away with it. After all she did not live there. But she didn't like to see Vi and Dorine stuck with everything, and so she helped out sometimes, especially when there was a good chance to talk. This fall seven people lived in the house, five men and two women. Vi was a couple with Rick and they shared a room. Dorine had been a couple with John, but he had broken up with her. Now he was seeing a girl who slept over occasionally.

Dorine had had to move out of his room, but she could not move out of the house. She could not afford a place alone. What she had done was to move the dining table into the living room and seal off the archway to the dining room with a rug. The kitchen connected with the living room directly so there was no problem serving and eating. The ex-dining room was noisy and Dorine could not go to sleep till everyone else in the house decided to go upstairs, but she settled for that just as she settled for being main cook and main dishwasher and main maid. She was not happy in the house. Vi was somewhat contemptuous of her, because she had no man and tended to be available.

"I'm the house whore," Dorine said to Miriam bitterly.

"Sex on demand. I wish I could live with you."

"I wish there was room." Though Miriam did not want a roommate, she determined to keep an eye out for Dorine and see if she couldn't do better for her. One man who cared would be an immense improvement on three who didn't (Rick having Vi, and John no longer interested). Phil was little better to her than the others. Coming in drunk and late, he might not bother to make it any farther than her bed, conveniently near the entrance. He would bring his groans and lamentations to her and she would wash him and undress him and tuck him in.

Dorine had dropped out of school because she could not relate to what she was supposed to be learning in psychology, her major. She was making an inadequate living in the typing pool of a local company. Everybody made fun of her because she had to wear dresses and nylons. The men were always putting her down for how she had to dress to go to work, as if she were too bourgeois to understand the relaxed way to dress.

Rick was a printer in a community shop where nobody cared what he wore or how long his hair was. Terry made some money performing, gave guitar lessons on a deal with a music shop, sometimes he made macramé belts and vests to sell on consignments in a shop on Brattle Street and part of the year he drove a truck for an organic food store. He always had four things going and between them he made it, day to day. Half the calls that came to the phone in the hall were for him, yet he hated to answer it. He was superstitious. He claimed Miriam was lucky for him and it was worth an extra twenty when she picked up the receiver.

John was still on unemployment from getting fired. Back when things were warmer and looser in the streets, he had used to deal grass and acid. But his sources had dried up and he did not like pushing hard drugs. He had found a straight job in an office. He had been fired, he was not sure why: so many people there were let go. While he was trying to get unemployment, he started dealing again. But feeling uneasy about ups and down and out of touch, he had been busted selling to a nark almost right off. Now he was waiting for his case to come up. Vi was the only one still in college, at Tufts. Eliot made some money doing carpentry, making furniture, putting up shelves and cabinets for people. He also got a small pension because his foot had been blown off in Vietnam. Dorine said he was the nicest to her now that John hated her—except for Phil sometimes—but his niceness was passive.

"I figured out what it is," Dorine said softly to Miriam, scrubbing the pot in which the potatoes had cooked. "It's because he doesn't feel he's a whole lot better than me. Because he's into a cripple thing. I try to make him feel good about himself, but I can tell that, coming from me, it doesn't mean much to him."

"You let them con you into accepting their evaluation. They use you and push you around and then, so they won't feel guilty, they say that's all you are."

"What am I?" Dorine shrugged.

"You're kind. You pay attention to others. You're sensitive and good-natured. You're smart. You have an attractive face and a beautiful body . . . Dorine!" Miriam put down the towel and turned the smaller woman to face her. "Ever thought of posing?"

"What do you mean? Sex pictures?" Dorine wrinkled her nose.

"No. Figure drawing for a class or a painter. I used to do that in New York to make money. I have a friend who's looking for a model. I'd pose for him but he's Jackson's roommate."

"You used to be Jackson's old lady, didn't you?"

"Last year. Anyhow, I just can't go over there and pose for Lennie and he says the light in my apartment is lousy."

"I don't know Lennie. Are you into something with him?"

"No! Jackson's roommate? That would be a bummer. But he's nice. I mean, if he weren't living there I might be interested." Actually she could not imagine being sexually interested in Lennie, thin sad rabbinical Lennie from Crown Heights in Brooklyn. She liked him as a cousin. She wanted him to get off the death trip he was wedded to, the dead blond he kept painting. Maybe he would love Dorine. She was pretty sure Dorine would love him. That might pull Dorine out of the house whore package, and even if it didn't work out all the way, it would start her off fresh. "Listen, would you do it? He's kind of depressed and lonely."

"You sending me over there to pose for him or fuck him?"

"Dorine, I promise you, it's you who'll make a pass at him.

Trust me. If you don't like him, what's an afternoon? If you like it, maybe I could find you a job posing, and you can kiss off the typing pool."

"That I wouldn't cry about, Miriam, believe me. Okay, set it up. Any evening."

"Has to be in the daytime, honey. Light! Saturday or Sunday?"

"Either one. I expect a big weekend with my laundry, and I should try to clean up this pigpen, but that's it."

"One thing. I know this sounds ridiculous. But you have to dial the number. If Lennie answers, I'll take the phone and talk to him, but if Jackson answers, you have to ask for Lennie."

"Miriam!" Dorine made her eyes wide. "After all this time! You had it bad for him."

"Every time I run into him, it's like nothing has healed. It hurts all over again."

"It's the same way with John," Dorine whispered. "When I know she's in there with him, I can't stay in the house. Sometimes I go over to Sally's, but if her old man's there, he doesn't want me around." Idly she picked at a stain on the drainboard. "Sometimes I get to staring at his new girl and I keep wondering how he could love me and then not. Is there something that gets used up?"

After the phone call to Lennie, Miriam strolled back to the living room. Rick and Terry were playing bluegrass with Sally's old man, who was visiting, and Vi was singing with them. Sally, a lanky redhead from Tennessee, was sitting on the floor out of the way. Eliot was nodding out in the corner, John had left, and Phil was sitting sideways across the old armchair with his long legs stuck out. When he saw her he made an impatient high sign and they both slipped out and up the stairs.

If Dorine did get involved with Lennie, if Dorine moved in with Lennie, if, if, if—she was such a *luftmensch*. But suppose. Then she would have a friend there, where she could no longer go. She despised herself for wanting so strongly to know what was happening with Jackson; had he another woman, was he happy without her? Phil saw little of him and they exchanged no confidences when they did meet. Dorine would understand her weakness.

If Dorine did move out, the pressure would mount on her

to move in. Everyone seemed to think it would be fun to have her in the house. She loved to have Phil nearby and to come over and hang out. But she had a strong feeling that the camaraderie would disappear if she were actually living here. She could accept each of the men in his roles and egotisms and passions and prejudices, so long as there was that necessary space. Any closer, and there would be first friction and then conflict. She had no intention of crossing the street to live.

Upstairs Phil showed her a song he was working on, played it through roughly on his pawnshop guitar.

GOING THROUGH CHANGES

You get bigger
and I get smaller.
I get shorter
while you get taller.
Oh baby, oh mama, where does it end?
What did I spend?

Baby, now I'm going down,
nice and easy, nice and slow . . .

"Sometimes I think you hate me!"
"It's just a poem, pigeon. You science types are so naïve."
"A poem you wrote."

You get stronger
while I get weaker.
Oh baby, oh mama, how far am I gonna bend?
Is it the end?

Once I had a name, I don't remember.
Every month is cold December
yet you wear a suntan.
When I ask, you say you can . . .

She got up and began to pace and he paused, his hand on the strings. "Come on, pigeon, we've fucked each other over a few times. It doesn't go away. Better I should love you in bed and put the anger in a song. Think you'd like it better if I knocked you around the room?"

"I think things are good between us, and then the poison comes out!" she held her head.

"Come on, what harm does a song do? I pay my dues."

"Words, words, you're so big on them! All right, go ahead. I can't stop you!"

"Why should you want to? They're my only way out of here, don't you see that?"

Sighing, she sat down on the bed. "I see that. I'm glad people like them and I hope that *macher* Hal does record your songs. But I wish you'd write nasties about somebody else for a change. I get tired of being the villain. Every man around here thinks I'm an absolute bitch to you."

"Baby, if you knew how little I care what anybody thinks. If I go through changes out loud, it suits me. Besides, it's made you a legend."

"Oh, great. I really dig that."

Phil grinned. "I think you do. You take care to live up to it."

Playing with appearances was a pastime he had taught her, starting that first summer in New York when they had played together in the streets and boutiques. Phil, always conscious of his audience, had taught her that consciousness. Still she was always first tuned to him when they played, for fear the game would turn into a destructive pavane, into a sudden catastrophe. Every time they went into public together, whether that meant simply downstairs into the living room on a hectic night or to a party or a concert or into the streets, she must always be tuned to that interaction with Phil. Yes, she was a scandal: they were both figures in their microcosm. Often people thought they knew her before they met her, and often she took pleasure in confirming their terrible expectations. Her public self at bad parties, at moments when she found herself on display, was not her but a mask. But sometimes the game threatened to trap her and she felt caught out there, exposed and bare and forced to act ever more provocative and extreme because she did not know how to slow down the pressure. Then she felt her life with Phil had turned her into a dancing poodle-woman that people expected to entertain them. Sometimes a sudden sense of shameful exposure would strike her raw. Then if she could dance she could escape it, if she could get close to Phil it would help, but if he were off from her, unreachable, then sometimes she did bad things: she ended up with men she had resolved to avoid, in just the ugly scene she had anticipated.

Bitterly his song said she had grown bigger and he had grown smaller. But she felt he vanished. Sometimes she lay chained to a skeleton. Sometimes he left her nothing, nothing at all except her noisy life clattering around her and herself crouching in the midst of it wondering why. Wondering who was she, this Miriam? What did all these people want from her, but to grab a piece and run off with it and gobble it down?

"Phil? Phil!" She started to tell him of the panic sticking through her chest like a long needle when, rising on her elbow, she saw the time. "Phil, you're late to work."

She was coming to know a secretary who worked at Tech Square, Beth, young and tiny. Their appearance together amused her; she told Beth they were Mutt and Jeff. While she was waiting for a free terminal, to go on the computer with her group's work, she would talk with Beth. At first Beth mainly tickled her—such a combination of intensity and ignorance, shyness and clarity—but quickly she began to like her. Above all she appreciated that Beth responded to her warmly and openly and seemed to admire her. Admiration from a woman was more of a gift than from a man: men never admired her so simply. They desired, they suppressed desire and resented, they acknowledged desire but felt unwilling to respond, so condescended. Phil came closer to liking her than any man she knew, and they had woven together such a complicated pattern, who knew any more what to call it?

Once while she was changing at Tech Square to go out afterward with a bass player she had met through Rick, Beth stood and watched her in the women's lounge.

"Miriam, what does it feel like to be beautiful? I mean it. Does it feel good?"

Miriam looked Beth in the eyes, a little threatened. She never knew what to do when other women began to be jealous. But Beth was really asking. "It feels better than being ugly. I like the attention."

"If I was a painter, you're what I'd paint for a beautiful woman."

"But once I wasn't, and someday again I won't be. And I'll still be me, and it will be like it was when I was fifteen and ugly and I'll still want people to admire me and want me, and they won't. Think of all the beautiful black women born in white cities before there was a black movement to let them see their faces in the mirror. Other people give you beauty and take it away. It's being given a ticket for a while to get away with what you want to do, to get the things you want."

"I want to be beautiful but not in a magazine way, not in a sexy way. I mean I want to like myself. I want to feel that I'm what I want to be."

"I think I am what I want to be."

"But you're always flirting, always playing games with people, always acting."

"That's just the social thing—how I act with men."

"I don't want to be that way with anybody," Beth said fiercely. Then she repeated it, maybe as much for herself as for Miriam.

Off she went to Rochester with Ryan and Owasa and Woods and Manganaro of her group. The meeting was mainly for biochemists, but there was a section on applications of computers and they were giving a paper on their work. She went partly because her name was on the paper and partly because she'd gone to only a few scientific meetings and still found them exciting. Because they would all be staying in a house that had been turned over to the conference and because she would be driving there with Owasa and Woods, it would cost little for what would be almost a vacation. She had never been in Rochester. Every time she got to visit someplace new, that was one more thing checked off the list of what she had never done, a small but measurable accomplishment. At the very least she would get to some parties, she would eat out, she would get to meet a lot of men and be amused.

Owasa and Ryan and Manganaro were all married, and Woods was friendly but gay; so she had simply omitted them from her calculations of pleasures to be enjoyed. Actually the only one she liked was Woods. Owasa she had respect for, he was very good, very fast. He had a faculty appointment already. Manganaro was plodding and out of his depth and bigoted and vain. He was handsome and left her unmoved. He never finished anything properly. Ryan was touchy but quick and always looking for an angle. When she had to instruct him about something—after all, she knew her side of the project, that was why she was working with them—he would begin to grind his teeth. She found that boring. Otherwise he was satisfactory company.

But Ryan had other ideas about his vacation as she found out the second night when there was a party in their quarters. She realized vaguely that he kept handing her drinks. He was always at her elbow with another cocktail. She was not used to cocktails, not used to anything but California wine and beer. She had no idea how much she was drinking except that she always had a glass in her hand. She was laughing too much, she was talking too loudly. No one in this group danced, they just stood and went ya-ta-ta-ta to each other. She felt as if Ryan were showing her off, this strange little man was suddenly pushing on her in some way she could not maneuver around. She was uncomfortable and she drank more, trying to regain her equilibrium. After a point the evening ran quickly downhill, everything seemed to tilt and run together. He was always at her elbow and everything else was up by the ceiling, swirling away. Everything kept receding from her. She was lying on a bed. Ryan was pawing at her. Pushing him away, she kept laughing. There seemed to be no one else around.

She kept trying to sit up and he kept climbing on her. His fox face sharpened, his chin was digging into her, his hands were strong claws tearing. He was getting angry. It felt bad. She could not bring herself to hit him. The laboratory politeness restrained her. She could not hit somebody on the group she was working with. She could only laugh and shove at him and try to get up. Her body felt vast and waterlogged. She seemed to be trying to move vats of blubber by remote control. Down there somewhere her huge legs in the depth of the bed. She could not hit a graduate student in the biochemistry department who worked on her group. She kept telling him he was a married man and he kept trying to force her legs apart.

She felt exhausted and nauseous. The elastic on her panties had given way long ago and he had actually got in for an instant. She began to be a little scared and said, "Okay, okay, let me get my diaphragm."

But he had a rubber. It was ridiculous. She had not seen one of those since the second time with Phil. The act was disgusting in a dry sort of way and it went on forever. Forever he was lying on her stomach pushing into her. It hurt but she was too sodden to feel strongly. It was a nuisance. She felt nauseous with him riding on her belly. She had to piss. His motion inside irritated her bladder. It went on forever and finally he pulled out. Presumably he had come, she got up at once and ran to the bathroom, stumbling till she found it. She could no longer remember where her own room was or how to negotiate the distance between. She could not even manage to find her clothes so, grimacing with resentment, she had to climb back beside him and go to sleep.

When she woke in the morning he was up already. She heard his voice talking on the room phone. She lay still and listened, alerted by the grate of triumph in his voice. "Five dollars, Al. Sure, come by on your way out to breakfast. You couldn't ask for more proof." He hung up.

A bet with Al. Hung over and sick to her stomach, she imagined making many holes in his body with a knife. She immediately dragged out of bed.

"Good morning, good morning, Miriam baby." Ryan was beaming. "How's the head?"

"Working." Scooping up her clothes as she went, she slammed into the bathroom and put herself together as quickly as she could work the zippers and buttons. But when she hopped out, Al Manganaro was already at the door. "Hey, how about some breakfast, Ryan? Well, well."

"I hear you have a bet with Ryan," she said sweetly, strolling past them swinging her leather pouch. "Gee, I wish I could help you decide who won, but since I passed out, I haven't the foggiest if I was had or not. I mean, you'd think if anything had really happened I'd remember—but maybe it just wasn't memorable. To breakfast?"

From that moment on Ryan was her enemy. The hatred was mutual but controlled, as both of them cared more for the group's work than for each other.

Lionel had let the flat near Nostrand go and taken a studio apartment in Brooklyn Heights. He said that it was convenient, and besides, the kids came home so seldom. Self-pityingly he said that to her, but she did not believe he would be pleased if they invaded. In fact, Allegra, faced with Christmas vacation and only invited to spend half of it with her boy friend, descended on her for the last four days. She gave up her bed to Allegra and slept at the commune with Phil.

"How come you didn't go to Lionel's? You always liked shopping Christmas vacations."

"The merry widower? He's in Florida visiting friends."

"So how come you couldn't borrow the key? I'm glad to have you, but you don't know anybody here. . . ."

"He told Mark and his roommate Loudmouth they could stay. And Mark told me I'd interfere with their social life. Isn't that rich?"

"I don't like our brother."

"He's going to be a success, though." Allegra was doing something elaborate to her hair with a wire brush, sitting at Miriam's desk. She spoke matter-of-factly. "He's the only one in the family with that kind of head—where do you think the *momser* got it? If you ask him why he likes somebody, like Loudmouth he rooms with, there's always an ulterior motive. . . . Do you like the way Dad is acting? I mean, really, do you?"

"I haven't been home that much. Every time I walked in the door of the old flat, a weight fell on me. I'd feel like I couldn't breathe."

"It was pretty depressing. But do you like his bachelor pad? It makes me uncomfortable. The same with his sideburns. And he's letting his hair grow—haven't you noticed? Every time I see him, he's sneaking to get it a little bit longer. And those shirts!"

"I guess that's how he wanted to dress. No more white-on-white specials from Grandfather." For years Lionel had worn white dress shirt irregulars with French cuffs from his father, who had been in the shirt business. They had always been baggy. Only Sonia pretended to think they were wonderful, very distinguished, she said. Even after Grandfather died, they had a lifetime supply. Mark had worn them too all through high school, but he revolted and said he wouldn't go to college if he had to wear them any more.

"So maybe he deserves purple shirts for a while. But he

embarrasses me." Allegra made her eyes wide. "He doesn't look like anybody's father. He thinks he's Marcello Mastroianni."

"Is he giving you money?"

"He puts me through school. Same with Mark. You're the only one off his back. He keeps asking me, 'When are you getting married?' As if I'm not trying."

"How is your boy friend?"

Allegra shrugged. "It's obvious if I marry him I'll have to put him through medical school. That sounds too much like Mama!"

"You're so young, Allegra, don't let them hurry you. Women who marry young, they always look sad to me in a few years."

Allegra frowned at the ends of hair, looking for splits. "Miriam, don't you get lonely? Don't you get scared?"

"I was lonely when I was younger. I have more trouble making sure I get the time alone that I need than I do finding people to spend time with. Scared of what?"

"Of being alone. Of losing your looks. Of getting old and not having anybody."

"Sure, sometimes."

"Well, I do often." Allegra threw the comb down. "What do you get scared of, big sister? You must be afraid sometimes."

"When I was younger I was scared that nobody would ever love me. I was scared of men, scared to talk to them, scared of being rejected if I showed I liked someone. I feel that less now. I support myself, and as soon as I finish the classes I have to take for my doctorate, I'll be working full time. I worry a lot about finding work I really want to do. I don't want to get stuck in some dead-end job. That's awfully easy for a woman. I don't want a job in a company where I'll be expected to go on doing shit work for years and never get a promotion and never get a chance to show what I can do. I don't want to go to work for the military or one of those big corporations. I don't even know if creative work in my field exists outside a university. But universities are tight and prejudiced against women. It's rotten hard for a woman to get a decent job around a university."

"Is that what you really worry about?" Allegra narrowed her eyes.

Miriam nodded. "I don't want to be poor, if the truth be known. I want to live comfortably. I'm tired of the half-life of a student. I want to be able to help my friends when they need help. I want to buy interesting clothes. I'm sick of eating in greasy spoons. I don't want a lot of money, Allegra, really. I just want a decent living. I want the things that make life pleasant. When I bought that reconditioned air conditioner for fifty dollars, do you know what a change that made in my life? This room gets hot in the summer, believe me, right up under the roof. I had enough hard times growing up."

"It wasn't so bad. You exaggerate."

"By the time you were growing up, it wasn't."

Allegra was still frowning. "But if you really get a Ph.D., who'll marry you? Dad says you're educating yourself right out of a husband."

Miriam's turn to shrug. "I can't imagine getting married before I'm thirty, frankly. I've too much wanderlust."

"But all the men will be gone by then."

"Good. I'll marry a nineteen-year-old." She laughed.

"You're still seeing Phil, after all this time! You might as well marry him. It's been years!"

"I'm not going to, Allegra, I told you that. Don't worry."

"What will you do with him when you do marry?"

"I don't know." Miriam hugged herself. "I can't imagine. But that's years and years away."

"I should send your little sister a bouquet, I like having you over here every night. But I wouldn't mind half an hour alone with her, I'll tell you true."

Miriam rose on her elbow and tapped Phil's chest. "No."

"How come?"

"No. No, because I used to be jealous of her. No, because I love her now and she'd feel bad."

"How do you know?" Phil put his hand under her chin. "Sometimes when she's holding forth I think she needs a touch of it."

"That isn't what she needs, and do you want to make me upset?"

"It might be interesting." But he left Allegra to her own devices for the rest of her stay.

She knew Allegra found her life bizarre and dangerous. She found Allegra's wan ambitions tedious. Still she clung to Allegra and Allegra to her. Miriam missed women in her life. She had a growing need for women friends, and she tried to reach out to other women and bind them to her by doing them favors, by trying to find out what they wanted and helping them to get it, as she had brought Dorine together with Lennie. She tried to discover increasingly, as time went on, what Beth might want.

Beth would be a superior sort of younger sister, with all Allegra's delicacy. Beth was a small butterfly, a warbler, the miniature deer she had seen once with Phil in the Bronx Zoo, a deer only a foot high—a nocturnal creature with huge eyes and bones that would snap in the hand. She was fascinated too with Beth's strange dry quality, cool and contained. Yet Beth was naïve and girlish too. There was a quality of will in Beth that was totally lacking in Allegra, yet beside her Allegra would have seemed sophisticated.

Like a squirrel, Beth carried about with her nuts and fruits to nibble on, and Miriam took to bringing her little delicacies for the smile that produced, a shining smile of surprise and delight almost too big for the thin freckled face. She liked to tease Beth: she could not help testing to see if Beth would be shocked. Beth seemed to want and to need nothing, but to live like a squirrel in the city eating her seeds and nuts and fruit and running to classes and concerts. As sexless as a child, perhaps, but Miriam liked that dry cool quality. It was a relief from her own vast yeasty sexuality. She wanted to think she might be as simple and as contained as that if only she decided to be.

When she saw Beth leaving the computer center with Ryan one day in April, she felt a sharp pain of loss. Her enemy was carrying off a new friend. He would poison Beth against her. He would damage Beth. He would use her and tear that clear integrity.

After the ugliness with Ryan, she was wary and careful with men at M.I.T. Indeed, her relations seemed to clarify. She had won admittance to a special seminar Wilhelm Graben was giving as his only contact with students while spending a few months at M.I.T. That in itself established a certain minimum of respect. It was also more exciting than anything else she had taken. He was one of the creators of the field, with a career in physics accomplished before he had encountered his first computer. He was urbane, witty, remote, still on the cutting edge of theory, and radiated a kind of amused power. She had almost a crush on him. Her work went well.

With Phil, things were bumpy. School had given a structure to his life that nothing replaced. He was drifting, tending bar and writing an occasional song, marking time, with his court case pending, always pending. Hal got two club dates and at each he sang a number of Phil's songs. Phil was excited by dreams of making it; he was ashamed and sure his songs were crap and he had sold out as a poet. Hal had a boat and they went sailing a lot during May. On the boat Hal was endurable, nautical and involved. Otherwise she found him rancid. He used others easily and moved on. His days were decorated with women. He had a chow who growled at everybody else and bit someone once a week, a dog he treated better than any human and fed raw beef. Putting up with Hal was a kind of penance.

That spring, with the invasion of Cambodia and the stepping up of the war, there were many demonstrations. Phil had nightmares and spent more and more time with Joe, who had gone into a permanent condition of rage. Joe was a chesty muscular guy with a brilliant smile set off by a thick brown mustache. His deep ringing voice carried through Going-to-the-Sun, with his loud descending laugh. But he was not sleeping that spring, or eating or teaching his classes, he was driven, burning, furious, and half the time his fury turned on those around him, who were at least within his reach. He was always telling Miriam how bourgeois she was.

No one who would not leave whatever they were doing and go with him on the streets that spring could escape his driven anger, and even minor political differences with those working with him blew up. The third week in May he stormed out of his apartment, leaving his wife Wanda and their little boy Luis and baby Johnny just at the crawling stage. For a week he hung around Going-to-the-Sun blowing hard, with two nineteen-year-old women doting on him. Phil had given him his room and moved in with her for a week and they were peaceful in the eye of the storm. In the meantime Wanda was running his Defense Committee, holding together the shaky coalition that his attacks threatened. On the eighth day of Joe's terrible reign over Going-to-the-Sun, Wanda arrived at suppertime with Luis by the hand and the baby on her back—a small chunky woman with dark wiry hair and intense black eyes—burning, worried, overworked, desperate, and strong as a mule. She simply arrived in time to eat supper. Joe began making a great fuss over his sons. And after supper, when it was time for Luis to go home to bed, Joe went with her. A simple division of labor, Miriam thought wryly, watching them depart: she loves and he permits himself to be loved.

Phil managed through the demonstrations not to get busted again, but Thursday he was clubbed and then gassed. Miriam sat up tending him. "If the enemy is the people who own banks and factories and the Pentagon, then I'm not the enemy. Am I?"

He rolled his head to and fro in her lap, under the icebag. "Who said you were?"

"You do. Your poems do."

"That's something else."

Gently she touched his swollen nose. "I wish we could lose our history. You worry me. . . . Why can't it be simple again? Without these reverberations of old pain."

His eyes opened. He lifted the ice pack. "Aw, pigeon, don't take it so hard. Everything hurts as we go, I don't ask that it don't. I don't want any other women I've ever seen, except for a change of bed now and then. I'm the one who likes you this way, remember?"

"Don't, Phil."

"You think it's over with him, yet you're still bleeding."

"Phil, it's over. But no matter what happens, ever, I won't cut you off again. I won't."

"Promise me." His voice was steely.

"I promise." She moved the ice pack back onto the swelling. "Tomorrow I have to go to work. . . . But we'll have Saturday together. Do you think you'll feel together enough to go to the street fair Saturday? On Garden Street, with music and goodies to eat and theater . . ."

"Together enough! Me, the original street-fighting man? Sure, I like carnivals. That is, if the weather holds good."

14

You Got to Feel It Spontaneously

In the morning she woke to the sunlight filtering through strawberry-bronze curtains she and Phil had made from sheets. Jackson still snored softly on his back. She raised herself on her arm to look at him, his sleeping face unguarded. His lowered eyelids were rosy. His lashes were longer than hers. Those silver hairs in his beard and mane glittered like real metal. These moments when she could contemplate him without being seen, without waking his wariness, were a gentle pleasure.

From that sleep she could believe he would open his eyes and his face would open too: he would wake as vulnerably open as he looked in sleep. Well, things were better. Yes, better. Yesterday had been trying, however. She had had a job interview in one of the firms just off campus, those electronic companies that nestled like piglets to the teats of M.I.T., on the same street as Draper Labs where they did simulations of wars and submarine battles. It had been hate at first sight. Then she had gone out for a second interview in the afternoon at Lincoln Labs. She did not want that either: too large, too hierarchical. She had come home glum and wanted to creep into his leanness and be supported. But Jackson had perceived her mood as a demand. He had backed off into his Who are you anyhow, woman? mode. She had had to pull herself together and put off worrying until she could be alone. Today when Jackson had gone off to his morning class she would be able to bring her depression out front and study it and figure how to live with it or deal with it. But through the evening she had to conceal her problem to be with him.

Dorine and Jackson and she had eaten hash brownies he had made till they were silly and easy giggling laughter swirled in the room. She and Dorine had danced together—Jackson would never dance but would glare under his brows at anybody who tried to pull him from his chair and tighten his muscles into rigor mortis. Watching them, he tilted back in his chair and smiled like an oriental potentate being entertained, and truthfully they were dancing in a few minutes not so much for the music or for each other as they had started, but to please his eyes.

Then they had all gone for a walk to get ice cream at Brigham's, where she had mocha and Jackson had butter pecan and Dorine had peppermint stick. Jackson had walked in the middle with his arms around both of them, unusually pliant of him. He made a point of never touching Dorine. Then they came back still happy and said good night to Dorine. At ten-thirty they had gone off to bed and made love until midnight and it was good, it was beautiful to be with him again.

His chest with the curly hairs rose and fell. Lightly she rested a palm against the skin, feeling the pulse. Beneath her hand his breathing altered. She felt that he was coming up through the layers of sleep. REM sleep: rapid eye movements under the blush of the lids. Dreaming about what? She had a pang of jealousy for the women in his head, more real than any flesh for him. Gradually she was learning how to love him properly. She was not letting her desperation force her into bitter cycles of retreat. She was not being coaxed into overtly trying to squeeze love from him. When he withdrew, she was learning to step back too. Yes, doing better. He would open to her. That promise was always there in the taut lines of his body, in the sad lines of his face, in the sandy wisdom of his eyes. Patience and accommodation. Living out her love day to day.

The eyes opened, blinked, focused. Caught her in the act of bending over his face. The eyebrows raised. He came alert so quickly. "Well. Are you putting a hex on me?"

"What makes you think I'd know how?"

"All women are witches."

"All men are pricks." She sat up and felt for her slippers under the bed.

"Where do you think you're off to?" He put out a long arm and pulled her against him. "Was a love spell. Mojo working."

"You can't bluff me. You have a ten o'clock class today. You wouldn't be tempted by ten naked maids in a row."

"Well, school's still something of a novelty. This aging boy wonder. I'm older than Higgins, my ten o'clock seminar man, and I can see that embarrasses him. He thinks I should be back on the Bowery waiting on the mission line."

"I knew the first time I saw you drinking grapefruit juice for breakfast that you liked self-pity in the morning."

"Woman, you don't know what's good. It takes the sweaters off my teeth."

"Have you tried a toothbrush?" She got away from him and hopped across the room. She wouldn't have minded bicycling over to M.I.T. a bit late. But once on such a cozy morning she had rolled over onto him and he had taken out that missed class on her for two days. He was convinced in his heart he was about to flunk out.

He skipped breakfast except for his glass of juice and a piece of toast eaten standing, but Dorine padded out in her cotton smock as soon as Jackson left, and they ate granola and blueberries together leisurely.

"Did Phil come in last night?"

Dorine dropped her gaze and nodded. "In my room."

"Dorine, don't start that guilty bit on me. Why shouldn't you take him in if you want to? You don't think I'm jealous, please, do you?"

Dorine made an effort to look at Miriam. "He makes me feel funny about it."

"Phil?"

"No! Phil?"

"Jackson, you mean. You know how uptight he is. You shouldn't let him get you down. I swear, somewhere inside he doesn't really approve of sex. It might be considered fun. He doesn't really approve of anything where the fact is more interesting than the theory."

"He says I shouldn't sleep with anybody while Lennie's in the hospital." Dorine stirred her very light, very sweet coffee round and round.

"He said that? Or you're just guessing?"

"He said it all right. With sadness, as if I were really being a shit. He makes me feel . . . so cheap."

"What business is it of his?"

"It was my fault. I mean, you and Phil had gone off to

that rock festival for the weekend. We were alone here and we were talking. I mean, I felt really close to him. I was talking about what happened with John and why it hurt so bad. How I got involved with Lennie and how I got into that trip last spring of really wanting him to marry me and what a shock it was when I finally said so and I learned he'd never even thought of it. I felt Jackson must like me a little bit, I mean, he listens so sympathetically. . . ."

She thought but could not say it was the role he liked: he liked listening and nodding and sympathizing a bit, giving advice.

"I thought, well, he can't find me completely ugly, to listen to me all evening practically. So when it was kind of late I asked him if he wanted to sleep with me. I didn't make a big thing of it. I just thought he might just as soon . . . he'd spent all that time . . ." Dorine trailed off. "I wasn't trying to poach on you. But he made me feel like a rotten potato."

"Dorine, don't let him get you down that way."

"He put down this quiet line about how Lennie is a friend of his and Lennie is in the hospital. I wouldn't have felt half so lousy if he'd just said, 'No, you don't turn me on.' But Lennie's been in the hospital since June, and I don't know if he's going to pick up with me again when he gets out. He keeps telling me he got hepatitis because he wasn't taking care of himself, as if I had failed him. He's grumpy when he's sick, and he just isn't that interested in talking to me when I hitchhike to New York. When I walked in he said, 'Oh, it's you.' His mother was there, and he hadn't even told her who I am."

"Being with Phil is between you and Phil. Jackson has nothing to say about it."

"But he watches me. Honest, sometimes I feel I have to sneak around. I feel his eyes on me. He makes such heavy judgments. He's always making judgments and telling us where we come short."

"He does that." Miriam poured more coffee for both of them. "Back when we were together before, when I broke up with Phil—"

"That was before I knew you."

"Yeah. Before Phil moved into Going-to-the-Sun—"

"For me, that place should have been named Going-to-Hell-Fast. I'm glad you got me out of there, honest. No matter how heavy Jackson weighs on me, I think a lot of him. I like living here. It's better with Phil, here. He's like a baby sometimes, and sometimes he just lashes out when he's had too much or he's upset. . . . But he can be sweet too. I know I should probably move out."

"I like having another woman in the house. They gang up on me. I'd go out of my mind with both of them if you weren't here to talk to. Besides, this place would stink, literally stink. The walls could fall in before either of them would wash a dish."

"Well, I'm good for something anyhow." Weakly Dorine laughed.

Miriam was lying beside Phil, on her side, tracing her finger slowly down his spine caressing each vertebra. "Where did you sleep last night?"

"Going-to-the-Sun. It was late and I was wasted, I just couldn't make it all the way over here."

When she had given up her room as a sign of commitment to the new order and their emergence as a family, Phil had talked of doing the same. But he did not like to break things off. He could not bring himself to tell the guys at Going-to-the-Sun that he was moving out on them. So he never did.

"You'll always keep one foot planted there, won't you? Makes me think you don't expect this to work."

"I expect nothing to work, ever. Everything human is an error. But I like having two homes. It's a hell of a lot better than having none."

"I wish we had a bigger apartment. Then we could each have a room."

"I think old Jackson wants Dorine to vacate so he can have his room. I don't think he expects Lennie to come back when he gets out of the hospital."

"I want Dorine here. I just wish we all lived in a bigger place. Sometimes I wish we had a house and a yard."

"Wow, baby, we can move out to suburbia. How about a nice split level with a family room in Wakefield? Or a colonial-age farmhouse with landscaping in Lexington or Concord?"

"They'd like us fine, wouldn't they?"

"We have enough trouble getting the rent together. Hey, get a job, get a job."

"I'm trying. I have nine tenths of the course work out of the way and the basic stuff run on my thesis. I just have to write it. But those programing factories turn me off. I don't want a dead-end job. They're so damned openly prejudiced in those corporations, the first thing they ask me is when I'm getting married."

"Why, you should smile sweetly, bat your big brown eyes, and explain you are already in a group marriage."

"Then they'd just ask when am I going to have a baby. Philip, love, I just don't know what to do. I wasn't that great a mathematician. Nothing besides computers has turned me on the same way. You can't decide to be talented in some field, you have to have the knack. *You* couldn't decide tomorrow morning that you're bored with writing songs, so you're going to compose string quartets instead."

"Maybe I will, a man of my vast and wasting talents. I could work at not composing string quartets just as hard as I work at not writing poems."

"You're always pumping some poison into your beautiful body."

"Now don't start with the 'Mother Mary, come to save us' bit."

"How come you didn't come home last night? I was waiting."

"You didn't wait long the night before."

"Oh, Phil . . . were you mad?" She wrapped herself around him, nuzzling. "Sometimes Jackson just doesn't pay attention to turns, and I never know if you're coming home or not after Finnegan's." Jackson had his ways of inveigling, not letting her catch him in a direct request that might break the gentle drift toward bed. "If you'd give me a call . . ."

He rolled free of her, resting his head on cupped hands, elbows spread on the pillow. "I am not going to call for an appointment. You want to be a call girl?"

"You're both so damned touchy about arrangements!"

"Who wants to get it up on schedule? The next performance of Phil and Miriam will be held at eleven-thirty sharply. Please be on ti-yum."

"It isn't a matter of making appointments. It's just a matter of my knowing that you want to see me."

"Well, I want to see you when I want to. Isn't that what wanting means? I am not going to get a goddamned ticket punched, like eating in a dormitory. If loving isn't spontaneous, then the last thicket of real man has been bulldozed at last. We get up by alarm clocks and we eat by the clock and we get relieved at work and piss by the clock. I am not going to be had like a pill."

"The two of you want everything so flipping spontaneous and then you get insulted if I can't second-guess you."

"That's loving, pigeon. You have to have a feel for me. You can't do it by contract."

"Philip . . . " She touched his chest, tanned that beautiful rawhide color he got, his skin so much darker than his hair. He went out a lot on Hal's boat. He was good with the boat, he had an affinity for wind and the sea. He sensed how to tack with his body as well as his mind, while Hal was still remembering the rules. People watching him said, "Oh well, growing up in Boston, he must have learned how to handle boats as a boy"; whereas he had learned only how to handle a knife and a woman and a needle. "Don't you think I am loving you?"

"Getting there. Getting there."

His skin tasted of salt. Salty, smoky, leathery taste from the sea, the sun, the day on the water. His eyes were the color of the sea as it had been today, with the waves making clean whitecaps tumbling over. Now they were fluttering shut and he was hardening under her lips and her fingers played over his belly and flanks. Body she knew so well, better than her own. Knew how to sense and to please, as if she had grown up curved into his side. When people fell in love, how could they want to trade in the people they had loved for those they were learning to love? She had let Jackson make her break off with Phil, like hacking off an arm. She must work to love Phil better, to insert herself between what he really wanted and his destructive energies, his self-hatred, his bitter ironies turning to bite them.

They made love slowly. When he felt himself about to come, he would stop her with a hand on her buttocks and she would wait and then slowly resume. He had not always the energy for that. But they both wanted to last together this evening. He had this night off and it was not yet completely dark outside.

"I wish we could get out of the city," she said beside him. Now the dark was complete and thick, the night still warm. "I want us to have a house at the ocean. Will I ever get a job and some money?"

"What's all this about houses and money?"

"Phil, wouldn't you like to get out of the city for a while?" She stroked his fine hair.

"Out of the city? Nothing but grass and cows. Now what would I say to a cow?"

"But you like the sea."

"I guess I would like to lie out on the sand someplace— maybe the Cape or Nantucket. Sand is the cleanest stuff —nothing like dirt."

"By next summer, providing I get a job, maybe we can swing it."

"Too tame." He was playing with her hair, twisting it on his fingers. "Why don't I ever get to go any place? Only places I've ever been are New York and out to L.A. and Tijuana. Only time I ever got out of the States was to Vietnam, gee, thanks a whole lot. I want to drink in sidewalk cafés in Paris. I want to swill beer at the Oktoberfest. I want to go diving with Japanese fisherwomen. I want to get laid by Eskimos. I want to bargain for hash in Marrakech, while liquid-eyed adolescents pray for my cock. And what do I do? Walk the dusty streets of Cambridge from Finnegan's to Harvard Square, intersection of a thousand private drives. A poet needs experience. All I get is a day older."

"We will travel, love. I've never been any place. I haven't even been to L.A. and Tijuana."

"Hey, gringo, you want to buy my seester? What would you do in Tijuana? We couldn't even smuggle dope in your brassiere since you don't wear a brassiere. That's what I did with Barbara, the bitch I was traveling with. Yes, I want to take off for Trinidad or Lima or Rio, pronto."

"On what I'm making this summer, how about a ticket to Worcester on a Trailways bus?"

"How about you get me a beer?"

"Phil, promise me one thing, a little thing."

"Anything that does not change the power balance of our electrical triangle. That's an instrument for a rock band, you know, electrical triangle?"

"That's the point. We aren't a triangle. There are four of us living here."

"What? Oh, Dorine. Our lady of marshmallows."

"You lean on her when you want to, don't you feel just a little chintzy putting her down? I like Dorine."

"Am I objecting? I get along with her. I don't mind."

"You don't mind her in bed either."

"So? Examine the ass on her sometimes if you need an explanation. John used to call her Bottom Round."

"She does all the work here and nobody ever says thanks, even, let alone helping her."

"Help her if you want to. She likes playing wifey."

"Phil, listen to me. I think you like her better than you let on—it's a status thing. Jackson wouldn't deign to sleep with her, so you pretend you don't care. She's warm and she's good to you and you like that. Why not be a little nicer to her sometimes, then? Let her know you notice she's alive too."

"Why don't you come down on him? He's the one making the frost to float in the air. I used to fall by her bed in Going-to-the-Sun, and I fall by here. Okay by me, okay by her. It's Jackson who tries to get her to feel that's Significant."

"I do try to talk to him."

"Sure you do. You find it easy to dump on me. You're scared to come down on him. I'm going to start throwing my weight around here and get a few rights for me for a change."

"That's something to look forward to, isn't it?"

15

The Champion versus the Hustler

"The hustler is a victim too," Jackson was drawling. "He eventually gets hustled by others."

"So is the champion defeated. Nobody wins all the time.

The hustler accepts that, but the champion doesn't."

They had just been shooting pool, which she had come to learn meant they entered one of their routines. She saw them together as never previously. Sometimes she appreciated the grace, the wit. Other times she felt subtly handled and thwarted and set aside. Other times she felt grossly put down, processed by them. Never in the good times or the bad times of their living together did she feel that she or Dorine was with them as they were with each other. If Phil was not demanding her attention or Jackson subtly commandeering her sexual energies, if one or the other was not trying to monopolize her before the other's gaze, they were playing together before her, in back of her, off where she could not quite grasp the issue or its outcome.

"Who's winning for, if there is no public? The hustler has only himself for an audience. The champion wants to win, the hustler to survive. You can't tell me those goals are equivalent," Jackson said.

"It's a question of butchery versus art. A question of hidden strength. If you're so insecure you can only enjoy your victory if it's public, there you are. But with the hustler, the style is as important as the outcome. It's the setting up of a relationship with the mark. The third time is more meaningful than the first. . . ."

They went on that way, yet Phil cared as much about beating Jackson at pool or whatever the game of the week was, as did Jackson did about beating him. Perhaps if she had had more brothers or been closer to Mark . . . Mark's relationship to Lionel had been bumpy. Lionel gave his favor to Mark and withdrew it for reasons of mood that only sometimes intersected with something Mark had done right or wrong. It was a household of shifting alliances. Mark and Allegra would combine against her, when she played heavy Mama. Mark and she would bully Allegra and refuse to take her along. Allegra and she would make common cause against Mark, who hogged the bathroom and left it dirty.

But Phil and Jackson reinforced each other even while they competed. Between them was high tension, playful relaxation, and no touching. She doubted they discussed her except in joking; yet her nightmare was that they would unite against her. That nightmare swelled from the way they would close ranks to punish her, to refuse, to tease in a way that passed closer and closer to unbearable pain. She wanted to be fully herself with each, but she felt kept in her place as they shared her, as they fought over who was really the smarter, more talented, sexier, more dominant male in the family.

What she called friendship with Beth, as they came closer, was a different animal than how they were with the guys from Going-to-the-Sun. When Ryan moved out, he had left behind a small black and white television that didn't work. Jackson and Rick, who had worked in a radio shop, spent all of two Saturdays taking the set apart. Now after a fashion it worked. Often she wished the volume did not work so well. Now the guys from Going-to-the-Sun would come to watch basketball or football and they would sit by the set drinking and betting and contradicting each other loudly. The main thrust of the football afternoons and the basketball evenings lay in that verbal game surrounding every play dimly visible on the grainy twelve-inch picture. Alone with her, Phil had contempt for jocks and fans.

"It's training to the American male to get your rocks off watching two guys pound each other, or twelve guys pound each other. You learn to let the peasants do the dying for you on the evening news. Shut up and take it, shut up and watch it, shut up and let it be done. They're the experts. Beat your palms together when they give you the signal." Yet Phil shouted and groaned and argued statistics with the rest of them.

Sometimes the game would be rained out and there would be nothing to watch but movies about the R.A.F. or Roy Rogers. Then they would get so stoned they could not speak coherently but fell dimly into giggles. As well as they all knew one another—Phil and Jackson and Terry and Rick and John—they could not seem to sit and talk, but must everyone be elsewhere, looking at something besides each other: if not the set, then the inside of their heads.

She tended to clear out and go over to Tech Square, where she had a desk. If Dorine was around they might go for a walk or to see a friend. "Why do they get into that?" she asked Dorine. "It's so mindless, I can't recognize them. My father wasn't into those sport rituals at all."

"Well, do you think your father was some kind of ideal?"

Miriam was startled. "Of course not. I see what you mean. His manhood was never in question because he was always

standing firmly on top of my mother and us. Maybe it's better
they should have their rituals."

"I just wish John wouldn't come. 'Hi,' he says, 'how're
you doing,' and goes in and sits down in front of the set.
Let's go see Sally."

Sally was pregnant and going to have the baby, although
the father had skipped out. She did not have enough money
to go to a doctor who would let her have natural childbirth.
Since she was big on doing things the natural way, like having
the baby to begin with, she had decided to have the baby at
home. She said, where she came from, lot of women had their
babies at home and they didn't make a big deal of it. Dorine
and Miriam were frightened of the possibilities, so about every
two weeks they went and argued with her for a while. All
that happened was that Sally got bigger and stayed just as
stubborn.

Sally was afraid that if she went into the hospital they
would take the baby away from her—maybe they would
put her under a drug and make her sign a paper—because she
was not married and had no money and did not intend to
put down any father's name at all. She didn't want her baby to
be registered or get a birth certificate. Then her baby would
never have to go to school and be taught to be stupid and if
he was a boy he would never be drafted. She had a fantasy
about bringing her baby up on her own, getting back to the
country where they would have a small farm and raising him
hidden away where he would grow into a beautiful person.
Sometimes she talked of taking her baby back home to Tennessee, but then she would say she just couldn't go back.

Sally never came to see them where they lived because of
what Jackson had said to her boy friend when she found out
she was pregnant. Sally could barely read and write; she had
only gone to school part time and had left school in the tenth
grade. "How would she know?" Jackson had said, and then,
"Well, it's the oldest trick in the world, I guess they don't
have to learn that one out of a book." Sally had a room in
the house of a married couple who were too strung out to be
of use. Miriam thought she could have three babies and they
wouldn't notice.

If it was a down to go and see Sally, it was usually an up to
visit Beth. Beth was still living in a funny dim room in a
dingy warren in Back Bay, ugly and crowded with books and

yet cozy. On the walls were notes Beth made to herself: NOBODY LOVES A DOORMAT, THEY JUST WALK ON OVER. THE MIRROR IS THE FIRST DAILY TRAP. CHICK—small, fuzzy, helpless, stupid, cute, lays eggs and in the end gets eaten. CAT—predator, active, alert, tough, independent, mean, quick. The language says one is predator and the other is prey. LOVE IS WHAT WOMEN DO INSTEAD OF KNOWING OR FIGHTING OR MAKING OR INVENTING.

"That's a new one." Miriam pointed to the wall. Every so often Beth painted over a section she got tired of. " 'Love is what women do instead . . .' Do you really believe that?"

"Sure," Beth said. "Don't you?"

Beth was finely made, small-boned, small-featured and colored in pastels, yet she seemed sure of her own identity. She seemed to have her own cry that she uttered through the confusions they all lived in.

"No! I wouldn't love more if I did nothing else—there'd be less of me to love with!"

"But you'd think it was even more important than you do now." Beth was sitting on her bed cross-legged in green corduroy pants and an orange sweater that did not really go with the pants and made her skin look sallow: no one with freckles should wear that shade of orange. It looked large and probably had been given to her. It was the waif in Beth. Miriam was always bringing her things too. She would have liked to show Beth how to dress but had somehow never managed to get onto that subject.

"Loving is just how I react, interact with another."

"Nonsense," Beth said cheerfully. She had a way of contradicting without malice that Miriam enjoyed. "What's called loving is part sexual service—mutual or not. Part of what I call life-support functions: all those daily jobs that make the house to function like cleaning the toilet and making food to appear and garbage to vanish and beds to be usable and floors to be passable and clothes to be wearable. That assure the house has in it what's used for blowing the nose and making the headache go away and putting salve on the sore thumb. Part is plain body servant. Part is emotional self-titillation. Playing dramas with, around, under another person to make you feel alive. That's what I see people meaning when they talk about love. That's what I used to mean."

"That's not loving, that's just living with somebody,"

Dorine said. "You can do all that and not be in love."

"Right, but why? Why sign that contract without pay, just for keep? Because you say to yourself you're in love. If you lived with another woman, would you take on doing all that?"

"Dorine does it all in our household, already."

"And aren't you a little bit in love?" Beth smiled at Dorine.

"It's just that I admire him a whole lot. I know he doesn't care about me."

"Jackson? Oh dear." Dorine's face hurt Miriam. Dorine's heart-shaped face with its look of resignation. Miriam saw Dorine suddenly as waiting on Jackson's attention, as waiting hopelessly, passively for him to like her, for him to grant her dignity as a person. It was seeing in Dorine the caricature of her own waiting. It was feeling the iron pain of wanting, wanting, wanting him to love her.

She began to cry and for a moment she could only sob while tears ran out. Beth and Dorine were staring. She could not even speak to reassure. She could only weep and weep, heavily. It seemed to her that her pain went deep into her childhood, plunging harsh roots into her earliest sense of self. It was the waiting for the good morning when Sonia would suddenly lift her back into her lap, the only loved baby again. It was the waiting for the good evening when Lionel would suddenly beam on her and love her as his own darling girl, would suddenly see how good she was and love her. It was the constant striving to prove herself worthy, the constant struggle to win the love that must surely come, that was surely promised her. It was Jackson's enigmatic face that must surely open, his eyes that surely must finally see her and love her and redeem her and accept her as his woman.

Beth came and put her arms around her, light arms enfolding. As Miriam sat in the kitchen chair, Beth was leaning forward over her, stroking her face and hair. Strange to feel Beth's softness. Not like a mother holding. Gentle firm hand on her hair and cheek. Slowly the tears eased.

"I don't know what got into me, to make me do that." Miriam scrubbed her eyes gently, blew her nose hard. "Really. It wasn't what you said, Dorine."

Beth backed off and went to sit on the bed. "You do know why you cried!"

"Oh, sometimes he gets to me. Sometimes I wish I'd never

met him." Even as she said that a desolation crept in her nerves. To live without him . . . bleakness, emptiness.

"I don't understand it. I like him," Beth said. "He's obviously a much better man for you than Phil? Can't you see that?"

"Leave off your broad didactic manner for the rest of the afternoon, would you, Bethie? Please?"

Dorine laughed nervously. "He's not always nice, Beth. He has a streak of meanness. I guess every man does."

"But you don't have a streak of meanness in you?" Beth was sitting lotus position, something she had recently learned to do.

"Not the same way. . . ." Dorine wrinkled her nose, surprised by the question. "I have bitchy days. I get fed up, especially at work."

"Do you act mean, then?"

"If I did, I'd be fired. You have the same kind of job, you know what I mean. They keep telling me to smile."

"So you come home and take it out at home?"

"No . . . I get depressed. Sometimes I just want to go to bed and lie there and never get up. I hate myself then."

"You turn it inward. Just as I do. But I'm trying to learn to get mad. Even if I can't express it directly, I want to know I'm mad. It's hard for me to express anger; all my life I've been trained to turn it inside."

"I don't have any trouble getting mad," Miriam said. She was feeling more herself. She was ashamed of crying. She had exposed parts of herself that were not appropriate. She spoke firmly, to make up for what had slipped out. "I had an interview the other day and this glib psych type started telling me how I could only expect a certain level of job since I'm a woman, implying what an unfeminine thing it was to have expectations that I might be paid what I'm worth or want to do something technically interesting. I figured I wasn't about to get a job there anyhow, so I let him have it."

"I wonder if you find it so easy to get mad when it counts?" Beth looked at her, head perched to one side. "I used to get mad sometimes at my husband. Then I learned not to. Because he was bigger and stronger and he could punish me, he could make it cost too much."

"I'm not married to either of them. I'm independent. Look, I'm not in the same bind other women get into—maybe I've been lucky. My work is at the center of my life, and no matter what happens with Phil or with Jackson, I go on doing that."

"That's true." Dorine sighed, holding out her hand as if to signal a halt. "I envy you that, I really do. What can being in the typing pool mean to me? It's a burning waste of time. A machine could type bills and invoices all day. Most of the girls, they're around my age and they hope to get married, or they're older and back to work. The kids are in school and the family needs the money, they can't get along on what the old man makes. It's not a salary you can live on. You can't have a life on it, not an apartment, not a car."

Beth said, "I'm trying to make a center to my life that isn't a man. My job's not quite as bad as yours, but it's nonsense too. But I'm trying to make a center in my own self."

"I don't know what that means," Miriam said. "But you seem to me to know who you are."

"Not yet. I'm trying. So much of it is undoing things. Finding that I'm not what people told me I was. I don't know, Miriam, maybe you don't have the same difficulties as Dorine with men, but I can't understand about Jackson. You should be so right together."

"Why don't you ask him?"

"I have. You know how he can play off his silences. I come away thinking what a boob I am to dare to ask. Or else I think I got an answer and it isn't till I try to say it over to myself I realize I got nothing."

"*Eppis.* Welcome to the club."

"Oh, he says some things. He says you won't be a real woman. He says you're afraid to be a real woman with him."

A shield buckled in her and she cringed. Scalding anger. How could that son of a bitch say that when she tried so hard with him? Real woman her ass. Scalding jealousy he would say that to Beth. "You know, if I ever said to him he wasn't a real man, he'd never touch me again. But he can say that about me. God help you if you're made of flesh and blood instead of moonshine and you don't exactly fit those idols he hauls around."

Beth leaned forward anxiously. "I didn't mean to hurt you. I don't ever understand what people mean when they say things like that. They're a real good way of putting each other down, that's all I know."

"Sometimes when you talk with him, I feel a little jealous. Isn't that silly?" Miriam said.

Beth looked stricken. "But he talks to me as if I'm a child. He's patronizing."

"At least he talks to you," Dorine said. "He just listens to my troubles like a shrink and nods his head."

"Bethie, I don't know why he makes me jealous. I'm never really jealous of Phil, who gives me six times the cause."

"Maybe you don't love Phil," Dorine said.

"Don't say that. I do. It's a different kind of loving, but I love him. I don't feel he's holding back on me the way Jackson does." Strange too to think that they would never sit around, the three of them, talking about Phil in the same way they did Jackson. Phil did not play the father, the judge, the external patriarchal conscience. "What Phil is, he shares with me. Maybe if you feel a man is really with you, then you don't get jealous when he's with someone else. But if he's not giving you what you want, maybe you mind everything he gives anybody else, even the time of day."

"I wouldn't know," Beth said. "Mostly I've been interested in men who hadn't anything to do with me. Most people don't notice me anyhow."

"I was sick with jealousy after John broke up with me. Sick." Dorine closed her eyes, lifting her face blindly. "I used to lie in bed knowing he was upstairs with her. I could have shared him with her, I really could, if only I'd felt he still cared about me. But to be thrown out like that. It made me feel used. That I was a thing he wanted and then got tired of. When he comes over with Rick, I still can't bear it. He acts as if nothing had ever happened between us, he just says hi and gives me a vacant look. He doesn't even see me. He doesn't care that I always leave."

"You shouldn't live there, I think sometimes," Beth said.

"But I want Dorine with me. I'd be lonely without her. And she doesn't have enough money to live by herself."

"Where would I go?" Dorine shrugged. "It's better with Miriam in the house. Being the only woman was bad. Ryan used to talk as if I was beneath contempt. Chlorine, he called me. I wouldn't go back to Going-to-the-Sun for anything. That was bottom."

"I don't know . . . I've been thinking," Beth said. "I've liked living alone. But now I'm thinking maybe I'd like to live in a house with other women."

"Just women?" Dorine made a face. "Like a dormitory."

"If they were women you liked? It doesn't mean you couldn't see men. In a house with other women, you couldn't end up like you were in Going-to-the-Sun. . . . Anyhow, I'm not trying to do it this week. But it's on my mind."

"But why?" Miriam asked her. "I think of you as being satisfied by yourself, being complete. I can't imagine living with a bunch of other women."

"Why? Why shouldn't we help each other sometimes, instead of always giving and giving and taking care of men and making them feel strong? I have nightmares too. I'm scared too. Going on from day to day trying to make myself be the kind of person I want to be, I need support. I want help. . . . I daydream too much. I make a new world in my head. I'm strong and heroic inside, where it's easy. . . . I've been going to a group of women that meet together at M.I.T. and talk once a week and that's made me think a lot about other women. . . . That, if we have the same problems, maybe we can help each other too. . . ."

As they went back home on the subway, Miriam puzzled why she disliked Beth's idea so much. Perhaps if Beth lived in a house with other women she would have less time to be her friend. She saw more of Dorine, but she cared far more for Beth. She admired Beth, which was rare for her to feel for another woman. Beth was different but equal. A desire to please Beth rode around with her always, along with the desire to please Phil and Jackson. She would buy Beth little gifts of a scarf or a bag of organic figs or some apricot leather to eat, just as she brought Phil poetry or wild shirts. For Jackson she bought books about ideas that people were arguing about—books by biologists explaining war as mammalian aggression, books inventing categories of social consciousness—and tobacco for his pipe.

To give presents was to tell a person you thought of him when you were someplace else. Beth enjoyed getting presents, as did Phil. Funny that they did not get along, when they both had certain direct childlike traits she liked. With Jackson, she would have to wait patiently and see if the item appeared in use or was dispatched to the limbo at the bottom of his closet. Then she blessed Phil and Beth for being able to say when they liked something. To ask for what you wanted, to be glad when you got it and sorry or angry when you didn't: how could she think that was a trait of childhood? Surely not of hers. Nobody in her family had ever been able to say "I want," "Love me," "Help me." Like Jackson. Silent struggle. Did she think that was more real, deep in herself?

"What sign are you?" Dorine was asking, and she made herself pay attention. "Your birthday was July, right? You're a Leo. That's a strong, fiery sign. That's you all right!"

"What sign are you?" Miriam asked politely. The subway train came out of the side of Beacon Hill past the Charles Street jail in the fading light, across the wide river. Plunged into the ground under M.I.T.

"I'm a Libra. Ruled by Venus, we like to make peace. We're easy to influence, since we see both sides of a question. . . . You make faces, Miriam, but I'm more like Libra and you're more like a Leo. Phil's a Pisces. Each of us resembles our own signs."

"We pick out those things that match and drop the rest. When's your birthday, anyhow?"

"A week from next Tuesday. I'll be twenty-two."

She had almost let it slip by. She felt a pang of guilt at not caring enough for Dorine. She would get her something nice. And the men: they must do something. She would talk to them.

The Fall Joint Computer Conference was held in New York and she went, job hunting. Staying with Lionel set her teeth on edge, but she had no choice. He complained to her incessantly about the young, meaning young women, how demanding and intolerant and immoral and spendthrift they all were. She could only suspect his recent romantic efforts had soured. He seemed puzzled and a bit listless. He kept urging her to come oftener to see him, though he asked her next to nothing about her life. It was too sad to confront with her old anger.

At the Fall Joint not much turned up. It was a poor time to be inexperienced and job hunting. The high point was when she maneuvered shyly up to Wilhelm Graben in the lobby, and he recognized her. After a pause of perhaps sixty seconds, he recognized her and even remembered her name. Graben was absolutely the most brilliant teacher she had ever had and a star in the field. For five minutes he chatted with her and even gave her some advice on her thesis, until they were interrupted. Then he squeezed her hand, saying in the Viennese accent that he never had when he was lecturing on technical matters, "So charming to see you again. Miss Berg, yes? Come down to Washington and I'll find a niche for you." That was an empty flourish and she knew it, but still she walked away in a glow of visibility. Even if she couldn't get a decent job, she was good enough so Wilhelm Graben remembered her.

The only job offer she got was from a shaky company in New Jersey. The idea of commuting every morning from New York or of living in New Jersey seemed equally depressing. And that would represent giving up on their struggle as a family. That was almost a tempting fantasy for a couple of days, but she could not do it.

Phil was tending bar. She was trying to decide whether she should work on her last paper for a class, get out her thesis, or read a journal. She wandered out to Jackson, studying at his desk, to get an idea of his plans for the evening. But he sat scowling at the door set on legs, closed on himself. She could work well in total oblivion to anybody on earth. Still she could snap from that work to attend to Phil or Dorine or him. She could break her concentration to let in light and sound and air, then return to work when the other's need was met, the problem solved or at least acknowledged.

But standing by his desk, she felt him making her embody the forces of chaos seeking to break through into the neat world of his studying. Standing there trying to find out if he wanted to sleep with her that night, all became tense and ridiculous, yet she could not shatter the web of myth. She was soft to his hard, warm to his cold, moist to his dry, dark to his light: they were total Yin and Yang in the living room. She felt herself becoming Irrationality and Distraction and the Temptress.

"You're an inborn Calvinist!" she shrieked at him.

"Any Calvinist would insist there are no other kind."

"Calvinist! Platonist! Spoiled priest! You just want to diddle your ideas. You're afraid admitting I'm human would wreck your damned hierarchy, your scheme of the universe! Why can't you work without erecting barriers around yourself?"

"Not all of us possess your ability to read and write standing on your head fucking, bitch. Now let me be."

"Ever notice that I insult you with idea names? When you want to insult me, you call me sex names."

"I am a traditionalist in my insults. While you stop to invent a weapon that will serve the occasion."

"I detect bias in your description, friend."

"I am not your friend, I am your lover. But not tonight."

"Jackson, how can you be the second, if you aren't the first? That's the whole trouble, I think."

"That *is* part of the trouble, you think too much. Talk too much too. Now clear out. If I get this done, I might even get a couple hours' sleep before I go to work in the morning."

He had a teaching fellowship. He liked teaching but would not admit it, pretending to find it intolerably boring. He worked hard on his classes some days and others he went off unprepared and ill-tempered. She could not remain standing by his desk turned into a petitioner, turned into a temptation. She went off furious, slamming the door of her room and hearing it echo in his head as proof of her irrationality and overemotional responses. She wrung her hands and paced, kicking off her shoes so he would not hear her.

How could he turn her around so? She had gone to him to get the evening clear. Now she was too angry to work. They both, both of them, wanted her at their total beck and call like an instant houri, but stuck up their backs and went lumpy with stubbornness if she attempted to get any commitment about time or arrangements, so that she might manage the ninety-two things she was also doing. How they turned things around, how they turned her around. Her anger was sour in her mouth.

When she woke up that taste still coated her mouth. She had overslept. Dorine was gone, Jackson was gone and she was late. In the dirty bathroom mirror misted from her shower and splattered with Phil's lather from a couple of days before, she looked at her morning face and brooded on her pores. She was twenty-four. Her face, was it not already coarsening? She squeezed brutally the pores in her nose, peered at the fine lines beginning to net her eyes. Soft skin under the lower lid. Twenty-four. At twenty-four Sonia was teaching and had just met Lionel. Now her mother was dead, dead. Would she die young? Sonia had not seemed young. She did not feel young, examining her chin in the filmy mirror. She wanted to weep for herself with no mama and aging already, with pores gaping like the mouths of graves. Aging —she too would age, every day she would age more and more and soon she would be ugly. Maybe defeat ran in the maternal milk, the maternal blood from generation to generation. This day she tasted her defeat and had no stomach for breakfast. Her life seemed to grow more painful and more difficult from week to week, more demanding. She was giving, yes, pouring out blood and milk and energy, loving and trying to help. And in herself she was starving. She was wretched.

She marched from the bathroom to dress. She was to go on the machine that night with a new program to debug: for hours she would not think about her life. She would not think about anyone, least of all herself. She would exist in her intelligence and those bright spaces of algorithm, her vast game with the machine. She was programing in LISP, a fascinating language. Only work seemed clean and firm this morning, only work gave pleasure. What was this woman-thing of loving and bleeding? He said she was not a real woman, ah, damn him rotten: he refused to love her. Yet only three nights before, him against her, in her. How he came into her. A wild loose ache remembering. Riding and riding and falling. With him she lost her mind a little whenever it was good. She rode off the end of her control into free-floating, free-falling gyres loosely open. She could not deny him. Love, she called out, love! It must come out all right, it must. They would work it out. She was trying so hard. It had to work out, it had to!

Phil promised on Tuesday to get Dorine some little thing for her birthday. On Thursday he was still assuring Miriam that he'd do it. Saturday: "Sure, sure, don't get on my back. I said I'd do it. What's the fucking hurry?" Monday she bought Dorine a pair of earrings and negligently Phil agreed to give them to Dorine the next day.

But Jackson would not, would not. "She is not my . . . I'm not responsible for her. She isn't mine."

"But it's her birthday. She lives here."

"Did I ask her to? She lives here because of you, don't you know that? She lives in your shadow, she clings to you."

"Jackson, you like so much to play the kind counselor. You listen and listen to her. But it's yourself you're paying attention to, your role. It's yourself you're caring about."

"What do you think you do? You think you care for her?"

"Not as much as I should. But I'm trying to."

"Bullshit! Did I give you a birthday present?"

"Yes. Oh, love, of course, I haven't forgotten."

"Then you have nothing to complain about. Dorine is not mine. I'm not going to act like an ass to make her feel like the birthday kid."

She made Dorine a cake. It was the first cake she had ever made from scratch, a chocolate cake with coconut icing. It took two hours to make and every mixing bowl in the kitchen, but she had fun. The cake was lopsided and the icing ran down onto the plate, but it tasted terrific. It tasted much better than she could remember Sonia's cakes tasting. It was just about the best chocolate cake she had ever had. She'd taken the recipe from the *Globe* and made up the frosting from what she remembered her mother or her grandma doing.

Dorine liked the sweater, and the earrings that were from Phil, and the whole cake got eaten. Every last slice. Jackson ate about half of it himself. "Chocolate cake is the only ideal cake," he said. "All other cakes would be chocolate cakes if they could."

After Dorine had shut her door, they both followed Miriam into her room.

"Well, well, and that were a noice cake, weren't it?" Phil sprawled on the bed, speaking with a fake British accent he affected when he particularly wanted to send her against the wall. "A bit dear, though. All that grinning and bowing and scraping we had to go through."

"Does it hurt you to be nice for an evening? Does it hurt that much?"

"The lady says we aren't nice," Jackson said loftily. "The lady is very, very nice. She wants us to work very hard to be nice so we may be worthy of the lady."

"Now look, you wouldn't do what I wanted anyhow, so why don't we forget it? I made the cake 'cause I wanted to. I didn't notice you refusing to eat it."

"See, I said it was an expensive cake," Phil drawled. "Want me to go screw her now, for a present too?"

"I see you mean to make it expensive to me, that you were both civil for a couple of hours."

"My man Jackson, what's civil mean?"

"The opposite of militant. It's a kind of service, the civil service. You pass a test to get in and you die to get out. Like marriage, I think."

"Thank your lucky stars, Jackson my man, because the lady could have made a bigger cake and asked us to hide in the filling. To step out kicking and singing 'The Eyes of Texas Are Upon You' or other old favorites of sister acts."

"You have a pretty good act going on top of my head." She leaned on her dresser facing them, Jackson sitting with his palms together upright in her desk chair, Phil sprawled on the bed. Phil was on speed or something that overwound him. His eyes glittered, his fingers jumped. Jackson had his mask-face on, his hands in an attitude of prayer.

"Whereas you prefer to do a juggling act." Jackson took out his pipe, tamping it on the arm of her chair.

"She aspires to a trained dog act," Phil said. "Poodles are easy to train, I hear."

"You want to just use her as you each see fit. Housemaid. Shoulder. Footstool. I'm not supposed to see and I'm not supposed to care, as long as you treat me a shade better!"

"The lady throws knives," Jackson remarked. "This is a versatile lady. And she doesn't feel appreciated!"

"It's not trained dogs, it's trained seals. They're the ones who applaud when you throw them a chocolate cake. They make nice fur coats too. Do you think you'd make a nice fur coat, Jackson?"

"We both know you would not, Boyle, because you're too thin-skinned."

"I don't know, dahling. I've been told I tan rather nicely." Phil was now into his equally obnoxious queen parody. "You just think you'd make a better coat because you're so wonderfully *hairy!* With a bath mat fore and aft, you brute. Think you're Kong himself."

"Look, the lady has turned her back on our act. Do you think we offended her? Something coarse we did or said?"

"Never!" Phil lifted one buttock and farted.

"Not us." Jackson made himself belch cavernously.

She would not turn. She leaned on her dresser, close to tears but too angry. A couple of rumpled scarves lay there, her extra lenses, a mirror, and lens fluid. A bottle of hand lotion and big hairpins. Her comb colored like a tortoise shell and a brush with wooden handle. The hand lotion promised that it would restore youthful softness to hands damaged by sun, wind, or detergents. Which reminded her that the dishes were not done and she could hardly expect Dorine to wash them after her own birthday celebration.

She walked out between them to the kitchen and began gathering the dishes. As she had expected, they slowly followed and quickly melted away when they saw what she was doing. She was still angry as she ran the water and the first thing she did was break a glass that slipped out of her hands in the sink. She had to feel in the soapy water for the jagged pieces.

All she wanted them to do was to be kind to Dorine. But they transformed that into some disgusting process of genteel manipulation. How could any woman resist feeling guilty when accused by even one man she loved? She was miserable. The way they united to punish her made her feel helpless. She could not defend herself, she could not explain. When they went into one of their routines she only wanted to run from them.

It was unfair. She was trying to get on better with women. Living with two men who constantly pushed and pulled on her, she felt a sharp need for women she could talk to about her life. It healed her guilt at not pleasing her men utterly, gave her a frame of reference drawn from other women's experiences. But her growing friendships with women got in the way of maintaining friendships with men. She had more trouble getting along with the men from Going-to-the-Sun. Before, she had compartmentalized her reactions. In one pigeonhole was how they treated her, in another was how they acted with men, and off by itself was how they treated other women. Then she had used to judge them as they judged each other, by how they treated other men, and of course how they acted to her. She remembered agreeing with Phil that John was a kind person: he was kind to Phil, certainly. He was kind to men and dogs and children, he was even pleasant with what he'd call strong women, though he never got involved with them. Other women he used up like a case of beer and then turned mean. Now she could not separate those judgments. She could not say any longer that John was kind. Even with Phil and Jackson she found it harder and harder to ignore the way they behaved with the women she liked.

She felt that this night they hated her, and she felt hateful. Her anger was a sharp taste in her mouth, hot and bitter as horseradish. It was hard not to want to blame Dorine for getting her into trouble with her men, yet Dorine had done nothing. It had been her idea. And her conscience pushed her to try to treat Dorine better and secure better treatment for her from them. She felt defeated and wronged and wrong, and still to blame, still to blame standing with all the day's dishes to do and her index finger bleeding into the dishwater, as seemed fitting. She hoped she would bleed all over every dish.

16

You Are What You Eat

"So now you'll have to get up every morning for work too," Dorine said across the breakfast table. "Regular old five-day-a-week grind. That should be a bringdown."

Out of politeness Miriam agreed. It would have been unfair to Dorine to insist that she did not dread going to work, that the long hunt for a reasonable job had depressed her far more. She was curious about Logical Systems Development, Inc., where she had at last landed a research job. "It's not one of those corporations run like a programing factory. It seemed pretty informal. Besides, how can any job hang you up if you stay loose about it? Nothing's permanent."

"But you're planning to get there on time. I see you looking at your watch."

"I'm new. I figure I'm lucky to get the job."

"So what's the difference whether you get there at nine-thirty because you're afraid to lose your job, or if you get there at nine because you have to punch in?"

"But did you notice the initials? L.S.D. I figured, what the hell, I'd make a crack about it. The guy interviewing me said they named it that for a joke, they had to give it a corporate name. They're all more research types than business types."

The Logical office shared a small building on Prospect with dentists. Indeed, she could hear the whirring of a drill through the wall by her desk. After sharing a cubbyhole with three other students, the offices seemed luxurious with carpeting underfoot and a big desk of her own in an office she shared with only one man; it was even furnished with a blackboard. The inner partitions in the space that Logical rented were made of wallboard and did not mute the flow of sound, but she was used to cramped quarters and a high noise level. The walls were a strange color that Jaime, a young man she worked with, called "spleen green." The carpeting gave her little shocks whenever she touched a metal doorknob. Her office mate, Fred Weathering, thought the office over-crowded. He muttered that when he was hired they had told him Logical would be moving out to Route 128 and a new building. She hoped they would not move. Now she could bicycle to work, and when the weather got even worse she would hitchhike.

Her office mate was balding around a scraggly brown beard that fell into two wispy points. He was married and had two children with a third on the way, and was just moving his family from a house in a tract in Woburn to a bigger house in a more expensive development in Lincoln. His desk bristled with photographs of his children.

Just about everyone had long hair or a beard or both, although some of them wore tweedy jackets and some of them dressed in leather and some wore jeans. Only the president, Abe Tyler, was confined to mere sideburns, although the secretaries were sleek and soignée and wore make-up, and the only other woman in the place who had a technical job dressed like the secretaries, department store snappy. Miriam was a bit outstanding in that setting. She was grateful for having been hired and determined not to develop the legend that had tagged her at school. When Fred asked where she lived, she said she shared an apartment with friends.

Although the technical staff looked hairy enough to have had the usual experiences of being hassled in the streets, threatened by police, pushed around, she could tell from their incessant talk that their life styles were pretty much suburban, with an overlay of hip clothes and dope and rock music. Most of them were married, most of them had children, most of them were buying homes and furnishing them way beyond their incomes. They spent warily, the worn copies of *Consumer Reports* circulating, but they were always buying something. They spent hours each day wandering with coffee cups through each other's offices—Chemex coffee made fresh by the secretaries every two hours—to trade puzzles and games and gossip as often as real work problems.

What had drawn her to Logical was that it was not a businessman's company at all. It had been started by and belonged to research types. Abe Tyler and Dick Babcock and Neil Stone had got together two years before to create a place where they could do the kind of work they were interested in without a lot of pressure from business-oriented types: a place where they could function in a good loose creative environment for the development of their science. Logical was an exciting company with a lot of good people who'd been drawn by their names—they were all of some reputation, especially Tyler, although of the directors only Stone had his doctorate. The relaxed atmosphere and the chance to do work that was far out technically attracted people too.

She would be working on a dynamite project that would be into pattern recognition and heuristic programing techniques, in the direction of artificial intelligence. It dovetailed beautifully with what she had been doing on her thesis. It was as far as possible from the dead-end programing jobs she had been offered. It was a chance to do something new and interesting that might even advance the state of the art. And she was to be paid for it a daydream salary, starting at ten thousand dollars a year. On that kind of money she should save half of it. Then she could quit or take a leave of absence and travel. She could make true all those imaginings with Phil. They could have a place at the shore the very next summer where everything would be clean and golden and baked by the sun, and Phil would look healthy again. He would be out of the city, away from Finnegan's, away from dealers, away from the bad scenes where he talked himself out instead of writing.

The compiler they were building with its sophisticated language would be a tool for people in the sciences who wanted to use computers but did not understand them, who would never have the time to waste learning an alien discipline. This sort of compiler would make it possible for a person to describe problems to a computer without being terribly precise, and the machine could work out the best way of proceeding. Whenever she thought of the possibilities inherent in the project, she felt excited, she had the feeling of being on the brink of something vital. It was a good sense, a high tight feeling in her chest. She had been right to wait for something meaningful; she was justified.

Fred was working on the same project and so was Jaime Lesander, a delicate-looking boy—she thought of him as a boy although in fact he must be a year or so older than she was. He looked like a perennial undergraduate with porcelain features under a frizzle of dark blond hair. He was gentle and whimsical and she liked him. He and Fred played Go. Jaime always won but he was willing to play because he kept hoping that Fred's game would improve. He brought Fred books in strange English, including a book of aphorisms translated literally from the Japanese.

Their boss, if that was the right word since he was generally less authoritarian than Fred, was Neil Stone. It was the custom for everyone to call him Neil, never Mr. Stone. He wore a close curly dark brown beard. His eyes were hazel with a lot of green in them—or perhaps the walls did that. He wore steel-rimmed glasses and rumpled sports shirts that seemed too large. Every morning he came in looking brisk and neat. It was one of his endearing characteristics that within an hour of beginning serious work his tie was awry, his shirttails out, his shoelaces untied, his fly unzipped, his cuff button fallen off. When he had to go off to negotiate a contract or represent the company, Abe's secretary Efi gave him an inspection and grooming. He was slender, wiry, of medium height. He was soft-spoken and moved quietly. Sometimes he would walk into her office and be standing there watching her before she was aware.

Once she heard Fred on the phone to his wife call someone The Cat, and she knew at once it was Neil. That made her smile. He was clean, quiet, graceful and quick as a cat. She even thought she saw a bit of the cat about his eyes, tilted slightly. He was still ruddy from the summer. His nose was long and aquiline; she wondered if he was Jewish. He had that nose Mark glared at in the mirror, her mother's nose. A shade more marked than her own. He was all in all a pleasant-looking man, in spite of his untidiness and the air he had of being about to lose a shoe or his pants. She especially liked when he smiled suddenly and his even white teeth showed in his beard. He had a good smile. His face crinkled up, his eyes danced, and his teeth gleamed.

Only his hands were nervous. Often while he was talking his hands would tap, tap with a pencil, with a piece of chalk, with a ruler on the desk. Or they would walk over each other like long-legged spiders. He was very controlled, his low voice, his measured graceful movements, his explanations famous for their precision. If he said there were six points to be covered he never stopped with five. There was an elegance to his presentations that pleased her aesthetically: he was a good man at the board. Logical had a weekly seminar and his were always heavily attended. She enjoyed their Monday meetings to discuss the project. He was very controlled, except for that nervous vitality leaking out through his thin restless hands.

"The truth is," she told Beth, "far from it being a drag, I'm happier at work than any place else."

"Things aren't better at home, uh?"

"Not better. It isn't what I wanted for us. I thought I'd be able to have a good relationship with each of them. But that isn't happening. They're sharing me. I don't know . . . I suppose it takes a long time to work out a good relationship with anybody and longer with three or four than two."

"But it's not getting better?"

"Maybe I'm too demanding. They both think so. I don't know what to think any more. I'm the medium but they're the message—that's what it feels like."

"Change your mind about living in a house with me and some other women?"

"Beth, what do you want that for? You're in a women's liberation group now, right? Isn't that enough support?"

"It's okay, but it's just a consciousness-raising group that meets once a week. They're students. They have different problems than I do, and it's no use pretending I don't feel that. They have families taking care of them, they have boy friends, and they'll have professions. None of them are alone the way I am. They just plain can command more money, more help. Some of them give lip service to feeling close to women who work, and then they come out with things about organizing secretaries and say things that show they think secretaries are stupid and naïve. . . . No, I don't feel I get that much help from them. I get frightened sometimes, I feel as if I'm fighting the whole world and I must be wrong because everything, everything in the streets and the books and the media, all says I'm wrong. I need a warm place too!"

One evening in middle November when Dorine called the hospital, she was told that Lennie had been released. Upset, Dorine spent several hours speculating why he hadn't let her know before she got up the nerve to call his mother's apartment. Lennie was there and she told him she'd hitch down to see him the next weekend.

Sunday night Dorine came back with a temperature. "I'm sick of myself," was all she would say. Other times she said she had caught a bad cold in the November rain. She did not go to work Monday or Tuesday but stayed in bed. Miriam brought her a radio to listen to WBCN and made soup and tea and toast, carrying breakfast and supper in on a tray. Dorine was collapsed, often weeping. Perhaps she was sick in order to be cared for. Although she was not really that weak, she would not read or try to sit up. She wanted to go back to her childhood and have her mother tiptoeing in to feel her forehead with a gentle hand, whispering concern about her for a change, instead of whispering to Dorine's father secrets and plans from which she was excluded.

Her throat was raw and her voice husky. It was Wednesday night before she wanted to talk about what had happened. "He's out of the hospital, all right. Got a job already."

"In New York?"

Dorine nodded. Her heart-shaped face lolled against the heaped pillows. Her hair was matted with sweat. "His aunt got him a job in the display department at Ohrbach's."

"He isn't coming back then? Does he want you to go to New York?"

"For what?" Dorine let her lids shut. "He's living at home and he's got a girl already. He used to go out with her sister. The sister's married and she brought Shirley to the hospital."

"Is he involved with her already? Are you sure?"

Dorine's eyes opened slightly. "So, he should wait? He's changed cities, so he changes women. He says she's sweet. She'll pose for him and worry about him. After he moves out into an apartment, she'll come and cook and do his wash. What do I care?"

"Dorine, what happened? Was he cold to you?"

"He came over where I was staying with my girl friend. We went to bed. Afterward he talked about Donna, the great love of his life. He isn't in love with Shirley, he isn't even pretending. It made me sick. Why should I go to New York? What does it matter, me or Shirley, we're the same, a piece of ass that takes care. I'm thankful he didn't marry me! He'd never have noticed the difference."

Thursday morning again Dorine did not get up to go to work, and when Miriam returned, Dorine was in bed waiting to be taken care of. Miriam began to be a little frightened. She did not say anything to Jackson, and Phil she could not speak to. He was taking so many things she couldn't even tell what he was on. He had drifted off into a morass where she could not reach him. He was seldom interested in making love, his anger flared out at random gestures, phrases that struck him cross-eyed. Miriam would worry about that tomorrow. For the meantime she had acquired a sick child who would not get up. She called Beth.

Beth came and shut herself up with Dorine. When she came out she said she was going to go ahead and look for a house they could rent: Beth, Sally, Dorine, and Miriam if Miriam wanted, and maybe Gloria from the Computer Center.

"But what has that got to do with it?" Miriam asked plaintively. "Lennie doesn't live here any more."

"That's only part. She despises herself. She plays servant. It has to stop." Beth stood with her arms crossed. Her hair was wet from the rain that fell for the fifth straight day, damp and lank against her cheeks. In jeans and an old shirt she looked like a little boy.

"Why do you think setting up a convent is going to help her?"

"Just a women's commune—why does that upset you? If she still wants to see Phil, she can. I don't think she will. I don't think she'll want to see anybody for a while. She has to learn to do things on her own terms."

"Bethie, what are you getting into? Want her to collapse on you? You want to play housemother to Sally and Dorine?"

"I'm not going to take care of them. You do that more than I do, Miriam. You even play mama with me. But I can't be mothered and I won't play mother. I need them to live with. I want to help raise Sally's baby. It's not so farfetched."

"You're lonely?"

"Yes. At night, in the mornings, when I'm down."

Before Beth left she had coffee with Jackson and told him about her idea, asking where she should look for a house. Miriam came and went, making mint tea for Dorine and carrying it on a tray with cinnamon toast. She felt ashamed, how she twinged sometimes when she saw Beth talking with Jackson. She could not help guessing that Jackson must also be drawn to Beth. There was a woman he might love, without all the disadvantages of her life and character. No competition, no history with Phil.

Perhaps she could use her jealousy to refine herself, to confront what she disliked. That night she said to Jackson, "I admire Beth a lot."

He looked at her blankly. "What?"

She repeated herself. "She knows who she is very clearly."

"She's a nice kid," he said without interest. "Young and naïve. Phil was quoting Dylan Thomas the other day, and it came out she thought he was talking about two guys: Dill and Thomas. Like dill pickles, I suppose." Jackson smiled tolerantly.

"She hasn't had an education." Miriam sat up very straight. "She sits in on courses, you know."

"She's a bit young and bugeyed. Just needs a few more times around the track."

"I thought you liked her."

"Sure. She's a nice kid. I guess she has a bit of a crush on me."

Miriam shut up. She should have been relieved. Her jealousy faded into light ashes and blew away. It should be a relief to feel nothing where pain had been. Why wasn't it good? That he could not see Beth at all—she did not think he was covering up, he would perhaps have been willing to let her taste her jealousy longer if he had known—disquieted her. What did Jackson see when he looked at her, Miriam, if he saw so little of Beth? A silly question, yet she could not grasp how he could look right through Beth and see nothing.

Dorine was packing. Phil took notice. But he said nothing to Dorine. To Miriam he said, "Well, Jackson can finally

take his room back and stop being a bloody martyr about sleeping on that cot. That's a lot more comfortable than the bed of nails I camp on." Meaning the sofa in the room with the hi-fi, where in fact Phil never did sleep, since if Jackson was with Miriam, Phil invariably crawled in with Dorine.

No, it was Beth he picked the fight with, when she came to help Dorine finish packing. Dorine had signed the lease. All the others had some gross liability in the eyes of the landlord. Phil had been making jokes about Beth using Dorine to get the house, and Dorine as landlady and janitor extraordinary. But he went at Beth as soon as he could confront her, not about Dorine but about a bombing at Tech Square. A bomb had gone off in the women's john, wrecking some plumbing and files in the office next door and damaging the ceiling.

"Well, I thought it was kind of stupid," Beth said, lowering her head.

"Oh?" Phil smiled broadly, bouncing a little on the balls of his feet. "How would you have done it intelligently? That should prove interesting to hear."

Beth swallowed visibly. Her adam's apple swelled. "Well, first, they didn't make it clear why they did it. . . ."

"I think that would be clear enough. Is there anybody left alive who doesn't know why our people bomb university buildings?"

"I should think a lot of the secretaries didn't understand. Now there's no toilet. We have to go downstairs."

"Oh, pardon me. The secretaries have to go pee downstairs, so of course it was stupid to bomb the computer complex. It's terrible how some of the boys who are drafted disturb the secretaries in the draft centers, too."

"They don't understand why it was done. We don't know what happens inside the computer. We don't know what that stuff is. You have to make things clear to people. The workers in a place never know more than their little piece." Beth sounded muffled and frantic. Miriam could see it was hard for her to argue. She could not quite look at Phil. She would glance quickly at him and then duck her chin again. Her throat sounded constricted.

"The workers who make napalm don't know what they're doing, so it's dreadful rude to fuss about it, picketing and boycotting and all. Your logic is marvelous, dear. I bet the

other secretaries think the same way, if that's what you call it."

"It isn't enough to be big conspirators." Beth's voice was shaking with anger. "If you don't explain to people the meaning of what you're doing, it's just to make you feel better."

"You, you? Darling, I didn't blow it up, I beg your pardon."

"Whoever did! It was a bad time. I've been trying to talk to them about how we really are workers and we ought to relate to each other and help each other, and not to who we work for . . . "

"That's what people always say, have you ever noticed? That's Jackson's line, the theoretical radical for whom any action in the real world is always incorrect. There's always somebody to criticize and say, 'If you hadn't rushed into it prematurely, if you'd gone on talking about it another six months, one year, two years,' as if people could win any battles sitting talking to each other."

"Phil, she didn't say anything like that. She was saying that if an act is supposed to mean something, that meaning had better be made clear. After all, it's hard to see how blowing up the women's john has clear strategic value."

"If that's what she meant, why didn't she say that? Big Mama Berg is taking over. Let her say what she means, if she means anything at all."

Beth had taken advantage of Miriam's intervention to flee to Dorine's room. Miriam followed. Beth was sitting on the bed's edge with her head on Dorine's shoulder, while fat tears slid down her nose. Dorine was wearing her sheepskin coat ready to leave.

"Shut the door," Beth hissed. "Shhh. I'm ashamed to react this way! Oh, I wish I was better with words!"

"Phil can talk circles around an auctioneer. I never get the better of him in an argument."

"But you can stand up to him! I put so much effort into breaking through the wall of fear, of doubt of myself, what comes out is an anticlimax. I'm such an idiot." She sat up and blew her nose.

"At least you try," Dorine said. "I don't even do that."

"Why do you get so frightened in a little argument?"

Beth blew her nose again. "It's crossing taboos. You know, asserting myself, contradicting somebody. Even to argue with

somebody means you're saying you're right and they're wrong."

"Not necessarily. Phil argues for the fun of it. He'll take a position just to contradict somebody else."

"But don't you see, that's the thing that makes it hard—that it's naked competition. A contest. Well, I wasn't brought up to put myself forward in open competition. I try, I kick myself in the behind until I open my mouth."

Beth and Dorine giggled together, Dorine saying, "How do you kick yourself in your own ass?"

Beth said, "Well, it's easier when you always have your foot in your mouth." They got up and began checking the room for objects Dorine had forgotten to pack, slippers beside the mattress, a drawing of her Lennie had done when they were first together tacked to the closet door.

"I wonder why I can argue, then? If it's upbringing? I come from just as male-centered a home as you do." Miriam drifted in their wake, feeling sorry for herself. Why did Dorine have to move out? She hadn't ever wanted Beth to take Dorine away, only to get her on her feet again.

"Oh, you believe in it, like they do," Beth said.

"Believe in what?" Miriam was holding herself. Leaving her, leaving her. People were always leaving her.

"Words!" Dorine spoke with surprising firmness. "All those words. That theorizing. You think it means something, just like they do. You can do it too."

"I wish I could," Beth said. "I want to be better with words. I want to be able to answer them back. But I don't believe that's how you do anything. I only want to use words as weapons because I'm tired of being beaten with them. Tired of being pushed around because I don't know how to push back."

"You're wrong if you think I take the conversations in this house seriously. Most of it is just playing around."

"I don't think so," Beth said slowly. "It's more. I think it's a way of putting things in their place and people in their place and keeping them there."

"Oh, Bethie. They argue with each other all the time. It's jaw exercise. It's Indian wrestling."

"In a society where people were ranked for Indian wrestling, people would practice it a lot. They're making a pecking order."

"Bethie, how come you argue with me so well? Aren't those words you're using?"

"I'm not afraid of you. You're my friend."

"How can you be afraid of *Phil?* You confuse verbal violence with something real. And don't you think Jackson is your friend?"

"If I'm not his equal, how can I be his friend? He treats Orpheus as more of an equal than me."

That night Jackson moved his stuff into the room that Dorine had been using. The room could not immediately regain its air of neglect, for Dorine had circumspectly cleaned it, but it took on that Spartan grimness of all Jackson's dwelling places. The mattress, devoid of sunflower spread, sagged. The walls without prints or posters stood bleak and grimy. Without curtains the window gaped on the wall of the house next door. Still for a week or so the room mingled their odors before the scent of her perfume, her bath powder and her sweat faded into Jackson's pipe and grass and socks and harsher sweat, the damp wool of his socks drying on the radiator and his boots wet from snow cooking beside it.

Phil had gone through weeks of excited castle building while Hal was cutting his first album that included Phil's "Hudson Blues":

> *The Hudson River*
> *runs deep but wide.*
> *That's Jersey's smoking*
> *on the other side. . . .*

He could taste the money he was going to make. He would get free of tending bar, life would be easier, looser, less haggard. He would get off the bottle, he would only dope for the goodness of it, no more deadening escape.

The record came out and faded into the record stores. It crept along. Everybody assumed that Phil in fact must be making a mint, but Phil received what amounted to one twenty-fifth of a cent out of the total royalties allotted to songwriters who couldn't command bigger fees: perhaps a more minute amount than his or her mind could grasp. It had come so far to something like $347. Phil had spent more than that celebrating the wealth that was to come to liberate him.

Still he could not quite relinquish his dreams. The album was still selling, though slowly. The song would turn to gold yet and he would quit Finnegan's and be born again. Late at night when they used to lie making love and sharing their minds, he talked into the dark obsessively of the time when Going-to-the-Sun had begun to play his songs and he had tasted a local celebrity. He wrote little now, he hardly ever sat down to work on a poem or a song. He had had a bad fight with Joe centered around the extent to which he was doing hard drugs, a bitter fight that had left Phil with a sour brooding anger, a sense that Joe no longer trusted him. Phil had got into the habit of spending more and more time in the bars talking. He had bar friends who got off on hearing him spiel, hearing him float intricate worlds of fantasy on the drifting smoke. That instant audience hooked him. Still, when Hal came to Boston in December to play some gigs, Phil's dreams revived. One night when Phil was invited to a party at Hal's motel, he dragged Miriam along after insisting he supervise what she wore. He had her dress flamboyant and sexy.

They had good hash and poor catered food. She danced for a while, but she had put in a long day at work and by eleven she wanted to sleep. She managed to avoid letting Hal actually corner her long enough to make a move. He had a girl with him, long and blond and silent, as he had his luggage and instruments and his golden chow, but he was obviously curious to try Miriam. Phil kept away. They had a small scene between them before he would leave.

When they finally got home he was moody and mean. "Aw, would it have hurt you to fuck him?" he said in the face of her sore joking. "You said yourself he's attractive."

"Abstractly. He doesn't attract *me*. Besides, I wouldn't go to bed with the grooviest man in the world while his girl friend is sitting there brooding on the whole show."

"Aw, come on. She wouldn't have said boo."

"I know it. That's what I mean."

"Aw, shit, get off it. You've gone to bed with plenty of studs for no good reason. This was a good reason."

"To you. Why the hell don't *you* fuck him?"

"You think I wouldn't, to get out of that bar?"

"Phil, you're being silly. My ass isn't worth that much to him. He's used to getting laid wherever he goes. It wouldn't do you any good, and it would nauseate me. Besides, you know damned well I'm not getting involved with anybody outside this household."

"What's the use of that horse shit? Do you think I care? Let Jackson lay his purity rap on the cat, makes as much sense. He's turned on by you because you're vital and sensuous and then he wants to put you in a can."

"Amen. But that's how it is. I have enough trouble dealing with the scene in this house."

"Sacrificing me to him again. He always wins. Have you noticed that? He thinks it's because he's Clark Kent, the All-American Boy. Pure as Ivory Soap, wholesome as Mom's apple pie. He can kiss my sweet ass."

"You never really fight. You say that to me. To him you'll make a joke. You fight each other through me. You never take each other on directly."

"Aw, your ass. I'm not afraid of Jackson. I can take him any time and he knows it."

"What does that mean? I'm saying you never talk straight to each other about what's wrong."

"We understand each other." Phil drew himself up straight to glare at her. "I said, we understand each other!"

"I doubt it. You both go out from your front lines and make signs at the other. You have rituals."

"Trying to make trouble between us. That's what you're always after." Narrowing his sea-colored eyes to squint at her, he shook his forefinger in her face slowly. His eyes looked out of focus.

"Phil, that's vicious nonsense. I want you to communicate. I want us all to understand and help each other. I'm tired of the two of you fighting your status wars through my body."

"She's tired." He pirouetted to the mirror. *"She's* tired. What has she done to get tired?" He flung himself on her bed, crossing his arms over his chest. Hollowly he intoned, "Here lies Philip Francis Boyle, a has-been in his twenties and now aging fast, about to pass that dreadful barrier to middle age. I talked it out. The body of Philip Francis Boyle lies in dribs and gobbets in all the bars and pads and coffeehouses and pissparlors of Cambridge. And the biggest, the juiciest part of all . . ." He rose on his elbow to tap Miriam's stomach. "The

Great Ear. The ear and the womb and the stomach. All absorbing bodies. All digesting bodies. Woman, you've swallowed me!"

"Oh!" She turned from him. "The black widow myself! Wow! Just wow! Your brains are full of metaphors spinning idly. That's about the ugliest thing you've ever said to me! If I'm so horrible, why don't you leave? You'd better get out while the going's good!" She seized him by the wrist and yanked at him, pulling him off the bed so he landed on his behind with a crash. "Now get out!"

"Ow! Owww!" Foaming and cursing he lunged at her. "That does it, bitch!" He swung at her and she ducked but not fast enough. His fist caught her in the face, hard enough to knock her down. She sat down in a heap, twisting her leg.

He stood over her with his fists trembling and she shielded her face, afraid he would hit her again. But something cracked then and he fell forward over her, mumbling and beginning to weep. "Just like my old man! My old man all over again."

Leaning back against the closet door, she held him. "There, there, Phil. We shouldn't do this to each other."

"Did I hurt you? I didn't hurt you, did I?"

"I think you sort of did."

"Yeah. There might be a bruise. Let me get some ice."

The next morning she had a black eye to carry to work. Everyone there immediately asked her what had happened. She said she had been mugged. No, he had not got her purse: she had screamed and fought back. The assailant had run off.

She was sure that if she had come up with an accident story—I ran into the door, I bumped into a post—no one would have believed her. But to say she had been mugged fit into everyone's urban mythology straight away, until Fred Weathering asked her, "A black guy, uh?"

"No," she said firmly. "He was blond and clean-shaven." But Fred looked skeptical. She liked Fred less and less. He had adopted a hearty avuncular manner toward her, but she could never quite relax. Between her and the men she worked with was the smelly memory of Ryan's and Manganaro's bet. With Jaime she did not worry because his passions had more to do with gadgets and games than women; and with Neil she had begun not to worry. He was quiet and clear: she could not imagine him speaking about women to any man at the office. He was almost old-fashioned in his consideration and his courtesy. She felt guilty when he questioned her about the mugging and scolded her for hitchhiking. He often seemed a little worried in his inquiries: it was partly his manner and the tone of his reserve. Not a man who pushed on anyone; if she had to have a boss she preferred it to be him. A good idea, a good piece of work produced an instant concentration from him that was a reward.

"Miriammmm," he said her name when he saw her passing and called her into his office, when he came to ask her something. His voice dwelt on the *m*'s, tasting them. With his quiet arrivals he aroused tension in Fred, who she had begun to suspect was working beyond his depth technically. He was a bluffer and not a good one, unlike Ted, Abe's favorite who held everybody spellbound at his seminars and often made one of the team to get contracts or to renegotiate contracts on which as usual they were not managing to come in on schedule. No, Fred bluffed desperately and therefore poorly and he could not bluff Neil. So he was uneasy and at times haggard. When he tried to bluff her, she had to fight to contain her temper. Working with Fred she felt held back, and she preferred it when Neil gave her a piece to do alone. She felt he sensed that and tried to arrange the work that way. The younger technical people were divided between the Abe Tyler claque and the admirers of Neil, including her and Jaime who talked about him a lot together. She found Abe square and impersonal. He had a way of looking without looking, not quite hearing you. She never felt that way with Neil.

She was talking with Sally on the phone, her legs in new boots propped up. She was running her fingers over their surface like the hide of a beautiful toad, interestingly rough, as she listened to Sally describe her physical condition in the ninth month. Lately Sally was enjoying her pregnancy, telling each sensation and change. She no longer feared giving birth alone.

"Dorine did a drawing of me last night. She did me undressed. Just plain looking like this great big hill of a woman. You can see it's me all right, peeking over the belly. I look uncomfortable but real proud. I put it up over my bed."

"I didn't know Dorine could draw. Did Lennie teach her?"

"Isn't that the limit? Like if I didn't ask her the very same thing. She gave me this real sad look. 'You think I'd have dared draw anything around him? Can you imagine what he'd have said?' "

"I'm embarrassed. So are you settling in over there?"

"There's lots of work, for real. Of course none of us knows how to do nothing useful. Between us we can't put up shelves or fix the toilet that runs all the time, or put in a ceiling light. We can't even turn up the pilot light on the stove that keeps going out. But we're learning."

"How?"

"Beth went to the library and got out a boy's book called *How to Fix Things Around the House*. She figured there'd be some book. Beth says there's always a book in the library about how to do anything."

"Now that Ryan's out, there isn't anybody who knows how to do anything useful here. That's one male role I notice both my men reject."

"But otherwise, you still like it, huh? We were kind of hoping you might move in. We have an empty bedroom for you."

"That's nice, but I do enjoy polygamy. It suits me."

Passing, Jackson had given her the usual ironic stare, the raised eyebrow and slight smile with which he always commented on her telephone conversations—though he spent as much time on the phone. But at the last sentence he turned and glared.

Getting off the phone quickly, she went after. "Now what was that dirty look for?"

"Polygamy, hm? I don't remember marrying again."

"That's a figure of speech. You don't imagine Sally understood me as saying we had a three-ring ceremony at the circus?"

"I'm sure nature child didn't understand much. Do you consider yourself married? To me? To us?"

"I consider I've made a commitment to this setup. You make it clear enough you don't want me getting close to anyone else. I don't consider it marriage, but I do consider us a family, de facto."

"A de facto family. So I'm a de facto husband." They

were arguing in the hall. He stood with his hands behind him as if to keep them out of sight, out of reach, as if to emphasize that he would not touch her.

It was cold in the hall with a draft whistling through. She held herself across the breasts, pulling the mustard shawl closer. "This is stupid. What's got you uptight with me now, all of a sudden?" He had made them a pleasant lunch of scrambled eggs with bits of cheese and tomato, and they had sat on at the table long after it talking out a fantasy about what they would do if she had a computer console in her room the way Abe Tyler and some of the big shots at Project MAC did—all the games they would play on a computer, all the work they would make it do for them. Now the damp wind from the swamps of his mistrust was blowing. Perhaps any time they were loose and easy together had to be paid for, soon.

"Marriage does not amuse me, strangely enough. I do not feel married. If I did, I'd jump out the window. Any window, any door, any fire escape, any loophole, any drain."

"Jackson, have I ever said to you I want to get married?"

"You don't have to."

"No, because you understand everybody better than they understand themselves, because you're so wise. Supposing I will get married in a few years. How in hell do you presume I'd marry *you*? What would I get but a lot of grief?"

"Pardon me." He drew himself up. His eyelids drooped, his mouth curled. "I expect you're shopping for a nice upper-middle-class hubby. A professor with tenure and good prospects to carry you out to Utopia. Surely out past Route 128 there's a fancy development in rolling hills called Utopia?"

Why did that immediately make her think of the men who worked at Logical and why did that make her feel guilty? His eyes cold, his body drawn up rigid, his voice edged with contempt: it was all no good. It wasn't better. Tears suddenly came loose in her. Gobbets of something raw and wet tearing loose. It hurt to cry, broken open. She could not breathe, she had to lean on the wall hiding her face in her shawl. "It's so bad! So bad!"

"Miriam." His voice was gentle. It came close. "Miriam?"

"I only want to love you, and it's so hard!"

His hand on her bowed head stroked back the hair. His arm encircled. Against his shoulder, against his body no longer rigid that supported her, she collapsed and hung and cried.

"Miriam, Miriam, baby, I don't know what it is. Why we strike out at each other. You start enveloping me. I feel you reaching out for more territory, pushing my defenses back. Then we're at war again. Miriam, I don't want to hurt you. There, it's all right now. Come here. Like this."

By the time the tears stopped—she thought of them happening to her like a storm—they were undressing, they were getting into bed. It was good, yes. But it did no good. Afterward when he got dressed and went off to his classes, she did not bother to put on her clothes but slunk across the hall and into her own bed.

Phil was visiting his mother in Medford and from there he would go to work. His mother always made him supper. He said she was a lousy cook but would never forgive him if he didn't eat until he was bloated.

Miriam stayed alone in her room feeling torn open. What was the use, what was the use? He did not love her, he would never turn and love her. Two wrongs did not make a right, and Phil and Jackson together were hell. And separately, what? Did anything in her life add up to more than a boil, a scab, a sore, a wound? Was Phil still with her at all? That was a joke. When was the last time they had been together in any gentle full way? He was with no one. He was killing himself gradually and making her his accomplice.

She loved Jackson, she loved him and she wanted to stop. God, it was loving a phantom locked in an iron man, a warm ghost that came and went in a tunnel of ice. She was impaling herself upon him and bleeding out her strength. Phil and his myths of the toothed vagina, the mother devouring her lovers. Well, she could make myths of the barbed penis, the rod of punishment that was bleeding her anemic.

Jackson would never open to her. He did not want to be together with her. He wanted her around, but at a distance. He wanted to be alone, and sometimes to let her in to visit his loneliness, as he invited her into his room, which remained mostly shut against her.

Why did she pretend so solidly to be strong in front of Beth and Dorine? Why didn't she break down and tell them she felt drained and defeated? But how could they help her? How could women help women? In other women she could

only see the potential threat that Jackson might turn suddenly to them, and she would die; or sufferers worse off than
herself. She must save herself. But how? She lacked the will
even to get up and do yesterday's sinkful of dishes.

17

Of Fog and Snow (Phil)

"I am your death," said the needle to him. The sweet white
snowstorm in the blood, the loving spoonful of oblivion with
its lush thunder of numbness would hit him soon.

"Shit, man . . ." Jackson was scowling.

"That's what it's called. Two points for the street smarts."
He was lying on Jackson's bed, partly to irritate him. Jackson
hated him to lie on his bed but could never think up a reason
to give. Putting Jackson uptight was amusing.

"I think you're out of control."

"Ha. Ouch. Fuck it. Who's in control? You and Miriam
are two of a kind the way you like to think you know what
you're doing."

"What's it for? That stuff is poison, and you're getting
creepy. Sticking a needle in your arm isn't even aesthetic."

"Yeah? You tell on me to Mama and I'll knock your
teeth out."

"You couldn't knock Orpheus down, wan one. Chinese
name, Wan One. But I tell nothing."

"Come on, man, last generation I'd have been a damn
alcoholic like my old man. I get by on a bit of this, a bit of
that. A regular butterfly. Hooked on nothing. I keep moving."

"Moving in narrowing circles."

"The moralist." He felt pissed. He had been enjoying shooting up. He liked the paraphernalia. There was a ritual proper
to it, like the pipe with opium, like the social booze scene.
He liked the white death's-head imagery of heroin—the
ghostly horse, the pale junkie, snow and skeleton inherently

poetic. "You're scared, man. You have your habits and you ride along in your rut. You have tobacco and dope and you won't touch a stranger."

"Unlike you, I get no thrill from spilling my brains on the linoleum."

"Aw, never mind." The wall of thunder. "Forget it."

The next night he had a dream. It woke him so he remembered it clearly. He dreamed he was naked with Jackson and they were touching each other's pricks. But when they went to fuck, they could not agree on who was to get to fuck the other in the ass. They kept arguing and shoving each other. Finally Jackson hit him in the nose and he woke up.

His head was still hurting from the fight at Finnegan's. Ugh, not to remember. He grinned at the dream, sitting on the edge of the cot in the front room. Orpheus slept at the foot, stretched out taut as a pulled bow. Once when Phil had had an erotic dream about Jackson he had told him. Jackson had been embarrassed, disgusted. A dream like that was a secret weapon: he would carry it around inside. Because he was not afraid of his own dreams and Jackson was. It was a true dream since they were always jockeying for position. A pleasant muddle of emotions stewed in him: a little excitement. His prick was still distended. A little superior amusement because he could endure to look into himself and Jackson could not. A little anger, because since Jackson refused to look at what he considered meaningless he was free of knowledge about himself that Phil would never be free of.

The dull pain in his chest brought back Finnegan's, bad from the beginning. He fingered the bruises. Joe had come in with a black chick, tough and flashy. When he tried to start up a conversation, curious, interested in her, Joe put him down: turned him into anonymous servant-bartender. Joe had told others he was a bad risk and cut him to his face . . . just because he was into skag a little bit. . . . Then Joe hadn't been gone five minutes when his old lady Wanda came in with Luis by the hand and baby Johnny, like a scene out of an old-time melodrama, looking for Joe. Their neighbor had just been busted on a bench warrant and she had their baby too and she was out of milk and no money in the house.

"Hey, you got any lic-rish for me?" Luis gave him a big golden grin and reached up at the bar. When Phil had been palling around with Joe, he always used to bring Luis licorice shoelaces.

Wanda was looking him in the eyes, a head shorter but giving him that fierce look, arms akimbo. "You telling me you haven't seen him today? Phil, you wouldn't lie to me in this trouble!"

Then his boss dumped on him for not kicking her out with the kids as soon as she walked in. He wasn't functioning well. He had to be on top, conscious, sensitive to what was happening all along the bar, who to cut off when and how: the meek wispy slobs drinking their way to the moment of explosion; the tough guys putting it in until they would slobber and cry about life and love; the casual arguments that could end with somebody on the floor; the okay pickups and the whore cruising; the stud pushing too hard on a woman who was trying to get drunk fast. He hadn't stayed on top, he had started out too tired, too dulled. Jesus, a fight he could hallucinate better than remember, chairs, bottles, a cop coming in. He had been fired on the spot, that much he remembered. Aw shit, he could use a vacation, he was bone-weary. Besides, let them see if they could find somebody who could handle that crowd the way he could, the wild mix of the drunk and the stoned, ups and downs and booze, with half of them perennially sore and ready to jump. Let the boss see if he could find anybody who could handle it night after night. He'd fucked up just one time, and that on top of missing a night the week before when he was strung out. Aw, the hell with it.

He did not feel sleepy. He went to the window, looked out at the empty night street. Carbon-paper sky with a sliver of moon like a nail paring. Ice on the sill, spikes of ice under the eaves. Padding through the middle room and hall, cautiously he pushed open the door of her room. Padding like Orpheus, who had followed him rubbing his legs and hoping for a very early breakfast—he stood over the bed. A sense of power came from watching sleepers. People asleep were supposed to look disgusting but they looked helpless. Jackson was snoozing on his belly, the pillow loosely clutched. She lay on her side, back to Jackson and facing Phil. Lightly he stroked her bare shoulder, slipping his hand under the blanket to stroke her breast, distorted against her by her crossed arm.

Groggily she stirred and after a moment opened her eyes.

He motioned for her to be quiet and get up. She went on gaping at him sleepily. He realized that she could not see him: she was too nearsighted without her lenses. He leaned close. "Come. Please," he mouthed in her ear.

Half asleep, she got out of bed and stumbled after him, catching up her robe from a chair. Silently he shut the door and drew her along toward the front. She resisted. "What's the matter?"

"Come with me. Come on, Miriam." He got his arm around her and drew her along pressing against him.

"Is something wrong?"

"Nothing's wrong." Brief flash of Finnegan's and the fight, his boss's face. "Just come with me."

She dragged her feet. "Was up late. Got to get up early. Let me sleep."

She was playing inert, hanging back and making herself squishy. He was put off, then interested. Someone only half there. He yanked her along to the bed and began to kiss her. In his embrace she slumped and yawned. "Phil, are you drunk? Let me go back."

"No!" He upset her onto the bed and fell over her. Soft yielding body. Normally she was so responsive, it was like making a stranger. He was hard and excited. Like a stranger in bed, a kind of rape. His excitement bore him forward. When he thrust into her, he was surprised that she was not dry, then realized that she had been with Jackson. That excited him more. He should have taken her right in the bed, should have let Jackson wake up to find him fucking her. He could have raped Jackson for that matter, lying there with his ass up. Her body under him hardly stirred. He came with a groan muffled by her hair. Lying in her, he enjoyed still the afterglow, the fantasy acted out. Then he realized she was already asleep under him. Would she remember? Funny if she didn't. Woke up in his bed with no notion how she got there. It was a joke he had played on both of them.

But when she did wake up she was ill-tempered. He pulled the covers over his head and let her storm off to work.

When he got out of bed, he was still feeling set up. Act out your fantasies: that was his motto. Blake's theory: unacted desires rot the soul. The lineaments of gratified desire. He felt gratified and even willing to face a breakfast and chew it for a change. He was sitting at the table dunking a stale

doughnut in coffee Miriam had made and skimming a science
fiction novel she had left there, when Jackson came through
on his way to the john, turning on the radio to the news as
he went.

"Seen Miriam this morning?" Phil asked slyly.

"No, she got up before me. What brings you out on the
near side of noon?"

Jackson didn't know his bed partner had been stolen.
Phil studied Jackson's face for signs of tension. Jackson just
looked sleepy. For a moment Phil was disappointed, but
knowledge is power. He waited for Jackson to re-emerge.

"What are you reading that crap for?" Jackson challenged,
looking at the slime monsters on the cover.

"Aw, you believe in high culture. If it had a quote by some
jackass like Irving Howe, you'd be willing to read it. What
disappoints me is the failure to imagine truly alien beings.
The men from Mars or Alpha Centauri are all human in
disguise or else they're in reptilian mode or insect mode or
pool-of-slime mold. Just green human beings with purple an-
tennae and four arms."

"Is that so illogical? Life has probably evolved every
place according to the same chemical laws. Now you figure
there are just so many niches to be filled in any ecosystem:
something jumps, something runs, something grazes, something gnaws, something preys on the little things that run in
the grasses, and so forth. Something that jumps has big jumping muscles. Something that grazes has a mechanism for biting
off and digesting tough fibers."

"You're uptight even in your imagination. You need to
think there's some logic to life, that it evolves according to
some neat scheme, a proliferating road map of forms with
major trunks and minor branchings and a chart that would
look nice in four colors."

"You find the notion of randomness exciting. You're one
of those people starts talking about random joggings of atoms
and chance mutations and you get a hard-on. You never use
concepts for what they mean but for some kind of nervous
thrill. Like the Victorians getting their rocks off by going on
about 'Nature red in tooth and claw.'"

"While you're scared of anything you can't sit on and control. I don't have that kind of middle-class separation of mind
and body. I groove on what I think, and I feel it in my mus-

cles. On my pulse, like Keats says."

"You mean you lead with your prick. Just like you did at nineteen. The longest adolescence on record."

Was he going to say something about Phil's coming birthday? He waited, tensing. But Jackson didn't go on. "Like you live in your head and you don't know what's happening in the provinces. There's a revolution out there and you don't know it. Like Louis in Versailles," Phil said.

"Freedom starts in the head, Phil—something you've never begun to learn."

"Man, you wouldn't say that if you were facing six months in the can, I can tell you that." Trial hanging over him, lawyer suggesting he cop a plea. Maybe he should look for a lawyer who'd do a more political defense: or would that get him longer? At the last minute he decided to go with Jackson toward the Square. He didn't feel like hanging around an empty apartment. A light wet snow was falling. Slithery feel of the wet flakes on his face raw from shaving, a damp cool caress. Flakes caught in his lashes. He wanted nothing, he felt empty and saintly and almost ecstatic in his emptiness. Fine to be up for a change on the bristly side of noon. He felt cut loose and floating. Yes, to want nothing, to need nothing, to be open and empty to every touch and smell and taste, every impulse shooting through the clean air. He had been fired into freedom.

Flakes melted on his outstretched hands. He took off the lined gloves Miriam had given him and balled them in the pocket of his pea jacket. He liked his pea jacket, the flatness of the wool, its smell, its navy color. He might have been a sailor. Now he could feel the snow lighting faintly on the back of his hands. Drifting along.

"How long do you think that girls' dormitory is going to last?" Jackson was asking. "I hear them every so often trying to get Miriam to join the campfire girls. Fat chance. If there's a dykey bone in her, it's buried pretty deep."

"They'll be yowling and hissing and tearing each other's hair the first time a man walks in. Let them eat cock!"

Jackson went on talking but he did not listen. He nodded and said hmm from time to time. He liked walking beside Jackson along Mass Avenue past the hip stores, he felt good and close to Jackson now. The tenseness had blown off in the clean air and they moved together inside their friendship like a

—

private sun shining, so many towns, so many scenes, always counting on each other. As Jackson talked on about classes and students and tests, he smiled and gave him a poke in the ribs. Good old Jackson, he would not have him one jot different.

After they parted he turned off into the Common, feeling that empty alertness in him like a perfect box he was carrying. Ready for anything: encounter, confrontation, adventure. The morning carried him bobbing and light on its surface. As he drifted he studied the bark of trees: trees rooted deep down in the earth, solid to his ephemeral passing, wood to his ghost. Lightly his fingers caressed the ridges.

For a while he stood looking at the snow so lightly coming to rest on the ground and feeling the cold settle on his skin. Then he felt someone's eyes. A girl was trotting toward him: Beth, Miriam's girl friend. He thought of pretending he didn't see her, but she was headed right for him, her lips already parted to speak. Plume of breath. Fluffy snow on fluffy light brown hair.

"Phil? Listen, I just called and Miriam's not home. Do you know her number at work?"

He shook his head. "Logical something or other."

"You don't remember the name?" Breathless, her eyes wide and pleading on him. Usually she was cool, withdrawn.

"Not offhand. I'm thinking. How come you're not at work?" He made a typing gesture.

"I got fired."

"Yeah? Guess what, me too. For what? Dropping your gum in the big machine?"

"Falsification of records. Oh, it's a mess. A detective came around and then they fired me. Jim—my husband—" She stopped and winced. "My husband! He hired detectives, him and my family—"

"Thought you were divorced?" Small-boned rabbit quivering in the cold. Wouldn't feel like much in bed. A mouthful. Snap. Both of them waifs of the storm, fired, in trouble with the pigs.

She made a wry face. "I pretended to be. I just ran away."

"But they can't fire you for being married."

Her hands flapped. "I gave them a false age, I pretended to be older and divorced, I pretended I had two years of college. Oh, it's stupid. I've been doing the job for a year. The detective came and saw me. I'm scared, I don't know what they can do to me! He said I committed fraud and that I stole the money—I drew it out of the bank and signed Jim's name. He says I'm a minor and legally the ward of my husband. I don't know which end is up, I'm really scared. . . ."

"Look, they can't make you live with somebody if you don't want to. Don't let them get to you."

"I don't know what to believe and not to believe! He says I could go to jail. I never thought they'd fire me and now I'm out of a job!"

Putting his arm around her, he brushed the snowy hair back from her face. "Calm down, take it slow. You can get another job. I'm in the same boat myself. . . ." He started to say he'd take her home when he remembered that crazy houseful of women. "Come on back to the apartment. Maybe I can find Miriam's number and we can have a cup of coffee and talk about it."

She pulled back. "I don't even know how to get a lawyer. I'm going back to the house and call Gloria at M.I.T. and see if she knows where Miriam's working. Would you tell Miriam to call me as soon as she gets in? Just as soon as she gets in, if I haven't got to her before then?"

"She's no lawyer. Besides, they can't touch you." He looked past her at the snow falling on the Common. Cold little bitch, ungiving. Clammed up tight when he tried to be nice. The only reason Miriam liked her was she enjoyed playing Mama to lost sheep. Baaa to this one.

Off she scurried without saying good-by and he strolled on, spitting elegantly at the base of a tree. Prissy little twat. No warmth in her, like a goddamn porcupine. She could run her own messages. Making a fuss about her little problems, when he was facing jail and out of a job too, and he wasn't running around flapping his hands and whimpering.

Then Miriam would go wailing over the phone and trying to find a lawyer and meddling and making a huge fuss. She would go tearing over to the women's house and they'd all carry on. Miriam was a giving woman, not like that hard little chick, but she liked to feel important fussing over people. The big social-worker act. If he had the bozo's luck to be married to her, he sure as hell wouldn't hire detectives to haul her back. Some people didn't know when they were well off.

What pissed him off was that she wouldn't yield anything. He could speak to her nice and easy, he would come floating into the kitchen and start rapping to her and she would not give him the least bit of warmth or support. Like she was scared she might let go of a touch or a smile or a spoonful of honey. She wasn't that cold with Jackson. Like Dorine, she was worshipful: because he wouldn't give them the time of day they thought he was a saint. Because Jackson sat and let them tell him their troubles and gave them those grave looks and never, never came on to them or put out a finger to touch them, they thought he cared. Whereas his standards for pussy were high and he couldn't be bothered. Except in a rare sadistic stretch like in New York with 4B, when he thought he was consorting with the proletariat. Jackson was too much sometimes.

But Beth made him sore. He was sure she could open up and give a bit of sweetness. Then she'd gone and got Dorine to move into that dykey setup with that crazy hillbilly about to drop her kid. When he thought of Dorine he felt the warmth of her backside in bed. He thought of slipping into her bed. Putting his arms around and feeling her. "Phil?" she would ask in that high sleepy trailing little voice. Like who else would it be? He liked to come into her from the back. Sex with Miriam was good, but it was interaction, he had to please her. He had to figure Dorine enjoyed it; after all, she never complained. But she never said anything and so he never had to worry and it was easy. He liked having her there, in fact, he liked it a lot. Jackson and Beth between them had taken her away. Jackson didn't have the sense to appreciate Dorine, just a nice warm piece of ass. Jackson didn't want any woman in the house who wasn't his and he didn't want Dorine. She was too easy to appeal to his pride of conquest. Yes, he was pissed at them both. Probably that's why he'd hauled Miriam out of bed last night. Dorine had been his for more than a year, not quite a relationship but sure a resource, and now the fuckers had messed up a good easy thing.

He sat on a bench watching girls. Indian woman in a pale pink sari with a brown woolen coat that looked the wrong size over it. Did you unwind them? He wondered if they wore panties. Liked the way she skimmed along but the coat was ridiculous. Across the street he saw a Radcliffe girl he had picked up once but he had not liked her snotty patter and he did not call out. She was talking with a bearded dude who was walking his bike alongside.

Beth had been Ryan's girl. That irritated him too. Giving with that bastard and not with him. Sometime he'd like to crack that shell. A thin kid, probably not much fun but easy to pick up and toss on the bed. Fuck her till you got some reaction out of that bony piece.

Suddenly he felt cold in his belly. Bad karma. Bad thoughts. He sat very still, hoping it would go away. First time in months and months he had remembered it, always each time hoping he would never remember it again.

That fall day it had been foggy since the middle of the afternoon; nudging each other in social studies and pointing to the fog creeping in as if they cared, for something to look at. What was fog to him then? He liked it because it slithered in, because it felt sneaky. It was a white night in the day. It made things strange. He felt invisible in the fog in a good way, slouching like a private eye.

The guys he hung out with then, they were not a gang but they had pretensions. Whose idea? Anybody's? The idea belonged to the streets. Pissed on all day in school, they were going to be men that night. The fog magnified sounds. In the dark you could hear for a long way but it was hard to tell where sounds came from. They were standing in an alley in a block of stores, half of them vacant and all closed by seven. The bus stop was down by the corner. It was around eight. He remembered hearing a churchbell beating dully in the thickened air. It didn't seem to come from anywhere in particular.

The first woman was with a man. "She's too old anyhow," Mike grumbled. Then two women together carrying shopping bags. The boys stepped out of the alley to get a look when they heard the voices. Mike said again they were too old. When the women saw them, they stopped and crossed over to the other side.

John said Mike was scared. Phil said he agreed with Mike, what was the use if they were dogs. Kevin said they were scared and what mattered was doing it. When they heard light footsteps next, Mike said this was it, no matter, and sent Kevin and Phil to stand across the street and the other two waited in the alley out of sight. It was a girl alone.

She fought hard but there were four of them. It was easy to subdue her and force her back into the alley. He remembered she had been carrying her schoolbooks in a cloth bag and she was carrying in it too a loaf of sliced bakery bread that spilled out; the paper tore and the smell of caraway and rye bread rose as the slices were trampled. Her glasses broke right away. She had large brown eyes. All he could remember of her face were her staring brown eyes that squinted with pain and welled tears and sometimes shut tight against what was happening. Mike gagged her with his handkerchief when they got her down on the pavement so he never did really see her face. Her hair was in a net pinned back. Probably she worked behind a counter, maybe she worked in the bakery that had made the bread, and had to put up her hair after school in the net. She had been hurrying home and had not bothered yet to take it off. The net tore quickly and her light brown hair, soft and light like Beth's, tumbled out and got wet and dark, stained from the pavement.

He was very excited at first. When he took his prick out like the others did, he was hard already. She was still struggling. At first he had held her from behind before they got her down and the idea of the power of it had made him feel high. It was still exciting to see her lying there and know they could do anything to her. John was tearing her clothes open like a daydream, like the things he always imagined doing. He wanted to get in her right away, but they had shot craps for the order before and he was third.

Mike said she was too hard to hold and fuck at the same time. John slapped her around but she was still fighting so Phil held her down on one side and Kevin on the other—they were third and fourth. John was feeling her breasts and then he started pinching them so she groaned through the gag and tears ran from her eyes. Then Mike said enough playing around, it was his turn first. He got on and cursed and told them to hold her legs farther apart but after a while he finally got in and came almost immediately. He said it was great and he was going to take a turn again after the rest.

It was John's turn and he got on and started twisting her arm and slapping her. It was kind of ugly. Phil didn't like to watch but he was helping to hold her down. She was getting messed up. John came but he still wanted to be fooling around. Mike said John had to get off, it was Phil's turn.

John took over holding her down.

She was bleeding, either because she'd been a virgin or because it was her period or just because they'd hurt her inside. Her mouth too was bleeding into the gag and her eyes were staring at him with horror. A gold chain around her neck was twisted to one side, cutting in. He found he didn't have an erection any more. Her body felt rigid with fear. When he prodded himself against her, she felt cold and oozy and he thought he could feel her pain.

It wasn't like he thought it would be, it wasn't like the daydreams where the woman yields and likes it and it's groovy. It was like four of them beating up on her. It was like his old man breaking his mother's jaw. He felt scared. He felt they could kill her. It would all be the same. They could break her legs and leave her in the street. They could slit her throat. It would be the same. He couldn't get it up. He felt cold all the way through and scared.

"She doesn't turn me on," he said. Then was the part he couldn't think about. He still couldn't bear it. They were all jeering at him, it got worse and worse. Kevin took his turn and then Mike held him from behind like they'd held her, and John masturbated him trying to get him hard so he would take her too. But nothing would happen. Then John said he was going to serve him right because he was just a woman too, he wasn't a man like they were, he was a cunt.

John took out his prick again and told Mike to turn Phil around and hold him. Then Phil went crazy and started fighting them all. God, he was scared. He had a knife but so did Mike, and John could take him, he knew it. He felt if they did that thing to him he would die. He fought berserk. He was kicking and punching and praying, he was crazy with fear.

Then the only lucky thing happened. A car turned into the alley. The minute the headlights came around the corner, they left the girl there on the ground and they all ran like crazy. It wasn't the pigs, it was only a car. They heard the brakes squeal and the guy shouting, but they ran out into the street and they got away easy. They never heard anything about it.

There was nothing in the papers, no police ever came around asking questions. For a long time he would think he saw the girl on the street and be really scared. Obviously she never reported it to the police: how could she? She was still in high school. If she ever told anybody she had been raped, that would blow her reputation forever, she'd be treated like a whore. Then his mother got married and they moved out to Medford where he had felt out of place but where he had stopped worrying about meeting that girl with the staring brown eyes.

Not a thing he liked to remember. He thought of it as unreal, not part of his life, except for what had almost happened. Jesus, that would have done him in. Still he was glad he hadn't taken his turn with her. It had nothing to do with sex. Each of them could have got laid that night if they'd wanted that. It had been a ritual, it was feeling powerful and being men together. And he hadn't made it. It was more like shooting pigeons with Kevin's air rifle than like fucking. More like waiting after a game to beat up some middle-class kid when they played Boston Latin. That was why he had thought, standing in the alley with his limp cock dangling, that they could kill her just as easily, because that would have proved they were men even louder. He never had told anybody. Oh, he'd told Jackson a long time ago. But he'd made the girl sexy and made it more of a stag movie scene. He had started out to tell it to Jackson straight, but it had turned in his mouth to something else. He always hoped it was buried for good. He did not like to remember how vulnerable and painful it had been to be a kid.

Funny how he had not been able to tell Jackson. He had started out feeling Jackson was the one person who might listen. Maybe one of the ways Jackson maintained a kind of dominance over his friends, his buddies, was that father confessor act. He had told Jackson how frightened the girl was. He had been able to tell Jackson about how he was excited at first and then scared and turned off. But when he started to tell the rest, it came out that he had not wanted to and the others had been angry. There was something about the way Jackson was listening, saying with a laugh at one point that he had never raped anyone except his wife Sissy, and grinning, that made the story come out with him being fastidious instead of scared shitless. Suddenly he felt Jackson's all-American suburban background there and thought, aw, your ass, they don't go out and jump some girl in the street when they want a gang bang, those ex-Boy Scouts, they hire some broad and call it a smoker or they get some guy's date

drunk at the fraternity. It's all legal, it's social. If he had told
Jackson how they nearly made a pansy of him, it would have
given Jackson more points finally.

He could have told Miriam about the impotence. She did
not make that big a fuss: good if he could get it up, if he
couldn't, next time he would. But if he told her about the
rape, she would identify with the girl. She would immediately
see herself seventeen coming home on a fall evening from the
library. She would say, "Do you imagine if that had happened
I'd have gone with you two years later in the museum?" She
would never understand that he still did not know, could not
tell if he felt guiltier for having taken part in the assault or
for not having been able to take part in the rape. He still
could not know. Part of him mocked the idea of manhood
that consisted of torturing a girl in an alley and part of him
judged with his peers that he was less a man for not being
able to get it up when they could. Part of him still thought
he had failed.

His cool clear high was blown. That little bitch Beth had
brought him down. His ass was frozen to the bench. Stiffly
he rose and strolled toward the square. Miriam, he wanted her
now: to fall into bed and talk. He wanted to feel cared for.
He didn't feel like fucking, he felt like being held and
cherished. But she was at work, every damn day now, never
around when he needed her.

Walking stiffly, like an old man: his ass still numb. Old.
Thirty creeping up on him: two months and he'd be over that
magic line. Like a lousy trick, a bad joke: he was still Phil
the kid. How could he be arriving already at thirty? James
Wright poem with the punch line, "You have wasted your
life."

So he started looking. It was rule one that you could
always find a woman. Men were off at jobs in the daytime but
women were around waiting. He cruised the square but didn't
see anything he fancied. He didn't want a Cliffee, he didn't
want to have to come on and impress, and he didn't want
someone strung out from a missed connection. A young
housewife was the ticket, someone who'd appreciate him.

There was a bike standing outside a tobacco store, fancy
humidor tobacconist. Not locked. Quickly he got on and
rode off. Aw, fine. The pavement was wet but not too bad.
Over the bridge and into Allston. Past all the new Harvard

stuff. He could remember the little houses here, nice sprawly working-class neighborhood with lots of trees and back yards and toward the end, when they were fighting the crunch from Harvard, big signs in front of every house about Save Our Homes. Long gone. Off down North Harvard Street strung with ratty-looking Christmas decorations in the direction of Brookline. Pedaling along, he found it a good English bike with lots of gears and nice handling in the slush. The warmth came back into his body and he felt alive. A fine edge. He left it outside a shop and walked on toward Coolidge Corner. Somewhere along here someone would cuddle him. Scent of bagels from a bakery, onion, garlic. Food smells from a delicatessen. He wanted a nice lunch.

Through the plate-glass window of a laundromat he saw Laverne Ryan, sitting disconsolately watching the dryer churn clothes past her gaze while her toddler kicked in his stroller. He looked her over, trying to decide. Her hair was pinned up and she was chewing gum. He could remember the elegant Laverne skinny as a clothespin but dressed to the nines. She was looking not exactly bedraggled but a little haggard. Still she was Ryan's woman, even if separated, and that counted. He owed Ryan a few small favors, indeed he did. Ryan wanted her back and he definitely would not want Phil messing with her. Besides, she looked like she needed the company.

"Laverne, what are you doing around here? It's fantastic to see you. Thought you'd moved?"

"No, still in the old apartment. It really is a bargain and moving's such a drag, and Bonnie's in nursery school here. What on earth are you doing in Brookline?" Surreptitiously she spat the gum into her hand, faking a polite cough, and he saw her stick it under the bench.

"Oh, I had a reading last night around B.U. Party afterward. You might say I just got up." He remembered she had been susceptible to the Great Poet come-on.

"Oh, a poetry reading? That's wonderful. I wish I'd heard, I'd love to have come. Though it's hard for me to get sitters. You don't look like you were up all night partying. I mean, you look . . . fine."

"So do you, so do you." He sat beside her on the bench, extending his arm along the back. She looked better close up, color in her face now. He lit a cigarette for her and she still had that neat little flip of her wrist. Hollow cheeks and soft blue eyes all attention to him. Her lips slightly pouted: pretty good. She was getting it on for him. "So you're on your own now? Won't pretend I'm sorry. You're too good-looking a woman for Tom Ryan, the old goat, you know that?"

She laughed lightly, giving him a dip of the lashes. "Oh? Who am I for then?"

"I should be so lucky to guess. I've been watching you a long time, a poor lonesome waif with his nose pressed up against the window. Longing for a kind look, a sweet word."

"Phil, you're something else. You've never been lonesome in your life for five minutes!"

"I'm lonesome right now."

"Go on. Partying all night. I bet some girl took you home from the reading, didn't she?"

"Ever heard of being lonesome in a crowd? Nobody took me home, Laverne. I passed out in a chair, and I feel like a ghost."

"Hey!" she shrieked. "Those are my clothes! Where do you think you're going with my clothes?"

The woman turned to survey her. "Why don't you watch your machine then? It's been off for ten minutes. Sitting there carrying on."

"Ten minutes, my foot. I looked away for an instant." Laverne collected her clothes and began to fold them into the cart.

"Laverne . . . how about lunch? Come on, have lunch with me. I'm starving." He probably had fifty cents on him, but he figured she couldn't go out with him carrying her laundry.

"Phil, I'd love to." She patted at her hair. "But Tommy would scream his head off. He gets awfully cranky. He hasn't had his lunch yet and he gets his nap after. I'd love to eat lunch with you but I just can't."

He took her arm. "How about making me some lunch then? It's silly to run into you after so long and lose you to a pile of sheets."

She laughed. "There's not much in the house. Some eggs."

"Eggs would be fine, don't fuss. Anything you eat, I'll eat too."

"Oh, don't bet on that. I eat yogurt."

"So I'll eat yogurt too." By this time he was pulling the clanking squeaky cart of laundry and she was pushing the stroller with Tommy in it. He couldn't imagine how she'd done both on the way there. Must have been quite a sight, Laverne in the middle and the cart behind and stroller in front like a choo-choo train.

"Oh, I know men don't eat yogurt." She gave him an arch look. She seemed nervous but willing enough to let him come along. She was still up on the hill behind Harvard Street on the ground floor of a three-flat house with faded-looking junipers beside the steps. She disappeared immediately to comb her hair and probably to change. When she came back her ash-blond hair was loose and combed out on her shoulders and her face looked more together and she was wearing a soft green sweater and well-fitted gray pants.

First she fed Tommy slop from a jar, spooning it into him in his high chair. Then she made scrambled eggs for them. He helped himself to a beer from the refrigerator. To judge from the water collected on top, it had been there awhile. She had one with him. She was nervous still but in an appealing way: she punctuated every few sentences with a short soft laugh. The laugh did not say she was amused but was an offering to him to be pleased with her, to let her please him, not to judge what she was saying if it was not pleasing. It was obsequious and playful. He felt better already. She had always been soignée and unapproachable, Ryan's wife. He touched her shoulder and her arm and once her hip, and although she laughed each time and pretended not to notice, she did not withdraw. He had another beer as she continued to sip her first.

"How about his nap?" he suggested. Time to get on with it.

She agreed, but Tommy, who understood at once, started yelling and banging. There followed half an hour of confusion. He lay down on the couch beside the white plastic tree with its lights blinking like a soft advertisement. He was mildly bored but contented, feeling her wanting him to be there. He did not feel specifically sexual response in her, not even when she came back from the kid's room and after hesitating, sat down on the couch where he beckoned her. Immediately he slid his arms around her, pulled her alongside him to kiss. She had said something about getting the daughter from nursery school at four. He did not feel in her body that she wanted him particularly but he sensed she was acquiescent. She felt obliged.

When he got his hands under her sweater—she wore a brassiere and it took him awhile to get the stiff thing off— she interrupted and said she had to do something, please, she would be right back. She trotted into her own bedroom. He followed, deciding why not use the bed. She was rummaging in the top drawer, red with embarrassment. "It must be in the bathroom. I'm so sorry! It'll only take a minute! Please." She ran into the bathroom and started pushing things around in the medicine chest. Apparently there she found what she was looking for because she shut the door and then in a while came out. In the meantime he took off his clothes and opened up the bed. She came out of the bathroom still dressed and stood there flatfooted till he got up and put his arms around her.

She was a green stiff-feeling woman, but he was gentle and patient. Maybe he was enjoying the idea of it better than the thing itself but she was pretty and Ryan's wife and it was a pleasant thing to do on a snowy afternoon. He had just got on her when the kid in the next bedroom started hollering. Then if she didn't give a quick buck and, mumbling apologies, cram herself into pants and sweater and run off. The cries continued, diminished, and finally turned off. By the time she came back, stripped and hopped in again, still saying her soft apologies, he was limp as a worm.

When she discovered that she seemed upset, though he couldn't see why as she hadn't taken more than a polite interest in the proceedings. But a few minutes later she was curled up in his arms crying and telling her troubles. "Before I married Tom, lots of men wanted to marry me and anyway lots wanted to go out with me. I still don't know why I married Tom, he's shorter than me, honest to God. He's a mean person; I used to think sometimes, that he just must hate me. . . . My family liked him, he even bought me a solitaire diamond. But now, with two kids, it seems like nobody cares for me any more. I got married so young, I hardly had a chance to enjoy it all, being young and pretty. I think I'm still . . . pretty?" Waiting for his reassurances. "But now I don't meet any men. How can I? I have to keep house and take care of the kids. I joined the neighborhood association but all those men are married. I even tried bowling! Honestly, all I meet are married men, and who wants somebody else's husband? Tom still wants me back. He's living with some

girl, I don't know what kind of slut she is to live with somebody else's husband! But he still wants me back. I don't know!
He's smart, after all, and they're his kids. And I don't really
believe in divorce. . . ." At that point the kid started crying
again. Up she hopped and dressed and ran off. Phil lay a
moment making faces at the ceiling and then he got dressed.

"Are you going?" Her face pinched with disappointment.

"No, no. Just thought we could have a cup of coffee,
something like that." Actually he had meant to go, but in
the face of her desolation, he couldn't. She thought she had
some real coffee but after looking in all the cupboards decided maybe she'd used it up when she tried to give a party.
Finally she made cocoa.

"I haven't had cocoa in years. Jesus, makes me feel like
a kid. Winters are different for kids. When was the last time
you touched snow?"

Tommy was up by now, so they bundled him into his outdoor clothes till he was round as an onion. Then they pitched
out the back door. There was about two inches of snow by
now, not much but it packed well. Phil tried to show Tommy
how to make a snowball but he was too young and just
squeezed it in his hand and laughed. Then they went back in
and she made more cocoa for him and Tommy to have with
animal crackers.

She seemed like a pretty good mother. Maybe because she'd
always been so soignée she didn't seem to mind when Tommy
splashed the milk and spat up the cocoa. Or maybe she was
in a good mood because he had stayed. Her cheeks were rosy,
her eyes seemed bluer and brighter, even if she did leave the
room every time she had to blow her nose.

They sat on the couch with Tommy banging blocks together and screaming and carried on a conversation when they
could hear each other. She cuddled up to him and showed
him a sweater she was knitting. It was a handsome fisher-
man's knit.

"Oh, I've made three little outfits for Tommy and a scarf
and mittens and a cute little hat for Bonnie and a blue
sweater for her, she's blond like me. I made myself a scarf
and a cardigan and a blue beret and a sweater from the same
yarn as Bonnie's, and a heather tweed sweater. If you really
like this sweater, I could make one for you."

"Sure I like it. But isn't that a lot of work?" Jesus, he suspected she really might do it.

"It makes me feel better. Knitting is something I know how to do. Then at the end of the day I can see at least I got some knitting done and at the end of a couple of weeks I have something to show for it."

He could imagine her in the four-room apartment halfway up the hill knitting away. Alone with her kids, knitting and knitting, covering the whole house in heather tweed. Knitting a big shroud for them. It was creepy. Still he kind of liked her. "Hey, you want to make some more cocoa? Without the marshmallows this time."

After they picked up Bonnie from nursery school, he hitch-hiked home. Jackson was making meat loaf with bacon laid on top and basil and onion inside, baked potatoes, good smells in the kitchen. "Jackson, old buffalo, where did you learn to cook like that, growing up in Sofa, Idaho?"

"I learned to cook from books, as anyone can who is willing—unlike yourself—to follow simple directions. A recipe is the codified knowledge of the experienced."

"Aw, ever ready to read wisdom in a grain of processed rice." He gave Jackson a poke in the arm.

"I learned to cook after Sissy cleaned me out. I didn't have enough of the ready to eat out and I got tired of frozen shit. I thought I was getting ulcers, but after I started cooking for myself the pains disappeared."

"If I talk enough, I don't notice what I'm eating—that's how I can stand the chow at Going-to-the-Sun. Here's Miriam."

Going to meet her, he followed her into her room. She was wet and cranky. "Ugh, what a day. That Fred Weathering is going to drive me out of my mind. I disagreed with him in project meeting and he told Jaime I'm a castrating bitch! Last time he had one of his dim ideas, I waited and told him afterward what I thought was wrong. He said, 'Well, if you thought that, why didn't you speak up when we were making the decisions?' Hey! What the hell did you mean routing me out of bed last night? I was yawning all day long. Was that supposed to be fun?"

Aw, she was in a foul mood. He felt a little uneasy, thinking she could read his easy afternoon lying around drinking cocoa. Got to get her into a better mood. "Hey, old lady, you know what score I finally evened up?"

She plumped down on the side of the bed, yanking off her wet boots and toweling some water from her mane. "What are you keeping score on now?"

"For you, baby. Old Ryan. Or have you forgiven all and turned the other buttock?"

"That miserable twit. I am not in a forgiving strain. Did you see him today?"

"Only by proxy. I ran into Laverne. He's trying to get her back, he's promising anything—"

"But he's living with one of the secretaries—Beth told me."

"Well, she might be living alone soon. He's working on Laverne. Anyhow, I picked her up, went back to their cozy domestic flat, and laid her."

She looked at him blankly. "That's supposed to be doing me a favor?"

"You're not jealous, baby. Tit for tat. Old Ryan'll chew his insides out when he hears it."

"Laverne never did anything to me. Ryan is my enemy, not her. She's probably lonely. How could you think using her sexually would make me feel good?"

"She's Ryan's wife. I figured that evened the score."

"She isn't Ryan. She's a person too. Oh, you make me sick!" Pushing past him, she stormed out. He followed, peeved and somehow thrust into the wrong. Still drying her hair, she dropped on a kitchen chair.

"You're late tonight." Jackson leaned one arm on the back of her chair. "Supper in five minutes."

"How can you be jealous of Laverne? It was just an afternoon's game."

"Jealous! I'm sorry for the woman. I'm sorry for all the women you pick up and use. How am I supposed to get along with other women, how am I supposed to have friends when I never know which of them you're going to cozy up to, fuck, and discard!"

"We've been together five years, and you still think I'm going to discard you?"

"No, I'm *different*. How am I supposed to explain to women who are my friends that I'm different but they're fair game? Take a bite of the apple and throw it away." She was really excited, waving her hands around and shouting.

Jackson made a cool face of disgust. "Nothing like a scene with supper to dull the appetite. What's all this emoting about? O Philip, what new sin have you committed against womankind?"

"Nothing. Just nothing!" He leaned on the refrigerator, folding his arms. "She came home in a foul mood from work and she's taking it out on us."

Jackson leaned on the back of her chair. "How would you feel if we took out our daily sufferings on you?"

"You do, and that's not what's up." She shook her head angrily. "Phil uses women and that's all there is to it! He told me about Laverne and expects me to say, 'Whoopie.' "

"Laverne Ryan?" Jackson went back to the stove, looking over his shoulder. "What about her?"

"What about her yourself. I met her on the street and spent the afternoon with her. She seemed glad for the company."

"She still separated from Ryan?" Jackson tasted the beans judiciously, added salt. "Not a bad-looking woman. Not bad at all. So where's the crime? You raped her on the kitchen floor?"

"I did not. I was more ravished than ravishing."

"I'm sure we all find you ravishing." Jackson came back to the table. "Have we a jealous female glowering on our hearth?"

"You're both crazy. That's not how Phil told it to me! He said he was getting revenge on Ryan by laying her."

"I was making a joke." Phil gave a long-suffering pout. "I can't even joke around here any more."

"Laverne is an attractive female. Do you feel you did harm to her person or psyche this afternoon of December 23?"

"I did not." Phil tucked his hand in his leather vest. "I might say that the lady in question appeared pleased with my company and other services. She fed me lunch and gave me cocoa and animal crackers."

"I would not say, then, that the scene could be interpreted as violent. Animal crackers?"

"Animal crackers and cocoa, your honor, once with marshmallows and once without."

"I find the defendant innocent of all charges brought against him. I assess court costs on the plaintiff for causing a fuss about nothing. Unless you wish to request that the defendant encounter less attractive females in his daily walks."

"I'm not jealous! You both twist everything! I'm sick of it!" She started out of the room. "I don't know if I believe you now and you were lying before, or the other way around."

Phil pulled himself off the refrigerator. "Jesus, I'm the one should be sore. Lying your ass. You've lost your sense of humor. You take yourself too damn seriously lately."

"And who appointed you my judge?" She rounded on Jackson. "I'm sick of being judged by the two of you. I'm sick of this life. It's ugly!"

"So if you can't take it, get out of the way," Jackson said coldly. He was angry by now, his anger transmuted into an icy rage coming down like a drill bit. "Enough scenes. Stay or go. Accept or get out. I don't like random scenes with my supper. I don't like women who carry on when nobody's hurting them."

"Accept or get out—that's just like you. Eat shit or starve. No chance of a human compromise. No chance of you coming halfway and giving in return. Do you think I'm crazy to go on giving and giving myself down a rathole?"

Jackson and his ultimatums: he was going to push her into a corner. All a bunch of noise. "Aw, shut up, the both of you. What's wrong tonight? Is supper ready or not?"

"There's the damn phone. Just a minute." Miriam ran to answer it.

"What's the big idea giving ultimatums?" Phil said softly to Jackson. "Enough with the melodrama."

"She's not going to push me around. This is my house and if she doesn't like it, she can pack and clear out."

"Yeah, and leave us fucking our hands? Come off it, you got her really mad now."

"No. I'm the one who's mad. No sexual blackmail. I want her to stop throwing her weight around. I'm not going to be abused by a chick every time she feels like complaining. You attach too much importance to her threats. You encourage her. You take all that gassing for real."

"Then what are you getting so mad about yourself?"

"Supper's ready. Let's eat." Jackson put the food down and Phil joined him. "You're the one she was digging into, anyhow."

"I didn't do a thing."

"Misunderstood again." Jackson looked at him with raised brows. "I wouldn't mind some time in the hay with Laverne."

"Man, she's available. She's the original bored and lonely housewife."

"Didn't she used to have some job downtown?"

"She's got two kids."

"Then what did you do, lock them in the closet?"

"The daughter was at nursery school and the son was napping. No sweat. She was eager for it."

"Hmmm. Where did you run into her, exactly?"

Phil laughed. "You wouldn't mind taking a walk there, right?"

Miriam came to the door, pushing her hair back with one hand. She looked even crankier. "Why didn't you tell me Beth was trying to get me all day?"

"I forgot. Like you have observed, I had a busy day."

"But why didn't you tell her how to reach me at Logical?"

"I forgot. Like I said. Now get off my back. I got more things on my mind than little girls with big mouths." There she was carrying on about Beth and she didn't even know he was fired too and in trouble.

"She went back with the detective, with her husband. I know they couldn't make her do that legally! She was conned into it."

"Sit down and eat," Jackson said with leaden calm. "Try chewing your food instead of us."

"I'm going over there. Now! And I'm moving out."

"Aw, Miriam, sit down and eat your supper and shut up. What's all this? Just 'cause we had a few harsh words—"

"I can't stand it! Phil, you're always on something now and it makes you paranoid. I can't forgive you for hitting me, I don't believe you won't do it again. A scene like that last night in the middle of the night, I think you're going crazy! And you, Jackson, you just take and take and you won't give. I can't stand it! Loving somebody who won't love back, it's a dead end, it's a trap, it's killing me!"

She stormed out of the room and he saw her limping down the hall halfway into her wet boots and trying to hurry. Then the outer door slammed. Jackson was being cool and trying to look bored. He could feel Jackson's anger coming through the calm like a high-pitched whine, like steel bearing down on steel. "Some more meat loaf?" Jackson asked. "There's plenty for us both, after all."

THREE

Both in Turn

18

That Which God Has Joined

Because events happened fast Beth had little time to think. She fell back on passive resistance, which worked poorly with Jim and the detective actively pushing and pulling on her, threatening and causing things to move faster than she could figure out the direction. When Jim showed up at the commune, she panicked. She did not want him in her life. She had a panicked, choking fear that if the detective and Jim marched around on her life, the fragile beginnings of independence and self and relationships that she had made, there would be nothing left. She did not want them to know her life. The more they threatened, the more she wanted to conceal. In her confusion and fear she agreed to go with them—anything to get them out.

Then the detective flew to Syracuse, leaving her to drive back with Jim in his car. During that seven-hour drive she repeatedly imagined, every time she used a toilet in a service plaza, running away. Always when she emerged he was grimly standing in wait. Every time she tried to start a conversation with him he grew angry and began to drive so erratically she got scared and shut up. Turning the radio loud, he drove staring straight ahead. Dreading Syracuse, nevertheless after a few hours she could not imagine a tighter hell than being cooped up with him clenching his jaws and driving, driving while the radio sang about love and sweet dreams and easy sex. The Stones sang of women who were under their thumb, while other groups beseeched girls to give their favors, be true, stop hanging on or go away. They all sounded like bad jokes to her. She remembered in the early days of her marriage rock music had seemed to promise her life and space and energy. Now it felt like her enemy, reinforcing in Jim images of how men and women were supposed to be.

The Massachusetts Pike turned into the New York Thruway and it was all the same nightmare of white road advancing before them and blurring to the sides. Two days before Christmas: the traffic was heavy. That morning it had snowed, but the expressways were clear until outside Albany. After dark the wind rose and snow came blowing at them. He did not slow and she was attacked by fearful images of collision. Out of rage he would smash them both into a viaduct.

They ate in a service plaza. He had a hot turkey platter and she had vegetable soup and a cheese sandwich. Chewing the tasteless cheese, she remembered the pill fight. Cold fingers closed on her throat. To have sex with him would be ugly but she was not sure what would happen. When she went to the women's room, she removed the pills from the container in her purse and worked them into the lining of her coat. Then she threw the container away.

Standing at the washbasin and scooping her hand for water, she took a pill and glared into the mirror. How pathetic she looked! She made a fist, grimacing. How had they found her? After a year and two months, she had felt safe. She hated herself for feeling safe. But maybe now he would give up when he faced her new self, her intransigence. The detective had hinted that perhaps if she co-operated a divorce might be worked out.

When they finally arrived she said, "You're in the same apartment? But please, I want to stay in a motel."

"We had a three-year lease. Where did you think I'd be?"

"I didn't think you'd want to stay out here."

"Did you think a lot about what I wanted?"

"Anyhow, I don't want to stay here. I came back to Syracuse to talk, but that doesn't mean staying here."

He came around to her side, opened the door, and pulled her out. "You live here, remember?" He yanked her by the hand.

She hung back. "No! I live in Somerville, in my house. I don't want to go in there. I'll come over tomorrow, but I don't want to sleep here. I don't want to be married to you, I don't want to be with you."

"You don't know what the fuck you want. And we are married, or did you forget that too?" He dragged her by the arm until they were inside. Then he let go and locked the door ostentatiously, even though it was only a chain lock and turning a knob. She sat down in the recliner, avoiding the couch. After all, she might as well act like company. But the act of sitting in his chair made her nervous.

"You want a beer?" He got himself one from the kitchen.

"Yes, please." Her throat felt dry.

"Oh, you learned to drink while you been gone."

"I just thought . . . water would be fine."

"Sure, you'd rather get high on drugs."

"What's with you, Jim? You smoke grass."

"I don't play around with those hard drugs, acid and speed and heroin and all that shit."

"What makes you think I do?"

"I read the detective's report, I know what you been doing. I know who you been hanging around with instead of me. Made a beeline right for it, didn't you?"

She found herself holding her breath. She looked away, around the room. "It's not even messy. See, you don't have to be dropping stuff on the floor. I mean, it looks nice."

"No thanks to you. I got a woman comes in once a week, a fat old spade who does some other apartments in the building, the super told me about her. Sets me back twenty just to have her for a day. Highway robbery."

"You got a tree too." Twenty a day, a hundred a week if you did get work every day. About what she'd got in the department store. A woman paid to do what she'd been expected to do every night for free after a day's work.

"I got it for you. I figured you'd enjoy a tree, like we're a real family for a change."

"Jim . . . I don't want to feel like a real family. I want to be back with my friends. Sally's going to have her baby any minute."

"Some hippie slut with no husband. Having a bastard. What's wrong with you? What do you think your own mother is going to say to all this stuff?"

"I'm sorry I married you, really! I don't want to make you unhappy. I didn't know what it meant. Everything was always pushing on me, get married, get married, get married—"

"You sure pushed me. You wouldn't give me the time of day without a ring. You sure changed fast." He pulled a balled-up paper out of his wallet. "It's all down here from that detective. You were screwing some professor who left his wife for you, right? Screwing him all the time in a house with a bunch of guys, maybe you were screwing all of them."

"No! It's not right! I didn't!"

"It's all down here in black and white!"

"Jim, I don't even go out with men now. Please listen to me!"

"You like dykes better." He shook the balled-up paper at her. "You're sick, you know that?"

"Dikes?"

"Women who go to bed together. Don't come on innocent with me any more, I'm on to you now."

She felt peculiar. Had the detective really thought that about the women's commune? Who was she supposed to be lovers with? She said slowly, "I don't think I want to be close to anybody that way. But I guess if I had to choose who to be with, maybe I would choose women right now. I never thought of it. You laugh at me for not knowing what that word means, and I am ignorant. Or maybe I would have thought of that before. That touching women might be different from men. But I don't want anyone to touch me."

"You think I'm going to believe all this crap, don't you? You think I'm pretty stupid. You think you got smart hanging around a college and screwing professors. That was the real big time, you think, and you can push me around. You got another think coming, girl. I was nice to you before, I tried to treat you like a goddamned valentine. Boy, what you put me through. You kept me hot and hungry for months. You were too good to put out. You must think I'm stupid, you must think I'm easy to put it over on." He stood, his hands open and sweating. "I had to pay that detective two hundred dollars and expenses and he flies all over the place and stays at motels and he don't eat peanuts. I paid through the nose. I paid to get you back and I got you back, and I'm not taking any crap from you. You made me feel like a piece of dirt, but you're going to take it instead of dish it out for a change."

He started for the chair. She got up and ducked behind, then made a run for the door. He caught her before she could get the chain off. He picked her up, carried her flailing wildly into the bedroom, and dumped her on the bed. Then he dropped on her. She remembered Miriam saying once, "Go on, I don't believe one guy can do it against my will—I'd just give him a kick in the basket." But Miriam was five feet nine. Beth was squashed under him, her thighs pinned, her hands clawing and pounding on his back. She was furious at herself.

She hated herself lying squashed and helpless while he forced her thighs apart. Why did women wear pants like tissue paper? Why must she hate herself for being hurt?

It hurt, him forcing his way into her, it hurt a lot. She chewed on her lips. It hurt and soon it must be over, soon. She waited for it to be over and tried to concentrate on turning hating herself into hating him. He was getting away with it this time, but she must not let him hurt her again. She was dry and tight and each thrust rasped and hurt more. He was making her a child. A child can say, *"No, I won't!"* And mean it passionately, with all her heart and body. *"No, I won't!"* But father or mother or teacher says, *"Yes, you will."* And they always win. A child can be sent to bed hungry, a child can be beaten, a child can be forced.

Her father used to whip her with a wooden yardstick that stood in a corner of the kitchen. She had never seen it used for anything else. Her mother would slap her face, would turn her over her knee to spank her. Her father always whipped her with the wooden yardstick. She would run before him screaming, "No, Daddy, no! No! I didn't do it! I won't do it again!" It hurt, like this. It humiliated, like this. It was disgusting to run that way, lying and promising and blubbering and she would not cry now, her anger would seal her.

Afterward she would look for bruises, sneaking into her parents' room to use the three-way mirror. She would love her bruises for the feeling they gave her of being terribly abused. But if anyone else noticed, the humiliation would return and she would die. Dolores was the only person she ever told. Dolores' father punished her with his fist. They whispered together and comforted each other.

Lying with him plunging at her like a club landing, she hated her father, for the first time consciously she hated him. Would it have been such a big deal to love me? Would it have cost you so damned much? You stingy skinflint. You wouldn't love me and you wouldn't love Marie and I don't think you loved Mommy by the time I was born. What would it have cost you? You think I would have asked for so much? You scared me witless I would lose my virginity somewhere, like losing a quarter out of a hole in my pocket, and then, god, you'd kill me.

Why didn't he come? He always used to come fast enough. She writhed under the raw scraping. Every time I used to be necking with a boy, the times Jim and I would pet, I'd be jerking around with fear. I would keep having this vision that you would suddenly appear and kill me. All I could think of was getting some man to take me away from you so I wouldn't be afraid any more and I wouldn't care any more that you didn't love me. That's all you ever wanted, to get me out of the house and married so you could wash your hands of me.

Her mouth tasted tinny, salty. Blood from the lip she had bitten through. Why didn't you raffle me off, one of those church raffles you loved where there's a chance at the turkey or a car? You made me so hungry for love that's all I could think of, somebody to love me and carry me away. Now look! Look! I suppose you call this love! Maybe it is, stripped bare. As Miriam would say, enjoy, enjoy. Why didn't she come? Why didn't she call me? She'd have known if I had to go with him. She'd have known if they could put me in jail. But she never called, she didn't come.

Finally he finished and rolled off. "How'd you like that?" She couldn't tell if he was being sarcastic. "It hurt."

"I'll bet. Go on, you liked it."

"It hurt. I don't like being raped."

He laughed as if she had made a joke. "Where do you think you're going?"

"To the bathroom. I hurt and I have to pee."

She locked the door and sat on the toilet to think. Her brain felt addled. Huddled there, she apologized for all the times she had laughed at lady wrestlers. She apologized for a day in late spring when she had passed on the Common a karate demonstration by some women. She had thought they looked ridiculous in their white suits, like walking laundry bags. The rigid chopping gestures and fierce noises had made her smile. Now she apologized to those women sweating and groaning and making explosive sounds from their diaphragms that spring day.

She asked forgiveness of the girls she had watched in high school playing field hockey and volleyball. She remembered telling Dolores, "Well, if I was a giraffe like her, taller than all the boys, I'd go out for sports too!" She asked forgiveness of the women she had judged big and awkward and ungainly, because they were not willing to be weak. She had believed herself superior because she could not, because she did not dare.

It didn't matter any more whether he could put her in jail or not. She felt sore all over. Her vagina burned, her womb ached from being pounded, her arms and back hurt. So did her head. She looked in the medicine cabinet for aspirin. Creme rinse for hair: now Jim never used that. She looked further, among the hair tonics and shaving creams and laxatives. Two yellow pills in a prescription bottle: three times a day after meals, Arlene Rogers. If he had a woman, why was he doing this to her?

Leaning against the bathroom window, she contemplated jumping. Ten feet. But she did not have her purse or winter coat and would not get far. He began banging on the bathroom door. Hurriedly she looked around for a good idea and then gave up and unlocked it.

"Let's go in the living room and talk," she said.

"I'm played out. I got up before sunrise to drive to Boston and I drove all the way back. I need sleep."

"I'm not sleepy. I'll sit up and read."

"The hell you will. I'm not trusting you out of my sight." He made her lie down with him, keeping his hand on her hip.

She waited. She waited forever until he slept and then she watched another hour go by on the clock. His hand had fallen from her. Then she began to ease out of bed. He woke immediately. "Where are you going?"

"To the toilet. Do you think this is school, I have to ask you before I pee?"

"I want you to ask me before you do anything. That way we'll get along fine."

He took a long time to go back to sleep. Again she waited and tried to slip out and again he woke. He was sleeping lightly, anxiety keeping him on edge. She told him her bladder hurt, which was true. She was too angry and scared to sleep. She kept berating herself for having agreed to return with him, for having panicked, for having let the detective scare her into believing she would go to jail if she did not come along. For letting them club her into submission with jail and her family and their sudden appearance. She had been afraid they would somehow get Sally into trouble, get the state to take her baby. Afraid they would hurt the women and break up the commune.

Would they hold together without her? How self-important even to ask. Anything that depended on one person wasn't worth doing. If it was working for them, they would hold it together. She imagined being back. Walking in the door.

Sally would say, "Wow, you made it just in time, girl! Almost missed my baby."

Not if that meant dragging Jim and maybe the police back on her trail. She could not go directly back. She must run first in some other direction. The state-line game. Farther, faster, in a new direction. She would go west, as far as Chicago, maybe farther. She would not return to the commune until she knew she was safe. If she got away from Jim this time, he had to let her go: but she had thought that the last time. Hate would be a thin motive for a long chase. Perhaps he had hired the detective only recently: perhaps it had not taken them long to trace her but rather only lately had he bothered to try. Before she left, she must find out.

Breakfast: "I'll cook eggs but not bacon. I can't touch or eat meat. I'm a vegetarian now."

"What kind of garbage is that? Just make me bacon."

"I can't cook or eat meat, Jim. I'm telling you." She grasped at a way to express it to him. "It's against my religion."

"What kind of a crappy religion is that?"

"I'm a Buddhist. I've become a Buddhist."

"You can unbecome one right now. You think I'm going to live on eggs, you're crazy."

"I don't care what you live on. I eat vegetables and fish and milk and cheese and eggs. But I can't cook flesh."

She thought he was about to hit her but he controlled himself. She remembered that control. "All right. Skip the bacon for one morning. Tonight we have meat, I'm telling you. I got a steak in the refrigerator. And tomorrow you fix a Christmas turkey."

If she was still here tomorrow, he could cook her a turkey. She fried eggs and made toast and coffee.

"Your cooking is as lousy as it ever was. You could patch a tire with those eggs."

"I don't like to cook. I don't ever do it."

"Oh, you eat out all the time, huh, like a millionaire?"

"I mostly eat raw foods."

"You really have turned into some kind of a nut!"

"Yes." She smiled at him. "You wouldn't like me at all. Jim, how come you made me come back when you already have a woman? Arlene Rogers."

"Who told you about her? What if I did? I got the stuff on you from the detective, in writing, so don't try to put anything over on me. Two wrongs don't make a right."

"But if she was living here with you, why not just go on?"

"She's none of your business, and she didn't live here. Don't put words in my mouth. Who told you about her?"

"I bet the detective had a hard time finding me. That's how come it took you so long. Because I covered my trail good."

"Think you're so smart? How hard is it, you think, to find Beth Walker? The electric and gas are in your name. It didn't take him but two, three days to find you."

"I put the deposits down. They made us give big ones too. I bet we'll never get it back."

"It's my money anyhow. You owe it from what you stole."

"I didn't think you were looking for me after all this time."

"I figured to get things straightened out. It's Christmas. Everybody gets to be with their family at Christmas."

"So go home to your mother." She cleared the table. "What happened to your girl friend anyhow?"

"I told you shut up about her. She's not hanging around, if that's what you mean. I never cheated on you when we were together."

"We aren't together. I came back because you threatened me with jail. Now I'm ready to go to jail. I don't want to live with you! I have my own life!"

"You married me and you better believe it, I'm tired of having a wife off in Boston. You were the one so hot to get married, and now you better start making the best of it."

Turning, she slowly took from the rack over the stove the biggest knife and held it out. "Maybe you think I can't hurt you with this, but I think I can." For good measure she took the second biggest knife in her left hand. "Maybe you think you can get this knife away from me, but maybe I can cut you with one while you're going for the other."

"What do you think you're doing? You're going to fight me?"

"A knife is just as sharp in my hand as it is in yours. I say I can manage to hurt you just like you hurt me."

"Put that down." He got up and started at her. She lunged. "Hey!" He leaped back. "Watch out!"

"I want to hurt you! I'll kill you if I can! Listen to me, I don't want to be your wife! I'm walking out of here!"

"I'll call the cops as soon as you're out the door."

"Call them! I'd rather go to jail than stay here!"

"You're crazy! That's what it is, you're crazy. That's why you ran away. That's what's wrong with you."

"Hooray! I'm crazy. And I'll cut you up!" Wonderfully she heard her loud voice. Astounded, she watched the wild knives she was waving. She who wouldn't touch meat. If she actually cut him, she would be destroyed with guilt, yet she waved and slashed away. It was almost fun to scare somebody else instead of always being a victim. "I'm walking out. I'm going to see a lawyer. I'm not going to let you use me the way you did last night, not ever."

"Sure, you go to a lawyer." He was being heavily ironic. "Fine. That'll knock some sense into you. I already been, so I know what you're going to hear. Go find out the cold facts, and then you'll come crawling back. If I bother next time."

Backing out the door with her coat on her shoulder, still holding one knife with her purse wedged between her arm and body, she did not dare relax her posture till she was down the steps.

"Merry Christmas," he shouted out the window. "I hope you freeze to death, you bitch!"

She had trouble stuffing the knife into her purse. Then she walked on rapidly. Syracuse was colder than Boston with a foot more snow and she was stuck out in the suburbs as usual. No bus, no car. By now she had learned to make do. She trotted out on the highway where she had used to hate to walk and stuck out her thumb. She passed up the first ride, with two men, but took the second with a woman, who brought her into town.

From a phone booth she called Dolores. Mr. Mendez answered. "Dolores? She ain't here. Who is this?"

"This is Naomi. I used to go to high school with Dolores. I'm back here visiting. Do you know where I can find her?"

"Oh, a high school friend. Dolores isn't living at home no more. She's with a girl friend, a nurse. You want her number?"

It was Saturday morning and Dolores was home. "Bethie? Beth Phail, I mean Walker. What happened to you?"

"Dolores, listen. I ran away from Jim, you know that?"

"Sure, honey, I heard. Not like you told me. But I figured you had another man, huh?"

"No, but listen, Jim came with a detective. He scared me into coming here. Listen to me, Dolores, for all I know, he's after me, maybe my family's after me, the cops may be after me for Jim. All I want is a place to hide for a couple days till after Christmas when I can call a lawyer. I won't feel bad if you say no. I won't get you in trouble, I promise. Before I start dealing with a lawyer, I can move out to a motel."

"Honey, it's okay, I won't tell Jim. I don't know what happened between you two, but like, I don't care. Let me clear things with my roomie."

She was off the phone for a while. "Bethie? She says okay. But you have to sleep on the couch. You got a car?"

"No, but I'll get there. Just give me directions."

Dolores was sitting on the couch drying her long black hair, smoking a cigarette, drinking a cup of light sweet coffee and dying a pair of shoes red, all at once and lazily, with her plump legs curled up beside her. She had on an orange and green shiny robe that changed colors as she moved, bound at the neck with gold tassels. "Yeah, isn't it something? A harem dream, you bet. It's Moroccan."

"Lebanese," her roommate said from the bathroom.

"My nutty boy friend gave it to me. It's from a head shop. I feel like something off a cigar box—you know, those stinkers my old man used to smoke. How are you, kid?" Dolores peered at her. "You got a bruise the size of a pumpkin on your arm. Jim do that?"

"And it hurts when I pee and my back aches and I feel so ashamed!"

Dolores clucked and sympathized but finally could not understand. "I can't see leaving a man when you don't have a man. What's the point? If you don't have anybody else, I mean, you don't have to be careful with me, why not stay with him? You used to like him okay."

"Dolores, you aren't living with a man, why do I have to?"

"My parents would murder me dead, you remember them. I had trouble enough getting this apartment. As it is my mother calls me up every day. I wish I could tear the phone out. Besides, I got a boy friend, Dan." She lowered her voice. "For a while Joan didn't have a man, she broke up with the doctor she was seeing, he was married anyhow, and it was a long time before she got herself another. We were at each other's throats."

Christmas Day both Dolores and Joan spent with their families. Staying alone, she did not answer the phone, caught up on sleep, took a long hot bath and washed her hair and clothes. She was decked out in borrowed things from Dolores, too big but comfortable. There was little to read in the apartment, and she did not feel like staring at the TV. She wished she could talk to her family. She could not get them out of

her mind. Neither could she call. She kept imagining her
father answering, like a bolt of judgment ready to thunder
down on her. She kept going to the phone and standing there
and drifting away. Her mother and Marie she could deal with.
But her father and Dick and the whole family massed as they
would be for Christmas dinner, that she could not hack. Even
to think of them gathered around the table made her feel
eight years old and wrong.

She wrote a poem on a pad of paper she found beside the
phone with SOMEONE CALLED at the top and a picture of
Cupid sending an arrow through a telephone. Her poem
went:

> *Everything says no to me.*
> *Everybody tells me no.*
> *Only I say yes.*
> *I have to say it again and again*
> *like a singer*
> *with only one song.*
> *Yes, Beth! Yes, Beth! Yes, Beth!*
> *Yes!*

That made her feel better. Folding it, she put it in her wallet,
with her old pictures.

Outside the snow was coming sideways and the temperature
had gone down to seven, the radio said between "White Christmas" and "Rudolph the Red-Nosed Reindeer." She decided
not to go for a walk. Except at work she had hardly been
bored since she ran away. Always there were books to read
and things to work on and lately always friends to talk to.
Sally, Dorine, Gloria, Miriam were on her mind, they were
with her daily whether she saw them or not. She was caring
for them and considering what they had said to her and
thinking about what they might do together. She felt that they
saw her as a person as nobody else ever had.

The novelty of boredom made it more irritating. How had
she used to pass her time? She could no longer daydream;
she could only worry actively about her situation, helpless
until she could call a lawyer and find out what Jim could do
to her. She picked up some magazines from the coffee table
and began leafing through.

They were not exactly like the magazines she'd read in high
school. There was more about sex and more about food. The

girls' magazines assumed you went to school with lots of boys you had to attract and know how to handle ("How to Say No without Losing Him"). These magazines assumed you had to go out and find men and spouted suggestions for joining activities where They would be sure to be found. They also seemed to assume that you went to bed. There was an article on female orgasm written by a male doctor, which had as its theme that every woman could have instant orgasms if only she wanted. Apparently this was for women who didn't want to go to the movies and see how the actresses did it.

There were articles about getting back in circulation after divorce, about making glamorous dinners for dates, about sewing clothes that would look more expensive than you could afford, about buying lots and lots more clothes in new styles, about meeting men at the office, about how roommates could spend their entire joint salary for a month giving a New Year's Eve party, and ten articles on Beauty. If she followed the directions in even one or two of them, the upkeep on her body would consume her entire free existence.

There were many stories in which women got men in various ways or lost them. Their problems were all with romance. The stories were sexier than those she had used to read. The effect of reading them was to feel discontented and sad and vaguely stirred up, as if lacking, as if something were wrong with her. Quickly she put down the magazine. By now it was getting dark.

The lawyer was short, balding with sideburns, and seemed slightly amused, though not enough to cover his being bored during the twenty minutes he granted her.

"Little lady, it is not possible for a husband to rape his wife." In fact, he explained, it was not legally possible for her to be raped at all, not even by a platoon of strangers.

"Now, you left your husband. This detective fellow has information on your involvement with another man. You were living in a so-called commune including a woman about to have an illegitimate baby. No court would recognize any act with you as rape. The reputation of a woman is considered by the court as relevant to the question of whether an act of intercourse is rape. Rape isn't a crime such as murder or robbery, little lady, a crime is committed whether the victim is a bank president or a lady of the streets."

"So if I'm not a virgin or the property of one man, I can't be raped, according to you?"

"Frankly, you couldn't proceed in any such manner. Under no circumstances could your lawful husband be considered as not having rightful access to you."

"But I left him last year. I don't live with him. Can he force me to be with him when I don't want to?"

"But you did not secure a separation. You are still man and wife in the eyes of the law. There is no legal way in which you can prevent him from entering your domicile. . . . As for a divorce, he can divorce you. You of course can contest it, especially if we locate witnesses on this Arlene Rogers woman. With a detective's report he is by far in the better position, especially if your abandonment preceded his involvement. You don't have a leg to stand on, little lady. Now of course if he proved agreeable we could proceed against him in the matter of Miss Rogers or cruelty perhaps. You claim he did hit you several times? Any witnesses? Anyone who saw your bruises?"

"Only on my arm now and on my . . . leg."

"Not too good, considering the provocation. Before you left?"

"I didn't go around showing them to people." How had they got into discussing divorce? She had come to find out whether Jim could force her to go back to him if he called the police.

"More's the pity, little lady. He could proceed against you in the matter of the desertion or in the matter of the adultery. Frankly, you are in a weak position. Though we could give him a battle. But if he doesn't want a divorce, we are in a difficult position to procure one, unless we can turn up some items to discredit his testimony. In any event, I wouldn't think you could do well in the settlement, I'll be blunt with you."

"I don't want money. I took half the account when I left."

"That was your mistake."

"That's what you think. I'd never have got away otherwise. Listen, I can try to pay him back that money if he insists. You go see him. You talk to him for me and find out what he wants. Make him understand I won't go back to him no matter what!"

"How will you pay me, if I may ask?"

"I have a checking account in Boston. I'll write you a check."

"I'm sure you'll understand if I wait till it clears to act."

"It will clear!" She clutched her shaking hands in her lap, full of reactions that prickled and burned within her. They made it so difficult. They made it so grimy and humiliating, every step. "I'll call you from wherever I am."

"It would be best if you left me a phone number and an address."

"No. I'll call. How long will you have to wait for the check to clear?"

"Five days ought to do it, one way or the other."

"I'll call you early next week then. Do whatever you have to, so he won't come after me again!"

"I'll see what we can find to proceed on, little lady, but I can't work miracles. You've left yourself in a weak position, a very weak position indeed." He held out his hand. "Now the check. . . ."

"Mama, you never gave me a chance to want anything else but getting married! I wanted to go to college. I wanted to be a lawyer, remember? You thought it was silly."

"You wanted to marry Jim, you were seeing him right under my nose—your sister Marie told me that. What do you think is going to become of you, the way you're acting? My own daughter, and you're turning out worse than Elinor!"

"Mama, that was too young to get married! I want to be myself, Mama, not Mrs. Jim. I want a chance to be me before I die."

"You were a lucky girl to find Jim, and you're throwing it away. He'll still take you back, he told me so himself."

"I don't want him back!"

"What kind of a man do you have in Boston, won't come to see your family?"

"I don't have a man, Mama. Don't you ever wish you'd had a chance to do something besides have babies and take care of us and clean the house and do the laundry and make supper?"

"I've had as good a life as any woman. I'm not complaining. Your father's a good man and he's taken care of us. It's my children who've been a disappointment to me!"

"Can't you believe I know what I want?"

"You're too young and silly to know anything. It's all those television programs and movies, you and your sister Nancy are full of nonsense. Every man has his faults. Jim may drink a little, all men do. He holds down a job—"

"I hold a job too. I'm not afraid to work."

"Jim will take you back, if you buckle down and swallow your pride and try to make him happy. You listen to me, Elizabeth, this is your mother talking. I just want you to be happy. I don't know how you're going to end up, Bethie! Your father won't hear your name! And you'll be lying in some alley with your throat cut like those poor girls you read about in the paper. Listen to me, Jim may not be perfect but he's your husband. If you go running around, he'll wash his hands of you. Then you'll find out nobody will want you any more."

"Mama, I didn't call for you to read me the riot act. I wanted to tell you I'm okay. How's Nancy, Mama?"

"All right. She has a boy friend. I keep an eye on her."

"I'd like to talk to her for a minute."

"She hasn't come home from school yet. She doesn't get home this early."

"I'll bet, Beth thought. She knew when the seniors got out. "When will she be home?"

"I don't want you talking to her. I'm having enough trouble with her already."

"Do you think I'd corrupt her? Oh, never mind, Mama, listen, I have to go now." She was struck, hearing both of them, how often people in her family told each other to listen. Listen to me, they kept saying, and nobody ever did.

"You never write! What's wrong with you? Do you want me worrying?"

"I'm sorry, I can't write for fear you'll tell Jim where I am. When this thing is settled, I'll write." She hunched in the phone booth, her bladder burning. Something was wrong. Dolores had told her to go to a doctor, but that would have to wait.

"We never had a divorce in our family. Tell me the truth, is there someone else?"

"Good-bye, Mama. I'm sorry you're unhappy about me. All my life I was unhappy till I ran away." She had a terrible urge to cry to her mother about her pain, about what Jim had done. Quietly she put the receiver back. She had no heart for arguing. Her mother could not comfort her and was truly scared; her mother was scared that if Beth stepped out of the safe role there could be nothing but disgrace and disaster and death.

Dolores lent Beth forty dollars and she hitchhiked out in

the direction of Chicago. Starting again this time with less
money, she went with greater confidence that she would
land on her feet. The worst out there was no harder than
it was back here, and she would survive.

19
A Little Strange and a Little Familiar

Beth did not return to Boston as soon as she had imagined
when she left Syracuse. At first she was afraid, and then she
had to make money to pay off Jim and the lawyer and the
divorce. That meant staying put at a secretarial job in the
sales department of a company that installed air conditioners
for offices and public buildings. It meant learning the small
devious means of sabotage clerical workers adopt at jobs they
hate. She began to realize why certain women at the computer center and later at Tech Square had never been able to
do their tasks correctly. She became dumber every day. Visibly
she tried, she smiled and fluttered and tried. An assumption
was built into the structure, into the roles, that she was stupid,
and that left space.

At her old job she had done whatever she was given as
well as she could. She had thought it necessary to work well:
it was behavior carried over from school, where she had been
trained to try hard and earn good grades. She had acted as
if that job was like being in school. Looking back, she knew
it made no difference. They would have fired her as quickly
if she had been the fastest typist in the East, and no more
quickly if she had been as dumb as she was supposed to be.
All these offices had a certain number of slots for women.
The private secretaries did far more than they were paid for
and identified with the men they served, wrote speeches,
bought presents, propped up egos. But in the typing pool she
got in more trouble for standing out in any way than for
losing letters, misfiling invoices, standardly misspelling words,
or taking half the afternoon to type one letter. The men who
could have you fired would do so more quickly if they noticed

you did not shave your legs than if you broke the Xerox machine.

Lunch hour offered no relief. In the little luncheonettes and cafeterias where secretaries went, they were expected to eat quickly and clear out. The restaurants where people were allowed to take longer for lunch were too expensive without an expense account. She hardly ever saw women together in them. Generally she brought her lunch. On nice days she could walk over to Michigan Avenue and sit on a bench, if nobody harassed her. What the women in her office did was to wander in the Loop window-shopping or drifting through the department stores. Essentially there was nothing to do except buy. On their lunch hours, they might spend what they made the rest of the day.

The pressure to dress in a certain way was high on this job. She learned the game of secondhand stores and the game of accessories, but she resented having to think about it. The receptionist, Karen, who sat out front alone, spent far more than she made on clothes, in styles the others had perhaps seen in magazines or on television, but she was always the first they would see in real life wearing such clothes. Karen had overdue accounts at three department stores and a couple of specialty shops on Michigan Avenue. She managed by sleeping with some of the executives and their clients.

The girls spoke of her as lucky, as having the best job. On most breaks Karen would sit on the bench in the women's john doing her nails and ignoring the conversation. Other times she joined in and told them funny stories about their bosses, but never if the private secretary of that boss was present. She knew girls in the pool would not tell on her. She boasted she never ate lunch if she didn't have a date, in order to stay thin. The family doctor had put her on amphetamines in high school to lose weight and they had burned her out, but she had kicked them finally. Now she just starved herself. She had to drink with the clients and that, she said, went straight to flab.

At Thanksgiving, Karen took an overdose of sleeping pills, almost died, and remained in the hospital a couple of weeks. She was let go from her job. Every couple of days Beth went to see her. No one else did. Karen said she had been involved with the manager who had got her her job, that he had promised he was going to get a divorce and marry her. But lately, when she pressed him, he had said he would never leave his wife for a whore.

By the time Karen got out of the hospital Beth had paid back Jim and the lawyer's fees and saved what the divorce was supposed to cost. She was free to quit and leave Chicago. Karen asked her again and again to travel with her to California. Karen did not want to go alone. Beth felt hesitant about going straight back to Boston. When she first came to Chicago she had called Miriam collect. Jackson had answered and refused the call, saying Miriam didn't live there any more. Beth did not know what that meant. After she had been working awhile and had some money, she went to a pay phone and called the women's house. An operator told her that number had been disconnected. Once again, after brooding over it long enough to work herself up, she called Miriam's old number. Jackson answered. He said Miriam had moved out to the women's house and he claimed to know nothing else, nothing at all. He was testy. She asked for Phil, and Jackson said shortly that he didn't live there any more either. That was that. She did not even know where to address a letter. Were any pieces left to be picked up? Any friends waiting? She might be rushing back to nothing at all. She had never traveled, she had never been West. She told Karen she would hitchhike to California with her.

Karen had turned on her old life. She cut her blond hair and let it begin to grow out brown. She dressed in jeans and army surplus. Beth thought that Karen could not help being beautiful no matter how she dressed, but in army surplus other people often did not notice. Karen had a face Beth thought of as Midwestern and Scandinavian. Karen laughed. "I'm Scottish and German. And Midwestern is an insult! It means I look like a cow!" Karen came from Green Bay where her father had a desk job in a dairy, and she had gone to college for three years at Wisconsin. "I don't know, I felt that the life in Chicago was corrupt but that was what it was all about. I thought the other girls were fools not to use their looks to get something. But now I think I was just worse used. He never came to see me once in the hospital!"

Beth thought Karen attractive with her high forehead and milky skin and fine features that seemed all gentle curves. But she generally liked the way her friends looked, that seemed to go with liking somebody. She certainly felt closer to Karen as she was now than with green eyelids and fountains of

bleached hair and know-it-all manner and bizarre clothing
that made her body a neon sign.

Aside from the flatness, the Midwest did not seem that
strange to Beth spread out under the shield of snow. The
first place that seemed exotic was Albuquerque, where they
decided to blow the money to rent a motel room and hang
around for a week. The second night they were staying there,
sharing a bed, after they turned the lights out Karen put an
arm around her. She was surprised and kissed Karen good
night, but Karen did not stop kissing her then. Beth was
frightened, more of the idea of what was happening than of
the fact. Karen was gentle. She sensed Karen would not
persist if she drew away. But how could she insult or refuse
her? She was Karen's only friend, her only connection: perhaps that was why Karen wanted to have sex with her.

When they got up in the morning, they had become
strangely and immediately a couple. Beth pondered that. They
had been friends, they had been traveling together. She
thought of her Boston friends as much closer to her. But by
that act in bed they became a couple. This was the thing that
Jim had accused her of, and now she was doing it. Now he
would say she was a lesbian. "Dyke" was his word.

The sex with Karen was the first consistently pleasurable
sex she had ever known. Soon she found out how passive
she was, how inexperienced in consciously satisfying a lover.
Karen could not take her pleasure and climb off. She had to
please Karen actively. That made her feel self-conscious,
awkward. Then she came to experience it as more natural
than just being acted upon. If she were more active with a
man, if it were mutual, it might be better as it was with
Karen: but she was not sure. Anyhow, the sex with Karen
was something they did together, and while she could not
abandon herself to it as Karen could, for the first time she
could initiate, she could *make* love.

Thinking about it, sometimes sitting in a car that had picked
them up and looking out at the vast landscapes of desert and
mountains and irrigated fields while Karen made conversation
to the driver or did a stint of driving, the label-thing would
attack her. She would think, Well, now I am a lesbian. She
would think she had to do something about her new identity.
It became a whole complication, whether she should tell
people or not tell, act out that she was with Karen or pretend they were not a couple.

They wandered until they came to San Francisco and there they stopped. In the Mission they found a house, mostly women although there was one man who was with one of the women and another man half living there. Karen made clear to the house that they were a couple. Several of the women had been in consciousness-raising groups and were not inclined to get upset over women loving women, and the house agreed that a couple of gay women would be good for them. Karen said they were being liberal, but it would do till they found something better.

San Francisco was beautiful as no place Beth had ever lived. On weekends Karen and she took long walks. They would pick out some hill from the map and walk around there. Those were good times. It felt like spring, although the people who lived there said it was winter. They said spring was when the fruit trees bloomed. Beth did not like the house as well as her own commune, and it made her miss her friends. It was more like Going-to-the-Sun, where Dorine used to live, a house where people slept and came and went and ate together and things somehow got done by somebody. Because this was a women's house, the food was okay and the house got cleaned and the men had to do an equal share. But the people did not get far into each other and did not make a common life. Nor did she and Karen move into larger relationships. They were a couple and Beth began to find that constricting.

If she loved Karen, it might be different. She liked Karen, but somehow that did not open into loving her. She asked herself if she were afraid. She did not know if that was it or if something cold in Karen held her off. Somehow Karen was more the man in their couple and she was more the woman, and Karen seemed to want it that way. In bed they were equal and that was good, but out of bed they were maybe not quite equal.

Karen easily took a hard line with her, telling her about the world and laying down axioms and criticizing her naïveté, and too easily she slipped into passivity. She felt her identity oozing away. Somehow she did not get the private space she needed. She had not wanted to live in a couple, she had known that, yet somehow she had eased into it. Why could they not have gone to bed without becoming a couple? Yet they had both begun to act that way the next day, and the very feeling they had that the world was against them, that others would punish them if they knew, cast them out, had made them in their travels close into a tighter knot. Beth thought more often of Boston.

She did not come to know the other women well, for she could not as easily reach out. She did not have as much time to read or think. Some precious strength was leaching away, not in a quick dangerous rush but slowly. Hesitantly she began to talk to Karen. Karen became frightened and jealous. She clutched, she fought. Then gradually Karen let go. They were still together but not so together. Karen began looking around in the house and at her job in the hospital, she went out to gay bars now and then. When the fruit trees began to bloom, Beth hitchhiked east again with another woman who was going to New York.

The house still existed but it took some time to find it, because it was not in the same place. Finally she located Gloria, who was living with her boy friend but knew where the women were. They had got kicked out. They were still in Somerville but had moved to Spring Hill, dropping off high and steep from the hospital into short dead-end streets called terraces, on one of which stood a run-down house with peeling white paint and a broken front porch. Dorine was living there with Sally and baby Fern. After Gloria left, a divorced woman, Connie, and her little boy David had moved in, and so had a woman named Laura. They had an empty bedroom still and they were glad to take Beth in.

Sally had gained weight. Beth thought she looked better, less gaunt and Orphan Annie-like. Her long red hair was braided and she sat down as still as anybody Beth had ever seen. She did not smoke or chew gum or play with her hair or chew her nails, she had no tics or twitches. When she sat, she sat.

The night Beth moved in, she stayed up late with Sally and Dorine. Dorine's color was better. Her face was sweet and heart-shaped under the frizzy bush of chocolate hair. Her eyes were not so often downcast, at least in the house, and she talked more, with short pauses but as she warmed up, vivaciously.

Sally said, "No, Jackson was putting you on. Miriam lived here for a piece right after you left. She helped me when I had Fern, she was pretty good. She always picks up little Fern and tells her, 'You know I saw you born, you little squirt!'"

"Why did she leave?"

Sally shrugged. "She didn't take to it."

Beth puzzled. She was so glad to be back! Dorine and Sally had kept her things in the basement. Now she had her books, her clothes, her scribblings, and the small familiar objects she had not touched since that afternoon she went with Jim.

"She didn't get that much into the house," Dorine said quietly. "She made more money than any of us. She was involved with her job. And she was in analysis the whole time she lived here. . . She went into a funk of deciding she was terribly self-destructive and needed help. . . . She was very warm with us and fussed over us, you know her way. But . . . she wouldn't let us fuss back. Maybe we couldn't help her. We weren't that together. . . . But she couldn't ask."

"Did her analyst think she should move out?"

"How can you ever tell what a shrink says? She could always pretend that to spare our feelings. . . . My parents had me in therapy for two years. . . . I always used to think how much it was costing, that I better say something interesting. He seemed so bored."

"However you spell it, it comes out the same," Sally drawled. "She got herself married."

"To Jackson?"

"Are you kidding?" Dorine made a wry face. "They never spoke again. He didn't waste himself trying to get in touch with her."

"She didn't marry Phil!"

Sally laughed. "Phil lit off for California. You could of run into him there. No, she married her boss, Neil Stone."

"What kind of guy is he?"

"Nice enough," Dorine said. "Quiet, bright. Obviously he's crazy about her. We all went to the wedding—they had a rabbi but it was pretty hip. Really, it wasn't a rebound thing. She'd been seeing him for months. They were already living together."

"I thought you weren't supposed to get married in analysis?"

"Oh, she isn't still in, Beth. She never impressed me as one of those people who go to a shrink for eight years. . . . Maybe the house was good for her, anyhow. Neil strikes me as a nice loving man and a big change for her. Completely un-macho."

"You liked him? Her boss." Beth could not imagine liking anybody put over her at work. "Is he a lot older?"

"No, he's one of those scientist types—like I'm trying to be!" Dorine laughed, for she had gone back to school. "Maybe he's thirty, at the outside. Doesn't look more than twenty-six. They were living in his little apartment on Broadway, but now they've gone and bought a huge old house in Brookline—I mean literally huge! I think Miriam wants to have children."

"Awful big," Sally said. "It used to be a rooming house and it's just like this old place, every little thing falls down if you look cross-eyed at it."

"I was over there with the two of them before they moved in, when they were getting some walls torn out," Dorine said. "Neil kept admiring the woodwork and saying it was structurally sound. I kept looking around and thinking, Wow, is this going to be a job. Go on, call her up. I know she'll be glad to see you."

They had two bedrooms down and three up. Beth had the smallest, in the back next to the bathroom. The kids, Fern and David, had the room to her right, painted with elephants and giraffes, and Sally and Connie shared the big front bedroom. It faced south, the sunniest in the house. They had hung the windows and lined the ledges with plants. The room was green and yellow and white, full of leaves and plants flowering. Sally and Connie preferred to share that room and have the children together next door. Beth wondered briefly if they were lovers, but they slept in bunk beds and did not act together. She wondered if she had lost some necessary innocence in dealing with women. But when she told Sally about Karen, Sally did not seem particularly surprised. She was mildly curious, more interested in why Beth had felt she had to leave Karen than in how they had become involved.

Beth felt that Sally, like herself, was sexually withdrawn, but that Sally was more at ease in her body. Sally was physically affectionate with Connie's boy David as well as with her own baby Fern, scooping them up to hug and kiss, tickling and teasing and playing on the floor, crawling around the living room on her knees.

Dorine had one of the downstairs bedrooms and Laura the other. There was nothing over those rooms but a low attic that could be entered through a door midway up the stairs, at the turn; that is, when the door could be pried open. On the other side of the entrance hall was the living room, furnished only with scattered blocks and peg sets and cushions, and a big old-fashioned kitchen where they ate and tended to sit downstairs. Upstairs everybody spent a lot of time in the room that Connie and Sally shared, because it was so pleasant. The women had been in the house for three months and had done the most urgent repairs. Everyone had fixed up her own room, but otherwise, only the kitchen and the children's room had received attention.

Borrowing sheets from the general supply, Beth spread out a sleeping bag in the room she painted red and white. Dorine said it looked like the inside of a candy cane, but this was the first time Beth had ever chosen what something was to look like. Miriam had made a lot of tie-dyed curtains when she lived in the house and left them when she moved out. Beth commandeered a pair for each of her windows. At Good Will in Cambridge she got a desk and chair, but a bed would have to wait till she had more money.

Sally did not work. She earned a little cash making clothes for people or on consignment for stores that sold things women in the youth ghetto made. She sewed smocks and long dresses and long skirts and loose blouses, often in a patch-work of pieces fitted carefully. Sally spent a great deal of time getting things for the house cheaply or free. Being the only one who did not regularly bring money in, she made up by what else she brought them. She found Beth a free bed the next week. Laura had given her car, a six-year-old Saab, to the house when she came, and they all moved the bed.

Sally's resistance was mute, stubborn, and total. She was utterly unco-operative with the economic system. Marvelously inventive in ways to survive without a job, a husband, a family, a name, her life was filled with making and ma-neuvering. Sally's mysticism was earthy, centered on cooking and feeding and growing plants and reading palms and her own body. She called herself Sally only: she said she had no last name because no woman had her own last name. Last names were to show possession and for the use of the state.   •

She read nothing. She did not listen to the radio or watch the small television Connie had brought with her. She doubted all information from out there. She trusted words little. More than anyone else in the house she touched. Yet there was little sexual in her touch: it was a form of caring and direct knowledge.

Once Beth heard Laura ask Sally, "Where do you come from?"

"Out of a woman's body." Sally smiled. "Just like Fern and you."

Her voice was not from Boston. It was from Tennessee. Both children hung on her when she let them.

Connie had been divorced by her husband; that is, she had agreed to the divorce and carried it out. "Was I supposed to keep him on a chain? He'd left anyhow." Connie smoked all the time and Beth could not have shared a room with her, she would have got sick. Connie was thin and avid-looking with large nervous eyes and glasses she took on and off and on and off. She taught seventh grade in Newton. She had wanted to be a writer, she had wanted to work on a magazine, she had wanted to do anything except be a teacher. She had a boy friend who was also a teacher and divorced, who taught high school social studies. He was active in recycling. He came over on a bicycle and told them they should not have a car. Beth had trouble accepting that because she was just learning to drive, and driving was independence. He was always cornering one of them in the kitchen and telling them they should wash and flatten tin cans and keep each kind of bottle separate. When he caught her, Beth always invited him to do anything he pleased with their garbage.

Dorine had returned to school part time to study biology. She had a theory that the next assault on people was going to be biological, that the power structure was going to do something hideous with genetics to breed a passive, idiot population of consumers, and that women had to take over biology before it was turned completely into a weapon. Dorine's room sprouted women's posters all over the walls. She told Beth for seven months she had been in a consciousness-raising group that had recently broken up, feeling they had gone as far as they could together. Several of them were working in a free clinic now. "Besides, this whole house is a continuous C-R group, you know?"

Everyone was aware of Dorine's tendency to become common maidservant, to do silently the tasks that others put off or forgot. Dorine herself would say out loud, "I'm doing it again, aren't I?" when she automatically began picking up after the children or clearing the table while the others were still chatting.

"Oh, my relationships with men . . ." Dorine sat at the

head of her bed with her legs drawn up, hugging them. Beth
sat cross-legged at the foot. "I don't know that I can say they're
better. They're shorter. Yeah, you might say that now I have
short miserable affairs instead of long miserable affairs. Sometimes I can see what's coming down in a couple of weeks
and break it off, instead of letting it go on and on like a
terminal disease, until the man gets nauseated and ends it.
I suppose that's some kind of change." She made a face.
"Nothing I would give a party to celebrate."

Laura was new to Beth, but at first she did not feel so. At
first Laura was always reminding her of Karen because of
wearing army surplus and acting loud and blunt and dog-
matic. Laura told people very quickly that she was bisexual.
She told that to Beth when they first sat down at the breakfast table together. Beth found herself shrinking, as if Laura
might suddenly reach out and dominate her as Karen had.

Laura did not become Karen more as the days passed, but
rather Beth began to see Laura. She was aggressive in her
speech. She talked loudly, she asked questions and contra-
dicted the answers. Even upstairs Beth could hear her marching in the front door. She would let the door bang open and
shout, "Hey, I'm home!" or "Back from the wars!" or "God,
what a shitty day!" at the top of her lungs. "Where the fuck
is everybody? What's happening? Let's get it on!"

Beth noticed slowly that Laura made noise as much to
give herself living space as to attack anybody. She was quick
to take offense, quick to withdraw, quick to sense insult. She
was perhaps the shyest woman in the house when it came
to speaking of herself except in comical or mock heroic
stories, and when it came to asking for anything at all.

Laura had worked on a suburban paper: she had essentially
written it and put it out. But when the paper went from
weekly to daily, the owners brought in a new editor to put
over her, because there could not be a woman editor. She
was expected to go on doing the same job at the same wages,
while he polished his editorials and lunched with business
leaders. She had quit. Now she was working for an underground paper. She fought all the time with the men on the
staff, but sometimes she won an inch, two inches. At least
she could let her sexual identity and her politics hang out,
she said, but often she was depressed about her battling role.

Her relationships with men consisted mostly of pickups
and brief adventures in which she was determined to remain

unexploited emotionally. She said that without the house she would go crazy. Her bisexuality seemed to Beth more a thing she would argue to other women as necessary to their dignity than something she pursued. However, Dorine told her Laura had fallen in love with a woman at the paper and that they had lived together for two months. While Laura was covering a demonstration in Washington, the ex-boy friend had got the woman back. Laura had been badly hurt, and she was still protecting that large sore. She was convinced she had been sent out of town intentionally.

Of the children Fern was the more physical, walking already and yanking at anything she could reach, tugging and tasting. Into whatever was left open, unlocked, ajar. David was the more verbal and moodier. Connie was always worrying aloud because he was the only male in the house. "Don't fret, I'm gonna fill up the house with babies," Sally said calmly. "I figure to have another little baby. Soon as I work through in my mind how I want to do it this time."

Because Beth was happy in the house and because the need for money forced her into a job as a typist downtown, and finally because the thought of Miriam married made her shy, it was awhile before she called. Miriam Stone, Mrs. Neil Stone, was her name. She had to find out that strange name before she could find her. Miriam Berg was no more. Women must often lose a friend that way, and never be able to find each other again.

Saturdays, Laura was teaching her to drive. She barked, she teased, she tried to make Beth grasp too many things at once, but she was overall patient and Beth was learning. Amazingly the car obeyed her. When she was married, she had got a learner's permit and Jim had begun to give her lessons. But the lessons happened less and less often after the first few. Since Jim kept the car with him anyhow, she did not push. Now it would be a piece her car too, once she had her license.

The next Saturday Laura had a conference to cover. Connie gave Beth a quick parking lesson in the morning before she took the car to run errands and drop David by his father's for the day. So Beth called Miriam and asked if she could come over. Miriam sounded surprised and pleased, but the conversation kept being interrupted by someone asking questions behind her. Beth felt shy on the phone anyhow. After lunch she took a house bike. It was a long bike ride but the day was cool and buoyant and sunny, to be enjoyed.

The house was on a corner lot, the lawn neglected and puddled. Freshly painted a dark gray with dark green trim, it was a big turn-of-the-century structure with a tower jutting out at the corner. In front the big maple was not yet in leaf and dense bushes made a bare and twiggy thicket on the side facing the cross street. It looked formidable because of the dark color or perhaps because, unlike their house, it did not seem to be standing ramshackle and wide open. She had a brief memory of childhood, of going to call on girl friends. In her neighborhood children did not ring the bell or knock. She used to stand outside and yell, "Do-lore-es! Do-lore-es! Come on out and play!"

Slowly she climbed the steps. At least they were as sagging as her own. A ladder and cans of paint with colors dripped down their sides stood on the porch.

"Beth! It is you!" Miriam hugged her, bulky coat and all. They made glad noises at each other as Miriam took her coat and they stood somewhat uncertainly in the huge high-ceilinged entrance hall. "Oh, the house. You don't really want a damn tour, do you? It's mostly a mess. Look, the beautiful woodwork, etc. Isn't it somebody's Moorish dream?"

All around the entrances to the living room, dining room and den off the hall and on the stairway were carved wooden arabesques. High on the stairway was a stained-glass window. The living room had a marble fireplace. The few pieces of furniture huddled together around the hearth as if for warmth, a couple of Danish chairs and a couch consisting of cot and bolster.

The dining room, in more usable shape, was furnished with big oak pieces, a round table on claw legs, a high glass-fronted cabinet. They drifted through to the kitchen. The front hall had been too imposing, the living room too empty, but the kitchen gave her a thread of connection. The stove was new and big with two ovens and the refrigerator too was new, but mostly the kitchen was old-fashioned with a pantry off it and a sagging floor covered with shabby linoleum showing older linoleum through holes. Miriam put on a kettle for tea and brought out some tins for Beth to choose. She picked Earl Grey for the lavender scent.

Miriam's lustrous black hair was loose on the shoulders of a dull golden Indian shift, embroidered down the front and at the hem with green and orange. That remembered warmth and kindness wove almost compulsively around Beth as she sat chewing whole wheat bread with grape preserves.

"Yes, I learned to bake bread. Bethie, you can't guess how sensual it is! It competes with fucking. The dough feels alive in your hands. Isn't it delicious? I'm serious. Don't I bake great bread?"

Different, yes, but how? The year and a half had calmed and burnished Miriam. Beth watched her cross to the cupboard. Her gracefulness had taken a stately turn. Beth thought she could guess. Miriam had lost self-consciousness, she had settled more into her full body. No longer feeling so observed from many sides, she did not watch herself with that same nervously sexual wariness. She was not hunter or hunted. She was actually at home. Was that the result of her marriage? Beth began to wonder if she generalized about marriage from too small a base. Could marriage be good for Miriam?

The bread was delicious. She stared at a pegboard studded with instruments whose uses were strange to her, choppers and grinders and whirls of wire and odd-shaped spoons. "Do you like to cook now?" Beth winced at the flatness of her question. It was a poor question for all that she wanted to pack into it. It stood for what she would have liked to ask outright. When she had last seen Miriam, Miriam had like her been fighting for her scrap of social dignity, survival as a person. Was it true then that a kitchen, a marriage bed made Miriam happy, this big dark gray house of Mr. and Mrs. Stone?

As if Miriam read something of her intent, she gave Beth a slow sweet smile. "Stay to supper and find out."

"But you never did like to cook. The whole issue of food was a war between Jim and me—when I was married."

"You were married. Sometimes I forget." Miriam dripped honey on a slice of dark bread. "I guess I was afraid if I gave any signs of liking the things women are supposed to I'd get stuck somehow. I wouldn't be taken seriously in my profession. I'd get even worse treatment from the men I was involved with."

"I don't enjoy 'life support' work. I don't mind if everybody shares it, but nothing will ever make me like it."

"But I feel good as a woman now—Neil's done that for me. I don't feel like I'm battling all the time in every area of my life. For the first time in my whole life, somebody really

loves me. I don't have to fight him, I don't have to be
struggling on that front. I can enjoy being a woman. So I
can do all kinds of things I never did, like cooking, like
baking. And they give real pleasure to people, and to me."

"Why did you get married? Did you really want to?"

"Yes!" Miriam clasped her hands on the table, leaning
toward her. "Oh yes, Beth, I did! I wanted so badly for some
man finally to gamble on me as a woman. Oh, you know he
hurt me so bad."

"Jackson?" Beth said softly.

Miriam nodded, "I was sick of being treated as a thing that
couldn't be trusted. Sick of being punished. Of being pulled
and hauled and held off. Yes, deep inside I wanted somebody
to say he really wanted me, really wanted to commit himself
to me and mean it. Not to hold back the words, not to hold
back the love, not to hold back his head or his hand or his
trust. It felt so good! It still feels beautiful. I kept thinking
at first, Neil doesn't really see me, he'll get disillusioned, he'll
withdraw. But he didn't. Sometimes I dance around here by
myself with joy. Thinking that I'm loved, finally I can love
somebody without being charged my soul, without paying in
blood." Miriam rose and came around the table to put her
hands on Beth's shoulders. "I don't mean to sound egotistical,
wrapped up and wallowing in comforts. It's just that it feels
so nice to be happy for a change."

"You moved out of Pearl Street that winter?"

"Apparently the night you left town. I had a fight with
them. I felt fed up in a final, bitter, ugly way and I couldn't
take any more." Miriam shuddered and sat down.

"I was angry with you for not helping me. I know it's
irrational. I couldn't get hold of you. But I was mad at you
because you weren't there to help me."

"I was angry at myself."

"I felt you let me down. But I don't now. If I hadn't let
them scare me, everything would have been all right."

"Why did you stay away so long? Did you go back to him?
Everybody thought you had."

"How could people think that! No. I was scared that he'd
trace me. I made up my mind not to come back until I was
free and clear."

"So you got a divorce?"

"It's a matter of time now. Everything's worked out and
I feel pretty secure. Part of me will always be a little scared

until I'm free. Miriam, even if I loved somebody, I'd never get married again. It's too scary."

"But that depends on the person. If you trust a man, it's not scary. If you really communicate, if you love and trust each other—I know Neil wouldn't want to hurt me. I *know* him."

"I guess I'd like to feel that way about somebody," Beth said doubtfully. "I guess I would. But I don't see what that has to do with asking the state to register you as a legal bind. If I trusted somebody and loved them, I'd figure they wouldn't need to be tied up with a contract."

"But sometimes you want to make a public statement, a public commitment about the way you feel. You want to be a family. I want to have kids with Neil, and sure you can do it the way Sally does, but not if you work at a job, not if you want your kids to get a good education. Sometimes you just want to stand up and say, 'We are a family. We are together.'"

"I could see some ceremony where you get married by saying so and divorced by saying so. But this is the patriarchal way, where you lose your name and become property. I've gone through it once, to be owned by somebody no matter what I want."

"If you loved a man a whole lot and trusted him, Bethie, it wouldn't feel like ownership. It would feel like loving."

"You forget, I had the same training in falling in love as you did," Beth said somberly, sitting up straight. "I did think I was in love with Jim."

Miriam gave her that sweet slow smile again and took her hand. "Thinking you're in love in high school, full of true romances, is not quite the same as growing slowly to love somebody when you've been through a few men and you have some idea who you are. You won't make the same mistakes." Miriam stood up. "Now, you must agree to stay to supper, because then we can run down to the fish market and get a nice piece fish to feed you. But if you don't and you won't, I have to put the roast in. Come, will you eat my married food?"

Beth stayed. "Sally said you married your boss. Doesn't it feel funny at work? You are still working, aren't you?"

"Beth, you're the limit!" Miriam put on her coat. "Marriage hasn't changed my personality! I'm more of a person now, not less, because I'm not wasting all that energy fighting those

I should be getting love and support from. Neil was head of the project I was working on. Naturally, I was put on a different project, and now I'm under Dick Babcock, not Neil. Worse luck."

"Do you still like working there?"

"It's a good place—lots of topnotch people, interesting vibes." But Miriam's voice lacked conviction.

Neil had been off playing his first game of tennis of the season with Dick, who was treasurer and office manager of Logical. He was taller and bulkier than Neil and broken out now in a heavy sweat, even his mustache wet and drooping and his face a dark red. "Ha, I'll get you next time," he was shouting as they came in. "Just out of practice. Too much booze."

"You should exercise in the winter. We lead sedentary lives," Neil was saying, kissing Miriam in the kitchen, rumpling her hair, cruising the top of the stove without interrupting his remarks. "Then suddenly one spring day you think you'll be an athlete. That's abuse of the body."

"Don't think you haven't put on a few pounds with home cooking."

"Too true," Neil said amiably. "Still, you know, a good regimen of exercise on a daily basis . . ." He went upstairs to shower and change. Dick ended up getting invited to supper too.

Coming into the dining room while Beth and Miriam were setting the table, Dick looked Beth over without subtlety and obviously decided he was not interested. At the table he talked company gossip. Beth, relieved not to be stared at any more, did not mind what they talked about, although Miriam kept making strenuous efforts to get the conversation onto more general subjects.

Neil was close to Miriam's height and built on a lean wiry mold. His eyes were greenish brown over a carefully kept dark curly beard, much curlier than the hair on his head. His face was young and mobile. He admired the meal out loud and urged Dick to express his appreciation, eating a little stooped with precise neat motions. "Bread, Dick, you must try some. This is none of your sawdust chemical-laden bread, full of alum and plaster of paris and formaldehyde. This is real bread that Miriam bakes herself." Everyone ate heartily and a great deal. Beth felt Neil accepted her presence, but without curiosity. "Oh, Miriam doesn't mind if you stay to supper," he had said to Dick in her presence. "She's always bringing people home. We feed half of greater Boston. Our favorite charity is our dinner table."

"It's her Jewish-mother syndrome," Dick said. "Eat, eat."

At the table they talked of a "jaunt to Washington" Dick had just made with Ted somebody, "to try to pry loose some funds for heuristic programing fun and games." They exchanged stories about a contract monitor who liked Logical and thought they were groovy and creative. She would do what she could to get them the contract, but they had an enemy there too. It seemed that Abe, Logical's president, had once crossed swords with that enemy's protégée at a Spring Joint Computer Conference seminar. Dick wanted to include Neil's name on the proposal they were trying to get funded, that would support Frank and Ted full time, but Neil said that his time was all used up on other contracts. "Unless you can slap me on as a consultant, it won't work. After all, you can't charge my evening hours, the government will never believe it."

"Not if they've seen Miriam, ha-ha." Dick took more of the curry. "She was our secret weapon to spring on old Logan—remember how she got around Wilhelm Graben, eh? But you put the quietus on that."

Miriam gave Dick a quick glare, then smiled politely and hopped up. "Time to get the pie out." It was apple with lemon and raisins and nuts. Beth had helped cut the apples and watched Miriam roll the dough. Now she followed Miriam into the kitchen. Miriam let the door swing shut behind them.

"That's my boss now." Miriam shrugged. "I can tell you don't like him."

"I guess he's all right. I mean, he hasn't said much offensive."

"Not much, it's just his manner." Miriam laughed. "He's a pig, but live and let live. He's between marriages. He gets married every five years. They have a kid, then the marriage comes apart. He's supporting two other households. I have to go to Washington with him next week on the current contract, only for a day, but I'm not looking forward. He wears on my nerves. He's not capable of treating any woman as an equal but if you're married, at least the jokes are less gross."

"Does Neil like him? They seem to be friends."

"They started the company together along with Abe, who put up what capital there was. Neil likes everybody, Beth. When he can't, he feels guilty."

"I used to be like that. Now I don't have any trouble at all disliking individuals. Sometimes I can even hate someone."

Miriam squeezed her arm. "Strong emotions and now some strong coffee. Everyone at Logical drinks it all day long. My kidneys are starting to go. Did you get your old job back at Tech Square?"

"Are you kidding? They fired me before I left. No, I have a dreary typing job downtown on Milk Street."

"That sounds like a waste of time."

"It isn't a thing you do because you like it, Miriam. It's a thing you do because you need money. You can get used to anything to make a living. I suppose being a prostitute is that way."

Miriam grinned. "How tough you're getting, just listen to you."

Beth shied away, embarrassed. "It's all service, isn't it?"

"Would you be willing to learn to be a programer? I could try to get you in. There's always a couple of what they call teeny-bopper programing jobs, tedious but I think less so than the typing pool. I'm sure it pays better."

"I'm tired of clerical jobs and I don't see a way to ever get loose. I'll try anything."

"All right, let me see what I can do." Putting the warm pie, plates, and the coffeepot on a tray, Miriam balanced it on her hip like a waitress and slipped through the swinging door to the dining room. Reluctantly Beth followed.

20

The Rhythms of Two Households

Beth quit her job on Milk Street and went to work at Logical Systems Development. Miriam found she could not get Beth hired as a programer—Neil was too scrupulous in technical matters to intercede—but did get her in as a keypunch operator. Well, the pay was the best yet and less subservience was demanded. Some months before, Logical had moved to new offices in what they called an industrial park on Route 128, in an area of rocky hills and reservoirs and many small computer and electronics companies. Miriam picked her up every day in her red VW. Miriam drove separately from Neil because she went to work earlier and left earlier, to start supper. Neil did not appear before ten. He had an elaborate morning ritual that Miriam described, driving and gesturing.

Beth sat with hands folded, listening. The rain that fell was warm and the landscape was softening. The first red of buds on maples had eased into pale greens. The rocks were wet, the lawns lush, the trees filmy with buds or sprouting little leaflets, the dogwood and cherries in bloom. Connie was teaching Beth the names of trees, along with driving lessons, when she alternated with Laura. Connie liked to go hiking—that was how she had met her boy friend—and she liked to know what things were called. When Beth walked with Connie she met on the street a towhee, a sugar maple, a Darwin tulip. Other beings crowded the spaces between human habitations.

When she was with Miriam, the space between things was filled in with human cries and colors of relationships; the needs, the hungers, the plots and plans of people they knew swarmed around them. With Laura, streets were political manifestations: on this block the scars of urban renewal showed, on that a particular corrupt combine owned apartment houses and gouged rents, here was the site of a busing controversy.

Miriam was telling her how Neil got up: "First the clock radio turns on soft country rock. Then he takes a hot shower and shaves at great length. He has a fancy electric shaver that looks like a racing car. In the meantime I stumble out and peer around and groan and swear and stagger to the kitchen. He appears bright and lively and clear-eyed. I can hardly stand it. But it's only the beginning. After breakfast, he exercises. I'd think he'd do them before. But no. Afterward. Canadian Air Force exercises. Anyhow I struggle into my clothes and go off and he's still hopping around in his underwear.

"Then he sits down and drinks more coffee and reads the morning paper and jots down technical ideas. He gets up extra

early so he can fool around for an hour and then sit drinking
coffee! Myself, I'd get up the last minute and skip breakfast.
But, oh well, that's marriage. Give a little here and there. He
cares a lot about that morning schedule. He imagines he
couldn't possibly have good ideas if he changed it around
just a little. Technical people are wonderfully superstitious,
have you noticed?"

"I like breakfast too. I like that kind of a meal—no fuss."

"Oh, he isn't fussy about breakfast—not much! A couple
of fresh eggs sunny side up cooked in butter to the exact point
of being cooked through but not overcooked. An English
muffin toasted pale brown and some Swiss preserves, say
black cherry."

"Married people eat too much."

"Beth, you're a puritan!" Miriam parked and hauled out
of the back seat the Greek bag she used for a briefcase. "Well,
here we go through the looking glass, *nu?*"

Neil had his office in the part of the suite called the
executive wing—although the "suite" consisted of a large
square divided by walls stapled to the floor. Abe, Dick, and
Neil had offices apart from the others in the new setup, with
Efi as their secretary. Two other secretaries sat by the entrance for everybody else to share. The directors' offices were
furnished with large walnut desks and sofas and Danish
chairs and big blackboards of real slate. Dick was the force
behind the changes. He felt their mode had lacked style.
Miriam had an office by herself now too, but it was an inside
office, windowless, the size of a bathroom. Miriam called it
the air-conditioned womb.

Beth was put to work in the largest of the inside rooms,
where the equipment lived. It housed the keypunch, where
she sat and typed as if on the typewriter, but the punch made
holes in cards. She also used a verifier, on which she typed
but no holes appeared, while the verifier checked that the
Hollerith codes had been correctly punched on the cards.
Then there was a line printer with a hopper where she fed the
cards in, a 407 that printed out the listings again.

She started with handwritten data or programs from the
technical people and put them on cards; then the 407 turned
it back to print-out again. She also worked an interpreter, a
duplicator, and a sorter on occasion, all simple machines that
did one thing and usually only one to the decks. Also in the
big room was a Xerox machine and a computer terminal

used over telephone lines to a time-shared computer in Boston.

The work was boring, but when she was not busy she could read. One of the worst things about the Milk Street job was something it had in common with her Chicago job: that when she had nothing to do, she was not allowed to carry out an activity of her own but must look busy. It was necessary above all, not that at every moment she must actually do anything, but that she must always be seen as appropriate. She could never sit and read at her desk. However, she could make notes to herself because that was typing. Here at least no one objected if she read occasionally. She could salvage some of that empty time. Lunch was no problem as she brought it and ate at her desk. Miriam was expected to go out with the technical staff, but every so often she would bring along leftovers and sit and gossip with Beth in the equipment room. Sometimes Miriam would eat only an apple.

"I'm gaining weight. You don't know, but I used to be fat. All through grade school and high school. Then for years I never put on an ounce. I thought I'd got rid of that problem forever. But now, I'd just about got plump before I caught it—I mean, I wasn't even watching my weight! Maybe it's getting older? You're always so thin, Bethie—it's the way you eat, a little fruit, a nut or two, like a bird."

"Why don't you eat less if you're worried?"

"How can I cook a gorgeous supper and not eat? I love to eat."

"Anyhow, you're not fat."

"But I could be. That's what scares me. Like my mother."

"Mine too. She's short like me and about as wide as she is tall."

"What is it, you get married and then you get fat?"

"I don't see what other pleasure she has, if you leave out the TV."

"My mother, you should have eaten her food, Bethie, you wouldn't talk about pleasure."

"I never thought whether my mother was a good cook." Beth sucked on the pit of a date. "Food was food, it was what Mother made. How much can anybody do with hamburger and hot dogs and meat loaf?"

"My mother, she had a no-fail method of killing meat dead. She'd start cooking it in the morning and leave it simmering on the back burner all day. I grew up thinking all meat was gray."

"Did she come to your wedding? You never talk about her."

"She's dead."

"You did tell me! How could I forget? Nobody close to me ever died."

"That was something really chewed over in therapy. I felt dreadfully guilty. I was so involved with Phil then. He was the sun and the moon to me, Bethie. Yet my mother made me feel guilty for wanting to be with him, and I couldn't get close to her. I had lots of old garbage to unload. My feeling my father rejected me. Trying to prove I was attractive with man after man. That hook of trying to make a man love you because you love him, the way I did with Jackson—"

"Did you want to get married with Jackson? Or was that just with Neil?"

"With Neil. He wanted to get married for three months, but you know me—I was scared."

"So what changed your mind?"

"Oh, I'd been grappling with those fears in therapy—that I wasn't worthy. That Neil couldn't really love me, but would withdraw. Like my mother, I'd love a man and he'd use me. Then I went down to Washington for a few days—that was when I was being shifted off Neil's project onto Dick's."

"They'd taken you off Neil's project *before* you got married?"

"I gather Abe had indicated that it made him uncomfortable. I was very involved with the work, they were my ideas too we were working on. But Neil agreed it was inappropriate. You know, he has all that elaborate set of professional ethics about what you do and what you don't do in the company and at meetings and in the journals. So they stuck me on the ABM project."

"Do you like working with Dick? I mean, how can you stand it?"

"Has he been after you, Bethie? Tell me if he bothers you, and I'll drop a word to Neil."

"He doesn't find me attractive and I plan to keep it that way." Beth made a face. "What happened in Washington?"

Miriam looked startled. "Oh, you mean changing my mind. We were separated for a couple of days and that gave me time to think about life without him. When I got back I just knew I wanted him—that I was willing."

"You missed him that much on the trip?"

"Well, like on the plane, I had time to think. I saw my life very clearly and I knew. I hear the boys coming back."

Jaime's high laugh in the hall, sharp, barking. Ha-HA! rising. He had yellow ringlets and a soft petulant droop to him. Beth liked him but he could not be communicated with past the level of a set of games that formed his contact with people. With Fred he played Go, with Neil, chess. He would drop by with a puzzle of wire or wooden blocks in his pocket that would then migrate through the company. The rest of the week as she was passing an office she would see somebody bent over it.

When he came in to drop off his programs to be coded on decks, he would play secret agent. He would be passing along vital secrets. Or he would play Bogart as detective. She sometimes had an urge to touch him that surprised her, to touch his arm or pat his cheek. If she would make it part of the fantasy she could touch him, but then it would not matter. There was no real way to touch Jaime, any more than there was a way to talk to him about their lives.

He cared a great deal for how he looked, for his pastel shirts with intricate and exotic patterns, for the fit of his pants, for the leather of his boots, but not with an eye to pleasing anybody else. He told her he thought everyone in Logical dressed like slobs . . . yes, like cretins! Dress was part of his aesthetic. That was his favorite word. "That's a very aesthetic solution!" he would say in admiration. Beth noted that most of the men had a way of indicating that judgment—pretty, elegant—their term of admiration for work that pleased them technically.

This was different from other offices she had worked in. The manners were casual, and self-indulgence was somehow assumed: that everyone wanted to be comfortable, that everyone had a certain right to play—every one of the technical people, that was. They were always talking about games. She found it hard to tell when they were talking about the projects of the company as everything tended to be discussed in the terminology of games and model building.

Several of the men had liked the old building in Cambridge better, where they had all appeared equal in the same shabby offices. Now the hierarchy was marked. They did not like that. Men who'd been hired since took the layout for granted. They thought the old-timers silly: Logical was a better place to work than most and why shouldn't Abe with the biggest reputation have the biggest office? Wasn't he president? He was building up a good technical staff, garnering prestige. Regularly people wrote papers and presented them at conferences and meetings. Though Abe was president, he had not ceased to do technical work and regularly co-authored papers.

Those who were not completely into the willful-child-games-playing-forever model—the more ambitious—thought they'd like to be in Abe's shoes, making lots of money, owning a prestigious little company, and still doing good technical work. Abe did not have his degree (by which they meant the Ph.D., she learned after questions Jaime found comical) but he had good connections with Harvard and was involved in a seminar there. He was reputed to be finagling for a degree granted on work he had already done.

Of the three directors, Dick was the least academic. He did more managing and less technical work, and his project to run was the anticipated governmental moneymaker with lots of low-level people stuck on it, the anti-missile piece of the action. He was the least respected by the staff, who gossiped about him with malice: his loud jokes, his poor taste, his technical gaffes, his overt pursuit of the dollar, his edginess with those who outclassed him technically, his crude sallies at women, his loudmouth poker playing in which he could bluff nobody, his five-year marriages and huge alimony payments.

About Neil she listened most carefully. He was the quietest director, the most academic in his orientation. He had his degree, as they said, and had been offered a post at Carnegie he had declined. He published frequently and had the longest bibliography. He did not like to go actively after contracts or to be worried about how to support the ever multiplying staff. Still his name and connections were useful. He had put back some of his salary into stock options. The stories about him were of the absent-minded professor sort—how he'd walk past Miriam without recognizing her. Stories of him stopping his car in the middle of the expressway to whip out a pad and jot down a technical idea.

Miriam was regarded as brilliant but erratic. People experienced difficulty in working with her because they could not follow her leaps. That irritated Fred and Dick, though not Jaime, who enjoyed bolts from the blue. But Jaime was not working with her any more, being still on Neil's project.

There were always what they called teeny-bopper programers in a large inside office doing the boring mechanical programing.

They did not care as much how she dressed, how she sat at her desk. Only Dick fussed about the businesslike atmosphere. He would lecture the secretaries and the teeny-bopper programers on being neater, more punctual, more subservient in effect—pleasant, he called it. The others mostly did not relate to her sufficiently to care. They came in with their demands and each one thought his own job always the most important and the work of the others garbage. They were always harried. The whole office seemed permanently months behind schedule. Their estimation dates on contracts were set optimistically and never accurate. There was a perpetual air of everything being about to collapse, emanating most intensely from Dick, who kept the closest watch on finances.

It was he who dealt with the bank. They never had enough money on hand to pay more than two months' worth of salaries, and since often the money for contracts came through late, Logical was usually into the bank for a tidy amount. She picked that up from the secretaries. When Miriam did not join her in the equipment room, often one or more of the secretaries did. They would not come if Miriam was there, seeing her as the boss's wife. They could not relax or gossip if she was in earshot.

Then Beth crossed into another universe and went home. The house was solvent nowadays. Connie had her teaching job and some child support. Beth was making decent money, by their standards. Laura got some money from the paper and some from her family. Dorine was in school and had trouble contributing: she just covered her school expenses with what she made modeling. She was supposed to put in eighty dollars a month but usually she could not. Sally never could. The disparities in what they gave had long ago been worked out; they had different levels of education and different handicaps and their earning power differed accordingly. From those who could, more must be asked. They had enough to pay the rent and utilities and eat pretty well and buy gas and insurance for the car and a gallon of California wine once or twice a week and a small amount of grass and soap and basic drugs and toiletries—very basic. They had enough for minor medical expenses. Connie and she were covered on the job and Dorine could use health service at school, but the others and the children were vulnerable to sudden high costs.

They haggled long over occasional purchases. Toys for the children: no dolls or dolls for both? Were guns an outlet for aggression or the channeling of energy into war games? Did competitive games teach skills or train for a society based on mistrust and cut thy neighbor?

When Dorine went home for Pesach she brought back a relic of her childhood, a green and white dollhouse of two stories with four rooms of furniture. The dollhouse touched off a battle.

Laura poked with a stiff forefinger at the little bassinet. "Training in consumerism. Move the furniture, get more, practice housewifing. Redecorate your kitchen."

Dorine was sitting bunched up with her pointy chin tucked in her sweater. "That isn't what it was like. I loved this house! It was . . . a theater. I had little china animals from an Easter basket—"

"What about an Easter basket? You just went home for Pesach," Connie said.

"My parents bought a little of everything, if you see what I mean. Pesach is with my grandmother. Easter is with the Easter Bunny. We didn't do the Chanukah trip but we did the Christmas tree."

"So they were training you to buy." Laura banged on the roof. "The most important training for a middle-class woman. How to discriminate between identical products. Brand-name loyalty. Buying as a hobby. Training in how many objects you can want for a house."

"Laura, it wasn't like that. I had these little china animals—dogs and cats and chickens and bunnies. In a way they were more real to me than people. I made up stories about them. That house was a world."

"Mmmmm." Sally shook her head. "Some little girls play mommy. Me. Right? Some play lady. Some play true love gonna come. He swoops down on his white horse."

"But I was wrapped up in the animals. My mother thought there was something wrong—animals on the couch, playing the piano, taking a bath. It bugged her. She bought me people dolls. A pink plastic mommy and daddy and baby. They had no character. I put them in none of my adventures. But I learned to keep them in the dollhouse while I was playing. The daddy in bed. The mommy at the stove. Then when my mother would ask what I was doing, I'd show her. Then she'd think I was all right and go away. I remember, most games I really enjoyed I had to pretend I was doing something else, because one of them would decide it was queer."

"Do you like your childhood, Dorine?" Beth asked. "I hate mine. But since it was me I have to accept it to love myself. Learning to love yourself, you found that at home. But you don't want to lay that on our children, do you?"

"But it wasn't bad for me—it was beautiful."

"In a private dream-trip way. Practice for being passive, living in wishes. Dorine, you can love the child you were and love our children too, without wanting to make them the same."

By the time they finished the debate Fern and David had found the dollhouse and were playing with it. Probably they were too young. The house survived, scuffed and scribbled over with crayon. But the furniture was reduced to shards of plastic and hunks of squashed metal in a week. They were constantly hearing a small crunch and looking down to see they had just stepped on a tiny pink plastic toilet or little white kitchen table on the stairs, on the bathroom floor, in front of the refrigerator. Dorine wept and wept about the destruction and then she let it all go.

Beth loved Saturdays. Lying in the bed Sally had found for her under a quilt Sally had made for her, she woke feeling like a beloved child. She had wandered and now she was home. Not that she had felt this way as a child—special, cared for, surrounded by people wanting her there—not often anyhow. In bed she tried to guess from the quality of light through the curtains Miriam had dyed whether the sun was shining, whether the day was cloudy. She listened to the small and sharp noises: to Fern's bellow of rage, to David's high yelp of pleasure, to the shower running and the phone ringing and the vacuum cleaner going. Today she must clean the upstairs bathroom and hall.

In the first house everything had been unstructured. Everybody had resisted making rules. "This isn't grade school, this isn't prison." So the women more thoroughly socialized to notice dirt, more thoroughly trained to sensitivity to the needs of the group, did the work and the women who were freer from that training did little.

While Beth was off in Chicago, they had gone through three systems. Now they had a new one. Nobody who visited

the house liked it—too structured—but they thought it was
fine. All jobs fell into categories. There were the shit jobs,
the jobs that provided little satisfaction and involved little skill:
dishwashing, disposing of garbage and trash, cleaning, laundry, shopping. Then came jobs that required mastering and
gave satisfaction: cooking, painting, putting up shelves or
doing carpentry, working on the car, sewing. Last there were
tasks that required dealing with others: landlord, doctors, insurance agents, the electric company. Each had to do some
jobs in every category. That way nobody ended up getting
all the jobs that involved creativity, nobody ended up doing
all the things that aroused anxiety and required aggression,
nobody ended up stuck with the repetitive tasks empty of
prestige or reward. They all spent time with the children.
There were specific times each was responsible.

The system was elaborate and visitors scoffed. To run
properly it required that every few weeks they sit down and
review the categories and tasks ahead. But they found it
took less time than when they had solved each day's problems any which way as they arose: finding that somebody
had to go for food and somebody had to cook it, when somebody else had the car already and was stuck because it had
no gas because nobody had cashed a check.

Saturdays she had driving lessons from Laura or Connie.
Today Connie was to give her a lesson if Fern's cold did not
get worse. All things were related. Beth got up and began her
yoga. Sally and Laura and Beth went Wednesday nights to
study yoga.

Downstairs Sally was kneading rye bread. Fern and David
were in the yard making mud pies, while Laura was turning
over the soil for a vegetable garden. The neighbor's yellow
dog watched through the fence, wagging his stumpy tail. While
Sally put the bread on the refrigerator to rise and sat down
to have tea with her, Beth ate breakfast. Sally picked up the
spilled caraway seeds from the table one by one with a licked
finger. Dorine was off posing. Connie was doing the laundry.
After breakfast Beth did her upstairs chores and then went
out to help put in the garden. Digging was good to do, though
soon her back ached. She was no longer shy with Laura. They
put in peas and onions, lettuce and radishes and carrots.

Laura's turn to cook: she cooked from the book, carefully, and made good meals. Sally cooked from instinct and
made good meals. Connie had learned to make many recipes

while she was married, and relied on memory and experience to good effect; but Dorine and Beth cooked with disinterest and rarely did anyone like their meals. Beth had abandoned her vegetarianism. She could not eat rare meat or meat by itself, but she did not want to set herself apart from the other women. She never cooked meat, but she had begun to eat it in mixed dishes. Since they ate a great many soups and stews, egg dishes and vegetable proteins, she could share most of the food.

Laura made goulash with noodles and green beans. Sally had baked fresh bread and for dessert there was brown betty. Laura said it was a feminist dessert. She made it with wheat germ and granola, currants and apples. Sally said it tasted like Christmas. They figured out she meant because of the currants. Saturday night they always had wine.

After supper Connie went up to dress for her boy friend, while Laura went to deliver an article she had edited. When she returned, Sally, Dorine, and Beth were making popcorn and working on their children's book. They were trying to make a storybook so that when Fern and David began to read they would learn from books free of stunting roles. Dorine was illustrating their story about a brother and sister named Sky and Maple who lived with their mother and their mother's sister on a houseboat. Sally, Dorine, and Beth got louder and louder and more and more excited working—it was especially their project. Writing and drawing storybooks for the children had been Dorine's idea, after she got over the fiasco of the dollhouse. Sally had found a notebook bound like a book to use.

They played the parts and tried them out before they added each scene. They argued fiercely over shoulds and shouldn'ts at each step. Beth could hardly wait till they finished and got to read it to the children.

Thursday Efi, the secretary Beth usually caught a ride back with, had the flu, so Beth left early with Miriam. She kept Miriam company while she was making supper. Connie would pick Beth up on the way back from her school, after a teachers' meeting.

Miriam was carefully and with obvious pleasure cutting up a chicken, dismembering it with a mean-looking boning knife. Beth watched; any job Miriam might have given her would have been more a favor than assistance, and Miriam would have interefered in the execution.

"Miriam, Laura's reading a book about Taoism. It has a story about a cook who never had to sharpen his knife because he cut in the Tao—between the bones."

"I'm not that good—yet." Miriam smiled. "Neil says I'm blood-thirsty because I don't like supermarket meat, all packaged in plastic wrap and labeled, wrong half the time. I'm glad you're here today. I was kind of low."

"About work?"

"A bit. And my period started. It was late and I kind of hoped maybe I'd got pregnant in spite of myself."

"Are you so eager? It's easy enough."

"Easy!" Miriam looked appalled. "One chance a month. One poor egg, journeying that distance down the tubes, forcing its way to the womb. It's lonely, it waits. Poor wallflower, down the drain."

"Does Neil want you to have a baby?"

"More than me, even." Miriam's dark eyes grew wide, thinking of something. "He feels he waited years and years to meet me. He has years of living to catch up on."

"But if you have a baby you'll have to quit work."

"Only for a while. I could afford to go back soon. I make enough to pay for someone to take care of the baby. Maybe then they'll be done with that damn project. I hate it! Can you imagine what Phil would say to me if he knew what I'm working on? Can you hear me trying to explain how I got stuck helping design systems for anti-missile missiles? Nobody else seems to feel the pinch. They just don't connect what they do with life in the real world. Even if you bring it up, they make a joke about everybody knowing it won't work anyhow."

"Couldn't you go some place else?"

"Not without making waves. And I doubt if I could get a good research job. The job market's tight, there are thousands of hot-shot programers on welfare. Oh, let's not shop talk. We so seldom get a chance to spend time together outside of there, let's not waste it."

Miriam sifted flour and herbs together, added lemon and wine, and put on the chicken. Then she washed her hands and tossed the apron over a chair. "Come on, let me show you where I love to sit. What I adore about these old houses are the niches and crannies. Can't you imagine growing up here playing hide-and-seek?" Miriam led her up the big trumpeting front staircase with its carved balustrade and strange Moorish decorations. Halfway up where the stairway turned in a U a window seat was set in with worn leather cushions, under a stained-glass window with smaller clear windows on either side.

Lozenges of lavender and amber and bottle-green light fell on Miriam's legs curled up on the bench. She had kicked off her shoes and sat scratching voluptuously between her toes, grinning at Beth. Her thick hair hung down brushing her legs. "Hey, how are you really, nowadays? Do you like living with just women?"

"I love living there. I've got used to not being alone—that was hard at first. But I can shut the door and be alone. The way we're trying to be together is important to me."

"Mainly I just didn't have the time to give to the house," Miriam said defensively. "I was in therapy, I was working hard at my job. I was very, very glad to have that house to move into from Jackson's. But there are so many hassles to group living. Instead of just going ahead and eating or buying something, the way I'm used to, we were forever having meetings and jawing about it. It just seemed an enormous waste of time on non-essentials."

"I don't think who does what work is non-essential."

"I don't know, I felt I was playing the man of the house. At the other extreme, Sally was everybody's wife and mother."

"But none of us are the husband."

"Independence has to rest on financial independence. If she wasn't in the house, she'd be on welfare. Not working puts her in an artificial position of dependency."

"Insisting everybody contribute equally is ignoring that we really do come from different places. Connie has a college education. She really can get a better job. Laura has a degree but being gay makes it harder. The rest of us have a poor capacity to earn. Dorine is in school. When she gets through, she'll make good money. But Sally never finished high school. Nobody in her family did. She had to take care of her brothers and sisters. It's silly and stupid to pretend we don't have different class backgrounds. Connie has more earning ability than I do, I have more than Sally, so why not admit that? Sally could kill herself waitressing six days a week and not make what I do taking it easy."

"Maybe you could send Sally back to school so she'd get her high school diploma. How about night school?"

"But Sally doesn't want to go to school. She hated school. She felt put down. She doesn't want to learn to sound middle class. She doesn't want to work in an office. What's the human value in trying to make her over to somebody they'd hire?"

"But how will she get along when she doesn't have all of you?"

"How would any of us get along? She does have us."

"Maybe if you didn't all think you had each other, maybe you'd have to look harder for somebody you could love."

"But I love Sally."

Miriam gave her that slow smile. "I bet you have a lot more loving in you than Sally can ever use."

"I don't want to love somebody that way, Miriam."

"*That way!* You're such a . . . a little spinster sometimes. I don't believe it's for real! When I think that prick Ryan represents half your sexual experience it depresses me."

Remembering for the twentieth time that she could not tell Miriam about Karen. She needed an opening wider than Miriam had ever given her. Miriam made so many assumptions. Loving another woman with her body was not one of the doors she left open—if she even saw a door there. "I'm open to many things, many people—maybe even a few things you're closed to—like the house."

"Yeah, but . . . they're not equal. To really love someone and be loved in return. I feel rich! It's indecent to be happy. It almost makes me guilty, Beth. Sometimes when I'm happy I remember how miserable I was and I remember all the people I care about who are still getting lacerated, and I feel guilty."

"When I wake up on Saturday morning in the house, I'm happy too, and when we are all together making our book for the children. I don't think much of the romantic drama."

"Neither do I. It's terrible to be struggling through relationship after relationship and losing and losing, every damn time. But loving somebody who loves you, it's a daily thing." Miriam laid warm fingers on her arm. "I want you to be happy too. I want you to have a full life."

"My mother used to tell me she wanted me to be happy but she meant the way I was supposed to be. When she said she loved me, she meant I was behaving okay. Often she told me she was disappointed in me—usually when something had touched me. A full life can be full of learning and doing and, maybe, even fighting."

Wake up! Love! Miriam crooned to her and leaned forward, more seductive than she realized. Smaller physically, shy and awkward and far less sensual, Beth could not imagine reaching out sexually to Miriam. She could not imagine how she would do it. Even the images in her head of sexual initiation all consisted of a male taking a female into his arms. Miriam *could* make love to her, but never would think of it. Nor must she. Not now, not ever. She wanted only to be everyone's sister.

"Sometimes you make me think of Neil, Bethie. Sometimes people like the both of you who are slow to open up have a lot more to give—as if you'd been keeping it in reserve. Come on, I have to check the chicken and put the rice on."

Her pace was quickening. Beth kept out of the way as Miriam chopped onions, melted a pat of butter, washed vegetables and tore them up for salad. Then, with supper once more in hand, Miriam went back upstairs two at a time and settled on the window seat to face her. This time Miriam drew up her legs against her chin, leaning her cheek on the window. Beth felt in her a waning of attention. One part of her was leaking through the glass into the street, watching, on the alert for Neil. A part was focused on the supper cooking. Only a part of Miriam remained for her, attentive and affectionate. It was as if she were already gone. She was not sorry to see Connie's car pull up since they were no longer together: Neil's approach was too close and Miriam was tuning herself to him in preparation.

The divorce was finally at hand. According to the agreement by which she had bought her liberty, she was to do the actual divorcing in court. Here she was appearing to cite all kinds of non-existent faults and crimes of Jim against this happy home. The major event was coughing up more money to the lawyers, paying court costs and memorizing what she was to recite.

Dolores let her sleep on her couch. Dolores was still involved with the same boy friend but no longer believed he would marry her. "I'm shopping around, shopping around," Dolores said.

She had dinner with her family. The evening creaked. Her mother kept talking about how many job openings there were in Syracuse, and how G.E. was always hiring secretaries and key-punch operators. Her mother talked about how many interesting young men were living in the neighborhood. Her mother kept talking about the empty room going to waste. Yet they hardly looked at her. They asked nothing about her life. Her father told her she was dressed like a hippie, which wasn't even true. Her mother kept staring at her chest and finally in the kitchen in a stage whisper asked if she were not wearing a brassiere—as if she had ever, ever needed one.

Her mother said how long she'd waited to see her own daughter and started crying. Nancy asked who was she dating and what kind of boys did she meet working at the computer company. Her father said that was a growing industry. There were longer and longer silences. Beth felt herself shrinking. Sunk in her family, afloat in a sour cabbage soup, she was leaking substance and turning mushy. They would disapprove her back to a child again and lock her in her room without supper. At ten-thirty, after several weeks at the dinner table over the sorry chicken that kept sticking in her throat, they spent an ice age in the living room. The television was on and her father's eyes kept flicking to it. They asked her questions and did not listen to the answers. Anxiety sat on them all.

Finally she escaped to Dolores. The next day she had to go to court. Surprisingly, Jim turned up sitting at the back. He did not have to. Perhaps he was afraid of the process, afraid she or the lawyer would betray him and he would end up tricked into alimony. Anyhow, he sat behind her and watched, hunched up.

Hers was the fourth divorce to come up. Each group of wife and witnesses sat with their lawyer waiting to be called. It was quickly over. The judge asked her one question directly, if Jim had been cruel. She almost muffed the answer. It felt funny to say that in front of him. Afterward, walking out with her lawyer, trying to escape his sticky, pudgy presence, when she saw Jim, she went over to apologize for saying that.

"It's a joke anyhow," Jim said. "They don't care about us. Just their money." They walked on a bit awkwardly in the direction of the parking lot. "You kept my name. I thought you'd take your own back."

"What is mine? My father's? I thought about that. I decided I liked you better than my father. Since I don't have one of my own, I'd just as soon have yours."

"I wasn't complaining. I didn't think there was anything about me you liked."

"I don't hate you, Jim. I just couldn't stand being married to anybody—not even you." The lawyer was standing just behind them. She did not want to get into his car.

"You want to have supper? Say good-by that way. It seems funny standing here with him listening. We could go someplace around here—there's a steak house two blocks over. I don't know if it's any good. If you're not doing anything."

"I'm not doing anything. I had supper with my family last night, and that was awful. But I don't eat steaks. We can look at the menu outside and see if there's anything I can eat."

"You still don't eat meat, huh? It's against your religion." Jim laughed. They looked at the menu posted on the red and gold window. It was an Italian-American steak house that had eggplant parmigiana so she went in with him. He had a steak with spaghetti on the side and they ordered chianti.

It was sad and funny. She still liked the way he looked. Not that he looked the same: like her, he was two years older and he looked less hard and less buoyant. She could see again the Jim she had seen: not shimmering with fantasies but the man she had been attracted to. Again she could like the foresty gray-green of his eyes and the chiseling of his nose and chin. Again she could like the strength of his arms, of his hands on the table, and not fear them on her.

It was funny, it was sad to sit at the table with him. She was dressed like somebody else for court, even wearing panty hose and a dress. Seldom did she sit at a table in a restaurant drinking wine with a man. She could see herself at eighteen eating pizza with Jimbo near their high school and rubbing knees under the table. Superimposed pictures with the out-lines blurring, like a cheap printing job of color on color.

"Gonna get married again?" he asked her.

She shook her head no. "I didn't like marriage, Jim. I don't like keeping house for someone."

"What'd you do? Go back and live with those women?"

"Yes. There are five of us now and two kids."

"And no men?"

She smiled. "One little boy aged four."

"You ought to make him into a real sissy," Jim said, without much edge. "I figure you'll marry one of those professors if you hang around the colleges there. Besides, where did you say you were working?"

"A computer company." She saw something then. Something leapt in her head and she sat up straight. She saw something hurting in him that she must stop, because the hurting was mistaken. "Jim, I didn't leave you because . . . I mean, I wasn't trying to turn you in on . . . a professional. I think you think . . . that what I want is a man with a college degree."

"Sure. You always were smart. Better than me in school. You always went in for books. That's the way it goes."

"No, listen, that's not it. I see what you think—that I don't want a man who works in a garage. I must want a man who works in an office. Who makes more money and comes home with his hands clean. But that's not it. Really."

"You think I don't get sick trying to get ahead? I don't want to be stuck like my old man doing the same job on the line for forty years until I drop dead. But they make it hard. They make it hard to get a start."

"I'm in the same place, Jim. I can't get a good job. The thing I have I got through a woman friend. I don't want any husband. I don't want to live in a family. I like living in a commune. I want to live my own life and do the things I want to."

"You think I'm such a dope I can't understand. But I can see the world's changing. But you see how far you get, how much you can really get away with." He ate his steak for a while. Then he got into a fantasy trip about how he was going to start his own garage. He was going to set up a high class garage and repair foreign cars, sports cars. That's where the money was, those guys with cars that had to be tuned all the time. He went on about how his uncle was going to finance him.

But her life must seem as much a fantasy to him, her ambitions as tenuous. Maybe he'd get his garage. That was likelier than that this society would let her live as she wanted and find real work to do and a permanent commune. It was blind to feel superior to Jim's daydreams when her own were so fragile.

When they were leaving, he touched her more than necessary, helping her on with her coat. His hands fell on her shoulders. Again she could read his feeling, that he was wanting her a bit, wistfully, wishfully, nostalgically. He was

wanting her to come back with him wherever he was living.
He said he'd given up the old apartment. Briefly she felt it
with her body. She was no longer afraid of him and she remembered now when she had loved him, she could let herself
remember it with more than her head again. But she did not
love him. She did not want to lie with her body. She did not
want to borrow him to prove to herself that she was capable
of sexual response her world called normal.

Instead as they came out onto the street and she waved to
a passing cab, she waited till the cab had stopped. Then
quickly she put her hands on his shoulders and rose up to
kiss him. "Take good care of yourself," she said, still hugging
him, and then hopped into the cab and shut the door.

21

I'm Good and I'll Prove It

Miriam was making black bean soup on a turkey-carcass base.
The big old kitchen was steamy with good smells. The turkey
had been roasted for Neil's parents on the weekend. She
could not persuade herself that she liked them, but they
could be worse. They lived in Harrisburg, Pennsylvania, and
the trip was too long for them to make often, as they had not
the habit of flying. His father was an optometrist, Sherwin
Stone; his mother, Emily, kept house. There had been four
boys and his mother often confused them in her memories
and in conversation: would call Neil Simon, his next older
brother. Neil was the youngest and his mother made a big
show of doting on him. Yet she was always saying, "But you
used to love lima beans," and he was always correcting her,
"No, that's Si, Mother. I never ate lima beans." Whatever it
was Emily doted on so loudly, so sentimentally, it wasn't the
man she was married to. Whenever Emily made such a
mistake, she would be flustered and upset, while Neil would
say in his calm voice that she should not worry. Sometimes
a muscle in his cheek would kick.

With his father Neil had long conversations about the computer business, especially about Logical. His father thought being director of a company was serious business. He was always trying to impress upon Neil that being a director was a burden under which he should stoop at least a little: appear to ruminate decisions. Always his father would ask him eagerly when the stock would go public. Neil had some stock from the beginning and some from options he had exercised since. She could not see why he bothered buying pieces of paper with no value, but that seemed part of the charade of being a corporation, along with having a lawyer write up directors' meetings that never occurred and keeping a corporate seal in Efi's drawer. Always Neil would answer that the corporation was operating on a shoestring, in debt to the bank, and if for some mad reason they ever did go public, he certainly would not advise his father to invest in them. His father, thin and gray—gray in skin and gray in hair—would take off his glasses, of which he always had at least one spare in his vest pocket, and polish them carefully, frowning.

Neil talked little about his family. He told her he remembered mainly trivia from his childhood except that it had been, he thought, normal and relatively happy. She had a grudge. She felt his long years of finding it hard to relate to others off the technical level, the training in being out of touch with his own feelings and not knowing them till they knocked him down—meeting his own emotions suddenly like a car bearing down on him in the street—was the fault of some powerful and pervasive atmosphere of repression in his family. Obviously there was a steady unremitting pressure to succeed.

Emily was pleased that she was Jewish and almost a Ph.D. Almost, almost. Neil's project had had a plausible relationship to her thesis, now moldering. Lucky she was working for a company and not a university. Nepotism rules would have forced her out of her own department immediately. At least in Logical she could remain in the company. Still Emily could not see why she should bother to get her degree, now that she was married. . . . She would work again on it, she would find time in the summer, when things were slower at Logical with people going off on vacation and taking off early and sneaking long weekends. She would use that ebb to steal the time to finish her thesis.

Yet she felt oppressed by Emily. Little jokes that offended her. Little references to the coming grandson to carry on the name. As if "Stone" were a name anybody had carried very long or very far. Miriam Stone, that should finish those awful old jabs about Venus Berg forever. But of course nobody around her even knew about that. Except Beth. But Beth ran over things like that, a clear stream that stayed clear.

Mother by surrogate, suggesting similar pressures from her mother yet not her mother, not her face, her voice, her hands. Touched that old wound. But she *had* been good, playing her role all weekend. Neil seemed pleased. He knew the amenities came hard for her. He did not require that she want to please his parents but only that she do it. She walked through the empty conversations and the necessary vacuous hours of all sitting uncomfortably trying to think of something to say and she walked through them all without bumping too hard into anything, while her head ached and her eyes burned with boredom. At last it all ended and they were once again alone together and everything returned to being simple.

The soup steamed and lazily she toweled her hair dry, shook it back on her shoulders, stretched, and stirred the pot. Saturday afternoon. Neil was off playing tennis with Dick, as usual. Neil thought it important to keep in shape. His slender neat compact body. A good body, under control and responsive. They made love a lot. That had been a pleasant surprise. When she began to feel attracted to Neil, she had felt that was because he was a good man, a man who might be loyal to her and kind and gentle, a man who would value her. She had talked a great deal with her therapist about exactly why she was interested in Neil, as opposed to the qualities that had drawn her to Phil and Jackson and dozens of others. They were good values this time, rational values.

After the first few times in bed, somewhat awkward and patchy, they had got into a good thing sexually. They made love frequently. She felt secure enough about their loving to admit that he was not as experienced in pleasing a woman, in exciting her, as she was used to. But what did that matter, by comparison with the lack of tension? Sex was not a battleground or a proving ground. It was just their way of loving. It was simple and frequent, and if he did not always seem to sense that she needed more time than he to come, the fre-

quency of the sex made it less frustrating on the occasions
when she was left hanging.

Once when she had talked with her therapist, Dr. Bachman, about her strong reaction to Jackson, that sense of being
sexually out of control with him, he had suggested that her
strong response was based on masochism, based on her satisfying with him a deep need to punish herself. At once she
had felt a strong shock of denial, almost a desire to laugh,
an absolute physical sense that he was wrong. But slowly she
had forced herself to an acceptance of what Dr. Bachman
said, because the phenomena of resistance had become familiar
by that time. Now that blind sexual spasm was a thing of
the past: her mature sexuality was calmer and sunnier.

When she heard a sound at the front door, she immediately
hoped it was Neil home early: then they would make love
this afternoon. She liked best to make love in the afternoon,
when she had her full energy. Walking to the door, she rejoiced in her body. Still smiling, she realized by the knocking
it could hardly be Neil, but her joy remained, though muted.
"Jaime. How elegant you look." She presumed on her leeway
as a married lady and kissed him. Jaime was so touchable-
looking, more than once a brief urge to get him into bed
had passed through her. Clearly, however, she saw his nervous
virginity. He was worse than Beth, really, who had passed
through sex like a patch of briars. She would make a bet
Jaime had never ventured in. Besides, mature love was faithful love, as Dr. Bachman had led her to see.

But Jaime liked to be caressed, now that she was safely
married. He kissed her back, tangling his hand in her still
faintly damp hair, curling as it dried. "What smells delicious?"

She swept him back to the kitchen with her. "Black bean
soup. Yes, you can stay to supper."

Jaime peered into the pot, slender, faunish, with yellow
curls trailing on his thin shoulders. "You see through me.
What are those vegetables floating around, then?"

"It's puréed at the end. Come sit and talk with me."

Jaime bowed his head in mock submission. "Why does Neil
play tennis with Dick? Dick's such a clod. How can Neil
tolerate him? Brain the size of a microdot."

"Neil doesn't like to judge anyone. When he suspects he
dislikes somebody he works with, he feels guilty. Remember,
he's known Dick for years. Maybe Dick was less of a clod
then."

"Neil is so much more . . . sympathetic, cultured. I'd think Dick would drive him to tears."

Miriam shrugged. Dick never ceased to rasp on her nerves. "Neil is a creature of habit. Habit frees him from the necessity of making small decisions all day long, every day. That freedom matters to him. He'll eat lunch every day at Orzato's, though the food is rotten, because it's less effort to go eat that rotten food than to search out new food probably as rotten. Playing tennis with Dick is what Neil does Saturday afternoons, weather permitting. Not to do so would require a decision and he would have to convey that decision to Dick. That might cause pain. Neil would rather walk on coals than cause pain. Which is one reason I married him, I think."

Jaime adored Neil. Jaime had enjoyed working with her, he responded with excitement to her ideas, they had never spent outside time together until she married Neil. Jaime had few friends. He had no way to make connections with people, locked into his work and his ego. But he could spend time in the house and slowly he began to talk a little. Idly she remembered that Jackson had used to boast that the Pearl Street apartment was a web, a net, a halfway house. Well, it had been a damned cold one: witness how they had treated Dorine. She was making a warm place here. Always lots of good food, always space and comfort.

Fortunately Dick had a date and did not stay to supper. If he had Jaime would probably have left and she preferred Jaime's company. After supper Neil and Jaime played chess. She wondered why she didn't. She had not played since that time with Jackson. The game remained invested with suspicion. Perhaps she guessed that if she brushed up a bit she might beat Neil and that would not do. Her therapist had always been suggesting that her need to compete with men was a product of her resentment of her brother and his superior position. Well, maybe, but it was hard enough to justify to everybody with all those notions about what women shouldn't do and be her scientific work. Work was what counted. So beyond that initial affront, she sought now to play women's roles.

After all, she need not be shut out from happiness and fulfillment just because she had a certain kind of brain. Just because she could think well about systems design did not mean she was doomed not to be loving, nurturing, and warm. Her life had hurt her, she had felt herself defeated till pain sang in her. Despair and dead ends and broken connections. Now she was through into her sun, but she was careful.

Learning to please Neil who had rescued her, she found she could please others too, in casual ways. It was a dance to bring food out and arrange it and serve it. How easy to do a small thing like asking people to supper. Neil enjoyed having the company without himself having to seek it beyond inviting somebody home. He was proud of the meals she set before guests and tickled at the compliments. "Do you eat like this every night?" Neil always answered with great innocence, "But of course."

By the time they went to bed Saturday night she was tired, what with the week's shopping, laundry, making supper and cleaning up. They made love but she could not concentrate enough to come before he had finished. Then she could not drift off. The longer she lay beside his sleeping body, the wider awake she became, the more uselessly alert. Finally she let her mind play over some of the technical materials she had been reading and pondering.

About three she hopped out of bed and tiptoed across the hall to her study—bleak, unfinished room she must paint eventually. She sat down and started to write, as quickly as her hand could move on the pad. Her brain was working in leaps, in great encompassing bolts of new material, and she could not transcribe her thoughts quickly enough.

About five she went back to bed. When the alarm went off three hours later (Neil liked to rise early even on Sunday) she felt she had been kicked in the head. Her good humor returned with the memory of her beautiful idea. Away with the missile nonsense, she would settle down to working on it today and get it whipped into shape. Yes, Abe had asked her just last week if she wanted to give a seminar soon, and she had said she would think about it—feeling small desire to haul out her neglected thesis. Unfinished business made her queasy in her conscience. But here was an idea that fed out of that material but was light-years past it and exciting enough to stun them all. She would get Abe to let her work on it. They could carry her on overhead for a while till they could get a new project funded. She did not mind working alone, although that could never be as exciting as the give-and-take of a really creative group. However, it would be preferable beyond comparison to being stuck on Dick's project.

Everything about the missile contract was political. She

had wasted a month generating ideas about machine design only to have it finally sunk in to her that since the contract for the hardware had already been let to UNIVAC, there was an unspoken pressure operating against any ideas Logical might produce. That is, UNIVAC was going to implement the machine design and was deeply unfriendly to ideas that didn't go with the predilections of their already existing hardware and their technical people. Logical's far-out suggestions for machine design were just a boondoggle, a baroque embellishment on the contract, and never intended to be implemented by anybody.

The technical people they had to deal with at Bell Labs kept changing. The old faces would disappear and new people turn up to deal with them who had no idea what they were doing and what had happened before. The same thing kept happening with their government contract interface, where people kept finishing their tours of duty and going off, leaving important pieces of paper lost in the works and requests unheeded and interim reports in limbo.

She hated the whole clanking apparatus and she hated the intended product. Now she had a way out. She would tell Abe Monday afternoon that she wanted to be scheduled for a seminar. There she would present her new idea and they would all be turned on. They had to: it was a breakthrough: a descriptive method that would be adequate for describing *both* artificial languages and computers. This it would do in such a way that an algorithm could translate automatically— without further human intervention—a program written in the artificial language into machine language.

This was the so-called compiler-compiler problem and it had never been solved. But she saw a way in. She could not guess—no way of knowing at this point—if her idea would work, but what a breakthrough if it did. Even if it didn't, she was sure the effort would generate interesting materials. What she saw was an intelligent method for partitioning up the possibilities—a pattern recognition approach which she hoped and believed would produce useful partitionings in each artificial language and which would then explore those possibilities.

What usually went wrong with such schemes was that a language developed for describing the syntax of other languages—like artificial or computer languages—lacked a semantic bridge between the two structures. Invariably that bridge had to be spelled out by a programer for each language-computer pairing.

But she was conceiving a super compiler-compiler that could simply be handed descriptions of five languages, five machines, and could handle specifications of which language was to be linked with which machine. Then the super compiler-compiler would accept programing and knock out machine code for the required case. The combinatorics involved made it a hairy problem. What she thought she saw was a method for making the partitionings, the choices, not blindly but heuristically: it was gorgeous if far out. But it just had to grab Abe. This would get her back onto something exciting. She had not joined Logical to do ugly boring nonsense mired in politics. Truly it made her sick. Even if she had been a right-wing nut she would have hated the project, since the probabilities of the anti-missile missile system working at all were abominably low. She had known that for months.

She was ashamed of her work. At odd moments she imagined trying to explain it to Phil, running into old friends, politicos, and bumbling through an answer to what she was doing. The contract stank, but she was beginning to realize everything around was sticky. Even the pure research she had been working on with Neil was funded by the Department of Defense, through A.R.P.A. In fact all the most interesting projects in computer science seemed funded by the Pentagon, when she came down to it. Only they could afford big machines and only they were interested in the techniques on the level of sophistication where she wanted to work. Thus to say something was at the cutting edge of the science was almost for sure to say that the military was paying for it, since nobody else could afford to.

Neil did not make those connections. He thought of the whole thing as what Phil would have called a vast ripoff: that the government was paying him for playing his elaborate and beautiful games. He saw no results in the newspaper from the intricate webs of logic he spun out. She shied away from confronting him. After all, she did not know what to propose as an alternate source of funding. Neil was a good person, a kind person, but he had not been trained to make connections in terms of social consequences. And if she were less blind, what difference did that make?

Well, the first step was getting out of the project she loathed.

Then she would gradually try to move herself into some
other area of expertise and research—a branch of computer
science not quite so dependent on fancy, vast, and expensive
equipment, so that somebody besides the D.O.D. could afford
to use it. She could not turn to Neil for help. He knew the
ins and outs of the computer field on a more intimate level
than she did, but her attempts to talk with him always ended
up either as technical arguments about the worth of somebody's ideas or as anecdotal histories on his part of brilliant
systems men. Nor could she tell him exactly what had
soured her. She would have had to tell him about her last
meeting with Wilhelm Graben and that she had no intention
of doing. That would upset him. It was meaningless. The last
gasp of a dying way of life.

The day of the seminar came. She had not been talking
half an hour when she had a strong physical sensation of
being bombarded by waves of hostility. She could not even
complete setting out her idea before the attacks began. She
seemed to have hit a bare nerve in almost everyone. Neil
of course disqualified himself: the only person who might have
understood the importance of the idea and followed her
argument. No, she was being paranoid. Jaime could follow,
Abe could follow, Fred and Ted should be able to follow
easily. Yet Fred was hardly able to be polite. The idea seemed
to affront him personally. He sounded angry as he argued
that her compiler would make improper partitionings and
never be able to escape. It would forever continue to try for
matches between the languages in a nightmare loop straggling
into infinity. He made it sound like a bad trip: a memory of
years before with Phil on acid, being caught in a small self-
enclosed universe where the same words repeated endlessly
and eternally, and she knew that never would she be able to
escape forward.

Ted sounded just as mad, though he spoke with arch sarcasm. He said how he thought it was wonderfully fascinating
to presume to solve in half an hour what was in its essence
an insoluble problem. One that a great many individuals of
vast reputation and experience had spent much time and
energy on. They all did enjoy a good science fiction tale now
and then, so why not a sci fi seminar? The junior members
of the research teams could always be depended on for a
bit of flying sauceritis. Perhaps every technical person was

entitled to an ego trip sometimes, but most of them would prefer doing it on their own time.

His sarcasm entered her like shrapnel. Her hands sweated into the chalk, dust compacting on her damp palms. She could not tell if he was angry because she had *presumed* to attack such a problem, or because *she* had presumed.

Jaime was the only one who seemed to want to grapple with the idea. His objections were in terms of whether the descriptive techniques were really adequate to all cases. She answered him as best she could and then the rout continued. When it was finally done she walked out quickly, shaking, and shut the door of her office. She had never seen anyone attacked that way. She could not believe the response. She had been sure the idea was exciting, but that excitement had been fury. Yet perhaps she was being defensive. There were large holes. She had been hoping by presenting the idea early to get criticism that would spur her on to rapid progress. Mostly, of course, she had hoped to get off the missile project.

She must confront Abe directly. He had not attacked her, he had only asked whether the number of possibilities could really be sufficiently reduced by the pattern-recognition approach. That was a serious question. She felt she had handled it well. She would appeal to him. Only he decided what they would take on as projects and what they would not.

Friday afternoon she got an appointment to see him. With the name Abe one would have expected a fifty-year-old Jewish businessman, a pudgy grandfather: but Abe was from Lincoln country and had been named by his father, a self-made agribusinessman. How he had ended up in computers was anyone's guess. He was a big-boned man with sandy hair and perennially squinted eyes of in-between color, a firm handshake and a just-folks manner that disappeared in a flash when he was annoyed or dealing with people he wanted to impress. He had a firm reputation and had been in analysis since before Neil had met him. It was said in the company that Abe had chosen Boston as a site for Logical, not so much because it was a fertile field for computer contracts as because that was where his analyst practiced.

Abe had a large family, the oldest in prep schools and the youngest still a toddler, all by the wife whom Miriam had seen only twice, dressed up for some occasion with the wives of other company presidents in a manner which cost a lot to no effect Miriam could figure out—beige linen dresses

that went into the wallpaper with the gaunt body. He lived
the farthest from the office, up almost into New Hampshire in
a farmhouse supposed to date from 1830, on which he was
always financing renovations. He had several acres and a palo-
mino. Abe held aloof from the rest of the company, although
all three directors had known each other well before they
formed it. He was opaque to her. He hated to fire technical
staff—leaving that, when it must be done, to Dick—yet indifferent to them as people. He was proud of how good an
organization he had built: his stable, perhaps.

From time to time he picked favorites known to be up and
coming. Ted had been especially favored for six to eight
months, because he had developed an idea they had incor-
porated in a proprietary product: a program they hoped to
market to other companies. Lately Ted had fallen from grace
because the idea did not work after they sold it. The program
did not do what it was supposed to—true of a great many
programs, perhaps most of them—but Ted had been caught
because the way it didn't work had become visible too quickly.
She had never been a favorite son in the company, but she
would not mind that position at all.

Abe heard her out patiently enough, though she had the
feeling his mind was only partially engaged. Where was the
rest of him? He sat behind his neat desk with his long legs
spread and his feet propped on a lower drawer pulled out,
fiddling with his pipe. Half the men at Logical smoked pipes.
This was a meerschaum. The tobacco had a sweetish smell
that tickled her nose. It was close in the office and she wished
that the windows opened. Outside it was raining lightly but
persistently. The sky looked low, sagging just over the expressway and about to fall in long filmy strands over the cars
beginning to clog it for rush hour.

"People weren't exactly unanimous behind this idea. I like
to feel my technical people are agreed that an idea has merit
before I would go pulling someone off a project he's already
on."

"But with any idea that has a certain amount of risk—
that involves taking a giant step—you can't have agreement
beforehand."

"It is an exciting idea, Miriam, and I'd be the last to deny
that, and we certainly got some excitement out of the boys
on Wednesday. But you know we're not a big outfit with a
lot of extra capital to bankroll our ideas. Even if this idea

does pan out, chances are it'd be too costly to have much commercial application. Now"—he held up his hand to head her off at the pass—"you know and I know we're here to do research. But we aren't in a financial position right at this moment to fund our own pure research off the cuff."

"It wouldn't take long for me to reach the point where we could see if it works or not. It really would be a break-through if I'm right. If I'm wrong, it wouldn't take long."

"I know that you feel strongly, and I wish I could give you the green light. Tell you what we can do. I don't want you to give up. I want you to go ahead and work on your idea on the side while you're on the ABM contract. Then in six months or so we can review your progress. I think we might have a reserve for developing our own technical ideas by then. You'll have your idea roughed out and filled in. I like to feel the staff is behind any idea we finance on the cuff, because it's a risk to all of us. But you're not to feel dis-couraged. Work on it, keep at it, and we'll see if we can't come up with something in six months, nine months. You don't want people to feel you can get supported on a project of your own because Neil threw his weight around."

"You know Neil would never do that. He didn't say a word in the seminar."

"You know that, and I know that, because we know Neil. But technical people are always apt to be a bit jealous." He stood, signaling her audience was finished. "Don't let a little criticism dampen your spark. Back to the drawing boards. I bet that in six months you'll have something for us to see."

"Look," she said with rising desperation, feeling herself backed out the door, "I really do feel out of place on the missile contract. What about Ted's project? Couldn't I work on a piece of that?"

"Why, Dick thinks you're doing fine. We're satisfied. You're too critical of yourself. As for Ted's project, it's one of those government contracts written for one full-time class three systems man and one part-time class five. You don't meet the specs. Be seeing you. Right. Any time."

That weekend she came down with a cold and Monday she stayed home from work. Immediately after Neil left and she snuggled down in their bed upstairs, in the corner room with the tower, she knew she wanted to be sick. Normally she would have gone to work with a cold. She rarely took to bed with anything less than the flu. But today she wanted to stay home and sulk.

Why not? What was a house for if sometimes she could not stay in it and not have to see anyone or pretend she was not hurt and furious and miserable? Why should she be so hurt? It was only a technical idea that had misfired. But a good one. Bastards. Jealous bastards. Nobody liked it when somebody else was the one to pull down a good technical idea. What they all loved more than anything was to be able to say about somebody what they did about Dick: that he could only manage, because he could no longer do technical work. Like saying somebody was impotent. In fact she had once heard Ted say that Dick couldn't cut the mustard any more, meaning do good work. Logical was supposed to be such a rarefied jolly pure atmosphere, ideal setup, small software outfit controlled not by business types but by the scientists themselves. But a company existed to make money. Money came only from certain sources. Those sources determined the work to be done, determined ultimately what people came to feel was technically interesting work.

She got up to make herself tea. Brought it back upstairs with an orange and an apple. Weighed herself with anxiety and climbed back into bed. This room could really be special, a retreat, if she ever got off her ass and fixed it up. Time, time, never enough time. The basic layout of the house was interesting, with that dramatic cascade of stairway and the marvelously well preserved woodwork. They had furnished the dining room with care and done a reasonable job with materials at hand on the bedroom and kitchen and Neil's study. But the living room was still basically empty—wasted.

At first they had lived in Neil's apartment. After looking for a while at larger apartments they'd decided to think about a house. Everybody else they knew had bought or built expensive modern objects out in the tracts, as Neil said, where they lacked doors to shut and sounds reverberated and nobody could be alone with his thoughts or work. A box of noise in a sea of mud: they both thought of the house that Fred lived in with his herds of children and exhausted whining wife. Not for them.

They searched until they found a big old house in a pleasant area of Brookline. They had not really decided to buy a house, to commit themselves financially, but in the course of looking they crossed that line. They could not afford it

but they would get by. Neil was optimistic about Logical.
The house was a mess. They had despaired of ever getting
the work done—not right, they gave up on that, but sufficiently so they could move out of the cramped bachelor quarters and spread out at their ease.

The house could be something people would enjoy, a house
that did not look like every other house, a good environment
—if she ever had the time. At least this weekend they must
get a couch. People put effort into everything except their
own pleasure. That driven Protestant work ethic, what was
she doing with it nattering away in her? Why try to be so
original and creative when, supposing she had got Abe to
back her work, any products of her effort must necessarily be
misused? The only kind of context where her ideas would
ever be applied was the military-industrial complex. Her
best ideas fed the war games. What was the use?

Oh, she knew who had made her see that, rubbing her nose
in it. Charming Wilhelm, who wasn't even radical. He was
just more civilized than the men she worked with. He had
a global sense of the society and how it fit together that only
politicos tended to have, and they lacked the facts generally.
Wilhelm had loads of fact.

Wilhelm Graben was of the older generation of computer
people who had created the field in the fifties, after his already
distinguished career in physics. He had come to the States
from Austria in 1938, in early adolescence, his father a
scholarly refugee. He was the most exciting teacher she had
ever had, and she had retained for years a special awe of him.
He told her he thought in English, though he sometimes
dreamed in German. He had a fine trace of accent that
vanished when he spoke of technical matters. He was perhaps
an inch or two shorter than her, almost bald, and the first
much older man she had ever found attractive. She had
found him very attractive. He projected a charm and a sexuality unusual in an older man and unusual among scientists, a
sort of sensual amused feeling tone, very civilized, ironic and
right on the beam. That he picked her out to pay attention to
flattered her.

She had been more or less living with Neil already. Neil
was pressing her about marriage but she was dubious. Neil
had asked, however, that she be assigned to another project.
Without enthusiasm she went along with the team to Washington for a presentation. Wilhelm appeared in some advisory

capacity. Her hands shook when it was time for her performance—she had been his student. She wanted desperately
to impress him.

They all had dinner together. She managed to ask him
what he had thought of her presentation, and he suggested
they might talk about it afterward. She had gone off with
him to his hotel room, giddy with his attention. He could
advise her. She had still been a believer in Logical, and he
had made it clear she sounded naïve. Pushing on her was
the judgment she would have to make about Neil, who could
not understand her hesitation and interpreted it as a lack of
confidence in him or his feelings. If she phrased her doubts
in terms of herself, he would tell her that she was humble
about her own best qualities. He wanted the ceremony, the
fact of marriage. He kept saying that it was easy to drift in
and out of relationships, to slam the door from the outside
when things did not go well, and at least the commitment of
marriage made it harder to give up. He wanted it to be very
hard for them to give up, he said.

She liked Neil's being in her field. She had had nothing but
misunderstanding and antagonism and unreasoning counter-
demands from Phil and Jackson. They had not understood
what she did, they had given her no comfort, no support,
and often they had not even been willing to listen. Oh, Phil
had listened, but his antagonism to technology was so pro-
found, his listening did little good.

But a man in her own field could understand her problems.
They shared a common basis for communication. They shared
pleasures and tensions. Perhaps she was attracted to Wilhelm
as another dimension of that feeling. But Willie had had two
careers already, both distinguished, and he was a star. Doubt-
less she felt curious about what lay behind the elegance and
the wit, even the arrogance. Following him to his hotel room,
she was quite aware of the tarnished elements in the attraction,
but curious, curious still.

He drank brandy. He carried with him a snifter in his
attaché case. "Oh, not crystal—clumsy, heavy glass—but of
an ample size for the nose. But a solipsist like myself carries
only one. I'm afraid we will have to rely on the hotel glassware
to serve you. Then you're not an aficionado of cognac?"

He talked and he talked. He had liked her presentation
but told her that almost no one else had followed it. "You
must learn on these occasions to draw nice-looking diagrams

on the board and give those diagrams snappy names. It does not matter that they mean nothing. You present too much material too fast. It annoys. I find you the most interesting of your group, but you'll never do anything in the field."

"Why not?" She stared, attacked suddenly through the cocoon of attraction and brandy and talk. "You think I lack the ability to develop good technical ideas?"

"On the contrary, you have an unusual intuitive mind— the best thing one can say about any scientist. But you're an attractive, a very attractive woman. So you'll do nothing. Why should you?"

"You're an attractive man. Why do you bother if all that matters is sex appeal?"

"Ah, that is not the same and you know it. Only homely women survive to accomplish in their field. Or perhaps a woman has the luck to become widowed. Who would ever have heard of Madame, if Monsieur Curie had survived? The husband stands in the light, the wife waits in the shadows."

"I'm thinking of marrying Neil Stone. We wouldn't be working together, though. Already Neil thinks we should be on different projects."

"If you were thinking seriously, would you be here with me? Perhaps. But what a waste. You admire Stone a great deal—I do not. But you are something far rarer in this country than a wife. You have the makings of a great courtesan. You will not find here many men to appreciate what you are, but the ones who can, will appreciate you a great deal."

"I . . . I don't think of myself that way." Her face froze. He was older, European, she must remember that he had a different frame of reference. "I simply like to follow my curiosities toward people sometimes."

"You would go much farther, my dear, as a grand courtesan—such as the hetaeras of ancient Greece, cultivated, highly regarded, a class of women apart—than as a systems analyst. You have too original a mind. You're sloppy, of course. And you lack that awareness of the opponent's responses essential to success. You stare into the depth of your idea and see fires. You neglect to watch the faces of the gentlemen in the room who control the budgetary decisions. That's a fatal error for you and for your idea. You forget that government people want only to solve their problems. The academics want only to stare at the head of a pin technically. They adore men like your fiancé, who pile up in their papers—and they write a great many tedious papers—enormous technical detail on some unimportant point. Mathematically exacting papers. Your academic prefers a nitwit who reasons very carefully about nothing to yourself, who have such large grandiose free-swinging ideas and go swinging them about the room, knocking over the ashtrays and the china of people's prejudices. Everyone prefers to deal with a closed mind, my dear, it is less challenging. Further, with someone like your fiancé or Ted Barnes who reasons in tiny steps, that reasoning is easy to check. Intuitive power does not make one popular! I know." He chuckled, sniffing the cognac. "But I take great care how I present my ideas, cloaking the leaps in minute spidery webs of mathematics. But I'm afraid that you lack that necessary patience. You don't understand the rules of the game. I suspect you're playing the wrong game altogether."

"I've heard you use that phrase so many times. Everybody's always talking that way at Logical."

"Intelligent people know they're playing games, and that makes life amusing. We all seek a technical situation in which we can play our own intricate and fascinating games, rather than the dull and shoddy games that the powers-that-be would have us play."

Why was she frightened? She did not think he could read the steel fear penetrating her chest. She was smiling, she was curled in a chair swirling the brandy in the glass. She could tell from his eyes drifting over her that she looked attractive. If he could see inside she would look like a rabbit crouched in headlights. He had hit a sore nerve in her. She did not want to think of herself ever, not even for five minutes, as a high-class whore trailing unraveled affairs across the landscape. That anyone could tell her that was what she was, that was how they saw her, and expect her to blandly agree threatened her profoundly. Made her feel backed against a jagged wall she thought she had left far behind her. What was she doing here? Perhaps he was right, that if she truly intended to live sanely and not bleed herself out in meaningless beddings she would not be here. Quickly she changed the subject. She got him into high instructional mode. She questioned him about the project she was being shunted into. "I don't feel comfortable working on software for missiles, frankly. I feel like I'm being hired by death."

"What nonsense. It's scuttlebutt that the system will never

operate. For instance, assuming that the computer technology works out perfectly—for the first time in history, perhaps—but assuming that, the crucial interface is that combination of radar equipment and computers. Now there cannot possibly in any real war situation be enough time to discriminate the raw data in the radar inputs about what would be real missiles and what simply extra junk floating about. All weapons are programed to fill the heavens with large quantities of objects that induce noise on the radar. Chaff for instance—aluminum foil—reflects radar beams quite nicely and produces responses that would indicate serious objects approaching. The electronic countermeasures will be jamming, with strong transmission at the same frequency that the radar operates on. . . .

"But forget military questions. Think about the most amusing aspect of the ABM. Now you are exploding, say, a five-megaton warhead to knock down a missile no bigger than a barn. Obviously, this does not require a warhead of five hundred million tons of TNT—Hiroshima was destroyed by twenty thousand tons' equivalent. Thus you can deduce that accuracy is simply not in it. They're figuring on exploding a five-megaton bomb to knock down a missile because they are not counting on being in the same state with it—states imagined to be lines superimposed upon the air. . . ." His voice was calm and mocking. She grew colder and colder. He thought all this funny. He had learned to live with it. Perhaps she would too. Or perhaps it was better to be a high-class whore than a high-class scientist. She sipped the brandy while the fumes crept up her nose and the room floated in the cold blackness of outer space and megadeaths.

"Defense, it's called. The rhetoric of defense, of course, is that human beings are being defended. But the type of weaponry we are discussing is absolutely useless in defending human beings. It would make little difference, I would imagine, to someone on the ground whether he was fried alive because an enemy missile exploded twenty miles to his right hand, or because one of 'his' missiles exploded as far overhead. The temperature on the ground would instantly rise several hundred degrees, in either case. Defense is defense of missile silos, not of people or the landscape, which would be eliminated. . . . But you must admit, the rhetoric with which American politicians address their constituencies about defense spending is amusing."

"The more you talk, the less I want any part. It makes me sick, truly."

"This project could be a computer man's dream, if the nitwits don't hamper too much. It's a chance, as Abe was saying loudly in his folksy back-porch manner, to get in on the ground floor of a whole new technology. I must say, I should rather have a top-floor view myself. However I may fault his use of metaphors, I cannot fault what he means. A string of identical large computers linked up to work on the same problems—it's a system designer's paradise. In what other context could we seize the chance to do anything as delightful? The economics of the thing are simply ridiculous, staggering. Nothing but defense could siphon off the money for so many king-sized computers lashed together."

"You think that, because the system is a large boondoggle actually considered as a weapon, it's not inhumane to work on it."

"I think that a scientist can only be a scientist—or perhaps also a lovely woman." He lifted his snifter to her. "We can never know what those who govern will do with our ideas. Our duty is to the state of the art—the cutting edge of knowledge. Now we have talked and talked and talked— I am a middle-aged man, certainly, and I talk a great deal too much. But not so old I am not ready to stop talking, my dear. Come."

Then indeed she felt like a whore, for the last thing she felt like doing was being touched by him. There being no question of her pleasure—her mind was frozen, her nerves jammed— she performed.

So she had left Washington scared. Scared she was becoming what Wilhelm had suggested. Scared of losing herself. Scared of falling into a mire of being used, abused, handled, disregarded, degraded. Miriam, twenty-five-year-old bag of sexual tricks and good times for busy gentlemen. Wilhelm disliked Neil, but then she was not sure she did not dislike Wilhelm. She felt chilled to the bone, frozen like winter mud through to her spine. She had indeed followed her curiosity into his elegance and cynicism and learned something, but the face this knowledge wore was the skull. Back to Neil, quickly. She could not read on the plane, she detested chatting with Dick, who sat beside her. Would he say anything to Neil? Unlikely. He could not after all be sure anything had happened. He could only suspect. She stared at the white masses of cloud and longed to be back with Neil instantly. Right now to fall into his arms and tell him Yes, Yes, Yes, quickly before he changed his mind and turned from her.

Side by side they sat on their new Danish couch, teak and black leather, with the new free-form teak coffee table bought at Harbor Design the week before and just delivered.

"You talked so long on the phone to our keypunch operator, I was afraid there would be nothing left for me," he teased her.

"How do you like the couch? Does it feel good?"

"Finally we can do a little living in our living room. I'm tired of sitting around the dining-room table all evening. Now perhaps you should do something about the windows? Draperies? Shutters? I don't care. Something interesting. Just so we haven't the present option of looking at the people's TV across the street or the inside of a window blind."

"We have to start going around to antique-junk shops to find another chair or two. Maybe a leather chair. Or something carved. I think we should have old pieces in the house too. But isn't this comfortable?"

"I told you—in all my years of sitting in people's houses on what they call couches, this is the only object I ever rested my behind on that didn't make it complain."

Miriam slid over and curled up, her head on his slightly bony shoulder. Neil put his arm around her. So good to know she could approach him without having to take atmospheric readings: that he would like to have her touch him, that he would not likely decide she was impinging or corrupting or undermining him by displaying her affection. "You let me love you—that's the nicest thing about you."

"The nicest thing about you is doing it. You're so funny. Why wouldn't I permit you to love me? Do you think I'm crazy? I know a good thing when I see one." His hand slid down her arm to cup her breast.

"Loving is great—everybody should have someone to love him or her. That's what this country needs."

"Indeed. I can't imagine either of us starting a war."

"I must say, I'm glad you're overage for fighting one." He did not know how some men measured out their love like platinum. In a general way he knew about her past involvements, but he would never quite understand. "Neil, you're good for me. You can't comprehend how much you mean to me—"

His hand tightened on her breast. "Before I met you, I was lonely, Miriam. Just as they say fish would have no word for water or birds for air, I never said to myself I was lonely because it was a constant in my life, not a variable. I never learned to reach out, to open up, to be with others. But as soon as you touched me, you opened me up."

"I want to make you happy. I want to be good for you. Sometimes still I mistrust myself. I think I can't possibly be what you want for the rest of your life, because you really are a good person, Neil, in a way I'm not." She curled up closer. "But I'm trying! Trying hard. . . . Are you happy? Am I succeeding?"

"Of course I'm happy. We're still learning about each other and how to communicate and how to please. I love you, Miriam, but I'm not capable of saying so in ten different ways. I don't have that gift of words. I think we're doing well in our marriage. I know that sometimes I'm awkward. I don't have practice in knowing what a woman likes."

"Practice on me. Practice makes perfect."

"There's one more thing I think about. . . . Here we are in our own house. A big house with plenty of room. I'm thirty, you're twenty-six. We're not kids. I was so late finding my own woman, we're behind for our ages. Shouldn't we start a family? It would get Mother off our backs. I know you don't like that needling. But they say it's harder to have a baby later on, harder to conceive, harder to carry and deliver."

She shrank. A child. Baby lying there in front of them, she tried to see it. But he was right, time was passing in her as well as outside. He wanted a child very much; she had promised him a child. Why not soon? After all, her efforts to get back into doing research that meant something had failed abjectly. Abe could save that six months crap for somebody who hadn't observed that the company was always short on money, always in debt to the bank, and that there were always favorites who alone got to play their own games, as Wilhelm would have said. By the time she had the baby and took off a few months, they'd be done with the missile contract. She'd get a crack at something good. In the meantime she'd finish her thesis, get her doctorate, and put herself in a better arguing position, with more leverage.

A baby in her arms. That whole adventure. To feel life in her quickening, to grow large with life. She would be a real woman then, she would be what they had all tried to prove she was not. Jackson with his carping. Becoming a mother, she would contain her mother and no more miss her and no more carry that old guilt. She would prove them all wrong. She would prove that Neil was right to love her and marry her, to take a chance on her. She would validate her womanhood. She would bear her own baby to love as hard as she could.

She saw herself stepping proudly through her pregnancy, ripe as a pear and glowing, full and bountiful as a sheaf of ripe wheat. Suckling her own baby. Her flesh moved. She would have Neil's child and he would love her even more, they would really be bound together securely, they would be a family. She would be strong for her child, strong in loving.

She could feel Neil waiting: patiently, patiently but with a marked tension. He wanted that from her, he wanted it badly. She would satisfy him. She would be a mother, a good mother, warm and nurturing and protective. Why not? "You're right, it is time. Okay, let's go upstairs and make a baby. Maybe we can get it together. It's about the right time of month, I think. Why not?"

22

In the Fullness of Time

Until the early fifth month she had not been visibly pregnant, she had borne the slight bulge encompassed within the curves of her full body. Thereafter she had begun to show but continued active and enjoying herself until halfway through her eighth month she took a leave of absence from Logical. She was feeling fine and could have gone on working, but she wanted off the project and she wanted to finish her thesis before the baby was born. The summer had melted away, leaving her little advanced, and she had not managed to get back to it since.

She looked forward to having days in the house to work on her thesis, to shop for baby things, to fix the house up. She felt as if she had not had a real vacation since she was nineteen. Always she had been in school or working or both. Always she had been engaged in making a living, worried about her progress in her work, anxious and responsible. Now she had only to wait: moving inexorably toward an event that was inside her and would happen involuntarily as weather and yet she had chosen that it happen. To meet a person who did not yet exist but was present. The heartbeat under her heart.

When she spoke, she called it "the baby." She did not want to assign a sex. If the child was a boy, he was to be named Jeffrey Thorne: Jeffrey after Neil's grandfather, Thorne after Abe's middle name. If the child was a girl she would be Ariane, after a name Miriam had read in a book. She wanted her daughter to have a pretty name, like the one she had always envied Allegra. Neil liked the idea of carrying on family traditions. He had in fact asked her if she didn't want to call their daughter Sonia. She had shuddered. Ariane— she loved that name. It was Greek, Cretan. It was a weaver-woman. Ar, to rhyme with far. Ar-ee-ahn. She had asked Neil's secretary, Efi, who came from a Greek-speaking family, how to pronounce it.

The house was too large for one person wandering through. At times it spooked her. Her fears would gather in corners and mutter. The fear of punishment: that her child would be born with something wrong. She tried not to think of that, but whenever she saw a blind woman begging downtown in front of Filene's, a woman in the subway with a strange livid birthmark on her face, a man missing an arm, that fear would grip her belly. Sonia had told her some people believed that thinking bad thoughts could harm the child. Sonia said she had listened to symphonic music a great deal while she was pregnant in order that her children would love music and please their father. Only Allegra could carry a tune. Those torturous music lessons, glacial afternoons chained to the piano. Mark had been forced to study the violin and always he had made it squeal like a mating cat.

Yet before she had taken lessons she had wanted to bang on

Aunt Yette's piano. Once in a great while Aunt Yette would play Brahms or Chopin. Aunt Yette made many mistakes, for her hands were arthritic. Yette would never play when Lionel was around, for he would mock her old-fashioned style. Grandma said Aunt Yette played with feeling. Lionel liked no one's playing but his own, although the piano was not his favorite instrument: it forced him to turn away from his audience.

How sour she was toward him. Everybody said she would mellow toward her own childhood after she had a baby, that she would understand her own parents. Reconciliation, too late for Sonia. Miriam had always thought she understood Lionel too well. Sonia had been more mysterious in the terrible pressure of her love and suffering, her loneliness in the midst of a loud unregarding family. Miriam carried with her unborn child her buried mother, whose forgiveness she would earn in motherhood.

"You're awfully moralistic about your father," Neil told her. He liked Lionel: they got on. They found each other fair-minded and agreeable. Lionel had come to visit with a girl friend, although he called this one his fiancée, Mrs. Fran Gutmacher, the widow of a doctor whose children were grown. She was carefully kept and corseted and rather shy, beaming and clinging. "You don't judge anybody else by the standards you use on him."

At first Neil had not really understood what he was getting into when she decided on the Lamaze method. But she had been sure she could get him involved. The idea of being knocked out while some doctor pulled out her baby was disgusting. Several wives of Logical personnel had had their babies by natural childbirth, and each recommended her own doctor. Dr. Foreman was not only willing to deliver by natural childbirth, but indeed set up his procedures on that assumption.

Sometimes she was afraid. Sonia had brought her up on stories of the pain of childbirth. Sonia had told her it was the worst pain in the world. Nothing else hurt that much. They were in the kitchen helping Mama make chicken soup. Allegra was cutting the carrots. She was chopping onions. Why had she always got stuck chopping onions? She was crying. "When you get older, then you'll cry for real," Sonia was saying darkly. "The reason why mamas love their babies is because they suffer so much to bring them into the world."

But the literature and Dr. Foreman assured her that fear

caused pain. If she were not afraid of the natural process of birth there would be no pain. She would not be passively delivered but would actively give birth. Neil and she together would bear their child. Until she was taken into the delivery room he would be with her. He was not allowed to be present during birth, which seemed bizarre to her. Why should he be with her during the labor, long and tedious and surely mostly a drag, and then miss the climax? They were trained to speak of everything in the plural—"when we go into labor"—then he was robbed of the actual moment.

Early in the ninth month she began to get so big that Neil teased her about twins. By the middle of the day her back ached. She felt like an obscene joke, the way people looked at her—as if she should not be out in public. Men made remarks, she was everybody's thing to comment upon freely. She felt like a wounded whale. Her pregnancy that had felt pear-shaped and glorious now crushed her, as if inside there were no more room for organs but only a giant kicking and writhing.

"You must be going to have a boy," Efi said, patting her stomach. "He's so active."

When she repeated that Beth got angry. "Will you do that to her? Dress her in pink and teach her to keep still?"

That Friday Ted and his wife Barbara came over for supper: roast duck she had made with a crisp skin, apple stuffing, bulghur wheat and broccoli with mornay sauce. For dessert orange mousse. Now they were all sitting in the living room. Barbara was admiring the new dark blue draperies and they were gossiping about Logical. Ted had not been interested in going along with her on the natural childbirth thing, Barbara said. Therefore she had had a spinal block to make sure at least that she would be conscious, even though she hadn't felt anything.

"But you know, after they did it, my legs went numb. I got scared, because I'd heard about a woman who was paralyzed for life because the spinal tap had been done wrong. So I kept saying to the nurse, 'Nurse, something's wrong, my legs are numb.' And she kept saying in that cheerful opaque way, 'Now, dear, everything's fine, be quiet.' But damn her, it never occurred to her to tell me right out that my legs were numb because the injection always does that."

She was not fond of Ted and Barbara, but in a sense these

evenings played themselves. Her job was to make the dinner a success and the house pleasant. Most of the time she was sunk into her body, lulled and communing with the child, who bobbed and swam and lurched there. For some time she had not been able to wear her contact lenses. Something about fluid balances changing. She had had to get glasses again. Neil did not like them. But he wore glasses. It wasn't fair of him to make such a point of not liking her in glasses when he wore them too. Well, after the birth she'd immediately start in wearing her contacts again. But the unaccustomed glasses seemed to move her a little more distance from whoever she was talking to. She did not feel attractive, and somehow that took away some of the energy she used to make contact with others. There seemed . . . little point in trying hard.

Watching Barbara, listening, she remembered she'd felt sure Neil would be brought around to natural childbirth. One of the reasons she had felt secure enough to marry him, to entrust herself (Sonia's mistake riding in her), was that she felt sure he loved her and felt lucky to have her. Had he not told her many times how lonely he had been? So she should be able to get her way a reasonable proportion of the time. She had agreed to have the baby now, so it had been only reciprocal for him to agree with her on the method: and he had.

When Ted and Barbara left, she dragged her heavy body upstairs after Neil. In ten minutes he was sleeping and she was launched on her nightly vigil. In the first months of pregnancy she had slept and slept and slept. She had dozed off in the office, head on her arms, in a movie theater once, often sitting in the living room. She had imagined she would snooze through her pregnancy, hibernating. But that excessive sleepiness had passed off and lately she could not sleep at all.

The baby was a night person. Soon as she got ready for bed he—it—started to dance. The moon must call to it. It thought her a ballroom. Or perhaps it had already started the Canadian Air Force exercises that Neil did. Not that she could find a comfortable position any more. She felt as if her bodily processes had taken over. She and the fetus inhabited this vast swollen body like mice in an old house, while the big dilapidated body farted and belched and had to piss every five minutes. Even if the fetus would sleep at night instead of the daytime, how could she sleep with having to pee every time she moved? She could not regain her warm com-

placency of the middle pregnancy. She counted the days until
the baby was due—in spite of Dr. Foreman's warning that
the baby would probably come late, she counted till she
would get rid of this overstuffed disgusting body that could
no longer do anything right—heartburn instead of digestion,
backaches, water on the knee and swollen ankles. Soon she
would have had her own body back, lively and properly
shaped, and then *she* would do the dancing.

Still she must have slept because suddenly she woke and
had to poke Neil in the shoulder, calling plaintively in the
dark. The muscle of her leg was bunched up like a tennis
ball, a hard painful knot of muscle cramping. Without fully
waking, Neil reached under the covers and, clumsy with
drowsiness, kneaded it, massaged until the muscle slowly relaxed and the pain ebbed.

Grateful for the easing of pain, she touched his cheek. He
was sliding back into sleep. Very recently they had ceased
making love. Neil and she had invented a theory that the
fetus experienced her orgasms, but lately it had seemed to
disapprove. Also Neil had become afraid they would hurt
the child. His desire seemed to be in abeyance—indeed, who
could desire her in her vast state?—although when she saw
his morning erections she found herself making edgy jokes.
If men and women each carried a baby half time, how
different marriage would be.

Though parking had become difficult she went every few
days to the women's commune. Sally, who was in her seventh
month, came to see her even oftener. She would not discuss
the father. Miriam had started out keeping a journal of her
thoughts and sensations, but she had found it monotonous.
Talking to Sally was more satisfying. Sally was on her second
child and that made her something of an expert, though she
said every child was a different journey.

They talked about the dreams that nobody else wanted
to hear. Miriam had dreamed vividly through her pregnancy
and Sally had been doing so the last month, as if by con-
tagion. Miriam felt as if she were describing a rich nocturnal
country sometimes more real than her waking life. They
wondered if their children dreamed inside. What would be
dreaming to someone who had no images? But the blind
must dream. Perhaps the embryos heard sounds or had motor
dreams as Miriam used to see in Orpheus, when he would be
chasing something or eating and little aborted motions would

jerk his paws and muzzle and his eyes would dart rapidly.

Miriam felt closer to Sally than she ever had. When Miriam had lived in the house she had sometimes taken comfort from Sally's presence, but oftener she had been at a loss for things to talk to her about. One of Sally's ways of making contact was by caring for someone, taking care—physically, emotionally. Miriam found it hard to accept nurture from another woman. That felt like childhood. After all, being supportive and helpful was a basic way she related to people too: it was as if she and Sally were both coming on along the same beam and thus had never been able to find in the other a reassuring response.

Now they revived each last detail of Fern's birth at home, when Miriam had assisted. They discussed Fern and David at length. Miriam was furious with herself for having paid little attention to Fern when she was in the house. Now she was trying to catch up on Fern's history. Suddenly she found children fascinating. She had liked children, sort of, but found it boring to discuss them. Now that she was to have a baby of her own, all other women's children assumed a vividness and a particularity altogether new.

Sally attempted to teach her to sew. Together they had made bright comfortable smocks for the last months of their pregnancy. Miriam's hands were awkward with the needle. Sewing made her twitchy and she was always pricking herself. In the meantime Fern and David would be running around screaming and giggling and tripping over things. It was amazing how many objects were around they could get hurt on. The house had to be childproofed.

Of course Beth was off at work during the days. Sometimes she would stop by on Saturday, but in general they saw less of each other. No more lunches, no more conversations on the way to work. Evenings of course Miriam was with Neil, and Neil and Beth had not managed to get to know each other. Once again the hierarchical situation at Logical made that difficult. Neil was never unfriendly to Beth; he simply did not quite see her. He did not mind her being around, but he never seemed to want to know her. He never asked Miriam why she liked Beth so much, thus providing her with an opening.

Not that they were as close as they had been. Beth lacked enthusiasm about her pregnancy, tending to want to talk about the same old topics. It annoyed Miriam. She felt as if

Beth accepted Sally as involved with babies and the kitchen and her own body, but was judgmental against Miriam for exactly the same thing. But then Beth had never been pregnant.

"Sometimes you make me feel like such a glutton, Bethie," she said, sitting forward with legs apart to rest her belly. "I want to be a good technical person and creative in my field, I want to be happily married, I want to be a good cook, I want to be a good mother and have lots and lots of babies— I want everything! You've pared yourself down. You refuse most experiences. You get the same mileage out of less raw data. It's very third world."

"Thinking in metaphors the way Phil used to! It doesn't look that way to me. It looks like you're cutting back. Becoming more withdrawn and private in your life."

"But, Bethie, what could be more real than having my own baby?"

"Alone. Inside a family. Just you and Daddy and baby makes three."

"But you'll come by. Won't you?"

"But it won't be my baby, the way Fern is."

"Do you really think of Fern as your baby?"

"Yes. I feel responsible for her. I help support her. I raise her. She loves and trusts me. It isn't intense as if I were her only mother, but intensity that way isn't necessarily good. She has five mothers. I think that's basically different from having one. Different not just in quantity but in kind."

"Is David your child too?" Miriam could not help the teasing tone in her voice.

"At first I never thought he would be. After all, he lived in a nuclear family for his first three years. I can see differences between David and Fern from that. But he's opened up. When I came back, he was still on the scared side of learning to live in the house. He's still more private than Fern, he turns things inward. But he's unlearning that. He's much, much more affectionate and less whiny."

"His home breaking up must be responsible for some of that whining. How can a little boy understand his father moving out? But do you really think it's good for him, growing up in a house with only women?"

"Do you want him to model himself on what male means in this society—John Wayne and the green berets, a stiff upper lip and a successful ulcer? Control and dominate anything that moves you or feel like a ninety-pound weakling if you can't. He'll grow up feeling loved and cared for and encouraged to feel, encouraged to learn to do things with his hands and his body and his head."

"Besides, you're going to tell me Sally says she's carrying a boy."

"I guess David's superimportant to me because he's the one male being I do love."

"I tell you, this big and unwieldy, I can't imagine doing it again. But I'm sure I'll change my mind. They say you forget. Discomfort is so undramatic to remember."

Beth rested her head against the glass of the tinted window —they were in the alcove on the stairs. "I hate Aldous Huxley! I don't care if he's dead, I hate him!"

Miriam sat up straighter. "What on earth is that about?"

"I read *Brave New World*. Connie gave it to me because I was saying women had to create a technology of birth— so we wouldn't have to carry babies inside. Everybody jumped on me—even Laura! Well, that book did it. It was a new idea then—that was when feminist ideas were still strong, before the counter-revolution was really on top. He got in and creamed the idea before it could have a chance. He made it be associated with horrible people and a disgusting society where sex was a commodity. And it's remained a nightmare joke ever since."

"But, Bethie, discomfort isn't a disaster. Learning to ski is uncomfortable, so is learning to swim. You imagine pregnancy is awful, but it's satisfying too. I can't imagine giving up bearing my own babies."

"But you have no choice. I'm not talking *Brave New World*. I mean that women could choose whether to carry their babies or to have the embryo produced in a controlled environment. That would eliminate most birth defects. They'd be caught early and another egg fertilized."

"Let's talk about something else." Miriam touched her belly.

"Like store-bought bread. People like you and Sally who like to bake bread could. But women who can't bear babies and who plain don't want to wouldn't have to carry them inside."

Miriam laughed. "Imagine! Where did baby brother come from, Mommy? Oh, we bought him at the department store."

"I'm thinking of something like a community incubator. No more miscarriages, no more premature births—"

Perhaps there was resentment that she had married Neil. Neil had been the most accessible of the directors. Not in an emotional way—he was always reserved—but available to play tennis and chess and Go, to run out after work for Chinese food. He had never objected to being called up at any time of the night with a hot technical idea. He had always been ready to listen and comment with his precise close reasoning to the matter at hand. Now the easy bachelor was gone. There was a feeling around that Miriam had caught him, cleverly.

Strange how they assumed that Miriam had got Neil to marry her. Beth assumed the opposite, that Neil had pursued Miriam until she agreed. They did not know how many men had been attracted to Miriam, she thought, angry at their presumption. She could not quite grasp a sense of Neil. He was pleasant enough looking, slender, hazel-eyed with a good warm smile that popped out of his neat curly brown beard. He was rumpled and gentle-seeming. He had a soft agreeable voice and never did she hear him raise it beyond what was minimally necessary to carry over background noise. Although he had a certain shyness, he also had confidence. Both Abe and Dick had something about them that said they needed to prove themselves constantly, though by different means. She sensed that Neil took a certain amount of admiration, of acceptance, for granted. The secretaries all wanted to mother him, to cuddle his untidy forgetfulness. She could imagine Neil backing off into space, sure someone would catch him. Maybe that had captivated Miriam.

Yes, a funny place, full of fussy and comfort-loving technical types who were selfish in different ways from the businessmen she had worked for. They were jealous and gossipy yet seemed largely invisible to each other as people. Just as they could not see Miriam. Miriam had told Beth that when she first came to Logical she had made up her mind not to bring her scandals and legend as femme fatale with her—but Beth thought she need not have bothered. These men were not sufficiently interested in human relations to care. They seemed to have wives as they had cars or expensive houses or garbage disposals or children. They had huge reserves of contempt for most people—drudges, fools, idiots—including the army of ordinary programers. They were into research. That was pure and fun and beautiful. That was not the kind of job Miriam had tried to get her hired for.

"Bethie, change the subject. I'm serious. I'm starting to feel nauseated."

"I'm sorry." Beth's light eyes regarded her with surprise and disappointment. The incubator was an idea she was absorbed in.

Ah, if only Beth would meet a good man! She had tried bringing Beth together with every unattached man she could think of. The only one she seemed to get on with was Jaime. Every so often they went to a movie, to the zoo once with Fern and David. But she could not fool herself that anything more was going to happen. She liked Jaime, she loved Beth, but she felt impatient. How could anyone settle for so little?

With Sally she felt differently. After all, Sally had a child of her own and another on the way. That was half a life. She could understand why Sally lived in the women's house. Her relationships with men had been brutal and abusive. Nothing much had changed since Sally was fifteen, when she had been raped by a boy she knew who gave her a ride into town.

The father of Fern had been a member of Going-to-the-Sun when they were into blue-grass music. That was big around Boston always, no matter what other fads came and went. He had found a status symbol in having a real hillbilly girl friend for a while. She was a decorative accessory to the group. In fact she could play acoustic guitar as well as any of them, though she would never sing for embarrassment if her boy friend was around.

Sally played for her sometimes, as difficult as she found it with her belly. Sally thought it sad that Connie didn't know any lullabies. She sang to both children. She thought it needful as changing diapers. Sally had brought over some good grass and they smoked some together. They were feeling relaxed. Sally wasn't yet big enough to be bothered and Miriam was feeling a little better since her baby had descended from just under her breastbone into the middle abdomen. It pressed more on her bladder but less on her stomach. She found it easier to balance herself.

At one point they went to look in the big bedroom mirror side by side, undoing their smocks. "Look now, it isn't fair," Miriam complained. "My nipples are so dark, and yours aren't. Look at that dark stripe down my belly. The doctor said it would fade some but never completely. How come you don't have a stripe?"

"I don't know. See my stretch marks? They're getting pink. Maybe because I'm a redhead and you're dark."

"I hope my breasts go down after I finish nursing."

"Wait till you breast-feed. It feels heavenly."

"Do you think they'll go down? I must be a size E. I feel grotesque."

"Oh, they'll go down. Nobody stays that big."

They closed up their dresses and shuffled downstairs, Miriam stopping to rest a moment at the window seat. She was short of breath. Then they continued to the kitchen. Miriam had decided she was sick of pink and blue, and they were cooking their baby blankets in a big pot of red dye.

"The stuff in the stores is so ugly." Miriam stirred the cauldron round and round with a big wooden spoon already dyed red. "All covered with cutesy hideous humanoid birds and bunnies. Why not yellow and blue and green and orange and purple? Beautiful colors, subtle prints. Who decides that everything surrounding a baby in the first years be unmitigated crap?"

"That's what comes out, you'll see." Sally leaned on the sink giggling. "Yellow crap, brown crap, white crap, black crap, crap, crap, crap, crap, CRAP!"

"Miriammmmm? Miriammmm?" Neil home early. He hardly ever arrived before Sally left. Usually she drove Sally home by four, but it was getting hard to fit behind the wheel. Today Connie was to pick up Sally on her way home from Newton.

With a little groove furrowed between his brows, he came into the kitchen sniffing. "Isn't that grass? Who's been smoking grass?"

"Oh, we have, love." Miriam went to kiss him. "I think there's a little left on the table, you want some?"

He jumped back from her. "Are you crazy?"

"What?" She stopped short. "Something wrong? You're home early. Did something go wrong at work?"

"Something's got to be wrong with you. What do you think you're doing, smoking grass when you're nine months pregnant!"

"Neil, I drink a glass of wine at supper, too. I wouldn't get drunk and I wouldn't get high. But what's the fuss with a little grass? It's not going to do anything to baby it doesn't do to me. Just turn him or her on a little."

"How could you do it? You must be out of your mind! You ask the doctor, go on, you call the doctor and ask him what you're doing to our child."

"Neil, you've got to be kidding. I'm not going to say anything to him. He might be cool, he might not. What's wrong with you? All of a sudden you sound like Straightman. Don't you smoke dope? You're scaring me, I mean it, and not for the baby."

She had never seen him so angry: it was the first time she had got him really angry. He did not threaten her; after that initial bellow he did not raise his voice. He simply continued repeating his point again and again and again, stubbornly, monotonously, inexorably until she had a splitting headache. She was furious with herself for crying when she was right. She was furious with him for suddenly coming at her all fierce and patriarchal, as if he had become somebody else. Here she was married to him and he was acting like a stranger. Worse, he was yelling at her in front of Sally, who thought men were brutes. Sally would go back to the house and tell the women—tell Beth, who hadn't got to know Neil; Connie, who obviously thought she was getting softening of the brain, so involved in babies when Connie was just building an independent life again; and Laura, who considered it Victorian to deal with men at all. Sally would tell them how Neil pushed her around. How he wouldn't let her—wouldn't *let* her —smoke grass when she wanted to.

"Neil, I haven't become a baby just because I'm carrying one. I'm an adult woman, your wife—not a child!"

"Then act like my wife. You're carrying my child, remember that. My child!" He heard himself and paused for a moment, to speak more softly. "I don't want our child born feeble-minded. I don't want him crazy with birth defects, chromosome damage. We work together learning natural childbirth to produce a healthy baby without anesthetic damage, and you go using drugs!"

"Neil, you've gone out of your mind! There's more stuff can damage your chromosomes in a loaf of store-bought white bread than in all the grass from here to Algiers, you know it."

"We don't either of us know, and I don't want you taking risks with our baby. After you have the baby, smoke as much as you want."

Oh, it was incredible! Shortly Connie arrived and Sally,

who had already put on her coat and gone into the hall to escape them, ran out without saying good-bye. The argument did not miss a beat. Supper burned on the stove which they stood squared off, and only the fumes of lamb chops charring broke through their trance or anger.

The argument went on. She could eat no supper. The food disgusted her. He sat there methodically spearing his chop and slicing the meat into neat squares, talking between bites. He would not cease battering at her and denying her quiet until she started sobbing and panting hysterically.

"You're a pig!" she screamed between sobs. "You're trying to make me sick! You don't care how upset you make me, so long as you get your way! You hate me! You have to hate me to treat me this way!"

"You disgust me. Look at you. Stoned out of your mind and blubbering! You're not fit to have a baby."

"I hate you! I hate you! I wish I'd never met you! What am I supposed to do, nine months pregnant with your child, and you treat me like this, chained to a self-righteous fink."

"Act like a woman instead of an adolescent idiot, for a change." He flung down his napkin and went off to his study, slamming the door on her.

Tears ran down her face until it was swollen and sore. Then she would pause for a while and sob dryly. Then the tears would resume. Above all she hated him for his ability to walk out. When they were quarreling, she could never tear herself loose from him, she could never leave him and walk off. She could not shut him out of her that way. She knew, and was tortured by knowing, he sat in his study working. He had banished her from his consciousness. It was so mean! She could not for one moment cease remembering that they had quarreled and that he had revealed he no longer loved her. He had withdrawn. Her misery felt vast and static as a lake of frozen lava. What would she do with the baby? What would she do with herself? What would become of them alone? He had pretended to love her and now he was abandoning her, with her looks shot, her belly huge, and her job gone.

Finally she could not stand it any more and she ran into the study where indeed he was reading a journal and began screaming at him. This time he did not give way to his rage but instead coolly he bored at her. Pressed and pressured until, sobbing again, she broke and agreed, promised she would not smoke. It was maddening to think as she lay in bed unable to sleep that she simply could not tell him that she had been occasionally smoking dope all through her pregnancy, having checked with women she knew that it was fine. Like wine and booze, a little was fine and a lot was bad. Avoid the hard drugs and tobacco. Avoid processed foods. She felt humiliated, as if she had put herself into a totally vulnerable position, and now he could begin to insist on his whims and his prejudices.

A week before she was due, Neil's mother arrived, announced only by her phone call from Logan Airport. Before Neil left to pick her up, Miriam made a stand in the hall. "If she's around I will not be able to have the necessary concentration to go through the Lamaze method in the way we're trained to do together. Now I'll be nice, but tomorrow you pack her on another plane. Suppose I start labor early? She goes back tomorrow, I mean it!"

After Neil left and she remained in the kitchen, she was ashamed. All the old mother-in-law jokes: how humiliating to act in type. Her mother-in-law might not be the world's most intelligent woman but she was well-meaning. Still, they grated. Emily had kept writing her, "hadn't she stopped working yet!" Making it sound almost obscene. Actually she had quit early and could have worked another three weeks or more, and she knew it. She had twinges of guilt. She hadn't set a good example. As the only woman with a choice position on the technical staff, she should have worked right up till she went into labor, so they could not use that excuse on the next woman who applied.

The first thing Emily said when she got through the door with her two suitcases—two—was, "What, you're still not wearing a maternity brassiere? You're going to injure yourself for life!"

"Mother," Miriam began. How the word caught in her throat. It meant Sonia. But Emily insisted. "I am used to doing without. My muscles are developed. I can support myself, even if I am as big as a barn."

"What does the doctor say about that?"

"The doctor has never said anything. I presume he's accustomed by now to patients who don't wear bras, as he must have become accustomed over the years to patients who don't wear corsets."

"Well, you ask him if you won't end up deformed. Haven't

you seen pictures of savages, women with their bosoms hanging down to their knees?"

Thinking Emily but saying, "Mother, they nurse their babies for five years."

"I'm sure I never heard of any such thing!"

"Mom, if there was anything wrong, Dr. Foreman would have said something," Neil assured her. "He's a very forward-looking obstetrician."

There seemed nothing neutral. Look at the new drapes, Mom, Miriam made them herself. And who hung them? Oh! Oh! Emily was as upset that she took a glass of wine with supper as Neil had been about the joint. The next morning Emily was still there and Miriam prepared to make a bad scene. But before she could work up to it, Emily made a mistake—a gross strategic error. Instead of getting into an argument with Miriam, Emily took on her son.

Neil was trying to explain the Lamaze method and how he would be helping Miriam through her labor. Emily was so shocked at the idea of him being present throughout in the labor room—it was as if he had said that he used the women's lavatory in a theater—that she expressed herself loudly. That did it. Miriam could sit back and watch.

All of that Saturday the argument continued. Neil was determined to extract from his mother an acknowledgment that their way of birth was superior. He was after his initial desultory agreement committed to it. He identified with the Lamaze method more heavily than she did. She remained a little skeptical, saying to herself, Well, if it gets really bad, I can always ask for something. But Neil cared. The ideology appealed to him: birth could be beautiful and natural if only you wanted it to be and mastered the proper techniques. They would give birth according to the rules and together. It was almost scientific. It gave him a role and a purpose. Emily had stomped right over that commitment.

It was amusing to see that inexorable pressure, the steady bore of argument, the voice not raised but never ceasing and never yielding, the firm and self-righteous insistence, all brought to bear upon some other woman. It was relaxing to see Emily waste her energy trying to change her son rather than his wife. She could simply sit back and mull over the stirrings of her child in her vitals. The next morning indeed Emily left, still insisting as she was firmly hustled out by Neil carrying both suitcases, "You're just like your father, exactly.

Both know-it-alls! Now I'm telling you, you ask your wife. Ask her if she wouldn't rather have a woman at that time, rather than some man who doesn't know a thing!"

It was a full week later, three o'clock on a Tuesday, when she called Logical. Efi said Neil was talking to Abe, could she call back? "No," she said firmly, enjoying herself. "Put me through now."

"Oho," said Efi. "Good luck. Are you packed?"

"For a week already. . . . Hello, Neil? We're starting, I think."

He arrived all arms and legs and nerves and immediately could not find the stopwatch they had agreed to keep in an obvious and convenient spot, which suddenly neither could remember.

As his plaintive voice came to her cursing softly and begging the watch to appear, she resisted the urge to go. He was always mislaying things. He would find it. She made herself stay put on the couch with one hand resting on the heap of her belly. Yes, definitely a contraction. She could feel the uterus harden as the pain . . . . the contraction came. She wished she had had supper first, but that was silly. Nobody was hungry during labor, she had been told, and from now on she should take only clear liquids. She remembered the horror story of Phil's about the first Mrs. Flynn, who had died under anesthetic from eating at a picnic. Miriam had gained fourteen pounds, not bad but not as good as she would have liked. If she had eaten as her body seemed to bid her, she would be as big as the elephant she felt like.

By the time Neil found the watch—on the dresser beside the bed in case she began in the night—and returned to time her, her contractions were occurring every fourteen minutes and lasted approximately twenty-five seconds. She felt them in the small of the back, although when she touched her belly it firmed each time.

The show had appeared before she called Neil, and now she had a steady discharge. She had Neil put on a Bach record and they proceeded with the breathing and timing they had been taught. Neil called the doctor and got him at home. When the pains were five minutes apart—slightly later than she had been told but she was in no hurry to enter the hospital—they went. She had cut her own pubic hair close with a nail scissors when the pains began being regular, having had Dr. Foreman write on her record that she would prep herself. She did not relish having her genitals shaved. She wanted to control what she could. Now she was tormented by the itch of forgetting something essential. She felt calm and excited. The contractions seemed larger than her body, not inside her but as if she were inside them.

Dr. Foreman hadn't got there yet and she was given her admission exam by a resident on duty, a tell-you-nothing doctor. "What is the dilation?" she asked him and he said in that don't-worry-little-girl voice, "Oh, you have plenty of time yet." Then the bag of waters broke.

The labor went on and on. Sometimes she felt exhausted and just wished the whole damn thing would end and forget the idiot panting and counting and carrying on. Contractions, my ass. It was pain and big pain and it hurt like hell. However, she continued. Partly she was ashamed to act as if she couldn't handle it, having gone this far. And she wanted to be awake, she wanted that desperately. What was the use in giving birth if she let them deprive her of experiencing it?

"But, Neil . . . it does hurt. It hurts. I'm telling you."

"You're fighting me. Go with the contractions. Don't panic now, Miriam. We're so close."

"I'm not panicking! I'm just telling the truth, damn it. Neil, it hurts."

"Contractions aren't pain. Don't forget now, don't tighten up and hurt yourself. Let me help you."

It was rhetoric. Pain was pain and calling it contractions didn't make it hurt any less. Wave upon wave upon wave. She panted and did her relaxations and did what she had been taught and she was angry. She did not scream, she did not cry out, she did not do any of the things she had been taught were shameful and ignorant. She panted instead of screaming. She counted instead of crying. She bit her lips and bit her cheeks and did what she had been taught and went on. On, in the ridiculous little hospital gown designed to rob her of all dignity. On, among the nurses and residents and doctors doing their business and processing her with as little nuisance to them as possible. On between the blank anonymous walls. She remembered Sally's birth. Perhaps she was not as scared as some of the women around her because at least she had seen birth herself, taken part in the birth of Fern in a roomful of women, singing and rubbing Sally's belly and kissing her and talking softly. Neil was with her, she held his hand, she held tight to him, but she could feel always his fear that she would not be good enough, that she would not be committed enough, that she would back down from the way they had chosen.

It went on and it went on and it went on. She still wanted to stay conscious though often, sinking in the pain she sought to go with, she could not remember why. Could remember nothing. Had no notion who or why she was. She felt herself weakening. Her body was big and strong but it was weakening. Yet she went on. To give up, to go under, would be to lose all the advantage of her hours of suffering, ten hours, twelve hours, thirteen hours, fourteen hours, fifteen hours since she had come into the hospital. Her stubbornness was a rock. She sucked the rock in her mouth along with a sponge. She felt she would die rather than let them knock her out. She had her rag of life gripped in her teeth. She wanted to stay in the light. She would not let go.

It went on and it went on and it went on. Finally, seventeen hours from the time she had checked in, she was taken into the delivery room. She was surprised, lifting her head to look around, that it was a small room. She realized that she had expected a very large room, from operations in television and the movies. The lights were bright but not inordinately. The operating table to which she was moved felt, looked, much like the table in Dr. Foreman's office where she had been examined frequently enough.

She experienced a strong urge to sit up, to get off the table and down on the floor. To squat. But they were strapping her down. That felt all wrong. She felt a strong compulsion to get off her back, to squat, but could not. She bore down where she was, although the urge to raise her whole body forward seemed almost as strong as the urge to push, to thrust. It was moving very fast now, it was plummeting heavy as a truck downhill: huge and heavy and out of control. It carried her, no longer worried, no longer afraid, no longer weak. Now, finally, now she pushed. She watched in the mirror overhead except when he was cutting her with the scissors. Then she looked away because it was terrible to see her tender genital flesh sliced through.

When she looked back, she stared and cried out because the head, the head was blooming there. Huge coming through her. Ridiculous. A dark wet head emerging from the nest of towels and large sheet that swathed her blood-dabbled, strained and still swollen thighs. In the mirror a pile of laundry was giving birth. A person was emerging. Then she was laughing, because it looked ridiculous in the mirror. Oh! For real, at last. The child! "I did it!" she cried out and Dr. Foreman said, "Of course you did." Foreman was reaching up, pulling, and the shoulder was out. The baby turned its head. She could not tell yet whether Ariane or Jeffrey was coming from her to the light. Red shoulder, slippery, glossy, moving, alive. The baby turned its head toward its shoulder, it was for real, alive, she saw it move! The other shoulder. Gradually, gradually, the baby slipped out of her, oh, beautiful creature thrust into the world glowing and bright.

Upside down he held her baby, using a rubber tube in its mouth and nose, and already—they had not even struck the baby if they really did that—her baby was crying.

"You have a girl, Mrs. Stone."

"Ariane!" She was flooded with joy. Her own, her child, her darling, her flesh and blood. "Give her to me." My daughter.

"Soon. We're not done with you yet."

"Oh. The placenta."

Exhausted and impatient, she lay in a puddle of small sensations. Foreman was mucking about in her, moving the uterus. She could feel herself contracting again. Expulsion of placenta. She no longer cared. She did not bother watching what they were up to but let her eyes close. When she looked again he had the placenta in his hand. He was telling her that her uterus had good tone. They had repaired the incision and were fussing with her baby. She was released and sat up on one elbow and came alert. "Is she all right?"

"That's what we're checking. . . . She's fine."

The nurse handed her Ariane, wrapped in a blanket. "Her head!"

"It'll round out in a day or two. Primiparous molding. The nose will recover too. In a couple of days, Mrs. Stone, she'll be pretty as a picture."

The Stones' song, "She's a Rainbow." Somehow Ariane was all red and blue and yellow and bright and moist. She was shining, already kicking and squirming. With her face screwed up she cried and cried but no tears came. Ariane, Ariane, monkey face, precious monkey face. Gray eyes? No one in her family. She was suddenly scared for an instant, somebody else, from some other year. Must be someone in Neil's family with gray eyes. Or maybe they were all born that

way, like kittens. They were trying to take the baby back.
She wanted to savor her triumph but procedures came first,
and she had to relinquish Ariane to the nurse and the nursery.
She sank back, too tired to argue or question, and was wheeled
to the semi-private room she would be sharing with two other
women who had just had their babies.

She was weary and spent. She had expected to feel good
afterward. She had expected to be rewarded for doing the
birth the right way. The baby out, her body back, joy to the
world. But she felt like something a truck had run over. Her
breasts hurt, huge and swollen and sore and hot to the touch.
She had not expected it all to feel so messy. She could not
quite rise to the moment but felt as if she were hanging in
dim tepid water not quite able to break through the surface
to fresh air. When the nurse got her up she walked, but she
did not feel right. Loose and sloppy with the stitches hurting,
her body did not fit her. She was sunk in a vast weariness,
illuminated by dull aches and occasional burning twinges.

She was glad to get out of the hospital, but she felt numbed
still. Felt alienated from herself, her body, Neil, even Ariane.
Least perhaps from Ariane. They were connected through
her breasts. Every few hours Ariane cried for her, every few
hours her breasts ached to be suckled. They were bound in
animal linkage and that bond was the most real thing she
could still feel. But she was frightened. She did not feel that
she loved her baby. This strange animal in her lap with its
smells and its loud cries, the fierce desires that shook it, she
was not quite sure what she was doing with it. They belonged
to each other through an animal bond but she felt so little else,
she was terrified.

When she looked sideways at Neil, she felt distant and
alien from him too. He was not bound to the baby by the
chain of feedings and hours, yet she could feel love loosed
in him toward Ariane. He hovered over her, crooning and
gazing, and very gently with the tips of his fingers caressed
her nose, her ears, her fingers. He babbled over her, he loudly
rejoiced, he truly found her outrageously beautiful. He demanded of everyone within range that they admire her. But
soon he left Miriam in the house that felt too big around her
and went to the office where she had used to go. She thought
of her old desk. She sat and wept for her baby, for herself,

because she was a bad mother. She did not love Ariane, she did not love Neil, and she could not stand herself. She was empty and harried and oozing and spent. Poor Ariane! Poor Miriam! They had all gone off and left her and what was she to do? All but this creature grasping her breast for food. Feeling like the youngest sister punished by the wicked witch in a fairy tale, the youngest sister turned suddenly into a crone for punishment, she clutched her baby and wept in the bedroom chair.

23

Motherhood Is a Woman's Creativity

Beth was stretched on the Danish couch, her cheek still numb with novocaine. She was off work because she had had to have a wisdom tooth out. "No, I don't want anything," she mumbled.

"The effort required to take care of children rises exponentially, not arithmetically," Miriam was saying firmly. "That's why when Neil starts on me about 'Let's have another real quick' I want to bang my head on the wall. Fuck Dr. Foreman and his pontifications. Fern! Put that down. Come on, give it to me, that's a sweetheart. Now what *schlemiel* left a pocket knife in the living room?"

Beth turned on her side. "Do you really mind having the kids Mondays and Wednesdays?"

"Sure, but I love having time to myself Tuesdays and Thursdays. I only wish I could stay here and work—it's so quiet. But that time Neil called and I was working here and Ariane was at the commune, that did it. Almost blew the whole thing."

"He doesn't like her to come over to our house, does he?"

"He had an extra-careful middle-class upbringing. His mother irons sheets and towels. He thinks the commune is dirty. I think he has fantasies about what goes on there. I avoid the subject. I mean, he can hardly say, 'Don't visit your friends with Ariane,' but he can raise hell if I leave her there and come back here, and he catches me."

Miriam now talked about Neil as if she were talking about the weather or the government, Beth thought. Neil was not a father like her father, she had to give him that. He was affectionate and warm with Ariane, he worried about her constantly. When he could get away with it, he would send one of the secretaries into Boston to get a specific creative plaything he had seen. He had bought a camera and photographed her smiling, sitting, crawling, crying, pouting.

"Besides, Bethie, your room is my haven. As soon as I walk in and shut the door I start feeling like me."

"But it's noisy, huh?"

"There's no way to keep Ariane from knowing I'm in the house. Still, I like your room. It's Pavlovian. When I walk in and see the candy cane walls, I start to be able to think."

"I like to know you've been using it." Sometimes Miriam left her little presents, a drawing, a cookie, a piece of fruit. Miriam could no longer give presents freely, for she had neither the time nor the resources, but she made do with what was around. Beth liked coming home from work to find a trace of Miriam, whether it was a rose plucked from the red rambler on the fence here or a long black hair unknowingly lost.

"Beth, poor baby, why don't you take another demerol? You look as if you're in misery."

"Anyhow, the novocaine's wearing off. It makes me scared I'll bite my tongue. At least I'm off work for a day and they can't dock me."

"Don't tell me it's reached the point where you'd rather have teeth pulled than go to work out there." Miriam disentangled Blake from a bunched-up rug. Sally's baby was an avid crawler already.

"Close to it. I suppose I should be grateful they retrained me instead of firing me when they switched over to the new system—"

"Don't waste your breath. A new girl takes a long time to train, not in the job itself, but in picking up a certain understanding so that you can catch an error now and then."

"I find data preparation boring. Oh, it's easier and quieter sitting at the keyboard and looking at the terminal like a miniature TV. I feed the machine directly over a high-speed line. I can see that it's more efficient using the tape cassettes than it ever was using cards. I edit right on the little screen. But before at least I had some variety. The company's grown so fast, I don't know half the men who hand me stuff now."

Miriam knelt to get David's ball from under the couch and to persuade Fern to give back Ariane's raggedy rabbit, its ear wet from chewing. Then she looked out the window toward the street, a gesture she usually made frequently as the afternoon moved toward five, five-thirty . . . but it was only three-thirty.

"Are you expecting Neil early?"

"No, what made you—oh, because I looked. Guilt. Listen, keep this to yourself, promise?" Miriam waited for a nod. "Maybe you should be thinking what you'd do if you lost your job. Neil keeps telling me not to worry. This fall he's teaching a seminar at M.I.T.—reflecting prestige back to Logical. But I know he's dickering for a position there. Don't ask me to pretend I feel enthusiasm. That's part of the reason I'm killing myself to finish my thesis before they come down on me with a nepotism rule."

"Why would I lose my job if Neil quits? I'm sure nobody remembers by now you got them to hire me."

"Of course not. They're losing the anti-missile missile contract—they've been canceled. That means half the staff are going on overhead in a month. So either they find another big contract fast, or they fire lots and lots of people. The directors are battling too—especially Abe versus Dick and the business manager Farley they brought in last year and gave so much stock."

"Well, the stock isn't real anyhow, is it?"

"Just paper. But something funny is happening. Neil *insisted* we buy a bunch more. We had a big fight. I thought it was the stupidest thing I ever heard." Ariane began to scream. Tears raced down her chubby face and she sat on her behind and howled. In empathy, Blake started crying too. Miriam picked her up to check her bottom, grimaced, and took her up to change. Her voice continued.

"Miriam, I can't hear you. Tell me when you get back." Beth remained on the couch.

David poked her in the side. "You sick?"

"I had a tooth taken out."

"A tooth like this?" he pointed.

"Way at the back."

"Can I see it?"

Miriam came running past to scoop up Blake, still crying, and carry him upstairs too.

"I didn't keep it, David. I'm sorry."

"I wouldn't never, never forget *my* tooth!"

"Bethie, come up. I never made the beds and talcum powder's spilled all over the bathroom!" Miriam added over the railing a minute later, "Better bring Fern and David."

Beth collapsed again in the bedroom in an old-fashioned easy chair Miriam was planning to reupholster sometime; it leaked stuffing on the rug. Miriam was making the bed, thanking providence she had remembered. "Such sarcasm, when you forget something. If I had to explain I'd have to go into a song and dance routine about why Fern and David and Blake are here, and that would blow my cover." Dashing around, she picked up socks that Neil seemed to have thrown here and there, dirty underwear, a used tissue, a bathrobe, a damp towel.

"You're stuck with all the housework now, aren't you?"

"You said it."

She had to follow Miriam into the bathroom where the baby powder had snowed. Miriam said, "Who was playing with this? David, who was squeezing the baby powder?"

"Connie says that talc may possibly be involved as a cancer-causing agent. It's closely related to asbestos—"

"Baby powder? Beth, living causes cancer. Just what I want to know." Miriam was down on her knees sponging the floor. Her glasses slid forward and she caught them in mid-air, gasping. "All I need to do is break my glasses today. These frames are too big. I swear my head was bigger when I was carrying."

"How come he doesn't help any more? He used to do the dishes some nights and clean the house with you."

"Because I'm home now and, as he says, what else do I do? I can't figure out how to argue. After all, he's supporting us now. He does work all day and I have trouble saying what I do. Time melts away. Sometimes I don't manage to get dressed before noon, though I'm up at seven and running every minute."

"Are you going back to work?"

"I started to tell you about Logical. We had this fight about him buying more of their Monopoly Set stock. He's always saying we don't have enough money. Honestly, Beth, I don't think either of us realized that when I stopped working our income would go down by a third."

"Let's go downstairs. I'm happiest lying on the couch."

"Five minutes, Bethie. I never did clean the bathroom this morning and the basin's full of hair and lather. Fern! That gate stays *shut!* Now, I mean it, Fern!"

"You were telling me about Logical, or about money?"

"I've worked since I left home. If I wanted a book or a pair of pants, I bought it. Honest, I find asking for every penny hard to deal with. It's like being fifteen again and having to ask Daddy for an allowance."

"Do you want to go back now?"

"You look so uncomfortable, come on, we'll go down. I'll carry Ariane and you carry Blake. Come on, Fern, come on, David. Mama's big fat baby girl! She's so round and squeezable, Bethie, such a pussy cat! She's just a ball of goodness, isn't she? . . . So Neil went and bought a bunch more, when the company's in trouble. He says he has to support Abe in the battle with Dick. But they're in trouble and they're going to get rid of a lot of people. They're way in debt and the bank's putting on pressure to come up with a plan. Or they'll go into bankruptcy. Anyhow, they wouldn't hire me back now if I came in and begged on bended knees."

"Logical's not the only place to work, you could get another job."

"It's a lousy time to look for work. Fred's still out of a job, isn't he? Besides, there has to be something better to do with my skills than design command and control systems. I've thought it through, Beth, and I realized something about the whole direction my work has been taking for years."

"You sound discouraged. Do you wish you were in another field?"

"I like working with computers. I think people need computers. What they replace is human drudgery. But I think I was into a kind of software only realizable on very large and therefore expensive machines. A lot of what I did was too theoretical for me to get a sense of what it might be used for. I'd be lying if I said I had a real sense of that. But just by the nature of who has money for that technology, you never get far from the Pentagon, you never get away from the C.I.A. or the intelligence community—what a euphemism! The only things that get that much spent on them are surveillance and war games and running the empire."

"So what does that leave you to do?"

"I want to start at the far end of that spectrum. I want to work on problems that are small-machine, small-system problems. Then maybe what I do won't necessarily be used to kill people, to burn people, to track people. Maybe it can be used for something at least innocuous, like keeping medical records, keeping track of a library. . . . But that puts another kink in getting back to work."

"Have you talked to Neil about all this?"

"Logical isn't into that kind of problem, and none of their customers are. He agrees the missile contract was a terrible mistake for Logical. After a while none of the good people wanted to work on it and they hired more duds to fill it out. They didn't come in on time, they ran over, they produced a piece of crap technically. But he still considers what he does too theoretical to have a relationship to anything in the real world, and he says I'm being narrowly moralistic. Like the Church persecuting Galileo. That scientists have to be free to pursue their science and can't try to second-guess what doesn't belong to the field. He says that, for a woman, naturally that kind of consideration weighs more, and I can't possibly be thinking of leaving Ariane alone already with some paid woman who wouldn't love her and would teach her bigoted ideas and wrong attitudes. . . . And he's right. I insisted I was going to find someone to care for her a couple of days a week. I interviewed six women. They cost a fortune, and, Bethie, I couldn't leave Ariane with them! They were . . . exactly as Neil said. Ariane's intelligent, Bethie, and sensitive. She could no more stand one of those women all day than I could."

"You feel guilty even about bringing her to the house twice a week." Beth was stretched out. Her jaw ached, she felt weak.

"Well, I'm responsible for her. When I walk out of the room she starts to scream. She's so young."

"That's the trouble. Sally isn't responsible for Fern and David and Blake."

"Of course she is. You think she doesn't care about her children?"

"I said she isn't responsible. We *all* are. She can do whatever she wants this afternoon. I don't even know where she is."

"Bethie, if the house breaks up, then Sally knows who's really responsible for Fern and Blake."

"The house won't break up. We're committed to each other." But Beth sat up, feeling a chill inside. She knew why Miriam had said that. Things had not been so easy lately, not easy at all.

The tension had started between Laura and Connie but it had spread out, it had run cracks and fissures into all the relationships. The equilibrium was no longer an easy jouncing but a crazy wild swinging between alienation and total embrace. "This is my family. My only family. I don't want things to go wrong." Beth lay on Dorine's bed. Of course she had come to Dorine. Gradually all of them had begun to depend on Dorine's strength, to see her as the most stable. Beth did not think Dorine quite understood why yet.

"Sometimes things do go wrong." Dorine was sitting at her desk collating pages of a paper. "Don't start to grasp. That makes you pretend things are better or worse than they really are."

"But why can't we be together again the way we were?"

"Because the differences *are* real. But we can try to work them through and maybe we'll come out closer. . . ."

The paper Laura worked on was folding: lack of money, splits in the staff, loss of circulation. There was rumored to be another paper organizing, but Laura did not think she wanted to join it.

"All journalists, even in the alternate press, develop attitudes. A knowingness that comes from spending your time writing about what other people are doing, and getting the sense you have a lot of savvy because you can see what's wrong. Anybody can put out a paper, and it's somebody else's turn. You can learn the skills in a couple of months. You master them in six. In a year you're probably as good as you ever will be, collectively. Then you get tired."

"That sounds wasteful," Connie said. Lately, whatever one said, the other had to contradict. It became a point of honor. "Suppose after I taught school for a year I decided I was tired of it and I was going to be a librarian. One of the excuses they give for not hiring women is that we aren't serious— won't stick with something."

"I read a study once that a teacher taught more in her first two years than she ever did again. I think anybody can teach."

"Anybody can stand in front of a class, if that's what you mean. I don't call that teaching."

"I don't believe in professionalism. I could teach, you could put out a paper. That is, I could teach if it wasn't that they don't hire gay teachers."

"Well, you can hardly expect parents to feel enthusiasm for that, especially with adolescents!"

"Sure, I might rape them all in the women's john, right?"

Bump, another confrontation. Again, again, again. A potlatch of energy that used to go into making the house pleasant, into the children and meals and talk shared: now burnt off in set pieces of mutual disapproval. Beth swore that each lay awake at night thinking of ways to insult the other. Things had begun to go wrong between them when Laura brought up at a house meeting having her girl friend Lynn move in with her. Laura was much happier lately, more vocal and outgoing and in general friendlier, which made the constant confrontations all the worse by contrast. She had been going to gay dances and talking a lot with women in gay liberation. For the first time, instead of occasional and generally miserable involvements with straight women, she was seeing other women who defined themselves as gay.

Connie had been absolutely opposed to Lynn's moving in. After a couple of days of vague protests about crowding and liking things the way they were, she came out with, "Well, if Lynn moves in, why shouldn't Ross? I mean, why should you be allowed to have your sex object in the house and I be forbidden mine?"

"Because she isn't my sex *object*—she's a woman. And if women can't care for each other, we're never going to change. You can't fuck the enemy and fight him."

Lynn had not moved in. The matter had simply been dropped, but it had left bad feelings. Perhaps the first roughness between Connie and Laura began because Laura truly adored David. She liked to roughhouse with him, she loved even his moodiness, she enjoyed the extra effort it took to open him up. She would get down on the floor with him and growl like a grizzly bear and roar like a lion. Sometimes he got hysterical with laughter or started jumping up and down. His energy burned in his face. He loved Laura. He loved her back passionately. He grew furious with her too and threw toys at her and hit her, as he never did his mother or any of them. Because when he wanted Laura's attention he wanted it: he did not forgive her for being busy or distracted or depressed. If he had four mothers he had only one Laura, his super playmate, his heroine. Connie would frown and say, "You're getting him too excited, Laura. He gets so overwound when you play with him, he can't go to sleep. He gets cranky and starts to bawl."

"There are worse things than crying. He knows what he likes, don't you, David—you dig Goliath. David-Ha-Ha, David the Big Cheese, David the King-Kang-Kong."

Connie's boy friend Ross disliked Laura on principle and indeed when Laura heard his voice she immediately got as loud and vulgar as possible. If she went into the room she enticed him into an argument on the politics of ecology. Laura could argue rings around Ross because she chose the subjects she was going to goad him into attacking or defending, and she knew much more than he did about the politics of the several suburbs from working on the paper. So she had the satisfaction of making him angry, and he had the satisfaction of making Connie uncomfortable about living in the house with a LESBIAN. He played upon her inherent uneasiness: was she being a good mother, was she fulfilling her duty, was she providing the right environment? Or would David grow up to be a drug addict rapist hood because of Laura and the commune? Laura described it that way, and it was cruel but not exaggerated. In truth Connie also feared that her husband would find out about Laura at some point and take the children from her in court. She clipped cases she read about women who had lost custody of their children for doing abortion referrals or living in communes the judge found distasteful.

Now Laura was going to lose her job and Connie was not pleased. Working on the paper had had some prestige connected with it and some money, though little enough. Beth told no one about Miriam's warning on Logical, but she might be out of a job soon herself. Connie was not about to support them all. Beth felt the house pulling apart. Yet out of the storybook project, the children's book they had been writing for Fern and David and for Blake too when he got older, something more exciting had emerged. After they finished the first book they began doing little plays together, at first for the children but lately, after the children were in bed, for themselves. They called what they did jamming. They would pick a theme and improvise together.

At least those were the words she picked to describe the process to Connie when she came home from seeing Ross and found them still up bellowing at each other. Improvisation seemed a cool male image, men who had mastered a set of skills and body of material exercising their competence. What they did was raw and always on the edge of being ridiculous. They did "The Date," "I have something awful to tell you, I've missed my period," "The Job Interview," "How Come You Don't Love Me Any More?"

What they did was funny. To hear a woman saying those things, that each had said a hundred times for real, was funny and painful. Violence seemed always about to break through the scenes. The power relations stood bare. The pregnant woman and her boy friend, the make-artist and the woman trying to please, the boss and the secretary: they were all at war. It was a theater of stark melodrama with lines that were extremely funny. People kept killing each other. The repressed, the unexpressed, the silent violence and pressures pushed through the roles. Sometimes they scared each other.

Sally got into it, Dorine got into it, Beth found herself screaming. Laura got into it too, but she did not seem to experience the loose rush of power, of strong feeling emerging as if from the walls and shaking them, that Beth felt and she was sure Sally and Dorine did too. Who would have believed that Sally could become a suave bored boy friend arranging an abortion on the phone and making his woman feel guilty for causing him trouble? She could mimic voices and accents and gestures. Once she had the scene straight—not the first time they would run through, not the second or third—then suddenly Sally would be into her role and talking in paragraphs. She would be full of words, Sally who could sit placidly for hours with her hands on her belly.

Sally looked younger when she was acting. Beth thought of her as being older, but she was Beth's age. Dorine got into it too, but she had other structures in her life now. She was becoming clear about what she wanted to do and why, and that gave her a different kind of strength than anybody else in the house. She worked brutally hard, taking a full load of graduate courses and working as a figure model. She was overextended. They all had to fill in for her. She could not quite carry her weight in contributing money, in doing her share of the housework, in fulfilling her share of child care. But she was important to them. Everybody wanted her to manage. Her clarity was comforting. Laura never started arguments with Dorine about her professionalism. When she left her books scattered about and Beth picked up an advanced organic chemistry text, she might as well have been looking at something in Russian. But the why was clear to her: women had to control their bodies: the technology of fertility and embryology and genetics would be putting more and more control over who would have babies, and when and how and what kind, in the lap of those wonderful people who had brought us Vietnam, the loaf of formaldehyded white bread, the hydrogen bomb, and permanent smog.

Beth felt strongly that she was lacking a similar purpose. She half hoped they would fire her from Logical so that she would have to think what she wanted to do. She needed something useful and good to sit in the center of her life. How could she go on selling eight hours a day pushing buttons to support the rest of her time, even for the house?

When she walked in the double glass doors at Logical, past the receptionists, she felt her body clench. She felt herself flattening to the low profile she must maintain. The organization was bigger, the hierarchy more rigid. Everything went through channels. Gradually decisions had come to be made invisibly, and recently there had been an ugly scene when Dick discovered some of the younger staff swapping information about salaries. At the same time, because of media jokes, everyone imagined that he knew something about the women's movement and felt free to tease her, because it was known she lived in a women's commune. They were free to make what they called jokes, but she was not free to answer, because she was a clerical worker. She was supposed to smile and make the little gestures that indicated appeasement, the little gestures half flirtation and half submission.

She was always being criticized because she did not smile enough. Her face felt frozen at Logical. She was expected to duck her chin or twist her shoulders and give that little laugh when she spoke, that little laugh that says, "Why it's only little ole me speaking." She had become so conscious of that little laugh that her throat would shut on it. She sat very still when they spoke to her, she thought of how calm Sally sat: she tried to wait them out. But she was too angry to be good at placidity.

Some of the younger technical people were too stoned to care. The directors did not understand this. The directors were of another generation and did not know the younger technical staff they had hired. The best young programer now that Miriam was gone, hired for her job, was Bill, and in the ten months he had been working there she had never seen him straight. He was a complete computer freak. He lived and breathed and ate and slept computers. Never in a million years would he question what his work was for, as Miriam had begun to. He never goaded her and he did not care whether she smiled at him or looked cross-wise. He brought his programs in and he might stand looking into inner space for ten minutes, he might even chat, but if she answered he never heard what she said the way she meant it anyhow. He was easy to get on with because he was totally out of contact: no friction possible.

To see him with Abe or Dick was high comedy. Neither of them understood Bill was stoned. He wrote good code and they valued him and he did not bug them about salary raises. He did not appear to notice anything, not office politics or infighting, and he never pestered them about stock options. They saw him as absent-minded from seriousness.

The network of dealing among the younger employees remained invisible to the directors. She bought for the house at Logical where the grass, the hash, the occasional tab of mescalin or acid were of higher quality and better price than in Cambridge. There was traffic too in the drugs the women's house would not touch, coke and quaaludes and barbiturates and speed. The secretaries bought with the technical people except Efi, who grew marijuana at home under purple lights. Everybody was a customer except the directors and the business manager. Even Neil was a customer, although he did not know it, because Miriam bought with the women's commune. Now that the baby was born Neil expected her to have grass in the house along with wine and scotch and ginger ale and beer. He did not ask Miriam where she got the stuff as long as it was satisfactory.

Beth had not come to like Neil any better. She saw him as Miriam's owner and disliked being in the house when he arrived, sniffing the air, perhaps cruising the stove, asking for Ariane and immediately beginning to dote and worry and cuddle her. "Oh, Ted's on his way. I told him to eat with us. We have to work tonight on a proposal for NSA. Why don't you put on a dress?"

"I doubt if I have a clean dress. Why didn't you warn me before I put supper on? Are you prepared to do a loaves and fishes miracle with four lamb chops?"

"I tried to call, but the phone was busy. Which I guess is why you don't have a dress to put on and Ariane isn't cleaned up. What you find to chatter about for hours to those women . . ."

"I was talking to Dr. Miller about Ariane's sore throat, if you want to know!"

He jerked around. Felt Ariane's forehead, cooed at her to open her mouth for him. "What sore throat? Where did she get a sore throat? Did you take her temperature?"

"How do I know where she got it? In the supermarket."

"Have you been taking her over to those children again? They always have colds. I've never seen that little girl, Feather, whatever her name is, when her nose wasn't dripping."

They were no longer polite, that was it. He did not use the same soft voice to Miriam he used to the technical staff. And he looked at his child the way he had used to look at his wife.

"Oh, he gets irritated with me," Miriam said, giving Ariane orange goo out of a jar as she sat giggling and banging in her high chair. Gouts of orange were splattered over Miriam's arms and spotted on her cheekbone and dabbed on her worn shirt. It was an old tie-dyed T-shirt, faded but pleasant, where the new stains came to rest with the old without rancor. "He comes home tired and he wants to relax, he wants sympathy and attention. He wants Ariane clean and bubbly and ready to be played with. I've been cooped up all day with the baby, and I want to talk, I want to use my head and my tongue. So we're already at war, with our different needs. I've become too emotionally dependent on him, I know it. I get two afternoons a week at your house and maybe Sally gets here once. Except for Saturdays I hardly see you. He's knocking himself out trying to save Logical and getting ready for his seminar this fall. If it wasn't for Laverne around the corner, I'd disintegrate from talking only baby talk. I never imagined I'd be friends with Tom Ryan's wife, but I couldn't do without her!"

"What do you talk about? She seems kind of pathetic."

"Oh, relationships. Our marriages, our children. She has three kids, including a baby, six months. The dependency thing. I don't think she's solved it either, but at least she knows what I'm fighting." Miriam pushed her glasses back. At some point they had dropped and the frames cracked.

Now they were held together at the bridge with tape.

"But you're getting your thesis done. Doesn't that help?"

"But it's taking me forever to type it. If I were still at Logical, I'd just give it to one of the secretaries . . ."

Yes, Beth thought, the staff did things like that.

"It's as if Ariane can't stand to see me at the typewriter, it's a signal for her to start screaming. I can hardly believe I'm close to done."

"Then what will you do?"

"Bethie, I can't think past the point of my degree. The house is always a mess, I haven't cooked anything new in months. I see the red dress I started making in the ninth month sitting upstairs. I never read a book. It's a miracle if I look at the paper. Neil asks me what I do all day, and it seems to me I chase my tail and that's about it."

"My life begins when I get home from work."

"They're not having much luck getting new contracts. Things are tight in the industry, companies going bankrupt."

"I almost hope they fire me."

"Why? What will you do?"

Beth shrugged. "I've been thinking lately maybe I'd like to do women's theater."

"You want to be an actress? You're putting me on."

"Don't sound so shocked. I think maybe I want to do women's theater with a group. That's different."

"You astonish me. I never thought you wanted to get up on a stage! You have a hidden side." Miriam was smiling.

"I want to act out things women need to express. You'd have to see what we've been doing. Miriam, would you come?"

"I'd love to!"

"Tomorrow night? Please."

"I'd have to get a baby sitter." Miriam looked dubious. "You never imagine how many things you won't be able to do."

"I think I do imagine."

"But don't you ever want to have your own baby?" Miriam hugged Ariane up out of the chair and nuzzled her, while Ariane chewed on her hair. Ariane was a fat curly child with black eyes and Miriam's skin. She was a child everyone wanted to pick up and squeeze. Two months older than Blake, she was much fatter and bigger and noisier. Miriam said, "She has the character of a jolly little Napoleon. A will of iron and lungs to go with it. She always wins. My father says she looks just like I did at her age, but I've seen photographs. I was a big baby, but sallow, rather melancholy. Just what I'd like—a child I could push around. But this tigress! She doesn't even sleep much. I think she uses solar energy."

"How come she has so many toys?" Both looked around. As far as she could see through the rooms and hall, toys were scattered, dolls, plush animals, square pegs to be pounded into holes, pull-toys, rings and stakes, busy-boxes, things on wheels. Ariane had more toys than the three children at the commune, perhaps six times as many. The house was going under in a breaking wave of scattered toys, and every time Beth came, something new was underfoot.

"Oh, Neil's always bringing her a treat." Miriam spoke apologetically. "She does have an awful lot, doesn't she? Her grandparents buy her toys too, so does Jaime. Even my father, who remarried by the way. The widow of a doctor. I tell you, after a few years of dating the kind of women he kept telling my mother she ought to be, he's gone and married another version of her. Another woman who adores him and thinks he's a wonder, and what is she? But this one has money. . . . And my sister Allegra, who married into peanut butter, has a baby now. We keep sending each other pictures. That's just a bad joke about the peanut butter. Everybody's married."

"My sister Nancy too. She ran away and married a guy who just got out of the Army. Knew him for two weeks. I don't care, it can be everybody, everybody in the world. Except me."

"Don't play innocent with me." Laura had her elbows planted on the kitchen table. "You told us about Karen. Why not come out of the closet? The first step in our liberation is being able to love each other, to give each other that love and support and tenderness we've given men. Men don't have to be gentle and nurturing because they can find a woman to do it for them. But all women are starved for tenderness. Come out of the closet and you'll feel stronger, you'll respect yourself."

"I'm not in the closet, Laura. I don't have any sex life, and I don't want one. I don't feel gay, I don't feel straight, I don't feel anything."

"Because you're afraid of what you do feel. Don't you

see, Beth, you're still concealing, you're still letting them make you ashamed of loving another woman. When you stop letting them make you ashamed and afraid, you'll be stronger, you'll feel good and beautiful in your love. Stand up with us and be counted!"

"But I don't know if I count!" Beth turned her face to and fro. She felt pushed. She was angry with Laura for trying to make her do something she didn't want to, and angry because Laura was succeeding in making her feel guilty.

"You're afraid. Somebody might see you. You might lose your job or lose your friends. Because that's what it means in this society. If nobody knows, cool. If somebody knows, they can treat you like a mad dog, they can lock you up and deny you a living. It's you they mean, Beth, you with Karen."

Beth turned her face in blind distress from side to side. She found it hard to look at Laura's accusing bright face. "I went to bed with two men, I went to bed with one woman. I don't think I wanted to go to bed with any of them! Maybe what I'd like to march for is the right not to have to. Ever!"

Laura leaned forward, speaking softly. "Was being with Karen like being with your husband?"

Beth shook her head no.

"Better? Was it different? Another woman loving you?"

Beth nodded. Added immediately, "But both men were different too. I want to stay as I am! I don't want to be with anybody!"

"Sometimes you want to pretend you're a child. Beth, Beth, you're equivocating. You're still in the closet and why? Are you still not able to love yourself, and therefore you can't really love other women? Or are you simply scared of what the society can do to you if you stand up and say you love women?"

"Laura, are you so sure you love yourself better than I love myself? Maybe I wish people would just stop going to bed with each other for a year! Maybe we'd all get straight in our heads then. We'd see what really connects us."

"Being turned on by that woman scared you. It scares you still, and so you want everybody to be afraid of each other the way you're afraid. Beth, loving is nothing to fear!"

"Yes, I'm afraid." Beth stood up. She felt pummeled and raw. Her hands and legs were shaking. Slowly she climbed the steps to her room to lie clutching her pillow, shaking.

24

Out of the Closet
and into the Frying Pan

Dorine marched in and sat on the side of Beth's bed. "Come on, Bethie, it's not like you to lie and sulk. Don't let Laura get to you. You know, she feels very embattled. Besides, I'm going to march with her, so she won't feel like nobody in the house is supporting her."

Beth sat up on one elbow. "You're marching with the radical lesbians? But you've never even . . . I mean, have you ever been involved with a woman?"

"Well, no. But I've thought about it."

Beth began to giggle. "You've sinned in your thoughts."

"I have thought about it. It makes sense to me. It just seems like somehow I can never do it, for real. Some deep awkward inhibition that makes it something heavier than it should be. But suppose I did meet a woman sometime I could love, who could love me? Besides, Beth, I kind of enjoy demonstrations. Long as I don't think I'll get my head bashed in or one of those blinding gases sprayed over me. I don't think this is going to be rough. It's just a march, with a lot of chanting and posters."

"I feel so mixed up, Dorine. I feel she's forcing me to decide something I don't want. . . . When I saw Jim the last time, I felt . . . almost as if I could remember how I used to want him. I could remember loving him. . . . I don't know, I'm more afraid of loving a woman now than before Karen. Then I didn't know it was possible, I never worried about it. I don't know! I don't know! My life is hard already!"

"I haven't slept with anybody in months, myself. Though I think about it." Dorine sighed. "I have a lot of dreams about fucking, and sometimes I have an orgasm right in my sleep, and that's really nice. . . . Do you masturbate?"

Beth shook her head, looking past Dorine.

413

"Beth, don't curl up when I ask you a question. I do. Don't you know how?"

"I don't want to."

"You aren't into your body."

"That isn't the only way! I like to walk, I like to swim and work outside!"

"I'm sorry, Beth, I don't mean to bait you. You're right to insist on being you. Your own way. . . . Speaking of complications, did you talk to Miriam this week? No? Then guess what. Go on, guess the least useful thing that could happen to her."

"Getting pregnant again?"

"Never mind, you don't have to guess. Phil is back."

"Oh." Beth sat up, putting her feet over the side of the bed. "Will that matter to Miriam? I mean, she's married now."

"But when an old friend arrives dirty, hungry, broke, and just altogether half destroyed, you don't say, 'Sorry, honey, I'm married.' I wouldn't exactly say he's pleased to find her domestic in Brookline with a baby. . . . But you know, they were more friends than lovers in the years I knew them."

"You've spoken to him?"

"Yeah, he called me. So I let her know and said, 'Do you want me to give him your number?' She started whooping with joy. Some people don't know when they're well off, Beth —including me."

"Why do you say it that way?"

Dorine made that funny bittersweet smile. "Beth, I told you a lie. I said I hadn't gone to bed with anybody in months? I went to bed with Phil this afternoon."

"But why? Oh, Dorine, you've been so strong lately. What did you go and do that for?"

"He asked me to come and see him and I said I'd stop by on the way back from my afternoon lab. He's staying at Jackson's. Bethie, it's funny—there they are, back together again. That marriage will outlast any we know. Anyhow, Jackson was at school, which was fine with me."

"I wouldn't . . . mind . . . seeing Jackson again. It's been a long time."

"That would be easy to arrange. Just stop by with me. Anyhow, Phil was there and we had a couple of beers together and we talked and talked and talked. I don't know, I felt good talking to him. I felt I was different and he could see that and liked it and I could feel differences in him, though I don't know what they mean yet. He's been through bad things."

"You mean you felt sorry for him?"

"No, I didn't. I don't know why I didn't. He kept telling me how great I was looking. Then he said, 'Hey, do you want to talk in bed?' "

"But why?" Beth's voice trailed upward.

"Well, if a man occasionally asked so outright and friendly about it, no pressure, just 'Do you want to?' right in the middle of a good talk when I'm feeling close, I might have a lot more sex. I felt right about touching him and I could give some clues to what would please me—that's new for me, Beth. I felt pretty mellow when we got up, good through my body and on top of things. I think I was still up on that when I got home and found Laura fighting everybody else in the house."

"So maybe you're marching because you feel funny about what you did with Phil."

"Not so, Beth. This time I feel I can like Phil and it won't hurt me. I can go to bed with him and he won't use me. Look, I'm not there available and defenseless. My life has its own structure now. I have to make so much money, I have to spend so much time in the lab, I have duties here in the house."

"So what do you want with him then?"

"Beth, Beth." Dorine put her hands on her shoulders. "Don't do that to me! Make me feel guilty for something I did that I wanted. Don't."

"But you've been so strong."

"But I can't be strong *for* you. We can be strong together." Dorine buried her hands in her curly ruff of brown hair. "All heterosexuality isn't necessarily a woman servicing a man. It's as if we can be friends now, real friends. I know he's still hung up on Miriam and that she means a whole lot to him. He's been broken and he's mending. And I can't give him much—not much time, not much energy."

"What can he give you?"

"Communication. A sense of play. The feeling mellow in my body. . . . I don't know about Jackson, about dealing with him. That's a test of strength. Being around Jackson used to make me feel like a piece of nothing."

"I wonder if I'd still feel attracted to him. The way I used to." Beth felt fierce with courage saying it out loud. "I don't think so. Besides, he's older now."

"So are you, ninny. So is supper. Come on downstairs and eat with the rest of us. There won't be anything left for us."

Beth paused in the doorway. "Why did Phil have to come back? Why couldn't he stay where he was! All he ever means is trouble."

"When you look at him, you won't ask why he came back."

On Saturday, Beth marched with Laura and Dorine. Her uneasy conscience made her go: what Miriam called her Puritan, the voice that made her feel that the more it cost to do something—the less she wanted to and the keener her fears—the more needful it was that she perform that act. But she did not enjoy the chants and the songs. Oh, part of her could watch Laura striding arm in arm with Lynn and another woman under the banner GAY IS BEAUTIFUL and see how happy Laura looked. Her face was flushed, her hair tumbled, her eyes bright with excitement as she marched, almost dancing along. Dorine was having a good time too, shouting and waving a poster and singing in her strong soprano with the other women. Beth's conscience could make her march, but her conscience could not make her feel truly a part of what she did not want to be doing. Her body felt tight and hard. She wished herself visible only to the women around her. She felt awkward around the men from Gay Liberation and was glad they were marching separately: they made her feel as if she were all elbows.

The march had been called partly because of recent police harassment but also, Laura told her, to influence the women's conference going on that weekend to give more space to gay women's political demands. After the demonstration they went off to the conference, at Boston University. Laura went to the gay women's meeting, but after looking through the nine workshops, Dorine and Beth decided they wanted to attend the one on women's theater. "Wanda Rosario. Haven't I heard of her? Does she write stuff?"

"I don't think so. . . ." Dorine frowned over the name. "I have a feeling it's Joe you're thinking of. Used to be a big *macher* in the Radical Alliance. Proponent of the student-worker line. Phil used to hang around with him. Remember Joe Rosario who got fired from Northeastern and there was a student strike? He used to drop by Going-to-the-Sun."

"Maybe she isn't his wife, then."

"He had a wife. I met her when we were bailing Phil out. What she'd have to do with women's theater I sure don't know. Anyhow, maybe we can find a group that you'll like." Dorine gave her hand a squeeze.

"Well, is that her?" Beth asked softly as they came in and sat down on the floor. They were late and the workshop was under way. A woman was setting everybody in groups to doing exercises with their voices and bodies.

"I'm not sure. . . . It could be her. No, it couldn't be."

For three hours they kept at it. It was exhausting and great. This woman knew what she was doing, she did not so much direct and instruct them as set them going together. They did some exercises with the group all at once, some things in small groups, some in twos and threes. They roared and bellowed. They sang. They drew air into their lungs and let it out in long, long groans and ululations. They beat time on the floor and on their thighs and they clapped in counter-rhythms. They danced and leapt and did slow circles. They became one another. They became parts of their own bodies and parts of their pasts. They were what they most wanted to be. They were animals. Then they were one big animal together. Then they were a machine. They were a cow together, they were a big snake, they were a wolf. They were a typewriter and a car.

The woman Wanda Rosario was small, almost as small as Beth, but heavier. She had a chunky body and wild dark hair, coarse and short and streaked with gray. She had huge dark eyes, a swarthy complexion, a sharp nose. She had blunt large spatulate hands that became totally other when she used them. They became birds, they became fish, they became flowers: they had no bones but were water flowing; they became knives and boxes and armor plating. They were weapons. They were puppets.

Her hair stood on end, her eyes blazed, her voice bellowed. Then it sank to a weird carrying whisper. She crackled with energy. She talked about women's music, the songs women sang, the dancing women had done together, the rituals of women's lives handed down from mothers to daughters for thousands of years from Paleolithic times and now destroyed. Women had had their culture stolen, suppressed. Women imagined they had never been poets or composers because their music had been anonymous and collective.

She talked about the need for women's rituals, for making each other strong, for giving each other power, for feeling each one her own beauty with each other. They must make their own strong clean rituals of giving birth and puberty and fighting and growing and sharing and dying.

She illustrated with a ritual from the Santería, explaining how the forbidden African goddesses and gods had been disguised under the names of Christian saints, had entered the bodies of women dancing, and had thus manifested themselves. In this dance she was the goddess of the sea. One of the women who was in her company beat on a drum. Both Wanda and the woman began to sing something back and forth between them, and then Wanda began to dance, swishing back and forth rhythmically an invisible skirt as she stomped and turned and moved her hips. And Wanda dancing became beautiful.

Watching her, Beth caught her breath. She could almost believe on the spot in possession, in the mystery of the Santería, because dancing Wanda was radiant with power and strength, Wanda was beautiful. A wanting touched her nerves. Did she want to be Wanda? She tried to imagine that. She was in the presence of a woman who could make hidden things real, who could make inchoate emotions leap into the flesh. She wanted—what?—to know Wanda? To be near her? To be part of what she did. Right then she knew what she wanted to do in the world. She knew. She wanted to work with Wanda, she wanted to be part of that theater group.

As the workshop was breaking up, Wanda answered questions. One of them was from somebody obviously thinking like Beth, but with more nerve. "Yes, I'm starting a new group. Some of us from the old Red Wagon will be the nucleus, and we already have a house in Roxbury where we can live and work. But this new group is going to be larger. We're going to use a lot more music and dance movement in our theater."

The group would work together until they had a common identity and a common style and a repertoire. She thought they should have three or four months of hard work before they could start performing. Providing they got started at once.

Beth worked her way to stand as close to Wanda as she could approach. A group of women were asking questions, discussing methods, telling each other and Wanda what their

groups were doing. They were arguing about whether anyone in women's theater should take on a role like Wanda's
of director, or whether everything should emerge from the
collectivity. Wanda's voice came occasionally through the
hedge of backs, sounding tired, sounding weary. She did not
defend her position. She sounded too tired to defend herself.
Beth waited and waited. Finally as Wanda was getting ready
to leave, sticking her head through an old horse blanket of a
poncho, Beth said in a voice that fled her throat like a mouse,
"I want to be in your group! I want to work with you!"

"Have you worked with any theater groups before?"

"No. Only in the house. We improvise together. I live in
a women's house."

"Come out to Roxbury tomorrow. You got the address?
Good. Do you work?"

"Yes, but I'll quit."

Wanda smiled wearily. She looked wan and empty. "Not
yet, please. Come and see how we are. See if you want to be
with us. We're just starting. Today, here, we were doing
simple exercises. Fun to do and loosens everyone. But we're
going to be trying to make theater that speaks for women.
That can pull women out of their solitary cells. I can't talk
any more now, I'm beat. But come if you want to. . . . Don't
be afraid. I do mean that you're welcome to come. . . ."

Dorine and Beth left the conference giddy and floating.
They were too wound up to stay for the plenary session, too
excited to sit still. They walked across the B.U. bridge, almost
skipping along. As they came off the Cambridge end, Beth
said, "You know, we should have stayed. There's a lot of
business to be covered today, decisions about day care and
health issues."

"You know we didn't want to. Neither of us ever say a
word at meetings anyhow, if there's more than ten people.
We're both too excited to listen to anybody. . . . Hey, you
want to stop by Phil's? You said you wanted to."

But as they were turning the corner onto Pearl, familiar
and shabby with its odd-sized frame houses crowding the
street, Beth felt guilty. "Taking our pleasure to them. We're
backsliding."

"It's the trouble in the house. You don't want to go back
right now and find Connie and Laura fighting, or Sally and
Connie not speaking. It's close to exploding. The kids feel it
the worst."

"We're making excuses. I'm giving myself a license for being curious because I think I found something today I really, really want to do. I think she's great, Dorine. She gives off energy like a little sun."

"Beth, it *is* the same woman, though I just couldn't believe it. When you were talking to her at the end, I looked at her close up. She has that big mole on her cheek. I remember that from the night at the precinct, when she was waiting for Joe and I was waiting for Phil—Miriam was on the computer. I remember thinking that she wasn't very attractive. To show you where my head was at in those days, I thought an important guy like Joe, I'd expect him to have a pretty woman. But Wanda was plain and she looked her age."

"She looks older because her hair's got gray in it. She can't be more than thirty-five. I looked at her hands and throat. . . . I want to know everything about her."

"I remember noticing when we were sitting together that she didn't shave her legs and I remember feeling superior, thinking she was a real slob. Thinking, how did she expect to keep a real righteous man like Joe, being so sloppy. Oh, men. Oh, women!" They were climbing the familiar dim stairway smelling of Orpheus' signature.

She knew ten minutes after walking in—oh, the room was much as it had been, the cat curled on a chair, nose tucked in his long dusty fur, one yellow eye checking them over, the web of extension cords, the dirty dishes and glasses overflowing with butts and the charred tobacco dumped from Jackson's pipe—that whatever she felt about Jackson, she felt it still. Phil was thin and quieter. She did not mind him as much as she had. He was easier to ignore, and he was paying attention mostly to Dorine.

Jackson looked . . . the same. She swore he was wearing the identical faded blue denim shirt. The sad lines etching his cheeks still drew her fingers. Dorine was much bolder. She was talking on, turning to Beth for support. Telling them about the march, as if daring them to say boo, talking about the workshop and the exercises.

"You're both looking tiptop." Jackson scratched himself slowly all over his chest. "Life in the nunnery seems good for the body and soul. Isn't that so, Felipe?"

"I always said I'd like life in a nunnery. It's the priests I never could stomach."

"I'm not a nun. Phil knows that already." Dorine laughed

and Phil pulled a long innocent face.

Jackson looked from one to the other, raising an eyebrow. "And what about you, Beth? Are you a blue nun?"

"Do you mean sad or pornographic? . . . I don't know what I think about sex." She would not look away from his sandy bloodshot gaze, though she felt her face heating slightly. She would not let him make her into a child.

"Why, you're not to think about it. It's not a thing that improves with thinking, Beth."

"You should talk, Jackson," Phil drawled. "That's all you do, think about it."

"Better than talking about it all the time, wouldn't you say?"

"Aw, go on, back in the Boy Scouts in Sofa, Idaho, they told you if you used it regular it would fall off. It's you should have been the junkie instead of me. That puts it from your mind for sure. Ride the needle far enough and you don't know what to do with a woman if she crawls in your bed."

Jackson let his glance trail over Dorine. "I don't know, we used to hear it all the time about the sexual revolution. Now, except for the homosexuals who've taken to the streets screaming, it seems like everybody else has given it up for macrobiotics or backpacking or freaking on Jesus."

"It was only a revolution for men." Dorine looked delighted with something. Somehow she had ended up standing nearer to Phil and farther from Jackson, leaning on the refrigerator sucking his pipe. "It only meant I couldn't say no without being told I was frigid and not with it."

"Don't bring your banners in here. Still, I want to know what Beth was doing out with the lesbians. You strike me as about as much of a bulldyke as my mother."

Beth found herself standing very straight with anger, and then she saw him smiling inside his face at her reaction. She took a deep breath and signaled with her eyes to Dorine to let her answer. "Not all women are into playing butch and femme. In fact, being with women is one way of getting away from those roles. Second, I don't have any particular sexual identity—"

"You used to have one in the old days, back with Tom Ryan," Jackson said, giving her a face of bland inquiry.

"No, I didn't. The only identity I had was loneliness."

"Hmm." His face stopped being funny. "A lot of people could say that about a lot of things that go on. It's kind of

bald, but that about wraps it up. . . ." His face went into
teasing again. "Still I can't imagine anything quite so provocative as you standing there looking at me wide-eyed, telling me
you just don't have any sexual identity."

She hated herself because her heart was pounding, because
she would have enjoyed punching him in the nose, and she
still found him attractive. She still wanted him to find her
attractive. It was entangled with her new and old fears about
touching and being touched. She had marched with the gay
women and now she was doing the best she could to flirt with
Jackson, because she felt pushed to untie at last that knot
she was satisfied to have tight inside her. "Doesn't seem to
provoke you to anything besides teasing me."

"Right on, Bethie." Phil was slumped in a chair with one
hand on Dorine's on the table. "Call his bluff. If Jackson had
a coat of arms, the motto would be KEEP OFF THE GRASS."

"And yours would be a bottle rampant. Your eyes are
bigger than your stomach and/or other organs. . . ."

"Four-thirty." Dorine stood up. "I cook tonight. I do little
enough the rest of the time. I have to shove off. If you want
to stay for a while, Beth?"

Beth shook her head no and followed Dorine down the
hall. Phil kissed the back of Dorine's neck, mumbling a
question. "Gee, Phil, I'm sorry. We made a rule not to have
men sleep over."

"Jesus, it is a nunnery. No men, like no dogs allowed. Do
you think we might rape the children or shit on the floor?"

"Easy, Phil. It's a rule because there are women in the
house more comfortable that way. It's a safe place. If men
treated women reasonably, we wouldn't have to deal with
women so fucked over they're threatened by any man just
being where they live. . . . If you want I'll come by Monday,
late. I'll call from the studio where I'm working and let you
know."

"Monday afternoon I'm going over to Miriam's but I'll be
back here for supper. Give a call. But that's some half-assed
rule. Suppose we made a rule, no females? What would we
do, fuck in a phone booth? Aw, it's like being fifteen."
Grumbling, he went off to his room.

Jackson followed them to the door, hands in his pockets.
"Good to see you, Dorine. And Beth. Any time you want to
come by and discuss your sexual identity . . ." He was smiling,
half coming on, half putting her down. "I think if we looked

for a while we might find you one."

"Do you think so?" She was shaking with anger. She stomped out the door and then turned in the hall. "You think you can stick your notions on my head like a paper hat that has to fit!"

He leaned on the doorway grinning. "I think I could have some fun seeing what fits." He bussed her on the forehead, then ducked in, pulling the door shut. Inside she could hear him chuckling.

She sat down on a step clenching her fists. Dorine hauled her up by the elbow. "My, my. I'm immune to him, that's my goodie of the day. I don't give a hoot about him. But you're not in that state, are you?"

"He thinks I'm a child. He thinks he can tease me and get back home safe. He makes me feel like a . . . nincompoop. I will call his bluff! I will!"

"Shh! Beth." Dorine took her hand. "You don't win arguments with a man in bed. You be careful. You get mixed up with him and raked over the coals the way Miriam was and I'm not going to stand for it! I'll kill him if he messes you up. Now you forget him."

"But I don't feel attracted to any other man I know. I have to find out."

"What's wrong with celibacy? You've been doing fine. What do you want to go messing around with him for?"

"You tell me. I'm only half grown, only half there. All right, maybe I'm gay, maybe I'm straight, maybe I'm bisexual. Maybe he's a way I could find out what everybody else seems to think I just have to know."

"Beth, be careful. I couldn't stand for you to get hurt. And him! He just shouldn't be given a chance to mess up any more good women."

"You're giving Phil another chance."

"But Phil's not the same. And neither am I. What I'm trying with him isn't what I ever had with a man before. I like Phil, somehow I do, I still do. He knows how to play. Except when I'm with him or sometimes in the house, I never play."

"Well, I'm not the same person as Miriam either."

"Beth . . . you know you've admired Miriam a whole lot. This wouldn't have a little bit of competitiveness in it?"

"I'd never have gone near him in a million years when she was involved with him. . . . I don't know, maybe he seems to count more because of her. How can I tell? . . . For once

I want to choose what happens with a man. I don't want to live with him, Dorine, I don't love him. But I find him so attractive I feel like a fool."

"That doesn't sound good to me."

"Don't worry, Dorine. Not about me. First Wanda and the theater group and then him, I feel as if I'm coming unstuck inside. Everything is breaking loose in me and bumping around. I'll never be able to sleep again. I can't even stand still. I don't know, Dorine, whatever it all is, at least it's exciting."

25

How to Fall Is as Important as
How to Get Up

One Saturday in early November, Connie moved out, taking with her everything she had brought or bought down to the toys that had seemed to be all the children's, and of course she took David. That was essentially the end, because none of them had the heart to look for someone else. The quarrels were too fresh, the force centrifugal, and they were all broke.

Connie married her boy friend and moved to an apartment complex in Waltham. That was the last they saw of her, except for arguments over who owed what on the phone, the gas, the electric bills. She developed a last-minute conviction that she was being taken for more than her share and wrote nasty notes. It sat badly in Beth's mind. Connie said she did not want them to see David any more. What David thought of all that they would never know.

Dorine decided she could not go with Sally and Laura and Beth into the women's theater house. Through a woman sculptor Dorine worked for she got into a mixed commune of some graduate students, a sociologist, two city planners, a couple of artists. There were no children. It was a well-built comfortable house and Dorine called it less protective than their old Somerville house but interesting, and she felt lucky to move in.

With Sally and Laura, Beth moved into the three-story rambling Roxbury house that had been a parish house and was already extensively changed—"remodeled" was too bourgeois a term for what had been done to it. It was strange but livable, and there were already eleven women and four children there. With their two, that made half a dozen and felt sometimes like a herd. Two of the kids were Wanda's, boys four and six. With so many children, so many women, so much activity—the exercises, the practicing, other children running in and out, constant work going on—the house could never be as closed as Beth's old commune.

Though no men lived there, a couple of the women had boy friends who stayed over and Jane was married, though her husband lived in New York. When he came, he stayed in the house. The phone constantly rang, among hammering and banging and children's intent voices. Some rooms were set aside on the top floor for people to work and read in silence, and a room was kept for meditation and yoga.

Beth had to grip herself hard not to bolt. She had never lived with such a crowd. She had liked living alone. She had worked on herself and learned to live with four other women and three children, with a room of her own and a door to shut that she often did shut. Now she shared a room with Sally in the midst of a tribe.

Because of the constant theater exercises and the acting out of feelings and the experimenting with touching and dancing together—because of all this traffic with the inner life, people tended to express what they were going through. Fairly early Beth stood up and tried to explain her trouble with the communal roar. She did not want to withdraw. She did not want to make everyone else into a Them, a block outside. But she needed help. Part of her still wanted to be separate and quiet.

At first she minded that when she sat down at the table she never knew who was going to be at supper. Someone who did not live in the house might be sitting right across from her. She found the looser style hard to adjust to. She missed the old house. She had loved to come down to meals knowing they would be there together, every day. It had been small and warm, and at the good times she had felt like an ideal daughter in an idealized family.

This was rougher. If she did not have a specific task as-

signed and she missed supper, no one would come in search
of her. The house was not a close-knit family but tribal. It
was a confederacy. The commune was not so loose that
nothing got done, like Going-to-the-Sun. The women were
always changing the place into something more exciting, more
comfortable, more inviting. Walls were always being painted,
furniture being repaired or made, posters going up and toys
created. Someone was always kneading bread or baking cookies. The food was good, lots of whole grains and fresh fruits
and vegetables. At the same time, since they always had
guests, it went quickly. If Beth blinked too long at a platter,
it was empty.

Though she could always go into a quiet room, the house
was not peaceful. It breathed a fierce energy. Sometimes Beth
felt as if she had moved into Wanda. She knew she confused her feelings about working with Wanda with her sense
of the house itself—it all blurred inside her. Never had she
worked this hard. Some evenings she dragged herself upstairs
and fell prone across the covers of her bed. She would wake
hours later with the light still burning, her clothes on, stiff
and confused.

Often after the sessions together, her body ached. Her
small weak body. An inferior instrument. Wanda called her
out on that attitude. "You have to stop hating yourself. Your
body will do whatever you teach it. It's a good body and
you must stop treating yourself like a bad dog that ought to
be whipped."

Sometimes her fatigue was good, was a sense of being well
used. Sometimes it was a fatigue of defeat. Wanda was trying
to teach them a way of falling from judo, so that they could
fall and not be injured. They must not clench their muscles
and freeze when they fell. Learning how to fall correctly
was the first step in self-defense, the first step in acrobatics,
the first step in a true physical ease that would improve their
dancing. But Beth felt as if that fear of falling went through
her brain, back into the base of her spine. Always she froze
and then hit hard, shatteringly.

Wearily again and again she tried. Wanda could coax her,
could order her, could shout at her, could sing to her in
that husky electric voice that she must loosen, that she must
trust, that she must relax and go with the fall. Still her body
tightened and when she hit the floor it hurt, it always hurt.

When she looked at her body in the shower, her brief sexual

fantasies of the early fall seemed ridiculous. She was marked
with blue and purple and yellow bruises. She ached. Fortunately she had a job where nobody looked at her: she
worked three evenings a week as cleaning woman in an office
building. She preferred it to secretarial work. Nobody was
around except the night janitor, who ignored her.

Wanda talked a great deal about energy levels. "Women
have been taught to dampen our own vigor. To cut back
and stay passive and keep a low profile. Most of the work
women do in this society has no beginning and no end. No
product. It's upkeep, maintenance, service, nurture. When
the work is done well, it's invisible. When it's badly done,
people complain. Typically our days are scattershot—ten tasks
going on at once and none of them such that one begins,
one defines a problem, one tries, one solves that problem, and
then one rests."

Wanda made them aware how they moved, how they rested,
how they occupied space. She demonstrated how men sat
and how women sat on the subway, on benches. Men expanded into available space. They sprawled, or they sat with
spread legs. They put their arms on the arms of chairs. They
crossed their legs by putting a foot on the other knee. They
dominated space expansively.

Women condensed. Women crossed their legs by putting
one leg over the other and alongside. Women kept their
elbows to their sides, taking up as little space as possible.
They behaved as if it were their duty not to rub against,
not to touch, not to bump a man. If contact occurred, the
woman shrank back. If a woman bumped a man, he might
choose to interpret it as a come-on. Women sat protectively,
using elbows not to dominate space, not to mark territory, but
to protect their soft tissues.

Further, men commented on how women looked and
walked on the streets. Women did not stand in groups ob-
serving men critically and aloud informing them of their
approval or disapproval, commenting that they found a man
attractive or ugly, that they wanted to use him sexually or
that they thought he could be bought for a price. A woman
walked with a sense of being looked at: either she behaved
as if being evaluated by men were a test and she tried to
pass it; or she walked with chin lowered, eyes lowered. She
pretended that, if she did not look at the men, the men could

not see her. She walked very fast, pretending to be invisible, deaf, dumb, and blind.

Beth's developing awareness made it hard to go to the drugstore. Sometimes she felt raw and sore. She remembered childhood fantasies about saying a magic word that made her invisible. Now she was personally invisible but visible as one of a class: girl, cunt, you there.

Once in a while Beth ate with Dorine at her new commune. It was an affluent, comfortable house full of well-educated women and men who talked a great deal and teased each other in ways Beth could not follow. It was a house in which many people were somewhat political and heated arguments were common. Dorine seemed at home there, but Beth was not at ease. She preferred Dorine to eat at her house. Dorine stopped by to see each of them, Laura, Sally, and Beth, and took the children out. Usually she got Fern and Blake for an afternoon on weekends. Dorine fitted naturally into their house, though she said it was too hectic for her to live there. Beth got to spend as much time talking with her as when they lived together. Laura she saw less of in the big house, because she was seriously involved with Lynn and spent as much time as she could with her.

Sally was accustomed to sharing a room, since she'd lived with Connie, but Beth found the lack of privacy hard to get used to. Slowly she learned to use the meditation room when she needed space around her no one could cross. Sally was relatively easy for her to live with, because she was still and had no compulsion to smother silence under words.

A fierce argument raged over whether they should have Christmas for the children. Wanda was in favor, feeling they should not give their children something to feel deprived about by comparison with children in bourgeois families. They would buy nothing but make presents. But other women were totally opposed. The argument woke Beth to the world outside. Weeks had melted past. The house voted not to have Christmas. Beth decided that it was time for her to go and see Miriam.

Wednesday afternoon when she arrived at Miriam's, Phil was bouncing Ariane on his lap and Miriam was running a load of laundry through and talking full tilt, sitting on the counter with her legs dangling. What was it? Miriam looked

less haggard. She was still heavier than was good for her,
but she seemed more focused. She was talking gaily, swinging her legs: she looked younger. The waterlogged, drowning, slow quality was gone. Her hair seemed alive, her body
radiated energy. Partly her face looked different, Beth realized,
because the glasses held together with tape had been set aside.
Probably, since she seemed able to see, she had succeeded
in breaking in her lenses again, after trying off and on in a
desultory manner for months.

"Oh, Beth, what happened to you? I thought you'd got lost
for good. What do you mean by disappearing from the on-
going soap opera of my life? Sally's more faithful, she at least
calls. I miss you guys—even more than I miss my two afternoons of liberty! But wow, do I miss them. I just got that
thesis done in time." She peered into Beth's face. "Where
did you get those bruises?"

"Trying to learn to fall properly." Briefly Beth explained.

"Oh, have I missed you. Look, Ariane's mastered sitting
up and she's started to creep like a midget racer. Hey, remember Phil?"

"Miriam is trying to make me jealous by going on how
she missed you, gone for two weeks." Phil bouncing Ariane?
Beth blinked. Yet Ariane bubbled and giggled till she drooled
and clung to him with stubby fists and sharp little nails. "But
Miriam won't give me my dues of admitting I was missed."

Phil had stayed skinny, gaunt and sharpened-looking. Still,
he did not look broken, as Dorine had implied. Wanda's
mystique about energy had taught her to be sensitive to
vitality and inertia. She felt a strong burst of energy coming
off Miriam, radiating heat and light and excitement. From
Phil she thought she felt a narrow intense beam, focused
back on Miriam. They seemed to her like sun and moon.
Yet, listening to them, she did not think that was how they
saw each other.

"Well, missed or not, I'm glad he's back, Bethie. He's
given me a good kick. Here I was sinking into domesticity,
fading into the breakfast dishes. Not that Ariane isn't an
amazing daily miracle. She doesn't miss a thing. But my intellectual level was settling at Dr. Seuss. I'd reached the point
where the highlight of my days was interminable gossip sessions with Laverne Ryan about whether Tom or Neil was
meanest last night and psychologizing our poor children to
death."

"You'd all deserted her to a life of suds and socks and Her Master's Voice. See, I told you for years, it's one thing to be playing earth mother to grown men. At least our diapers don't need changing. But you wanted a real baby—"

"Instead of you frauds. Look at my darling. You have to admit you're no competition. She's twice as smart and twice as pretty!" Miriam wiped Ariane's mouth, beaming at her.

But Ariane began to cry and Miriam had to take her. Phil said, "I'll admit item one. She's here. She's on the scene, we have her now—"

"I like that *we*. Listen to him!" But Miriam no longer was. She was trying to comfort Ariane, who was lost in cranky wailing. "It's past her nap time. I'd better take her up. Not that she won't howl, she hates to be deprived of your company. She'd give me away to the Salvation Army to keep you in the house. Come on, mama's baby, time for your nap. Now don't fight me!"

Ariane screamed all the way upstairs as Miriam carried her kicking and bellowing. Left in the kitchen with Phil, after a while Beth asked, "Are you still living at Jackson's?"

"Sure, I'm basically lazy. I want a home made for me." He smiled at her. "Still don't know why I resisted setting up house with Miriam all those years. Was I real sensitive and ahead of my time refusing to domesticate her? Or just scared?" He shrugged. "By now, what does that matter? It's a whole new ball game."

"Does Jackson ever see her?"

Phil shook his head heavily. "He never asks me how she is. If I mention her, he doesn't answer. He knows I see her regular. I tell him I'm coming over. But he won't ask one thing. What a pious fraud he is, what a stiff one!"

"You didn't stay together long after Miriam moved out."

"We were pissed at each other. I blamed him, and he thought I was a stupid prick to be caring so much. Or he was letting on that's how he felt. Miriam was so far into Freud she couldn't talk English, doting on that mercenary shrink. I just lit out. Decided it was time to be moving on. A bad scene all around." He shook his head as if he had water in his ears, scowling.

He asked her about the theater group, about Wanda in particular. "You come back and find the whole landscape turned upside down. Joe was always running around, but I never thought he'd leave her. He made such a fuss about the boys. She used to depress me because she'd make me think of my mother—stoical, strong, putting up with hell and never asking pity, a real workhorse." His gaze stayed on the swinging door Miriam had gone through, until she came back through it.

"That was Neil on the phone. You can both stay to supper tonight, loves, because he won't be home till late. He's meeting some computer types from Palo Alto at the airport and they're having supper at Tech Square. So stay and stay, and we'll have some roast lamb from yesterday cold—made it with lemon and mint and rosemary—and I'll make us a Greek salad with feta and black olives. We'll have good bread I made and lots of wine—it will be lovely. I can whip that up in five minutes, no cooking to do, and be with you the whole time."

Phil went to stand by Miriam, resting his head on her shoulder. "Notice that we get leftovers. Scraps from yesterday's table, crumbs, cold meat, used rosemary—"

"It sounds wonderful!" Beth said with fierce loyalty. "I don't want her cooking for me."

"Beth has a rule, have you noticed?" Phil gestured with his free hand. "Nobody can criticize you except her."

"Laverne is jealous because you're here all the time, Phil. She thinks it's shocking. She's been gossiping about me. I bet she wishes you'd drop over there."

"It's only right I should oust her from your affections. After all, she did me dirty once, by indirection. Anyhow, I'm on her right side now. I'll have you know I've been invited to her big Christmas blast."

"So? Even *we* have been invited." Miriam dodged away from his hand. "Would one of you stick the wet clothes in the dryer? I want to sit down peacefully and not feel responsible for a thing."

Phil was frowning at Miriam, so Beth after a moment moved the clothes. "You're invited? I assumed not. So, do you feel like chatting with your other old roommate? Christmas is a little early for Auld Lang Syne."

"What are you talking about?" Miriam froze. "Him?"

"None else. He's invited. He has a soft spot for Laverne. I guess more for the way she used to look . . . like the soft spot on a rotting pear. Don't give me the big stare, pigeon." He took her chin in his hand.

She ducked away. "Why didn't you tell me sooner? Before I'd accepted!"

Beth said, "It would bother you so much to see him?"

Miriam did not answer.

"Son of a bitch!" Flapping his thin arms, Phil strode up and down the kitchen. "I should never have let him near you!"

Miriam laughed. "Oh, my dear, letting and not letting was never your long suit. I'm not complaining in retrospect. I'm sure I'll have to see him sometime. But they know, don't they! I bet Tom is behind this. He loves to be nasty. God, he hates other people to have feelings, it brings out his sadism to feel somebody else is happy . . . or unhappy. He hates me. He hates you too."

"So long as ass-lickers like Tom Ryan hate me, I know I must be doing something right."

"Why can't you just tell Neil you don't want to go?" Beth said. "He never seems to like parties. I've heard him say he only used to go in hopes he would meet a pretty woman, and now he has no reason to go at all."

"But I *argued* with him! I liked the idea of getting dressed up and dancing. Lord, Phil, I haven't danced in a year or longer! I used to imagine my legs would drop off if I went a week without dancing."

Beth insisted, "Just tell him you've changed your mind."

"On what excuse? He hates irrational changes."

"But Neil knows about Phil and Jackson—doesn't he?"

"Oh, vaguely. Ancient complexities, what do they matter?"

"She means the straight man abides few adventures more interesting than he's had," Phil drawled. "I'm in the house under false pretenses." He tousled Miriam's hair as he passed.

She shook away from him. He touched her often, compulsively. Unable to reject him, Miriam chose to treat it as a form of teasing or pretended not to notice. "Don't be melodramatic, prick. He knows you're an old friend and we used to be sort of involved."

"Sort of? Anyhow, I can fix things so neither Jackson or I actually gets there. Better yet, since he wants to go, why not fail to get a baby sitter? Or develop a toothache after supper?"

"The baby sitter! Phil, you're still a genius, even if you pretend not to think so any more. It makes me angry to think of that lizard Ryan setting a booby trap. And Laverne, she's supposed to be my friend, even if she's jealous. She knows I wouldn't want to see Jackson, we've talked about him. I'd love to spike their guns!" She shut her eyes a moment. Then, bending forward with a grin, "Philip, we are attacking. Go dial your number. Go on. Beth, give me your hand and some moral support."

Watching her carefully, his eyes never leaving her face, Phil said, "Jackson, hi there, man. Listen, an old friend wants a word with you."

Miriam took the phone, swallowed, and said briskly and very fast, "Hello, Jackson? This is Miriam Stone. Listen, you're going to Ryan's party? . . . I thought so. Phil said as much. . . . Could you do me a favor? About nine, say, tell Ryan I told you we can't make it. We tried and tried but couldn't get a baby sitter. I've been calling Ryan and he isn't home, or I'd tell him myself. . . ."

After a medium pause she snorted, nodding into space, and her voice became natural. "I rather suspected he had visions of a confrontation. Be sure everybody hears! Say it loud! Well, good-by. . . . Sure, good-bye." Quickly she hung up, looking over her shoulder as if afraid of being caught in the act, looking at the window. "I'm wonderful if I say so myself. Quick thinking, quick action, and I hope Tom dies of disappointment. Jackson jumped out of his skin when he heard my voice."

"You spend two months refusing to phone me there for fear he'll answer, and then you let Tom panic you into calling him."

"It wasn't so bad. It's out of the way now. It wasn't so traumatic, when you come down to it." Miriam sashayed into the living room and flung herself on the couch, drawing up her long legs. "I still wish I could have gone and danced. The only time I wear a dress any more is to go to the pediatrician's. You know what? I'm going to give a party. A New Year's party. I'll bring it up with Neil tonight."

Phil sat down beside her. "You're feeling uppity after talking to Jack the man."

"I've been an idiot to make such a fuss. Why should I care? I'm married, I have a life of my own and a family, my child. How can he hurt me? He's the same old Jackson going along in his rut. Does he even have a girl?"

Phil propped his head against her. "Him? Not on your

life. He leers at Dorine occasionally, that's about the size of it."

"Hey, is Dorine avoiding me because you're involved? Come on, Phil." She gave him a gentle push. "Don't lean all over me, I get enough of that when Ariane's up."

"Don't be a cold mean bitch. It's little enough I get from you."

"Is she avoiding me? It's silly. Just because she's involved with somebody I used to see—I mean, one can hardly avoid that in these parts. I hate to think she may feel things are sticky."

Beth said, "I think she was worried you might mind."

"Nonsense." Phil put his head on Miriam's lap. "Dorine knows I am faithful to you in my fashion. Besides, if you haven't seen her, it's because you don't make appointments six weeks in advance. I get ten minutes in a phone booth with her now and then. At least I'm allowed in her bedroom these days. It's a very unselective house, they even have m-e-n. She's killing herself according to some ideal of how a liberated woman should act. Eighteen hours a day in the lab, four to pose for money, and that leaves a whole two hours for eating, sleeping, fucking, and taking a crap. She calls that living and thrives on it."

"Dorine and I have practically changed places. . . ." Miriam spoke slowly. Her hand touched Phil and drew back. "It's strange, Beth. As if all our lives had no inner shape. . . . But of course that's nonsense. I don't know why I said that. I don't want to do the kind of work I was doing at Logical. People are the most important thing to me. My marriage gives me emotional security. . . . I think I'm better for you now, Phil, than I ever was when we were involved, because—"

"Now we aren't involved?"

"You know what I mean. Don't you think I can be more helpful?"

"I'm trying to stop my slow-motion suicide. I think you're trying to help me, as much as you can with both hands tied behind your back."

"Phil! That's silly. Beth, I'm right, aren't I?"

"But you can't be as close to any of us as you were," Beth said reluctantly. "You're not out there with us. You can't see us except at fixed times. Your life is structured around this house."

"Things are changing! With Ariane no longer an infant,

I can take her along. I know I wallowed in domesticity. But I'm not withdrawing now. I think I can be a better friend because I'm not so needy and greedy myself. I'm not on the make for me. I really am bored to tears with the couples game."

"Dr. and Mrs. Stone present . . . another perfect sumptuous dinner, brought to you in living color and stereo yawns!"

"I just realized I don't like *any* of those people. I'm sure Neil doesn't. It's just that he can't make himself dislike anyone. He truly does admire those academic cutthroats. If I say Graben is a backbiter and cheats on his wife, Neil says, 'But oh, he's sure to win the Nobel prize in five years. . . .' He hates to criticize anybody, he thinks it's terrible to analyze people and talk about them. He calls it picking. I'm sure if he could hear us half the time he'd be shocked, we'd sound like vipers. . . . You know, he just doesn't notice. Like we're over visiting Ted and Barbara and it's clear there's a war on, he's blatantly putting her down all evening till I hardly know where to look. But Neil just doesn't see. When I say something afterward, he's so surprised. He has a filter in him that blocks out what he thinks are the wrong things to see. It's that gentleness in him. Even when he's bored, he's good-natured about it. I get nasty when I'm bored. I want to kill somebody."

Phil tilted his head back to look up at her. He still had it halfway on her lap. "And why do you think it took two years for you to figure out how much those people bore you? Is that called hypnosis? Or is it called fear? Or being out of touch?"

"But I didn't mind! Being married to Neil really is nice, Phil. He loves me, he wants to take care of me—"

"Do you need a lot of taking care of these days?" Phil asked.

"Neil enjoys inviting people home for dinner and knowing they'll be impressed. . . . I mean, I could do it, so why not, I felt for a long time. It seemed like an easy way to make people feel good. . . . It wasn't till recently I realized I don't care if those people like me or not. They don't know me, they don't care about me. I'm just Mrs. Stone, and Mrs. Stone is like Mrs. Jones, except she sets a better table."

"What's happening at Logical?" Beth asked. "Funny how

unreal that place is now that I've escaped. Are they going
bankrupt?"

Miriam shrugged widely. *"Some*thing's going on. Neil's
going on the M.I.T. faculty next year, though nobody out on
128 knows that yet. Abe forced Dick out. Can you understand fighting over control of a sinking company? Neil's
doing what he always wanted—getting out of industry into a
university. He'll do consulting, of course. But Logical's still
in debt and in trouble and everything's hanging fire. Those
guys he's seeing tonight are connected somehow. Maybe Abe
and Neil are getting a contract from them at the last minute.
They're from some West Coast-based schlocky company.
The sooner Neil's out, the better."

They had a noisy picnic supper in the living room and
Miriam put on rock records. Phil kept trying to turn up
the volume, while Miriam kept telling him they had to keep
it down for Ariane. Miriam danced awkwardly at first. Beth
found it sad to see her moving with clumsiness. But by the
time she had danced to one side, she was in touch with the
music. Watching Phil and Miriam turning, playing to each
other, closing a pattern and opening it up, Beth thought that
Phil and she were like piggy banks for Miriam, repositories
for parts of her self not quite forgotten but unused today.
Marriage was peculiar: that one day a woman became somebody else, lost her name and habits. Did Neil refuse, or did
Miriam censor those parts of herself she thought inappropriate? How would Neil react if that repression began to fail?

A year ago, six months, even two months before, Beth
would have watched from a chair. But she was learning to
move. She was still too shy to dance close to them. She went
apart, turning away to face the window. Outside the street
was white under the street lights. Apparently the snow had
stopped falling. But Miriam would not let her stay in the
alcove by the windows. Miriam came dancing over, seized
her hand, and made them form a circle. They danced around
and around faster and faster, until Beth got dizzy and sat
down hard.

Then the door opened and Neil came in, briefcase in hand,
shaking off snow and stamping his boots in the hall. "Hello?
. . . What's going on?"

That instantly guilty look. Miriam seemed to turn girlish.
"Neil? Hi there, we were just . . . dancing. Beth and Phil are

visiting. . . . How come you're back so early? Didn't the men from Palo Alto come?"

"They'd eaten on the plane and they weren't ready for supper yet." He glanced from one to the other coldly, with a minimal nod. "You've eaten already?"

The plates were still sitting on the coffee table. "We had a little snack. I wasn't going to make supper, since you were going to eat with them. . . . Is something wrong?"

"They're downtown drinking now and all I've had since noon is a couple of rancid anchovies and an olive I fished out of a martini. My head aches. Could you dispense with that tinny music?"

Hurriedly Miriam flipped the switch. He dropped his briefcase in his study, then turned back, hand to his forehead. "Honey," she said, "I'll get you some aspirin." She started for the steps.

"I'd rather eat. I think it's a hunger headache. We sold Logical. Let's have a bite to eat—some of that lamb would do."

"I'm so sorry, Neil. We . . . ate that. I didn't think it would be so good by tomorrow . . . so I thought . . ."

Neil glared at Phil, slumped gracefully in the doorway. "Oh?" He sat down, forcing his head into propped hands. "Anything, then. Anything at all you didn't get around to disposing of?"

"I'm so sorry. . . . Listen, I can whip up an omelette. How about an omelette with herbs? A bite of cheese? There's that good bread I made yesterday." How diffident she was with Neil. Had she set him up as her conscience? Did she fear the turn of his judgment against her? Beth could not figure it out, that tremulous apologetic wavering before his solid north, an outpouring of excuses and explanations. Somehow Miriam had given over an essential part of her identity to him, to feeling sure he loved her, and she feared a glacial movement of his judgment against her. Standing before him, Miriam wrung her hands involuntarily, tense and awkward. "Listen, I could open a can of good pâté, and you could have that on bread."

"You aren't planning to eat with me?"

"Of course I'll sit down. I had a snack."

"Did you happen to notice I told you that we sold Logical? Or aren't you interested?"

"You'll tell me all . . . who'd buy Logical? I mean . . ." She threw a look at them, pleading. "Honey, wouldn't you like the pâté?"

"We'll be going." Phil spoke with sulky dignity. "Come on, Beth honey, I'll give you a lift."

Phil drove especially fast. As she clung to the door, Beth could not help thinking how little she had yet done with her life. "Shit, shit, shit," he was muttering, executing turns in wide stylish four-wheel drifts.

Beth worked up the courage to say, "I thought you were into a slow suicide. Anyhow, if you won't drive slower, let me out."

"I am in complete control of this car." But in a couple of blocks he did abruptly slow down. "Okay. You don't like me much, do you, Miss Bethie?"

"No. I never thought you were good enough for her."

"And how do you rate Mr. Clean?"

"Lower," she said truthfully. "She's backed into the wringer."

"He could have married anybody! That's the trouble, he thinks he did. Man marries one of the finest pieces ever walked the ground, a girl with guts and imagination—most women have imaginations like pencil sharpeners—and what does he care about? *Is supper ready?*" He drove on through Roxbury, but instead of taking her left to her house he turned right and drove up to the top of Fort Hill and parked there, by the old tower.

"I don't think he's a bad person, any more than my husband was. He's probably kinder and more responsible than you are. It's just what he expects of WIFE. He can't treat her any way than as a high-class domestic servant, because that's what she is ninety per cent of the time. He feels entitled to her undivided attention whenever he needs it, and when we're in the way, he hates us."

"You know, Bethie . . ." He tapped the wheel. "Sometimes you seem to expect that if you said a nice word to me I might rape you on the spot. Is that it?"

"I don't like you. I don't trust you. You use women for . . . sustenance. . . ."

"You don't like me," he said with melancholy bravado. "You think I'm some sort of gigolo."

"I think you're involved with Dorine, so what do you want with me tonight?" The gates of her sympathy were rusted against him. Her throat felt dry as if to let out an extra word would be dangerous.

"The iron sense of property women . . . some women . . . have. See, Dorine's been correcting me." He rubbed his hand over his face. "I'm here because I didn't punch him in the jaw. . . . Dorine doesn't want much of me. I have to do it her way or not do it, and I'll take that but I can't take it very far. The permanent condition is, she isn't with me, she's at work. And I'm still in love with Miriam, always, Dorine knows. It's a permanent condition like being Irish and talking too much and having my tonsils out. My tonsils won't grow back and I love Miriam. But I'm telling you, it isn't given to every man to have a second chance with the woman he wants. I swear I have one. He has her but he's going to run it into the ground. I fucked up before because I was into that slow suicide scene. But I'm going to take her and that kid, and he can suck his big toe."

"She won't leave him. She wants to be a good woman. That's why she had the baby, to justify her. She wants to be good and she needs to have him love her."

"He doesn't love her. He hasn't idea one about who she is. So she panicked and fell into marriage like you'd jump off a bridge. But she's coming back to life."

"Does Miriam know you still . . . love her?"

"Love, love. Ariane loves banana, mashed up. Neil loves roast lamb, medium rare. Phil loves Miriam. Does she know I go crazy not able to touch her except like a puppy dog, no. She'd feel guilty. She's always feeling guilty about something. I should have realized at some point the got-to-get-married respectable bit would grab her, she grew up in Flatbush. Should have been watching. I was so stoned all the time I couldn't tell my ass from a wall plug. You keep your mouth shut too about this."

"It's all hot air." Beth huddled against the door. "I wouldn't tell her anything to upset her. I want to go home. I have work to do tonight. Go find Dorine!"

"She'd let me, let me come and whimper about Miriam. For that reason I don't. I go to Dorine to see Dorine. You don't comprehend that. Never mind." He started the car. "I think if you ever smiled at me your face would fall off. Jesus, I wonder what Wanda makes of you? If the rest of the troupe is like you, I bet she's dying of chills and anemia! Well, Miriam always likes pallid girls around who don't compete and make her feel like Mama."

"Do you think she lets you come except for pity? She thinks she's helping you."

"She needs me. Life was getting dull. She fell for me the first time because I made things interesting, I turned her on to her body, the world, her own energy!" He had talked himself out of his depression. His voice was silky and amused. "Now I find her right back in Flatbush, stuck, boxed, sinking into daydreams and routine. A second chance, I'm telling you, born again. Once again *she* needs *me*. I'm not fantasizing this time, I'm playing it through step by step."

When Beth came in, Wanda seemed to have been waiting for her, for she called her into a room on the ground floor where they often worked. Wanda was wearing a dark red shirt; she seemed in a good mood though a quiet low-key one: banked coals. "Have some glögg. It's a hot mulled wine drink with spices. Smell. Isn't that lovely?"

Beth, still cold from huddling in the car while Phil orated to the stars, drank her first cup gratefully and let Wanda pour her a second. "It's only hot wine. So you're upset because you think Phil's trying to hurt your friend? Frankly, I've never really seen Phil hurt anyone. A bit parasitic. Lazy. Full of dreams and role playing and bad poetry. But Dorine says he's changed. You don't think so?"

"I guess I don't care." The wine slid down, hot and spicy, warming her through. "I don't care if he's supposed to be changed. I don't believe it."

Wanda was resting her hand against her cheek, smiling slightly. Her eyes, deep-set and almost black, rested on Beth affectionately. "Phil used to disappoint women a lot. He charms easily and disappears with ease. Water. He flows away. But he doesn't do that much damage. I think I'm something of an expert on what kinds of men do the most damage . . ." She stopped smiling. Her eyes went a little opaque, her gaze fixed past Beth. "Sometimes men do change, Beth, and then your anger is obsolete. People tell me Joe is different. That political defeat and the destruction of the context we all worked in have made him human. Maybe that's true, though I wouldn't care to find out close up."

"It hurt you bad when he left you?"

"Yeah." Wanda grinned crookedly. "Probably would have hurt more in the long run if he'd stayed. . . . But I'll tell you how I felt when people first started telling me he's changed.

How nowadays he doesn't stomp over women with his boots on. How he actually listens to other people's opinions. He doesn't think any more he's organizing a woman by fucking her. He doesn't insist he was born with the right line. . . . Well, for years I tried to make him more human. But I was furious when people told me that, I was bitter with fury. I was angry at him for daring to improve. He'd hurt me and our sons, and he had no right, no right to try to be a good person any more. . . . Do you feel what I'm saying?" Wanda poured more glögg in her cup.

Beth sipped the wine, frowning. "Phil never hurt me."

"Maybe he sums up things in men that have hurt you."

"He talks too much. He turns everything into words and makes it change in words, but nothing changes. He blurs things. Miriam is somebody who can do real things; how can she ever have wanted a man who can't do anything?"

"When she could do things herself, what did she need a man to do them for? Why should women always have to love men who seem to be on top?" Wanda chuckled in her throat. "If I lived with a man again, I think I'd like a nice warm unambitious country boy. . . . Truthfully, when I go to New York, I always see an old friend of mine. He runs a shop where a lot of movement stuff gets printed. He's a nice middle-aged fat widower with good politics and a good belly laugh, and I love to be with him. . . ."

Beth did not particularly relish the idea of Wanda running up to New York to spend time with a fat old printer.

Wanda was saying, "But with Joe, I wanted him to remain the villain. That he should begin to change after leaving me I couldn't allow. I wanted to have a good conscience in hating him. . . . But think what I'm saying. That he should go on the same way hurting other women. That if he wasn't mine, let him do no good to nobody. . . . I've had to learn to control that resentment." Wanda was smiling again. Her teeth were wide apart and strong-looking. Her eyes were shining with laughter that Beth thought had been melted in them like spices in the wine. "I'm just going on. . . . You're looking sleepy."

"It's the wine . . . I think I drank too much. . . ."

"Come on, stand. Yes." Wanda pulled her up by the arms. Beth felt herself bouncing loosely to her feet. "Now, over you go!"

Beth found herself on the mat. She lay a minute in surprise. She did not hurt. "What happened?"

"I threw you and you fell correctly. Beautifully. You didn't think what to do, so you did it. Now, again." Wanda pulled Beth to her feet and they turned around each other. Once again Wanda threw her and she found herself on the mat, lying on her back and laughing weakly, in contented silliness. Again and again and again Wanda threw her until she learned to feel the falling, to feel herself doing what she had been taught but had never before done. The glögg sweated out of her. She felt clear.

"Enough. I think you won't forget." Quickly, lightly, Wanda leaned forward and kissed her. "Go to bed."

Beth walked into her room. Sally was sitting on her bed repairing a stuffed monkey that was leaking fluff from the base of its tail. Beth walked in and, spinning around once with a grin of joy, let herself fall. Correctly. Then she lay on the floor and grinned at Sally.

"I'm a fallen woman at last! I know how to fall!"

Sally beamed at her and went on sewing the monkey's tail back on.

26

Mohammed Comes to the Mountain
and Finds It Stone

"Don't try to make me somebody up there," Wanda said with quiet anger. "On some higher level. I'm older than you, yes. I have a few things to teach you that you want to learn, though most of it is in you already. But I'm not existing on some easier, calmer level. If I'm older, I'm also more spent. I have less reserves, less to spare. I'm a woman the same as you are, and it isn't easier for me to fight and to survive and to get things done than it is for you! It makes me angry when you pretend it's different for me."

"But you know so much more. You never wonder who you are, I know you don't!"

"Beth, it's recently I stopped being only Joe's woman and mother of my kids. That's all I was for years, and don't forget it. Joe, my kids, and radical politics were my life, in that order. I wasn't on my own list of priorities."

"But now you do know! You do! I feel you're pretending. Because I know you're stronger than me."

"You mean I'm louder. How do you know I'm stronger, Beth? Because you haven't seen me break yet?"

"You don't get this angry at the others . . ."

Wanda shrugged with a tired smile. "Think I ask more than you can give?"

Beth was embarrassed. "It takes me a long time to do what I have to, sometimes. Like learning to fall."

"Think how much slower I am. You're twenty-three. I'm thirty-seven. In a year you won't have any more to learn from me and you'll be able to take over a great deal of what I do."

"Me? I couldn't. . . . I'd feel paralyzed."

"You're learning to move and express and think in motion. I'm telling you, in a year. Oh, don't look terror-stricken. The group will be functioning by then, everyone will be doing what I do now. I couldn't stand it if I thought I'd have to hold everything together forever. I need more time for my boys. This way can't last, I couldn't sustain it. It wears me. Then I get to feeling sorry for myself and I want to be coddled and cuddled and fussed over. Here you are wanting me to feel like a strong woman from a circus all the time. In many ways you're stronger than I am, Beth, you just don't know it yet."

"I don't believe that! I'm learning to do things I never imagined I could begin to do. I find working with the group beautiful. I think the theater we're making is a powerful force, that makes women's truths visible and moving. But I don't have the . . . imagination, the power you have. I learn to do what I'm taught and sometimes I get an idea. That's all."

"What has imagination to do with strength? My imagination makes me afraid in the dark. It makes me constantly fantasize ten thousand ways I could lose my boys."

"Are you afraid in the dark? I mean really."

Wanda grinned crookedly. "Yes, Beth. Really and truly. Those few evenings I'm here alone, every sound turns into a burglar, a prowler. I never can sleep in a house alone. I just lie awake seeing the shadows turn into monsters. I've been that way ever since I was a child, and I'm still that way. . . . I remember nights when Joe didn't come home and I'd lie there seething. Then when I'd finally hear him, I'd pretend to be sleeping. So he wouldn't be mad."

"Oh, you remind me of Miriam. She makes such a fuss about things she does badly. Like she used to make a big thing of not being able to cook. But it's all nonsense, because when she decided she wanted to, she could. She acts out her clumsiness to disarm people, so they won't hate her for all the things she does well. You're playing that game. You're saying, 'Forgive me for being creative, see, I'm scared of the dark and being alone.' "

"I'm saying, 'Because I do something well, don't expect me to do everything well.' Don't think I'm not scared. Believe me, I find all this hard. I'm still lonely and somewhere inside it's cold."

"You have your kids, you have all of us and the troupe."

"By my age, you don't take much for granted because it's here today. I have fewer options, Beth. It'd be hard for me to get a job. I have no place to go back to. Every choice I've made to fight for change has cut off a few more choices and escapes."

After Wanda left, Beth felt she had failed her. Had been lacking in response. She sat on at the table with her chin dug into her chest. It was so much easier for her to respond to Women than to another woman. She did not know whether she was more afraid she could not respond to Wanda or that she could. She did not even know how to tell if Wanda wanted her to open up as a friend or as a lover, or if there was a difference.

She found it easy to love Wanda when they were all working, easy to feel her, easy to express affection; and difficult when they were alone. The more confidence Wanda expressed in her, the more scared Beth was, as if any respect were a burden more terrible than the contempt she was used to. Sooner or later she must fail Wanda, because who was she? Only Beth. She tried to fight that self-fulfilling prophecy of disappointment. She was able to do more and more that she wanted to, and to want to do more yet. But still there were many little worms of self-hatred and doubt and fear nibbling on her. She struggled against those voices of despair. But the struggle never seemed to be over. Each little victory was a little victory and nothing more. Sometimes she imagined herself giving up. Collapsing. She would fall down and refuse to get up. She would huddle in a catatonic knot and never again would she force herself to do one single thing.

Wanda had told her once about the pillar saints and she thought what a magnificent cop-out. She would run off to a desert. She would sit on the top of a pillar in rain and sun and sleet and never again do anything whatsoever except contemplate the air and the inside of her mind.

She wanted to love Wanda, yes, but safely, without demands, from a distance. She wanted Wanda for her own loud, strong, vigorous dark Madonna. Part of her froze and tucked in when Wanda wanted to make demands back, when Wanda wanted to talk about her aching legs or to worry aloud about her sons or to be sullenly angry and defeated: when Wanda asked her to be her friend.

New Year's Eve the troupe, now calling itself Traveling Women's Theater, did a performance at a community center. Afterward, Beth went to Miriam's party, as she had promised. The house throbbed light and music and every room felt crowded. She found Miriam in the kitchen talking closely with Dorine, by the sink full of empty bottles and glasses.

"With women like you and me, Dorine," Miriam was saying, shaking back her hair with a wide gesture, "it's a race between outgrowing your adolescent masochism or having it outgrow you—consume you utterly. It's awfully lonely after a while being the bighearted earth mother, on tap, loving a man who can't see any good reason ever to marry you!"

"But I think I have it licked. I don't need to hurt to feel I'm connected to somebody. I don't only admire men who piss on me. Really. I'm into my own work and I haven't that much energy left to embroider things and brood. . . . Hi, Beth. How did the show work out?"

Together they drifted back toward the living room, where the phonograph was roaring. Just at that moment Laverne, regal in a long bottle-green velvet dress, made an entrance with Tom trailing behind her with a small, inturned smile, watching the reactions to her. She was beautiful and artificial as an orchid from a florist's refrigerator. Beth found her strange to regard, as if Laverne had become something to hang on the wall or pin to a Christmas tree: all green and gold, with her hair like wood and her eyelids green and her lips shiny and her face frozen in an expression of simpering disdain aimed at no one. She walked to be admired. Tom ambled along to the side and a little back, almost parodying her progress and watching for admiration.

He had her back. He had her dressed as she should be. He was exacting a tribute from the others and from her, a slow revenge for the year of separation that would not be any the less enjoyable for the fact that she would probably never recognize it. Her glance touched Beth and switched away. A moment later Tom gave her a big smile and his hand dropped heavily on her shoulder, he kissed her before she could dodge away. "How are you doing, Bethie? Long time no see." He did not wait for an answer. Laverne had paused at Phil, lounging in the doorway with a glass in one hand and the other playing with the fringe on the vest of Sue, a secretary at Logical who was flirting almost desperately with him. Laverne stood until she had drawn his attention. She had just begun to talk to him when Tom took her elbow and led her onward.

Just beyond, Jackson was shaking hands with Neil, both smiling with good will and great malaise. Jackson questioned Neil about his work, older student trying to put the younger professor at ease. Neil seemed to be explaining something at great length. That mutual pretense for Ryan had forced Miriam to invite Jackson and him to come. Beth stood awhile holding a glass and looking for anyone she knew free to talk, anyone at all she could look at, to escape the nakedness of standing alone at a party. An hour earlier she had stood among strangers and acted a baby, acted a bear, acted a secretary, acted an unwed mother. She had roared and wept and flung herself down. She had spoken at length. She had died. Before all those strangers.

But now she was Beth with a stiff smile stretching her leather face into a grimace. She was the single most conspicuous person in the room, with no one to talk to. She would stand there, a neon wallflower, and no one would address a word to her but people would saunter back and forth through her bones.

She wished passionately that she were back in the commune, in her room. She could not escape the archway. There was Miriam dancing now with Phil, they were being haughty and languid and menacing. They were flirting and acting out an elaborate seduction. They were doing karate without touch.

Miriam was laughing with her body while her eyes shone and her hair stood on end. She was hot and flushed. Joy radiated from her like steam. She was totally enjoying herself, having forgotten the party and everyone, including Neil. Beth enjoyed watching them. It gave her something to do that explained why she was standing alone.

Then she happened to glance at Neil. He was trying to look amused but not succeeding. He looked irritated, he looked worried, he looked scared. Perhaps he had never seen Miriam dance; it did not fit into their life together. He looked at her as if she had taken leave of her senses and begun throwing dishes around the room. His forehead puckered in a taut seam.

Miriam danced with anyone willing. After a couple of numbers, Phil would go off for a drink and pause to check out Dorine. Sometimes they danced. But Miriam never sat down. She was high on the dancing. She could have been the woman Beth had seen so long ago, dancing at the street fair in Pakistani pants and a top with no back. She imagined Miriam dancing with Traveling Women. Miriam radiated energy, as Wanda did when they were on. Miriam was more beautiful dancing than she ever was still: and Neil did not like it. He saw that she was paying him no attention, that she did not act like his wife and the mother of his child. She was so involved in dancing she had nothing left over to care what she looked like or who watched or whether her hair was flying or she was sweating or whether other people at her own party were enjoying themselves. This was not the sort of party where everybody got going. Mostly these people stood talking and observed the dancers as if they were an exhibition.

"Really, look at her," Sue said to Efi. "You'd think she could dance with her husband once in a while, for form's sake."

But Neil did not dance. He did not know how. The crease on his forehead deepened, he fidgeted with his beard and looked lost and unhappy. Tom was talking with Jackson but his eyes stayed on Laverne dancing with Ted from Logical. Laverne had only three motions but she made sure she looked graceful doing them. Ted danced as if his behind were on a bumpy road and his arms disconnected halfway down. He kept his eyes fixed on Laverne's belly and grinned without mirth. They made Beth nervous and she turned back to Tom and Jackson, who had shifted. She could see Jackson's sad emblematic face turned to the dancers. He too was watching, watching Phil finish his beer and come to claim Miriam.

Miriam paid attention always to the music but she did not pay that much attention to any of her partners except Phil. Beth wondered if anyone could see them and not know they had been lovers for a long, long time. They played. Between them was sensitivity to one another's intentions, and a humor expressed through both bodies. Parodies were picked up at once and refined. Neil stared and frowned and brooded. She felt coming off him not so much jealousy as fear, fear of the sudden unknown wild woman, dismay, roles confounded.

Several times Beth caught Jackson's eyes but he did not approach and she could not seem to move. She felt stifled. Not only was she literally choked with the smoke and pounded by the loud music and loud talk—everyone was shouting and a few people from Logical had noisemakers— but she found herself rooted by the archway. She had nothing to say to these people. She felt awkward and ugly and, yes, sorry for herself pinned like a plain brown moth to the arch. Everywhere men were on the make looking over the women and making their selections for the remainder of the night. Everywhere men and women cooped in constricting marriages were wriggling through the night's narrow cracks. What had she come for?

Phil and Miriam were swooping back and forth among the other dancers, doing a sort of war dance, when Miriam swung too wide and her outflung arm caught Tom, standing close by. His drink spilled forward on her. The glass fell and broke.

Neil pushed forward at once, grasping her shoulder. "Now look. You've spoiled your dress."

"The cleaner will get it out. I can change. I'm sorry! Let me pick up the glass."

Dorine ran off to the kitchen. "I'll get it."

"Well, don't stand there dripping." Neil urged her out of the room ahead of him. "Running to and fro, bouncing around like a child. How much have you had to drink tonight? Didn't you see how people were staring?" His voice was low but it had an edge that would cut paper cleanly.

"I was just having a good time. . . . The dress isn't ruined . . . I'll change. . . . It's only a glass, Neil."

Dorine knelt picking up the pieces and mopping at the spilled liquor. Neil was still pressing Miriam through the crowd to the stairway, his hand in the small of her back. "You act like a child allowed to stay up late. Hurling yourself around and trying to make everyone look at you. Really, when you drink too much you become an exhibitionist!" Up the stairs they went and out of the party. Neil no longer looked sour. Miriam looked upset, confused, but Neil looked relieved. His forehead lost its seam of tension. Beth did not think that Miriam would dance any more that night. Upstairs he went to select the dress she would put on, and when Miriam came down again Beth suspected she would be feeling in the wrong. She would be ashamed. Already as Miriam climbed the steps the swing was gone from her walk. Embarrassed, she hurried out of sight, just ahead of Neil.

"Did you see that?" Phil asked her. "Papa spank. Jesus."

Jackson turned abruptly from Jaime, who was showing him a wire puzzle, and headed out of the living room. Beth watched him go to the study where the coats were piled and then she went after him. "You don't have to speak to me tonight," she said at his elbow. He jumped, turned and saw her. "Just so long as you take me along."

He cleared his throat. "A bargain. Can you find your coat?"

In a clumsy rush to avoid speaking, for she did not know what to say, forcing herself upon him in panic and despair, Beth stuffed her arms any which way into her jacket and muffled herself in her scarf and pulled on her gloves and trotted after Jackson. He stiffly held the door wide and they went out without saying good-by to anyone. Striking across the lawn of unbroken snow to the corner, his step was long and loping. The boom of the music drifted muted from the windows that laid out piers of light on the snow.

"I hope you don't mind walking," he said gruffly. "No choice. Unless you can fly like the little bird you sometimes imitate? . . . Now why did I go there? Why? Don't tell me. In fact, don't talk. At midnight I turn into a scarecrow."

As they passed under the street light Beth looked sideways. What on earth was she doing with him, tall, unspeaking, his head bowed into his collar for warmth, his hands jammed in the pockets of his stained worn trench coat which was all the coat she had ever seen him wear, spring, winter or fall? It was cold and they had a long walk ahead. She was glad for her jacket, her only luxury: it was a quilted nylon navy

blue jacket, lightweight and warm in the sharpest wind, filled
with down: a blue padded jacket that always made her feel
irrationally but pleasantly like a Chinese peasant.

Another block and another through streets of black
shadow and white snow, in cold like a frequency too high
to be heard that attacked her nerves. She felt like giving
him up. But where would she go and how would she get
there? As they were crossing the Charles, the church bells
and sirens and car horns announced the end of the year,
the beginning of the new. He did not pause or look at her.

With sharp assertion she put her arm suddenly through
his. Startled, he tightened the stance of his arm. But she
could think of nothing to say. Without a word he was taking
her back to Pearl Street and that, after all, had to be what
she intended in leaving with him: although she could never
tell him that she had had nothing so much in mind as to
escape the party where she had no small talk, no ready flirtation, nothing to do except watch and experience a growing
discomfort. It was the commerce of sexual selection and
manipulation, prancing and infighting, that made the whole
room menace her, shouting this was how things were, ugly,
eternally ugly, and never could they be changed. She could
not tell him that she had not so much intended to pick him
up as to change what she was stuck staring at. As they turned
onto Pearl Street, she dragged on his arm. He looked down
then and cleared his throat. "Want to come up? For coffee?"

To get warm. "It's so cold tonight." The small victory of
forcing speech out of him sapped her defiance and she was
glad to follow the bleak stained tails of his trench coat upstairs. He walked into the apartment snapping on every light,
past the neat cot with the Mexican blanket, past the doors
of his room and Phil's. Now slowly he went before her down
the step to the kitchen. On the table a chessboard stood with
a partially played game. He looked it over cursorily before
stowing it on top of the refrigerator. Then he put on a pot for
instant coffee.

"Who do you play chess with now?"

Eyes the color of dark honey under his raised brows. "She
did teach me to play. . . . Oh, John or Rick, from Going-to-
the-Sun. But I always beat them. I've got much better. Do
you play?"

Beth shook her head no. "I have no talent for playing
games."

"That could be refreshing." His smile lit and was gone. He sat down across from her. He wore one of his blue work shirts, the button gone from one cuff and that sleeve partly rolled up, leaving his forearm bare, sallow and hard as knotted wood. "It bothers you to see Tom with his wife?"

"Tom Ryan?"

"I don't mean Tom Thumb. Thought you didn't play games?"

"I just couldn't believe you meant him. I don't like the way he looks at his wife, that's all, and he doesn't mean well by Miriam."

"I saw you looking at them." With a somber knowing half-smile. "It's hard to forgive yourself for being wise afterward."

"Tom? That meant so little. Are you wise afterward?"

He got up. "Come on, I'll put on some music. What would you like to hear?"

"Mainly you talk. I'm tired of the inside of my head tonight." Beth followed him to the living room.

"No more rock music. Seems like we've forgotten to listen to anything else for seven years. I used to be into jazz. I used to love baroque music. That's how we'll welcome in the new year—with something sane and joyful, like Torelli." Then he took a seat in his swivel chair by the door-made-desk.

Beth kicked off her shoes and lay on the cot, propping the pillows behind her head. If he found her position provocative, let him act on it.

"You were looking sad tonight. If it wasn't Tom, who is it?"

"Just me. That party brought out all my fears. All the little worms." Beth heard her voice shaking and clenched her hands in futile annoyance.

He flicked a burnt match into a cup, sucking on his pipe. "Cry if you want to. You sound close to it."

"Will you comfort me?"

He contracted to stillness. "I wouldn't know how."

Beth smiled. "Then what's the good of crying?"

"I thought women were supposed to enjoy that sort of thing."

"Oh, did you, now? That must be a comforting idea for *you*." She looked at him through her lashes. "You get ten points for turning the conversation on me right off. I wasn't the one who hightailed it out of there. I just came along."

"For the ride?" He ducked his chin, smiling. "Some scotch? Nothing to mix." Unfolding himself to his feet, he fumbled under the desk and came up with a bottle. Beth reached out. Jackson started to hand it to her, then paused. "Glasses." He brought in two shot glasses, holding hers quivering with scotch till Beth got up to take it. Then he sat down on the cot, stuffing the pillow away behind him and resting his feet solidly on the floor. "You go sit in the desk chair."

"Why?" Beth stood over him grinning.

"Because I said so. Behave."

"I was comfortable."

"I wasn't."

She sat down beside him. He finished his shot and put the empty glass between, frowning with all the lines of his eyes and mouth, like the intricate grain in good wood. "Don't provoke me, Beth. Something will happen."

"Let it. What on earth else are we here for?"

"No." He took his head in his hands. "Will you please not make matters worse?"

"Why is that worse? Why bring me here?"

"I don't know." He spoke into his hands. "I'm guilty sometimes of double-think. I wanted not to be alone."

"Well, you aren't." Firmly she took hold of his hands and, kneeling, tugged them from his face. "Don't you find me at all attractive?"

"Shut up. Drink your whiskey."

"Fine idea." She drank off the glass, gagging. "We can both get a little drunk and then it will be all right."

"I'll put you out!"

"Miles from my home, in the cold and the snow?"

"Then stay and be unhappy with me. But do it quietly like a good person and listen to Torelli." He leaned back, his eyes half closed, his fingers tensed around the shot glass propped on his chest.

She listened, but the wall was hard. After a while she let herself down, resting her head on his thigh. Slowly his hand came down to burrow in her hair, stroking, wandering, knotting around the roots. Strong wiry hand, cold at first, taking warmth from her. She lay still, concentrating on the music and his hand. She had guessed right, she did like for him to touch her. Gratefully she lay under his hand, which slid to her nape, held in a stronger grip, then withdrew to the hair and the safety of that fleshless caress.

Yes, it would be like that, cool, quiet, remote. She could share a part of her life with him and he would not crush her. She imagined a relationship with him that would be almost ascetic; they would come together without pressure now and then and they would talk a great deal. He would not overwhelm her or threaten her, but rather quietly they would be together. He did not seem to want much of the world's goods. She thought she felt in him some fastidious, reluctant, Puritan iron that would not swamp her with demands. Miriam had wanted him to love her, to want to marry her; but she only wanted a tangential cool caring. Slowly she turned toward him, her cheek against his thigh, and gently touched his chest with her fingers.

"Behave, or I'll put you in the desk chair." He gave her hair a sharp tug.

"Ow! It won't do to treat me like a mischievous child. You'll have to talk. Why not?"

"I don't love you."

She banged her head vindictively on his thigh. "What makes you think I want you to? Is it still Miriam?"

"It's me, me, the way it's always been!" He tangled his hand in her hair and turned her head so she could no longer see him. "I'm much older than you are, Beth—"

"Too old to go to bed with me. I understand—ow!"

"I do not provoke!" He pulled her hair again, laughing deep in his chest.

"I do!" She sat up. "Stop that or I'll fight back!"

"I though you were already. By the way, why don't you grow your hair out? It would be even softer."

"Why, would that remind you of Miriam too?"

They faced each other hostilely. At his movement she jumped, but he picked her up and, standing easily under the burden, started across the room. "Anything human reminds me of something." Dropping her in the desk chair, he stepped back. "I'm not treating you like a child, I'm treating you like a woman. You've sneaked and grown into one. That's the exact trouble."

She stopped her ears. "Don't flatter! I hate it! If you wanted to, you would. You just don't want to, and that's all."

Leaning against the desk, he waited for her to put her hands down. "I can't take advantage of a mood and a reaction—"

"Why not? I'm willing to."

"Nine out of ten men would be too."

"Don't you dare congratulate yourself on your virtue! It just means not giving me what I ask for."

"Besides, Phil might come home."

"We can go in your room and shut the door."

"No! No! No!" Gesturing widely in dismissal, he banged his elbow on the desk. "You don't know who you are yet. I know myself too well."

"You don't know me."

"Can't you imagine what it's like after you've run through yourself? I know the gambits open to me. There are some I won't repeat. The pain outweighs the pleasure." With a heavy shake of his head he went to the next room, where the needle had been beating its head against the record label, and put on a Bach cantata. Reaching into the bookcase, he pulled out his stash and began rolling a joint.

"What are you scared of? I'm not going to make big demands or expect much."

"That's what they all say"—he passed her the joint, holding in the smoke and the end of his sentence—"the night before the morning after."

"Oh, don't be so pseudo knowing. We're going on tour soon. Isn't that safe enough? Only the king who murdered every woman he slept with had a surer thing."

He grinned. "If you kept this up for a week, I bet I'd give in. . . . I can't imagine you being an actress."

"I'm not, in an individualistic sense. I don't think what we do would mean much to you."

"Does it mean much to you?"

"Yes!"

"So fierce. See, you are young." He rolled a new joint.

"Wanda's your age. Commitment isn't always naïveté."

"Maybe she's a slow learner. . . . You must imagine the world is covered with time and time is thick. Very thick. There have to be a great many people to burn up that time . . . like candles slowly eating the oxygen in a room."

"If we expect little and take what we can get tonight, why will we be disappointed?"

"You can't expect as little as I give. You don't see me."

"I could say the same. What do you want?"

"Nothing I can have." The record played. They smoked down the second joint. "The night's ration. All things in measured poverty. Besides, in its way it's been pleasant. We've distracted each other."

Whether it was the dope or the Bach or simply fatigue, she was more relaxed. But not yet defeated. What would he do if she reached over and kissed him?

"Why are you smiling?"

"Lean forward and I'll tell you."

The wary, affectionate glance of an old adversary/friend. Time seemed to have flattened, as if she had been trying to seduce him for years, and there was pride in her persistence as in his denial.

At length he stood. He rose and stretched to the ceiling, scratching himself thoroughly all over his chest. "You sleep in here, on this good old cot. This is a virtuous house, and it's time for bed. I gather that Phil is not going to honor us with his presence tonight."

She lay restlessly at first, dully colored geometric shapes forming on her tired eyes. However, it was from a sound sleep she woke to make out after a moment Jackson, in briefs and undershirt, standing like an indecisive stork at the foot of the cot. As he remained there still, brooding on her from the dark, she finally whispered, "I'm awake."

"Well, go back to sleep. It's good for you."

"Why are you up then? Come in and get warm."

"I had to piss."

"In my room?" She sat up, the sheet slipping forward. "Are you cold?"

"As the grave." His grin was skeletal in the moonlight. He took hold of her foot through the blanket and squeezed it. "So cold nothing will ever warm me. Good night, sweet Beth, and pull those covers up." She heard his chuckle as he padded away, and the dry creak of his door as he shut it.

Clutching her knees, she sat up staring into the dark. From her lack of success she certainly couldn't plan on making it a habit to seduce men. She felt her first attempt a total failure. Sighing with disgust, she lay down again. The whole commerce between men and women was too complicated and exhausting, composed of boxes and blind alleys and dead ends. She should have gone from the community center back to the house with the rest of her troupe and had a nice warm celebration. They would have been drinking warm glögg and rehashing the performance and dancing together and eating gingerbread that Sally made. She should have been with them, her tribe and her children, but instead she had been pursuing the cold ghost of a fantasy. Though she woke again twice in the night, no one walked through the dark toward her.

27

Like a Great Door Closing Suddenly

Miriam felt alive again. She felt as if she had been sleep-walking in twilight and now she had burst through a filmy but stifling barrier into full light. For the first time in a couple of years she had no trouble losing weight. She even had less difficulty sleeping, although the easy sleep she had known seemed gone forever. The inability to sleep during late pregnancy had melted into the early months with Ariane, when she had had to stumble out of bed for the 2 A.M. feeding and the 6 A.M. feeding. She woke at boards creaking, voices in the street, branches scraping the siding, slight sounds that never reached Neil beside her. Her nerves had been retrained. Even asleep she felt responsible and strained to hear her child.

Neil felt the energy in her and seemed worried, mistrustful of it. She could feel him watching her. Most of his comments took the form of whether she was doing enough for Ariane. She tried to use her new energy to come closer to Neil, to capture a new intimacy, but somehow she had not managed to show him what she was trying to do, and he saw her attempts as irrational demands.

"What do you mean, be more open? Open about what? I'm not withdrawn, I'm thinking about a technical idea."

Yet she could not feel him loving her as before. Sometimes when she pushed on him to be closer, more open, they quarreled. Usually then she would cry and they would be reconciled. Neil never wept. She did not think he thought the more of her for crying. Perhaps he took it as a sign she was sorry she had pushed on him.

Ariane reached out like a vast hot wet fist and clutched

her. "Mommy," said Ariane. She was Mommy. She was the source of warmth and food and comfort, she was a blanket, she was a breast, she was the heart beating. That felt good. She was also hateful Mommy, tyrant Mommy, Mommy the wall to be pounded on. Ariane was a year old. She was lovely with dark brown curly hair and enormous brown eyes, chubby and vigorous and loud. She wanted what she wanted with an instant passion, a compressed willfulness that came down on Miriam like a club. She could not believe she had been that forceful a baby. Ariane wanted with a passion that amazed Miriam. Ariane wanted to grab at a scarf that Dorine was wearing, wanted to clutch a shiny lighter a guest had used and dropped on the coffee table, wanted to touch, to taste, to handle—wanting entirely, with her whole passionate body, violently craving.

Ariane was good-natured and laughing and rosy. She was also quick to lose her temper. She would pound with her fat fists. She would grow red in the face and scream. How she could scream! Miriam got a headache in five minutes from Ariane's screaming. Neil would slam out of the room and shut himself in his study, telling her she was spoiling their child. If all else failed Ariane would hold her breath. She would hold her breath until she was blue in fury. See, she said, with her body, I am killing myself to punish you! Hateful Mommy! Hateful Daddy!

How could such a small body contain such will? "My little tiger," Miriam crooned, cuddling her. Ariane talked now, some in words and some in sounds. She did not yet walk. She stood from time to time and sat down hard on her behind with a yelp that frightened Neil. She was an active creeper but seemed to have no desire to walk. That worried Neil more than her, for he remembered Sonia reminiscing that she had been close to a year and a half before she walked. He insisted she ask the pediatrician what to do. But when Ariane fell, he rushed to her in a fear that Ariane caught at once, and cried harder.

Somehow Ariane did not resemble what Miriam had imagined a baby would be. She was cuddly but her character was strong, passionate as the heroine of a grand opera. You came out of me, Miriam brooded over her daughter, but she did not understand how Ariane could be hers and Neil's. She was healthy and fierce. Whenever Ariane was not sleeping, she could be heard singing to herself, talking, yelling, screaming, burbling, laughing, roaring. Daily she learned new words, and Neil was proud. He loved to show off her new ability to talk and talk before others. Everyone said how bright and darling she was. When she spoke, both of them shut up to listen.

It was ridiculous to be jealous of her own baby: no one ever before had been so unnatural. She was deeply ashamed. But sometimes she was jealous of the attention Neil paid Ariane in the precious evenings, the precious Sundays. All those hugs and kisses she would have liked. She felt a maid-servant to her child, invisible behind the stroller, behind the playpen. She was appalled to find herself so selfish, so weak as to be jealous of Neil's pride in Ariane. Sometimes, un-guarded, she remembered her depression on coming home from the hospital, and guilt laid her flat. Something vital was lacking in her, obviously. She had tried and tried to be a good woman, but something must be missing. All those people who had told her she was not a real woman, flawed, they had known something. She imagined Ariane turning and telling her what a bad mother she was.

She loved Ariane. She never had to be told to hold her, to cuddle her, to caress her. She had never loved anyone so much. Ariane had for her a radiance, always. When she picked Ariane up and held her, words gushed from her. Love rushed from her in silly sweet names: Bundle of Life, Tiger-Tiger Burning Bright, Ketsela, Chickadee-dee-dee, Ary-annie-poo. Ariane was what she was working on instead of the anti-missile missile project, and no sane person could deny that Ariane was a better way to spend her time and energy!

Yet days spent cooing and babbling to Ary-annie-poo-poo-poo, cleaning, washing dishes, doing laundry, changing wet pants, saying No-No and mopping up spilled food, left her weary and untouched. Exhausted and mentally starved. When Neil came home she fell on him with teeth and claws, hungry for love, hungry for meaning, starved for intelligence and stimulation and content—ravenous for the world outside.

Neil felt entitled to rest and pampering. "After all, I pulled us out of financial disaster. I had to tread a careful path, but I brought us through." The West Coast firm had bought out Logical, name, equipment, staff, and contracts, with a two-for-one exchange on the stock: now Neil had considerable stock in that company worth real money on the exchange, though he was legally bound not to sell any of that stock for two years. But at current prices his stock was suddenly worth a hundred and fifty thousand dollars: that silly paper. She felt stunned and way outside. So that was how you made money in software: you sold out an ailing company. That was why Abe and Neil had forced Dick out. In the meantime Neil was extracting himself slowly from the company, would soon be consulting only at a handsome price while teaching at M.I.T.: the sort of setup he had been wanting all along. He complained of the strain of learning the departmental situation at school while managing the politics of withdrawing from Logical. He felt good but over-taxed.

Often after supper he went into his study and didn't come out. Sometimes one or more of his graduate students appeared to work with him, closeted there. When he emerged, he wanted her there. "Don't you want me to succeed now? Ever since I got my degree, I've been wanting to get back into a good technical university, but I'll have to carve out my own niche. It's a competitive atmosphere, don't have any illusions about it." He often seemed to forget she had spent years in that department. "They're great snobs about people who've worked in industry, when there isn't one who could live in the style they're accustomed to, if they didn't do con-sulting. . . . Still, it's a better atmosphere. No more worrying about the bank, about how to pay all those salaries every month. But the adjustment isn't easy, and I expect help from you. Isn't this what you want me to do? You were the one who was so down on Logical. Now you complain when I work late. This is an exciting step forward, but it's monstrously hard. Do you want me to fail?"

Then everything cleared. She found her face again, her self: Phil came back. Oh, Phil was still Phil, still Philip-sparrow, helpless and in bad shape. He talked out his life in castles of floating words, he was reforming himself and his existence as usual. But he was there: he looked at her, he saw her, he gave her back to herself.

She was half grateful to Tom Ryan in retrospect for still thinking enough of her to try to upset her. Most of the pro-fessors and computer professionals she met looked right through her. Married women were twice invisible. No one heard what she said in arguments. She might say something startling or witty or even rude, but the conversation would go on. This is Mrs. Stone, and hello, Mrs. Stone, what does your husband do?"

Well, what did she want them to ask? What *she* did? Change her daughter. This is Mrs. Stone, née Berg, who used to be in the artificial intelligence lab at Project MAC, who used to do research on heuristic programing techniques, who used to be a person: why, she even has a doctorate, moldering in a drawer.

She kept hovering mentally before that closed study door. It was all right for Neil to do that. It was acceptable for Neil to be selfish about his time and his energies and his desires, to withdraw and preserve himself. It was all right for him to emerge demanding love and comfort and amusement. Because he was the breadwinner.

But by virtue of ceasing to earn, Miriam ceased to be able to be selfish. She could still remember her exacerbated anger with Philip just before that last argument on Pearl Street, because he had dared to wake her in the middle of the night when she had to go to work in the morning. Her time had become valueless. When a person is paid for her time, she thinks it worth something. But Miriam worked all day and was paid nothing but her keep. To think she had dared yell at Philip for abusing her, for getting in the way of her work. How uppity she had been, how wonderfully sure of her own worth in at least that area. Every pay check had validated her pretensions.

But Phil restored her continuity. He spoke to her individual mind. He remembered how she had been. They could go on anecdotally for hours. Phil said they had gone soft. "Jail made a gossip out of me and housework has done it to you." But for all that, they continued with vigor.

California had broken something in Phil. Perhaps he would mend, perhaps he could not. In bits and pieces he told her, not once but again and again. If talking about their mutual past was sociable and comforting, talking about his recent past terrified him. His face would tighten, the color would leak from his voice. His eyes would go blind and he would lick his lips. The Philip who had come back to her was not the man she had left. He was beautiful to her as Ariane was beautiful—both radiant creatures whose every gesture charmed her—but he was not the same expansive prince of fantasies.

He had really gotten into smack in Berkeley, really strung out. He had been busted, he had kicked in jail cold turkey where he had no choice, and he had served his time. He had come out at last, but with something missing.

He treated himself with a new wariness, as if he had discovered he was made of glass. He did not even drop acid or mescaline. He smoked grass and he drank wine and beer. He would touch nothing else. He was afraid. "It's in me. My old man was an alcoholic. Maybe it's all genetic. A piece is missing, a chemical piece. Dorine says that could be it."

"She said it was theoretically possible."

"I have the feeling that if I touch smack again I'll go right back where I was. I want it. I want to be there. That's the truth."

"If only you'd eat. You're so skinny. All bones. You were never this thin before. It isn't healthy."

"Fasting is good for you. It cleans you out. Every time I think I'm getting sick, I go on a three-day fast and take vitamin C and fluids and I don't get sick. It feels beautiful inside."

Miriam found Phil's new health regimen silly. She fed Phil as much as she could, but he remained skinny. He said he needed loving, not so much bread and butter.

"Dorine loves you. What more do you want?"

"You know what more. A lot more. Dorine likes me. And you, do you get all the loving you want?"

"I have to go down to the market and get meat for supper. You want to come along or stay here with Ariane?"

Phil was a source of strength and excitement, but he had the uncanny ability to put his finger on her sores. Not enough loving. Maybe no woman at home ever felt she was loved enough. Loving for a living, for a profession. The central terror of her life was that Neil would stop loving her. Every time she heard neighborhood gossip about husbands who up and left their wives, she wondered. Laverne always passed on those stories. Their loving was not what it had been. Neil got angry if she said that. "After all, we both have other things to do beside sit around and moon at each other." But she felt . . . not so cherished. They made love less often. They made love less often than she wanted to. A week, ten days, two weeks would pass. From jokes that Laverne made, she knew that her problem was hardly unique. Everything she read on the subject suggested that if he was losing sexual interest in her it was her fault. She was not actively seductive enough. It was true she had let herself gain weight, but she had lost most of it. She tried to find time to exercise and sometimes succeeded. Oftener she got to dance with Phil to the phonograph, and that was a good workout. Her problems felt dull to her, housewives' problems. They were jokes that comedians told on television and cartoons depicted in magazines.

But Phil had snapped her out of her lethargy. She was finding her way out of the magic circle of inaction. One night she even sat up and finished the red dress she'd started when she was pregnant with Ariane and spending afternoons with Sally. She was thin enough for it to fit her: another small benchmark.

She put on the new/old dress that had sat upstairs in pins for fourteen months and greeted Neil in it. He seemed pleased to see her prepared so formally to greet him, although he pretended to be suspicious. "Sure there isn't some little thing you want?" Indeed, the evening went as it was supposed to. He did not work, they listened to music together sitting on the couch, sipping sherry. They discussed Ariane and his department. From her days as a student, she passed on some stories and observations edited because she did not want him telling her she was picking at people again. He showed her the rough draft of a paper he was writing, and she worked out some examples and changed the structure around. The pencil jumped across the paper. For such a long time she had done nothing technically. He was excited by one of her examples and said she had really been a help.

On the couch he sat with his arm around her. They even went up to bed early and made love, although he could not forbear bringing up the matter of the son it was time to be starting, when she went to put in her diaphragm. He did not go on about it and they made love well. Maybe he was right and she did not try hard enough to please him. Still the evening felt . . . artificial, manipulated. She had pleased him and he had loved her. Working on his paper had felt good. Why wasn't she taking more of an interest in his courses and his research? But she wanted something of her own to do too.

Neil and Phil did not like each other. It was best if they did not meet, so it did not become an issue. Phil had to be managed so he didn't confront Neil, for he enjoyed irritating him. She did not of course see Phil secretly, but she simply did not call Neil's attention to how often she let Phil come over, how often they went out in the afternoons together. She was a neighborhood scandal but she did not care. Let the women she had used to sit with in the playground with their carriages give her those knowing looks: what they knew were lies and she did not need them any more. All their talk of how to stop thumb sucking and what to do about head banging! She had her poet back.

"I'm not a poet any more, face it. I wanted to *be* a poet, but not to write poems, because that was work. The whole way I was using words was sick—to manipulate people and the world. To control. To make my fantasies materialize."

"I liked your songs. Except the awful ones about me."

"I can't stand any of them. I don't want to use my head that way any longer."

"Well, what do you want to do?"

"I'm learning carpentry. I want to work with wood. I want to do simple useful things with my hands and keep my rotten fucked-up head out of it. I don't trust how I use words."

"Forever, you just want to build shelves and cabinets?"

"Maybe I'll learn to make furniture. I have an idea for a bed that would be beautiful, Miriam. I just know I don't want to use my head in that old controlling, conning way any more. Don't you think I manipulate you less? Don't you think I'm straighter with you?"

In a way. There was always an oblique struggle. He wanted her and she could not let him express that directly. She could not let that come out or it would be bad. She would have to reject him. If things did not stand out there between them bald and stark, they could go on and after a while he would forget the old nostalgic wanting. She had to see him. She wanted to feel she was helping him.

But the struggle could not get too close to the front of her attention. Somewhere in her Phil was still Phil and it was natural to touch him, it had always been natural. She never let herself think about being in bed with Phil, but her body remembered him. Old sensual memories drifted up along the nerves, murmurs of old good easy and communicative sex, natural and sensual. It was not to be remembered. Occasionally she dreamed of him, vividly. She enjoyed her sexual dreams: no one could make her guilty about what she felt in sleep.

She must not let them argue openly because she had no reasons except that she was married to Neil and he would not want her to. Neil expected her to be faithful. She had promised to be. That fidelity in that sense was a meaningless concept to her, alien, peculiar, was something she must never

let herself be enticed into discussing aloud. She was afraid
to argue with Phil, that she might not be able to defend Neil's
position. But if she gave in to Phil and to her fidelity to herself and him, then she would be guilty before Neil. Neil could
always make her feel guilty anyhow, and she would lose
some essential ground to resist the heaviest of his pressures.

"I don't like living with old Jackson any more," Phil complained, sitting sideways on a chair. "We're bound in different
directions."

"What direction is he bound in, except around his own
dead center?"

"Don't kid yourself. I find the new motivated scholar on
the make a bit of a drag. I'm telling you, he's going to crawl
back on his belly into the middle class through the doors of
the Ph.D. and rest there, hard-working and moral at last
by his own endeavors. The prodigal son. His parents are
pleased that he's teaching and passed his orals."

"Why am I not more surprised? He'll fit in."

"Maybe because that ties in with why you took him
seriously? Besides, being with him pushes me back into my
old way of using words, of dealing with people. Sometimes I
find myself responding to his bantering and making some kind
of put-down joke about Dorine. I know I don't feel that way,
but I do feel like an asshole if I make a point of not wanting
to talk about her like that. I feel like I have to defend the
relationship. He has a way of looking ironic and raising one
eyebrow. . . . Or the way he jokes about me not going to
Finnegan's. I keep telling myself, You don't have to measure
up. Fuck it with being a man according to Jackson."

"Then why don't you move out? I think there is something wrong in the way you're friends . . . in the way you
love each other. It's . . . oblique and competitive. It hems
you in."

"Why can't I move in here? All these rooms. Conspicuous
consumption. Or does The Man mean you to fill them up
with kiddies?"

"He wants more. . . . Phil, don't start teasing me about
moving in. He'd never put up with that and you know it!"

"Why not? Couldn't he use me? I could polish his shoes."

"Quit it, Phil! I mean it!"

"Alas. I know you do."

If she yelled loud enough, Phil would stop, just as he would
not persist in trying to embrace her if she gave him a good

push. But it was temporizing, keeping the globes flying through the air and never colliding. Still she could remember the first months with Ariane when she had been ground between the rigid schedule of Ariane and the rigid schedule of Neil, with no time, no space, no energy for herself.

"Is he ever jealous of me?" Phil asked her.

"Why would he be? I've never given him cause."

"Nevertheless, he is. Isn't he?"

"Jealous?" She paused, unable to find the word. "He doesn't get hot angry that way."

"No. Just coldly, persistently. Like a head cold."

"You just don't understand each other."

"Are you so sure?"

Not jealous. Possessive. They were not the same. A couple of times Neil did something that upset her, yet she could not confront him. Twice, a week apart, he came to bed quite late, after she had been asleep awhile. Always of course she awoke and spoke to him, asking him how his work had gone. Once ten days ago and once just last night he had responded by moving over and beginning to make love to her. Half asleep, she had forgotten both times to get up for her diaphragm. She suspected Neil of doing it intentionally, to get her pregnant. But she could not make an issue of it. They made love so seldom in comparison to what she would have liked, she could hardly complain. She had taken to going to bed every night now with her diaphragm already in, but that depressed her, made her think of the fact that probably that night they would again not make love. He said that she looked lovely half asleep, tousled and soft. She wondered if she was less threatening then. But she remembered too how he had loved her when she had been carrying Ariane, how tender, how concerned. . . .

In her high energy, she finally replastered the upstairs hall. She answered letters from her father's new wife—they were buying a condominium in Long Beach on the Island; from Allegra, who sent pictures of her new baby; from Neil's mother with requests for yet more pictures of Ariane; from Sally and Beth. They were on the road with the women's theater troupe. They wrote postcards from Bangor, Maine, and Attleboro, Vermont. In Bath they were busted for indecency. Later, snowed in, they sent her a letter together. Sally wrote:

You can send us a note at Goddard, we'll be there in a
month. Use the address of that commune. Tell us how you
and Ory Ann are and everybody, I wonder about Phil
sometimes with Dorine, what is happening? Though I
think Dorine knows how to take care of herself.

Dorine is worse than us at writing, she don't have time,
and I know we are not so good. We have a new children's
play we do that we like a lot, you could call it a kind
of fairy tale, it has a lot to do with how we are thinking
about when we were children and our own children.
The children are all in it as well as us. We are having a good
time traveling women like our name although people
think we are a pretty queer bunch. I never lived like this
from place to place, I see why gipsies like it. Fern at
first did not like being on the move so much though Blake
could not be better. Fern likes it too by now.

Beth wrote:

We are really a group now. Wanda was right when she
insisted we would all come to take over things she did in the
beginning for all of us. It is an exciting thing to grow
together this way, Miriam, I wish you could be here
with us. We make many mistakes still. We have an awful
tendency to get so into a new thing, to perform it
before we are ready.

In Utica last week we did a terrible show, a bomb.
It was a new piece we were still working on. We went
ahead and did it anyhow. Why do we do things like that, all
of us, when we say we know something isn't ready and
then we do it? It got off to a slow start, like glue. We lost
the audience and we could feel that. It seems as if we
responded to that by elaborating more, desperately, and
slowing the piece down even more and it just got worse and
worse! It was awful.

But we worked on that same piece (called "The Day the
Mirror Broke") for a whole week. We had this house
to work in and we have really got into it. Now it's one
of our best things and I *know* when we do it next time it
will be fantastic and powerful.

Sally is playing the guitar a lot these days and she is
good! She wrote songs for the children's play. It is nice too,
but I am less involved in it than Sally is. I want so bad

for you to see us. I can imagine you with us, dancing
and banging on the drums and chanting. I love Wanda
and I love the troupe and I wish you were with us.

I love Wanda a lot. I mean that for real! Do you understand? Don't think because she is so much older than me
that it is like mother and daughter, it isn't. It isn't anything
like anything. It is just us together inside the looser us
together.

Miriam dreamed and dreamed of something real and
external to do. She could not go back to work. Every time
that subject came up she had to agree with Neil that Ariane
could not be turned over like a puppy dog to some hired
person to sit with. She did help Neil with his papers more,
but he had regular assistants for the classes and on his
project. They regarded her as an intruder. Moreover, Neil
wasn't writing papers about the kind of research she wanted
to get into. It was all the big machine stuff she had washed
her hands of.

Whose idea? Phil perhaps thought of it or maybe she did.
She could fix the time—she had been making rye bread
and Phil decided he wanted to take a turn kneading the
dough. Then he found he liked that. It turned him on. So they
made a loaf for Phil too. Then Phil had been talking about
how great homemade bread was and how healthy it was to
eat whole-grain bread. He had been on a long slow suicide
trip, but now he was going to live with respect for his body.

It was true Phil told over his vitamins like a rosary. Once
when she was in Cambridge they had stopped at Pearl Street—
an afternoon Jackson taught—and on the kitchen table stood
rows of Phil's pills: bottles of vitamin E and vitamin A in
long oily amber capsules; bottles of desiccated liver and
vitamin C plus bioflavinoids, dolomite mineral, lecithin and
yeast tablets and kelp. On the breads, anyhow, they could
agree. They both doted on dark breads, rye and graham
flours, buckwheat, made with molasses or honey, eggs and
wheat germ.

They decided to bake bread and sell it. It was a daydream
at first to figure out the cost and how they would go about
distribution. But the more they discussed it the more passionately Miriam wanted to do it. At least she would be doing
something. She would make a little money. She would be
the bread woman. That was nothing Neil could get upset

about. It wouldn't take her out of the home or away from
Ariane. It was healthy and womanly and it even had a good
smell associated with it.

Three times a week they began to bake and distribute
bread. Monday was rye bread and Wednesday was graham
bread and Friday was mixed-grain bread. Phil and she drove
around and got health food stores to agree to handle their
bread. Phil had long conferences with people he knew in the
food co-ops in Cambridge and got two co-ops to agree to put
bread on their lists for a week or two to try it out.

"We can't figure on making money at first," she said with
cheerful pragmatism to Phil. "Not till we've built up a demand, a market. Then we can increase our quantity till we
break even and then pull ahead."

The bread business gave a rationale for their being together. They were in business, they were partners. Miriam relaxed a bit. She no longer had such a sense of juggling her
life. Phil had been properly plugged in. She did not even let
herself get too worried when her period was overdue. It had
happened before. Phil and she screamed at each other, they
made huge messes, they had catastrophes. But they enjoyed
every crisis. They had never before worked together.

Distributing the bread provided a wonderful excuse for
running around and seeing all her old freak friends, the
communes, the whole Cambridge scene. Sometimes of course
a non-event happened. A couple of times he kissed her
before she could remember why not. Basically she always
had Ariane between them.

Every so often the subject of Phil would come up with
Neil. There seemed no way she could say to Neil, "Don't
worry about Phil! I love him but I don't take him seriously."
Phil was the only person beside her baby she could play
with. About Neil she brooded as usual. Somehow Neil had
become a subject she studied. Sometimes she detested herself
for thinking in circles about him. Why couldn't they live
together in some easier, looser manner? Why must she always
be "understanding" him? He didn't spend that effort studying
her, he didn't need to. He knew what he expected of her and
only grew worried when she failed to provide it.

If only Neil would understand that she could not take
Phil seriously. Phil could hint around, but he could never
support Ariane and her. He wasn't cut out to be a husband
and father. When she was younger she had been able to

afford Phil because she was supporting herself. If only Neil would stop bothering about Phil and let her have his friendship and the bread business and a little joy and excitement in her daily life.

One of the project heads at Tech Square, Hardwick, gave Neil a piece of frozen venison. Hardwick had killed a deer in Maine and had had it in his freezer but had decided they would never finish it.

Neil was sitting at the dining-room table having the tail end of his Sunday breakfast—café au lait made with the milk heated just to scalding and the French roast fresh ground in the blender and some of her bread and jam. The way he sat was neat. His body was compact and she was always wanting to reach out to him at times like these. He remained physically attractive to her in a cozy immediate sense: she was always wanting to touch him. How often now she reached for Ariane instead, afraid of rebuff.

"Why can't we have croissants? That's a real French breakfast." His tongue touched his lip. "Lovely buttery croissants."

"But you didn't like the ones I got at the bakery."

"They weren't croissants. Just brioche dough in crescent form." He sipped the last of his coffee, daubed his carefully kept curly beard with the napkin. Then he smiled at her. Instinctively she leaned forward, still wanting to touch him. "Why don't you see if you can make them?"

"Neil, I think they're an all-day affair. You have to roll out the dough and chill it. Butter it and roll it out and chill it again and again."

"You spend all day making those breads." He visibly withdrew. Hurt? Ruffled?

"But that's my business."

His voice armored itself in mockery. "You sound like my grandmother, who used to live on the edge of Harrisburg and raise chickens. Don't you think it's a little unnecessary? We're better off than we've ever been." He mocked, but his eyes were sulking.

She did not want to argue about the bread making. "I can try to find a recipe . . ." How could he act as if she'd rejected him? Sometimes he really confused her. She cursed her mother-in-law for teaching him love was being cooked for, fussed over, provided for with cleanliness and considerable martyred bustling.

"Imagine driving up to Maine and dressing yourself in scarlet and tromping around the woods shooting cows and dogs and each other," Neil was saying. "Hardwick is so sure he's a hero for executing a deer—as if deer could shoot back! Then he won't be bothered to eat what he's killed. Probably his wife doesn't know the first thing about how to roast something that doesn't come wrapped in plastic from the supermarket. First we'll thaw it and age it a bit— let it get high. Or should you do a marinade? Anyhow, Friday night when they're here we'll serve it back to them. Poetic justice."

"You invited them for Friday? That's one of my bread days."

His eyes took on that little-boy sulk. "Friday is a traditional time to have people over. It's the weekend. If you must play at being a baker, do it another day next week."

She remembered believing when she had been getting to know Neil that his unwillingness to shed blood, his contempt for hunting and fishing and fighting, were a refusal to play traditional male roles. She did not think that any more. He disliked violence in words or action; he preferred a quiet tone of authority. After all, losing your temper was a poor tactic for getting your own way, as she had found out time and time again with him. Her emotionality would be used against her.

Phil lost his temper often. He would blow up and at times he used to threaten her with his fist. She remembered how furious she had been that time Phil had actually hit her. It was horrible to be hit. But to struggle with Neil was far more difficult, Neil could get angry, very angry, but never lose his temper, never lose his sense of strategy in the argument, never lose sight of his goal. She felt weary before him often enough, because he never seemed to doubt his habits or his taste or his predilections or his morality: he seemed to feel through and through that what he liked must be right. When she scratched granite, underneath was more granite. Something in his family and his training gave him that advantage over her, that quiet dreadful surety, the conviction of propriety and sense of moral superiority as a weapon. She could feel hurt, she could feel outraged, she could feel furious: but she could never muster that cool daily self-righteousness. It defeated her time and again. She had married him for his strength, and perhaps that was the source of it.

Friday of the roast venison and evening dinner party: she had marinated the meat as he had told her. As Neil suggested, she had looked up venison in *Larousse Gastronomique* (a Christmas present) and was referred to roebuck. She had no idea what cut of deer she had or how old the deer was, so she tried to adopt a medium strategy among the various ways of preparing lean pieces and tender pieces and tough pieces. Friday was the day they made health bread with four kinds of flour, her personal favorite though Phil preferred their rye.

They got started in plenty of time. Ariane was in an irritable, coddle-me mood, cutting a new tooth, but Phil succeeded in making her laugh a lot. The dough rose well, the second rising was up on time, and the pans went into the oven. The house smelled good. Phil was in a sunny mood and not pushing her at all but singing at the top of his lungs. Ariane was trying to walk that day and falling down a lot and screaming, but every time Phil or she came running and got Ariane moving again before she took her fall seriously. Outside the rain was coming down. The snow was gone and the first green things poking out. Miriam even managed to get time to wash her hair while Phil kept an eye on the first batch baking, and she got Ariane into bed for her afternoon nap so she wouldn't be cranky when Neil got home and could stay up a bit for the company.

The bread was in both ovens, the second batch baking while the first batch cooled, when Miriam heard an awful thump and then Ariane's scream. She did not know how she got upstairs, she was so frightened. Ariane lay on the floor beside her crib, twisted so that Miriam was sure she had broken her leg. Miriam ran to her, seized her up. Somehow Ariane had stood in her crib and climbed on the bars and managed to fall out headfirst. This was supposed to be a crib no child could fall out of, but Ariane had climbed up and fallen and struck her head. She had an ugly sore red spot that was going to be a bruise on her forehead and she was weeping and weeping hysterically. Miriam carried her to the bathroom, shouting at Phil to get out of the way, and sponged her baby. By and by it was clear that Ariane was not badly hurt, but there was that ugly bruise and she had been frightened. The falling had scared her as much as the bump, perhaps, and she clung to Miriam.

The oven had a buzzer that went off when the time was up, but in the turmoil they must not have heard it. Finally Phil said, "What's that?" He might have meant the smell or he might have meant the steady penetrating buzz that had obviously been going for a while, because the whole load of both ovens was burnt. It was not so badly charred it could not be eaten, but it was too burnt to deliver.

They wasted some time berating each other. Finally they realized there was no time to do anything good. The bread had to be delivered in time for the co-op pickups and there was no short cut in bread making and rising. They decided to cut the loaves in half and deliver half a loaf for each loaf ordered, and to give refunds on half the price.

"Fuck it. Last week we broke even for the first time!" Phil got on the phone to make sure their solution was okay with the co-op co-ordinators. They were behind schedule and she started cutting and bagging for delivery. Neil came home to the kitchen full of burnt bread, smelling like a fire, with dirty bread pans covering every flat surface, the burnt loaves only half carried out by Phil, who had just got off the phone. As soon as she saw her daddy, Ariane burst into tears and started wailing tragically. "What have you done to her!" he shouted at both of them. He got the idea she had been burnt in a kitchen catastrophe and he was not to be disabused of that until Miriam had told him three times step by step what had happened.

"Oh, this is lovely, this is charming, this is just what I need!" Neil did not raise his voice. Slowly he paced the kitchen, cutting deliberately in the path of Phil, still toting bags of burnt bread to the garbage, and Miriam, who was finishing bagging the half loaves. "What kind of madhouse is this? It stinks! It's filthy! I come home and find my child wounded. What's going on here?"

"Neil, please. Accidents happen. She isn't badly hurt—"

"Are you a doctor? How do you know? She was terrified."

"If she's going to learn to walk, she has to fall sometimes."

"Are you going to justify her injury? Are you going to say it's a good thing for her to fall on her head? Perhaps she'll fall down the steps next time you're too busy to keep an eye on her. Have you gone mad?"

"Neil, you'll frighten her more by carrying on. I'm sorry she hurt herself. I was scared myself. But she'll fall many times. She was trying to get out of her crib."

"Why weren't you on hand? What is all this nonsense? Just what do you think you're doing with this garbage all over the house? This is a sane thing for my wife to be doing?"

"This is our business! I want to do something! It doesn't take much time and this is the first time something's gone wrong."

"How many things have to go wrong before you learn? A professor's wife peddling bread from door to door. I'm tired of the mess and the confusion. Hardwick will be here in an hour and a half, and look!"

Miriam was surreptitiously signaling to Phil to leave, but Phil was being stubborn. He folded his arms, scowling. "Why are you afraid of him, Miriam? What are you so afraid of? What has he done to you?"

"Shh, Phil." She tried to wave him out. "Take the bread!"

"What does he do to make you so afraid? I demand to know why."

"Who are you to demand anything?" Neil turned on him. "What are you? What are you doing here? Why don't you go home, if you have a home?"

"Neil! He's my friend. He's here because I asked him."

"Well, why do you? This isn't a hotel or an orphanage. I've heard things about this man. I've heard he was put in jail in California for selling drugs."

"Not selling, possession," Phil drawled. "Do get your facts straight. Jail's an interesting place to visit, but I don't think you'd like to live there. Miriam knows that. I think everybody in Boston knows it except you. You'd know it too if you had any curiosity about other human beings."

"Everybody in Boston seems to know quite a bit about you. I don't want to. I don't want you around my child. I don't want you around my wife. I don't want you in my house. I don't trust you and I don't see why I should put up with you any longer. You're nothing but a parasite!"

"Neil! Stop that. Phil's my friend!"

"I'm here because she wants me here." Phil made that shaggy butting motion of his head. "I'm not going till she wants me gone. I care about her in a way you couldn't conceive of—you academic prig with your iron sense of property! You cold slimy eel wriggling through the university bottom. You don't want a woman, you want a fucking domestic staff, housekeeper, butler, nanny, pastry cook, gamekeeper, wine steward. Why don't you fuck a robot?"

"Phil, shhh! Both of you!" She waved Phil to leave. "Phil,

please leave! Leave, before you make things worse!"

"They can't be worse, don't you see that yet? How much will you take? What's wrong with you, pigeon? Wake up!"

But finally, finally, because the bread had to be delivered, Phil walked out with his chin in the air. Then she had to go dashing around the kitchen dumping the dirty bread pans into the pantry out of the way and getting supper started and picking up Ariane's toys from every place and trying to remember what she had planned for dessert. Neil had gone into his study and slammed the door.

When the Hardwicks arrived, supper was not yet ready, she was still wearing her pants smeared with dough, and when they finally sat down to the boasted feast the venison was tough and dry. She still could not tell whether she had undercooked it or overcooked it, but it was miserable. Everyone chewed and chewed and chewed the meat. Hardwick and his wife Elaine kept making terrible insincere compliments on the sauce. The meal dragged on while she picked at her plate.

When the Hardwicks finally left, Neil went up to bed without a word and she followed. She could not face cleaning up yet. She felt exhausted and curiously numb, detached from a body that felt bloated. In the bedroom she looked at Neil sitting on the bed naked clipping his toenails. He did not look at her. The teeth of the mechanism met neatly and the waxing moon of nail fell in an arc. She felt a great reluctance to get into bed, to lie down to whatever was coming. She looked at the calendar on her dresser, she brushed her hair. She could feel him behind her bunched over, gathered into himself. Yet he did not begin the cold rational attack, the listing of her errors. He said only thickly, his voice furred with emotion, as he shut out the light and lay down so that no part of him would touch her, "I don't want that man in the house."

"Neil, he doesn't come to see you. He's my friend. I'm working with him."

"I don't want him in my house. I don't want him near Ariane! I'm not making a request, I'm telling you!"

Her throat closed. Some deep new anger in his voice, a gathered violence pushing on her. After a while he added, "If you don't have sense enough to understand that men of that sort aren't suitable friends, I'll make the decision for both of us. I'm telling you this: if he comes in this house again, I'm calling the police! I'll take Ariane and stay in a hotel with her before I'll see that man around my daughter."

She lay awake all night. She was two months overdue, she was pregnant, she knew it. She could feel that quickening knot. She was embarked again. She felt as if he had said to her, "I require your right arm," had drawn a knife and performed the amputation. She knew she was bleeding. She knew she was hurt badly. But she could not feel anything except a vague surprise at how things were going in her life.

She would see Phil sometimes, but out of the house. More lies, and he would be far from the center of her life. They would not work together. She would have no bread business. She would lose him, finally. Phil would not accept being sacrificed to Neil's anger, he would not forgive. She could not forgive herself for sacrificing him, but she did not see how she could fight Neil and win.

It was different from what she had expected, so different. If she concentrated, she could remember how she had felt. She had thought Neil was lucky to get her because he was lonely and lacked skills for being close to others, and she would be close to him and help him be in touch with his own feelings and his body. She had thought she was lucky, because now she had made it as a woman, she was loved, she was safe, she was cherished and wanted. She had imagined both of them working in their field in mutual admiration and support. She had imagined that since he loved her, of course he would make some compromises: she would be able to get her way on things that mattered to her, a reasonable proportion of the time.

It seemed to her that every man she had loved had tried to protect himself from her as if she were a dangerous monster. She lay on the bed like a half-finished meal. She: who was she? Mrs. Neil Stone. Vessel carrying embryo. Miriam Berg was dead. Miriam Berg had many troubles but she had been someone to be, a person anyhow. Mrs. Stone was nobody in particular. She would not be missed, except by Ariane. Phil was right: Neil could replace her by *Larousse Gastronomique* with pushbuttons.

Lying beside Neil, she was frightened. She did not feel loving toward him, she would have liked to hurt him. But she did not dare. He had threatened her for the first time with leaving her. That was the first time he had said he would go, he would take Ariane and go. But what scared her

most in the thin dark was that he would cease loving her
even as laxly as he had been doing. In striving to survive as
a person she had angered him, she had injured him in his
sense of how things should be, and his withdrawal might last.
He created a clear unequivocal moral world of man and wife
in which she ran before his judgment like a rabbit.

As she rested her hands on her belly she had a fantasy
that she had loved Phil one afternoon, so that they had con-
ceived this baby. Phil's baby. It was empty nonsense; yet as
a fantasy it was consoling and she cherished it. This baby
is dedicated to the one I love, she thought, the one who will
never forgive me. Then she thought, I mean me.

28

Caught in the Net

After two months of being on the road, Traveling Women
rented a house on twenty-odd acres in New Hampshire, near
Berlin. They rented it early enough in the spring to get a
garden in. Sometimes they were all there for a day or two,
sometimes for weeks. One or two usually stayed home and
so did the kids. The garden had to be tended and watered,
the kids had had enough of living out of duffel bags. Everyone felt the need for a center. They renamed themselves the
Round Earth. They took turns staying home when the troupe
was touring.

Although the farmhouse was drafty and out of repair and
nothing worked well for long, Beth loved the house. It had
only one bathroom—impossible. There were too many of
them. Laura rigged up an outdoor shower at the hose connection. When the weather was warm enough, that relieved
some congestion. They dug a pit toilet and built an outhouse
over it. They began to construct a sauna bath.

Life on the farm was rough and makeshift, but they were
learning to do many things new to them. Several of them
could work on the truck, they all worked the land, they

fixed up the house. Money was in short supply. They still did a mixture of free and paid performances. Sometimes they played outdoors. Sometimes they performed in university auditoriums. Sometimes they passed the hat to the crowd that had collected, sometimes they got a nice cashable check from a bursar's office, sometimes they were paid in fruit or vegetables or maple syrup, sometimes they got only a place to sleep and a meal.

They were uneven, but their lows were not as bad as they had been and their highs were much higher. They were still learning how to use their bodies, how to use their voices, how to use their minds, how to pick up the vibrations from an audience and use them to carry the audience further. They were still learning how they felt and how to express it and create with it.

When Beth got up in the morning, she felt good. She would run outside barefoot or in tennis shoes. She would run outside and stare at the mountains and laugh. It seemed amazing that she should feel so good, that she should live with people she loved and work together with them. That she should be allowed to love Wanda and be with her. The air was clean, the birds came and she remembered Connie, who had always known their names, and wondered what had gone wrong and how David was and if he remembered them. Selling vegetables on the road one day, she made a little money and bought for the children—for Wanda's boys, really, Johnny and Luis, because they were the only ones old enough to use it—a book of birds with big colored pictures.

Beth freckled and then finally tanned for the first time. Often they worked outside naked. They were becoming less awkward when they did physical labor, although some of them, Sally for instance, had never been awkward. They raised their vegetables organically and picked berries and made preserves and kept chickens for eggs—Rhode Island Reds with feathers of bronze and stormy characters. She had never considered that chickens were actually birds, like robins and bluejays: they had their lives, they interacted, they had dramas and depressions. They would become broody and have to be snapped out of the blues by being dunked in water. Their rooster really did crow in the mornings and sometimes in the afternoons too. He was beautiful and arrogant. All their chickens were beautiful. They had also a black goat named Harriet. She gave milk which they used

as it was and also tried to make into cheese. Their cheese
was foul and slimy, but they ate it anyhow and kept trying.

They had a calico cat who came one day pregnant and
now they had three kittens also. There had been a fourth but
it was hit on the road by a car that did not even slow down.
Mother Jones was the calico, the kittens Snow, Rudy, and
Lucy Stone. Even the chickens had names, but Beth could
tell only the rooster and one of the hens whose tail hung
funny. She called them all Here Chickie, Chickie. If they
thought she had food, they came; otherwise they looked at
her, head cocked, and went the other way.

Luis and Johnny were passionate about naming. They
were in the process of mapping the world and naming everything. They loved to have long conversations about Mount
Heobalbalus and the Valley of Zombies and Boot Hill. Every
anthill on the twenty-three acres they had named and scrawled
on a map in seven colors of crayon. Luis in particular would
get very mad if they refused to use what he considered the
right names of places.

He was the older. He was brown-haired and curly and
big-boned. He was handsome, perhaps already a little vain,
loved his new (to him) two-wheel grown-up bicycle, was
quick-witted and good with tools. At seven he took a certain
amount of responsibility for all the rest of the children.
Johnny was small and skinny and dark. In the summer his
skin tanned so dark Beth did not always like the way people
looked at him in the village. He had Wanda's huge eyes. He
was quieter and shyer and Beth's favorite of all the children.
He loved the animals. He cried all day and all night when
Nick the kitten was run over. Beth always felt he took everything in and forgot nothing. But spending so much time running in the fields and the woods with the other children, he
got rougher and easier as the summer progressed. He lost
some of that excessive soulfulness. He seemed to brood less.

School was awful, something had to be done. They had
to set up a free school for the kids. They got into planning
that with some of the other communes in the area. The other
kids taunted them at school. And they learned so many un-
truths. They learned less than they did at home and they
hated it. They picked up bad habits. But Wanda promised
Luis that, by the fall, they would have solved the problem
and he would not have to go back to the local school, on
the yellow bus.

Mornings. Beth woke, Wanda beside her in the jangling old bed. The shade had fallen off again and the sun streamed onto clothes dropped on the braided rug Sally had made. Wanda slept with her hand palm outward, shielding her eyes from the sun. Beth had to pick up that hand and move it to kiss Wanda good morning. Wanda's hair—coarse black and streaked with white that shone like metal in the sun— tumbled on the pillow. In the strong sun her skin was coarse, the grain of her face very visible. Loving Wanda stretched her like a big bass drum: loving Wanda was fierce and huge and made her feel about to break open like an overripe fruit, as if she loved more than she could contain. She waited for Wanda to open her eyes, deep-set, intense black eyes. Burning in her tanned face.

They were together in the house and separate in the house. The house did not exist to reflect or contain or support them, any more than it did Jane sleeping in the next room with her husband Eric, who was with them for the summer. Sometimes the needs of the troupe and the house let them be closely together, made a common substance of their lives; sometimes the needs of the group pulled them apart.

She had to control her desire to stand over Wanda with teeth bared, trying to keep the world at bay. Wanda had wanted to be loved, Wanda had asked her for intimacy for a long time before they had begun to love each other. But Wanda had been loved before. Once upon a time Joe had loved her in the early years they were together. Wanda had that skill of finding people here and there who would love her eventually. But for herself, Beth was convinced that Wanda was her miracle, and that there was no other possible chance for her to love equally and passionately and with her whole heart, if she had not this small dumpy dark throaty woman to hold. Wanda was her wren, her witch, her fire, her rose, her wilderness, and her nest of sweet repose.

Wanda needed to reach out to others. There was the man in New York she saw when they performed there, the radical printer who lived on Morton Street. Beth hated that street. If she was silly enough to insist on asking, Wanda would say matter-of-factly that yes, she had gone to bed with him. He was an old friend and she liked to be with him.

She wanted to know everything about Wanda. Especially at night before they fell asleep, they would discuss the day's problems and interactions. Other times they would exchange some year—their fifteenth, for instance. Wanda had been born in Queens but her family had moved out to Farmingdale on Long Island. Her father was second-generation Italian, a conductor on the Long Island Railroad who wore an American flag pin on his uniform and an AMERICA LOVE IT OR LEAVE IT bumper sticker on his Ford. Wanda's only brother had been blown apart in Korea and had died slowly in an army hospital for three years. Her father had closed himself off from all of them in his grief, turning it at last into a cold angry patriotism that explained his loss and the emptiness of things. Her mother, from a Polish family, cleaned and cleaned and spent a lot of time in church. Wanda had been sent to a parochial grade school, but the public high school. Her mother in particular wanted her to be a schoolteacher. She said it was something Wanda could always fall back on. Her parents mistrusted books but stressed the importance of going to college to get a decent job. Frequently on Sundays they had gone to her brother's granite slab to leave a potted geranium and avoid each other's eyes in anguished embarrassment.

As a child Wanda had been very religious. One of the nuns, Sister Mary Theresa, thought she might have a vocation. Wanda had not wanted to go to the public high school. There she had been visible chiefly as a quiet studious girl who would cross the stage on honors day to receive awards for being the girl on the library staff to work the most hours in the semester, or the hall guard with the best attendance record; or to stand and recite in earnest throatiness speeches on Sportsmanship and Making Democracy Work and Citizenship in the Halls. She was always collecting money for starving orphans in Greece or Radio Free Europe (picture of wan children behind barbed wire) or UNICEF or birth defects (picture of deformed child standing on crutches). She sang in the glee club and choral society.

Maybe Wanda's love for singing led her astray, because when she went away to college and became a teacher the way she was supposed to, she spent a lot of time folk singing. Although she had absorbed rhetoric about individualism and free enterprise and the Crusade against Godless Communism, she did not retain her parents' racism so well. God must love all little children, including little black children trying to go to school. She got involved in civil rights. Wanda's first serious boy friend, at age twenty-one, was a black organizer from St. Louis. She began to teach the fourth grade, but her summers off she spent in the South. Her father threatened to shoot her and to have her put in an insane asylum or in jail. When she went to jail the first time, it was in Birmingham, although in a funny way the trooper who busted her reminded her of her father. Wanda's two younger sisters, who thought she was crazy, both lived on Long Island.

Wanda got out of jail weighing ninety-four pounds and calling herself a Christian Communist. That was the summer of '63. Her non-violence died in Mississippi in the summer of '64, along with Chaney, Goodman, and Schwerner. Wanda could not trace every step of her changes. By the time SNCC expelled its whites, she was already involved in anti-war activity and with Joe. She met Joe at a meeting of the Fifth Avenue Peace Parade Committee, where he was representing a Lower East Side organization and she was representing a committee of teachers against the war.

"You know, I was never much to look at, but I was pretty noisy!" Wanda would laugh, making the bed jangle. "I fell for him like a ton of bricks, Beth. I didn't even have the dignity to play hard to get. I of course didn't know I was only the four hundred and fifty-second woman to do that. If we hadn't been on the same side in a big political battle—the losing side, need I add—I don't know if I would have seen him again after the first night."

They were lying side by side facing, the candle beside the bed throwing the hill of Wanda's hip on the wall. She lay with one hand tucked under her face. "Joe used to always be organizing women by fucking them, but that wasn't the scene between us. I guess he liked me at first because—well, he almost admired me. I'd earned some campaign ribbons. I had my credentials—do you see? I was a comrade, so he treated me with a little respect. This of course is before we were married. We weren't even living together. I was living in Brooklyn where I was teaching, and he was living on Avenue C."

"You got married because you got pregnant?"

"Beth, I didn't even call myself a Catholic by then. But when I found out I was carrying, I just couldn't have an abortion. I just couldn't. Not Joe's child, not my child. I couldn't! The thing is, he felt the same way, you know. We'd been seeing each other for a long time by then, but as soon

as we got married everything changed, Beth, everything!
Then too, that coincided with changes in the movement and
a lot more macho prancing and street fighter heroics. Things
just got worse and worse. As Puerto Rican militancy developed, that was good for him, he wanted to relate to that,
but I'm not Puerto Rican and he'd act as if he were ashamed
of me. Then he got a teaching job at Northeastern. Coming
to Boston removed me from the political context where I
had an identity separate from his. Here I was, Joe's old lady
with the brats, and Joe was out playing wild Latin guerrilla
and going to bed with his students, and I was becoming the
burden, the nag, the bag. Yeah, the old lady."

"Now you're my old lady."

"Not any more than you're mine. Don't butch me, you
little freckled would-be turtle! Who ever heard of a ticklish
turtle?"

Slowly Beth was learning to be physically affectionate, to
be able to comfort and hug and kiss and put her arms around
the adults she lived with, as well as the children. Still there
were times when her skin prickled and she had to be alone.
They had put up a tent out back in the woods that was the
alone-place. Probably Beth used it more than anyone else.
Living so closely and working so meshed with others abraded
her nerves at times so that she would find one day that she was
sore with noise and proximity and must withdraw for a day
to grow her patience back.

They had made special friends with a commune in the next
town, who were farming seriously. The commune had been
started by a couple of former SDS women who had known
Wanda, and in fact told Round Earth about the house for
rent. There were five women, four men, two babies, and a
six-year-old. Round Earth and Bleak House traded food
and skills and books and information. They rented tools
together and both used them the same day. They bought
together things they could not afford separately. They visited
back and forth constantly.

Since Round Earth traveled so much, this was not quite as
important to them as to the other commune, but it was important enough. Bleak House was their often captive audience to try out new works from the crude beginnings. The
men there were the first men Beth had been real friends with.
Everyone in that house had been through a year and a half
of fighting their old attitudes and consciously trying to play

equal and looser roles. Men who had been involved in such a struggle were different in obvious and in subtle ways. They had different manners and different anxieties. In gross ways the house was unlike other communes: the men cooked too and the women also chopped wood and the men took care of the children and the women climbed up on ladders and worked side by side repairing the roof. One of the men, Alan, did needlepoint for pleasure. He was also accurate with a rifle. He taught Wanda how to shoot. Beth wanted to learn but, for a month, couldn't get herself around to being able to ask him. Finally she accepted Alan as her teacher—maybe because he was a vegetarian and did not shoot birds or rabbits. Learning to touch and to accept touch from the men at Bleak House was delicate, was gradual. If she had not the constant experiences of the troupe on the road to remind her how oppressive the rest of the society was, sometimes she could have forgotten, traveling between Round Earth and Bleak House.

All the people in Bleak House had been what Wanda called movement heavies. Bleak House was decorated with the paintings by six-year-old Tamar and with pictures of Madame Binh and Chief Joseph, with a Wanted poster on Nelson Rockefeller in Spanish, with an Outlaws of Amerika Weather-poster with the big bright rainbow. All the people in Bleak House thought of themselves as revolutionaries and saw themselves as enlisted for a fight that would last twenty to thirty years. Most of them spent a lot of time trying to make connections among the freaks who had moved to the country, trying to start alternate institutions like food co-ops and free clinics, and trying to build a bridge of communication to the local people.

Wanda was glad that Beth liked the people at Bleak House. She said maybe Beth wouldn't have two years before: that they had always been good people but then they had been desperate and frantic. Now they were settled in for the long haul. Several had served time and almost everyone considered it a possibility. Yet the manners in the house were gentle and warm, as if they were women and men who had learned to consider each other with care. The babies were the only tyrants. No one could deny them. Beth learned to be with them as friends, men and women, in a slow but finally abundant acceptance, like the tendrils on a grapevine growing.

There were wild grapes at Bleak House and they made conserve together. Alan said they were fox grapes. One afternoon when the grapes were ripening and they were picking them—two days before Round Earth was to leave for the first of their fall tours—Wanda and she made love in the scent and shadow of the vines, their hands and mouths purple and sticky and sweet.

Making love with Wanda was natural. All the hardness had been in letting herself open up, letting herself respond. They were close physically, in bed and out—no sharp differences. Wanda had taught her to love with her body, to express with her body, to know with her body. There was no border between nuzzling affectionately and making love. They were loving each other working, they were loving each other making a play, they were loving each other when they were teaching new women stiff and tight and frightened in their bodies, women who thought themselves weak, how to move, how to fall, how to jump, how to shout.

She felt as if sensuality born only in her genitals at that first tentative touch had spread through her. Into her arms, into her chest, into her belly, into her buttocks, into her back, into her thighs, into her neck, into her cheeks and her forehead and her nape and her forearms and her toes and her insteps. With whole bodies they made love. There was no question that they could please each other, no need to ask or wonder who would come when or how.

It was loving. She loved Wanda as Wanda was. She could not imagine Wanda younger or with unlined skin or with her hair all black or her waist tiny as she said it had been before she bore her children. She felt jealous sometimes when she met someone, man or woman, who had known Wanda before. But she fought that. All that living had gone to cure this salty woman to just the right taste for her. Wanda did not close her off from others, did not hold her in a box-shaped intimacy, and she fought herself not to clutch. It was a sureness. She was a tree in strength of love, she dreamed, standing high on a hill in New Hampshire and hung with flowers and fruit at once.

In May, a year after Round Earth had first come to New Hampshire, they visited Boston. Bringing Ariane and a new baby, Miriam came to an afternoon performance. Ariane sat pressed beside her, sulkier and thinner and taller of course, a delicate lovely-looking child who was given to pouting. She was two years and three months old, almost frightening with her articulate babble. *"No"* was her favorite word that afternoon. Obviously Ariane did not remember any of them and when Sally bent to kiss her, she kicked and began to wail that she wanted to go home!

Miriam was looking distracted with Ariane hauling on her and baby Jeff squirming in her lap. He was a fat beamy infant, lighter than Ariane had been at his age in hair and coloring, with Neil's hazel eyes. There was no time to talk, with people milling around and old friends to speak to and Ariane tugging on Miriam's arm, stomping her foot and saying, "Now! I want to go home now!"

The next day Beth went out to Brookline to the big gray house for lunch. Miriam made her a cheese omelette, then sat at the table watching her eat with her head propped on her hands. "Oh, I'm on a diet. I'm always on a diet. Since my last pregnancy. Isn't he a chubby little darling? I'm glad he was a boy, Beth, I mean it. At least Neil's off my back now about making babies. One of each kind seems to be adequate. I know it really is better for Ariane to have a sibling—I always felt sorry for only children, except for the moments in my childhood when I wished I was one. But, being the oldest in my family, I think I can get into her feelings and try to make it up to her."

Of necessity Beth observed the children a great deal: Ariane interrupted the conversation freely and frequently, and always Miriam stopped whatever she was doing or saying to listen to her and answer her with full seriousness. Beth felt differences between Ariane and Fern, Ariane and Luis and Johnny, Ariane and Tamar. Receiving a huge share of Miriam's intelligent and concentrated attention from morning to night, Ariane was far more intellectually and verbally precocious than the commune children, but not as emotionally mature. She was more imaginative, fey, sensitive, and demanding, and far more seductive. She seemed already feminine. The commune children looked more to each other and less to adults, and were at the same time surer of adult attention. Always someone was available, not one of a couple to be seduced from each other, entrapped or forced into granting precious attention. Love did not feel like a scarce commodity or exclusive interaction. The commune children looked grubbier, hardier, scabby and banged up more. They seemed generally more physical in affection, in exploration, in aggression, in play.

"The way you say 'He,' " Beth remarked, "you sound like my mother talking about my father to Marie, my married sister. . . . Isn't it funny I always say 'my married sister' though Nancy's married now too." So am I, she wanted to add. Wanda pressed on her. Beth felt invisible to Miriam because she had not explained her life.

"Oh, you know, marriage is struggle. It's never what you expect." Miriam reached out to put an arm around Ariane, who ducked away, grimacing. "You just never anticipate what things you'll have to give up to keep it together. I think we've reached a modus vivendi and have a good strong marriage, finally."

"You always say that! Every year you say, 'This is a good marriage, it's not nearly so bad as last year.' "

"Growing up in a tight so-called happy family, he has fixed ideas about how wives are supposed to act, how I'm supposed to show I love him. . . . He needs, he wants a quiet, controlled, contemplative life and that's been hard for me to provide, because I'm not naturally that way. . . ."

"Why should anybody provide somebody else with a life? With Wanda—with the commune—we don't provide each other a life—"

"With that many people it must be different. I *try* to be helpful. The only interestng work I do is when I help him prepare a presentation or write a paper."

"Does he give you credit?"

"Are you kidding? Besides, what would it matter if he put my name on? Only the principal author—the guy whose name comes first—gets credit. That's true even when some graduate student wrote the whole thing. So? What else is new?"

"Don't you see Phil any more at all?"

"There's no use my pretending I'm not married part of the time and that I can have my old friends . . . and Neil really loathed the bread business. He can think up ninety-two reasons not to do anything! He kept saying, 'Suppose somebody gets sick from your bread, suppose you drop a hair in, suppose you don't deliver on time and somebody sues!' He's a worrier! He's always thinking what might go wrong. He's making Ariane that way, and it bothers me. She's naturally a brave, curious child but she picks up his fears."

It was hard to get Miriam onto any other subject. "So you don't see Phil any more? But you do see Dorine?"

"I say hello to him sometimes. He's living in Dorine's commune. Neil knows I go to see Dorine, he just doesn't know Phil's in the house. Dorine's my best friend—I lean on her. Who else can I really talk to? Phil and I don't have much to say."

"I don't like Phil, we rub each other wrong. But you were friends for so long. Did you get tired of him?"

Miriam looked at her hands for a long time. "Far from it."

Ariane interrupted, pulling suddenly at Miriam's hair, hard. She persisted till Miriam let her climb in her lap.

Beth asked, "Then how could you agree never to see Phil? If Neil decides not to like me, would you never see me? Or Sally?"

"It's not the same, Bethie, you know it isn't. I couldn't fight Neil. I was already pregnant with Jeff! Suppose I'd said, 'Fuck you, man, I'll see who I feel like'? All he'd have had to do was say, 'Fine, bye-bye.' "

The fear in Miriam's voice confused her. She never imagined that Wanda would leave her.

"Bethie, I love him, and besides, he's the father of my children. It would have been so masochistic to alienate Neil just to keep an old boy friend hanging around. . . . Though I did make a private protest, for my soul's sake."

"You mean, not out loud to him?"

"Don't tell anyone! It was stupid. Right after the doctor told me I was pregnant, I went to see Phil while Laverne still had Ariane. I went to bed with him. Just that last time, so he'd know I didn't feel indifferent. It was something I owed him."

"Only that once? Did you feel guilty?"

"No. . . ." Miriam shrugged. Ariane had climbed down and gone to stand at the window. "Just sad. It was so furtive, a drag somehow. Being scared the whole time somebody would come in. Sure enough, the minute we were dressed, in came Jackson. And, Beth, he had a woman with him. A blond who'd been his student. There he was being ironic and distant with her and there she was eating him up with loving eyes. It turned my stomach. . . . The next time I heard from Phil he was living with Dorine in that commune. He likes that house, he makes furniture, he has another guy to work with. It's actually handsome furniture. Really, it's not what I would ever have imagined for him, but he's thriving. And he's involved in something political with other ex-cons. . . . He said to me once very formally, 'I've made a commitment to Dorine.' "

Beth tried and tried to talk about the commune, about Wanda. Miriam was curious and asked questions about how they worked on their plays and how they took care of the children. But Beth felt her shy away when she tried to talk about Wanda.

"She's so much older than you," Miriam said, "isn't it sort of a mother thing? I understand that you admire her, but . . . "

"No, no! It's not like that." Impressions flooded her. She could see Wanda with her hand on her hip saying, "Women are always trying to push each other into the mother role or accusing each other of taking that over. I won't be the one who has to give and give like a personal soup kitchen and who isn't allowed any weakness. Most women act as if they're terrified that some so-called strong woman will make 'demands' on them. Then they'll suddenly be six and in mother's pocket again. I don't want a wife, I don't want to be your angel mother or your demon mother. I just want to be your loving friend. And I think you're strong enough to carry your share of the load."

Remembering, Beth still could find nothing to say except, "No, it's not like that! Women can be more to each other than mother and daughter or client and helper or competitors."

Going down the street after lunch, she felt angry at herself for being unable to say a thing that was so simple and so important and so beautiful as what Wanda was to her and she to Wanda.

The next morning Beth went down to Goddard extension early where they were holding a workshop, to set up. A while later Sally came flying in and said that something was wrong, she did not know what, but some man had come with an official paper, a subpoena for Wanda, and that Wanda was seeing a lawyer. They would have to do the workshop alone. Beth was scared. Was it the children? Was someone trying to take the boys away? Was someone trying to close their new school? She was too worried about what was happening to spare energy to worry about whether she could handle her share of the workshop without Wanda. She just went and did it. It was learning to fall all over again.

Twenty-three women turned up. A great feeling of energy

and power and joy built up through the warm-ups and the scenes and the organisms. She worked then with a small group, lying on their backs with their heads together in the center, like an open flower. She taught them breathing exercises and how to let out the air and sustain their voices. She had them groaning and bellowing and ululating and singing openmouthed. By the end they were all dancing together, making their own music by beating palms on their bodies.

When she got back to where they were staying and walked in, the air was different: it was like running into a wall. There was a metallic taste of fear that sang in the air, there was the rough frenzied whirring of confusion. Even the house cat was affected and crouched on the highest shelf with his fur on end. Laura was sitting bunched up in a chair, white-faced with tension and so tight Beth could feel her muscles aching when she looked at her. Nobody knew whether Wanda had been arrested or what, but that morning a subpoena had been served on her to appear before a federal grand jury. Anita, a woman from the law commune, had been called and gone to investigate. Anita called back and told them the situation. A grand jury was supposed to be investigating how deserters from the Army got assistance in surviving in the States or getting across the border into Canada. Wanda's ex-husband Joe, who had been working with G.I.s since the summer before, was probably the target.

"Then it's okay," Beth said. "She hasn't seen him in three years, so they can't do anything to Wanda. She'll just tell them that she hasn't seen him and she doesn't know anything about what he's doing, and they'll let her go."

"Anita says it might not be that simple," Laura muttered. "She says that might not be the only thing they're after."

"But Wanda doesn't know anything about Joe at all!"

Laura shook her head. "That isn't necessarily so, Beth. Even you know some things about Joe."

"I know I wish he was dead! It's so unfair for Wanda to get into trouble for something a man did she hasn't had . . . a penny or a kind word from in three years!" Beth paced the small living room. "But what else could they accuse her of?"

"It isn't like a regular jury. They're older, richer white people always, and they even run a credit check on them. They're to bring in indictments that the government wants. Ninety-five per cent of the time that's what they do—agree to prosecute. But Anita says that mainly they're a device for investigating. They're a way of forcing people to testify about each other. The F.B.I. can't force you to talk, the police can't, though they try. But a grand jury can send you to jail if you don't answer their questions."

"But Wanda doesn't have anything to do with Joe any more. So she can say that and they have to let her go!"

"But you don't love him, you hate him! He hurt you. He walked all over you and left your kids. Are you going back into that good-woman masochism for the sake of a man who used you as a punching bag?"

"It isn't for him, Beth. Though I'd enjoy seeing him cooked in a pot on the stove on a slow fire, I wouldn't enjoy seeing him on trial. I don't want them to win—the state, the machine."

"But you have to choose what's important! If you don't answer their questions now that they're giving you immunity, they'll send you to jail for contempt. Then you won't be with us, you won't be with your sisters—and you won't be with me!"

"Come on, Beth . . ." Wanda was trying to make her smile. "I'll sure enough be with my sisters. You don't think they're going to put me in a men's prison, do you?"

"Why did you take the Fifth? They just asked you about being married to Joe! That's a matter of public record."

"Bethie, try to understand. Don't roar at me so. If you answer any question on a subject, they have a right to force you to answer all other questions on that topic. If I answered any questions about Joe, even admitting I knew him, they could ask other questions." Wanda buried her face in her hands. "It's a blessing I had Anita! They wouldn't let her come into the room with me. It's scary, Beth, believe me. You act as if I had a lot of time to decide what to do. I couldn't have my lawyer in there, so I insisted on going out in the hall to talk to her after every question. They wouldn't let me write the questions down, but I'd remember them the best I could, and sometimes I'd have to go back and hear them again. They tried to intimidate me, telling me I was a real unco-operative witness and that would be held against me. Bethie, it's scary. You're in there with them, nobody with you, not even your lawyer. And they've invented this funny maze full of traps. If you say one word wrong, if you say the formula just one word off, it's like some bad fairy tale magic, they get to chop off your head. They make up the language and the formulas and you have to do it exactly right in the right order. If you don't say it exactly so, you're caught. It's like being forced back to eight years old, in grade school, and the adults get to make up all the rules. And every time you think you're safe, they hit you with a new rule you didn't know about. So that, whatever you do, you're wrong."

"But why can't you just tell them the truth? Say you were married to Joe and now you're divorced and you don't ever see him any more. You don't know what he's doing, and that's the truth. What do you care anyhow what happens to him? Why should you go to jail to keep him out?"

"I won't help them! I don't have to hold him on my back any more. I don't have to service him in bed and board and be his practical-side old lady who has to think about rent and feeding the kids, freeing him for big thoughts. But he isn't my worst enemy. The corporations that poison the rivers and make war profitable and the state that makes war—those are my enemies. This society taught him to take women and use them and throw them away. It taught him you marry a woman and then she gives you children and everything your heart desires till you trade her in on a prettier, younger model. This society taught him what it means to be a man—the fist, the balls, competing, winning, putting everybody down. In order to survive where he grew up, in order to be able to do something good at all, a Puerto Rican in white society, he became the knife that cut me. A gentle man, a passive man in East Harlem, Beth, he'd be crushed. He'd be rotting in a state mental hospital. He'd be a junkie. Joe made it as he could, but he never set the price of making it. He got to be a university professor, imagine that. Nobody else in his family got through high school—"

"I never got to college, but that doesn't mean I have a licence to stomp people."

"That he stayed radical means something. He made it in the white man's world, but he didn't pretend to think white. He didn't change his allegiance. That's why they're after him, that's why they want to break him. Well, Joe's not my friend, and I don't know, if he was lying on the floor, that I wouldn't stomp. God, I have scars from him. But they're my enemies much worse than he is."

"But if you don't answer the questions now they're forcing immunity on you, they'll put you in prison. They'll put you in prison and there's not one thing I can do! They'll separate us. You haven't seen Joe in three years. How much harm can you do if you answer the questions? You don't work with deserters, you don't know that much about what happens."

"This is a fishing expedition, Beth. The questions they want to ask me aren't just about deserters. They're asking about the whole web of connections in the movement. They want to know who's friendly with who, who lives where, in what commune, who sleeps with who, who gives money. They want to fill in all the missing connections so that people can't disappear underground any more."

"But they must know all that anyhow, they have all the phones in the country tapped!"

"Don't exaggerate, Beth. They don't know everything. Even when they 'know,' half of what they know is garbage and they want confirmation. Look, the questions they're asking me include every address I've lived at since the year zero. Who else lived there? What vehicles have I owned and who borrowed them? Who was at the women's conference last year in Boston and where did they stay? How did I travel from Boston to New York for the health care demonstration that summer? What meetings did I attend in that fall that plotted riots, demonstrations, or street actions—all lumped as one! Lots of questions about Bleak House, Beth. Who's stayed there in the last year and for how long and exactly when. When people were gone on journeys and when they came back. I can't answer those kinds of questions, I can't!"

"But it isn't illegal to have demonstrations."

"It is when they call it inciting to riot. Or conspiracy. Look, you can talk about stealing a parking meter. Now swiping a meter is probably a misdemeanor. But conspiring to commit a misdemeanor is a felony. . . . How many times have you sat around the living room while people went on a fantasy rap about shooting Nixon or blowing up the Pentagon . . . or hijacking a beer truck? Well, that's conspiracy. That's how they tied up the Panthers. Every time you say out loud, 'Gee, I'd like to stick a knife very slowly in Henry Kissinger,' you're in trouble. Maybe an informer says to you, 'Gee, how'd you like to stick a knife slowly in Henry K.?' And you say, 'I surely would enjoy to do that.' Conspiracy, understand?"

"People *don't* always go to prison. A lot of time juries see through what's happening."

"Yeah, but before the trial they've had you in jail, 'cause

they set bail so high on political people. So even if their case is made of cream cheese, you've spent two years in jail by the time the jury turns you loose. Your friends spent money they didn't have to get you out and defend you. And whatever you were doing that made them want to lock you up, you aren't doing it any more."

"But this isn't a real jury. Anita says the judge decides if you're in contempt, and they can put you right in federal prison. You'll be in their hands. They can kill you!"

"They don't want to kill me, I'm a little fish. They want information. They say right out loud that they want to spread paranoia and mistrust. They can only put me away for the duration of the grand jury. Six months, a year."

"We've only been together a year! Is that nothing? We can run away. We can go to Canada."

"Love, they're watching us. And what about the kids? Do you think, if we got away, they'd let us get near them? I am not going to lose my kids because I'm scared to spend six months in prison. I have to know that you're with the children. Otherwise I can't stand it."

"Wanda, without you the group will fall apart!"

"Then it's time for it to stop. Time for the women to take what they've learned and go out with it."

"I can't accept it!" Beth clutched herself. "I hate it! You've fallen into the good-woman trap! Sacrificing yourself for him. You don't really identify with the women's movement, not deep down, or you wouldn't care about him! You'd do what's best for us."

"What's best for us is not to let them use the courts to terrorize us. What is worse is to help the war machine hunt their prey. I believe in a separate women's movement so we can be in control of our own political destiny, and our own struggle. Because nobody ever liberated anybody else for real. Because the only people who care about women's issues are women. But I have to believe in making alliance with other groups who are fighting too, because we do want to win."

"By going to prison in their place."

"It's nobody's place to go! Or everybody's to imagine she might have to. Beth, it's only six months or a year. I was in jail for a week once and it was awful but here I am. Don't you think to make a revolution we might all have to be willing to do at least that?"

"Why can't we get away? So they're watching the street. We can go over the roofs. We can go straight to the kids."

"It's hard, Beth, being a fugitive. Hard and hard and hard. Think about it. We'd have to change names and appearances and use false I.D. Hard to hold a job, hard to survive. We'd be alone. For six months, it's not worth it. I'll know that you're with Luis and Johnny and you're waiting for me, and the time will pass. . . ."

"So now you say it's too late. Too late to live our lives, too late to be together, too late to work with our group and love each other. But not too late for you to be a martyr!"

"Beth, Beth, don't hurt me! I don't want to be a martyr. I feel like somebody being run over slowly by a big truck! Don't you think I'm afraid? Don't you think I'm scared out of my mind?" Wanda's face began to quiver and wizen. Then the tears burst out. Beth began to cry at the same time. She threw her arms around Wanda and hugged her close. They held each other, their tears running together down each other's cheeks, salty on each other's lips.

Wanda burrowed close, her hands convulsive and taut on her back. "Beth, I'm so scared you can't believe it. So scared! Scared of being hurt. Scared of being beaten. Scared of being inside and going crazy. Scared of never getting out. Scared I'll give in and talk and hate myself. Scared of being separated from the boys. Scared of losing you. Scared of what this will do to Luis and Johnny. Let me go, I've got to blow my nose." Wanda pulled from her and walked back and forth rapidly, clenching and unclenching her hands. "Got to get control. Hold on. Help me to hold on."

"Why? It does hurt. It hurts so bad."

"Because I'm afraid already. Beth, I keep remembering things . . ."

"Remember us. Think of us!"

"One time in New York I ran into one of the Young Lords with a little girl, about Ariane's age. Such a pretty little girl, but she didn't talk, she didn't say a word. I was teasing Jesús, was she his, because he wasn't married, and he got very proper and dignified and explained he was taking his turn with her while her mother worked. She was the daughter of one of the New York 21. Her dad had been jailed waiting trial on one of those incredible hundred-thousand-dollar bonds just before she was born, and he'd never seen her. He'd never been allowed to see her! All those years taken away from his woman and his child, and who can give that back? I'm so scared they'll take the boys from us."

"Because we're lesbians."

"Courts always take gay women's children. Because we're not a family they recognize. I'm scared, Beth, scared!"

"I will try to hold everything together. I will try." Beth took Wanda's hands and unclenched them. Wiped the tears from her cheeks with her finger tips and her mouth.

"There's still a chance they might not get the contempt. Anita's trying to quash the whole thing. But there will still be ways we can communicate. I trust Anita."

"I'm trying to trust her. And you. That you know what you're doing."

"Then go to the boys. Leave for New Hampshire now! Quickly. Don't hang around. If I get off, you'll know it. If I get sent to prison for contempt, Anita will tell you how to communicate with me. I'll put you down as my cousin or something."

"Don't talk that way, Wanda."

"It's the only way I can talk. Take care of everybody for me, for all of us."

29

Everything Comes to the Woman Who Doesn't Wait for Anything

Summer when you love somebody and you're with them, Beth thought, it envelops you in green and lush and wet and warm. It seconds your love-making. It gives you flowers and fruit that tickle your senses to open wide. It gives you grass to lie on and streams to bathe in together. It gives you the sun to warm your bare bodies. It gives you moonlight to talk by. But summer when your lover is seven hundred miles away in a federal prison, it's just a hot corridor to get through, somehow.

She tried to scrub away her self-pity. She was not alone.

She must stop sulking and brooding and lying awake in an empty bed. She must care for those she loved too, her sisters, the children, especially Luis and Johnny. The first month back at the farm she felt closer to them than ever, closer especially to Luis. Johnny, being small and vulnerable and emotional, she had always felt close to, but the more competent Luis—almost her size at eight and growing daily—it had taken this loss to bring them to each other. He was protective and big-brotherly toward the other children, and now somewhat so toward her as well. That was hard to accept and yet she found herself finally moved by it. There was something of sexual stereotyping in his assumption of big-brother roles, yet something too of simple good will and gentle care for others. At eight he was far from naïve and watched his tongue with anyone from outside. Sometimes he fantasied about his father out loud. The bitterness Wanda had shared with Beth she had never spoken to them. Luis remembered his father far better than Johnny did, who would sometimes ask about some man, especially about pictures of cowboys, if his father looked like that. Luis was proud that they had not succeeded in serving a subpoena on Joe, who had disappeared and was still invisible. He was not underground—he had not changed his identity or his appearance—he had simply removed himself to friends in San Antonio and was watching the progress of the federal grand jury that had pulled in Wanda. Beth knew because Wanda knew: Joe had communicated with her right after she got to Alderson. That same week someone had telegraphed Beth two hundred dollars from Albuquerque, with a happy birthday message for the kids. Gee, thanks, Beth said to the image of Joe the Mustache in her head: can you spare it? But they certainly needed it in the house.

It was July before the state came down on them and the children in a custody fight. Beth was at Alderson visiting Wanda when it began. Wanda's parents asked for and got the court to award Wanda's children to them. Round Earth was supposed to leave for a trip through upstate New York the next week, but Beth balked. She panicked and then ground to a halt. She had run frantically from town to town finding a local lawyer, who told her she could do nothing. She spent hours on the phone to Anita pleading with her to produce a solution, till Anita started screaming with frustration that she had five clients in prison already, and she could not invent laws for Beth's sake. Round Earth was coming apart at the seams: no money to pay the rent, their lives jangled too much to fit with the older material. Laura took off first, going to New York with Lynn to join a gay women's printing collective. Some of the women decided to go on working together in Putney, Vermont.

Sally could not decide what to do. She wanted to go on working with the group, but she did not want to take the children out of the free school they had started. Fern particularly wanted to stay in the school. Sally and Beth took Fern and Blake, cat and kittens, Harriet and the chickens to Bleak House, which had lost two people to the grand jury. Sally decided she would live at Bleak House but spend some time with the theater group. Fern was enthusiastic because she knew the children from school and Tamar was her best friend and there were also two dogs and rabbits at Bleak House. Fern was thin and sinewy at four and a half, with sandy red hair and freckles over freckles. She galloped like a colt, all legs and giggles.

Beth moved in to stay with Sally and the kids and to brood. She did not want to be responsible for anything or anybody, since she had lost, she had failed her charges. Since the court had taken custody she had not been able to see or to talk with Luis or Johnny. Now they were in Farmingdale with Wanda's parents. The thought of that tortured. How every day must be to them. But they were hardy and together. The last time she had seen them, being led out with their hair shorn and dressed in new plaid shirts and dark pants, Luis' a little too small on him and Johnny's a size too big, Luis had given her the clenched fist salute. Luis, take care, take care!

At Bleak House she shared a room with Sally as they had in Roxbury. Sally talked far more now, but Beth talked less. She felt wrecked, cast up on an empty shore to harden under the sun and salt. She wanted to be quiet and heal. She wanted to think—but not yet. Instead she had bad dreams of pursuit and flight, attack, more flight. Or worse, she had good dreams and then woke to find them deception. The only time she cried was at night, in the dark, when she woke from dreaming of Wanda—Wanda picking beans between the rows into a sieve and popping a tiny sweet one into Beth's mouth, Wanda sticking a rose behind her ear and dancing in the kitchen with Luis to Sally's guitar. In the humid afternoons she would hear the bobwhite calling and remember

Johnny imitating them: he loved the birds that said their
name, chickadee, bobwhite, towhee, peewee, whippoorwill.
Luis and Johnny had never managed to see a whippoorwill,
though summer evenings they could hear them madly shrilling.
One night the boys and Fern had tried for an hour to find one
by its voice and came back lumpy with mosquito bites. . . .
Fern would wind her arms that freckled like Beth's own
around Beth's neck and tell her not to be sad, that she loved
Beth and when she grew up she would go break down the
prison walls and bring back Luis and Wanda and Johnny and
they would all live at Bleak House together with Harriet and
Rudy and Snow and Mother Jones. Beth felt broken. She
could not seem to rouse from her lethargy.

Fern and Tamar talked of Luis and Johnny as if they were
in prison like Wanda. At odd times Beth flashed the image
of Wanda's iron-gray father gripping Luis by the upper arm
and hauling him off while Wanda's mother came pittering
after, clasping her beaded purse hovering over Johnny's head
as he tried to turn and wave.

Sally and Alan tried to persuade Beth to work in the free
school, but she could not engage herself. Something very
tentative was happening between Sally and Alan, not yet
sexual, perhaps never to be, that had something to do with,
how they both related to the children.

Perhaps Beth would have stayed on and on at Bleak House
because she felt broken and it was easy to be there, easy to
stay with her own momentum destroyed and her sense of her
life deflected. But in October a letter came from Anita. The
grand jury in Boston was still sitting and had subpoenaed a
new wave of witnesses. By now opposition was beginning
to be organized and a massive effort to get out publicity on
what was happening and to raise money for defense was
going on. Laura had come from New York to help, and
Anita asked Beth to do a couple of mailings with them. In
the back of Beth's mind as she went was the hope that somehow Anita would have discovered some legal route to get
Luis and Johnny back.

She worked in the office occupied by the defense committee and slept at Dorine's Wednesday and Thursday nights.
Dorine was very glad to see her, affectionate, eager to help,
running over with news and excitement. She had a good
fellowship and an interesting job and she was active in a
radical caucus of women in life sciences. Phil and Dorine

had separate rooms, separate lives, but the mannerisms of a couple who trusted each other. Beth felt ashamed first, that something about the way Phil would rub Dorine's back, something about the way they discussed choices each had to make, reminded her of herself with Wanda; second, that they made her feel desperately alone. When they went off to Phil's room, leaving her to the big hard bed Phil had built for Dorine, she felt as if her flesh could sense them making love, exchanging, like the paramecia Dorine had been working with and talking about, information, protoplasm, energy from their days.

The fishing expedition had caught a mixed bag: Catholic left, old SDS people, pacifists, women's movement, Socialist Workers' Party, gay liberation, Progressive Labor, academic liberals, and some old Peace and Freedom Party members. Many of them were untouched by the struggles of the women's movement, and would walk into the office, treat Anita, who was heading defense, as the secretary, and persist in addressing all remarks of content to Bruce, a second-year law student who was doing footwork. They would bristle on contact with Laura and Lynn. They stepped on Beth coming and going.

Friday night she found herself attending a general fund-raising party to which half of Cambridge had been invited, at the house of a professor of sociology attached to some institute attached to Harvard. It was a large white house on Sparks Street, surrounded by old maples that had turned orange and scarlet. Severe and shuttered outside, inside it was fancy and jammed with people wearing long glittering dresses and dungarees. It was catered and waited upon, and Beth felt violently uncomfortable.

Beside herself, twitching with nervousness, wishing she could shut her eyes and wake up back in her bunk at Bleak House, she crept into a corner by the rum fruit punch. Having had no lunch and no supper, she ate canapés on crackers and drank. Holding a glass was something to do. These elegant people chattered and shrieked like macaws. This was the other end of the world from Round Earth, from Bleak House: yet these people had money and therefore she was served up to them to question and stare at, a wild aberrant little lesbian whose lover was in prison. With curiosity they looked her over when they did not overlook her. It pressed in upon Beth what a distance she had traveled beyond what she had been raised to, like a chicken escaped and become a wild bird. Who had ever heard of a wild chicken gone to scavenge in the woods with the partridges and woodcocks and hawks? So she held glass after glass after glass. . . .

And woke in the morning light. Woke alone, queasy and stupefied with blood turned to sour milk, remembering nothing. Then after a bit she recognized the cot, though the room seemed strangely larger, lighter. "Jackson! Jackson!"

He came in wiping his hands on his pants. "How are you feeling?"

"You wouldn't believe it. I don't."

"Haven't you ever been hung over?" He sat on the bed's edge to stroke her hair back with a hand hot and damp from dishwater.

"Is that what I have? But I feel sick."

"But you were sick. On the street, on the porch, in the hall, on the steps, in the car. There wasn't enough left in you, fortunately, to throw up at this end of the trip."

"How disgusting." She buried her face in the pillow. "What else did I do?"

"Do you really not remember? Or do you just want to wallow in it?"

"Go away. I'll get dressed and come to the kitchen." Combed and dressed, she sat eating scrambled eggs. "I can't understand how I got so drunk!"

"I can't understand how anybody who drank conservatively seven glasses of hard booze can wonder . . . The mind goes out but the body goes on and so do the jaws. And the consequences."

"What on earth did I do that you're sitting there with that smile remembering?"

"Well, you didn't hit anyone, though you did kick one man."

"Me?"

"You. You insulted—again conservatively—ten or twelve gentlemen, including particularly your host, whom you compared unfavorably to a bottle of library paste. You said a bottle of library paste had more backbone and more taste."

"I said that?" Beth covered her face. "At a fund-raising party I went up to people and randomly insulted them? I couldn't do that!"

"There was nothing random about it. You were sitting in a corner by the punch trying to finish it and you looked

distraught. Men would come up to you and you'd fix them
with a stare and say something deadly."

"I can't believe this. . . . Did I say anything to you?"

"Only that I was afraid of you. . . . And that I shouldn't
make such a fuss about going to bed with you. After all
you'd seen me undressed already, on Memorial Day." He
grinned. "Don't make such gloomy-faces. Have a beer, you'll
feel better."

"I couldn't feel worse." Inside or outside.

He opened one for her and one for himself. "Drink it
slowly."

"Why are you so amused this morning?" She glared at
him. "And how come you brought me home after all that?"

He smiled and smiled. "Why, it's becoming something of
a habit, once a year bringing you home from a party or
other disaster."

"Wanda is my lover. Do you know that?"

"You said that too last night, at appropriate intervals. You
know, it's been interesting, watching you. Who'd ever have
expected the turns and turnabouts? So you think you've
found a sexual identity at long last? What a spunky little
thing you come on as, all teeth and claws and big brown
eyes."

"You're laughing at me. But I think it's true, what I said
. . . that you are afraid."

He rubbed droplets off the bottle with his thumb. "Why
should I be?"

"I wonder myself."

"As the aging virgin said when she fell off the cliff backward, hurry up and ask me again."

She looked up from her beer and he was watching with
a new, even warier smile. With a shiver of surprise and dismay, she came slowly around the table to stand before him.
Had she ever expected him to agree? She could not quite
remember why she had wanted this to happen. But here she
was and Wanda was far away behind walls and bars. This
was old but unsettled business.

Still sitting, almost casually he reached out and touched
her cheek, caressed lightly her face, her hair, her nape. His
sad, perplexed, and faintly challenging face had finally lost
its smile or swallowed it inside. They looked at each other a
long moment, their bodies not yet touching, both holding
their breath and partly antagonistic. Then with a short dry

laugh he reached out and pulled her onto his lap, wrapped her tight in his arms, and kissed her slowly and quite consciously.

After a while he picked her up and carried her out of the kitchen. "How light you are. Like a child."

"I'm not a child."

"Don't I know that? Children don't turn me on." Kicking the door open, he carried her to . . . it was not the mattress. The bed was large and solid-feeling. This room was somehow different. Wooden blinds, blue draperies on the windows. Trying to control her clumsy nerves, she got undressed as he did.

Lying with him in the new bed, she felt as if hot and cold currents were flowing through her, mixing, separating, clashing. Point Lobos with Karen long ago. Sleeping bag among the cypresses. Drapes on the half-open window flickered to and fro over Orpheus, who sprawled on the sill grooming his sooty fur. She met the cat's agate stare, a little disconcerted. Watching. And Jackson was watching her, his eye sandy and shallow and thoughtful, opaque as the gaze of a horse. Gentle, the word kept pattering in her head, he was being gentle with her. He was slowly and expertly and carefully turning her on.

She did not want to allow him that much dispassionate control and worked stubbornly to subvert it. But he was determined and all around her and expert. It was sex like an argument, like a proposition, like an explanation: he wanted only her acquiescence to take her along. The pleasure was an argument.

As if to leave nothing at all to chance he went down on her until she came before he entered her. It was almost embarrassing, to come with him still so in control, so attentive, so conscious. Yet it was working. When he pushed into her she was alive to him. She was acutely conscious of what she felt and did not any more quite distinguish him from her in the pushing. Slowly it went on and on and on, slowly until she came, violently, and found herself back to herself, marvelously loosened and at ease.

Then something in him loosened too. More was involved than his moving differently, harder and more rapidly for his climax. The looseness stayed in him as he lay on his back, yawning. He fell asleep for a while, snoring softly. She lay on her side regarding Orpheus, her hands tucked under her face. Like Wanda; she was lying on her side as Wanda often lay. Orpheus stared back for a while. Then he got up, stretched, yawned, and come over to the bed. He hopped up and lay down between them, purring.

She was surprised at herself. Surprised that she had gone to bed with him while Wanda was in prison. Possibly she was still angry at Wanda for being willing to leave her for any reason. More probably she had been attracted to Jackson for so long that it was a question that would go on asking itself till finally answered. She felt she was learning something new about herself—not perhaps what Jackson thought he was showing her, but something.

When he woke, he reached out and pulled her over on top of him. "How's the sexual identity this morning?"

"More varied. Are you always so sure of yours?"

"Feel." He gave Orpheus a nudge. "What do you think you're doing in bed? Think I'm going to cut you in for a piece of the action, you old tomcat? Out! Go find your own pussy."

She laughed and her hand slid lower. "See, now I have you by the balls. I do remember that man saying that's all every woman really wants. Was that the one I kicked?"

"Yes, in the shin. You said that would do as well."

"You found all that attractive!" She stared at him, straddled. "You do. Isn't that perverse?"

"It amuses me. By and by we can have a discussion about how awful that is."

On top she could come more easily. They were both looser, more passionate, more spontaneous. She forgot to watch whether he was watching and he lost his ironic control and writhed under her and grabbed her behind and moaned.

After she had taken a bath, at lunch of sardines and to-matoes in the kitchen, she said to him, "The apartment is different. Isn't anyone living here with you?"

"Years of roomies have worn me down. Besides, with rent control this place is a bargain and I'm not quite so hard up. I've got a job teaching at the U. of Mass. in Boston. I'll never get rich but it's a far cry from washing dishes or sweeping floors or getting a graduate student stipend a family of gerbils would starve on. My wants are few. I eat a little better, I can afford to have the place to myself—that's the major luxury— I feed Orpheus chicken livers, I buy a better tobacco mixture and better booze. I bought a piece of furniture or two. That's it."

"What strange journeys lives are. You started in the middle class, you dropped out, and now you're slowly returning."

"My father would call this a slum. He'd think I was living in squalor. and the difference between last year and this wouldn't be visible to him."

"But that difference is visible to you. And tangible."

"Beth, virtue isn't pain. You'd learned that by now, I thought."

"Too true. I think I've reacted so far to my old masochism, I don't even respect sacrifice when it's vital, maybe. . . . Okay, like you, I live kind of ascetic. I truly don't need a lot of fat between me and things, padding, waste."

"Neither do I, by and large. I've simply replaced the few things I want by others better in their type—instead of an old mattress, a real bed. I haven't expanded those things that I do want."

"I have." She picked at the sliced tomato. "I really have. There are human things I need I didn't used to. To hold and be held, to feel myself doing good work, to feel myself with others that I love, to be able to say out loud what I think and feel . . ."

"What are you going to do now?"

"Call the defense committee and find out what's on today. I have to hang around Boston another few days to help."

"Stay here. Why not?"

"Do you want me to?"

"Sure."

"It would amuse you?"

"It would amuse me. Better, it would please me."

"You've stopped carrying a torch for Miriam, is that it?"

"Well, you can hardly dream about a portly housewife with a couple of kids. I wouldn't know what to do with her. Once while Phil was still sponging on me, I saw her here. That was before his Christ the Carpenter routine—"

"You don't think his life is better now?"

"That woman has turned him into a house husband. He's besotted. Anyhow, a couple of months ago I saw Miriam buying a shirt for her hubby in one of those overpriced shoppies in Harvard Square. I say hi, she says hi. Nothing. No fire in her. She's just a busy lady with a shopping list and a crying brat on her arm."

"You don't like children and you don't like grown-up women."

"Right now, I like you. I like a little steel, a little fire, a little ice. Something that bends but doesn't break. Something that fights back so you know someone's there and not just a puddle of warm glue. I don't get it off with glue."

"Jackson, you are so incredibly arrogant, sitting there telling me what you like and what you don't! Well, now, I like chocolate but I don't like vanilla, and tutti-frutti's fine, but you can keep the lemon sherbet. I'm a human person, you pig!"

He laughed deep in his chest. "Exactly. Now the girls I've been silly enough to mix with in the last year or two, they might expose some energy in class. But as soon as you take them to bed, all resistance collapses. They become marshmallows."

"That wouldn't be because you were careful to please them so as to get them off guard, so they stopped being defensive and wanted to please you, now, would it?" She folded her arms. "It's a power trip, and they were Uncle-Tomming too crudely for you. You go in for uppity niggers. It gives you more sense of having overcome."

"You believe in being in touch with your feelings. I'm doing the same. I've been down in the gutter, Beth, and now I'm out and seeing clear. I have a little energy left from surviving to try for what I want. Surely a man is less oppressive who likes a little vinegar than one who wants nothing but sugar, sugar, sugar, all day and all night."

Beth was struck by how unlikely her old fantasies of being with Jackson had become. She had made him up in part, while believing she was shrewd in perceiving him. A quiet industrious poverty in which they would each remotely and hermetically dwell. "You're a white man from the upper middle class and even after you fell from grace you can be saved. Not on your father's terms, sure, but on your own. Now take Miriam. She's only been off the job market what—three years? But she's scared. She isn't sure she could make it for herself and her kids. Then there's Sally, my friend. If she tried real, real hard, she could get a job as a waitress. What options do I have? When I was on the inside of the system, I was doing tweeny jobs for peanuts. Now I couldn't tell you how I get by."

"Beth, don't start rattling some class consciousness you

learned from a book. I've been poorer than you'll ever be. I've been down and out like you can't imagine. I've been to the bottom of New York and the bottom of Mexico City— and you can't dream up a bottom more mean and dirty and violent."

"But I wouldn't be here if I'd been there. Women don't recover. We don't get a second chance. We're too expend-able."

"On Skid Row you see a few female losers, but you see a lot more men. And in jail its ninety per cent men."

"Right now that isn't too real to me, as you might guess. But it's just different trash cans. Men get thrown in jail, women get pushed into mental hospitals. There you don't even learn survival skills and how to be a better criminal. You get drugged into forgetting why you were angry and what you knew." She sat back suddenly and shook her head at him. "You're getting a real bargain if I stay here, you know? I'm replacing both Phil and Miriam in your domestic economy. You can argue with me and I'll fight to the end, and then we can go to bed too."

"My sentiments exactly. Are you still saying 'if?'"

Sunday, Monday, Tuesday, Wednesday and still she stayed. The defense committee finished the mailings she had been working on. Laura and Lynn went back to New York.

"It's amazing how you turn me on," he told her in bed. "Seeing as how you resemble a *Playboy* centerfold less than I do. Though I will say you have nice legs."

"Listen to you! Always competing. You're managing to feel superior because you're fucking a woman who doesn't have a fashionable body! You can even extract points from this!"

"Points and pleasure and insults too. What more could I ask?"

She amused him. He was keeping her and feeding her and petting her, like Orpheus. He felt he could afford her. She sensed by Thursday that he wanted her to move in. He would not quite come out with it, but he seemed to circle around and around saying so. "You don't eat much. You don't take up much space. You wear pants and a sweater and boots. Why, you're the economical size woman. Eat like a mouse and roar like a lion, now that's what I call an efficient use of energy. Very little fuel lost in that system."

The sex was different: not better or worse than with Wanda.

Being with Wanda was easier. Somehow they were loving each other and they pleased each other without calculating about it. The difference with him made it more intense. When she came, she had that sense of losing control, of being swallowed into her orgasm and then floating up to the surface again light and loosened. But making love with Wanda was loving. It was one of the ways they loved each other, and all day long there were other ways. Touching was loving like talking was loving like working together was loving. They made love to intensify the loving and then went about their business.

With him there was not the loving. And they had no other business.

Friday she told him she was leaving to hitchhike first to New York and then to Alderson. He tilted his chair back and looked hard at her. "What for? Just a visit?"

"I have to think what to do next."

"Think here. Why not do this next? You're already here and you've already let go of what you were doing."

"Look, I have a commitment to Wanda. I think I could have loved you. It would have been different. I prefer the life I'm living to somebody else's. . . . I do think I could have, before. . . ."

"I think you could now. You haven't said love and neither have I. We don't know each other. Live with me, a month, two months, three months. Take what's in front of you. Now you're the one who's afraid."

"Yes. Because if we lived together like that I'd try to make you love me."

"Do you have so little faith in yourself to think you wouldn't succeed? Don't you think I'm ready by now, ready for a woman?"

"I think you want that interesting, intimate struggle. You'd find that stimulating. I think I don't want to face in toward somebody and make them my struggle—not even you, Jackson. I don't want *you* for my life. With Wanda, we have problems, we fight, but we aren't each other's problem. We work together. I don't want to love a problem. I don't want that difficult, interesting relationship. I want to love somebody and face outward and struggle to change things that hurt me and hurt others. I don't want to be fighting the person I'm supposed to be with."

"Don't you think you're enough of a person by now to

take on a real relationship with a man? Sure, it wouldn't be cozy, it wouldn't be easy. What is, that's worth anything?"

"The theater troupe was just as real as arguing with you, Jackson. Can't you see? You want me now because I don't love you yet."

"Because things didn't work out with Miriam? I did care for her, Beth, but it was the way she was demanding. The way she pushed me made me clam up."

"You push on a woman until you have her loving you. Then she isn't anything to win, but a demand. Don't you see it would be the same way with me?"

"No. You're not the sort of woman with a real taste for complication and bringing the neighbors in and wanting to be a soap opera heroine that Miriam was. I think things would be pretty straight with us. I think we'd fight a lot—"

"But you'd win?" She shook her head. "No. I don't want to fight with you inside a household. I'd rather fight City Hall. I'd rather fight the system that made us both."

He shook his head slowly. Leaning back, he looked at her beneath half-lowered lids. "I don't want to see what's going to happen to you."

"You won't. But can I give you a dependent? A mate for Orpheus?"

"Oh, you still believe in heterosexual relationships between cats?"

"They'll have to work that out. But if I bring you Lucy Stone from the country next time? She's a beautiful calico, and I think she'll be needing a new home. Too many kittens there."

They had coffee together in silence, a reiterative sadness thickening the air. As he sat with his long hands clasped over his cup, seeking the steam, she could no longer tell what he was thinking and, more important, she knew that he would not any more allow her to find out.

She picked up her cloth bag of underwear and socks, stuck her wallet in her pocket, and kissed him good-by. He would not let his mouth respond. Behind her he walked to the door. "Good-by, Beth. If you lose that identity again, you know where to find it." As she went down the steps, she did not hear his footsteps walking away.

30

Plot of the Wild Chicken
Breaking Through

She did not really hitchhike to Alderson. After she had been in New York for five days Laura found a car for her to borrow. Laura offered to come along, but Beth said no. She wanted to talk to Wanda as nearly alone as luck would deliver.

The weather held. That made a great difference. Eight-thirty Thursday morning she drove in the lower gates. Hitchhiking was bad because all the towns around were hostile to the women in the prison and their visitors, and the chances of getting stashed away under some local ordinance, or any count they wanted to dump on her, were high. She even had to stay in a motel. Of course one of the side punishments of the way prisons were set up was that they were usually in places hard to get to and stay in if you didn't have money, and only your friends and relations who could take off from work and had transportation could ever get to see you. A lot of the women in Alderson were poor black women from Washington, D.C., who ended up in West Virginia for convenience in sticking them somewhere, since everything done in D.C. was a federal offense.

With no gun turrets, no barbed wire, just a mesh fence around it, Alderson was a genteel prison. She drove up the winding drive past the warden's house to the inner gates, where she parked by the visiting room. Alderson looked like a college campus or a boarding school for girls: trees and red brick buildings, the dormitories called cottages. Most of the guards were not in uniform. Wanda had remarked that it reminded her of high school: the dress codes, the sexual hypocrisy, people going steady and jealousy rampant, the insistence on being ladylike and prissy, the total arbitrariness of the rules, under which at times they would come down on prisoners for minute infractions, and other times they would let much go by. . . .

Waiting while they checked her name on Wanda's list, Beth tried to smile, tried to answer the questions politely. If they took a dislike to you, they would keep you waiting half the day. They would not call Wanda till they felt like it. Wanda was a troublemaker, they said, and once when Beth had come she had been turned away because Wanda was in seclusion in Davis Hall. Seclusion was their soft name for solitary. She had been locked in a strip cell for challenging a screw who was hassling another woman.

So she waited and waited, clutching her arms, staring at the wall, watching the door. She might wait two hours and then they would come and tell her Wanda was in Davis Hall again. Hall . . . like a girl's boarding school. Then suddenly, coming in behind a guard, Wanda. Thin. Very thin. Sallow. Prisoners did not get outside much. They used to do gardening and farming, but it wasn't considered ladylike enough, so those jobs weren't passed out any more. . . . Wanda's face broke into a huge grin of pleasure. They were allowed to kiss. They were allowed to kiss each other once at that first sight and once when Beth left. In between it was a matter of who was on guard. And the weather. Today the sun was shining. It was a gorgeous blue and yellow early November day and the prisoners and their visitors were allowed to go outside. All the way down Beth had kept saying under her breath over and over again, 'Just let it be sunny, just let us be outside together.'

She took Wanda's hand as they went out. The guard was watching them but did not say anything. It was all a matter of who the guard was or how the guard felt that day.

"You're so thin!"

"The food is shit, love. I can feel myself slipping toward malnutrition day by day. I can get mad about it. No vitamins, no minerals. Just carbohydrates. The institutional all-starch diet!"

"I was so scared you'd be in solitary again." She took Wanda's face in her hands. The guard took a step toward them, making a sign, and quickly she dropped her hands.

"I fight them. I have to, Beth. They turn us into children. The whole place says we are bad wayward children and they're going to break us real slow. It's a soft, slow oppression. They're always telling us to be *nice*. . . . I was on six o'clock lock for two weeks but that isn't the end of the world.

I try to play it on the line where I don't get sent to Davis but I don't get depressed. We get stagnant. It's a slow loss of pride, a leakage of self. . . . If only I could see the kids. . . . What did Anita say?"

"That we haven't a chance of getting them back. The courts have never once given custody to lesbian parents, even if you'd never been in prison. We have too many counts against us. Being poor alone would do it. She said to forget it . . . as if we could."

"That's what she said to me. I asked her to dig more. See if there wasn't some way, any way. . . . I asked her, if we separated, would they give me the kids back."

"Oh." Beth felt as if she were going blind in her body. Stone.

"Beth, once I had the kids back, I figured we could go away and that the basic problem was to get Luis and Johnny. Beth, don't look like that. Anita said it didn't matter. A lesbian past and a prison record are sufficient. There is no legal way we can get our children back."

Beth's gaze went to the horizon. Down in this valley, valley so low. She felt wizened, crushed. She felt a vast weight coming to bear on her. The word "oppression" came to her, not as a movement catch phrase—the oppression of women, the oppression of gay people, third world oppression, working-class oppression—but as the real weight of the system, of the hostile state crunching her under. "Why do they do this to us? We're so little."

"The family is the stone of which the state is built," Wanda said dryly, "or didn't you believe our own analysis? . . . Beth, understand, I have to get Luis and Johnny with me. I know what it's like for them there. I know my father will punish them daily for being my children, for being alive and vital and earthy and strong. He's going to try to crush us in them. I can't rest while they're captive. I just can't."

Beth tried to shake out of her numb grief and listen. "But Anita says we can't get them back."

"Legally. But I'm going to do it anyhow. To run away with my own children."

Beth wrung her hands. "Do you wish we'd run away before?"

"We would have been hunted by the F.B.I. A child custody thing just isn't that big. My parents don't have the money to track us with private detectives for months and months. . . ."

By 'us' I mean me and the kids."

"You don't want me along." Beth grabbed Wanda's hand. Cold as hers.

"It won't be easy being a fugitive, even a small fish one. We'll have to be alert and wary all of the time. We'll need false I.D. We won't be able to do theater, maybe for a long time."

"It won't be easy?" Beth laughed. "Easier together than not. We can't let them bust us up. Besides, you need me to arrange everything. What do we do first?"

Other prisoners and visitors sauntered past, a fat black woman about forty with two women who might be her sisters. A guard walked behind them.

"Oh, it's not so bad since I'm off that stupid secretarial job," Wanda said in the same voice. "I'm doing tutoring. Helping the Puerto Rican sisters learn the pig's English. Actually I kind of like it. I get to talk Spanish a lot. Did you see Roberta? She's been working nine months on one of those big fancy flags. We make those big flags for special orders, and seals with eagles in satin. Nine months of women's slave labor. Lot of anger gets sewn into one of those banners. Nine months. She could have had a baby, she says. She has one, but she had to sign it away in the spring."

"Isn't she kind of old to have a baby?"

"Old?" Wanda looked startled. "She's eight years younger than me. This is her third time in. Hustling and skag." Very casually she looked around. "The kids write me sad wooden letters, obviously censored. My father won't give them my letters. . . . You'll have to see Luis anyhow. But exercise care."

"What's the first step in our running away?"

"Do you want to be a fugitive?"

"I feel like one anyhow. I want to be together with you. Loving each other, we're always fugitives."

"That's romantic and metaphorically true. Being real fugitives is something else." But Wanda was sounding cheerful. "Beth, helping the kids escape is one thing. Going with us another."

"Not so. I've crumpled up since you went in. I'm ashamed of myself, how little I've done. But I'm awake now. I truly am."

Driving back to New York, she felt small still but no longer crushed, no longer helpless. Quick as a mouse and slippery and wary. She must first create new identities for all of them, and find a home in another city. Then she must figure out a way to pick up the kids without Wanda getting caught in the process. She would need help. She would need a whole lot of help. Then she hitchhiked to Boston and began.

She would never have guessed beforehand who would end up in her scheme. Who would want to help. Who would be clear and able. Who would be trustworthy. For several weeks she worked on new identities: Wanda was a widow named Marie; she was divorced and named Cynthia, called Cindy. Luis was Robert; Johnny was Mark. Then she went to Cleveland to prepare the lives they would assume. The grand jury had not subpoenaed any new witnesses and was preparing indictments. Soon it should be finished and Wanda would get out of prison. Beth must be prepared on the day Wanda was released. Once Wanda was known to be out, the children would be watched more carefully.

Briefly she saw Luis twice. It was cloak and daggerish on the flatland of tract houses, but he enjoyed it, like hide-and-seek. And understood. She was coming to have a new respect for Luis, for children generally: that they were people in a fuller sense than she had quite grasped. They could never speak for more than ten minutes.

"Oh, they make us go to church and confession and all that stuff. It's no worse than school. The teachers here, they sure are cross to kids. It's full of crap. If I use words like 'crap' the old man hits me. What I hate the most is when the old man gets excited at night and starts talking about Joe and Wanda. How they're rotten dirty, the dregs of the earth. The old lady's not as bad as he is. She says to us when she tucks us in that she's sure our mother loves us anyhow. . . . Do you *believe* it?"

"Is Johnny okay? I don't know if you should tell him you saw me or not. . . . What do you think?"

"I'll see. He cries a lot. He cries for everybody." Luis looked superior. He had continued to grow and put on weight. "He cries for Wanda and you and Sally and Fern. He cries for his girl friend and Rudy his kitten and Harriet the goat. But I tell him we're going to break out one of these days."

"We won't be able to go back to New Hampshire, Luis. Probably not ever."

"But we can do lots of things. We'll be okay. I'm not scared. I'm only scared of having to stay here. He hates us. He's always making threats about where he's going to send me, how he's going to take us away from each other. He's going to send me away to some school where they'll make me be a soldier, and keep Johnny at home. Can they draft kids now? Can he do that? The old lady says it costs too much. . . ."

"Military school? It isn't getting drafted, don't be afraid. It's just an extra strict kind of school. But we'll get you before he can do that. Promise!"

"When? Will she come for us?"

"No. It will be me and maybe somebody else. If I appeared suddenly one morning when you guys were walking to school and I looked funny—maybe I would have a wig on or my hair dyed? Do you think Johnny would get in the car or would he be scared?"

"Are you kidding? Would we get in the car? Ha! That's a joke. The hard part is when you come and you talk to me and then you go away."

"I'll maybe come once more and tell you to expect us, but maybe not. Maybe we'll just come with a car one morning. I think it won't be more than a month now. It's to be right around the time Wanda gets out. So when you hear them talking about that, you'll know to be expecting us. Then a friend is going to take you to another city and you'll have to both wait there with that person for us to get there the next day. But you'll know we're on our way, and that first night, you'll get to talk to us on the telephone so you know for sure we're on our way. Okay?"

"Got it!" Luis put out his hand to shake hers. He was into being very controlled these days. She wanted to seize him and hug him hard, to let her feelings out and share his. But no doubt he needed his stoicism. As Wanda needed her sense of struggle. She shook his hand and held it as long as she dared.

Beth asked Miriam if she would do a small errand. To her astonishment, Miriam insisted on taking a much bigger part. She would meet Laura and Wanda on the Connecticut Turnpike where Laura would bring Wanda from Alderson on the day of her release, and she would bring Wanda to Beth at Miriam's house, where they would hide overnight and disguise themselves. Miriam entered passionately into the planning. "Suppose they were my children? Of course she has to get them back!" Miriam brushed the heavy hair back from her eyes, frowning. "For once I don't mind the risk, Beth. I want to do it! Maybe I even need to do it!"

"But Neil wouldn't go along. Why do you want to take risks for us?"

"You think I always lie to myself. Sure, I've done a lot of that for years now. But oh, Beth, after a while the pain gets through. The pain gets through! I have so little self-respect left I need to prove to myself I'm still here. I can't even love my children right if I'm a dishrag."

"Are you very unhappy?"

"I was much unhappier with Phil and Jackson. Now . . . it's just nothing. It's being dull and bored and servile. I feel as if my life is over."

"Wanda's eight years older than you. She began another life when she was thirty-five."

"Come on, you call it the women's movement, but what do you have for an ordinary woman? I'm not twenty-one, I'm not attractive. No one looks twice and I don't care. I love my two children and I see them growing and changing and I see the world closing in on Ariane already. I see it. How nervous she is to please. But what have you got for me? I love my kids and I don't burn banks down or run around the streets with picket signs."

"You're beginning to understand how trying to be a good woman has oppressed you. It isn't me who's making you feel the weight that's crushing you."

"Yeah, sure. I feel it. You call it oppression, I call it pain!"

"Pain is individual. Internal. You think it's your problem, your fault. You still see it as private. If you were in a group with other women, you'd find out that what you think of as your private problems are common as Social Security numbers and fillings. You didn't mess up, you didn't fail. You don't have to feel guilty. You can fight it!"

"So help me, then. Face it, Beth, I'm no kid. I'm the mother of two children. I wouldn't let them go for my life to live over again. They're the world to me, Ariane and Jeffrey. They're far more mine than they are Neil's, for all he wanted them so much. He's so proud of himself spending time with them on Sunday afternoon."

"You keep saying you're not young. So maybe you won't catch another man. Is that it?"

"What have you got to replace it? Come on. I'm not about to start having relationships with women. Maybe that works for you. Okay, I'll believe it on faith. It's like a joke to me. I can't be turned on by another woman. Maybe I'm too old to change. Maybe it's been too easy for me to make it with men. What am I supposed to do then? You think I'm going to run off to Vermont and join a traveling circus? Beth, I can't. It isn't in me. Maybe I could have at nineteen. But my kids are real people too. And they're damned sure what they want, from day to day. Loud and clear."

Beth paced around the table. "I can't give you a one, two, three answer. I hear what you're saying, and I know it's real. But I can't present you with a replacement for Neil. He's security, he's your income, he's your love, he's your insurance policy, he's your government, he's your sex life, he's your society in one."

"You can say, go to work. Okay, by now I'm scared. I've lost my confidence by attrition, that beautiful technical arrogance. I haven't stood on my own two feet and presented a technical idea in years! I haven't even spoken in public. I've lost my cool. There's a depression in my field. Route 128 is a disaster area—companies folding, thousands out of work." Miriam shook her hair back, sighing. "And what does it mean, I quit because I didn't want to hire my brain to the military. Now I'll go back and take the same kind of job. Who am I kidding? I do less damage darning socks." Miriam was getting excited. Words gushed from her. Beth had the feeling that Miriam had been brooding and studying her situation for months but had never spoken a word. Her voice rose, thickening, and the words spouted. "And suppose I get some job, by the time I pay child care, what do I have left? Even if I get something from Neil. I gave him grounds for divorce once myself. I wonder if a smart lawyer like Neil would hire couldn't make a lot out of Phil. . . . I wonder . . . Anyhow, suppose by some miracle I get enough child support to pay for day care. How can I celebrate turning my children over to enforced baby sitting? Most women who do it can't get any other kind of work. It's lousy for the kids. And I'd come home at night tired. What would I have to give them?" Miriam sat down as if exhausted, then bounced up again. "I hate to sound like a bragging, pushy mama, but

Ariane is . . . brilliant! She has an incredible mind. She's full of insights. Did you look at those montages she's doing? She goes part time to a really free creative nursery, but the tuition is high. . . ."

"The whole ball of wax sticks together. That's a Wanda expression. You set your own terms that make the problem insoluble."

"How did Wanda managed to work in the theater with two boys? I guess they're old enough to be in school."

"Everybody took care of the children."

"I don't know. . . . Different women have different ideas about child rearing. I wouldn't care for Laverne imposing her notions on my children, any more than she would like mine."

"But, Miriam, you can't have it both ways! If the kids are solely your responsibility, then all you can do is hire the time of a woman who won't love them. If others care about them and therefore care for them, you can't have complete control."

Miriam looked dubious. "Most people are such pigs about children."

"I'm going to think about what you asked me. I can't come up with magic. My answer is going to be dull and practical. . . . I'm going to bring you things to read and some lists of groups that exist."

Phil and Dorine volunteered to take the boys to Cleveland. They were meeting in a Greek restaurant on Massachusetts Avenue where the bouzoukia music on the jukebox made background and they talked softly. It was early and un-crowded. Beth would be picking up Luis and Johnny and then turning them over to . . . Dorine and Phil? She must decide. "I don't feel good about your doing it," Beth said to Dorine. "What you're working on, what you're doing with your life is important. I don't want to get you into trouble."

"I'm not sacrificing myself—I don't expect to get caught. And, Beth, who doesn't have something precious in herself that deserves to be protected? Besides, Phil and I function well together. We both drive, we're used to night driving. I know we can do it. We can't control the off chance, but we won't take extra risks. Each of us knows how the other thinks and reacts—which is good when we may be dealing with emergencies."

"But *you*," Beth said to Phil. Still tanned from the summer, he looked healthy. Thin but not gaunt. An edge was gone from him. At the same time she sensed him more directly. She remembered the wall of glass she had felt between him and the world, except for Miriam, long ago in the coffeehouse. She could not quite make sense of the shifts and alterations—appearance? habit? "Why do you want to do this? We've . . . never got along."

"Disliked each other self-righteously."

"Well?"

"Dorine wants to, for you. And I always thought Wanda had plenty of guts. But how do you think you'll understand?"

"I have to trust you."

Phil grinned. "And I have to trust you worked this thing out well enough so we won't be caught. You don't know how much I don't want to go back inside."

"You served time." She tried to feel that with her mind.

"That's part of it. I used to know those kids, especially Luis. He's a real fine kid. And nobody with all their marbles would doubt Wanda is one tough mother." He shrugged. "You take the risk I might fuck up. I take the risk your plan might be full of worms."

"You keep questioning that. Because a woman can't possibly plan an action?"

"Don't call me names without provocation. Anybody not a mental case worries when they take risks. You think if you were a man I'd say, 'Yassah?' Come off it."

"Of course, you've always been scrupulously fair with women, all these years, so I ought to believe in your sudden conversion."

"You don't think Dorine knows what I'm like?"

"Every woman's man is an exception," Dorine said. "I have to say that before Beth does."

"Are all men bad and all women good? Or are there differences?" He shook his head heavily and then leaned back. Dorine was sitting with her arms folded across her breasts, keeping herself from interfering. "Make up your mind. Trust me or don't. I don't have enough self-hatred left in me to take a whole lot of kicking."

"Why do you want to? Is it for Dorine? Is it because you were in jail? I can't feel you. And I can't play with Wanda's life by spreading a thick coat of good will over everything and saying, 'It's so nice you want to do this that I'll take it like a lollipop.'"

"Do you ever know just why anybody does an act? Did you really understand why Wanda went to jail rather than testify?"

"Yes, I do think I finally understand that! Being politically naïve isn't like being female, it changes." With what? Having exorcised her anger at Wanda for leaving her for any reason? Taking action herself that carried risk?

"Well, it's a nice clear action. Suppose some bastards had taken me away from my mother? It could have happened to her just for being poor and alone."

She stared at him. "Do you think doing time changed you?"

"What kind of question is that? . . . You're a thing in their power. They can beat you, strip you, starve you, take away your letters and your pictures and piss on them and tear them up in front of you. Tell you what to read, deny you paper and pencil, bust you for staring. They can take your health away real slow or break your back in two minutes. 'Desperate' just has no meaning till you're inside. Then nothing ever is the same again. Not touching a woman, not taking a crap or looking at the sky or buying a paperback or smiling in the mirror. . . . Doing *Time*. While people outside give up on you. Go on and live and forget you and take your woman or your kids away and let them have absolute mastery over you, mastery to death."

"You think the effects were all bad? You never spoke to me for real before. Talking to communicate, not to manipulate. You always tried to make me give you something."

"How the hell do you presume that's jail and not Dorine? This woman is strong. And stubborn. We've been struggling and struggling with each other. Jesus, there are more direct ways to change your habits!"

"Beth, he's done a lot of his changing here." Dorine turned to Phil. "I think you came back with less . . . structures . . . but you might have rebuilt them into something harder." Dorine unclasped her hands from that protective, restraining clutch across her breasts.

"We're all so divided and put down, it has a funny side," Beth said softly. "Your ex-con, poor-child oppression. My female, lesbian oppression. I guess we might try to pull together instead of across the table."

Phil poured them all more retsina. Beth found she was sitting back. Her muscles felt sore, as if she had been holding up a weight. Why were they all suddenly easier? Beth knew she was going to agree that they would take Luis and Johnny to Cleveland. With the confrontation relaxed, Dorine began to interact with both of them. Beth watched Dorine and Phil together. Then she decided to bring that up out loud. "Do you think of yourselves as a couple?"

"Well, yeah," Phil said. "Loosely. In the context of the house."

"The center of my life is what I do. But I don't have to be quite so inhuman about it now. I don't need to prove to myself any longer that I can study, that I can work, that I can do research. I'm over the first and second humps—"

"There are no camels with these humps," Phil said. "We're done proving to each other what we don't need, and now we can enjoy what time we get. Sometimes we're in different cycles and we can't bring it together. She's more into her head, I'm more into my hands. I need to make real objects, useful objects. Beds people lie on, fuck in. Babies' cradles. Chairs. Desks. Tables. But we're both back from the extremes of that dichotomy too."

"What does that word mean? I don't follow you."

Dorine said, "For so long I hadn't used my mind except to invent rationalizations and brood on my sorrows. When I began to work, I became superrational and supercontrolled. I didn't want to enjoy my body. I was scared of being captured by the old passivity."

"Yeah, remember that first year? Sex measured out like holy water. I was like to die."

"Now I don't need to blot out everybody to be able to work."

"Aw now, my head trip was never control, I should hardly need to say—"

"Ha," Dorine said, wrinkling her nose. "You tried in your devious way. You were just too stoned to be good at getting power."

"Listen, growing up where I did, the way you felt like a man was by hurting, by beating, by putting down. Well, I identified with my mother too much to make it that way. Now, there were two models I saw, the champion, the hustler. The champion fights to win. The hustler wants to win too, but in such a way that it looks accidental. He doesn't cream an opponent, he cons a mark."

"Women have a soft spot for hustlers, that's why you did

so well." Dorine smiled sideways at him. "Because the hustler isn't alien. All women hustle. Women watch faces, voices, gestures, moods. The person who has to survive through cunning. Flattery, charm, manipulation . . ." Reminiscently she turned to Beth. "One of the things that used to hook me on our first rotten go-round was that I felt that Phil needed me, needed my sympathy, my caring."

"But I hustled women too. Aw, I hustled in the Army, I swear I hustled Jackson out of his marriage, I hustled into graduate school . . ."

"To listen to him tell it, you'd think he had it made!" Dorine said.

"Well, I was never a grade A hustler because my fantasies took over. They interfered with my ability to scan. The structures I built in my head got more and more real and what I tripped over in the street less and less important. Drugs helped. They helped a lot. They numbed me to the pain of losing and losing."

Beth said, "I couldn't learn to hustle. So I was a victim, a loser. But that isn't the whole universe! We can get outside of roles, finally! We can!"

"Mother Mary, I'm trying." Phil grinned. "But what a long slow tortuous winding it is."

"Jackson plays the sage but he's really a champion type, isn't he?" Beth said, remembering, remembering. "He has to win."

"We don't see each other much. I can't stand the smell of modest success. And I don't wrestle with him in the old way, I don't secretly want to be him. . . . But don't you have to win too? I'm counting on that."

"In the plural. That makes a difference. I can't define a victory that would be just for me . . . except the immediate one of getting my family together."

"Being with Phil makes me more, not less, Bethie. Try to see. We have separate problems and we have to solve them, each of us, but sometimes we keep each other warm and sometimes we help each other to survive, to see, to try. Now we can ask each other for things we want, at least sometimes. You know?"

Beth looked from Dorine to Phil. "Maybe it's the retsina. But I feel as if you want me to bless you. I'm only me. What you want, you do. I only want you to help me to get my love and our children together."

Dorine took her hand. "But we'll be helping you go away from us. After that, when will we see you? What can we do except send money? When will we ever sit down and eat with you again?"

"When we win," Beth said very softly, "we'll *all* sit down at the table."

Sally had come down to Boston to wait for Wanda to be released, imagining that Beth and she would go down to Alderson together to meet Wanda. Beth had to send her back immediately.

"I want you to be someplace where twenty-five people see you have nothing to do with this."

"But when can we be together again? Fern misses you."

"I miss you. As soon as it's clear how hard Wanda's parents are going to push trying to find us . . . If it's not bad, then you'll come. Soon, let's hope."

"Fern says she wants to spend half the year with you and the theater and half at Bleak House."

"But we won't be able to do theater, Sally. Maybe never again. But you will. And when things are clear, you'll come and see us with Fern and Blake and then decide. Maybe we'll have our family again."

"I want to go on adding people. I'd sure like Alan and Tamar with us too. I don't want to give up anybody, and yet we're always, always saying good-by to each other and moving our houses."

"Well, at least we didn't break up from the inside this time."

"Sure enough, but it hurts just as much."

"Not the same. It's missing, but it's not feeling wrong." Still, when Sally kissed her good-by and left, Beth wept and wept.

She lay on a bed in the back room of Miriam's house, her hands cold and wet on her belly. She could not seem to get warm although the sun shone outside. It was a warm day for February, the temperature in the high forties, the radio said. She monitored the news, not expecting anything but fearful always of disaster. Miriam had taken her children to Laverne that morning with a story about shopping to do. The shopping had been done already, the bags were in the car. Then Miriam had driven to intercept Wanda. Beth had arrived at the house at three alone. If anything went wrong, if Neil came home early, she would prevent them from coming. They called in regularly from pay phones. She did not answer unless the phone rang once, stopped, then rang again. Then she picked it up but didn't speak. If Neil came she was to walk out and wait in a shopping plaza.

She had pulled up to the curb and called to Luis and Johnny. They had come running, Johnny shrieking and Luis looking both ways and trying to appear casual and then at the last moment jumping forward and starting to yell himself as soon as the door shut. They almost deafened her as she drove off and begged them to get down in back and be quiet till they were out of the immediate neighborhood. "Now as soon as we get to Queens, you're going to hop in the VW bus with Phil and Dorine and change into the clothes there and they'll tell you everything else to do. From now on, you call me Cindy. Now what's your name, you there?"

"Robert!" shouted Luis.

"What's your name, hey, you back there?"

"Mark!" Johnny paused a minute. "Can I have another name? I want to be called Dean."

"Well . . ." Beth said dubiously, "you could be Mark Dean. Dean could be your middle name. Why do you want to be called Dean?"

"That was his teacher in general science in the fall," Luis said. "Johnny, I mean Mark, liked him. I had him too. He was okay."

Now they were somewhere in Pennsylvania . . . hopefully. Luis had said to Phil, "I remember you. You used to bring me licorice!" She felt an anxiety so vast and pervasive it sat on her like an ocean of cold black water. How could she imagine she was adequate at inventing a plan that would work? She felt weak and small. When she passed a mirror, she turned away sick. There were many mirrors in this house. All showed a small woman wringing her hands, scampering to and fro bent over, hunched to her belly like a poisoned mouse.

Her mouth kept filling with saliva. She would choke on her own saliva. Her fault, everything. All would go wrong. She hated this huge house. It made noises to itself. It muttered and creaked and clanked its plumbing. It made footsteps to climb the stairs. It made tapping in its walls. It made someone to be trying the doorknobs. It made closet doors to open and voices to call her name.

She tried to tame the house by moving in the Round Earth. She reorganized the public space, the quiet space, the children's special areas. Through the house she wandered, but always she saw Miriam's life there. A basket of Neil's shirts waited to be ironed. On the calendar in the kitchen Miriam's hand had made notations about people coming to dinner and what was to be served. Shopping lists. Toys, toys, toys. As she had promised Miriam, she had tried to answer the question about alternatives that would appear real to Miriam. She felt that Miriam had been disappointed in the nature of her answer. She had brought Miriam the latest copy of *Workforce* from Vocations for Social Change, which listed jobs existing in alternate institutions, free clinics, free schools, collectives working on community problems. Maybe Miriam could find someone to work with who could use her skills. If she could not find anything to do immediately, Beth had hoped she would get an idea of possible directions, a new way of thinking about her work.

She had brought Miriam a list made up by a women's project of child-care facilities available with annotations on what was known about them. She brought her the *Women's Yellow Pages*. Basically she was hoping that lists of alternate possibilities would set Miriam in motion, turn her outward from circling in helplessness. She brought her names of Boston people who tried to create networks of information and connection, who tried to plug people with skills into projects that needed those skills. She brought a list of some communes, not too radical, with both men and women and children in them, that Miriam might visit. She brought addresses of people who helped others find communes or start communes. She brought names and addresses of women's liberation groups and projects and women's centers. She brought women's newspapers and journals and pamphlets and articles.

Miriam looked at all that paper, pamphlets and lists and directories, and thanked her hollowly. She carried them away and Beth did not see them around. But that afternoon Beth finally found them as she wandered in desperate aimlessness through the house. They were all in the children's room on a bureau. At least a few of the items looked thumbed.

She did not know if she had failed Miriam substantially, or whether she had merely failed to excite her curiosity. Maybe slowly Miriam would warm to the approach she was suggesting. Beth could not guess. Perhaps Miriam had not wanted such concrete minute responses but a general answer that would immediately change her life; or a rhetorical answer she could dismiss, that would prove to her that nothing could change, for there was no place else to go.

Again Miriam called in. They must be close. She paced the downstairs, too excited to wait above, fearful she would miss a last-minute invasion of Neil. Finally she scrambled up to the window seat, where so often she used to sit and talk with Miriam. Knees to her chin, she watched the street, seething with anxiety and scalding hope. No, it was a trap. They were trapping her now. How stupid not to have them speak on the phone. Wanda was back in Alderson. They had caught Dorine and Phil and Miriam. She had ruined everyone's life. It was all over.

She heard the car. She ran down as the car pulled into the garage behind the house. She saw only Miriam in it. Only Miriam. But as Beth raced to the back door to open it, Wanda came trotting across the yard with Miriam, Wanda in dark plastic-rimmed glasses and a brown wig. Thin, thin. Came running to her and hurtled through the door, knocking her off balance. Wanda hugged her hard, hard against her, Wanda light but solid in her arms. Soft in spite of her thinness, her wiriness. Hugging each other till it hurt.

"Now, now, look at you!" Wanda scolded. "Don't bawl like a baby. Come on, we have to get upstairs. Don't cry, love. Ah, come on, you're getting me soaking wet!"

Wanda began to cry too then. She did not cry often. Beth always thought Wanda's tears were rusty. That crying hurt her as much as whatever made her cry. Wanda's face would wizen up, fold in on itself, then the tears would ooze from her clenched eyes and sobs would shake her. As soon as Wanda started to cry, Beth stopped and began to soothe her. Arms around each other, tottering like ancient and senile ladies, they swayed dangerously up the steps with Miriam pushing on them and clucking and hurrying them along to the back room where they were to hide for the night.

The layout of the house favored them. The back room was at the top of a straight narrow back stairs. Probably it had been a maid's room, for it had its own toilet and old-fashioned wash-basin that the Stones had not got around to replacing. It was nominally the guest room, where relatives slept when they visited. Basically it was the lumber room, absorbing everything unnecessary and superfluous and broken.

Both the master bedroom and the children's room were to the front of the second story. On the other side of the wide central hall were the bathroom and a narrow hall leading back to the rear stairs. Off that hall was the room that Miriam had been trying to turn into a bedroom for Ariane. Jeff was supposed to keep the room next to them as the younger, and Ariane would get her own room. The walls had been replastered and the ceiling and two walls painted, when Miriam had last bogged down. Across the hall was their hiding place.

Immediately underneath them was the kitchen. Miriam had covered their floor with spare blankets and towels and rags, to muffle their movements. "But mainly you should just stay in bed. You need the rest. Remember, the floor creaks. When anyone's in the kitchen, I'll make enough noise for you to hear, but don't count on that! You must be quiet. Unless somebody is running water hard, like the bathtub, don't flush that toilet."

Wanda bounced on the bed. "We won't make any more noise than mice do, but I hope you oiled the springs! God, I'm glad to be out. Beth, Beth! It's so beautiful outside! You're so beautiful!"

"You've been in too long and you have no sense. Now come sit in this chair. We have to use some awful stuff on your hair and make it brown."

"Brown, huh? How about I have red hair? I always wanted red hair."

"You'll like what you get. First Miriam's going to cut it. You're just like your son, who isn't satisfied with his name but wants a better one: none of you ever are pleased!"

"See, four years in the women's movement and I'm dyeing my hair and getting it done. Away with gray! Lord, love, do you think the kids will know us? Are they all right really? Those awful wooden letters they wrote me!"

"They're going to call here from a pay phone in the next half hour."

"Half an hour, Beth! Are they really all right?"

"Cindy. You better start practicing. Sometime late tomorrow we'll be with them."

Miriam finished cutting and Beth began mixing the dye. It was beautiful to touch Wanda, but wrong to alter her. She wanted to bury her face in Wanda's exposed nape but continued carefully working on her stiff hair.

"You both look so happy," Miriam watched from the doorway. "But you'll always be afraid. They can catch you at any time and take the children back. How can you act so happy?"

"We've been criminals since we began to love each other," Beth said. "We're always hiding a little."

"We're together," Wanda said. "We have a freedom more real than the right to walk into any police station and swear out a warrant against our neighbors. The freedom to act and to fight. That's a lot more than I had this time yesterday. That's a lot more than I've had most of my life."

Miriam shook her head. Then she went out, leaving them to their privacy, locked the door and slid the key under. Finally they were together again, even though for the moment Wanda could only sit on the bed's edge with awful-smelling brown glop foaming over her head and smile. "Give me your hand at least, Beth. Take off those ridiculous gloves, you look like a gynecologist."

"Obstetrician. Just gave you two huge boys." Beth took off the gloves that came with the dye and washed her hands carefully.

"Are you scared?"

"Sure. Always. But now I know we can fight. And sometimes, sometimes, win." She could feel between them the physical shyness of their first attempts to love each other, the shyness of long separation. Awkwardly Wanda lifted her arms, gesturing to Beth to come. She knelt in front of Wanda and took both her hands and held them to her mouth.

31

What Shines

"Before Jeff was born you stayed home with me all the time, didn't you, Mommy?"

"How come you ask that, Ariane-poo? I'm with you all the time except three afternoons."

"But you were. When it was just me. Then you stayed home all the time."

"No, I didn't. You've forgotten, but when you were little, even younger than Jeff is now, I used to take you to a house to play with other children. Just as I do now."

"You did?" Ariane regarded her with suspicion. "You really did? You're putting me on."

"Twice a week. Your mother was writing something then for the university."

"Aw, go on! You never did!" Ariane slapped at her. "At Chris's house?"

"No, this house was in Somerville, not here."

"I don't like Chris. He hit me yesterday."

"Did you do something to him? Did he hit you hard?"

But Ariane turned away, swinging back and forth, back and forth from the handle of the refrigerator. She was slender and fragile with dark brown wavy hair well past her frail shoulders. Her hair was one of Ariane's many vanities. Lately she had become a petulantly, guilefully feminine child: reminding Miriam somewhat painfully of Allegra. She was no longer fierce and pouncing, though her will was as strong as ever. But in competing with baby brother, she struggled for Neil's love. She craved being admired. She was studying how to make guests pay attention. Evening after evening as she fought the nightly battle to stay downstairs, to delay bedtime as long as possible, she became a more outrageous flirt. She climbed into laps, she kissed strangers, she told stories at the top of her lungs, she sang popular songs and did dances imitated from television in the middle of the living room.

"Mommy, what's pride?"

"That's feeling good about something you've done. For instance, I feel pride that I organized the play group."

"Mommy, Chris's mother says pride is a sin."

"Mmm. Laverne says things like that. That's all right, love, we don't want everybody to be just like us."

"How come you call her that? Isn't she Chris's mother?"

"Of course, and Tom's and Bonnie's too. But she has a name of her own. Just as I'm not only Ariane's mother and Jeff's mother—"

"Yes, you are! Yes, you are!" Ariane swung back and forth on the handle of the refrigerator until the door swung open.

"Shut it, Ariane. Come back, Ariane, and shut it. You opened it. Please."

Very slowly and elegantly Ariane shut the door. "Is it a sin to have the play group?"

"I wish you would get off of this sin thing. The only thing I'd call a sin is hurting somebody. . . . People have different ideas. People think and like different things. Differences make the world go round."

"Daddy says it's the sun."

"What? . . . Oh, the earth goes around the sun. Do you understand what he's talking about?"

Ariane nodded solemnly, making circles with her hands—imitating something Neil had done? "Buzz, buzz, buzz."

"What's that?"

"Buzz. Buzz. Buzz. I'm a busy bee going around."

He was what people called good with his children. He did try hard to teach them things, but he got annoyed if they were not interested. He grew more involved in the course of his exposition than in their reactions. His disappointment was crushing. Ariane was already learning to pretend to understand. The rewards for that were better than for actually trying to follow and asking questions that showed she didn't understand. Quickly she was learning to perform.

Some of the time freed by the play group Miriam spent trying to read back into her field. Trying to develop some expertise in information retrieval systems on small computers. But even her old proficiencies were proving useful. Dorine was at the point where Miriam could help. To a limited extent they were working together.

Miriam was also teaching a course at a free school in Cambridge. Called Computer Jargon and Manipulation, it was intended to demystify the uses and abuses of computers. She was enjoying it immensely. But then her eight students could not call her bluff. Neil was always asking what she told and explaining how she had it slightly wrong. She was teaching them what they needed to use machines and get around them, and that sufficed. Of course she was not paid, but at least she was doing something. She was also compiling a private list of computer access codes—the codes by which anyone with simple equipment like a teletype could dial into time-shared computers and borrow a little of that expensive time. She did not know why she was making the list, but she had the feeling that by and by she might find a human use for such keys to the mint.

The next afternoon when she had dropped Ariane and Jeff at Laverne's she drove the old Saab—it had been Neil's but he had replaced it with a new sportier one—to Dorine's commune in Allston off Commonwealth. She had used to come here ostensibly to visit Dorine, but really to keep some touch with Phil. Now she came to see Dorine. They worked hard for two hours. Then Miriam took a moment to ask obliquely, "I gave you some money. Did it get through?"

"I saw them. They're doing okay, though they're a little lonely there. But you know them, they won't be isolated long. They're living sparsely but their spirits are good."

"I liked having them in the house. It made me feel strong."

"Well, hold on to that a little. You *are* strong."

They got a lot done and Miriam forgot to watch the clock. She was downstairs calling Laverne to say she would be twenty minutes late when Phil came in from work. He greeted her with a big grin, they exchanged a couple of sentences, and she saw him take the stairs two at a time to find Dorine. . . . She preferred being gone before he came, for she felt a little sad when she saw them together. Between her and Phil were no vibes at all. But then she wasn't in a period when she felt like creating vibrations with anybody.

When she went up to say good-by to Dorine and fix the next time, they were standing together at the window, arms around each other, while Dorine poured out plans for the summer. "The Woods Hole thing is sure, it's really going to happen! We can be on the Cape till after Labor Day. Si has a boat we can borrow. I'll be working but it won't be like work. I've never lived near the ocean!"

"We've never really had a vacation," Phil was saying. "A chance to slow down. We'll have to find a house. Maybe Jerry and Frankie and some of the others would share one? What kind of a boat?"

"Maybe I'll come and see you with the kids," Miriam said.

"Oh, you say that but you won't do it. Why don't you?" Dorine said.

"Yes, but leave Mr. Clean at home." Phil grinned.

"He wouldn't come anyhow. . . . But I will. You'll see." Getting in her car, she wondered to herself if she really couldn't take the kids and visit them. Phil was gone, gone for her. She hadn't been able to choose him. But there remained, astonishingly, good will.

Cindy and Marie were living with the boys in a narrow frame house on East 128th Street in Cleveland. They had a little upper back porch they made plans to eat on in the summer, and a back yard they shared with the family downstairs, graduate students with a baby. Since Cindy and Marie were keeping odd hours—they worked a few nights a week cleaning small office buildings—they baby-sat for the Greenes in return for tolerance. Tolerance of their living arrangements, tolerance of the kids' noise and heavy use of the yard, tolerance of their new dog, a black and white stray whose limp was almost cured, named Dean. Dean was still nervous and yapped at night sounds, but he was fattening and settling. Cindy, who had never before had a dog, was crazy over his woeful eyes and stood up for Mark's right to sleep with him. Dean made up for all the animals Mark could not have in the city.

They were short on furniture. Aside from beds, they were stocked with tables and cushions. Robert and Marie were building a couch, so far resembling a vast low table. Marie said they were going to stuff it with Dean's hair, he shed so much. Mark liked that idea. He kept combing Dean and saving the hair in a matted ball till Cindy persuaded him to stop. For three weeks Dean looked unusually well groomed.

Their jobs were badly paid female labor not covered by social security or paid vacations or sick leaves, but work that brought them into contact with virtually no one. Dorine was working and sent money. They got by. As soon as the ground thawed, they put in a garden. In February they had pored over the luscious pornography of the seed catalogues, the opulent tomatoes, the rotund squash, the juicy greens. Robert, with his neat handwriting and his passion for drawing maps, made a master plan of the garden in crayons and ink. Orange for carrots, green for spinach, yellow for corn. They wanted to grow everything in a space the size of their livingroom. Now the peas and lettuce had broken ground.

"It is more work, just four of us," Cindy complained. She had just hauled the laundry through pouring rain. Marie was cooking and Robert washed vegetables for a salad.

"We get lonely with no kids," Robert said. "If we can't go back to New Hampshire, how come at least we can't live in a commune? There's one across the street down two houses, though they aren't political at all. And they don't have kids. Just old people."

"All of thirty. Rheumatic every one," Marie said dryly. "As long as my parents have detectives on us, we'll stay put. Maybe by fall. Can you put up with us old folks till fall?"

"How's the soup coming?" Cindy asked.

"Almost there." Marie tasted critically. "Salt. Chives." She pinched from the plant on the sill over the old porcelain sink.

"I have a meeting tonight at seven-thirty."

"Your consciousness-raising group."

Cindy did not feel she particularly needed her consciousness raised at that time, but it was a way to meet women and become slowly, cautiously involved here. Marie was spending some time working in a community day-care center.

"Tonight I work, but tomorrow we have to decide whether we're going to that meeting at the clinic," Marie said, her dark eyes raising the question they must settle soon.

Sitting down with bowls of potato soup, Cindy and Marie and Robert ate while Mark rattled on about his day, talking non-stop till Marie urged when he paused for breath, "Come on, honey, eat a little too." After supper, sitting over coffee, they returned to the topic they had been mulling for a week.

"All right, as a paramedical in the clinic, I might be a little more visible." Marie waved her hand and Dean, who had not yet been fed, wagged his tail hopefully and came sniffing.

"More than a little more." Cindy hunched forward.

"But I never did anything with health before. And sometimes we have to do what we want. The easiest way to protect ourselves is to do nothing political—and then whatever is the point!"

Cindy smiled. "Oh, you want to play doctor! And so do I—I'm coming around to it—only let's not kid ourselves it isn't risky."

Robert said, "Then you won't have to be cleaning women. I'd rather take care of people than scrub floors any day."

Marie took out a quarter. "Robert, flip it to see which of us trains first. Heads or tails?"

Cindy won the first chance to train to work at the clinic. "Ha! Now we'll see who gets to wear the white shirt in this house!"

Miriam had to get the kids fed before she started Neil's supper, as Jeff was too young to eat fancy food and Ariane would not. Jeff was chubby and placid and ate well. Ariane was suspicious of food. She ate hot dogs, hamburger, broiled chicken, eggs soft-boiled or scrambled, cream soups, tuna fish, cottage cheese, and American processed cheese. She ate asparagus and corn. That was it, except for everything sweet and rotten. Neil and Miriam had fierce arguments about who was responsible for Ariane's non-eating habits.

Neil came home as she was giving Jeff his bath. For a while he watched. "You pick him up too much. You're spoiling him."

"Neil, I don't hug him one bit more than Ariane. You're getting hypercritical, I mean it! You don't hug him enough!"

"You can't coddle him as you did Ariane. Look how spoiled she is. He can't grow up being a crybaby."

"Ariane is a beautiful child! I want Jeff to be gentle and loving. I want him to know touch and kindness and warmth are good!"

"You know as well as I do what an overprotective mother, a possessive mother, does to a son."

"Do you know what a cold judgmental father does to any child?"

"I don't think anyone except you finds me cold and judgmental. . . . Did you go to Dr. Bachman this week?"

"If I find any fault with you, as you do with me continuously, then I must be sick in the head—"

"Continually. You mean continually, not continuously."

"I mean if I'm not utterly pleased with everything you think I must be sick. I need adjusting. Off to the plumbers."

"Did you see Dr. Bachman?"

"I see him, but I don't think he sees me."

"What is that supposed to mean?" He folded his arms with a sigh. "Let me guess. You now have such insight that you can see more in your psychoanalyst than he can see in you. Doesn't that strike you as . . . unlikely?"

"I'm not going to him. He's your policeman. He did a job on me once. At that Christmas party, Neil, I saw him with his wife."

"She seemed harmless enough. Pleasant. Pretty in a faded sort of way. Or did I miss some deep meaning?"

"I watched him with her. If that's what he thinks marriage is, no wonder he can't help me! Neil, I don't need him to cluck and hem at me and lead me to green pastures of rumination. I need something useful to do in the world! I need some work, interaction with people, adult conversation, some ideas, some fresh air!"

"I don't understand how I'm supposed to be stopping you. I don't know what you do all day long, but from the way this house has been looking of late, it can't be much. Is Ariane's room ready for her yet? They're getting too old to share a bedroom."

"Jeff is fifteen months old! You're so uptight!"

"Ask Dr. Bachman about fifteen months, if you can bear to ask, given your late omniscience in everybody else's field!"

"Neil! Can't we stop this? Please!"

"I don't recall starting it, Miriam. I don't think I have hard words with anyone in the course of a day when I must see some hundred students and colleagues and staff. Whereas how many arguments have you got into in the course of the last two weeks?"

"I find your colleagues hard to take, now I don't sit back and keep my mouth shut. God, that fascist talking about population control!"

"If I could interrupt, I wonder if you managed to get supper tonight?"

"I thought we'd eat at seven-thirty."

"I have to be back at Tech Square."

"A project meeting? You didn't tell me."

"I have a new assistant, who's of some use for a change. Helen's no genius, but she's willing to work. I have a quarterly report due to NSA next Friday. We'll have to work double sessions the rest of this week. That ought to wrap it up and then we'll get Greta to run it through the typewriter."

Ariane begged to sit at table with them for the grown-up meal, since they were eating early. Not that she would eat. Neil said she might if she minded her manners. So Ariane sat at the dining-room table perched on the phone directory and an atlas, playing grande dame at three and a half a lot better than Miriam could at thirty-one.

Neil winked at Ariane. Delighted, she winked back. Then every time he turned in her direction she winked and giggled until he became annoyed. "That's enough, Ariane. Don't you know what enough means?"

"It's not enough! Daddy! Look at me!"

Finally she threw her spoon into the tureen of cream and

mustard sauce, splashing the table. Neil ordered her out and Miriam had to take her from the table crying. It was not that Neil was truly strict with the children. He never hit them. He believed in a happy permissive childhood, but he grew irritated if they trespassed too heavily on his routines. Then he pushed back, and Ariane in particular would grow hysterical at the rejection. She clung to Miriam, sobbing.

When Miriam came down, Neil had finished supper and her own chops were congealing in the cold sauce. A momentary nausea made her carry the plate into the kitchen, but a thrifty impulse sent the food into the refrigerator instead of the garbage can. Neil was whistling as he collected his briefcase. He was cheerful again but his cheerfulness passed over and did not warm her. They had quarreled without making it up. After he had gone out and she watched his new blue Saab dart off, she remained in the dark of the stairwell looking out at the street corner, the big maples with their new leaves tossing in the wind under the streetlight.

It was completely worse now that she didn't break down. The mechanism of quarrels and reconciliations had been based on her compulsion to come to him afterward; her inability to stand being shut out in the arctic cold beyond his love. He withdrew and she came after, to submit, and then they could be gathered together again. But she could not do it any more. She judged herself by new standards as Ariane grew older: she must set an example, she must be a good human being, for her daughter if not for herself. She could not teach what she could not at least weakly exemplify. Being Neil's aching concubine always ready to cry for forgiveness did not quite fit in, with the children growing able to watch them together.

For her the tear of the quarrel had to be knit in lovemaking. After their worst quarrels they had made love most passionately. But now Neil often said he was tired. He said if she worked all day she would not have so much extra energy at night. She said that when she had had a job they had both had the energy to make love. He said his project was more serious than Logical and took more out of him. So things went around and were no more resolved.

There must be a new way through to each other. To cut through his defenses and confront him. Somehow to touch him again.

Alone. She imagined being alone. A bogeyman nightmare.

She saw herself waking alone in the night with nobody to hold her, nobody to care. Dr. Bachman had loved to hear her dreams of anxiety those three times she had let herself be shamed into going back.

She had been looking up at a big beautiful Christmas tree hung with shiny globes. Dr. Bachman asked her to remember back into her childhood. But they had never had a Christmas tree. This was too perfect to be a real tree. In each round ornament she saw the room reflected and herself. A red world with a red Miriam, a green world with a green Miriam, a silver Miriam world, a gold Miriam world, long worlds of elongated giraffe Miriams, fat flattened Miriams, Miriams with gyroscopes revolving in their bellies, tinsel Miriams, shimmery translucent Miriams. She had reached up to choose, understanding she must pick, must pluck. Then it had fallen on her. The tree of selves had fallen forward, catching fire, burning her. She had wakened in terror.

Another time she had dreamed she was sitting in Finnegan's and Phil was supposed to meet her there. Then someone had come and told her that Phil had gone to California and was not coming. He had run away from her. She sat there in Finnegan's terrified, alone with all the people screaming and laughing to each other. All looking at her sideways, because she was sitting alone wearing her old bathrobe. She kept saying to herself over and over, "But he promised to meet me, he promised to love me, he promised!" Now there was no one.

How had she used to live alone? Of course she had the children. Silly to think that way. Neil did still love her. He was angry at her and knew no way to release that anger directly, so it stayed inside converted into that quiet cutting hostility, that carping, that insistence on her conforming to his family's standards. She must cut through his layers of expectations and self-righteousness and open him up to her again. She had reached him once. Why couldn't she get through now?

She had to try, with all her energy! Holding herself by the elbows in the stairwell, she watched the maples dashing in the wind. A sound like water rushing. A dark sure energy rose in her. He would love her again, he had to! She was a good woman, she had had his children, and they were beautiful, they were precious, they were the flowers of life itself. She could feel them asleep now above her, baby Jeff pulsing

like a luminous starfish in his crib, the life in him measured
and steady, beaming. He had been a colicky baby, he had
driven her mad. But once that was over he had blossomed
into a plump succulent morsel, a fat placid teddy bear. Even
his first teething had not really broken that wonderful loving
calm. His first word, after "mommy," had been "good." He
had reached out and touched her face and said what she was
still convinced was the word "good." Now of course he
babbled constantly. He stood early and beamed on the world.
Early he learned to walk on his sturdy legs. Only he would
not give up his bottle at night. He still insisted on sucking.
She imagined Jeff pulsing steadily in his crib like a warm
orange star.

Ariane was that blue-white star that shone blindingly and
then flickered almost out. She was the more intense. She had
nightmares and visions and tantrums. She drank in the tensions and terrors of the house through all her pores and
crystallized them into her fear of the dark, her fear of loud
noises, of thunder and the subway, her fear of large dogs and
trucks. When something attacked her sensitive nerves, there
was no way to comfort her. Her panic was total. She needed
love and love and love. She needed it and sometimes all the
loving Miriam could give her was inadequate and faded
into the vast maw of her fear and was swallowed up without
giving light. Other times Ariane gave out joy like a fountain.
So sensitive to nuances, so sharp in her senses. She painted
beautifully and made montages with scissors and paste. She
sang songs she made up in a clear piercing voice like a
warbler.

They had come out of her and they were. Different, new,
strange, barbaric and then civilized beyond her. Creatures
not her, yet hers.

She tried, she tried hard with them. Now she had to get
some time away to remain alive, but she was still trying hard.
Neil must know that inside. There were bad seasons and
mean seasons and seasons of ice and cold, of parching heat.
But there was so much life beating in her, she felt as if she
too must shine on the dark there in the stairwell to any being
with eyes to see the shining she saw in her children. She
would not pulsate a full rich orange, she would not coruscate
blinding white and blue, but she would emit a dim warm red
glow—not so bright as she had used to, perhaps, but steady
and a bit brighter than it had been in a few seasons. She

felt strong in her love, stronger in her self, stronger in the connections she had somehow preserved through attrition. She felt in herself Wanda's strength for her children; maybe not the greater strength it would take to put herself first, but the strength to fight for them, by all means. So she was not alone, but connected to them, and connected still to Beth and Wanda, not only through the money she secreted from household expenses for them but in her daily thoughts, her sense of them as a counterexample to defeat. Connected to Dorine, connected still in a muted, never to be complete way to Phil. Connected to Sally, who wrote her halting but faithful one-page letters. Her students at the free school. Whoever she was preparing her access codes and information retrieval expertise for. Out of such connections she could weave no security, no protection against her worst fears. But of such connections were wrought an end to the slow relentless dying back she had known, and the slow undramatic refounding, single thought by small decision by petty act, of a life: her life. That life shone too, dimly but with considerable heat, banked coals in the dark.

32

Another Desperate Soprano (Helen)

Helen had not intended it to happen. She believed in playing by the rules, and the rules did not include going after a married man. After all, she knew how bad that could hurt. Jerry had caused her enough pain during the two years they had been married to last her just about the rest of her life on that score. On the other hand, working with Neil, she couldn't exactly be rude to him. She liked him. She wasn't compelled to pretend she didn't. The rules didn't demand she lie in her words or her behavior. She did like him. He was the nicest man she knew, always cheerful and soft-spoken and gentle, with a kind word.

But she hadn't gone after him. The only thing she could

charge herself with was inviting him up that night for a cup of coffee when he went out of his way to drive her home. Home to her dreary studio apartment on the bad side, the dark side, of Beacon Hill. But he so obviously wanted to come in for a minute, to go on talking. She had had no idea he would make a pass at her.

She could say to herself that she should have resisted. Oh, sure, fine. She wasn't made of transistors and circuits. She was lonely and hard up. Why should she have to do all the resisting? She didn't ask him to make a pass, but how was she supposed to play the Sunday school saint with him holding her against him with that sweet smile and she could feel his erection?

A piece of luck that picked her to happen to, a ripe apple falling in her lap. There might be some girls too good to grab it, but they'd had more luck in their lives than she'd had. She was a bit older than many of the men she met on the job. Many of them were still in school, and besides, too often they reminded her of Jerry. All long hair and dopy smiles and follow the line of least resistance and useless to the core. She couldn't cope with that any more.

She had been lucky to get this job and she knew it. There was Aunt Maryrose, who'd raised her, daffy in the nursing home and eating up half her pay. Not that she begrudged it. Aunt Maryrose was all the mother she'd had. But Helen squeaked along and lived in her dim narrow studio with linoleum on the floor and the toilet in the hall. She had a beagle named Albert Hall left from Jerry and mice in the kitchen and unpaid bills from work done on her teeth and the nursing home calling her all the time complaining about her aunt.

Life gave her little room to swing her weight in. She had to watch everything. She watched what she ate, what she spent on carfare, what she spent on her body. She had to calculate everything. Nothing had been given her. And the last rotten abortion had cleaned her out for months. Twenty-four years old and three abortions. She would never go through another. If she had twins she would not go through that again. She would kill herself first! No matter if months went by and she never even kissed a man, she took her pills religiously. One a day, hope and pray. She could get pregnant from sitting on a man's lap, she swore.

So she'd given in that February night. So? He wasn't a

rat, he wasn't sick, he wasn't vicious, he wasn't mean. He was
a good-looking, well-set-up man ten years older who had a
soft job and earned a good living and was shopping around
for another woman. If it wasn't her, it would be another next
month. Now she was into the soup, she might as well fight.
Otherwise she'd just been had again. Again. He said his wife
did not love him. She was demanding, selfish, thought only
of herself. He wanted to be loved.

It was a chance, such a skinny chance. Then over spring
vacation she saw Mrs. Stone at a party. A loud overweight
woman in a dress that had been in all the stores three years
ago. A sloppy woman who didn't even wear a brassiere and
laughed at the top of her lungs. She was arguing about military
research with Dr. White, who was a project head, just as if
she knew what she was talking about, leaving Neil to wander
around the party and flirt with her.

Now Helen was to see them on home base. This was her
scouting expedition. She had to drop off the typed report to
him as soon as Greta finished it. After she collected the report, she stopped at the women's lavatory to look at herself
very carefully, before going down in the elevator.

She had a sharp way of viewing herself, detached and
almost hostile. She was five feet six, one hundred twenty
pounds. Morning and night she weighed herself. She had
lightened her hair to a natural-looking ash blonde, worn
shoulder length and softly waved. She had learned that men
around M.I.T. did not like heavy make-up, and she had
changed to brands that produced more subtle effects. Every
time she got a job she had to change something to keep up
with what was expected. She also knew that Neil liked her
in light grays, greens, blues, cool pastel colors that suggested
to him what he sought in her. His wife was evidently the
orange and purple sort.

When she found the house, Neil was watching Walter
Cronkite and Mrs. Stone was feeding the children in the
kitchen. Mrs. Stone was not nearly as fat as she had thought
at the party, and she looked almost pretty smiling at the
little girl, who was telling her a story about a cat named
Annie-poo. But she was wearing an old pair of corduroy
pants and an Indian shirt that had seen better days—had
once been bedecked with mirrors but had lost most of them
and faded unevenly. Indeed Mrs. Stone had large blue stains,
probably paint, all over pants and shirt and in her hair.

Helen could see up close that there were a few long white strands among the black in her hair—nothing a touch-up wouldn't have caught, but evidently she did not bother. She was not keeping up with Neil. So often women didn't. Helen felt a little anger toward the woman: didn't she understand that Neil spent his time around women who were young and pretty?

No, it was the children who would represent the obstacle. The boy was a baby, fat and splattering food in all directions and babbling incoherently about banana. He was cute enough, and if he hadn't been so daubed with food she would have picked him up to hug. The girl was lovely and awfully precocious.

"Do you work with my daddy? Are you a professor too? I rode up and down in the elevator where my daddy works and I saw all the electric typewriters in a room and when I pressed it went XXXXXXXXXXXXXXXXXXXXXXXXXXX!"

Neil could not hide his pleasure at seeing her, even though she tried to avoid meeting his gaze in the house. His face quickened, he seemed to grow more angular and boyish, his eyes kept moving to her and staying there. She was afraid that Mrs. Stone would notice, but she seemed beyond noticing anything, running from the stove where pots were bubbling to the little boy, dabbing vegetables on himself and the wall, to Ariane, who was at the table singing to herself about a big pink froggy instead of eating her chicken.

What to do? Should she get pregnant as a means of forcing the issue? Or didn't she have to? So hard to know. She did not want to push him more than she had to; he complained of his wife as pushy and demanding. He had been moving steadily toward the final commitment. He had even spoken of the settlement problem, saying no matter what happened they couldn't be too strapped, because he had a lot of stock in some company and it was all in his name. He had made a bad mistake, he said, choosing the wrong kind of woman, but didn't he deserve something besides fighting and contests of will and a wife who kept trying to change him to somebody else?

When she left, Neil walked her to the door and stepped outside. Right there on the porch he risked kissing her, he held her desperately against him and kissed her. "I can't stand this," he said. "You come in and then walk out. I'll think of you all night. Listen, Saturday. Can I come Saturday? We have to talk seriously."

She walked down the block. It was getting dark and it would take half an hour at least to get home on the subway. Then a steep walk uphill at the other end to her dreary studio, ho-ho, as they called it, where Albert Hall would be dying to get out to do his duty in the street and her supper of frozen chicken pot pie would be waiting to be popped in the oven. Then the phone would start ringing and the head nurse from the home would be on her back about how they had had to give more sedation to her aunt. It was a hole in the wall, a horrible place, and she hated Aunt Maryrose to be stuck there. Weeping in her bed and incontinent. Polite word for a nasty fact. She said they wouldn't help her to go to the bathroom when she had to.

Well, she wouldn't be in her rotten studio long and she wouldn't be alone long. She swung her arms as she walked and she wasn't even afraid of the dark shadows of the hedges and the passers-by who always looked so sinister after the sun set. Everyone deserved a little happiness. There were obstacles, there were difficulties, but he wanted her. He was quite used to getting what he wanted. So unlike Jerry, he was strong in his own quiet way. Her first marriage had been a disaster, but she thought her second had to be better, with her so willing to work and work at it, unlike some women. He was beginning to love her, he was wanting her, and soon she would not be alone any more.